THE CHILDREN OF THE GODS
SERIES BOOKS 53-55

DARK MEMORIES TRILOGY

I. T. LUCAS

Also by I. T. Lucas

PERFECT MATCH

The Children of the Gods Series Sets

MEGA SETS
INCLUDE CHARACTER LISTS

TRY THE CHILDREN OF THE GODS SERIES ON AUDIBLE
2 FREE audiobooks with your new Audible subscription!

NOTE FROM THE AUTHOR:
Dark Memories Trilogy is a work of fiction!
Names, characters, places and incidents are products of the author's imagination or are used
fictitiously and are not to be construed as real. Any similarity to actual persons, organizations and/or
events is purely coincidental.

Published by Evening Star Press

EveningStarPress.com

ISBN: 978-1-957139-14-2

DARK MEMORIES SUBMERGED

THE CHILDREN OF THE GODS BOOK 53

GERALDINE

*G*eraldine applied a coat of gloss over her rose-hued lipstick and examined her reflection in the mirror.

Ageless was the look she was going for, but there was no hiding the fact that she looked way too young to have a thirty-four-year-old daughter. So far, she'd somehow gotten away with it, but the older Cassandra got, the harder it was to pull off.

When people remarked on Geraldine's youthful appearance, she usually responded with a simple thank you, and more often than not, that sufficed. Some went further though, asking what her secret was, and for those she had a rehearsed reply—she stayed out of the sun, applied sunscreen every morning, and moisturized day and night.

Since that was what people expected to hear, they accepted her answer and moved on. She was just a simple suburban mother who wasn't important enough to justify further inquiry.

Soon, though, she would be forced to add plastic surgery to her arsenal of answers.

With a sigh, Geraldine pulled a brush through her hair.

Where did the time go?

For most people, that was just an expression. For her, it was a reality she had to live with. Huge chunks were missing from her memory.

She didn't remember being a child, or who her parents were. It was as if she'd been born an adult, and even after that so-called birth, much of her life was hazy.

Geraldine remembered waking up in a rehab center with a mind that was nearly a blank page. Later, after she'd relearned speech, she'd been told about the head trauma that had supposedly been the cause of her amnesia.

No trace of it remained, but from time to time, she felt a phantom pain on the left side of her head, and she imagined that was where she'd been injured.

Then again, she imagined many things that weren't real.

It was so frustrating to have a brain that seemed perfectly normal and yet didn't work right.

And why the hell wasn't she aging?

Did it have anything to do with the injury she'd sustained?

Geraldine didn't know how old she was when she woke up in the rehab center, but thirty-six years later, she looked exactly the same as she'd looked then.

She lived in fear of discovering the cause, and even more so of being found out. People would pay a fortune to analyze the secret of the fountain of youth hidden in her body.

Hopefully, the fake IDs she'd gotten over the years were confusing enough to throw potential investigators off her trail. So far no one had followed her, so her strategy was working. She also didn't use credit cards, paying in cash whenever possible, and she had no property listed under her name either.

Thankfully, Geraldine also never got sick, so she didn't need to see any doctors. She'd even delivered Cassy at home with the help of a midwife.

Well, not having medical insurance had been the main reason she'd chosen to do it that way, but she was so glad she hadn't gone to a hospital. They might have taken blood samples and discovered the abnormality that was keeping her young.

At the time, she still hadn't known that there was something wrong with her other than the memory loss. But in retrospect, not having money to spare had worked to her advantage.

Raising a daughter alone and having no formal education, Geraldine found it impossible to get a well-paying job, so money had always been scarce.

She'd supported herself and Cassandra by making quilts, for which she had a natural knack. The proceeds from selling them had covered her expenses, but medical insurance had been a luxury she couldn't afford.

All of that had changed once Cassandra started working at Fifty Shades of Beauty. Now they both had medical insurance, and quilt making had turned into a hobby rather than a way to earn a living.

It was nice to create just for the sake of creation without having to work long hours or rush to complete a project so she could pay the rent.

Her quilts were beautiful if she said so herself, and while she still had been selling them, they'd been snatched up no matter what price tag she'd put on them.

The last one Geraldine had sold fetched over seven thousand dollars, an extravagant sum that she'd been sure no one would pay.

Nowadays, she only made them for fun or to give out as gifts to her friends.

In part it was to humor Cassy, who insisted that her mother no longer needed to slave over the sewing machine, and in part it was because her quilts were a calling card that someone might trace back to her.

It was safer not to advertise her work.

"Mom!" Cassandra yelled from downstairs. "Are you ready? Onegus will be here at any moment."

"I'll be right down!" Geraldine took one last look in the mirror, checked that her eyeliner wasn't smudged, and fluffed up her hair.

She and Cassandra were meeting Onegus's mother for lunch, and Geraldine didn't want to be outdone by the woman. She wasn't nearly as beautiful as Martha, but Geraldine had been told that she resembled Elizabeth Taylor, who had been called the most beautiful woman in the world, so there was that.

Except, the definition of beauty had changed since the legendary actress had been a star. Nowadays, tall leggy blondes with strong jawlines like Martha were all the rave, while petite brunettes with hourglass figures and small chins were not.

Still, she and the mother of the man Cassandra had fallen in love with had a lot in common. They both looked much too young to have children in their thirties, they each had only one child, and both had raised them without a father.

Onegus and Cassandra becoming a couple and introducing their mothers to each other seemed almost serendipitous.

Here was another woman, one who lived across the ocean from her, who also somehow defied aging. Had Martha been the victim of a freak accident as well? Could that be the explanation for both of their unnaturally youthful appearances?

Not likely.

Perhaps good genes were responsible for their youthful looks after all. And if not, perhaps Martha knew the secret and could explain why aging didn't seem to affect either of them.

The get-together would be a good opportunity to ask. Martha was returning to Scotland Sunday evening, so today was Geraldine's last chance.

Opening her purse, she dropped the lipstick and the gloss inside, closed it, and headed downstairs.

Cassandra was waiting for her at the bottom of the staircase. "You look beautiful, Mom." Her gaze swept over Geraldine's dress and matching heels. "I love the polka dots. Who knew that they would make a comeback?"

The small white dots contrasting with the navy blue was a classic pattern, as was the cut of the dress. Martha would have a hard time finding fault with Geraldine's outfit.

"Do you like it?"

Cassy had as good an eye for colors and patterns as she did, and she trusted her opinion.

"I love it. The puffy skirt and cinched waist make you look like a cover model on a fifties fashion magazine."

"They do?" Geraldine smoothed her hand over the skirt. "I didn't realize that. Should I change into something else? I don't want to look old-fashioned."

She just wanted to look older.

Cassandra shook her head. "It's perfect on you."

"Thank you." Geraldine lifted her hand and cupped her daughter's cheek. "Tell me the truth. Are you and Onegus going to announce your engagement over lunch?"

Cassandra smiled nervously. "I've already answered that. Did you forget?"

Her daughter knew that comments about her memory issues upset her, which indicated that questions regarding Cassandra and Onegus's possible engagement had hit a nerve.

"I didn't forget. But you took half a day off from work, which you rarely do, so accompanying me to a lunch meeting with your boyfriend's mother must be very important to you. What else am I supposed to think?"

It wasn't only that. Cassandra had been edgy ever since the change in plans had been made. Geraldine had been supposed to meet Martha for lunch on Thursday, just the two of them, and then Martha had called to reschedule it for today so that Onegus and Cassandra could join them.

The phone's ringing saved her daughter from answering. "It was the gate," she said after ending the call. "Onegus is here."

2

CASSANDRA

*T*alk about being saved by the bell, or the ring, as was the case.

Tucking her purse under her arm, Cassandra opened the front door just as Onegus pulled up to the curb.

"You both look spectacular." He held the back passenger door open for her mother.

"Thank you." Geraldine smiled at him. "You're very kind."

"I'm just truthful." He opened the front passenger door for Cassandra. "You okay?" he whispered as he kissed her cheek.

She nodded even though she was far from it.

Cassandra was anxious and worried.

Were they doing the right thing with her mother?

The plan had seemed solid when they'd come up with it. Bring Geraldine to the clan's hidden village, confront her about her immortality and the family she'd left behind, and have her admit that she'd staged her own death by drowning. Roni would be there with Geraldine's fake driver's licenses as well as family photos of her with her older daughter, the one she seemed to have forgotten.

Was it all an act?

Was her mother aware of not aging? Did she remember having another family a long time ago? Or had she really lost her memory and didn't know either?

Confronted with her immortality and her past, Geraldine might spiral into one of her episodes. It didn't happen often, but when it did, her mother would become incoherent, babble nonsense and jumbled sentences, and cry for hours.

Sometimes it took days to bring her back to normal, or as normal as she got.

"You're tense," Onegus said. "Do you want me to put on some music?"

"I would love some," Geraldine said from the backseat. "Did I tell you about Cassy's dad? He was a musician."

"That's a new one," Cassandra whispered.

When her mother felt nervous or insecure, her stories got even more fantastical than usual.

One of Geraldine's two favorites was the one about her father working for the Ethiopian embassy. In one story he was the ambassador, in another an aide, and in yet another variation an analyst. But at least that story was pretty consistent. In all versions, his name was Emanuel, he was tall, handsome, and had a great smile. Her mother's other favorite was the brain surgeon she'd supposedly met in the hospital while recovering from her injury. He was brilliant, the head of the neurosurgical department, and a favorite of the nurses. His name changed from one telling of the story to another. Then there was the astronaut, who made an appearance once or twice a year, and a host of many others that had been one-time guests, like the musician she'd made up on the spot right now.

Onegus reached across the center console for Cassandra's hand. "What kind of music did he play?"

"Jazz, sometimes Blues." Geraldine sighed. "Every night, I sat in the back of the club and listened to his band perform. When he was on break, he would come to sit with me, and we would share a drink and talk and laugh. At the end of the night, after they were done playing, he would dance with me."

"Was he famous?" Onegus asked. "Maybe I've heard of him?"

Onegus was playing along, which was helping Geraldine relax. Getting deeper into her story mode always did.

"His name was Luis." She looked out the window. "He and his band weren't famous. They were young musicians, but they were good."

As Geraldine dove into her fantasy world, making up club names and going on about the famous actors and actresses coming to see Luis perform, Cassandra closed her eyes and tried to calm down.

The stress about the upcoming confrontation was stirring up her inner destructive energy, and if she didn't find a way to relax, she might blow something up.

Given that they were in a moving vehicle, that was extremely dangerous. Not so much for her mother and Onegus, who were immortal, but Cassandra was still human, which was another reason for her mounting stress.

She should have started transitioning already.

But that was a worry for another time. Right now, she needed to get the swirling turmoil under control.

When her energy blasts discharged, they mostly shattered glass and clay containers, but they could also melt electronics. Hopefully, she'd be able to hold it in until they reached the village, where she could aim the blast at a glass or a pot.

Given how elaborate Geraldine's story was becoming, her mother was nervous as hell, but at least she didn't notice when the windows started turning opaque and Onegus took his hands off the wheel.

They were nearing the village, and the car's computer had taken over. For the remainder of the trip, the windows would stay opaque, so they wouldn't know where the secret entrance to the underground tunnel was.

When the car entered the tunnel, Geraldine finally noticed that something wasn't right. "Where are we? Why did it get dark all of a sudden?"

"We are in a tunnel," Onegus said. "I hope that you're not claustrophobic."

"I'm not. But where is this tunnel? I didn't know there was one in this part of the city."

Right then, the car came to a stop, and a moment later, Cassandra felt it going up. They were in the elevator.

"What's that?" Her mother's tone was bordering on panicked.

"It's just a lift to an upper-level parking," Onegus said.

"Oh." Geraldine let out a breath and slumped in her seat. "It's in one of those underground parking structures."

"Precisely." Onegus turned to her and smiled reassuringly. "We are almost there."

3

KIAN

From his spot at the head of the conference table, Kian watched the open door, waiting impatiently for the rest of the council members to arrive and take their seats.

His office was the last place he wanted to be while his wife and newborn daughter were home, inundated with the never-ending throng of well-wishers. Syssi's parents were there to help, but so was Okidu—the reason why a council meeting was unavoidable less than two days after Allegra's birth.

Thinking about the cutest kryptonite in existence, Kian smiled. Since the first moment he'd seen her tiny face, he'd been overwhelmed by the love he felt for her and known that he would move mountains for her.

If it were up to Kian, he would have taken a paternity leave and stayed home with his baby until she was old enough to go to college.

The feeling of holding her in his arms was indescribable. It flooded him with such enormous amounts of oxytocin that he felt as high as if he'd taken a drug. Then again, the cuddling hormone was precisely that. It was nature's way of ensuring that mammals took care of their young.

Had it been like that with Beatrix? The human daughter he'd had with his human wife over nineteen centuries ago? Kian couldn't remember. But for the first time ever, he could think of her name without feeling a pang of sorrow in his heart and churning in his gut.

He'd paid a dear price for marrying a human at nineteen, and an even bigger one for having a child with her. Foolishly, he'd believed that he could hide his immortality and all it entailed from her, but it had been impossible. When his wife had become suspicious, faking his own death had been Kian's only option.

Lavena had suspected that he was a sorcerer, or a demon, or whatever other nonsense humans had believed at the time, and she'd feared him enough to share her suspicions with others. If she had, the villagers would have hunted him down, and he would have been forced to kill them all.

She'd left him no choice.

After faking his death, Kian had watched over his wife and daughter from afar, helping whenever he could without revealing himself. He'd watched Lavena remarry, had watched Beatrix grow to adulthood and have children of her own, get old, and die.

It had been the most difficult time of his very long life.

"Are you ready to begin?" Shai asked softly, his blue eyes full of compassion and understanding.

His assistant wasn't an empath per se, but he was incredibly attuned to Kian's moods. Had Shai realized that Kian had taken a trip down memory lane?

"Aye." He nodded at his assistant. "Let's begin."

While Kian had been distracted by his memories, the last council members he'd been waiting for had arrived.

"This is council meeting number 473," Shai announced. "Aside from Onegus, all council members are present."

The chief had a prior engagement, and since the meeting was informative in nature and the council wouldn't be voting, Kian had excused him. Besides, Onegus already knew about Okidu and his gift. Amanda, William, and Bridget were in the know as well, but they'd come to take part in the discussion.

That left only Brandon and Edna out of the loop, or maybe just Brandon.

Kalugal had somehow found out about the gift, and he had no doubt told Rufsur, his second-in-command, who in turn had told his mate, Edna.

Kian still hadn't figured out how Kalugal had found out so quickly, but he was determined to get to the bottom of it. If Kalugal was spying on him, that was a major breach of the accord.

Although, if the spying had been done out of curiosity and not with malicious intent, Kalugal could claim that it hadn't been a breach and get away with it. At least legally.

Kian's anger and mistrust would be personal, which was much worse.

"Some of you know what's on the agenda and why I have summoned you less than two days after my daughter's birth. Arguably, it could have waited until Monday, but I didn't want those of you who haven't heard about it yet to feel left out."

He looked at Edna and then at Brandon. "On the morning of my two thousandth birthday, Okidu presented me with a very special gift— the blueprints to build more of him. For months, he has secretly been filling up thirty-six thick handwritten tomes with instructions and schematics that have been hidden inside his operational memory." Kian waved a hand at William. "Don't ask me what that is. I'm sure William can explain it better."

Edna shook her head. "I'm not interested in hearing the details of how it was hidden. What I want to know is why it was hidden in the first place, and how it was retrieved nearly six thousand years later. I was under the impression that the Odus were found with their memories wiped clean."

"They were. Okidu doesn't know who encrypted them nor why. He rebooted after his drowning incident during Carol's rescue, and the reboot released those hidden memories. Along with the schematics, the reboot also released a new operational protocol that enables Okidu to better understand feelings and to make more autonomous decisions. One of his first decisions was to reboot Onidu, so he could help him write down the instructions and have them ready in time for my birthday. He tricked Onidu into submerging himself in the bathtub by telling him that Amanda had commanded it."

"Oh, boy." Brandon groaned. "We are in big trouble."

Kian nodded. "My sentiment exactly. We now have two sentient cyborgs, who are indestructible and dangerous, and who have the emotional intelligence of toddlers."

"I disagree," Amanda said. "I watched Okidu with Syssi and Allegra. He's very protective of both. Every time someone stops by to congratulate you and to see the baby, he hovers closely and makes sure that they keep their distance because they might be carrying germs on their clothes that are dangerous to the baby. This is precisely what our mother programmed him to do—to protect her children, and by extension, her grandchildren."

"I noticed." Kian turned to William. "Did you have a chance to go over any of it yet?"

Given how red-rimmed the guy's eyes were, he hadn't slept since the journals had been delivered to his office in the lab.

"The amount of information is staggering, and most of it is new. It will take me months to go over the entire thing. Maybe even years." He removed his glasses and rubbed his eyes. "I still haven't deciphered all that's contained in Ekin's tablet. My progress is in step with humanity's. I can't do it all alone."

In a way, Kian was glad. If a genius like William needed so long to decipher the information, Kalugal couldn't do anything with it even if he somehow got a hold of it.

Not that he was going to.

"What do you plan to do with the information once it's deciphered?" Edna asked.

"I don't know yet." He leaned back in his chair. "I'm glad that we have plenty of time to think it through and don't have to rush our decision. Even if we decide not to build any more Odus, the technology contained in those journals might usher in a new technological era, a quantum leap in our knowledge, and by extension, humanity's."

4

SHAI

*O*nce the meeting was over and the council members left, Shai stayed behind to wrap things up. He added the recording he'd made to the archives, wrote a summary and put it on Kian's desk, and lastly, cleaned the conference table with a disposable wet wipe.

"I'm heading home to have lunch with Syssi." Kian pushed away from his desk. "Would you like to come along?"

It was an invitation that neither of them expected Shai to accept, but he still appreciated Kian for extending it.

Shai had already seen the little princess, and although he wouldn't have minded getting another look, someone had to stay in the office. With Kian gone, probably for the rest of the day, it was up to him to answer emails and handle phone calls. The more he could take care of without involving Kian, the better.

"Thank you, but I'll just grab a sandwich at the café. Are you coming back to the office?"

"Not unless I have to. Call me if anything urgent comes up."

"Sure thing." Shai smiled. "Give Allegra a kiss from me."

Kian's expression turned softer than any Shai had ever seen on him. "I will."

When the door behind his boss closed, Shai let out a breath and walked over to Kian's desk. Booting up the computer, he sat down to read over the emails that had accumulated during the meeting. None required Kian's immediate attention, but a couple needed him to read them over, and he marked them as such. He answered the rest himself.

The truth was that he could have taken care of the other two as well, but it would have been overstepping his position.

Kian wouldn't have minded. In fact, his boss would have been happy if Shai took more responsibility upon himself, but that was precisely what Shai didn't want to do. He was a great administrator, and with his excellent memory, he was a good assistant. But there was a difference between remembering all the chess moves his

13

boss had made since he'd started working for him and coming up with new ones of his own.

Shai wasn't an entrepreneur, and he didn't have the guts to make decisions that might lose the clan money. He was perfectly happy with his job of keeping Kian organized and ensuring that his boss had all the facts he needed to make good business decisions.

Some might have thought of him as lacking ambition, but that couldn't be further from the truth. Shai's dreams were big, but they didn't include running the clan's businesses, or any other business for that matter. He'd minored in economics, so he wasn't clueless, but his real passion was movies. For now, however, writing screenplays was a hobby rather than an occupation.

L.A. was full of wannabe screenwriters who waited tables and worked in phone rooms. It was even embarrassing to admit that he was part of that group, which was why Shai never talked about it.

The main reason he never mentioned his stories, though, was that they were too personal, a way for him to tell what was in his heart, his soul, without actually telling it to anyone. It was a form of therapy.

Would anything ever come of it?

Maybe. At seventy-eight, he was a young immortal, and he had plenty of time to write his masterpiece. If he so wished, he could spend centuries on perfecting his craft. On the other hand, his immortality was also a major impediment for crafting his screenplays.

The advice to novice writers was to write about what they knew, and that was what he was trying to do. The problem was that without the immortal element, it was a struggle to convey what he was feeling and the motives behind his actions. All the alternatives he'd come up with fell short of the emotional impact the real story had.

He'd toyed with the idea of writing the truth under the guise of a paranormal or science fiction story, which would have solved the problem of authenticity, but not anonymity. It ran the risk of his clan members figuring out that he was telling his own story, and that needed to remain a secret.

Shai had managed to hide it for twenty years, and he would keep doing it until it was no longer relevant. The thought of that eventuality saddened him, but there was nothing he could do about it. As the saying went, he'd made his bed and now he had to lie in it, but despite all the difficulties, he didn't regret it.

On more than one occasion, Shai had been tempted to throw away the story that had been eating at him for two decades and write something completely unrelated, a fresh one that he could show Brandon and get his advice.

If Brandon liked the story, he could get Shai's script in front of the right people. Other aspiring screenwriters would have sold their soul to the devil for the Hollywood connection Shai had.

Oh, well, it was what it was.

With a sigh he pushed the chair back, got to his feet, and grabbed his laptop on the way out of the office.

The line at the café wasn't long, and as he got to the counter, Wonder greeted him with a bright smile.

"Hello, Shai. The usual?"

"Yes, please." He pulled out the clan's credit card and handed it to her. "It's not busy today. How come?"

She shrugged. "The guests are leaving soon, and many have chosen to spend time with their loved ones in the city. There is a better selection of eateries." She put his favorite sandwich on a plate and handed it to him. "Others are visiting Syssi and Kian. Everyone wants to see little Allegra. I'm not complaining, though. Wendy took time off to take care of Margaret, and Callie can only work a few hours a day. I'm managing by myself, but I like it when it's quiet and I can take a moment to actually talk with my customers."

"You are one tough lady. A real survivor."

That got a big grin out of her. "Thank you. Frankly, though, I would have also liked to take time off. Annani wanted to spend time with me, and I had to take a rain check. Once Wendy is back, I'm taking a day off."

"Did you get to see Allegra?"

Wonder nodded. "She's so cute and so tiny." Smiling, she leaned closer. "We have a betting pool going on. Those who say that she looks more like Kian than Syssi, and those who think that she looks more like Syssi than Kian. In three months, when Allegra's features become clearer, the winners will be announced." She motioned at the two small baskets at the far corner of the counter. "Team Kian is the one furthest out with the blue ribbon tied to it, and the other one with the pink ribbon is team Syssi. Choose one and put a quarter in it."

"What do the winners get?"

Wonder chuckled. "Being right. We will use the money to order custom-printed onesies for Allegra. Depending on which basket collects more quarters, it will either say Daddy's Girl or Mommy's Girl."

"Nice idea." Shai walked over to the collection baskets and dropped a quarter in each. "I can't decide who she looks like more, so I'm hedging my bets."

"That's cheating." Wonder handed him the cappuccino.

"I really can't choose." He took the plate and cup. "Thanks. If I don't see you again today, have a great weekend."

Shai walked over to one of the tables that was nestled against the hedge. The thing had grown so tall since it had been planted that it provided lots of shade at this time of day. He put his coffee and sandwich on the table's right side, the laptop in the middle, and sat down.

Perhaps he should write Wonder's story instead of his own. It was much more interesting, and Wonder had nothing to hide from the clan. Besides, humans would love the Wonder Woman twist.

5

GERALDINE

*A*s the elevator lurched up, Geraldine forced herself to stop hyperventilating and breathe normally.

The whole cloak-and-dagger thing was bizarre enough to be one of her fuzzy memories. She never knew whether they were hallucinations, vivid dreams that she remembered as if they had been real events, or whether they'd really happened—just not the way she remembered them.

Except, she'd never hallucinated in real time before. It had always been a recall problem. Was her condition worsening?

"Relax." Onegus put a hand on her shoulder. "We are almost there."

Should she be excited or frightened?

The car had gone through a tunnel and then entered an elevator that had gone up several levels. After they'd parked, they had to take another elevator to go from the parking garage to the actual village.

What kind of people built their neighborhood on top of a mountain with no road leading up to it? The place was inaccessible unless one knew where the secret entrance to the tunnel was, and elevators took people from the belly of the mountain up to its surface.

As the elevator door opened, Geraldine forced a smile. "You go first."

Onegus held the door from closing. "Ladies first."

"Come on." Cassandra threaded her arm through hers. "There's no reason to be scared. The place is gorgeous."

"It must be. It's guarded better than the mythical El Dorado." Geraldine half expected to find the buildings covered in gold.

Instead, she found herself in a glass pavilion that housed some kind of exhibit and was surrounded by greenery.

"What are the things on display?" she asked as they walked toward the exit.

"Archeological artifacts," Onegus said. "My cousin Kalugal is a collector. He'll stop by later to say hello."

16

As they exited through the pavilion's sliding doors, Onegus pointed ahead. "This is the village square."

On one side of it were several buildings that looked like offices or served some other public function. The square also housed a café, a playground, a pond, and a sprawling grassy area that was perfect for large gatherings. It was difficult to see details of the structures on the other side of the lush greenery, but they looked like residences.

"What do you think?" Cassandra asked. "Isn't it beautiful?"

The wistful tone in her daughter's voice was a big fat hint as to why they were having the meeting with Onegus's mother here and not a restaurant in town.

Apparently, Cassandra wanted to move in with Onegus, and she wanted her mother to fall in love with the place, so she would want to move in with them.

Wasn't going to happen.

It would be difficult, but Cassandra was a grown woman, and she didn't need her mother to live with her and her boyfriend.

"It is so peaceful here." Geraldine glanced at the playground. "Where are the children?"

"Would you like to stop at the café?" Onegus asked instead of answering her question.

"Are we meeting your mother there?"

"I thought we would grab a cup of coffee first." He smiled sheepishly. "My mother is running a little late."

Geraldine lifted a brow. "I thought that she was staying with you during her visit."

"She and the other guests are staying in a building that my family owns downtown. Since it's so close to the venue, no transportation needed to be arranged. They just walked across the street."

"I see."

She wondered whether it had been a hint that mothers and their grown children shouldn't live together.

"I haven't been to the café yet," Cassandra said. "I would love to check out the place."

"We are lucky that there is no line." Onegus ushered them forward. "Usually, the place is packed at lunchtime."

"Why isn't it today?" Geraldine asked.

"Because of the visitors. People are spending time with their family members, going shopping, and checking out the restaurants in town. I bet Wonder is happy."

"Wonder?" Cassandra arched a brow. "I've never heard of anyone named Wonder. Is it a nickname?"

Onegus chuckled. "That's the name she chose for herself because she resembles the actress who plays Wonder Woman. The new version one, not the old one."

"Oh." Cassandra glanced at the girl. "She really does."

"Let's catch a table before it gets busy again." Onegus led them to a table but didn't sit down. "I need to order at the counter. Do you want anything with your coffees?"

"Do they serve cappuccinos?" Cassandra asked.

"They do, and they are excellent."

"Then I'll have one. But I don't want to eat anything before lunch."

"I would like a cappuccino as well. Thank you." Geraldine waited for Onegus to leave before taking another look around.

Several of the tables were occupied, all by good-looking people, but the one who caught her attention was a young man sitting near the hedge delineating the café's enclosure.

He was blond, with skin as pale as Onegus's, but she couldn't see his face because he was bent over a laptop, typing away on the keyboard. He was smartly dressed though, in a white dress shirt, a white and blue checkered tie, and a gray vest. A brown jacket was draped over the back of his chair. It was bit much given the warm weather, but he probably worked in an air-conditioned office.

Was he an attorney? Or a banker?

Nowadays, those were the only occupations that required men to wear ties to work.

"You're staring, Mom," Cassandra whispered.

"He's a good-looking man."

Cassandra's lips twisted in a smile. "I didn't know blond guys were your type."

"I don't have a type. It's about what's on the inside. I like interesting men, men who are passionate about something or have an interesting life story. Otherwise, they are a bore."

Leaning back, Cassandra crossed her arms over her chest. "So looks have nothing to do with it?"

"Of course, they do. I'm an artist at heart, and beauty nourishes my soul. But it's much less important than a person's character."

Just then, the man lifted his head and looked straight at her. His stare was so intense that Geraldine felt herself blush.

She hadn't blushed in ages.

Then again, she might have forgotten her other blushing incidents.

Gathering her wits about her, she offered him a friendly smile and waved.

For a long moment, he just kept on staring, but then he smiled and waved back.

"What are you doing?" Cassandra hissed. "Are you flirting with the guy? You've just gotten here."

"I'm not flirting." Geraldine huffed out a breath. "I'm just being polite."

6

SHAI

Beautiful.

Shai had to force himself to look down and pretend that he was back to writing. He couldn't concentrate, and what was worse, he couldn't remember what he'd written before he'd sensed her looking at him.

That had never happened to him. He remembered everything. Always.

Who was she? Where had she come from? She wasn't one of his Scottish relatives or a resident of the sanctuary.

Was she a Dormant?

His heart sank at the realization that for a new Dormant to be in the village, she must be someone's mate.

She was already taken.

When a shadow fell over him, he lifted his head again, surprised to see Onegus grinning down at him.

"Pretty, isn't she?" the chief whispered.

Shai nodded. "Very. Who is she with?"

The chief put a hand on his chair's back and leaned closer. "Her name is Geraldine, and she's Cassandra's mother. We suspect that she's already an immortal, but she might not be aware of it. She's about to learn the truth soon."

Shai had been so focused on the mother that he hadn't noticed Onegus's mate sitting next to her. If he had, he might have deduced that there was a connection.

"Would you like to come say hello?" Onegus asked. "Just don't mention anything about immortals. We want to ease her into it."

Shai swallowed. "Then perhaps I better not. I don't want to blurt out something accidentally."

Onegus chuckled. "You've never blurted out anything in your life." He leaned even closer. "Geraldine is not with anyone. This might be your chance before all the other unmated males find out about her. Come and introduce yourself."

The chief playing matchmaker was disturbing to say the least. Was he trying to find a mate for his future mother-in-law?

Shai hadn't been aware of Onegus liking him that much.

But the chief was right about one thing. Once the other males found out about Geraldine, there would be a stampede to get her attention, and Shai would be left in the dust.

It was no coincidence that the Head Guardians had gotten their fated mates first. The Fates' intervention had played a part, but it hadn't been just that. These males were the kind females swooned over. The buff, tough fighters that movies were made about.

The upstanding heroes.

The defenders of the clan.

Shai was none of those things.

With a nod, he pushed to his feet. "How should I introduce myself?"

"As yourself. Shai, personal assistant extraordinaire." Onegus clapped him on the back. "Don't worry about it. I'll introduce you."

That didn't sound like much, but that was who he was.

"Your order is ready!" Wonder called from the counter.

"I'll help you carry it," Shai offered.

As they picked up the coffees and headed toward the table, Geraldine smiled the entire ten seconds it took them to get there.

"This is Shai," Onegus introduced him. "And this is Cassandra, my better half, and her lovely mother, Geraldine."

Shai dipped his head. "A pleasure to meet you both." He shifted his eyes to the daughter. "I saw you at the wedding and at Kian's birthday, but we haven't been introduced."

"Please, take a seat." Cassandra pointed to the fourth chair at their table. "There were so many people at both events, and I only talked with a few. It will take me forever to get to know everyone."

Geraldine's eyes were still on him, a charming blush painting her pale cheeks pink. She had the most extraordinary eyes, a unique shade of gray-blue that seemed to glow from the inside. If she was indeed an immortal, that wasn't surprising, but the reason for the glow was.

Shai was no stranger to human females' attention, but rarely from one as beautiful as Geraldine.

Her beauty wasn't what drew him to her, though. Despite her youthful appearance, Geraldine wasn't a young girl, and yet there was a sweetness and an almost child-like innocence in her gaze that he found both endearing and sexy as hell.

She turned her gaze to her daughter. "At least you remember the faces of everyone you meet. With my tricky memory, I remember some people vividly even though I met them years ago, and others I forget the next day."

Shai frowned. "Maybe those you forget are just not memorable."

She smiled brightly. "Perhaps you are right. I'm sure that I will not forget you. You are very handsome."

Cassandra made a choking sound, and Onegus chuckled softly.

"Thank you." Shai bowed his head. "I will never forget you either, and it has nothing to do with my photographic memory. You are beautiful and charming." In a move that was completely uncharacteristic of him, he reached for her hand. "I have

20

to admit that I'm smitten." He brought her delicate hand to his lips and kissed the back of it.

"Oh, my." Geraldine put her other hand on her chest. "Aren't you the charmer."

He wasn't. Perhaps he'd been possessed by the spirit of Casanova because this wasn't like him at all.

"I'm so sorry." Onegus's mother's arrival interrupted the special moment. "I forgot how horrible traffic is in Los Angeles. Especially on a Friday. It was bumper to bumper almost the entire way."

"No worries." Onegus rose to his feet and kissed his mother's cheek. "We had a very pleasant time while waiting for you. Would you like a cappuccino?"

"No, thank you." She sat down on the chair that Shai had pulled out for her from the next table over. "We should probably head to your house. Connor is waiting for us with lunch."

"We can stay for a few minutes longer," Onegus said. "Connor texted me that he needed a little more time to get everything ready."

"Good." Martha let out a breath and turned to Geraldine. "So, what do you think about our mountain-top village?"

"It's lovely," Geraldine said.

7

GERALDINE

*G*eraldine was glad that Martha had been too busy providing excuses for her late arrival to notice Shai holding her hand. He'd let go as soon as she'd arrived, presumably to get a chair for her.

Not that Geraldine had anything to hide, but she didn't want Martha to think that she was a man chaser and was flirting with the first guy she'd met in the village.

Onegus's mother wasn't an easy woman to get along with, but Geraldine was determined to have a good relationship with her. If their children were going to end up together, they would become a family, and Geraldine wasn't about to let small differences or pet peeves sour things for any of them.

So what if Martha was a snob through and through? No one was perfect, and the woman had her redeeming qualities.

"How are you enjoying your vacation so far?" Shai asked Onegus's mother.

"I'm having a fabulous time, thank you." She leaned over to pull him in for a quick one-armed embrace, which was surprisingly affectionate for a cold fish like Martha. "I'm so happy to be here for all these joyous occasions. First, the wedding, then Kian's very special birthday, and now the little darling that was born ahead of time, so we can all get a look at her before going home."

Martha hadn't added Onegus and Cassandra falling in love to her list of happy occasions, but maybe it was just an oversight.

"Have you seen Allegra already?" Shai asked.

"Not yet. I want to stop by their house after lunch. Who do I need to coordinate the visit with?"

"Syssi's mother is in charge of funneling the guests. No one is allowed to stay inside the house for longer than five minutes. After that, the guests are welcome to mingle in the backyard for as long as they wish and then leave through the side gate."

"Smart." Martha smiled. "I like Anita. She's a take-charge kind of woman."

"That she is." Shai chuckled. "She bosses everyone around, including Kian, and he takes it without batting an eyelid. I don't think he tolerates even his own mother doing that."

"We should get moving." Onegus put a hand on his mother's shoulder. "Connor texted me that lunch is ready."

"It was nice seeing you, Shai." Martha rose to her feet. "Say hi to your mother for me."

"I will." He turned to Geraldine. "I hope to see you again soon." He offered her his hand.

"Me too." She placed her hand in his, enjoying the gentle way he clasped it.

As Shai returned to his table and the four of them headed toward Onegus's house, it occurred to Geraldine that everyone was talking about their mothers, but no one was mentioning fathers. Well, except for Kian, the birthday-bash guy, who had just become a father himself.

Martha threaded her arm through Geraldine's. "Isn't it pretty here?"

"It's beautiful. Very serene." A little too serene for her taste.

The café was nice, and meeting Shai had been even nicer, but the rest of the place was too quiet. The gated neighborhood she and Cassandra were living in wasn't much better. People mostly stayed in their homes, and hardly anyone walked the streets unless they had a dog.

Geraldine liked their old place better, even though it was a tiny apartment in a shabby building that faced a major street.

Noisy children played in the hallways, people used the pool and the small fenced-off playground that was in the center of the building complex, neighbors talked to each other, barbecued together, and watched over each other's kids. The grocery store was a walking distance away, and so was the bakery.

"That's my house." They went up the stairs to the front porch, and Onegus opened the door.

"Something smells good," Martha said. "Did Connor make grilled chicken?"

"Among other things." Onegus held the door open for them to come in.

Inside, Geraldine had expected to see Onegus's roommate, the composer Cassy had told her about, but no one had mentioned that there would be another couple joining them for lunch.

"Mom, this is Roni, and this is Sylvia," Cassandra introduced them. "My mother, Geraldine."

The lanky young man looked at her with a strange expression on his face. "Hi." He walked up closer and looked down at her. "I'm Roni."

She smiled. "And I'm Geraldine. It's nice to meet you."

Looking uncomfortable, he rubbed his hand over the back of his neck. "Do I look familiar to you?"

Her smile wilted. "Have we met before? I might have forgotten. My memory is funky. I sometimes forget things that I should remember." She touched the side of her head. "I got injured a long time ago, and I forgot my entire life before that. I had to learn to talk. But that was long before you were born, so I couldn't have met you then."

He shook his head. "That's okay. We've never met."

So why had he asked her if he looked familiar?

Was he a celebrity she should recognize?

A smiling young man wearing an apron walked out of the kitchen. "Let's eat first and reminisce later." He offered Geraldine his hand. "I'm Connor, Onegus's room-mate, and the guy who makes sure he eats."

"And I'm grateful." Onegus clapped him on the back. "If not for Connor, I would live on sandwiches and frozen pizzas."

"Ugh." Martha shuddered. "I heard that Callie plans to open a proper restaurant. You need a place with proper food in here." She tucked a long strand of hair behind her ear. "We are lucky to have a central dining room in the castle, with proper meals being prepared three times a day."

Geraldine gaped. "You live in a castle?"

Martha waved a dismissive hand. "It's just our community's nickname."

Geraldine was about to ask about what kind of community Martha lived in, when Connor started herding them toward the dining table. "We can talk over lunch. I've been slaving over a hot oven all morning." He shifted his gaze to Cassandra. "I also hope that Callie will open her place, but it's not certain yet that she will, and it might be a while until we have a full-service restaurant in the village. In the meantime, you'll have to take over my job and make sure that Onegus is fed."

Cassandra lifted her hand. "Not so fast. You can't quit yet. First of all, Onegus and I are not moving in together anytime soon, and secondly, if he has to rely on me to feed him, the poor guy is going to remain hungry. Does the café deliver?"

Connor laughed. "It doesn't. I'm afraid that the only other option is frozen dinners."

"Gross," Sylvia said. "I'm so lucky that my mother cooks for Roni and me."

Again with the mothers. Did no one in Onegus's family have a father? It was on the tip of Geraldine's tongue to ask, but it occurred to her that it wasn't good etiquette to inquire about something that might be a touchy subject.

"*Bon appétit*, everyone." Connor motioned at the salad bowl. "First course is Caesar salad with garlic bread. Second course is chicken piccata with a side of pasta."

"Sounds delicious." Cassandra handed Onegus a bottle of white wine. "Can you uncork it?" She smiled at Martha. "A meal like this requires a glass of wine."

"I agree wholeheartedly." Martha lifted her glass for Onegus to fill.

It was a little after one in the afternoon, which Geraldine considered too early even for wine. Was Cassandra nervous about something?

Perhaps she and Onegus were planning to announce their engagement after all.

8

CASSANDRA

The conversation during lunch was stilted, with Martha and Geraldine the only ones chatting away as if nothing was amiss. Geraldine didn't know that anything was, but Martha did, and Cassandra wondered whether she just didn't care or was doing a great job of acting.

Roni kept sneaking covert glances at his grandmother, but other than that, he and the other three immortals had barely said a word. Instead, they were concentrating on consuming large amounts of Connor's superb chicken and side of pasta as if it was their last meal.

They were probably afraid of blurting something out before it was time.

Cassandra was still racking her brain, trying to come up with the best way to steer the conversation smoothly and gently onto the subject of her mother's immortality.

Martha folded her napkin over her plate, signaling that she was done. "Speaking of art, Onegus tells me that you are a gifted quilt maker."

"Thank you." Geraldine smiled at Onegus before turning back to Martha. "I don't know if I'm gifted, but I was good enough to support Cassy and myself by selling them."

That was fake modesty. Her mother was a gifted artist, and she knew that.

Martha pursed her lips. "I don't know much about quilts, but they look very time-consuming. How many did you finish in a month?"

"I usually made them pretty large, a six-foot square was typical, and with how intricate the patterns were, they took many hours to make. Most months, I managed only two, and when there was a large expense coming up, I stayed up late and squeezed in one more."

"How much did you sell them for?" Roni asked.

"When I first started, I didn't know how much to ask for them and offered them for a few hundred dollars. When they were snatched up, I raised the prices a bit, but I was afraid to ask too much and kept the price tags under a thousand dollars. Then I went to a quilting competition and saw how much other quilters were charging and hiked up my prices. Toward the end of my quilting career, I was pricing them at as much as seven thousand, and people still bought them. I was fortunate."

"Did you make a name for yourself as a quilter?" Martha asked.

Geraldine smiled sheepishly. "Not at all. I sold them under several assumed names."

Martha arched a brow. "Why?"

Damn, the woman was a good actress. Despite knowing the answer to that, her questions seemed genuinely curious.

Looking uncomfortable, Geraldine shrugged. "I preferred to stay anonymous. Frankly, I was trying to avoid paying taxes. I just couldn't afford it. As far as Uncle Sam is concerned, I don't exist."

Cassandra stifled a groan. What if all the suspicious stuff her mother had been doing didn't have anything to do with her immortality but with avoiding paying taxes?

Onegus put his fork down. "At first, you were making so little that you probably didn't owe any income tax."

Geraldine's eyes widened. "Really? I didn't know that. Not that it would have mattered. I figured out pretty quickly that I could charge more."

Martha's forehead was wrinkled as if she was struggling to solve a complicated puzzle. "I still can't believe that someone paid seven thousand dollars for a quilt made by an unknown artist, no matter how beautiful it was."

Cassandra chuckled. "Maybe my mother had a rich secret admirer."

"Not likely." Geraldine reached for her glass of wine. "Almost none of the people who bought my quilts knew who I was or even saw my face. The admiration was for my creations, not for me."

Martha leaned closer to Geraldine. "You said almost none of them, which implies that some of the clients knew you."

"I participated in one competition in person."

"So, how did you sell the quilts before the internet became a thing?" Roni asked.

"Catalogs." Geraldine smiled at him. "They existed long before the internet, and people ordered things from them, including quilts."

Onegus pushed to his feet and started to collect their plates. "Who wants coffee, and who wants tea?"

Cassandra followed him up. "I'll help you clear the table."

"Tea for me," Martha said.

"I'll have tea as well." Geraldine rose to her feet. "Can someone point me in the direction of the restroom?"

"I'll show you where it is," Sylvia offered.

Roni pushed to his feet. "I'll make the coffee."

Cassandra waited until the door closed behind her mother to ask Martha, "Why are you so interested in the quilting business?"

"I have a hunch." Martha got up and helped carry the remainder of the dishes to the kitchen. "Perhaps I'm wrong, but I really don't think anyone would pay such an amount for a quilt. It reminded me of a novel I read. A guy who was in love with a painter bought everything she put up for sale to support her and help her career. What if Geraldine had someone like that?" She looked at Cassandra. "Does your mother keep accounting records of any kind? Since she sold her quilts through catalogs and later online, she had to mail them. Perhaps she kept the names and addresses of her clients."

"I sincerely doubt that. Even if my mother kept them initially, she probably discarded them when we moved to the house we are living in now."

"That was a long shot anyway," Roni said. "How are we going to break it to her that she's my grandmother? Should I just pull out the photocopies I made of her old driver's licenses?"

"Not yet," Onegus said. "I suggest that we start with questions about her good health, her strength, and her enhanced senses. Hopefully, that will ease her into the subject."

9

GERALDINE

*B*y the time Geraldine returned to the living room, coffee and tea were served, and her six lunch companions were seated around the dining table and looking at her with somber expressions on their faces.

Cassandra included.

Her daughter had been tense since the day before, and it seemed that it was contagious because the others had caught it.

Geraldine didn't know what to make of it. Cassandra's tension might be related to work or to Martha, and Onegus might be anxious about his girlfriend and mother getting along.

But what about Roni and Sylvia? Why were they even there? No one had explained why they were invited. Was one of them Onegus's cousin?

Connor was the only one who didn't look stressed or anxious, but even he seemed to be expecting something.

Why the somber expressions?

She'd deliberately stayed away from recounting any of the memories that she wasn't sure were real, so it wasn't about her questionable sanity either.

Stifling a sigh, Geraldine sat down and reached for her teacup. So far, it had been an enjoyable gathering, and she'd felt comfortable with the three new acquaintances she'd made, as well as with Onegus and Martha.

Holding his coffee cup, Onegus leaned back and leveled his intense eyes at her. "Raising a child alone is difficult. What did you do when you got sick?"

"I don't get sick often." She touched the side of her head where the phantom of her old injury sometimes still throbbed. "Other than the amnesia that is. Unfortunately, I've never fully recovered from that, and I still experience gaps in memory from time to time."

"Did it happen when Cassandra was a baby?" Martha asked.

"Luckily, it did not." Geraldine rubbed her temple. "Motherly instincts must have overridden my memory issues."

28

"What about other injuries?" Roni asked. "Did you ever cut yourself while working on your quilts, or stab a finger with a needle?"

That was an odd thing to ask. "I don't remember that ever happening, but I might have forgotten. What does that have to do with raising a baby, though?"

"Not much," Martha said. "What about your recovery after giving birth to Cassandra? It must have been difficult to take care of her without help."

"Not at all." Geraldine smiled at her daughter. "Cassy's birth was easy. Even the midwife I hired said so, and I was almost as good as new the next day."

For some reason, her lunch companions, including Cassandra, looked exasperated. Had they expected different answers?

She turned to Martha. "Was it different for you? You were alone as well."

"I wasn't alone. I had my mother and my aunts and cousins with me."

This time Geraldine could no longer hold her tongue. "Your family seems to be devoid of fathers. What happened to them? Does it have anything to do with those enemies you are so afraid of?"

It would be so incredibly tragic if they had all perished in wars with those enemies.

Letting out a breath, Onegus put his coffee cup on the table and leaned toward her. "Before I answer that, I have a few questions that might seem a little odd, but I would appreciate it if you answered them."

"Okay…"

The entire conversation was strange, and Geraldine felt that she was being interrogated. Was Onegus an undercover Internal Revenue agent?

Geraldine shook her head. That was an absurd thought even for her.

"Is your hearing better than that of other people?"

She frowned. "I don't know how to answer that. I've never had my hearing checked."

"How about your eyesight?"

"It's very good."

"Better than most people's?"

"I don't know about most people, but my friends have commented on it on several occasions. I can read the small print on prescription medications that they cannot."

"What about your sense of smell? Can you smell people's emotions?"

"Is that even possible?"

Onegus sighed. "Then I assume it's a no."

"Why are you asking me these questions?"

Cassandra took her hand and clasped it between hers. "Because we believe that you are immortal, and immortals have superior senses."

Her heart racing, Geraldine yanked her hand out of Cassandra's grasp. "What kind of nonsense is that?"

"Did you look in the mirror lately? You look younger than me."

As panic seized her, Geraldine's throat constricted. It was one thing for Cassandra to question her ageless appearance, but it was another thing to do it in front of other people.

She forced a chuckle. "Martha also looks younger than Onegus. Does that make her immortal?"

"It does," Martha said. "Except for Cassandra, we are all immortal. Welcome home, Geraldine. You have found your people." She smiled. "Technically, we found you, but the result is the same. You're among friends, and you no longer need to run and hide."

10

ONEGUS

*O*negus watched the blood drain from Geraldine's face, and as she turned gray, Cassandra wrapped her arm around her shoulders.

"Breathe, Mom. Inhale, keep it in for a second, and exhale. That's good. Keep going."

Geraldine looked shell-shocked, and the six of them were holding their breath along with her, hoping she wouldn't spiral into a psychotic episode.

"Do you want a glass of water?" Martha asked.

Geraldine shook her head. "How? How did you all become immortal? How did I?"

So she'd known, or had at least suspected, but she didn't know how.

"It's in our genes," Cassandra said. "Immortals are the descendants of the gods from mythology. There are probably many who carry the immortal gene but don't know it. They are called Dormants, and if they don't get activated, they live out their lives as humans. The mothers pass on the gene to their children, though. And since you are immortal, I carry the gene, and Onegus can activate it and induce my transition."

"How?" Geraldine asked again.

Her eyes were wide as saucers, and Onegus could hear her heart pounding from across the table. He doubted anything they said would even register, but even though she might suppress the entire conversation and pretend as if it had never happened, he'd asked Kalugal to stop by later and compel her silence.

There was a small chance that Geraldine was immune, but he wasn't worried. Even if she told everyone she knew what she was about to learn, no one would believe her. The fantastic stories she weaved worked to their advantage.

"Sex and venom," Martha said. "For a female Dormant to transition, she needs an immortal male. Do you remember hooking up with someone and then feeling sick a day or two after?"

Onegus didn't want to embarrass his mother by pointing out that it wasn't

31

constructive to ask Geraldine if she remembered something that happened thirty-five years ago.

Cassandra's mother shook her head as if trying to wake up from a spell. "What do you mean by sex and venom?"

Martha let out an exasperated breath. "For an adult female Dormant to be activated, she has to have unprotected sex with an immortal male, and he has to bite her and inject her with venom."

"Bite?" Geraldine's eyes widened. "Like a snake?"

"Precisely." Martha waved her hand in his direction. "Show her your fangs, Onegus."

Thankfully, he'd trained his fangs to respond on command, either to elongate or refrain from doing so.

Onegus smiled broadly, letting Geraldine see them grow.

Gasping, she clasped a hand to her chest. "I must be hallucinating." She glanced at her teacup. "Did you put something in my tea?"

This wasn't going well, and they hadn't told her about the family she'd left behind yet.

Onegus doubted that Geraldine could take much more before losing her marbles. Perhaps he should call Kalugal now, have him compel her silence, and take her home to rest.

"There was nothing in your tea." Cassandra took her hand again. "Come on, Mom. It's not so difficult to believe, given what I can do. At least now I know where my strange power comes from."

Geraldine shifted her saucer eyes to Onegus. "Can you also blow things up with your mind?"

"I can do other things. Immortals possess a variety of paranormal abilities. Sylvia's talent is similar to Cassandra's, though. She can fritz out electronics, but without blowing them up. They only malfunction for as long as she wants them to."

"What about you? What's your special talent?"

He grinned. "Charm. Not every immortal has a paranormal talent."

She turned to his mother. "And you?"

Martha shook her head. "There is nothing special about me."

As Cassandra snorted, her mother shifted her eyes to Roni.

"What about you?"

Roni swallowed. "I'm one of the best hackers in the world. But I don't know if there is anything paranormal about my ability. I'm just brilliant."

That got a smile out of Geraldine. "Is lack of modesty part of being immortal?"

"Nope." He looked at Onegus. "What about the other thing we wanted to talk about?"

Onegus shook his head. "I think that's more than enough for one day."

The guy looked disappointed, but he nodded. "Next time, then."

"What other things?" Geraldine asked.

Onegus smiled. "Would you like to hear more about how immortals came to be?"

"Yes, please."

Martha lifted her hand. "First, we need proof that Geraldine is indeed immortal. What we know so far is not conclusive."

Roni opened his mouth to argue, but she waved her hand to shush him. "Humor me. I just want to make sure before we tell her all of our secrets."

Geraldine nodded. "I would like to know for sure as well. I noticed that I wasn't aging, but I don't remember ever having been bitten by a man with fangs." She touched the side of her head. "But then I don't remember many things."

"It's easy to prove or disprove." Martha rose to her feet. "I will need to scratch you, though. Is that okay with you?"

"Why?"

"If you're immortal, your skin will heal immediately. If you're not, it will heal at a normal human speed of recovery."

"Okay." Geraldine extended her hand. "Just do it fast."

"No problem."

Moving with immortal speed, Martha gripped Geraldine's hand and scratched it with her pointy ring.

"Ouch!" Geraldine pulled her hand back and covered it with the other. "That hurt."

"Put your hand on the table, Mom. Let's see how quickly it heals."

When Geraldine lifted her hand, there was no mark. It was as if Martha had never scratched her.

"It's gone." Cassandra lifted a pair of puzzled eyes to Martha. "Are you sure that you scratched her at all?"

Martha took a paper napkin and wiped her ring on it. It left behind a tiny blood-stain. "I'm sure."

Geraldine stared at her unmarred hand. "Whenever I got accidentally scratched or burned, and there was no mark, I thought that I imagined getting hurt. But I've just healed incredibly fast."

"Incredibly is right." Martha sat back down. "That was fast even for an immortal."

"What does it mean?" Cassandra asked.

"That means that your mother is genetically very close to the source." Onegus turned to Geraldine. "The less diluted your blood is, the faster you heal."

11

GERALDINE

*G*eraldine rubbed the area of her injury, trying to soothe the throbbing. "I don't understand what you're talking about. What is the source?"

"Perhaps Geraldine is like Wonder," Martha said. "She might have woken up from stasis one day, and then later met..." She stopped mid-sentence. "Cassandra's father," she continued. "Maybe she's from the gods' time."

"She's not," Roni said.

They were talking about her as if she weren't there, but Geraldine was too stunned to object. Besides, while they talked among themselves, she could think.

"Are you sure?" Cassandra asked.

Roni nodded. "Very. I checked."

Martha let out a breath. "Okay, so much for that hypothesis. Perhaps it was Geraldine's mother who was like Wonder. Do you have anything on her?"

Roni shook his head, then added, "It's also possible that the information was planted. I'm not the only super-hacker out there. But who would have the motive?"

Still thinking about Martha's strange comments, Geraldine barely registered Roni's about hacking. What did he mean by that?

Shaking her head, she turned to Martha. "What does the girl working at the café have to do with me?"

As one, they all turned to look at her, their expressions startled as if they'd forgotten that she was there.

"Wonder is ancient," Sylvia said. "She's from the gods' era, which means that her immortal genes are not as diluted as most of ours are. She probably heals as fast as you do."

"Gods' era? When was that?" Geraldine asked.

"Wonder is over five thousand years old," Sylvia said. "But since she was buried alive and went into stasis, she didn't actually live for five thousand years. She woke up not too long ago, and she also suffered from total amnesia. She regained her memories, though."

Geraldine shuddered. "Buried alive? Who did that to her?"

"No one," Onegus said. "It happened in an earthquake."

"Oh." That was a little less harrowing, but still. Geraldine couldn't imagine the terror the girl must have felt. "How did she stay alive for all this time?"

"Under certain conditions, immortals can go into stasis," Connor explained. "It's a form of hibernation."

"Do you think that it happened to me?"

"Or your mother, or her mother before her," Martha said. "That's still considered close to the source."

Roni seemed to be bristling, and Geraldine had a feeling that he knew something about her that the others didn't want him to disclose.

Did she want to know?

Perhaps later. Right now, she was already hanging by a thread and couldn't think about handling anything more.

Had Martha really scratched her? Maybe it was just another illusion? Perhaps they were trying to confuse her on purpose?

"You'll have to excuse me for a moment." She pushed to her feet. "Nature calls again."

When Sylvia started to rise, Geraldine waved her down. "I know the way."

On her previous visit to the bathroom, she'd seen a pair of nail scissors on the vanity top. She was going to use them to make a proper cut and see for herself.

After closing the bathroom door and locking it, Geraldine lifted the small scissors and debated how to do it. She could prick her finger, but maybe that wouldn't be conclusive enough. She needed a larger cut, but that was going to hurt.

"Don't overthink it," she whispered to herself. "Just do it."

Easier said than done. It took her another five minutes or so to gather the nerve.

Sucking in a breath, she dragged the pointy tip over her palm, making a long, shallow gouge.

It hurt like a son-of-a-gun, but only for a couple of seconds, and as Geraldine stared at the self-inflicted wound, she didn't even dare to blink lest she miss the healing process again.

The bleeding had stopped as soon as she finished dragging the sharp point over her palm, and right before her eyes, the skin was mending at a rate that looked as if she was fast-forwarding a video recording.

How had she never noticed that before?

How could she have gone through life not noticing things like that?

Could she had simply forgotten?

Perhaps her memory lapses had to do with things she couldn't understand and therefore had suppressed?

As Geraldine washed her hands and soaped the scissors, a knock sounded on the door. "Are you okay in there, Mom?"

"Yes. I'll be out in a moment. Do you need to use the bathroom?"

"I'm just checking on you. You've been in there for a long time."

"I'm okay." Geraldine put the scissors at the exact spot she'd found them.

She hadn't been gone that long, had she? What if her perception of time was warped, and that's why it had seemed as if the wound had healed so fast?

Geraldine lifted her hand and examined her palm. It was as smooth as it had been before the injury. No matter if only a minute had passed or an hour, it was still humanly impossible to heal that fast.

12

CASSANDRA

*W*hen Cassandra returned to the living room, Roni was still pouting like a kindergartner.

He wasn't happy about having to wait for another day to reveal his familial connection to Geraldine, but he had grudgingly agreed after Sylvia had talked some sense into him.

The guy's emotional intelligence had a direct inverse relation to his IQ, which meant that he was clueless. Anyone with a smidgen of empathy could see that Geraldine was on the brink of collapse.

In fact, Cassandra had been worried that she might faint in the bathroom, but she'd sounded fine.

"Is your mother okay?" Onegus asked.

"Yeah." Cassandra sat down next to him. "I think she needed a moment to herself."

"She's obviously close to breaking and needs to go home and process everything she's learned. I called Kalugal." Onegus glanced at the hallway before leaning closer to her. "He could have done it over the phone, but I wanted him to take a look at your mother. He was the one who unknowingly induced Eva, who is about the same age as your mother. Perhaps he induced her as well."

"Could that explain her rapid healing?"

Onegus shook his head. "It could explain an effortless transition that she might have not noticed, but not the healing. If she was very young at the time of the hookup, the transition might have felt like the flu to her."

As her mother emerged from the hallway, Cassandra reconsidered her earlier evaluation of her mental state. Geraldine looked ready to keel over.

"Do you want to go home, Mom? You look like you need to lie down."

"In a moment." Her mother sat on one of the armchairs, her little purse on her knees, her hands on its rigid handle, and her eyes staring into nothing.

Cassandra wasn't the only one who noticed.

37

Martha pushed to her feet. "Let me get you something to drink. I think strong coffee is in order."

Geraldine didn't respond.

That was bad. Geraldine didn't even babble, which was usually the first sign of her being anxious or nervous or just out of her element.

She'd gone straight to catatonic.

As Martha came back with the cup of coffee, a knock sounded at the door.

Connor opened the way, and Kalugal sauntered in. The guy looked just as dashing and handsome as she remembered from the wedding and Kian's birthday.

"Hello, everyone." His cultured voice somehow filled the space with renewed energy, and as Geraldine turned her head to look at him, he smiled at her and dipped his head. "And who is this beautiful lady?"

Did it mean that he didn't recognize her?

That was good news, right? At that stage, Cassandra wasn't sure of anything.

Her mother rose to her feet and took his offered hand. "Geraldine Beaumont. And you are?"

"Kalugal, Onegus's distant cousin."

"It's nice to meet you." Geraldine tried to pull her hand out of his, but he held on. "Come sit with me."

Kalugal's tone had carried a quality of undeniable command, but Cassandra wasn't sure whether he'd used compulsion on her mother. If he had, it must have been very gentle, which was good. With Geraldine's fragile mind, any sort of manipulation might have an adverse effect on her.

As Kalugal led Geraldine to the couch, she sat down and crossed her feet at her ankles.

Still holding her hand, Kalugal sat next to her. "So tell me, Geraldine. How did you turn immortal?"

"I don't know."

"Do you remember ever getting bitten?"

She shook her head.

"Did you ever dream of encountering a sexy vampire?"

Smart man. Many of her mother's fantastic stories had started as dreams.

Geraldine smiled. "I've read *Twilight*, but I don't like either of the love interests. Edward was made from marble and was cold, and Jacob was just a boy."

Kalugal laughed. "My thoughts exactly." He leaned closer. "I didn't like Bella either. She was too whiny." He smiled. "I love my hardheaded woman. My wife knows what she wants and when and how she wants it."

Geraldine sighed. "I love that song." She started singing softly. "I'm looking for a hardheaded woman. One who'll take me for myself..."

He leaned closer. "It's an old song. It gives away your real age."

"I don't know how old I am. Do you?"

"I know my age, but I don't know yours."

"Is there a way to find out?"

He shook his head. "Since our bodies don't age, we have no age markers."

"That makes sense."

Cassandra was happy to see that her mother had shaken off her stupor, probably thanks to Kalugal and his easy charm. Geraldine was a big flirt, and she always perked up when engaged by an equally flirty guy.

As Kalugal scooted closer, she either didn't notice or didn't mind. "You know that you can't tell anyone about us, true?"

Geraldine nodded.

"If you do, you'll put yourself and your daughter in danger."

"I know. Ever since I've noticed that I wasn't aging, I've been careful."

"Smart." He patted the hand he was holding. "But just to make sure that you don't accidentally tell anyone, I need to compel you to keep it a secret. You can think of compulsion as a stronger form of hypnosis. It's not going to harm you in any way, but it's going to keep us, you, and Cassandra safe."

"Are you asking my permission to compel me?"

He nodded. "I'd rather have your consent."

"I'm okay with that, but it's really not necessary. Who am I going to tell? My book club friends? They'll just think it's another one of my fantasies."

"Do you have many of those?"

She winced. "Regrettably, I do. Sometimes I have a hard time differentiating between what I've dreamt and what has really happened." She chuckled. "And what's worse, I feel compelled to tell people about it. So in a way, I know what compulsion feels like."

"Interesting." Kalugal smoothed a hand over his short beard. "Perhaps you should talk with a therapist."

Her mother's eyes widened. "I could never do that. What if the therapist figures out that I'm much older than I look?"

"You can talk to the clan's therapist. She's an immortal."

Geraldine's shoulders sagged. "Perhaps I will. But not today. I'm exhausted."

"Of course." He patted her hand again. "Let's get the compulsion part over with so you can go home to rest."

13

SHAI

*W*hen Amanda had called Shai, asking him to meet her at the café, he'd jumped at the opportunity. It wasn't because he was eager for the extra work, or because he thought that her idea to organize an impromptu party in honor of Allegra's birth was such a great idea, although it was, but because it had given him an excellent excuse to return to the café and get another look at Geraldine.

After learning about immortals, which Onegus had hinted was the reason for inviting Cassandra's mother to the village, she would probably be too shell-shocked to notice him, but he would settle for having another look.

When Amanda entered the café's enclosure, he rose to his feet to greet her. "Good afternoon." He pulled out a chair for her.

"Thanks for agreeing to help me." She kissed his cheek. "Everyone is so busy that I didn't know who to turn to."

So, he was the last one on her list?

That wasn't right.

"Thanks." He grimaced. "I was wondering why you asked for my help. You've never done so before."

She sat down. "Your job is too important for me to bother you with things like that, but my usual helpers are either guarding the guests or spending time with them. Without the Odus's help, Callie can't cook for seven hundred people. Do you have any ideas?"

"Of course."

He'd come up with several on his way down from the office. "Kalugal's men are not busy, and I heard that Atzil is a good chef. But an even better idea is to mobilize Jackson's resources. The celebration doesn't need to be a sit-down event with full catering. A nice selection of pastries would do, and Jackson has an entire factory full of people he can put to work on a rush order."

"Can he do that on such short notice? I'm sure he has other orders that he needs to fill."

"I've already checked with him, and he said he could do it if we let him know within the next hour or so."

"It's a go. Tell him to send the bill to me."

Pulling out his phone, Shai texted Jackson. "It's done. I'll ask Kalugal to assign several men to the task of organizing the tables and chairs and whatever else is needed. Where do you usually get your party decorations from?"

"I'll take care of the order, but I will need one of Kalugal's men to deliver it." She leaned back in her chair and smoothed a hand over her pregnant belly. "Are you sure Kalugal will agree to loan you his men?"

Shai smiled. "I can be very persuasive when I need to be. Kalugal is a smart man. He'll realize that doing me a favor means I'll owe him one in return."

"You're a lifesaver." Amanda waved hello at Wonder. "Not only with the party. You're keeping my brother from losing his shit, and we all owe you thanks for that." Smirking, she tapped the tip of her nose with a long-nailed finger. "Tell me the truth. Was it you who put those loungers on the roof for him to relax with his cigarillos?"

Kian, Amanda, and everyone else had been trying to figure that one out for months, and so far, Shai had managed to keep his part in it a mystery. But he needed information, and he was willing to trade his secret for it.

"I'll make a deal with you. If you tell me everything you know about Cassandra's mother, I'll tell you who put them up there."

"If you know, that means it was you."

Shai crossed his arms over his chest. "Suit yourself. But you'll never know for sure unless I confirm, and it's going to bug you."

"Fine. I don't know much about Geraldine, but I'll tell you what I've heard if you promise not to repeat it. I don't know how much she was told if at all, and I don't want it spreading all over the village and someone blurting something out to her."

He lifted his hand in a three-finger salute. "Scout's honor. Not a word to anyone."

Amanda leaned closer. "Did Kian share with you that Cassandra's mom is Roni's long-lost grandmother?"

Shai frowned. "He didn't."

Kian didn't keep anything from him, so it was surprising that he hadn't mentioned it. "When did he find out?"

"Tuesday. But it's not surprising that he forgot all about it, given what happened the following day. He had other things on his mind—Okidu's gift, Syssi's parents' earlier than scheduled arrival, and the birth of his daughter."

"Yeah, yeah, I get it."

Still, if Kian had found time to tell his sister and probably the rest of the family, he could have told Shai, the guy who'd been keeping him sane for the past twenty years.

"Anyway, Geraldine has serious memory issues. She suffered a head trauma before she had Cassandra, and she doesn't remember having an older daughter. No one knows what happened to her or how she turned immortal." Amanda chuckled. "Wouldn't it be funny if Kalugal induced her transition as well? She's about Eva's age, and maybe they attended the same college." Her eyes widened. "I bet no one thought to check that out. You should look into it."

"If I'm asked to help, I will. I don't want to butt my nose into someone else's business."

She laughed. "That has never stopped me."

As a prickle of awareness made Shai look up, he saw Onegus and the two ladies heading in his direction. Cassandra had her arm threaded through Geraldine's, and she seemed worried. Her mother looked pale and was leaning on her, which was probably the reason for Cassandra's pinched expression.

Without thinking, he rose to his feet and waved.

"Who are you waving at?" Amanda asked while turning to look over her shoulder. "Speaking of the devil. No wonder you wanted to find out more about Cassandra's mother. She's gorgeous."

When Cassandra waved back but didn't change direction and kept walking past the café, he rushed after them.

"Are you leaving already?"

Onegus nodded. "Cassandra and I still have work today."

Geraldine smiled at him. "Hello, Shai. What a nice surprise to bump into you again."

"Indeed." He stifled the urge to reach for her hand, pull her out of Cassandra's hold, and wrap his arms around her.

She looked so fragile. So lost.

Instead, he turned to Onegus. "Amanda and I are planning a party in Allegra's honor. If you can join us for a few minutes, we can provide you with the details. We also need your input as far as security goes."

It was true, but not the real reason Shai invited Onegus to join Amanda and him.

The chief was Geraldine and Cassandra's ride back home. If he stayed, so did they.

14

ONEGUS

*O*negus was glad to see Geraldine perk up. The woman was a harmless flirt, enjoying male attention even when it was as innocent as Kalugal's. No wonder her favorite fantasies revolved around Cassandra's make-believe father.

Perhaps those were daydreams? Or real dreams that her mind perceived as reality? Did she remember telling different versions at different times?

The good news was that Geraldine had tentatively agreed to see Vanessa, who might be able to figure that out. The bad news was that by tomorrow, she might forget she'd agreed to see the therapist.

Perhaps humoring Shai and joining him and Amanda at the café was exactly what Geraldine needed right now. It would help her shake off the shock of learning that her suspicions had been right and that she was immortal.

"Would you like to stay in the village for a little longer?" Onegus asked her.

"I would love to. It's so nice out here. The air is so fresh, and it's so quiet."

"Wonderful," Shai said. "Let me introduce you to Amanda."

Pushing up to her feet, Amanda smiled and offered her hand to Geraldine. "I can see the familial resemblance. Cassandra looks like you, and so does…" Thankfully, she'd seen Onegus shaking his head and stopped.

"So does who?" Geraldine asked.

"Never mind." Amanda waved a hand in dismissal. "You remind me of one of the actresses who starred in *Charlie's Angels*, the original series, not the movie. What was her name?" Amanda frowned. "It's on the tip of my tongue."

"Jaclyn Smith," Shai supplied. "One of the most beautiful actresses to grace the small screen. But in my opinion, Geraldine looks more like Elizabeth Taylor than Jaclyn Smith."

"You are right." Amanda gave Geraldine a once-over. "Like Taylor, you are petite and have a beautiful hourglass figure. You also have a similarly heart-shaped face with a delicate chin and sensuous lips."

"Oh dear." Geraldine fanned herself with her hand. "That's such a huge compliment and completely undeserved. I'm not nearly as beautiful as either of those actresses."

As everyone got seated, Onegus decided to give Amanda and Shai a short update about what Geraldine had learned earlier. "I'm sure you are wondering about what Geraldine knows, and whether it's safe to mention immortals in front of her."

Shai let out a breath. "That would be helpful."

Onegus looked at Geraldine. "Perhaps you want to tell Shai and Amanda what you've learned?"

She lifted a brow. "I don't know if I can. Kalugal compelled me not to say anything about the inhabitants of this place or even its general area."

"Good point." Kalugal hadn't included exceptions like Eleanor had done for Cassandra. "Geraldine suspected that she wasn't aging, but she wasn't sure why or how. Today, she finally got the explanation she was searching for. We didn't have time to cover a lot of ground, and things got a little overwhelming, so we decided to continue another day. So far, we covered what Dormants are and how their genes are activated, meaning fangs and venom."

Hopefully, neither of them would mention Roni.

He turned to Cassandra and her mother. "Did I forget anything?"

"You forgot the most interesting part," Geraldine said. "How quickly I healed and what it implies."

"Right." Apparently, Geraldine wasn't as forgetful as he'd thought. Her memory issues seemed to be selective. "It was only a scratch, but it healed so fast that it was gone in about a second."

As Geraldine turned to him, there was sudden confusion in her eyes. "Where is Martha?"

"She went to visit a friend," Cassandra said. "She hugged you and said goodbye."

"Oh." Geraldine touched the side of her head. "I forgot."

"You must have been distraught," Amanda offered.

"I was." She nodded. "Very much so. I couldn't believe that I've spent all those years denying what was right in front of my eyes. Whenever I got scratched, or burned my fingers on a hot pot, or bumped into something, I convinced myself later that it didn't happen, or that I imagined it hurting more than it had because no marks were left. How could I have dismissed all of that as lapses in memory?"

"Maybe that's the cause of your memory issues," Cassandra said. "Maybe the head trauma never happened. You couldn't reconcile what you were witnessing about yourself with reality, so you chose to forget the things that were irreconcilable."

Geraldine shook her head. "I remember the rehab center vividly. I stayed there for a long time."

"What if you imagined it? Or dreamt it?"

"I don't think so." Geraldine put her hand on the side of her head. "Sometimes, it still hurts."

"That's not likely," Amanda said softly. "The physical injury should have healed completely."

Geraldine nodded. "I know. It's like phantom pain. Like a distant memory of something that happened a long time ago."

"Speaking of distant memories," Amanda said. "Did Kalugal recognize you?"

"Why would he?"

Amanda smiled. "It has become a joke. He was quite active back in the day, so we thought that he might have been the one who induced your transition."

Shai's eyes blazed as he grumbled, "It could have been any clan member, or any of Kalugal's men for that matter, or even a Doomer."

Onegus nodded in agreement.

"When are you moving to the village?" Shai asked Cassandra, probably to steer away from the subject of Geraldine's possible inducer.

She cast her mother a worried look. "Not anytime soon. My mother needs time to process things before she can make up her mind."

"Move in here?" Geraldine's voice rose by an octave. "Living here is like living on the moon. I won't be able to invite my friends over or even tell them where I live. I can't do that." She turned a pair of panicked eyes to Cassandra. "And what about our house? Don't you love it? You worked so hard to be able to afford it."

Cassandra put a hand on her mother's shoulder. "Don't worry about it. We are not moving unless you want to. For now, we are just going to visit the village often and get to know our people."

Geraldine released a breath. "That, I can do. And if you want to move in with Onegus, that's fine with me. Just promise to come by the house at least a couple of times a week."

"We will take things one day at a time, Mom," Cassandra said softly. "I might need to stay over for a few days when I transition, but then I can come back home. Until you are ready to move, Onegus can stay with us whenever he can."

Cassandra's words must have gone over Geraldine's head because she just smiled and nodded.

"You have to come back on Sunday," Amanda said. "For the party. It's a great opportunity to mingle and get to know people."

Geraldine's eyes shifted to Shai. "I love parties. I'd love to come."

Mingling could be a good idea, but first, they had to tell Geraldine about her life before the amnesia. The problem was that she wasn't ready for that. The other option was to warn everyone who knew about the connection between Roni and Geraldine not to say anything about it in front of her.

15

SYSSI

$\mathcal{A}$s the door to the master bedroom opened, Syssi adjusted the shawl she'd draped over her shoulder, then let it drop when she saw it was Kian.

She'd escaped the well-wishers to breastfeed Allegra in peace, leaving Kian to play host.

The intimacy was precious. Syssi loved the little sounds of pleasure her daughter made as she fed, the feel of her tiny mouth and tongue on her breast, her little hands holding on. It wasn't something she wanted to share with anyone but Kian. Not even her mother, and not even Annani. Maybe later, when Allegra was a little older.

"Did more people show up?"

"Kalugal and Jacki."

She let out a breath. "It's tiring to host people while taking care of a newborn. I'm grateful for being immortal and needing only a little sleep. If I were human, I would have collapsed."

"Just say the word, and I won't let anyone else enter the house." Kian walked over to her glider and sat on the matching ottoman.

"We can't do that. Most of the guests are going home either Sunday evening or Monday. They want to see our little princess and wish her well."

"I'm amazed how well she tolerates it." Kian smoothed his hand over Allegra's tawny soft hair. "The sounds of conversation don't bother her. She just sleeps right through it."

As Allegra let go of Syssi's breast, uttered a cute little burp, and fell asleep, Syssi kissed the top of her head. "She is such an easy baby. Most feedings, I don't even have to burp her. She does it herself."

Adjusting her nursing top, she got up and put their daughter in the rolling bassinet that served as her temporary bed.

"Should I turn on the monitor?" Kian asked.

Syssi shook her head. "Let's wheel the bassinet to the living room. People are coming to see her, not her image on the screen."

"I don't care what they want. I want what's best for our daughter."

Smiling, Syssi lifted up on her toes and kissed Kian's cheek. "I believe that all the goodwill and love directed at Allegra is beneficial to her. I imagine her like a sponge, absorbing it all and getting stronger."

He wrapped his arms around her and pulled her closer. "I will never argue with your beliefs and gut feelings. You are the seer."

Kian hardly ever argued with her about anything, which sometimes made her uncomfortable. Everyone needed a sounding board, and not everything leaving Syssi's mouth was golden. The one exception had been his insistence on her refraining from summoning visions during her pregnancy. Initially, they hadn't seen eye to eye on that, but eventually Syssi had conceded that he might be right and that it was best not to risk it.

"Speaking of my abilities." She pulled out of his arms. "I need to call Madam Salinka."

"Not yet. You're breastfeeding."

Syssi laughed. "That has nothing to do with it, and you know it. But what I eat does. Did Okidu make lunch? I'm hungry."

Kian nodded. "He made sandwiches and is feeding our guests. By the way, Amanda had an interesting observation. She said that she watched Okidu during the visit, and he was very protective of Allegra."

"Of course, he was. I told you that we have nothing to worry about. Okidu is an asset, and I'm very happy to have him around. Did William make any progress with deciphering the journals?"

"Not really. He said that it would take him months, if not longer, and frankly I'm glad. If William finds it so difficult, no one else stands a chance. So even if someone somehow gets their hands on the journals, they won't do them any good."

"I'm not sure about that. William is brilliant, but he's just one man. A team of computer experts might be able to decipher the journals faster." She pushed the bassinet toward the door. "But we don't need to worry about it because the journals are safe in William's lab, right?"

"I definitely hope so." Kian opened the door and took over pushing the bassinet through. "I increased security in the lab, which was no small feat given how busy the Guardians are."

As they entered the living room, everyone lowered their voices, and Jacki rose to her feet. "Can I take a look?"

Right away, Okidu walked over to the bassinet and stood guard.

Syssi smiled. "Sure."

"She's adorable. I wish she weren't sleeping, so I could hold her." Jacki's eyes misted with tears. "Can anyone explain why I'm tearing up?"

"It's the damn hormones." Amanda sauntered over. "I cry over TV commercials."

From the couch, Dalhu nodded to confirm.

Kalugal walked over to his wife and wrapped his arm around her shoulders. "I think Allegra looks like Syssi." He turned to Kian and smirked. "Do you know about the silly betting that's going on at the café?"

"What betting?"

"There are two collection baskets. Those who think that Allegra looks like you put a quarter in one, and those who think that she looks like Syssi put a quarter in the other. The winning basket will determine whether the custom onesies they'll order will say Daddy's or Mama's girl."

"That's ridiculous," Anita said. "Allegra is a perfect mix of both her parents."

Behind her, Shai nodded. "I think so too." He walked around her mother and peeked at the bassinet. "The party in your honor is tomorrow at noon, but I bet you're going to sleep through it as well."

Syssi turned to him. "What party?"

He cast Amanda an accusing glance. "I thought that you spoke with Kian and Syssi about it."

"I've just gotten here. Same as you."

He shook his head. "It's not going to be a major production. Jackson is supplying pastries, and Kalugal's men will help set up the village square with tables and chairs."

As Syssi turned to Kalugal, he dipped his head. "I'm glad to be of help."

Heaving a sigh, Syssi plopped down on one of the chairs. "I don't want to sound ungrateful, but it's exhausting. Thank the merciful Fates that it's just one more day."

"When are you moving into your new house?" Amanda asked Kalugal and then looked at Syssi. "That's another reason to celebrate. We can have a housewarming party for Kalugal and his men."

"I hope it's not going to be for at least another week."

"Don't worry. It will take much longer than that," Kalugal reassured her. "I hired Ingrid to help us with the interior decorating, but she won't be available until all the guests are gone. She said that she can have our place furnished in two weeks provided that we accept her recommendations. If we choose fancier stuff, it might take months to get here. But once it's ready, we are definitely going to host a house-warming party."

Jacki sat in his lap and wrapped her arm around his neck. "I have an idea. Perhaps while we wait for our house to be ready, we can go on one of your archeological digs."

His eyes sparkled. "Do you really want to? It's not as exciting as it sounds. It's hot, there's lots of dirt involved, and most of the finds are insignificant."

"If it gets too hot, you'll take me to the hotel. I'm starting to develop village fever. I need to get out of here."

"I have a better idea. We can go to China and investigate the Mosuo people's connection to the Kra-ell. I've already contacted a local archeologist, and the guy applied for a permit."

"Smart," Kian said. "I doubt the Chinese would have granted a permit to a foreigner."

Kalugal smiled. "I can make them believe that I'm a local. I've impersonated Chinese businessmen before."

"Do you speak Chinese?" Syssi asked.

"I'm fluent."

Kian arched a brow. "Why didn't you mention that before?"

"I assumed you knew. Besides, I have no intentions of joining your team if that's where you're going with it. The Mosuo intrigue me, but I have no desire to chase after the Kra-ell."

16

GERALDINE

*W*hen Geraldine and Cassandra got back home, Geraldine went up to her bedroom, removed her pretty polka-dot dress and matching heels, took a shower, and got in bed.

"Are you going to be okay?" Cassandra stood in the doorway, the strap of her large satchel slung over her shoulder.

"I'm tired. I'm going to take a nap." She glanced at the clock on her nightstand. "It's after three in the afternoon. Are you sure that you need to go to the office? Can't you just work from home?"

Cassy sighed. "I wish I could, but Kevin wants to see me about next month's advertising campaign, and after all the time off I've been taking lately, I can't say no."

"Are you coming home after that?"

"Of course. Where else would I go?"

"Oh, I don't know." Geraldine pushed up against the headboard. "It's Friday. Isn't Onegus taking you out on a date?"

Cassandra shifted the strap to her other shoulder. "I think he exceeded his quota of time off as well. But if he can get away, I'll ask him to come over, and we can have dinner together. After you rest a little, I'm sure you'll have a ton of questions for him."

"It can wait until tomorrow." Geraldine stifled a yawn. "Enjoy your evening without me."

Cassandra eyed her for a moment before nodding. "We'll talk about it later. Call me if you need anything."

"I'm fine, Cassy." She forced a smile. "Stop worrying so much about me."

"I can't help it. You've learned some earth-shattering things today, and I really don't like leaving you alone when you are so emotionally drained."

"All I need is a nap, and I will be as good as new. I promise. Come give me a kiss before you go."

Cassandra lowered her bag to the floor, walked over to the bed, and gave her a tight hug. "I love you, Mom."

"I love you, my sweet Cassy." She kissed her daughter's cheek and then the other one. "If I'm still sleeping when you come back home, wake me up."

"I will." Cassandra kissed her once more.

After the door closed behind her daughter, Geraldine got comfortable and closed her eyes. She was mentally exhausted, but sleep eluded her.

Shai's handsome face kept popping behind her eyelids every time she closed her eyes. He seemed like such a nice guy, a really kind soul, and that was so rare.

She'd been with many men, most of whose faces she couldn't remember. There had been only a handful who she'd actually enjoyed spending time with, talking to, but no one had ever tugged on her heartstrings or made her want to build a home with him.

Those she'd enjoyed, like Emanuel and Luis, left behind fond memories, but she wasn't sure whether they were real. They kept popping up in her dreams, but she didn't know whether she'd actually met them or if they were figments of her overactive imagination.

Probably the latter because they were too good to be real. Handsome, charming, fascinating, gentlemanly.

With a sigh, Geraldine turned on her side and hugged her pillow. Maybe moving into the village wasn't such a bad idea. She had a feeling that Shai would be one of those males who would leave a lasting impression on her.

Maybe even more than that.

After all, he was immortal, so her secret was safe with him, and she was no longer raising a child, so there was nothing preventing her from having a lasting relationship.

Would Shai agree to meet her in the city?

Were immortals allowed to venture out?

Cassy could probably answer many of her questions, but she was gone and wouldn't be back until much later. But even if she was around, Geraldine was too tired and too confused to ask questions or make sense of the answers.

Perhaps the entire thing was another one of her fantasies?

She might wake up after her nap and realize that she didn't remember any of it, and then dream about it the next night.

It had happened to her so many times before. Entire days would disappear from her memory, and when she tried to reconstruct them, things didn't add up. She couldn't trust any of her memories.

Sometimes her dreams seemed more real than what she could remember of her life, especially those that were recurring. Like walking with Emanuel on the beach, or the cot in the fisherman's cozy hut, or the caring doctor…

Slipping into those familiar themes was like changing into a set of well-worn pajamas and hugging her favorite pillow. It was comforting, calming.

It was her happy place.

17

KIAN

"*T*he good thing about the party tomorrow is that the throng of visitors has dwindled." Syssi's father handed Kian a beer. "Whoever hasn't visited yet figured they would do so tomorrow."

"Thanks." Kian took a swig. "The sign that Anita hung on the front door was an effective deterrent."

It said that visiting hours were over, and to come say hello at the party. Syssi hadn't been happy about turning people away, but her mother had put her foot down, for which he was grateful.

Hopefully, Syssi had listened to Anita and was taking a nap together with Allegra.

"Onegus is on his way, but I'll talk to him outside."

Adam took a swig from his bottle and winced. "This stuff is strong." Nevertheless, he took another swig. "Onegus is your chief of security, correct?"

Kian nodded. "He couldn't be at the meeting this morning, and I need to speak with him."

Her eyes barely open, Anita walked up to Adam and leaned against his side. "I don't know about you, but I'm beat. I'm going to take a nap."

Adam put his beer on the kitchen counter and wrapped his arm around her middle. "The jet lag is still affecting us. Is Annani coming over later?"

Annani and Alena had spent the entire morning with them, but after lunch, Annani went back to her scheduled meetings.

"My mother and sister are visiting Edna and Rufsur, and after that, they are having dinner at Amanda's place."

Stifling a yawn, Anita covered her mouth with her hand. "If you don't need our help, Adam and I would love to catch up on some sleep."

"Of course. Thank you for all your help."

Anita smiled. "It's our pleasure."

When the two left for their bedroom, Kian let out a breath and headed to the backyard, where he could finally have a few moments alone.

He had just enough time to get comfortable on a lounger and light up the cigarillo he'd been craving all day long. As he took the first grateful puff, Onegus opened the patio doors and stepped outside.

"Good afternoon, Kian." He walked over to the other lounger. "You look tired."

"I am. Get yourself a beer from the fridge and come join me out here."

The chief hesitated for a moment and then shrugged. "My day is not over yet, but one beer is not going to affect me."

Kian wasn't about to argue with that.

A couple of moments later, Onegus returned with a Snake Venom bottle and sat across from him. "How did it go this morning?"

"The good news is that it will take William months to decipher the journals."

"Why is that good?"

Kian took another puff from his cigarillo. "Because we can take our time and don't need to decide anything now. Did you find out how Kalugal heard about it?"

Onegus shook his head. "There were no listening devices in the ballroom. After the first comb through, I had the place locked down and guarded, and the guys swept it again twice. He must have been eavesdropping on someone's conversation."

"The only ones who knew about it were at the meeting that morning, and no one remembers talking about Okidu's gift with Kalugal or any of his men close by."

"What about Jacki?"

Onegus shook his head. "Perhaps the Odus talked about it among themselves? Or maybe Onidu mentioned it to someone? You only told Okidu to keep it a secret."

That hadn't occurred to Kian, but it was possible. "I'll have Amanda check with him." He lifted his bottle and took a small sip. "What about Cassandra's mother, aka Roni's granny? Any progress with that?"

The sliding door opened again, and Syssi walked out, holding the baby monitor in one hand and a bottle of water in the other. "Hello, Onegus."

Kian stubbed out his cigarillo and scooted sideways to make room for her on his lounger. "I thought that you were taking a nap."

"I lay down for a little while, but I couldn't sleep. I wanted to enjoy a quiet moment alone with you."

"Should I come back later?" Onegus asked.

"I'm sorry." Syssi smiled apologetically. "I didn't realize how that sounded. I didn't mean you. I meant the never-ending throng of people wanting to see Allegra." She waved a hand. "Don't mind me. Keep talking about whatever you've been talking about."

"Cassandra's mother," Kian said. "She met Roni earlier, and Onegus was about to tell me about her reaction to the news."

The chief grimaced. "We didn't get to that. Learning that she was immortal and that we were as well was shocking enough for Geraldine. She didn't look like she could handle anything more. We decided to wait to reveal Roni's identity and give her time to absorb what she's learned so far. I asked Kalugal to compel her silence."

"Did he recognize her?" Syssi asked.

"He didn't, and none of his men recognized her picture either. Roni has already checked with all the relevant clan males when he first investigated his grandmother's disappearance, meaning those who were in the USA the entire period from the year Geraldine reached the age of consent and up until her supposed drowning. So, we know that her inducer wasn't one of ours either." Onegus cradled the beer bottle between his palms. "The only remaining explanation is an encounter with a random Doomer. But things get even stranger than that. To prove Geraldine's immortality, my mother scratched her to see how quickly she healed. It was much quicker than any of us had anticipated. Geraldine must be very close to the source."

"Damn." Kian had the urge to light up another cigarillo. "Do we know anything about Geraldine's mother?"

Onegus shook his head. "We need to question Roni's mother, but since she was only twelve when Geraldine supposedly drowned, she might not know much about her family's history. Roni's grandfather is another source, but from what I understand, he's estranged from the family."

Syssi frowned. "If Geraldine is close to the source, then so is Cassandra. Shouldn't she have transitioned already? When did you start working on it if I may ask?"

"At the wedding, which was almost a week ago."

"Maybe you didn't have enough time to bond?" Syssi asked softly.

"We bonded. Cassandra and I both felt it."

"Then it's probably going to happen very soon." Syssi wound a lock of hair round her finger. "Perhaps Cassandra's ancestress is a survivor like Wonder. It's possible that other immortals also went into stasis and woke up thousands of years later. Wonder said that there were no other immortal females in her caravan, but maybe theirs wasn't the only one that got swallowed up during the earthquake. There could have been others that Wonder didn't know about. I really need to start summoning visions again. There are so many mysteries, and it seems that I'm the only one who can find the answers."

"There are other ways to solve them," Kian said. "I don't want you exhausting yourself trying to solve all the clan's mysteries. Jacki has visions too. She saw Wonder's caravan go down after touching a figurine of her."

"Yeah." Syssi turned to him. "And that's another mystery we didn't solve yet. Who carved that figurine? I bet it was another survivor, one who knew Wonder when her name was still Gulan."

18

RONJA

*A*s Ronja pulled the chocolate cake out of the oven and put it on the cooling rack, Lisa bounded into the kitchen, her long ponytail bouncing from side to side. "Can I have a slice before I go?"

"It's too hot to cut. And where, may I ask, are you going so early on a Saturday morning?"

"It's after nine, so it's not that early, and I'm going to Merlin's."

On weekends, Lisa hardly ever emerged from her room before noon. "What's at Merlin's house?"

"He invited Parker and me to do an experiment. He has a whole laboratory in his kitchen, and he brews potions in there." Lisa chuckled. "You should see the place. It's like a mad scientist's lab and a college frat house combined."

Ronja narrowed her eyes at her daughter. "And how would you know what a college frat house looks like?"

Lisa rolled her eyes. "Movies, Mom. I live in a village full of immortals, and I'm driven to and from school either by you or by Parker's mom. Where could I have seen a real frat house?"

"I don't know." Ronja pretended to still be suspicious. "Teenagers are devious. You and Parker might have played hooky."

She didn't really think that they had, but it wasn't unthinkable. Parker was in love with Lisa, who pretended to be clueless and not to notice. The boy might go to great lengths to impress her.

"Parker?" Lisa chuckled. "Are you kidding me? He would never play hooky. He's so serious and straitlaced. He wants to be a Guardian like Magnus."

Ronja smiled. "Parker is a good kid. You're lucky to have him as a friend." And perhaps more in the future.

"Yeah, I know." Lisa glanced at her watch. "I'm late." She cast the cake a wistful look. "When will it be ready to cut?"

"It needs to settle for about twenty minutes and then go into the fridge for at least another half an hour. You can come back for it and bring Parker along."

"I don't know how long the experiment will take."

"The cake is not going anywhere. I'm not going to eat it all."

"You'd better not." Lisa kissed her cheek. "Bye, Mom."

Merlin's house was only a five-minute walk away, but Ronja had never been invited for a visit. The only time she'd interacted with the strange doctor was at Kian's birthday, when, out of the blue, he'd invited her to dance. It had been a surprisingly pleasant experience, and it had whetted her appetite to get to know Merlin better.

He was a doctor, so she knew he was smart, and his weirdness didn't bother her that much. Her first husband had been a little strange as well, and so had the other doctors she'd known back in the day. Perhaps not as colorful as Merlin, but they all had some oddities.

Perhaps that was something that afflicted super smart people.

During her short sojourn volunteering at a hospital, Ronja had been exposed to quite a lot of them, and then she'd gotten to know some of them better when she'd married Michael. There were the get-togethers in their house, the country club they'd all belonged to, and the conferences in exotic places.

Damn, she still missed those days.

The stupid dinner parties, the summer house, the trips abroad. If not for Michael's infidelity, it could have been a charmed life. She'd tried to live with it, and maybe if she hadn't loved him so much, she could have tolerated his philandering the way the other doctors' spouses had, male and female, but it had hurt too much.

Once David and Jonah had gone to college, she'd ended the marriage.

Ronja often wondered if the sleeping around was a professional hazard. Was it because doctors were such competitive people? Was there an internal engine driving them to do more, get more?

Most had Type A personalities and were difficult to get along with, many were conceited know-it-alls, and only a select few were motivated by a calling to save lives rather than the prestige and money.

Another possibility she'd pondered was whether dealing with sickness and death, day in and day out, prompted them to squeeze every ounce of pleasure out of life, with no regard for those they were hurting in the process.

The self-absorbed attitude probably afflicted successful people in other professions as well, but she suspected that doctors, especially surgeons, were worse than most. Pilots had a bad reputation as well, and probably for the same reasons. Theirs was also a demanding occupation with an aura of almost mystic proportions that only a select few were able to pursue.

The sense of superiority led to a sense of entitlement.

She shouldn't generalize, though. Her perception was probably colored by Michael's infidelity. It was easier to blame his profession than to consider the alternative.

Nevertheless, Ronja couldn't deny that she had a thing for doctors, even a quirky one like Merlin, who seemed to do everything to shatter the stuffy and self-important image his colleagues were known for.

Except, other than the two dances at Kian's birthday, he hadn't shown any interest in her.

Not that it was surprising.

She was an older woman living among immortals. How long did she have left before the last vestiges of her attractiveness were gone? Ten years at the most?

Not even that.

She was fifty-seven, which was awfully close to sixty. Why would Merlin want her? He might be God knows how old, but he looked as if he were in his early thirties, and despite his atrocious attire and crazy hair, he was quite handsome.

Still, he'd called her a pretty lady and had flirted with her shamelessly during the two dances they'd shared. What if he was waiting for her to make the next move?

Should she?

Eyeing the cooling cake, Ronja smiled.

Lisa had given her a great excuse for initiating a visit. Once the cake was ready to cut, she was going to take it over to Merlin's place.

As the saying went, the way to a man's heart was through his stomach, and her delicious chocolate cake was an express highway.

19

MERLIN

"My arms hurt," Lisa complained. "Can I take a break?"

Merlin chuckled. "Keep rolling and shaking. Otherwise, all the hard work you've put into making this ice cream will go to waste."

"I can shake both," Parker offered gallantly.

Lisa blew out a breath. "It's hard enough to shake one jar, let alone two."

"I'm an immortal already. I'm at least four times stronger than you are."

"True that." She handed him her jar and turned to Merlin. "I can't wait to become immortal. I wish there was a way to induce girls that didn't involve sex. Can't you make a potion that could do the same thing?"

As Parker's face got red, Merlin moved to block her view of him. "If I could, I would." Motioning for her to follow, he cut through his messy living room to the kitchen. "Would you like a glass of water?"

She cast him a dubious glance. "Do you have straws? I know that they are bad for the fish and all that, but how else is Parker going to drink? He can't hold the glass while shaking and rolling two jars at the same time."

Merlin doubted that Lisa's concern was about Parker's ability to drink. She could relieve him for a couple of minutes. It was probably more about the state of the kitchen in general and the dishes in particular. The pile in the sink reached all the way to the faucet, and there wasn't a single clean glass or plate in the cabinets.

"I'll fish out some glasses." Merlin reached with his hand into the soapy water.

"Careful." Lisa chuckled. "Something might bite you."

"Nah." He pulled out one glass and went back for more. "The detergent prevents bacteria from growing." He was about to launch into a scientific explanation when his doorbell rang. "I wonder who that might be."

"I'll get it." Lisa rushed to the door.

As she pulled it open, the first thing Merlin noted was the chocolate smell that overpowered the strong scent of bleach that he'd poured into the sink.

"You brought the cake!" Lisa exclaimed. "You are the best, Mom."

Merlin had just enough time to dry his hands with a dishrag, when the object of his desire, his daytime and nighttime dreams, walked into his living room, holding a baking pan with a chocolate cake inside of it.

Ronja was stunning, a slightly older version of Marilyn Monroe, including the blond curls, the pouty red lips, and a curvaceous body that made a male's imagination go naughty places—places it had no business going.

She was a human who was too old to transition, not to mention a grieving widow.

He shouldn't have flirted with her at Kian's birthday, but she'd looked so sad, and he couldn't help the urge to do something to cheer her up.

Big mistake.

Memories of those moments with her still haunted his nights and distracted him during the days. Holding her so close, his hands roving over the sides of her soft body, his nostrils full of her feminine scent, the sound of her laughter—

What was it about her that drew him to her with such ferocious need?

The long stretch of abstinence was probably to blame.

Merlin had been buried in his research, and other than taking breaks for Sari's wedding and Kian's birthday, he hadn't left his home lab in weeks. He wasn't as desperate for female companionship as some of the other clan males, but the latest stretch had been too long even for him.

"Hello." Ronja took a quick glance around and forced a smile. "I hope that I'm not interrupting. I thought that I'd surprise the three of you with a freshly baked cake. It was still hot from the oven when Lisa left, and she made me promise to save her a slice. Instead, I decided to bring the whole thing over."

Ronja sounded nervous, which caused Merlin's protective instincts to flare to life.

"It will go great with our experiment." He took the pan from her hands. "The kids are making ice cream."

Turning around, he looked for a place to put the pan down, but every surface was covered with either laboratory equipment or books.

Ronja must think that he was the worst kind of a slob, and she wouldn't be wrong. Normally, he hardly noticed the clutter and the thick layer of dust covering the things he didn't use often. But seeing it through her eyes made his ears heat up with shame.

"Here." Lisa moved a stack of books to make room on the table. "You can put the pan down." She scrunched up her nose. "I'll wash a few plates and forks."

RONJA

*M*erlin's place was a disaster. He and Parker were immortal, so Ronja wasn't worried about them eating in that filthy kitchen, but Lisa was still human, and she definitely worried about her daughter touching anything in there.

"Perhaps we should eat the cake at our house," she offered. "It's only a few minutes' walk away."

Merlin's face reddened with embarrassment. "We can eat outside. I think I have paper plates somewhere. Or we can use paper towels."

Lisa arched a brow. "For the ice cream? I don't think so." She headed into the kitchen.

Ronja turned to look at Parker, who was holding a jar in each hand and was shaking them vigorously.

"Five more minutes. Right, Merlin?" the boy asked.

"Let's see." The doctor looked at the substance that had coalesced in the jars. "That's about right."

"Here are the plates." Lisa walked out of the kitchen. "Sparkling clean. Do you want to wait for the ice cream to be ready? Or do you want to eat the cake now?"

"Let's wait for Parker to be done," Merlin said. "And then we can top the cake with the ice cream."

"Sounds good to me." Lisa put the clean plates next to the pan on the small table area she'd reclaimed from the clutter.

Merlin walked over to the front door and opened it. "When it's ready, bring a couple of chairs out. Ronja and I will wait on the swing." He motioned for her to follow.

The swinging loveseat was covered in dust, but that was nothing compared to what went on inside the house. The guy needed a live-in housekeeper or an Odu.

After Merlin had cleaned the thing with a corner of his lab coat, Ronja gingerly sat down.

He rubbed a hand over his long beard. "If I'd known that you were coming over, I would have tidied up a bit."

A bit wouldn't have done it. To make the place presentable, he would have needed an army of maids working all day long.

"I'm sorry I didn't call ahead." Ronja offered him a tentative smile. "And you don't need to apologize. I'm sure you have more important things to do than cleaning."

Heaving a sigh, he lifted his coattails and sat down next to her. "Back in Scotland, I had a lady who kept my house from falling into such a disgraceful state of disarray. She also cooked for me. Regrettably, that's not an option in the village."

"I didn't know that they allowed humans in the castle."

"I didn't live in the castle. Other than the very rare birth, there wasn't much need for my services there. I had a clinic in a nearby town and a cottage that I rented. I offered my services to humans, who actually needed them much more than my fellow clan members."

"How did you manage to hide that you were not aging?"

He ran a hand over his long beard. "This helped. It's hard to figure out a man's age when he's covered in white hair. But I also moved around. Every decade or so, I would close shop, go back to the castle for a little bit, and then open a new clinic in another town, claiming to be my own son or nephew. Some people suspected that I was the same person, and there were rumors about me being a sorcerer." He chuckled. "My unconventional attire and hairstyle contributed to the aura of mystery."

She laughed. "I bet. Is that why you dress like this?" She waved a hand over his purple pants and orange shirt.

He made a face, affecting confusion. "Why? What's wrong with what I'm wearing?"

"Nothing if you are color blind." She frowned. "Are you?"

"No." He put his arm on the back of the swing. "Color blindness is a genetic condition. The light-sensitive cells in the retina respond differently to certain colors. Depending on how sensitive they are to the wavelengths of light makes certain people perceive certain colors differently than others, or unable to differentiate between shades of the same color. Complete color blindness is very rare."

"Fascinating," Ronja breathed.

Did getting aroused by smart med-talk make her weird? And did Merlin know how sexy he was when he slipped into his lecturer mode? The intelligence, the confidence, the passion—those were the things she found most attractive in a man.

"Indeed it is." He grinned. "The intricate universe that is the body is a never-ending source of fascination for me. There is so much to be learned, so much we don't know yet." Regarding her with fondness in his eyes, he reached for a lock of her hair. "What makes us perceive beauty? Are we preprogrammed to find certain features more attractive than others? Is curly hair sexier than straight?" He wound the lock on his long finger. "Scientists would like to reduce everything to natural selection, the survival of the fittest, but not everything fits so neatly into the models describing evolution."

"How do you explain that?"

He leaned closer, his clean scent contradicting his disheveled appearance. "Chaos," he whispered conspiratorially. "Did you know that a chaotic system doesn't mean what most people think it does?"

It seemed that Merlin had figured out her weakness for smart talk and was exploiting it to the max.

"What does it mean?" Her voice sounded embarrassingly husky.

"Chaos is a dynamic system that just appears to be random, irregular, or disordered, but it is actually governed by underlying patterns, repetitions, feedback loops, etc. Chaotic systems are highly sensitive to changes in deterministic laws, which in layman's terms is called the butterfly effect. A small change in one state of a deterministic nonlinear system can result in large differences in later states."

Sexy, smart man. She wished she knew enough about what he was telling her to engage him in a stimulating conversation, but she'd understood only about half of what he'd said. "I'm afraid that went over my head. I heard the analogy of a butterfly flapping its wings on one side of the world causing a hurricane on the other side, but I don't know what it means."

"It means that it's impossible to predict the future because we live in a chaotic world. Every small change in the initial condition, even a tiny error in measurement, can produce wildly diverging outcomes. It's as true for the stock market and for traffic as it's true for the weather."

She let out a breath. "Perhaps it's also true for relationships."

"Now that went over my head."

Ronja chuckled. "Of course, it did."

Very smart people often lacked emotional intelligence. Michael had been a perfect example of a brilliant man who'd lacked the most fundamental understanding of human nature.

Merlin wasn't like that, though.

He was empathic and kind, and with some guidance, he could learn.

21

ONEGUS

*A*fter escorting the Clan Mother and Alena from Edna's house to Amanda's, where they were going to stay throughout their visit, Onegus felt as if a weight was lifted off his shoulders. They were back in the village, and they were not leaving until it was time for them to return to the sanctuary.

Thank the Fates for Amanda, who'd saved the day and invited them to stay with her. The original plan was for the Clan Mother and Alena to stay at Kian's. But after Syssi's parents had arrived earlier than scheduled, taking residence in Kian and Syssi's house, Onegus had feared that Annani would want to stay in the downtown building for a few days longer.

Amanda had made his job a lot easier by eliminating the need for the ramped-up security in the downtown building, which allowed him to leave Magnus in charge until all the guests went home.

Normally, Onegus wouldn't have cared where he worked, and his old office in the Keep was just as good as his new one in the village, but given the situation with Cassandra and her mother, he was grateful for the flexibility to spend more time in the village.

Geraldine was back home though, and Cassandra was at work, which freed him up to schedule a meeting with Ella, Jin, and Mey. Perhaps Ella could form a mental bridge between Mey and Morris, who was fluent in Chinese and Mandarin and could translate the echoes that Mey picked up from the walls, or even with Emmett, if the echoes were in the Kra-ell language.

When he walked into the café's enclosure, Ella, Vivian, and the sisters were already there.

"Good morning, ladies." He pulled out a chair and sat down. "I'm sorry for being late. I escorted the Clan Mother to Amanda's place, and it took longer than expected."

"No problem," Jin said. "We used the time to experiment."

"And?"

Jin shrugged. "We are still working on it."

"Not successfully." Ella sighed. "When I communicate with my mother, it's like talking on the phone. With others, it's just impressions and visuals. I can guess quite accurately what Jin and Mey are thinking, but I can't hear their thoughts."

That was disappointing to say the least. "I checked with Michael, and he said pretty much the same thing. He can get a better reading on humans, but with immortals he barely gets anything."

Jin leaned back and folded her arms over her chest. "There was a kid named Andy in the government program that was a strong telepath. I don't know if he'd be able to read immortals, or even if he can read actual thoughts, but I think it's about time we brought those people over. What's going on with that?"

The last report Onegus had seen about the government program had been a month ago, and he'd been too preoccupied to remember to check what was going on with those potential Dormants. Two of Kalugal's men and two Guardians were taking turns monitoring the facility at all times and communicating with Director Edwards, but since they hadn't reported anything new, he assumed that there was nothing to report.

"It got shoved down the priority list, I'm afraid. They completed their training a while ago, but with the changes the program has gone through, they haven't been dispatched on missions yet. The plan was to approach them when they left the government facility."

Jin frowned. "I'm starting to suspect that it was never about recruiting paranormals and training them for spying missions. That was probably only the cover, a way to get the government to fund the project. I think that Roberts and Simmons were only interested in their crazy idea of breeding super-humans, and that's why none of us was ever sent on missions. What better way to ensure that people hooked up than keeping them locked up together in a facility that was isolated from the outside world?"

Mey shook her head. "Then why keep it going? Roberts no longer has Eleanor to compel the couples to procreate."

"That's the whole point of what I was saying. He doesn't need to. If he keeps them isolated long enough, it will happen naturally. Who else are they going to hook up with?"

"Good point." Mey nodded. "So how are we going to get them out?"

"By now, they are probably being allowed to visit their families," Vivian said. "Can't we approach them during those visits?"

Onegus lifted his hand. "That's a discussion for another day. Right now, they are not a top priority. Finding the Kra-ell is."

Jin smiled. "For you, the top priority is Cassandra's transition. I heard that she and her mother visited the village yesterday, and that her mother is a confirmed immortal. What's the deal with that?"

Damn the clan's rumor machine.

Then again, he shouldn't be surprised. People had seen them stopping by the café.

"It's a long story. Geraldine doesn't know who induced her transition or even when. She claims that head trauma caused her amnesia and subsequent memory issues."

Jin lifted her chin and looked down her nose at him. "If you brought in the other trainees, Abigail might have been able to help. She's a healer who specializes in diagnosis. Spenser could read Geraldine's aura and maybe you could have gleaned some information from that."

"I get that you want to bring your friends to the village." Onegus sighed. "And I want that too, but now is not the time."

"Oh, look." Vivian smiled and waved. "It's Margaret and Anastasia. I haven't seen Margaret since she went into transition."

"Come join us," Ella called them over.

Resigned, Onegus got up and pulled two chairs from a nearby table. Evidently, today's meeting was not going to be fruitful.

As the two stopped by their table, Vivian asked, "How are you feeling, Margaret?"

"I am great. My knee is completely healed, and I feel like a million bucks." Margaret spun around to demonstrate and then sat down. "Wendy stayed with me the entire time. She'll be back to work on Monday."

"Good," Jin said. "Wonder wants to spend time with Annani, but she's stuck holding down the fort by herself."

Onegus pushed to his feet. "I'll leave you ladies to catch up. I need to get back to my office."

"Of course." Vivian smiled up at him. "I wish Ella could have been more helpful."

"That's okay," Mey said. "If the mission gets postponed again, I can double down on learning the languages, so by the time we leave, I might get good at both of them."

Jin snorted. "Yeah, right. You might be able to ask for directions and order a meal, but not much more than that. For some reason, we are both linguistically challenged."

22

GERALDINE

*G*eraldine reached the end of the page of her romance novel when she realized that she hadn't actually been reading. Her eyes had scanned the words, but her mind hadn't absorbed them.

Had yesterday's trip to the immortals' village been real? Or had she once again dreamt up something that had never happened?

It wouldn't be the first time or the last.

On the one hand, the memories were vivid and felt different than her other hazy recollections. But on the other hand, they were more bizarre than anything she'd been accused of making up before.

Except, this time Cassandra had been there, she had a witness, but the opportunity hadn't yet presented itself to bring the subject up casually.

Geraldine had planned on doing that last night, but Cassy had come back home late and had immediately gone up to her studio. This morning, she'd grabbed a cup of coffee and had gone back up to continue her work.

It was past one o'clock, though, and Cassy needed to eat.

Geraldine knew just the thing to lure her daughter to the kitchen. An avocado toast with a sunny-side-up egg on top was one of Cassy's favorites, and the smell of frying eggs might bring her down.

As the first egg landed on the pan with a satisfying sizzle, the door to Cassy's studio opened, and a moment later, Geraldine heard the patter of her daughter's bare feet rushing down the stairs.

"Good morning." Cassandra walked into the kitchen. "Or rather good afternoon. But since I didn't have breakfast yet, let's call it morning. Are you making avocado toast?"

"Indeed." Geraldine cast her daughter a smile. "I hoped that the smell would bring you out of your cave."

"It did." Cassandra pulled out a chair next to the kitchen table. "How are you holding up, Mom?"

That was a good but vague opening. "I'm still trying to wrap my head around what I learned yesterday."

"Yeah." Cassandra sighed. "It's not easy to find out that what you've suspected for years is true and that you are immortal. It sounds like fiction."

Geraldine let out a breath. "I wasn't sure yesterday even happened. Thanks for confirming it for me."

"Oh, Mom." Cassandra rose to her feet, walked over to her, and pulled her into a tight embrace. "It must be so confusing for you." She looked down and smiled. "You've always been so gentle with me. Even now, you're still holding me so softly. Give me a squeeze. I won't break."

Tightening her embrace, Geraldine kissed Cassandra's cheek and then pushed her away. "The eggs are starting to burn."

Cassandra frowned. "You didn't squeeze hard at all."

"Yes, I did." She turned the stove off and ladled the eggs on top of the two avocado sandwiches. "I squeezed as hard as I could."

"Unlikely. As an immortal, you should be much stronger." Cassandra walked up to one of the potted plants flanking the patio door.

"I can hardly move it." She crouched next to it, wrapped her arms around the pot, and hefted it an inch off the floor before putting it down. "Your turn. Try to lift it."

"Don't be silly. I can't lift that thing."

"It's just in your head. You think that you can't, but you can. Immortals are three times as strong as humans."

Geraldine eyed the plant. "Perhaps just the males are stronger."

"Just do it, Mom."

There was no arguing with Cassy when she was so adamant about something.

"Fine." Geraldine walked up to the pot, braced with her knees, and tried to lift it. The thing didn't budge. "I can't."

"Try harder."

She did, getting all flustered from the effort, and managed to move it a little, but not lift it. "That's the best I can do."

Cassandra frowned. "That doesn't compute. I need to ask Onegus if some of the immortal females are as weak as humans."

"First, let's eat." Geraldine washed her hands in the sink and sat down to eat her toast.

"Maybe they were wrong." Cassandra washed her hands as well and joined her at the table. "You were holding your hand, so I didn't see Martha's scratch. Maybe it was so light that it didn't break the skin?"

With a sigh, Geraldine put the sandwich down. "The same thing occurred to me, so I repeated the experiment. Remember when I went to the bathroom right after Martha said that I must be close to the source?" When Cassandra nodded, she continued. "I found nail scissors in there and used them to cut my palm. I made sure it was deep enough to bleed, and the wound disappeared right in front of my eyes."

"I don't get it." Frowning, Cassandra took a big bite out of her toast, and then another, until it was all gone, and she dabbed her mouth with a napkin. "You said that your other senses were nothing special either. Is that true? Or were you lying to cover up your oddities?"

"It's true. Maybe I'm a different kind of immortal, and my only superpower is fast healing."

"Or maybe you've been suppressing your supernatural abilities for so long that it became ingrained, and you can no longer use or even acknowledge them."

"I'm not aware of doing that."

Geraldine was getting tired of the whole thing. Of talking about it, thinking about it, being questioned. Couldn't they just go back to the way things had been before?

She was immortal, but nothing had changed about her other than getting confirmation and discovering that she wasn't the only one. It was a big deal, but it didn't mean that she had to change her life completely because of it.

She liked her life just fine the way it was.

Cassandra loaded the toaster with two more slices of bread. "Onegus told me that he sensed in you the same kind of energy that I have, just weaker."

"I'm not aware of that either." Geraldine finished the last of her sandwich and washed it down with a sip of water. "Are you seeing him tonight?"

Cassandra nodded. "I might spend the night at his place, but I'll be back early in the morning. I still have work that I need to finish before the party."

Geraldine wondered how long Cassandra would still make an effort to come home. She would be spending more and more time with Onegus at the immortal village and coming home less and less.

The thought made her heart squeeze painfully, but that's how it was supposed to be, and she shouldn't begrudge Cassandra her happiness. Children grew up and had a life of their own apart from their parents.

Maybe she should start planning for a future in which her daughter wasn't the pivot around which everything circled.

"What do you know about Shai?" Geraldine blurted.

"Not much. But you'll have a chance to talk to him tomorrow." Cassandra smiled knowingly. "He's quite handsome, and he seems to like you."

"I know. I hoped you had more intel on him that you could give me."

When the toast was ready, Cassandra dropped it on a clean plate and brought it to the table. "I was exposed to this world for the first time on Wednesday. I got to know quite a few people, but there are still so many I didn't." She smiled. "It's a whole village of people like us. If we move in there, you will no longer need to hide who you are or be afraid of someone finding out that you're not aging. You'll be safe."

It would be nice to live with no fear, but it would also be lonely. She had good friends that she didn't want to lose.

"I'll think about it. In the meantime, can you ask Onegus about Shai? I want to know the kind of man he is before I see him again."

"What's the fun in that? Get to know him and find out for yourself."

Hopefully, her daughter's smirking expression didn't mean that Shai had been planted by Onegus and Cassandra as bait to lure her into moving to the village. That would be very disappointing.

Geraldine liked the guy, and she hoped that he liked her back.

23

KIAN

The café was nearly deserted when Kian walked in and pulled out a chair. In the village square, Kalugal's men were arranging tables and chairs for tomorrow's party.

One of these days he needed to get Kalugal alone and coax him to reveal his plans. He could dangle the Odus's technology as an incentive, but he had no intentions of sharing it. If the journals contained breakthrough technology in other areas, he might throw a few crumbs Kalugal's way, but not enough to enable him to create an army of Odus.

Two sentient Odus were more than enough to keep Kian awake at night.

He had left Syssi and Allegra napping at home, with Anandur and Brundar hanging around just in case Okidu did something out of character. Posting them to guard his home had left a sour taste in Kian's mouth, and he would have never done it if it were only him in the house, but he wasn't taking any chances with his wife and daughter.

As he saw Amanda heading his way, he stood up and pulled out a chair for her. "Good evening." He kissed her cheek. "How are Mother and Alena doing?"

"Nathalie and Andrew came over with Phoenix, and they all went for a stroll around the village, which I'm sure Dalhu was thankful for. The poor guy ducked into his studio the moment they walked out. He's not used to having guests in the house."

"Say the word, and I'll arrange for them to have a house of their own for the rest of their visit."

She waved a dismissive hand. "Don't be silly. First of all, it's about time I hosted them for a change, and secondly, Dalhu needs to get used to having people around."

Kian chuckled. "Annani is not people. She can be exhausting."

"He'll survive. Tomorrow evening, she is posing for a portrait for him. I can't wait to see them spending several hours together. It's going to be exposure therapy for Dalhu. After that, Annani won't make him nervous anymore."

"Don't bet on it."

She shrugged. "Enough with the chitchat. You probably want me to get down to business so you can go back home."

"Syssi and Allegra are napping again, so I'm not in a rush."

She nodded. "I tried to get Onidu to cuss, and it didn't work. I even gave him a direct order, and he still refused, apologizing profusely for being incapable of obeying my wishes and repeating the words I told him to say. The only time I managed to get him to utter a cuss word was when I tricked him with words that sounded like it but were not."

"Give me an example."

"Clatter-fart."

"What's that?"

"A blabbermouth."

"Are you sure it's not a cuss word?"

"It's not. And neither is cockapert, which means impudent or saucy fellow. There is also cockchafer, which is a large beetle, dik-dik, which is a small antelope, and fuksheet, which is a sail that's attached to a ship's fukmast."

Kian laughed. "Where the hell did you find those words?"

"The internet." She smirked. "And I didn't get to my favorites yet—the ones Onidu refused to say even after I showed him the dictionary to prove that they were completely innocent."

"I can't wait to hear them."

"Sackbut, which is a brass instrument similar to the trombone, and skiddy-cock, which is a small bird."

"That's good." He laughed again. "And I don't mean as in funny. Evidently, Onidu is obeying his base programming even after becoming sentient."

She nodded. "I watched Okidu like a hawk the last couple of days, and he hasn't done anything suspicious. On the contrary, he's overly protective of Syssi and Allegra, to the point of being rude to those who come to see the baby."

"I've noticed." Kian sighed. "I wish there was a way to test it better than asking them to cuss. But it's not like I can command Okidu to punch a clan member to see whether my command can supersede Mother's programming not to harm her family."

"Right. But maybe you can tell Okidu that you declare him and his brothers official clan members, and then ask him to punch Onidu. They are equally strong, so the damage won't be significant."

"That's actually not a bad idea, but I need to think it through."

She huffed. "You shouldn't sound so surprised. All of my ideas are good."

"Naturally." He stifled a chuckle.

Some of Amanda's ideas were completely nuts, but he wasn't going to bring up the witchy ritual of dancing naked in the woods, for which she'd managed to rope a number of clan females, including Syssi.

Thankfully, his sensible wife had refused to disrobe, or at least that was what she'd told him.

"Where is William?" Amanda asked. "Wasn't he supposed to meet us here?"

"He was." Kian pulled out his phone. "I'll send him a reminder text. He probably forgot. The guy is obsessed with deciphering Okidu's journals."

"I'm not surprised. What's in them might revolutionize science."

William showed up ten minutes later, looking like he hadn't slept in days, which he probably hadn't.

"Sorry for being late." He pulled out a chair. "I lost track of time."

"So it would seem." Kian pushed to his feet. "Let me get you some coffee from the vending machine."

"Thanks, but I'm good." William motioned for him to sit back down. "I've been drinking gallons of coffee to stay awake."

"Any breakthroughs?" Amanda asked.

"I deciphered several of the symbols, but there are many more." He took his glasses off and wiped them on his shirt. "I know some of the gods' old language, but I'm far from fluent. I wonder if the Clan Mother would be willing to help me."

"I'll ask her," Amanda said. "She doesn't have the patience for technical stuff, but if you make a list of words, she'll translate them for you."

He nodded. "I know Annani hates dealing with anything that has to do with numbers, but I'm desperate for a shortcut. I can't wait to sink my teeth into this."

Kian put a hand on his shoulder. "There is no rush, William. Go home, get some sleep, and stop obsessing about this. I don't care if it takes you a year to decipher the journals. What's in them might be more trouble than it's worth."

24

MERLIN

*A*s a knock sounded on Merlin's door, he flung the thing open and grinned at his two helpers. "Good morning, my dear apprentices. Thank you for rising early and arriving ready for work."

He'd told Parker and Lisa to wear clothes they didn't mind getting dirty and promised them a hundred bucks each for their help.

Parker cast him a wary look. "Good morning. You said that you desperately needed our help. I hope it's important enough to drag me out of bed at seven in the morning on a Sunday."

"It is." He motioned for them to come in. "I'm in desperate need of reorganizing my living quarters, and I'm willing to pay handsomely for your combined efforts." He motioned at the new bookcases he'd gotten from the storage room in the underground. "I hope most of the clutter will find a new home in these."

Lisa eyed him from under her blond lashes. "Do you want us to move your stuff?"

Merlin could understand her confusion. Before, he'd told them not to move a thing without asking his permission first. His place might be a mess, but he knew where everything was.

"That too." He smiled sheepishly. "But to reorganize things, we need to clean up first. Or is it the other way around? I'm really bad at this."

Parker groaned. "I don't even clean up my own room, and you want me to clean this?" He waved a hand at the cluttered living room. "You need an army for that."

"I know. And you are it."

"What prompted the sudden urge to clean?" Lisa asked. "You didn't mind the mess before."

"Your mother's surprise visit made me realize the unseemly state of my abode. Frankly, I was embarrassed."

Lisa's eyes smiled with understanding, and that made him uncomfortable. She was just a kid, and this was about her mother.

"*Cherchez la femme*," the girl stated sagely. "If not for women, men would still be living in caves and wearing animal furs." She turned in a circle. "And here is the proof." She patted Parker on the back. "Come on. We can do it." When he arched a doubtful brow, she chuckled. "We can at least try to make this place semi-presentable."

"Thank you." Merlin bowed from the waist. "I'm in your debt."

"A hundred bucks is a generous payment, but you can throw in some chocolates from your stash as a bonus."

"Deal." He offered her his hand.

"Can I organize things any way I want?" Lisa asked as she shook on it.

"As long as it makes sense and I can find things with ease, it's your call."

She nodded. "It's going to take a while, and I doubt that we can be done before the party starts. It's at noon, and we will need to shower and change."

The party was the reason he wanted it done. Ronja was going to be there, and he intended to court her. If things went well, he would invite her to share a cup of tea with him after the party.

"I think the three of us can make it in four hours."

Parker looked doubtful, and so did Lisa. "Do you want us to do the rest of the house as well?" she asked. "Or just the living room?"

"I'll tackle the bedrooms and bathrooms. You do the living room and kitchen."

"Okay." Lisa clapped her hands. "Let's do it."

Leaving the kids in the living room, Merlin walked into his bedroom. First thing he did was collect discarded clothing from the floor and carry it to the laundry room. Next, he picked up all the sticky notes and other pieces of paper that he'd used to jot down his nighttime ideas and tucked them inside a nightstand drawer.

With that done, he looked at the bedding that hadn't been washed in Fates knew how long and then tackled it with gusto.

As he took off the duvet cover, his long beard got snagged on one of its buttons, and as he yanked on it trying to get it free, the button snapped, hitting his knuckle and bouncing off to roll under the bed.

Damn.

Merlin didn't want to know what was under there. He hadn't vacuumed under the bed since moving into the house. Twisting his beard into a knot, he bent down and reached for the button, but it had rolled too far under the bed for his arm to reach.

With a sigh, he pushed the bed away from the wall, uncovering a mountain of dust underneath. Thankfully, no roaches scampered from the clumps of dust, but some of it got on his beard.

Perhaps it was time to get rid of it.

The reason for growing it so long in the first place was no longer relevant, and neither was the waist-length hair, or the overly colorful clothes.

Many decades ago, he'd adopted the style as a costume, a persona he'd assumed while living and working among humans. Focusing on his odd looks, people hadn't noticed his other oddities, or had just dismissed them as part of his general weirdness.

Eventually, though, the look had become part of his character, and he had no intention of giving it all up and becoming a bore.

But perhaps he could tone it down a bit. He wouldn't cut off all of his long hair, but he could trim it and braid it or tie it back with twine. He hated shaving, so he wouldn't get rid of the beard entirely either, but he could trim it. The clothing he couldn't do much about without going shopping, but he could look for the few items that were free of stains, and if he could find the iron and the ironing board, maybe he could also give his slacks a quick press.

That was a lot of work just to impress a lady, but Ronja was worth the effort.

For the first time in a very long time, Merlin was interested in a woman for more than just casual sex.

She had an inquisitive mind and loved to learn. Heck, she'd actually gotten turned on when he'd explained things to her, and that had never happened to him before.

Most women tuned him out when he got going about science.

So perhaps he was being stupid for wanting to pursue a Dormant who was too old to induce, but Ronja was too good to pass just because she wasn't going to live forever.

Besides, he might find a way to prolong her life somehow.

After all, he was the potion maker, and despite what many of his kinsmen thought, his potions weren't a hoax.

25

ELEANOR

"*I* don't want you to leave." Emmett pulled Eleanor into his arms. "Do you really have to go?"

"I don't have to, but I should." She leaned into him and kissed him on the lips. "You're a politician. You should understand why it's important for me to attend this party and show that I care."

The truth was that she did care. Kian was a decent guy, and Syssi was one of those rare pure souls, or at least that was Eleanor's impression. She didn't know the boss's wife well, but she considered herself a good judge of character.

Not that she was infallible, but others thought the same of Syssi, so it must be true.

"When you are with me, this place is tolerable. I hate being alone in here."

Poor guy. He didn't look so good, and she wondered whether it was the lack of sunlight. He was well-fed and well-loved, but he didn't have room to move much, and the artificial illumination got depressing after a while.

She should talk with Kian about it. The government facility she'd lived in had a much better lighting solution, one that mimicked natural light, and the buildings also had windows that overlooked the wide central avenue. It hadn't been claustrophobic like the tiny, windowless apartment she and Emmett now shared.

"We'll talk about it when I come back." She kissed him lightly again and pushed on his chest.

With a sigh, he let go of her. "Don't flirt with anyone, and don't let anyone flirt with you."

She arched a brow. "So has spoken the guru of free-love?"

"That was the old me. The one who's never been in love and had no friends. The new me is a jealous alpha-hole."

Eleanor laughed. "Have you been reading Vivian's romance novels in secret?"

She'd brought a bunch of well-used books Thursday night, but Emmett had sneered at them, saying that he wasn't going to waste his time on romantic nonsense.

Looking sheepish, he nodded. "I couldn't sleep last night, and I wasn't in the mood for anything heavy, so I picked up one and intended to skim through it. Three hours later, I was still reading. I couldn't put the damn thing down."

"Did it get you randy?"

"I don't need smut to get aroused. I just found it fascinating on a psychological level. It gave me a valuable insight into how females think."

"You see? I told you that you can learn a lot from romance novels."

"Yeah." He smirked. "I learned that human females are confused about what they want. The heroine craved the dominant leader type, the alpha of the shifter wolf pack, but when he acted in accordance with his character, she called him an alpha-hole. She still had sex with him, though, and a lot of it, so I assume that she, or rather the author of the book, is attracted to these types of men despite their possessive tendencies and lack of charm and sophistication."

"Well, don't read too much into it. It's one thing to fantasize about a macho dude who's a powerhouse in the sack, and it's another thing to live with a jerk. I for one am not interested in alpha-hole jerks."

It was just slightly untrue. She liked assertive men, just not assholes.

Emmett grinned. "You should consider yourself lucky because you have found the perfect male. I'm a dominant leader type who is also charming and sophisticated and not at all a jerk."

She snorted. "And also so incredibly modest."

He looked her over. "I'm the best male for you. Remember that when the clan males swarm over you." He smoothed his hand down the curve of her hip. "You look too good to go to a party alone."

Her outfit was nothing special. Just a pair of skinny black jeans that hugged her curves, and a cropped, loose blouse that draped nicely over her breasts.

"Thank you for the compliment, but I'm not going alone. Peter is coming with me."

A soft growl started deep in Emmett's throat. "That's even worse. Don't fall for his we-are-just-friends act. He wants you."

Rolling her eyes, she tapped her nose. "He doesn't. If he did, I would have known, right?" She patted his shoulder. "Peter and I are work buddies. That's all."

"If you say so."

"I do. Read some more romance novels while I'm gone. You might learn something new."

As Eleanor opened the cell door and stepped out, she found Peter leaning against the wall with his phone in hand. "Ready to go?"

"I was waiting for you." He locked Emmett's door with the app. "You look good."

"Thank you. So do you."

"This old thing?" He waved a hand over his form-fitting dress shirt and slim jeans, then draped his arm over her shoulders. "Did you get Allegra a gift?"

She grimaced. "Was I supposed to? There was no time."

"I didn't either. We can stop by a toy store on the way."

"Are there any left? Everyone is buying everything online these days."

Peter pressed the elevator button. "As Anandur likes to say, you can find everything you need at Walmart."

2 6

CASSANDRA

On the way to the village, it got awfully quiet in the car once Onegus had exhausted his arsenal of amusing stories. Cassandra was in her head, thinking about the party and the plan to meet up with Roni at Onegus's place once it was over.

Perhaps they shouldn't mix the two and should wait to tell Geraldine about her forgotten family some other time.

That was going to be so much worse for her mother to hear than learning she was immortal.

Geraldine was so excited to go and had taken such care to look good, probably in hopes of meeting Shai again, that it would be a shame to spoil her good time. On the other hand, waiting with it felt like sitting on a ticking bomb. It wasn't a question of whether it was going to explode, only when. Perhaps the best thing would be to play it by ear.

Roni wouldn't like it if they postponed his big reveal for yet another day, but he'd live. Her mother's well-being was much more important than Roni's disapproval.

As usual, Geraldine picked up on Cassandra's anxious energy and got anxious as well. Any moment now, she would launch into another one of her stories as a way to cope with the uncomfortable feeling.

"Did I ever tell you about the fisherman?" Geraldine asked.

Did she know her mother or what?

Cassandra turned to look at her. "I don't think so. Was he my dad?"

Geraldine laughed. "No, silly. I met your father much later."

"So, who was the fisherman?"

"The fisherman was a good Samaritan. He helped me." Geraldine rubbed her temple. "I don't remember much, not even his name. I only remember him as the fisherman. Sometimes I get flashbacks, like sitting on the sand and watching the waves, or the cozy one-room cottage he lived in. I slept on a cot in front of the fire-place, and I felt safe. I don't know why I didn't feel safe before, though."

Cassandra waited for the rest of the story, but it seemed that was it. The ones Geraldine told about her supposed fathers were much more elaborate than that. Perhaps she was just starting on the fisherman scenario and hadn't worked out all of the details yet.

As her mother shifted in the backseat, her cotton skirt rustled. Today, Geraldine wore another fifties-style outfit. A white short-sleeved blouse with small pearl buttons in the front, and a bell-shaped skirt with big red flowers printed on a white background. A wide red belt cinched her tiny waist, and matching red kitten pumps adorned her small feet. The handbag was red as well.

"But enough about that." Geraldine sighed. "There is so much I still don't know about being an immortal." She looked at Onegus through the rearview mirror. "Cassy tells me that I should be stronger, and that I should see and hear better, but I don't. Do you know why that is?"

"I don't," Onegus said. "I should conduct a survey among the transitioned Dormants. Perhaps some of them didn't get stronger or get sharper senses either. All I know is that each Dormant is different."

"Why is that?" Geraldine asked.

He shrugged. "I guess it's because they have different ancestors. All of my original clan members are descendants of one goddess, our Clan Mother. The newly-found transitioned Dormants descend from different gods."

"Are any of the original gods still around?"

"Only two who we know of," Onegus said. "Annani, our Clan Mother, and Areana, her half-sister."

"What happened to the other gods? Did they go home?"

Cassandra found it interesting that her mother assumed the gods came from somewhere else, a faraway home. Geraldine wasn't into science fiction and thinking of the gods as aliens shouldn't be the first explanation that popped into her head.

"Regrettably, they didn't," Onegus said. "One powerful god declared war on the others and bombed their assembly with a weapon of mass destruction. Annani and her sister were the only goddesses who were absent from the city when the bomb eliminated their people, including the god who launched it."

"That's so sad." Geraldine sighed. "But maybe more gods were absent from that meeting, and they survived as well?"

Onegus shook his head. "The assembly was called to pass judgment on the rogue god. The judgment was passed, but then deliberations continued, and it was mandatory for all the gods to attend. Annani ran away, and Areana was on her way to wed that rogue god. That's how the two of them survived."

Cassandra turned toward her mother again. "If there were more gods out there, they would have probably left clues to their existence the way that the Clan Mother did. Some of the technologies we enjoy today were leaked to humanity by her descendants, and those gods would have recognized that."

"But if the clan lives in hiding, how would those gods have found it? From the little that you've told me so far, I gather that the gods are not omnipotent or omniscient."

Geraldine had a point, and Cassandra wanted to acknowledge that. "I agree with my mother." She turned to Onegus. "The clan had advanced technology only because Annani took her uncle's tablet, and it contained some of it. The other gods who might have survived didn't have it. Imagine that a catastrophe happens, like a solar flare that destroys our electrical grid, and for some reason all of humanity loses its memory except for the three of us. Would we know how to reconstruct all that lost knowledge?"

"We wouldn't," Onegus agreed. "But others that are educated in those fields would."

"Yeah, but did all the gods know how to build their advanced gadgets? I bet they didn't. In an advanced society, there is too much knowledge for one person to carry in their brain. People have to specialize. Those other surviving gods could have been artists, or historians, or musicians. They wouldn't know the first thing about putting together the simplest gadget."

Onegus smiled. "That's true. But our Clan Mother is convinced that no other gods survived. When she left the assembly, all the other gods except for her sister and the rogue god were present."

Cassandra wasn't willing to give up yet. "Perhaps she wasn't the only goddess who decided to run away. The idea might have occurred to someone else who followed in her footsteps. Some might have even been dispatched to find her."

Casting her an amused glance, Onegus took his hands off the wheel, and the computer took over driving the car. "We can play around with what-ifs all day long, but without concrete proof, it's an exercise in futility."

2 7

ELEANOR

"*Where* are they going to put all the presents?" Eleanor turned to glance at the huge teddy bear sitting in the backseat of Peter's car.

"Not our concern. They can exchange whatever they don't need. Besides, I bet not many will bring toys."

It had been difficult to decide on a present for people who had everything, so Eleanor had let Peter convince her to go for something silly—like the adult person sized teddy bear she'd ended up getting. He was cute, and if she had a daughter, Eleanor would have loved to put a giant teddy in the corner of her room, so she could sit in its lap when she was a little older.

Yeah. She would have a child right after she'd finished painting her picket fence white.

"What's the sigh for?" Peter asked. "Do you miss Emmett already?"

"I feel bad about leaving him alone." She turned to Peter. "Do you think Onegus would approve taking him to the pool and to the gym? I don't know if you've noticed, but he doesn't look good."

Eleanor knew that she would outlive Emmett, but even with his shorter Kra-ell lifespan, he was still too young to show signs of slowing down.

Peter cast her a sidelong glance. "He should be fine. We are feeding him according to what he said his nutritional needs are, and you are fortifying his diet with your blood."

She waved a dismissive hand. "He takes too little for it to make a difference."

The tiny sips Emmett took were part of their sex play and had nothing to do with his nutritional needs. They provided him with a quick boost, but that didn't last long. Perhaps if he took more he would get better, but so far he'd refused, jokingly saying that he didn't want her to get anemic.

Eleanor appreciated his concern for her, but it wasn't necessary. Her immortal body would replenish what he took in no time. Still, even if she managed to convince him to take more, her blood was no substitute for sunshine and physical activity.

"Emmett is wilting in that cell."

Peter grimaced. "You've negotiated the best accommodations in the dungeon for him, and that's still not good enough?"

Eleanor crossed her arms over her chest. "He needs sunlight. Even prisoners in high-security jails get to be outdoors every day."

"Immortals don't need sunshine."

"Our kind of immortals might not need it, but Emmett is different. We don't know where the Kra-ell came from. Heck, we don't know where the gods came from either. It makes sense that they are somehow related, but they are very different. I think that the gods came from a place with little light, and that's why they were so sensitive to sunshine. The Kra-ell seem to be more naturalistic. Emmett mentioned that they prefer to hunt for their food whenever possible. I bet they came from somewhere hot and sunny."

Surprisingly, Peter nodded instead of arguing like he usually did. "Emmett is olive-skinned and dark-haired. More pigment is needed to protect from bright sunshine. The gods and the Kra-ell could have originated in the same solar system but lived on different planets."

"Or maybe a planet with a locked orbit. One side always sunny, the other always dark."

"I see that you've been reading."

"A little. Do you think we can arrange for Emmett to get some sunshine from time to time? Maybe we could take him up to the roof and let him soak up some rays."

He looked at her from under lowered lashes. "Did you bond with him?"

"Not yet. Why?"

"Once Emmett bonds with you, Kian might consider letting him into the village. The mate-bond guarantees loyalty."

"Well, it didn't happen yet." She let out a breath. "It didn't happen with Greggory either, so maybe something is wrong with me."

"Greggory wasn't the right guy for you."

She arched a brow. "And Emmett is?"

He shrugged. "I don't know. You tell me."

"I'm not sure. Maybe the Kra-ell can't bond at all. Emmett was unfamiliar with the concept, so maybe it just can't happen between us."

"Would that be so terrible?" Peter asked. "Humans don't bond, and yet they form life-long, loving relationships."

"They also cheat on each other and get divorced."

"Not all immortal couples bond either. We were lucky so far, and I suspect the Fates had a big hand in it, but fated mates are supposed to be rare. In Annani's time, most immortal couples had arranged marriages. Very few mated for love, and out of those even fewer found their fated mates and bonded."

Eleanor huffed out a breath. "Figures that I would get the short end of the stick. I must have been born under an unlucky star."

"Don't say that." Peter reached for her hand. "Would it be so bad to just love and be loved because you and he chose each other?"

"I want the bond. I need it."

"Why?"

"Because I've been burned one too many times. I want to know that my chosen partner will never cheat on me, will never desire another, and will always stay by my side."

"I want that too, but I'll settle for finding love with a Dormant or an immortal who I'm not related to."

"That's your choice. But it's not good enough for me. I want it all."

28

SHAI

*K*alugal's men didn't need Shai's supervision, but they provided him with a handy excuse for hanging around the café and the village square while he waited for Geraldine to arrive.

"Is the angle alright?" Ruvon, Kalugal's tech guy, pointed at the big screen he and his friends had mounted on a moving scaffold at the east corner of the village square.

"Is it connected to the server?"

Ruvon nodded. "I tested it, and everything works. You have top notch equipment here."

"Put a video on. I want to take a walk around and make sure that the screen is visible from the entire square."

"Give me a moment." The guy cut through the grass to the equipment shed.

Kian was wary about parading Allegra in front of the guests, and the solution was to record her while she was awake, piece the clips together, and run them on a loop on the big screen. Syssi's father had volunteered to be in charge of the video recordings and the stills, compiling the assortment of images during the previous day. He'd promised that he would be done with the montage in time for the party.

The screen would also broadcast live interviews with the guests. Ella was in charge of that, together with her sidekick Tessa. After the party, Adam was going to make a montage of those as well. It would be a wonderful souvenir for Syssi and Kian, and also for Allegra when she was old enough to watch it.

As a music video started playing on the screen, Shai walked around the square, checking for blind spots.

"Turn the screen another five degrees," he told Ruvon.

When it was done, Shai gave the guy the thumbs up.

Was there anything else that could enhance the montage?

After all, this was Shai's first movie production, so he should put some more thought into it. Except, there was no time, and his mind was only half on the job he'd been tasked with. The other half was on a sexy new immortal whom he intended to charm the panties off at the party.

Shai chuckled. That was just a silly expression.

Even if Geraldine was that easy to seduce, it wasn't that kind of party. But she didn't look like the type who did hookups. She looked very prim and proper, like a debutant from the fifties. On the other hand, she was a mother, so she wasn't a blushing virgin like the girls he'd met in his youth.

He wondered how old she was. Did she even know?

Onegus had said that she was about Eva's age, which would be perfect because that made her only six years younger than Shai. But according to Amanda, Geraldine didn't know how she'd become immortal, and she didn't even remember having an older daughter. The woman probably had no idea when she was born. She could be any age.

Perhaps Roni's mother would know. If they were lucky, she might even have Geraldine's birth certificate.

Was Roni's grandfather still around?

Her family believed that she'd drowned, so even though her body had never been found, she had been declared dead, and her husband had become a widower.

Still, it was messy. What if Geraldine recalled loving her husband?

"Hey, boss." Atzil, Kalugal's cook, walked over to him. "Should I start taking out the trays? It's almost time."

Shai glanced at the buffet tables. The soft drinks were kept cold in buckets filled with ice, and one of Kalugal's men was standing behind the bar table and arranging glasses in neat rows.

Everything was ready. The tables were set with tablecloths, the chairs were slip-covered in white fabric with pink bows tied at the back, and the screen was in the right position. The only thing still missing was the montage itself.

Shai glanced at his watch. "The guests should start arriving in fifteen minutes. You can take the trays out but leave them covered until the last minute. I don't want bugs to get into the pastries."

"No problem, boss."

"Thank you, Atzil. Your help is greatly appreciated."

The guy waved a dismissive hand. "It's my pleasure. I wish I could have cooked for the event, but there wasn't enough time."

Shai smiled. "Next time."

Atzil lifted a finger and pointed it at his chest. "I'll hold you to that. For your next event, hire me instead of that stuck-up Gerard. He's good, but too frou-frou for my taste, and the size of his servings is a joke. A man can't get full on those tiny fancy dishes." He patted his washboard stomach. "I like hearty meals, savory."

Shai chuckled. "You sure don't look like you eat all that you cook."

"Oh, but I do. I burn it off weightlifting." He flexed an impressive bicep. "You have a nice gym down in the underground. You should give it a try."

"Someday I will."

"If you need someone to show you the ropes, I'm available. Until Kalugal's new house is fully furnished and ready, I don't have much to do. I used to cook for everyone, and now it's just my roommates and me, and Kalugal and Jacki." Shaking his head, the guy walked away.

The chances of Atzil finding Shai in the gym were slim.

Shai was naturally lean, and he wasn't into body building. His only form of exercise was walking around the village at night, and he didn't do it to get in shape. For some reason, his thinking process improved during his walks. He'd come up with many ideas for new storylines on his walks.

The problem was developing them into scripts.

His desk drawer was full of half-baked ideas and beginning pages of screenplays that would never see the light of day because they weren't the story that he needed to tell.

Until he got that one out of the way, he was stuck.

2 9

GERALDINE

*W*hen Onegus parked the car in the village's garage, Geraldine pulled a compact mirror out of her purse and checked her hair, her eyeliner, her mascara, and her lipstick. Everything looked just as good as it had when she'd left the house, but perhaps a coat of gloss was needed to refresh the color.

She pulled out the tube and brushed a thin coat over her red lipstick.

"You look great, Mom," Cassandra said as she opened the passenger door for her.

"Thank you." Geraldine took a deep breath and squared her shoulders. "It's important to make a good first impression, and I will be meeting many new people today." She smiled. "I'm a little nervous."

Cassandra threaded her arm through hers. "Don't worry. I'll be with you the entire time."

It was nice of Cassandra to want to shield her, but Geraldine had flirting with a certain handsome immortal in mind, and that wouldn't work if her daughter remained glued to her side.

"That won't be very productive." She let Cassandra lead her toward the elevators. "I need to find my own way among these people, and having you running interference for me is not going to do me any good."

"Let's play it by ear, then."

"Agreed."

As they walked out of the pavilion, Geraldine stopped to admire the transformation of the village square. Tables and chairs were set up on the lawn, white and pink colors dominated the tablecloths, chair slipcovers, the balloons, the banners, and every other piece of decoration.

"It looks so festive." She resumed walking. "I'm glad that we arrived a little early. Not many people have arrived yet."

In fact, it looked as if only the staff were there, and none of the guests had arrived.

"I needed to get here early." Onegus smiled apologetically. "I don't anticipate any trouble, but I need to check with my people in the security room."

While the two talked, Geraldine scanned the place for Shai. For some reason, she'd had a feeling that he would be waiting for her, but perhaps it had been wishful thinking because he wasn't there.

Cassandra kissed Onegus's cheek. "My mother and I will be fine. It's not assigned seating, is it?"

"It isn't. The party is buffet style, and it's not even a full lunch. There was no time to prepare anything elaborate."

Geraldine looked at the set-up and wondered what they would have done if there was more time. It looked fancy as heck to her.

"Go." Cassandra patted Onegus's arm. "We will find a place to sit and wait for you."

When he walked away, Geraldine scanned the area again.

"Are you looking for Shai?"

There was no reason to hide her interest. "I thought he would be here."

"Let's sit over there." Cassandra pointed at a table that was shaded by a tree. "The advantage of getting here early is that we can catch the best table. It's going to get hot out here pretty soon." She wiped the sweat off her forehead as she pulled a chair out for Geraldine. "I'll get us something to drink."

"Thank you. I'm starting to feel thirsty."

As Cassandra headed toward the bar table, Geraldine put her purse on the table and looked in the direction of the café where she'd met Shai at two days ago. The tables and chairs had been moved to the grass, and the place looked empty without them. No one was behind the counter, and the glass display was empty, but the vending machines in the back looked fully stocked with pastries and sandwiches.

She wondered how they were delivered to a secret village that no one knew about. The proprietor must be a villager, as must the two girls who worked there. But where were the pastries and sandwiches made? Was there a commercial kitchen somewhere on the grounds? And where did they get electricity and water from? To be hidden, the village had to be off the grid.

What was taking Cassy so long?

As Geraldine turned to look in the direction of the buffet tables, she saw her daughter talking with Amanda, the gorgeous brunette that had been with Shai at the café when Geraldine visited the place on Friday. The guy next to her looked like someone Geraldine wouldn't have wanted to encounter in a dark alley.

He was so tall that he probably needed to duck to pass through a standard doorway and also turn sideways because his shoulders were so wide. What had his mama fed him?

When the three looked her way, she smiled and waved, and when they started walking toward her table, she rose to her feet to greet them.

"This is my mother, Geraldine." Cassandra made the introductions. "You've met Amanda already, and this is her partner, Dalhu."

"A pleasure to make your acquaintance." Geraldine offered her hand to the enormous guy.

"Nice to meet you." He shook her hand with surprising gentleness and then pulled a chair out for Amanda.

"I love your outfit," Amanda said as she sat down.

"Thank you." Geraldine adjusted her skirt. "I thought it would be nice to wear something colorful for a summer party."

The truth was that she'd wanted to wear something pretty that would catch the attention of a handsome guy, who apparently hadn't been as impressed with her as she was with him.

30

SHAI

"That's good enough, Adam." Shai looked at his watch for the umpteenth time. "The guests are already arriving, and I have a huge screen in the middle of the village square with nothing on it."

"Give me one more moment," Syssi's father murmured. "I just need to align the beginning of this song with this clip, and then I'm done."

He'd said the same thing about the other ten clips.

The guy was frustrating the hell out of Shai. Talk about a perfectionist. Shai was an amateur compared to the retired sales rep turned nature photographer.

Apparently, they had a lot more in common than Shai had realized. Adam had spent his working years earning a living as a pharmaceutical rep, but his real passion had always been photography and cinematography. In his younger years, it had been a hobby, and Adam hadn't believed that he was good enough to make a living doing what he loved.

Now that he was retired and money was not a concern, he was working on a documentary that he and his wife were financing themselves and hoped to sell to one of the networks.

"It's done." Adam closed the laptop. "You can hook it up to your screen."

"Thank the merciful Fates." Shai grabbed the thing before Syssi's father changed his mind and decided to further tweak the montage. "And thank you." He rushed out of the office building.

Geraldine was probably already there, and he'd not only missed her arrival, but he also couldn't look for her until this last nuisance was taken care of.

"Here you are." Ruvon greeted him with his hands on his hips. "About bloody time."

"Wasn't my fault." Shai hooked things up and started the recording. "How does it look?"

Ruvon glanced up at the screen. "Good. What about the sound?"

"Coming up." Shai increased the volume. "Good?"

Ruvon nodded. "I'll take it from here."

"Thank you." Shai cast him a grateful glance before turning around and scanning the tables for Geraldine.

"There you are," he whispered.

She was sitting with Cassandra, Amanda, and Dalhu, and Shai didn't think twice before bee-lining straight for her.

"Hello." He pulled out a chair. "May I join you?"

"Of course." Geraldine beamed at him. "I thought that you would be the first one here, since you're the party organizer and all that. And when I didn't see you, I got worried."

Shai felt like he'd just gotten taller by an inch or two.

Geraldine had searched for him. She'd been worried about him. It looked like she was interested in him as much as he was interested in her.

"I had last-minute things to take care of. Allegra's granddaddy was taking his sweet time making a montage of her first days." He turned and pointed at the screen. "Behold, Princess Allegra."

Geraldine looked up. "Oh, how precious." She put a hand over her chest. "I wish I could hold her." She smiled apologetically. "I adore babies. If I could, I would have a dozen kids."

"You might get lucky and have another child," Amanda said. "Being immortal has its perks, but it also has a downside. Conception is rare."

"Oh." Geraldine's smile wilted. "So if Cassy turns..." She looked up at her daughter with wide eyes. "I can't say that word."

"You can say long-lived. That's what I did when Eleanor compelled me to avoid certain key phrases."

Apparently, when Kalugal had compelled Geraldine's discretion, he hadn't included provisions for when it was okay to say those forbidden things.

"Long-lived." Geraldine smiled. "Ha, it worked. So, what I was trying to ask was whether Cassy's transition into a long-lived person would make it difficult for her to conceive."

Amanda nodded. "Regrettably, the answer is yes. But we have a fertility doctor that came up with a solution that might help speed up the process. Personally, I don't get what's the rush. We are immortal, and time passes differently for us. Eventually, most females conceive. It just takes more time."

Dalhu took her hand between his paws. "The rush is necessary because the clan's enemies are procreating at a much faster rate."

"Who are those enemies?" Geraldine asked. "Cassy mentioned something about Onegus's family having dangerous enemies."

"That's a story for another time," Amanda said. "This is a joyous occasion. I don't want to talk about upsetting subjects."

Geraldine looked disappointed.

Perhaps this was his opportunity. "Would you like me to give you a quick tour of the village? I can tell you about these pesky enemies while we walk."

Her eyes brightened. "I would love that." She pushed her chair back. "How much time do we have before the official party starts?"

"Plenty," Amanda said. "This is a casual get-together, and the only official thing planned is Kian's speech and maybe Syssi's as well. But that's not going to happen until everyone gets here." She took a quick glance around. "So far, fewer than half of the guests have arrived, and it will take another hour until they are all here, seated at the tables, and ready to hear Kian's speech."

Thank you, Amanda. Shai cast her a grateful smile. "We will be back long before that." He offered Geraldine his arm. "Shall we?"

3 1

GERALDINE

*A*s Geraldine threaded her arm through Shai's, his scent washed over her, and she briefly closed her eyes. He wore cologne, but it was a mild scent, and underneath it she detected the fresh smell of soap and his own unique masculine scent.

She could tell a lot about a man from just that, but it had nothing to do with paranormal abilities. Geraldine couldn't detect emotions in his scent like Cassandra claimed she should be able to, but there were other simple things that any woman could deduce if she paid attention.

His cologne was good quality, but not one of those pricy numbers that cost as much as a mortgage payment, and he hadn't sprayed himself with too much of it either. That told her that he was modest but not cheap. The clean smell of soap indicated fastidiousness with cleanliness, which was not only attractive but also a requirement. She would never date a guy who failed the smell test. And the good natural scent he emitted meant that he was conscientious about his diet and didn't subsist on junk like so many single men did.

"Don't forget your purse." Cassandra lifted it and held it out to her.

"Can I leave it with you? It's pretty, but it's heavy."

The purse wasn't big, but the leather was rigid, and the handle was small and kept sliding off her slim shoulder. The only reason she'd chosen it for today's party was that it matched her outfit so well, and she wanted to look pretty and well put together for Shai.

He was a smart dresser, so he would no doubt appreciate a woman who was one as well.

"I can carry it for you," he offered.

"That's so sweet, but I can't let you carry something so feminine."

Reaching with his long arm, he snatched the purse off the table and hung it from the crook of his elbow. "I'm man enough to carry a lady's purse."

Dalhu chuckled, Amanda snorted, and Cassandra gave him a nod of approval.

"A true gentleman." Geraldine patted his arm. "Or is it gentlemale?"

She'd read a paranormal romance about vampires that used that term.

"We are part human, so we use the term male and man interchangeably." Shai started walking. "In fact, after so many generations of human fathers, we are probably mostly human."

Geraldine frowned. "On Friday, when Martha scratched me to see how quickly I healed, it happened incredibly fast. They said that it was because I was close to the source, and they also suggested that I might be like Wonder, who, thousands of years ago, went into something called stasis and woke up only recently."

Not sure whether her recollections were real or imagined, Geraldine cast a sidelong glance at Shai to check whether he was frowning or arching his brows.

"That's an interesting hypothesis," he said.

His lips looked so incredibly kissable that she wanted to stop talking, wrap her arms around his neck, and pull him down for a kiss.

But that wouldn't be very ladylike of her, and Geraldine wanted to leave a good impression. Shai wasn't like the random guys she occasionally shared her body with. Those fleeting encounters were necessary to satisfy the unrelenting hunger that refused to subsist on self-pleasuring alone. She didn't care much about what those men thought of her.

Shai was potentially a game-changer. Not only was he an immortal who she didn't need to hide her secret from, but he also appeared intelligent, interesting, and kind. In short, he was the kind of man she could see herself spending her life with, building a home with.

Being devastatingly handsome was just the cherry on top.

Up until now, she thought that men like him existed only in her fantasies.

Talk about getting carried away.

She'd only just met the guy, for goodness sake. All those good qualities she attributed to Shai might be the product of her wishful thinking. Before deciding that he was the one for her, she needed to get to know him better.

Shifting her eyes away from his handsome face and those perfect lips of his, Geraldine dove into telling him the rest of what had transpired at Onegus's house the day before. "Roni said that I couldn't be like Wonder, but I don't know what he based that on. Everyone took his word for it, though. Then Martha suggested that perhaps my mother or grandmother had been the ones who had suffered a fate like Wonder's. That would still qualify me as being close to the source."

"That's possible. If anyone can find out, it's Roni. He's an exceptional hacker, and he can get into any government server."

"That's not going to do him any good because he doesn't know my birth name, and I can't help him with that. I suffered total amnesia before having my Cassy."

Geraldine rarely shared that information with anyone, let alone a guy she'd just met. Even when she said it was the result of a head trauma, which was a physical injury, people assumed that there was something wrong with her mentally, and men scampered away. No one wanted to deal with a crazy woman.

"How did it happen?" Shai asked.

She lifted a hand to her head. "Frankly, I don't know. They told me in the rehab facility that my amnesia must have been caused by head trauma."

"That's actually a clue," Shai said. "You must have been induced after the rehab.

Otherwise, they would have seen on your CT scan that there was no physical damage left and would have assumed that there had been no injury."

"Now that you mention it, I don't remember them doing any scans. I don't think they had those machines back then." She smiled up at him. "When were those scanners invented?"

He halted and looked up as if searching for the answer in the clouds. "It was invented in 1967 by Sir Godfrey Hounsfield. The first patient's brain was scanned in 1971 in Wimbledon, UK, and in 1973 the first scanners were installed in the US. I'll spare you the rest of the history, but thirty-something years ago scanners were available and used to scan brains. They might not have been available everywhere, but with a severe head injury, you would have gotten one for sure."

Geraldine remembered Shai mentioning that he had a photographic memory, but she assumed it was for faces. No one could remember random details like that unless they were studying that specific topic for a test. "Did you look up the information after you learned about my injury?"

He shook his head. "I didn't need to look up anything. I never forget what I read. I can recite the entire article, which I read in 2005."

"Is that your special talent?"

"Photographic memory is rare, but it's not limited to immortals. Who knows? Perhaps humans who possess the ability, or rather disability, are Dormants."

"How can you say that's a disability? Take it from someone who can't rely on the veracity of her recall. It's a gift."

As understanding flashed through his eyes, Shai resumed walking. "We are not supposed to remember everything, but I admit that it has its uses. I had an easy time at school and at college. And since I read all of Kian's correspondence and go over every contract, I'm able to help him with details whenever he needs them. I'm better than the computer's search and find function."

3 2

SHAI

*A*s Shai had intended, Geraldine laughed. "I love it. Search and find."

The topic had gotten too serious, and that hadn't been part of his plan when he'd invited her for a walk.

Why had he done it? What were his intentions? To lure her into a secluded spot behind some bushes and kiss the living daylights out of her?

Yeah, kind of.

He'd promised her a tour, but he hadn't pointed out anything. He hadn't even acknowledged the people they were passing by, pretending that he hadn't seen their smiles and hand waves.

"What is it that you do for Kian?" Geraldine asked.

"I'm his personal assistant."

"Like a secretary?"

Damn, he hated when people assumed that.

"It's a little more than that. My job is to make Kian's easier. I read through contracts and prepare summaries to save him time. I even answer some of his correspondence for him, unless it's something that requires his attention and is above my pay grade."

"That sounds like a very responsible job. I hope your boss appreciates what you do for him."

"He does."

Nevertheless, Shai was a glorified secretary, and Geraldine was probably not impressed even though she pretended to be.

Would she be impressed if he told her about his screenplays?

Probably not.

A well-paying job was a far greater accomplishment than pipe dreams.

"What about you?" he asked. "What do you do?"

She shrugged. "I'm retired. I supported Cassy and myself by making quilts and selling them. Nowadays, I only make them as gifts."

"What do you do with the rest of your time?"

"I read, I watch television, I go out with my friends. I belong to three different book clubs."

"That sounds like a lot."

"It's a great way to meet new people who are interested in the same things as I am. I've made some very good friends." She looked up at him and smiled. "I didn't do any of that when Cassy was growing up. We lived in the city, and I kept a low profile because of my memory issues. I couldn't befriend people and let them find out that I had a problem. I was afraid Cassandra would be taken away from me. When she turned eighteen and started working, I joined my first book club. I figured that it was a good way to make friends, and if things didn't work out, I could just stop going to the meetings and find a new club. I was still making quilts back then, so I didn't have a lot of spare time, and that club met only twice a month, so finding time for it wasn't a problem."

Geraldine must have been so lonely during the years Cassandra was growing up. His heart ached for her.

"So when your daughter was young, you didn't have anyone to turn to for help if you needed it?"

"I had help." She touched her hand to her temple and rubbed it.

"From whom?"

"I don't remember. I just know that I wasn't all alone." She lifted a pair of sad eyes to him. "I might have made it up to comfort myself."

Once again, he'd made the mistake of diverting the conversation to topics that were upsetting to her, which was the opposite of what he wanted to do.

"You've done well. You managed to raise an amazing daughter. Cassandra is talented, successful, and she loves and appreciates you dearly. As long as it didn't involve murdering anyone, whatever you needed to do to make it through was justified. You are a survivor."

The truth was that she had killed someone—herself—and that had probably been in the name of self-preservation as well.

Geraldine squared her shoulders. "I guess you are right. God knows I didn't have a lot going for me. I might have been educated before the amnesia and could have had a well-paying job. But I had to relearn everything, including speech, reading and writing, and I didn't have any marketable skills. I had to support myself somehow, and the only thing I had an aptitude for was quilting, which I discovered in the rehab. The therapist said that I might have been a quilter before my accident and that I retained the muscle memory. But quilts are also a form of art, so maybe I was an artist before."

"That's possible. When did you stop making quilts?"

"When Cassandra got promoted and started making enough money to buy a nice house in a gated community, she didn't want me to continue selling my quilts. She wanted me to start enjoying life."

"And have you?"

Geraldine smiled. "Oh, yes. I made many good friends, and I have a rich social life."

That wasn't the answer he'd been interested in. She'd already told him about her friends and her book clubs. What he wanted to know was whether she had a boyfriend.

The answer to that was most likely a yes.

Geraldine was beautiful, sensual, passionate, and she wasn't shy. She'd probably dated many humans. Not that it was any of his business. He hadn't been celibate either, and those possessive feelings were uncalled for and quite disturbing. He wasn't one of those chest-thumping males who didn't know how to relate to a woman in any other way than dominating her.

He was a gentleman.

Geraldine smoothed her hand over her skirt. "I can also buy nice things now, which I couldn't afford before. But the truth is that I loved sewing outfits for Cassy and me. It was one more form of artistic expression."

"You can still do it if you want. In fact, you could go to fashion design school or art school. You have all the time in the world to pursue any path you may desire."

As long as it was a predominantly female faculty, he was good with anything she wanted to study.

Damn, he needed to stop thinking like a caveman. Even if Geraldine wanted to become a firefighter, he would somehow subdue the possessive beast and support her decision.

Right. When pigs fly and cows sing at the Metropolitan.

"I don't need to go to school for that. Cassy only took some online classes, and look how successful she's become." Geraldine pulled her arm out of his and took his hand. "The future looks much brighter now that I don't have to live in fear. It's such a relief to finally find out what's wrong with me." She chuckled. "I guess that what's right is more fitting. Immortality is not an illness or a disorder."

33

RONJA

$\mathcal{H}$olding a can of soda, Ronja scanned the tables looking for a glimpse of white hair and a splash of either purple, orange, or yellow, Merlin's favorite colors.

She needed to have a word with the doctor.

He'd summoned Lisa and Parker to his house for some project that had lasted only a few hours and paid them a hundred dollars each, which was a lot of money for a teenager, and she wondered what they'd had to do to earn it.

Lisa refused to say what the mysterious project had been about, but she'd said it had been absolutely necessary, and that Merlin would have paid much more if he'd hired adults for the job.

If he'd used them as guinea pigs to test his potions, she would have his head no matter how charming he was or how attracted she was to him.

"Come sit with us." Vivian waved her and Lisa over.

Magnus wasn't with his wife, which wasn't surprising since he was supervising the shuttling of guests from the downtown building to the village, but Parker was there, and so were Ella and Julian, Bridget and Turner.

"Hello, everyone." Ronja pulled out a chair. "Since two of the village's three doctors are here, I assume that there are no new patients in the clinic."

"Thank the merciful Fates." Bridget leaned her head on Turner's shoulder. "I was enjoying my vacation during the celebrations. I didn't expect to have a transitioning Dormant and a baby arrive the same night."

"How is Margaret doing?" Ronja asked.

"Great." Bridget lifted her head and glanced over her shoulder. "I saw her arriving with Bowen a couple of minutes ago. She looks amazing for someone who's just gone through her transition. I think she's the first patient I've seen who has gained weight during the initial stage instead of losing it."

"I'm glad to hear that." Pretending to look for Margaret, Ronja scanned the other tables and then shifted her eyes to the pathway. "Where is everyone? It's already twelve-fifteen, and the party should have started."

"There is no rush," Ella said. "It's an impromptu party." She pushed to her feet. "But I have a job to do, and I'd better get started. I'm supposed to interview the guests and record their good wishes for Allegra." She pulled out a microphone from an equipment bag that had been resting by her feet on the floor.

"Who wants to go first?" Ella asked.

Bridget lifted her hand.

As Ella tinkered with her equipment, Ronja glanced at the path again and nearly choked on the sip of soda she'd just drunk.

If not for the purple pants, she wouldn't have recognized the young man making a shortcut through the grass and heading her way. Still not sure it was Merlin, she reached into her purse for her glasses and planted them on her nose.

It was him alright, but he'd cut most of his mustache and beard off, leaving behind a neatly trimmed white-blond stubble.

The man was gorgeous, but whereas before she could see herself flirting with the doctor, or maybe even having a little fling with him down the line, she couldn't conceive of it now. Before, he could have passed for someone just a little younger than her. Now he didn't even look thirty.

"Is this the medical conference table?" Merlin cracked a joke as he pulled out a chair without asking anyone for an invitation.

"It is now," Julian said. "I like your new look. I might even let you in the clinic now that you are not a walking health hazard. That two-foot-long mustache and four-foot-long beard belonged on a wizard or a biker, not a doctor."

As everyone around the table murmured their agreement, Merlin turned his smiling blue eyes on Ronja. "I don't really care about the peanut gallery's opinion. I only care about yours. What do you think?" He smoothed his hand over his jaw. "Is it an improvement?"

Ronja was speechless, and that didn't happen often. He was flirting with her so unabashedly that it could seem as if they were already a couple, when it couldn't have been further from the truth.

Right. Tell that to her hormones, which had gone into overdrive when he'd talked about science stuff. It only occurred to her after the fact that he must have smelled her arousal with his damn immortal senses.

No wonder he thought that she was ripe for the taking.

It was so embarrassing. Then again, Merlin had made an effort to look good for her, so it wasn't as if he was taking her for granted.

But maybe it had nothing to do with her? Perhaps he'd just gotten bored with his old style and decided it was time for a change?

"You look very handsome, and also very young. What prompted the makeover?"

"You." He grinned like a cat about to pounce on the canary. "I wanted to look presentable enough for you to agree to go out on a date with me."

Ronja was afraid to look at her table companions, but since no one was talking, she knew that they were all listening.

She chuckled nervously. "You didn't need to chop off your beard to have coffee with me in the village café."

Leaning toward her, he took her hand. "I was thinking about a proper date. A restaurant in the city, maybe a little dancing. I heard that By Invitation Only has a dance floor and that the music is soft and romantic. Not the kind they play in clubs these days."

Fates, how was she going to wiggle out of it without embarrassing him in front of everyone?

"I don't know what to say," she murmured.

"Say yes."

She could go on one dinner date with him. Maybe it would be easier to turn him down when they didn't have an audience.

"Okay." She smiled. "When?"

His grin was triumphant. "I need to get new clothes, and I would love for you to be my fashion advisor. Are you busy tomorrow? We can go shopping, then we can catch lunch somewhere, and then we can come back here for a little rest and then go out again in the evening."

Bridget cleared her throat. "There is no way you can get reservations at Gerard's on such short notice, not even with Kian's clout."

As Merlin's grin turned into a disappointed frown, Ronja squeezed his hand. "Don't forget that I'm an old human. After a day of shopping and lunch in town, I won't have the energy to go out again. I will need at least three days to recuperate."

That was only a slight exaggeration. She would probably be good to go the next day.

"Then I'll cook dinner for you at home."

Lisa burst out laughing. "Oh, Merlin. You were doing so well. Why did you have to spoil it with that offer? You couldn't cook if your life depended on it."

Ronja had forgotten that her daughter was there, witnessing Merlin's courtship attempt and apparently finding it amusing.

Well, it was kind of absurd. Ronja was fifty-seven years old and looked like she could be Merlin's mother. There was no way she would go out with him on a date anywhere other than the village.

Merlin cast Lisa a reproachful glare. "Thanks for busting my cover. I wanted to get takeout and claim that I cooked it."

For some reason, Ronja hated to see Merlin disappointed.

It wasn't like it used to be with her first husband, the father of her twin older sons, the man she still thought of as the big love of her life.

Ronja had always been acutely aware of Michael's displeasure and desperate to gain his approval. He hadn't been an easy man to please, and most of the time, he'd been unhappy about one thing or another. Throughout their nineteen years of marriage, she'd done everything she could for the occasional fond look—anything that could make her feel as if they were okay as a couple. That he cared for her. That he didn't think of her as a nuisance.

With Merlin, it was different. It wasn't a need to appease him. The guy was so upbeat and positive that Ronja couldn't stand to see him unhappy.

"That's okay." She patted his hand. "You can come over and have dinner with Lisa and me. I'll cook."

Even if Merlin was the greatest chef, there was no way she could eat anything in his filthy house.

He shook his head. "I was so excited to spend an entire day with you that it didn't occur to me that it would be too tiring for you. I'll get takeout, and I want you to come over to my place." He leaned to whisper in her ear, "I have something I want to show you."

"What is it?"

"It's a surprise."

34

KIAN

*I*t was a good day, Kian thought to himself as he leaned back in his chair and looked over the festive village square. It was teeming with people, celebrating yet another happy occasion.

Naturally, the happiest for him was the birth of his daughter, which had miraculously coincided with his two-thousandth birthday.

The best birthday present he'd ever gotten.

In the distance, he could see Alena circulating between the tables where her children were seated. They were all scattered throughout the square, her daughters sitting with their children and grandchildren and great-grandchildren and so on. Her sons sitting with their sisters.

None of them were young, and all of them still lived in Scotland, which was one of the main reasons she and Annani had stayed at the downtown building. It had been a unique opportunity for Alena to spend time with her thirteen children all at once.

Most of the guests were leaving after the party, some the following day, and things were going to return to normal, or as normal as it ever got in his part of the clan.

Somehow, trouble seemed to stay away from Sari's part and routinely land on his doorstep, but since that was also true of blessings, he wasn't complaining.

So far, David was the only Dormant the Scottish arm of the clan had been blessed with, and Kian hoped it was just the start. But if the Fates demanded balance, and more Dormants meant more trouble, then maybe Sari could wait a little longer.

Her people were not ready to handle conflicts, and it was partially Kian's fault.

When he'd summoned the retired Guardians to join the war on trafficking, he'd depleted Sari's troop reserves.

They needed to revisit the idea of her moving her people into the village, and he planned to do it over the private family dinner he and Syssi were hosting after the party.

"Is the little princess going to sleep throughout her party?" Anandur said, pulling Kian out of his thoughts.

"It would seem so," Syssi said.

Oblivious to the noise around her, Allegra slept peacefully in her baby carriage, her angelic face turned toward Kian. He and Syssi tucked the stroller between their chairs, with the table blocking access from the front and Okidu standing guard and blocking it from the back.

That way, all of Allegra's admirers and well-wishers had to keep a proper distance, but they could still see her sweet sleeping face on the big screen mounted in the east corner of the village square. The screen was divided into two sections, with one running Adam's montage on a loop, and the other displaying Allegra in her stroller.

"You're blocking the camera's view," Andrew admonished the Guardian. "Your ass is filling half of the screen."

Anandur turned to look over his shoulder. "Sorry about that." He stepped sideways.

Syssi glanced at their daughter, her eyes full of love. "I can't believe that she's sleeping through all this ruckus."

"That's very good," her mother said. "She's used to hearing people talking around her from her time inside your belly, and it's comforting to her. Babies shouldn't be whispered around."

Pulling out Alena's vacant chair, Anandur sat next to Kian. "It's time for your speech. Everyone is here, and some of the guests need to leave soon to make it to their flights."

Kian nodded. "I need Alena and my mother to return to their seats."

"I'll get them." Anandur rose to his feet.

When he left, Kian leaned toward Syssi. "I want you to go first."

"Why? Because you didn't prepare a speech?"

"I never do. And if you cover all the bases, I'll take the microphone and say what-she-said and be done with it."

Syssi laughed. "No, you won't."

"Okay, so I'll thank everyone for coming and then add what-she-said."

Anita frowned at them. "Go on. I'll keep an eye on Allegra."

"Shouldn't we bring her with us to the podium?" Syssi asked as she got to her feet. "After all, everyone is here because of her."

"No need," Anita said authoritatively. "They can see her on the screen." She moved to Syssi's seat and put a protective hand on the carriage's handle.

"Shall we?" Kian offered Syssi his hand.

Smiling, she took it. "It reminds me of our wedding. All that's missing is a wedding gown and the song you chose for us."

"I can take care of the second part." He leaned closer to her ear and started singing softly, "I'm hooked on a feeling, I'm high on believing, that you're in love with me—"

As they got to the platform that had been erected under the big screen, Shai waved at them from his command center that was hidden between the bushes, and a moment later, the music stopped.

It took a few more moments for the gathered crowd to quiet down, and when they did, Shai walked over and handed Syssi the microphone.

"We are blessed beyond measure to celebrate the birth of our precious daughter with our beautiful, loving family and friends, who have cheered us on and supported us on our journey to become parents. Thank you all for joining Kian and me today on this most joyous occasion. A big thank you to Amanda and Shai for pulling off the impossible and organizing this party in two days. To my mom and dad, thank you for taking a break from your important work to be with us for Allegra's first month of life." She blew them an air kiss. "To Annani, the best mother-in-law I could have ever hoped for, thank you for creating this large, beautiful family and enabling this celebration in the first place. I love you all."

As the crowd cheered and clapped, Syssi turned to Kian. "To my mate, my husband, the love of my life, thank you for giving me the best possible gift, to love and cherish forever." She lifted on her toes and kissed him.

Their family and friends erupted in another round of cheers and applause, and when Syssi let go of his mouth and handed him the microphone, he turned and grinned at the crowd.

"I don't have much to add," he said. "My better half already said it all." It was slightly better than what-she-said. "Thank you for joining us in celebrating Allegra's birth. I hope many more are still to come, not just for Syssi and me, but for all of you."

As Annani stepped up on the platform, the cheering resumed once more, and when he handed her the microphone, they stopped, and a reverent hush swept over the village square.

"My children," she started. "It fills my heart with joy to be here today and welcome another granddaughter into the clan. Each of my children and grandchildren is dear, each one is special, each one is loved for who they are. May the Fates bless us with many more."

3 5

GERALDINE

"Isn't she magnificent?" Cassandra whispered in Geraldine's ear as the Clan Mother stepped down from the platform and floated away. "And to think that I thought she was an actress covered in glitter." She chuckled. "I must have been more drunk than I realized."

Geraldine smiled and nodded.

The goddess was indeed very beautiful, and her glowing skin made her spectacular, but Geraldine's mind was somewhere else.

She was walking on a cloud.

Actually, she was sitting, smiling, and pretending as if she were listening to the conversations going on around her. When the party had officially started, Amanda and Dalhu had moved to a different table, and Roni and Sylvia had taken their place. Another young couple had joined them, a guy named Nick and his wife Ruth.

Or was it his girlfriend?

It was hard to tell with immortals. They all looked young, and they all called their partners mates, which could mean many different things.

The last couple to join them was Sharon and Robert. Or was it Roger? So far, he hadn't said much.

Roni seemed tense, but Geraldine was too preoccupied with thoughts about Shai to pay attention to anyone's mood.

Regrettably, Shai couldn't join their table because he'd been called to assist his boss, but memories of their walk together were enough to keep her mind on his handsome face and his kissable lips and his gentle eyes.

Geraldine couldn't remember when she'd been so excited about a man, but that didn't say much, or did it?

Her foggy recollections of Emanuel and the other men who populated her dream world were pleasant. They gave her the impression of fun times, good company, and transience. None of it had felt as if she'd been in love or had bemoaned the relation-

104

ships ending. If there had been one to start with, it had been nothing but a summer fling, and one of those men had given her Cassy.

Which one, though?

She didn't know, which had turned out to be very fortunate.

At the time, Geraldine hadn't known that she was immortal, and if she'd included Cassandra's father in her life, he would have noticed that she wasn't aging. Instinctively, she must have known that she needed to keep moving around and avoid long-term relationships—romantic or otherwise.

Things were going to be different with Shai though, and not just because he was an immortal and her secret was safe with him. She'd felt the connection from the first moment she'd seen him, a sense of familiarity, which hopefully only meant that they fit well together and not that she'd met him before and had forgotten.

They'd exchanged phone numbers, and Shai had promised to call her.

He'd been called away to assist with the screening of the guests' well-wishing, so they hadn't had time to discuss the where or when or what. But the important thing was that he'd asked her out, and she'd said yes, and they were going out on a date.

Geraldine didn't care if it was as simple as a walk on the beach. She just wanted to spend time with Shai, and maybe get that first kiss she'd been so sure they were going to share but hadn't.

Several times during their walk, she'd caught Shai looking at her lips, and a couple of times she'd been certain he was going to kiss her, but regrettably it hadn't happened.

How disappointing.

If Shai still acted shy on their upcoming date, she was going to take matters into her own hands and kiss him for all he was worth.

"It seems like the party is winding down." Onegus rose to his feet. "I need to get to my office and check on the guests' transportation back to the downtown building and other locations." He put his hand on Cassandra's shoulder. "Connor can take you home, or you can stay at our house and wait for me to be done."

Geraldine wondered whether 'our house' meant Connor's and his, or had Onegus meant that it was also Cassandra's?

"How long will it take you?" Cassy asked.

"It might be a while. Probably until the last of the guests departs. It might be an hour or two. You have enough time to watch a movie if you like. Thanks to our Hollywood connections, we have all the latest releases on our server. Connor can show you the selection."

"Or I might entertain our guests with a little concert." Connor turned to Roni. "Would you and Sylvia like to join?"

"We would love to," Roni said a little too enthusiastically as if he'd been anxiously waiting for the invitation.

Something was going on with the young hacker. Had he and Sylvia gotten into a fight?

Connor turned to Ruth and Nick. "What about you?"

Ruth shook her head. "We'll take a rain check."

Cassandra turned to Geraldine. "It's up to you, Mom. Do you want to go home? Or do you want to stay for a little longer and listen to Connor play his compositions on the piano?"

Geraldine knew her daughter well, and Cassandra looked like she expected her to say that she wanted to go home, but the truth was that Geraldine was having a fabulous time and was in no rush to return home, especially since she had nothing planned for the rest of the day.

Besides, if she stayed longer, Shai would be done with whatever he'd been called away to do, and they might go for another walk. The kiss she so desperately craved might happen sooner rather than later, and she was impatient for it.

Well, not just that, but she would settle for a kiss. Good things came to those who waited, right?

"I'm having a good time." She smiled at her daughter. "Let's go to Onegus's house."

Cassandra nodded, but something that looked like worry passed over her eyes.

Roni let out a relieved breath. "I'm ready to leave."

Onegus leaned down and kissed Cassandra's cheek. "I'll come as soon as I can, but you can start without me."

Cassandra grimaced. "I'd rather wait for you."

"I don't want to wait," Roni said.

"It's not your call," Cassandra bit out.

For some reason, Geraldine had a feeling that they weren't talking about waiting for Onegus to watch a movie or listen to Connor's performance.

Something was going on, and she wasn't sure that she wanted to find out what it was, but she wasn't going to worry about it either. After all, they had already delivered the most shocking piece of information and also confirmed her immortality. What could possibly top that?

36

CASSANDRA

*C*assandra dreaded what was coming. She could have used Onegus's strength and reassuring presence to shore up her resolve, but he wasn't there, and she doubted she could drag things out until he arrived.

Hopefully, Connor's performance would take a long time, and when he was done, she could suggest a movie. The question was whether she could keep Roni in check.

With most people, it wouldn't have been a problem, but her nephew wasn't intimidated by her.

As Connor sat on the bench and flipped the lid up, Roni cast her a questioning glance.

She shook her head and mouthed, "Patience."

Thankfully, Connor had her mother's undivided attention, so she hadn't noticed the exchange.

"My most successful scores are in the horror genre," Connor said before playing a few bars.

Cassandra stifled a nervous chuckle. Had he done that on purpose? The short intro seemed perfect for the occasion.

"And this is from another movie." He played an intro that was even more chilling.

"I've got goosebumps." Geraldine rubbed her arms. "Music is such a powerful medium to convey emotions. Sometimes I think that the only thing separating us from the primates is our ability to produce music. It's a touch of the divine."

"Parrots and other birds can also make music," Cassandra murmured. "Are they touched by the divine as well?"

Her mother cast her a reproachful glance. "Maybe they are."

Roni humphed. "If primates had the right vocal cords, they would be singing as well."

"Singing is not the same as composing entire symphonies," Geraldine said. "Besides, who says that only humans and long-lived people are touched? Every living thing has a little spark of the divine in it. Even a blade of grass."

"I agree," Connor said. "But now I'll play for you one of my more upbeat compositions." He started a merry tune.

When he was done with the piece, he lifted his hands off the keyboard and dipped his head, as if he'd just performed on stage.

Everyone clapped, with Roni just going through the motions and Geraldine clapping the loudest.

"Which movie did you compose it for?" her mother asked.

Connor smiled. "*The Party Girl Next Door*. Regrettably, the producers didn't like it, saying it wasn't romantic enough, and made me compose something else."

"Wasn't that movie a comedy?" Cassandra asked.

"It was a romantic comedy with emphasis on the romance. I thought it was more funny than romantic, but what do I know. The producers have the final word." He turned sideways on the piano bench. "Can I make you something to drink before I continue to the next piece?"

"I would like some tea," Geraldine said. "But if you show me where everything is, I'll make it." She pushed to her feet. "Who else is up for tea?"

As Sylvia and Cassandra raised their hands, Roni crossed his arms over his chest. "I just want to be done with this, but I'll take a beer."

Cassandra glared at him, but Roni just glared back.

Impudent kid. She was his aunt, and he should treat her with more respect.

When Connor and her mother stepped into the kitchen, Roni walked over to her and leaned down. "You're not doing her any favors by dragging this out. Let's just rip the band-aid off and be done with it."

As the energy swirling under Cassandra's skin rippled in warning, she felt her forehead bead with sweat. "Don't push me, Roni." She dabbed at her sweaty brow with her sleeve. "I'm not in a good place right now."

Sylvia frowned. "Do you need to go outside and blow something up?"

"Not yet. For now, I've got it under control." She blew out a breath. "I just wish I knew how to do this right."

Roni chuckled. "I'll just call her grandma and give her a hug. How about that?"

"Is your grandmother coming for a visit?" Geraldine walked into the living room with a box of teabags.

"She's already here," Roni said.

Here it comes. Cassandra swallowed, wondering who was going to explode first, her or her mother.

"She is?" Geraldine put the box on the coffee table. "Why didn't she come to our table to say hello?"

"She did."

Her mother frowned. "Did I space out and not notice?"

Cassandra reached for her hand and gave it a tug. "I suggest that you sit down. Roni has something important he needs to tell you."

37

GERALDINE

*H*er heart pounding a wild drumbeat against her rib cage, Geraldine sat down. "What's going on?"

Roni sat on the coffee table facing her and braced his elbows on his knees. "You are my grandmother. Your real name is Sabina Bral, and you supposedly drowned thirty-seven years ago. Obviously, your body was never found because you are immortal, and you are right here with us."

For a long moment, she just gaped at the young man, waiting for him to say that it was a prank. But as his gaze never wavered and his lips never lifted in a smile, bile rose in her throat.

Impossible.

If she was the young man's grandmother, then his mother or father was her child, and it wasn't Cassandra. Geraldine wouldn't have forgotten the birth of her grandson. Besides, Cassandra was too young to have a son his age.

Roni looked to be twenty, or maybe twenty-one. He was an immortal, but that meant that he could be older, not younger. Cassandra would have been twelve when he was born. At that age, she hadn't even gotten her monthly cycle yet, so she couldn't have gotten pregnant.

Perhaps she'd been married before suffering the head trauma and her husband had a child from a previous marriage? A son or daughter who later had Roni?

The boy couldn't be her biological grandson. Geraldine would have known if she had another son or daughter. Even with the amnesia, a mother would have known deep in her heart, would have felt that something was missing, an unrelenting pain of loss.

She'd felt it often enough, but it wasn't an ache, it was just a big hole where half of her life had disappeared.

"You must be mistaking me for someone else."

"I have proof." He pulled a bunch of folded sheets of paper out of his shirt pocket and handed them to her. "See for yourself."

109

With hands that trembled, she took the pack and unfolded the pages.

They were photocopies of driver's licenses, and three of them she recognized because she'd bought them and had used them. They were under different fake names, but all had her picture on them. The oldest one, the one with the name she didn't recognize and a face that she did, that was the clincher.

Except, the face was hers, but it also wasn't. There were slight differences. Maybe it wasn't her?

"She looks a lot like me, but not a hundred percent identical. I don't think it's me."

"It is you." Roni pulled out another folded page and handed it to her. "This is a picture of you taken only a few days ago. I ran those from the three licenses and this one through a facial recognition software, and it confirmed that they are all of the same person."

Cassandra's arm wrapped around her shoulders. "Don't beat yourself up over this, Mom. Something bad happened to you, and you lost your memory. You had to relearn how to speak. How could you have possibly remembered who you were before the accident?"

Geraldine shook her head. "How could I have forgotten about having a child? Or children?"

Her eyes were filled with tears as she lifted them to Roni. "How old are you?"

"Twenty-two."

"Am I your paternal or maternal grandmother?"

"Maternal. You couldn't be my paternal grandmother. The immortal gene only transfers through the mothers."

"Oh." As she lifted her teacup, her hands shook so badly that the liquid swooshed from side to side, some of it spilling on her hand. "Is your mother here in the village?"

"No." He shifted his eyes from her. "I wasn't born into the clan. They found me and induced my transition. My mother is still a human, and my parents don't know where I am or what happened to me. They probably assume that I'm hacking for the Russians."

"Why?"

"It's a long story, and I'm sure you have more pressing questions that you want to ask me."

She did, but she didn't know where to start. A name might jog her memory. "What's your mother's name?" She couldn't refer to her as her daughter yet. She hadn't internalized it.

"Darlene. My mother's name is Darlene."

"Is…was I married to her father?"

He nodded.

A cold chill slithered down her back. Was she still married? "Is he still alive?"

"I don't know. I've never met him. The dude is or was a survivalist. One of those loons who live in bunkers and prepare for Armageddon."

"You're a hacker," Cassandra said. "You can probably find out if he's still alive, right?"

"Not if he lives off the grid like those loons usually do. They might not report deaths."

"What's his name?" Geraldine asked. "Maybe it will jog my memory."

Roni scratched his head. "Rupert, or Rudolf, or Randolph. Something like that. I don't remember, but I can find out."

None of the names evoked any emotion from her.

"How old is your mother?"

"She's forty-nine. She was twelve when you drowned."

Geraldine shook her head. "Nothing sounds even vaguely familiar. Can you tell me more?"

Roni let out a breath. "I don't know much. I have family photos if you want to look at them. My parents scanned all the old photos and uploaded them to the cloud, so I was able to download them. There is one picture from your wedding, and several pictures of you with my mother."

Geraldine wasn't ready for that. As long as she didn't look at the pictures, she could cling to the illusion that none of it was real.

"Does your mother have any siblings? Did her father remarry?"

"No to the first one, and I don't know the answer to the second. My mother didn't talk about him."

"Did she talk about me?"

He nodded. "She told me that you were a gifted quilter. Some of your quilts hang in our house, and others she kept in a box and aired twice a year when she did her big cleaning."

Some of the heaviness in Geraldine's heart eased. At least her daughter remembered her fondly.

"How is she? I mean, does she look anything like Cassandra or me? Is she a good person?"

"Let me show you the pictures." He pulled out his phone and started scrolling. "Darlene looks a little bit like you, but she's not as pretty. I guess she's an okay person, but she and I never got along." He handed her the phone. "Although some of it might have been my fault. I wasn't an easy kid to deal with."

As Geraldine didn't make a move to take the device, Cassandra reached for it. "I didn't see the pictures yet. Roni mentioned them when he first told me that you were his grandmother."

Cassandra had known and hadn't said a thing?

How could she?

The sense of betrayal left a sour taste in Geraldine's mouth. "How long have you known?"

Cassandra averted her eyes. "Since Tuesday. Onegus suspected that you were immortal. He sent Roni your picture, the one taken at the restaurant, to run through facial recognition software. Roni recognized you right away. By then, he'd been searching for you for years, ever since he'd discovered the different driver's licenses with your picture on them and realized that you were alive and still looked the same decades later. The discovery that his grandmother was an immortal was how the clan knew for sure that Roni had the immortal gene and could be induced."

Geraldine understood only bits and pieces of the information dump, and what she did was confusing.

"How did they find Roni in the first place?" She turned to Cassandra. "How did Onegus find you?"

"I already told you how we met. It was at the charity gala."

Geraldine wasn't sure she believed that. Cassandra had sat on what she'd found out for days. What else was she hiding?

She closed her eyes. "I don't know what to believe anymore."

3 8

CASSANDRA

*C*assandra clasped her mother's hand. "I didn't tell you right away because I knew how hard it would be for you to discover that you had a daughter who you don't remember. I wanted to ease you into it. The plan was to tell you everything on Friday, which was why Roni and Sylvia were here. But you were so rattled after learning that you're immortal that I decided to wait. I wasn't even going to tell you today, but Roni was impatient." She cast him a reproachful look. "His empathy needs some work."

As Geraldine squeezed her hand in silent forgiveness, the front door opened and Onegus walked in.

"I came as soon as I could." It took him one look at Geraldine and her to realize that he was late for the big reveal. "Can I offer anyone a glass of wine?"

Her mother lifted her eyes to him. "I would appreciate it. Thank you."

"Does wine affect you?" Roni asked. "Because it shouldn't. Immortals metabolize alcohol quickly."

She shrugged. "I like the taste, and since I never tried to get drunk, I didn't expect anything else." Glancing at the phone in Cassandra's other hand, she made no move to reach for it.

"I think you should look at the pictures." Cassandra offered her the device. "Maybe they will jog your memory."

Geraldine nodded. "Let's do it together."

Onegus returned with two bottles of wine, and Connor brought the wine glasses. He passed them around, and then Onegus did the pouring.

As Geraldine lifted hers with a hand that still shook, Cassandra patted her knee. "Are you okay?"

"Not really, but let's see those pictures. Maybe something will pierce the veil and release those memories." She lifted her other hand to her temple. "I want to believe that they are still there, and that I just can't access them. That gives me hope that one day my mind will heal, and I'll remember my life before the accident."

Unless the amnesia was mental rather than physical, her mother's memories were most likely gone forever. But Cassandra wasn't going to say that. Hope was a powerful thing, and taking it away could have a devastating effect.

She shifted her gaze to Roni. "Is the phone locked?"

"I disabled the lock before handing it over. You can just open it."

Sylvia cast him a curious look. "You never unlock your phone, not even for me."

He smirked. "Are you jealous? Do you think that I'm hiding messages from secret girlfriends?"

Her lips twitching with a suppressed smile, she crossed her arms over her chest and pretended to glare at him. "You'd better not."

Leaning over, he kissed her smack on the lips. "You know where I am every minute of the day. Besides, we are bonded mates. It is virtually impossible for me to even think of another. Not that I ever would. I have the best of the best."

Watching the exchange, Geraldine sighed. "That's so sweet."

Provided that it was genuine, it really was. If Cassandra had witnessed a similar thing in the human world, she would have rolled her eyes and called it fake. Immortals were different, but she still wasn't sure if the bond was a good thing or a crutch.

Fidelity should be a choice.

Cassandra wrapped her arm around her mother's shoulders, opened the phone, and together they leaned back against the soft couch cushions.

She was curious to see what her sister looked like, but the picture Roni cued to be the first was of her mother and Roni's grandfather on their wedding day. Except for the sixties hairdo, Geraldine looked exactly the same as she did now.

The groom was tall and gangly and looked a lot like Roni.

"Anything?" Cassandra asked.

Geraldine shook her head. "Absolutely nothing. It's like looking at a stranger."

Cassandra didn't know if her mother was referring to herself or to her husband, but she didn't ask. Instead, she flipped to the next picture, which was her sister as a baby.

"Cute." She cast her mother a sidelong glance to check her response, but there was none. She flipped to the next one. Darlene was about five in the picture, and she didn't look like a happy kid.

"She looks like Roni," her mother murmured.

It was true. Her sister had the same expression that was at once sad, angry, and condescending.

The next picture was of her mother and sister on the beach. Darlene was about seven, and both mother and daughter were smiling and looked happy.

"That's a nice picture," Geraldine said. "But it still feels like looking at strangers, except one of them is my doppelgänger." She lifted her head and looked at Cassandra. "Maybe I had a twin sister? An identical twin who really drowned?"

As all eyes turned to Roni, he nodded. "Some identical twins can fool the facial recognition software, but my mother never mentioned an aunt who was her mother's identical twin."

"Maybe she didn't know." Geraldine's tone was hopeful, and her entire demeanor changed. "Maybe we were orphaned or abandoned as babies and adopted by different families. Back then, they separated siblings." She took in a deep breath and then released it slowly. "It's such a relief to have an alternative explanation. I really couldn't conceive of having a daughter who I have forgotten about."

39

ONEGUS

*O*negus hated to squash Geraldine's hope, but the twin hypothesis was unlikely. It was also easily verifiable.

"I'm sorry, Geraldine, but the likelihood of you having a twin sister who was also a gifted quilter is very slim. This is a very particular hobby that not many engage in."

The woman looked as if he'd just poked a hole in her balloon, deflating and slumping against Cassandra's arm. "Identical twins also might share aptitudes for the same things." She didn't sound as if she believed it herself. "Maybe my sister was also artistic. Many women quilted back then."

"You were also a strong swimmer," Roni said. "My mother told me that they couldn't believe that you drowned. You went swimming, and no one started worrying until an hour had passed. They searched for you for days. If you knew back then that you weren't aging, that might have been a perfect way for you to stage your own death. Something unexpected could have happened along the way, like perhaps hitting your head on something, drowning for real, and going into stasis. Someone could have found you, or you could have washed ashore far away from there days or weeks later. In the meantime, you were declared dead, and no one was looking for you anymore."

"Roni's theory is plausible," Onegus said. "You could have lost your memory as a result of the blow to the head, or the stasis, or a combination of both."

Heaving a sigh, Geraldine nodded. "I have vague memories of a fisherman." She looked at Cassandra. "I told you about him on the way here, didn't I?"

Cassandra nodded. "It fits in with Roni's hypothesis. He could have found you floating in the water, or lying on the shore, and took you in."

"A good Samaritan," Connor said.

"The question is, where do we go from here?" Cassandra wiped her forehead with her sleeve. "Is it hot in here? Or is it me?"

Onegus frowned. It wasn't that hot, and as an immortal who had been born in Scotland, he was sensitive to heat and didn't enjoy the Californian summer.

115

"It's a little warm." Connor pulled out his phone. "I'll turn on the air conditioning."

Perhaps it was a little on the warm side.

"I love technology," Geraldine said as if she hadn't just discovered something as monumental as a forgotten family. "You don't even have to get up to turn on the air conditioner. It's all controlled by phone applications."

"I can do it with my mind," Sylvia said. "And if Cassandra learns to focus her energy, she might be able to do it as well."

"It's magic," Geraldine murmured. "What if I can do that too?" Her eyes widened. "What if Darlene can do that? You said that the immortal traits pass through the mother, so if Cassy has them, so should Darlene."

"Not everyone inherits the same traits," Onegus said. "And the various talents can also pass through the father. It's just the immortality gene that passes exclusively through the mother."

"I just thought of something," Sylvia said. "If Geraldine is close to the source, then Roni is as well." She looked to her mate. "You should have transitioned easily, but you didn't." She turned to Cassandra. "It took several attempts by several immortals, and in the end, only Kian's venom was potent enough to induce his transition."

"I was sick, remember? I had pneumonia." Roni ran a hand over the back of his neck. "Doctor Bridget said that it had prevented my transition, and that Kian's bite had coincided with my body finally being strong enough to go through it. If not for that, I could have transitioned after the first attempt."

Chest-thumping aside, the kid could be right. But it was irrelevant as far as his mother went. Forty-nine was too old to attempt transition.

"We chose not to approach Roni's mother for two reasons," Onegus said. "At the time she was forty-five, which we strongly believed was too old to attempt her induction, and she was happily married to a human, which I assume she still is. Since then, we've had a forty-six-year-old male Dormant transition, but he almost didn't make it. He was in a coma for over two weeks."

"So what do we do?" Geraldine asked. "Do we just leave it at that?"

"What do you want to do, Mom?" Cassandra looked at her mother with worry in her expressive eyes. "Do you want to find out what happened? Or do you want to put it behind you and go on with your life?"

Heaving a sigh, Geraldine closed her eyes. "I want to meet my older daughter. I want to talk to her, to hold her in my arms, but it's impossible. How am I going to explain who I am?"

"We can pretend to be distant relatives she didn't know about," Cassandra offered. "At first, I wanted to get a fake ID and pretend that I was an FBI investigator looking into Roni's disappearance. But your twin sister hypothesis gave me an idea. We can say that Sabina had a twin sister and that we are her daughters." She smiled. "From different fathers, of course. If she did one of those mail-in DNA tests that are so popular now, we could say that we did it as well, and that's how we found her."

Roni straightened in his chair. "I can find out if my parents have done one of those tests. And when you go to see them, maybe you can convince them to meet you at a location that will be safe for me to join. It has been four years since I've gone missing. I want to see my parents again and find out whether they were the assholes I thought they were when I was growing up or was it me."

"Oh, Roni," Geraldine said softly. "The truth is probably somewhere in the middle, and it's very mature of you to try to patch things up with your parents. You should never give up on family."

40

CASSANDRA

*Y*eah, unless that family tried to get rid of you.

Her mother's survivalist husband was a suspect, and Cassandra was determined to get to the bottom of his story as well.

Had he benefited from a life insurance payout following Sabina's death?

Had he been an abusive, possessive psycho, who tried to murder his wife because she'd wanted to leave him?

One of Cassandra's friends from school had lost her mother like that. The mother asked for a divorce, and the next day the father shot her, called the police, and then shot himself in the head. It was premeditated murder, and the reason he called the police before offing himself was to make sure that the mother's death would officially be declared before his. That way, he'd inherited their joined property as her husband, and in his will, he'd left everything to his son from a previous marriage, leaving Cassandra's friend with nothing.

Out of pure hatred, he'd done that to his own child.

Some people were capable of doing horrific things for all kinds of crazy reasons.

Thinking about the cruelty and injustice made her angry, and acts committed by those who were supposed to cherish and love their partners and their children were the worst. Those evildoers deserved a special place in the deepest levels of hell.

The destructive energy simmering under her skin was reaching explosive levels, but now wasn't the time to go outside and blow things up.

She needed to calm down.

Cassandra wiped the sweat off her upper lip.

The air conditioning vent was blowing air right at her, which should have cooled her down, but she still felt hot. It was the damn energy's fault, and instead of letting it boil over, perhaps she should follow Sylvia's advice and blow up a couple of glasses in the backyard.

Except, even at explosive levels, her power had never produced heat before. Maybe she'd caught something at the office.

Could one get scarlet fever at thirty-four? Because in addition to the heat, Cassandra felt as if ants were crawling all over her skin. She needed to scratch her arms and legs so badly, but she would never dare do that with her mother sitting right next to her. According to Geraldine, scratching in public was not something a lady did.

Since scarlet fever was unlikely, maybe she was allergic to something?

Yeah, she was allergic to evil, and it was hiding somewhere in her mother's past.

"I want to find out what happened to you." Cassandra conceded defeat and, as inconspicuously as possible scratched her left arm. "When we go to visit Darlene, I intend to grill her about her father." She cast a glance at Onegus. "Are you going to help me, or do I need to take Connor with me?"

Onegus frowned. "Are you feeling okay?"

"I'm a little hot." She scratched her arm again, not caring about the reproachful look from her mother. "It's the energy. It needs an outlet."

"I'll adjust the thermostat," Connor offered.

Onegus didn't look convinced. "Other than the heat, what else are you feeling?"

"I'm itchy." Cassandra gave up on trying to be inconspicuous and attacked both of her arms with her long nails. "I feel like a thousand fire ants are crawling all over my skin. I must be allergic to something."

"Or you might be transitioning." Onegus pushed to his feet, walked over to where she was sitting with her mother, and crouched in front of her. "Let me check your forehead." He touched his hand to her clammy skin. "You're burning up."

"I am?" She put a hand on her own forehead.

It didn't feel hot, just sweaty. "I don't feel as if I have a fever." Poison ivy was more likely. The itchiness was driving her crazy. "It feels like a bad allergy."

Onegus pushed to his feet and pulled out his phone.

"Who are you calling?"

"Bridget. I'm pretty sure that you are transitioning."

At that point, Cassandra didn't care what was going on with her as long as someone put her out of her misery and stopped the itching. At the rate she was scratching, there wouldn't be any skin left on her arms.

"I wasn't itchy," Roni said.

"What did you feel?"

"Nothing. I was tired, I went to sleep, and I woke up three days later. I was ten pounds lighter, but an inch taller, bringing my height to six feet and two inches. I also gained an inch and a half in shoulder span." He cast a smug look at Sylvia. "From a dork, I turned into a hunk. Well, not right away, but eventually."

She slapped his arm. "You're still a dork. But that's what I love about you."

"Only that?"

"Among other things."

Onegus ended the call and put his phone in his pocket. "Bridget will meet us at the clinic." He offered Cassandra a hand up.

Normally, Cassandra would have argued that there was no need to rush and that she was feeling fine, but maybe Bridget could give her something for the itching.

"Okay." She took his hand and let him pull her up.

"I'm coming with you." Her mother rose to her feet as well.

"Sylvia and I are coming too," Roni said.

Connor walked over and pulled Cassandra into his arms. "Good luck." He let go of her and turned to Onegus. "Keep me posted, will you?"

"I will. It might be a false alarm. None of the other Dormants were itchy, but then each one has exhibited different symptoms."

As Onegus opened the front door, the five of them spilled out onto the front porch.

"I just want the damn itch to stop." Cassandra scratched at her arms again.

"I'll distract you," Roni offered.

She winced. "Not with slam poetry, I hope. I'm feeling gross enough as it is."

"No, just something funny that happened when I woke up after losing consciousness. Bridget asked me if my sense of smell got better. I told her that I liked her perfume. She asked me to go deeper and try to discern other scents. When I focused, I smelled her happiness, and I also smelled her arousal. For a moment, I thought that it was about me, but even as conceited as I was, I knew it couldn't be. Besides, I was taken." He wrapped his arm around Sylvia's waist. "Imagine how embarrassing it was to admit that."

"What did the doctor say?" Geraldine asked.

"That I was right on both accounts. Her mate transitioned a few days before me, and she was still on a honeymoon high."

"It's a nice story," Geraldine said. "But I'm glad that I can't smell anyone's arousal. I kind of like the guesswork. It's more exciting."

"I agree," Cassandra said. "But it's no longer relevant for me. I found my one and only, and I know that he loves me."

41

KIAN

*D*inner was winding down when Amanda's phone rang.

She frowned. "Sylvia is calling me. I wonder what she wants." She pushed away from the dining table and took the phone with her.

She shouldn't have bothered. Kian could hear her happy squeal loud and clear.

"I'm on it. I'll bring it over in a little bit. We are just finishing dinner."

A moment later, Amanda walked into the dining room with a big grin on her face. "Sylvia called to ask me for a change of clothes for Cassandra. She's transitioning."

Annani clapped her hands. "How wonderful. Another happy occasion to round out this week."

"Why didn't she call Mey or Jin?" Lisa asked. "They are both as tall as Cassandra."

Kian wondered the same thing. Not that he minded. He couldn't care less about Amanda's wardrobe, but it was strange that Sylvia called her and not one of the other statuesque ladies. She and Amanda weren't close friends.

"Jin and Mey are escorting Arwel and Yamanu's mothers to the airport. They won't be back until much later," Syssi explained.

"We should get going as well." Sari sighed. "It was such a pleasure to spend time with you all that going back home feels bittersweet."

That was just the opening Kian needed to start his campaign. "You should revisit the idea of moving your people into the village. I bet there are rivers of tears flowing right now as people say goodbye to loved ones. Wouldn't it be so much better for everyone if we all lived in the same place?"

Sari heaved another sigh. "I struggle with my decision almost daily, but I still think that staying in Scotland is the right thing to do."

He shook his head. "I worry about you. You've been lucky so far, and you've fared better than us, but since I took away most of your Guardians, you don't have enough defenders."

"What has prompted this sudden worry?" David asked.

Kian didn't want to admit to his superstitions, but he didn't have a ready excuse that would have sounded better. "At the party, it occurred to me that my arm of the clan seems to attract all of the trouble, while your arm of the clan stays trouble-free. But then it also occurred to me that we've been blessed with many Dormants, while you were blessed with only one. It would seem that the Fates demand balance, and our blessings have come at a price. I'm more than willing to pay it and keep discovering new Dormants, but I can't say the same about you. Your people cannot handle trouble, and it's partially my fault because I lured the retired Guardians away. And since that's on me, your lack of Dormants might be as well."

Chuckling, Sari shook her head. "I have news for you, brother of mine. For better or for worse, you are not the center of the universe. In the same way that you can't take credit for the influx of Dormants, you can't assume blame for our lack of them. It's just the way it is."

"Just give it some more thought. I would love for you and your people to move in here with us. Kalugal's section is ready, and once the furniture gets here, he and his men can move out of the houses in phase two, and with the purchase of the building 3D printer, our new section is going to be ready much sooner as well. In six weeks or so, the village will be ready to house all of your people with room to spare."

She pushed to her feet and put a hand on his shoulder. "I truly appreciate the invitation, and it warms my heart that you are so eager to have my people and me here, but all I can promise is that I will give it some further thought."

"Fair enough." He rose to his feet and pulled her into his arms for a fierce hug. "I'm going to miss you."

"Then call me, and we will video chat."

"It's not the same." He let go of her to pull David into a bro embrace. "It was good seeing you." He clapped his brother-in-law on the back.

"Same here." David did the same.

It took another fifteen minutes for everyone to say their goodbyes, and when David and Sari left with Okidu to go to the airport, Kian's other two sisters were wiping tears from their eyes, and so were Ronja and Lisa.

Annani let out a long-suffering sigh. "Parting is always such sorrow. But we will see each other soon. After I'm done here, I intend to fly to Scotland."

"How long are you staying?" Anita asked.

"Not long. Perhaps a week or two." She glanced at Ronja. "My plans are flexible, but I do not wish to overstay my welcome."

42

GERALDINE

Geraldine sat next to Cassandra in the clinic's small patient room and held her hand.

The doctor had given Cassy something to calm the itch, and it made her sleepy. Thankfully, she wasn't unconscious, which Geraldine had learned was what happened to most transitioning Dormants.

Supposedly, it was a good sign, but she was worried nonetheless. What if Cassandra suffered a memory loss like she had?

Well, at least she wouldn't be completely lost because she could learn about her past from her mother and her boyfriend. Or rather mate, as the immortals referred to their partners. Even if the transition caused Cassandra to lose her memory, she wouldn't be in as bad a situation as Geraldine had been.

Or was it Sabina?

The name didn't evoke any emotion from her. It was the name of a stranger. Perhaps it would help to think of that woman as her twin sister even though she probably didn't have one?

At a certain point in the past, a split had happened. The woman named Sabina, who was mother to Darlene, had indeed drowned, and a new woman named Geraldine had been born.

Prompted by some instinct that made her fear discovery, she'd used many other names, but in her mind, she'd always been Geraldine. Who'd given her the name?

Had it been one of the therapists in the rehab? One of the doctors, perhaps?

Her memories from that time were foggy. Heck, most of her recollections weren't clear. Thank God she'd never forgotten Cassandra. Ever since she'd been born, Cassy had been her rock, her safe harbor, her tether to reality.

As a soft knock sounded on the door, Onegus rose to his feet and opened the way.

"I brought sandwiches and coffee," Roni said quietly. "How is Cassandra doing?"

"She is asleep, but she's doing well. Bridget is not worried."

Roni let out a breath. "I'm glad." He handed Geraldine a wrapped sandwich and a paper cup. "I didn't know what to get you, but a tomato mozzarella is always a safe bet. I also brought sugar for your cappuccino if you like it sweet."

He handed another sandwich and coffee to Onegus. "I got you the same thing." He pulled two sugar packets out of his pocket and offered them to Geraldine. "You can use one of Bridget's tongue depressors to stir it in."

"Thank you."

Geraldine wondered what a doctor taking care of immortals would need a tongue depressor for. They didn't get sore throats.

A few moments later, Bridget poked her head through the open door and frowned. "Take the party out to the waiting room, please. This is a patient room."

"Sorry." Roni smiled sheepishly.

Reluctantly, Geraldine rose to her feet and followed the guys out of the room.

The truth was that she was hungry and thirsty. She was also uncomfortable. The pretty red belt she'd cinched around her waist was digging into her skin, and she couldn't wait to take it off.

Maybe she could bother the nice doctor for a pair of scrubs. If she was going to spend the night sitting in a chair, she should at least dress comfortably.

After devouring the sandwich and finishing the delicious cappuccino, she felt almost as good as new and was ready to go back to Cassandra's room, but Doctor Bridget shook her head at her. "From now on, no more than one visitor at the time inside the patient room. You and Onegus can take turns."

Onegus cast Geraldine an apologetic look. "You can go to my house and rest a little."

"Thanks, but I prefer to stay here until you are ready to trade places with me."

He nodded and ducked into Cassandra's room, but he left the door slightly open, so Geraldine could still see Cassy from where she sat in the waiting room.

Roni moved to the seat Onegus had vacated. "Sylvia is coming over with a change of clothes for you and Cassandra."

"That's so nice of her."

It was a very thoughtful thing to do, but she doubted anything of Sylvia's would fit either of them. Cassandra was much taller, and Geraldine was both shorter and slimmer. But anything would be better than the form-fitting shirt and tight belt she had on.

"Yeah. Sylvia is the best. She called Amanda and asked her to lend stuff to Cassandra. They are about the same size."

"Can I ask you a question?"

Given his guarded expression, he probably thought that she was going to ask him about his parents, but he nodded nonetheless. "Go ahead."

"How did they find you? How did they know that you were a Dormant?"

His shoulders losing their rigidity, he grinned. "They needed a hacker with access to a government database." He rubbed his hand over the back of his neck. "At fifteen, I was already one of the best hackers in the country, but I was also a stupid, cocky teenager. I hacked into a secure government server just to prove that I could, and I got caught. They offered me a deal. I could go to a juvenile correction facility, or I could work for the government. I would even get paid, but I would have to be supervised twenty-four-seven. Naturally, my parents and I chose the second option."

"That must have been difficult. Did you go to school?"

He shook his head. "They provided me with a tutor. For the first three years, I lived at home. One suit took me to and from the government facility I worked at, and another suit stayed in the house to watch me. It wasn't easy for my parents or for me, and at eighteen, I asked for a place of my own. Their solution was an apartment inside the facility I worked at. It gave me a little more freedom, but I still couldn't hang out with people my age or meet girls." He chuckled. "I wasn't much to look at, so I doubt I would have gotten a girlfriend even if I went to school and didn't have an agent glued to my ass at all times. One day Andrew, Syssi's brother, approached me with a project that he wanted me to do for him after hours."

"How did he find you?"

"He worked at the same building. He still does. Anyway, what I asked in return for the favor was for him to smuggle a girl in so I could get laid."

Geraldine gasped. "What did he say to that?"

"He didn't like it, but I told him that it was either that or no favor. Long story short, Sylvia volunteered. Her ability to manipulate the surveillance cameras in the building was a big plus, and Andrew told her that it was up to her to decide if she wanted to cure me of my virginity or just thrall me to believe that she did. Luckily for me, and for reasons that are still a mystery, she actually liked me and decided to deflower me."

"Was she the one who discovered that you were a Dormant?"

"Nope. It was thanks to you. The favor that Andrew asked of me was to run a proprietary facial recognition program through every state's DMV records. The program was designed to find driver's licenses that had the same face on them but different names on different dates. Imagine my shock when the program spat out three licenses with your picture on them. The first one had your real name on it, so I knew it wasn't a doppelgänger. The reason Andrew wanted me to run the program was to flag potential immortals. Since you were an immortal, there was no doubt that I was a Dormant. The clan sprung me free, and here I am. End of story."

"That's why you didn't keep in touch with your parents. It wasn't because you didn't get along with them. It was because you lived in hiding."

He nodded. "It was a combination of both. I couldn't see them, so I convinced myself that I didn't want to. But the truth was that they were lousy parents. They didn't even come to visit me in the hospital when I got pneumonia. My handler and his wife sat by my side, but my own parents didn't bother."

Geraldine shook her head. "That's unforgivable. But maybe they couldn't come? Or maybe no one told them that you were sick?"

"It's possible. I was so out of it at the time that I don't remember what went on. After I got sprung from the hospital, my parents were closely watched, but perhaps enough time has passed for the guys in suits to give up on finding me. Andrew says that as far as he knows, no one is watching my parents' house anymore, but that doesn't mean that I can just walk in there. The agents assigned to my case might have left listening devices and hidden cameras all over the place."

43

KIAN

*O*ut in his backyard, Kian opened his humidor box. "Ladies and gentleman, help yourselves."

"Don't mind if I do." Syssi's father pulled out a Fuentes Opus X and then glanced at the closed patio door. "Anita will bite my head off, but I can't resist. I haven't smoked one in years."

"Then perhaps you should start with their Short Story." Kalugal pulled out the smaller cigar and handed it to Adam. "It's also an excellent cigar, but it won't knock you out like the Opus X."

"Thanks." Adam accepted the suggestion and handed the bigger one to Kalugal, who gave it a sniff and smiled.

"Andrew?" Kian offered his brother-in-law the box.

"No thanks. I'll pass." He lifted his bottle of Snake Venom. "That's poison enough for me."

"Eva?"

"No thanks. But if you have those small cigarillos that you usually smoke, I would love one."

"Sure thing." He pulled the flat box out of his back pocket and handed it to her.

When he offered the box to Ronja, she shook her head. "Thank you, but I have my own poison." She pulled a box of cigarettes out of her purse.

Dalhu turned him down as well, and Bhathian took out a Short Story.

Kian would have preferred to smoke alone with Kalugal and ask him point-blank about his long term-plans, but it would have to wait for another occasion.

Andrew took a swig of his beer and then put it down on the side table. "Have you heard anything from Lokan and Carol?"

Kian cut off the head of the Short Story. "They are still settling in. It will take time for them to start their side hustle. For now, they need to keep up the entrepreneurial façade."

126

A dreamy expression on her face, Eva held the cigarillo but didn't light it. "I could see myself sinking my teeth into an operation like that."

Bhathian wrapped his arm around her shoulders. "Patience, my love. Enjoy being a mother."

"I do, and I'm not in a rush to go back to industrial espionage, but I miss it. I miss the elaborate disguises, the excitement—"

That got Ronja's attention. "That sounds so fascinating. Were you a spy?"

"I was a private investigator. Cheaters cheat not only on their spouses. They also cheat on their business partners. That's what I was hired to find out and provide proof of."

As Kian sprawled on a lounger, Kalugal joined him on the other. "So, what's the progress with your China team? When are you deploying them?"

Kian took a puff of his cigar. "Probably in two weeks. Maybe even longer. Mey and Jin could use more time, and frankly, my head is not in it."

The truth was that he was having second thoughts about the whole thing. According to Emmett and also Stella, the Kra-ell didn't know about other immortals, and if they hadn't bothered him so far, they probably wouldn't. Why poke a sleeping bear?

Perhaps it was better to leave them alone.

"Who's going?" Kalugal asked.

"It's not finalized yet. Why? Did you change your mind and want to join the team?"

"Not at all." Kalugal puffed on his Opus X. "I find the Mosuo much more interesting, and since Jacki wants to join me on that expedition, I don't want to be anywhere near anything dangerous. But I think that you should include Stella in your team. Richard told me that she's fluent in Mandarin."

"Arwel suggested her as well, but all she can do is translate, which Morris can do just as well. You bring other capabilities to the table."

"True, but since I'm not interested, you should consider Stella. Don't underestimate the power of a good-looking woman. Women always make better spies. Even when they ask a lot of questions, women seem less suspicious to men, who will always volunteer more information than they should when they want to impress a beautiful lady."

"Jin and Mey are also beautiful."

"But they don't speak the language even though they look like they should, which will make people resent them. Besides, Stella has several qualities that neither of the sisters has."

Kian lifted a brow. "Like what?"

"She can lie convincingly. That's the most important one. She's kept Vlad's father's identity a secret for over twenty years. She also looks more fragile and less threatening than a Guardian or even Morris, who looks like an army sergeant." Kalugal smiled. "If the men she's questioning are the good kind, she will bring out their protective instincts. If they are bad, then they might assume that she's an easy victim, but we both know that couldn't be further from the truth. Under her soft, bohemian, artsy disguise, Stella is a predator with sharp claws."

Kalugal's assessment of her was spot on.

"If I send her, I will have to send Richard along as well. How are you going to manage without him?"

127

Kalugal shrugged. "The building project is almost complete, and the furniture is on the way. My men can take care of whatever is left to do. If you want him to supervise your new building project, he's yours."

Maybe that was Kalugal's motive behind pushing Stella's participation. He no longer needed Richard's services, and that was an elegant way to get rid of him.

It would have been easier to just say so outright, but that wasn't Kalugal's style.

"I'll take Richard off your hands. I have plenty of building projects outside of the village that I can use him for, so he won't be out of a job once the village's newest addition is done. An experienced supervisor is an asset, and they are not easy to find."

44

ONEGUS

*A*fter the short break in the waiting room, Onegus sat beside Cassandra, watching her sleep and listening to the various noises the monitoring equipment was making.

He didn't know what the different numbers and graphs meant, but as long as no alarm was going off, he hoped that everything was progressing as it should.

Cassandra looked so much more peaceful in repose that it was hard to imagine the rapid changes going on inside of her body. When awake, Cassandra's expression was rarely relaxed. In part, it was due to her Type A personality, which made her driven and uncompromising, and in part it was due to the inner energy she was constantly managing. It wasn't an easy supernatural power to live with, but hopefully she would learn to control it better, so it wouldn't control her.

Sylvia managed to be chill and easygoing despite her power. Then again, it could be that it was the other way around, and her power was more controllable because her mellow personality didn't constantly feed it.

As the door opened, he didn't need to look over his shoulder to know it was Bridget. She'd come in a couple of times before, looked at Cassandra, checked the monitors, and left without saying a word. By now, he recognized the scent of the soap or shampoo she used, which was a mix of vanilla and coconut, and the way she opened the door, which was decisive but quiet like the woman herself.

Once again, she looked at Cassandra, checked the monitors, and then turned on her heel and made to leave.

This time he wasn't letting her go without getting some answers. "What's going on, Bridget?"

She turned to him with a surprised look as if she hadn't noticed him sitting there. "I'm worried about Cassandra's stores of energy. I would have preferred for her to start transitioning on empty, but she came in loaded."

He glanced at the monitors. "Can you see it on the readouts?"

"I don't have equipment that monitors that, but I can feel it. Her blood pressure is dangerously high, which is why I hooked her up to the equipment even though she's not unconscious."

He glanced at Cassandra. "Could have fooled me. She's been asleep for hours. And what do you mean by dangerously high? Is she in danger?"

"Cassandra is sleeping because I gave her a relaxant in the IV. I don't want her blood pressure to go any higher. And dangerously high only means that I need to monitor her closely. She's young and healthy, so I'm not too worried."

When he raised a brow, she cast him a reassuring smile. "Cassandra is in a controlled environment under a doctor's supervision. I'm not going to tell you that you have nothing to worry about, but there is no reason for alarm."

Not the answer he wanted, but he would take it.

"Shouldn't we wake her up?"

Bridget shook her head. "Sleep is good for her."

After the doctor left, Onegus disregarded her advice, rose to his feet, and softly kissed Cassandra's forehead. She didn't wake up, but she smiled in her sleep, which was good enough for him.

He'd gotten a reaction.

Sitting down, he pulled out his phone and checked his messages. He'd turned the thing to vibrate, and it had been buzzing in his pocket nonstop. After reading through dozens of good-luck wishes from his Guardians and others, he'd stopped checking his messages, but it was time he took a look in case someone needed him. There were more good lucks, many with emojis of fingers crossed, and some with hearts and kissy faces.

The one he'd been waiting for, though, was from his mother. *How is Cassandra doing? When can I see you? Unless you want me to change my flight and stay until Cassandra transitions, I need to leave for the airport soon.*

He typed, *Don't change your flight. I can see you right now. Come to the clinic.*

It was nice of her to offer, but there was nothing she could do to help, and he didn't need handholding.

The return text arrived right away. *I'm in the waiting room.*

Rising to his feet, he pocketed the phone and walked out of Cassandra's room.

The small waiting area was packed. Geraldine had changed into a pair of leggings and a T-shirt, courtesy of Sylvia no doubt, who was sitting with Roni and wearing an almost identical outfit. His mother sat next to Connor, Arwel and Jin stood because there was no more room to sit, and through the clinic's glass door, he could see Yamanu and Mey standing outside.

"Thank you for coming." He clapped Arwel on the back. "But there is no need for you and Jin to wait around. I can keep you updated."

Arwel nodded. "Bridget has already given us an update. Jin and I will be in the café with Mey and Yamanu for the next hour or so. If you need us for any reason—a change of clothes, a cup of soup, whatever—just holler."

He chuckled. "Thank you. If I need anything, I'll send you a text."

When Arwel opened the door, Onegus smiled and waved at Mey and Yamanu, and when the door closed, he let out a breath and turned to his mother. "I'm sorry that I can't take you to the airport myself like I promised."

"Don't be silly." She pushed to her feet and pulled him into her arms. "Connor is taking me. Please, keep me posted. Don't wait until Cassandra transitions success-fully. I want to know about every little change."

Of course, she did.

"I will text you with anything that's relevant." He kissed her on the cheek and then on the other one.

Letting go of him, Martha wiped at her teary eyes. "Promise that you will come to visit me. Together with Cassandra and Geraldine." She forced a smile. "Geraldine can't wait to see the castle." She got closer and whispered in his ear, "Maybe I'll play matchmaker."

"Don't make any plans. Mother and daughter wouldn't want to live far apart, and I have no intentions of moving back to Scotland." That was most likely what his mother had planned.

Besides, Onegus had a feeling that Geraldine was already taken. He'd seen her when she'd returned from her walk with Shai.

Cassandra's mother had looked like a woman in love.

45

SHAI

"*I* can take it from here." Adam motioned for Shai to get out of the chair.

It had been two hours since Cassandra had arrived at the clinic, but Shai had learned about it only when Syssi's father came over to help him with the editing of Allegra's keepsake montage.

"Thank you." Shai vacated the chair. "I would have stayed to help you, but I need to go to the clinic."

Adam waved a dismissive hand. "I don't need any help. In fact, I prefer to work alone, and the only reason I let you even touch it was because of the family dinner I had to attend."

"When you're done, just close the door behind you. No need to lock things up."

Lifting his head from the keyboard, Adam smiled. "That's nice. Any other place with this much expensive equipment that wouldn't have been smart. But I guess no one has a reason to steal anything here, and you have only two teenagers in the entire place, one of them a girl, so pranks are not an issue either."

"They are not. Good night, Adam. And thank you again for doing this."

Syssi's father waved him off. "This is what I love doing. Now, leave me alone, so I can work."

With a nod, Shai headed for the door. It was a little strange to have someone working in his office, using his equipment, sitting in his chair. Usually, no one ever came in. If Kian needed him, he called, and Shai went to him.

Stepping out the office building's front door, Shai debated whether he should stop by the vending machines first and get Geraldine and Onegus something to eat and drink.

Maybe a better idea was to check with them first. After all, the clinic was next door to the office building, practically sharing its front space with the café, so it wasn't like he had a long walk. It would have been nice not to show up empty-handed, though.

Several Guardians were sitting in the café, some with their mates, no doubt to provide emotional support for Onegus.

His heart squeezed for Geraldine.

Not counting a grandson she didn't know she had, Geraldine had only Shai to offer her support during a difficult time like that. Her daughter was transitioning, and he hadn't known about it until five minutes ago.

Why hadn't she called him?

He would have dropped everything and rushed to her side.

Then again, Geraldine probably thought of them as mere acquaintances.

Shai intended to change her perspective very soon.

As he pushed the door open and entered the clinic, Geraldine turned and looked at him, a beautiful smile blooming on her face. "Shai? What are you doing here?"

"I'm here for you." He sat next to her and took her hand in his. "I only learned about Cassandra entering transition five minutes ago. Otherwise, I would have come sooner."

"Thank you." She squeezed his hand.

"How is she doing?"

"The doctor says that she's doing well. She didn't lose consciousness, but she's sleeping a lot. Bridget gave her something for the itch and also something to relax her, or maybe it's the same thing. I don't know much about medicine." She smiled sheepishly. "Aside from my time in the rehabilitation center, I didn't need to see doctors. Cassandra was always a healthy child, and aside from immunizations and other things required to attend school, she didn't need medical attention either, not even a dentist or an orthodontist. She had perfectly straight teeth." Geraldine stopped to suck in a breath. "Look at me, talking up a storm. I do that when I'm nervous."

She was adorable.

He patted her hand. "Don't apologize. You have every right to be nervous. Transition is scary. I bet Onegus is anxious as well, but he puts on a tough face because he's the chief."

"I know." She leaned her head on his arm as if they were an established couple. "Roni and Sylvia were here, and then Sylvia left and Roni stayed." She waved a hand over her clothes. "These are Sylvia's. It was so thoughtful of her to bring me a change of clothes so I could be comfortable. Roni sat with me for a little longer, but I told him to go home. He said that he would come later to check on Cassandra and me."

Had Geraldine been told about being Roni's grandmother?

Probably. Otherwise, she would have wondered why he was being so attentive to a couple of strangers.

"He's a good kid," Shai said. "A little prickly, but his heart is in the right place."

Geraldine scrunched her nose. "Did you know that I was his grandmother?"

"Yeah. Amanda told me."

"It feels terrible," she murmured. "I have another daughter and a grandson, whom I know nothing about. I keep thinking that they made a mistake, and that it wasn't me. Perhaps I had an identical twin sister who was also into quilting." She waved a hand. "Roni said that an identical twin could have fooled the facial recognition software, but he used my quilting to poke a hole in that theory, saying that even if I had a twin, it was unlikely that we were both quilters. Then Roni said that his grandmother had been a strong swimmer, and that she could have used her ability to stage her own death. But I'm not an avid swimmer. I can do a few laps in our home pool, but never in the ocean. I'm scared of the deep water, which is sometimes so murky that it's impossible to see what's hiding in it, the currents, the fish, the jellyfish." She shuddered.

He wrapped his arm around her shoulders and drew her closer. "Drowning would make the ocean scary even for a strong swimmer. You might not remember it, but your subconscious does."

She shook her head. "It's all circumstantial evidence. The problem is that even a DNA test won't prove that I'm not Roni's grandmother. Twins have nearly identical genes."

Her twin hypothesis was far-fetched, but he wasn't going to say that. With Cassandra transitioning, Geraldine had enough to worry about.

Shai's job was to offer comfort and support. "Whatever the truth is, Onegus will help you figure it out. It might also help to approach it from a different angle. Instead of thinking about the memories of your daughter that you lost, think about the new ones you will make once you reunite with her."

46

GERALDINE

*R*eunite with Darlene?

Geraldine couldn't envision that happening. She couldn't tell her daughter who she was, and even if she did, Darlene was not going to believe her.

Unless there was a way to induce her older daughter's transition, despite her age, and make her an immortal, she couldn't be told the truth.

Or maybe she could? What if Kalugal did to Darlene the same thing he'd done to her? He could compel her to keep the existence of immortals a secret.

"You're right." She turned to Shai. "I can tell my daughter the truth, and then Kalugal can compel her not to say anything about it."

"You don't need Kalugal for that. He was brought in because you're an immortal. Since your daughter is a human, Eleanor would suffice."

She frowned. "Why not Kalugal?"

"He's a big shot. Eleanor is not."

"I see." She rubbed her temple. "Is she the one who compelled Cassy?"

"Yes. She's a recently transitioned immortal, and we suspect that she also comes from a strong line. Compulsion ability is rare, and she's a strong one. She also transitioned quite easily despite being on the older side of the spectrum."

"How old is that?"

"Forty."

"Darlene is forty-nine. Is it too late for her?"

Shai nodded. "I'm afraid so."

"So maybe she shouldn't be told. It would be terrible for her to learn that she missed her opportunity."

As the door opened and Onegus stepped out with a smile on his face, excitement bubbled in Geraldine's heart.

"Cassandra is awake, and she wants to see you. She also wants a cup of coffee, but I need to ask Julian if that's okay."

It took Geraldine a split second to remember that Julian was Bridget's son and also a doctor, and that he had taken over the night shift not too long ago.

With a quick smile at Shai, she pushed to her feet and rushed into Cassandra's room.

"Oh, sweetie." Happy tears misting her eyes, she walked into Cassy's spread arms. "I was so worried about you."

"I was just sleeping." Cassandra rubbed comforting circles on her back. "I'm told that I'm doing better than most transitioning Dormants, so you really shouldn't worry."

Straightening, Geraldine wiped the tears away and took Cassandra's hand in hers. "So I've been told as well, but I'm your mother. It's my job to worry needlessly."

"Don't." Cassandra squeezed her hand. "I'm fine, and if I didn't lose consciousness so far, I probably won't." She glanced at the IV drip. "Bridget gave me something to relax, so I will most likely fall asleep again soon, and so should you. I don't want you to sit in the waiting room all night. Onegus can take you to his house, and you can sleep in his room or on the couch in the living room. It opens up to a queen sleeper."

"I don't want to leave you."

A stubborn expression on her face, Cassandra shook her head. "If you don't go, I'll keep thinking about you torturing yourself in the waiting room, and I won't be able to relax. Onegus is going to stay here with me." She moved to one side of the bed. "It's going to be a tight fit, but he can lie down next to me."

She'd known the day would come when her daughter would find a man and choose to rely on him rather than on her mother, but she wasn't ready to be replaced yet.

Geraldine heaved a sigh. "The last thing I want is for you to get upset. But I won't be able to sleep while being away from you. Maybe the doctor can find a cot for me, and I'll lie down in the waiting room."

"Onegus's house is less than a five-minute walk away from here. If anything happens, not that anything would, he can call you, and you can jog over here in under two minutes."

"Two minutes is an eternity compared to one second."

"Nothing is going to happen to me. Tomorrow, the doctor is going to perform the fast-healing test to confirm my transition into immortality, and I'll be out of here. Hopefully in the morning, but more likely in the afternoon."

"Fates willing." Julian walked in with Onegus. "But I'm afraid that you can't have coffee yet. The best thing for you right now is to go back to sleep, and I suggest that you stop fighting to stay awake."

Cassandra waved a hand at Geraldine. "I'm awake only because I'm trying to convince my mother to go to Onegus's house and lie down on a bed instead of sitting in the waiting room. If you can convince her to leave, I'll be able to relax and fall asleep."

As all eyes turned to Geraldine, she lifted her hands in surrender. "Fine. I'll go." She shifted her eyes to Onegus. "But you need to promise that you'll call me with every change in Cassy's situation, no matter how small or what time it is."

He put his hand on his chest. "I promise. For small things, I'll text you, but if anything important changes, I'll call you."

"Text me every time Cassy wakes up or just opens her eyes or murmurs in her sleep. That will be reassuring to me."

"I will."

47

SHAI

*G*eraldine walked out of Cassandra's room alone and closed the door, leaving Onegus and Julian behind.

"How is she?" Shai asked.

"Bossy as usual." Geraldine sat down. "She wants me to go to Onegus's house and sleep on his couch, and she won't take no for an answer. She said that knowing I'm in the waiting room would prevent her from relaxing and falling back asleep, which Julian said was the best thing for her."

"You can come to my house and sleep in a comfortable bed." Preferably his, but Shai wasn't going to be that forward. "My roommate is staying at the downtown building until all the guests are gone, and he changed his bedding before going, so it's all clean for you." When she looked hesitant, he added, "And my place is closer to the clinic than Onegus's. I'm the first house as you leave the village square. If need be, you can get back here in under a minute."

"Sold." She offered him her hand. "Let me just tell Onegus and Cassandra that I'm leaving with you." She rose to her feet, walked back to the patient room, and knocked on the door.

As Onegus opened the way, she told him and then pushed past him into the room.

The chief pointed a finger at Shai and mouthed, "Behave."

Shai smiled. "Always."

Behave could be interpreted in many ways, and his interpretation did not exclude seduction.

Shai doubted that Geraldine would be in the mood, but snuggling on the couch and a kiss goodnight seemed reasonable to expect.

A moment later, Geraldine stepped out of the room and kissed Onegus's cheek, making him promise to call with any news. She picked up a bag that contained the clothes she'd worn before, and then they were out of the clinic.

As they walked toward his home, Shai reached for the bag. "Let me carry this for you."

Smiling, she did as he asked and took his offered hand. "It's not heavy, and you said that your home is right next to the clinic."

"It is. But I can't pass up an opportunity to be a gentleman." He lifted their joined hands and kissed the back of hers.

"Your mama raised you well. Is she one of the visitors?"

"No. My mother lives here in the village. I was born in the United States."

They walked up the steps to his front porch, and as he opened the door, Shai was glad he'd left the house tidy that morning.

"Welcome to my home." He switched the lights on. "Can I offer you some tea? Or something to eat? Or both?"

"Tea would be nice." She sounded hesitant, and he wondered whether she was uncomfortable being alone with him in his house.

"First, let me show you where you'll be sleeping." Perhaps that would ease her mind that he didn't have any nefarious plans for her.

He walked with her to Thomas's room and turned the lights on.

"Thankfully, my roommate is neat as a pin, which is probably uncommon for Guardians. Most of them are messy like frat boys." He put the bag with her clothes on the dresser.

"Are you sure he will be okay with me sleeping in his bed?"

"I'm sure. He's not going to be back until Tuesday evening, which will give me plenty of time to change the bedding again and launder it."

"I don't want to be a bother. Perhaps I should sleep on the couch. You can give me a pillow and a blanket, and I'll be fine."

"It's no bother." He took her hand and led her back to the living room.

"What kind of tea would you like?"

"Do you have anything herbal?" She followed him into the kitchen.

He filled the electric kettle with water from the filter.

"I'll show you what we have." He pulled a box with assorted teabags out of the drawer and opened it for her inspection.

"Tough choice." She flipped through the bags with one long-nailed finger. "Ginger-lemon. That sounds interesting." She pulled out the teabag and handed it to him.

"I'll have the same." He pulled out another teabag and returned the box to the drawer.

Geraldine sat on one of the barstools. "Are you close to your mother?" she asked.

"It depends on what you define as close. We have dinner together once or twice a week."

His relationship with his mother was good, but he didn't share all of his secrets with her. He'd been tempted on several occasions, the need to share his burden with someone momentarily overwhelming common sense, but that would have been a mistake he would have later regretted.

"In a restaurant?"

"Mostly at her house." He opened the fridge and pulled out an assortment of cheeses. "She enjoys cooking for me."

"That's pretty close." Geraldine eyed the cheeses with interest. "I guess that living in the same neighborhood eliminates most possible excuses for not meeting at least once a week."

"My mother and I used to do that even before we had the village." He pulled out a box of crackers and added it to the assortment of cheese slices. "I lived in the Keep, and my mother had a small house she shared with another clan member."

"A keep? Like a medieval castle?"

Shai chuckled. "It's a high-rise in downtown Los Angeles, not a medieval castle, but it served the same purpose. Kian built it with the intention of housing the entire clan, but since most preferred to stay in their own homes, only the Guardians and a couple of the council members moved in there. Most of it was rented out to humans, and the clan reserved only several of the top floors, but we have an extensive underground facility there that is still in use." He poured the hot water into the teacups and put the platter of cheese and crackers in front of Geraldine. "After our enemies somehow discovered one of ours who worked in the Bay Area and murdered him, Kian ordered all of the council members to move into the secure keep and strongly encouraged everyone else to do so as well. Most did, but even though the building is luxurious, people were not happy to live in a steel and glass tower, and Kian decided to build us a village."

"I bet you enjoy living here more than you did in the tower downtown."

"I do."

48

ONEGUS

Onegus had intended to close his eyes for a moment, but at some point he must have dozed off, waking up with a start as the alarm went off.

His heart hammering wildly, he jumped to his feet expecting the worst, but Cassandra was breathing normally, her chest going up and down, and the only indication that something was off was the frown on her face.

A split second later Julian burst into the room, looked at Cassandra, then at the monitors, then back at her. "She must have dreamt an upsetting dream and fritzed out the equipment. The readouts are all over the place, but her heartbeat and breathing are normal."

The doctor's confirmation of his observation was reassuring, but Onegus's heart was still drumming wildly against his rib cage, refusing to settle down. His body was ready for a battle against a nonexistent enemy.

Julian put his hand on Cassandra's shoulder and gave it a gentle shake. "Wake up, Cassandra."

Her eyes flew open. "What happened?"

"I assume that you had a bad dream which resulted in an energy surge. It messed up the equipment." He turned toward the monitors and started flipping off switches until all the alarms stopped blaring. "I hope it was just a momentary glitch and that they will go back online."

"I'm sorry." She lifted a shaky hand to her forehead.

"Not your fault," Julian said. "I'm going to increase the relaxant dose in your drip, and once you're more relaxed, I'll turn the equipment back on." He opened a cabinet and pulled out an old-fashioned manual blood pressure cuff.

She nodded. "Can I have one little cup of coffee before you do that? Coffee doesn't make me jittery, and it doesn't have any effect on my energy. If anything, it relaxes me."

"Interesting." Julian wrapped the blood pressure cuff around her upper arm.

"Were you ever diagnosed with attention deficit disorder or have difficulty concentrating in school?"

"I was never diagnosed. I did well in school, just not in anything that had to do with science." She smiled sheepishly. "I spent those classes doodling fashion designs."

"What does that have to do with craving coffee?" Onegus asked.

Julian unwrapped the cuff and folded it up. "The energy blast helped. Your blood pressure got lower."

"That's good." Cassandra rubbed the spot the cuff had been wrapped around.

"To answer your question, Onegus—" Julian pulled out a stool and sat down. "Caffeine has a calming effect on the ADHD brain. The theory is that the brain of people who suffer from the disorder has an overabundance of dopamine transporters, or re-uptake inhibitors. They carry away dopamine too fast, creating a shortage of it. In turn, that affects serotonin and norepinephrine. The combined effect is a reduced ability to focus, especially on tasks that the person doesn't enjoy, a lesser ability to control impulsivity, and it even messes with the awareness of time. Caffeine stimulates dopamine production in the brain, temporarily filling up the gap created by the rapid depletion of dopamine. It also stimulates adrenaline, which has the opposite effect on people with ADHD, calming them down instead of riling them up."

"That makes so much sense," Cassandra said. "When I try to bottle up anger or frustration, it only gets worse, and the pressure increases. But if I get into an argument, letting the steam out, I relax."

"Precisely." Julian crossed his feet at his ankles. "ADHD people are stimulation junkies. The adrenaline surge temporarily fills the gaps, allowing them to feel calm and focused. That's why as kids they start arguments, and as adults they work in trauma centers and other high-stress environments. People with ADHD can function well in situations that would mentally exhaust others."

"Wow." Cassandra reached for the remote and lifted the back of the hospital bed to a reclining position. "That explains so much about my character." She chuckled. "If our character is determined by our brain chemistry, then free will is an illusion."

Julian nodded. "It's true to a certain extent. You are given a set of tools, and it's your choice what to do with them. Awareness is the first step. A clever person makes the most of what they are given and finds a workaround for problem areas." He pushed to his feet and rolled the stool back under the small counter. "Although I have to qualify that because smarts is a tool as well. The bottom line is that we have some wiggle room."

Cassandra smiled. "For me, the bottom line is that I can have coffee. In fact, I'd rather drink plenty of it than take a relaxant in the form of medication. Coffee seems more benign."

"True." Julian headed for the door. "But it's also much less effective and unreliable. It's not a substitute."

"Can we at least wait a bit?" Cassandra pleaded. "I hate this drug-induced sleep. It makes me feel groggy and sluggish."

Julian hesitated with his hand on the handle. "If your blood pressure remains stable or goes further down, I'm okay with waiting. But we can't risk it if it goes back up."

49

CASSANDRA

*C*assandra's eyes rolled back in her head. "Coffee from a paper cup has never tasted better."

Onegus sat on the edge of her bed. "You are easy to please, my love." He kissed her cheek softly.

"Right." She chuckled. "There is a picture of me next to the dictionary definition of high maintenance. But at least now I have a medical excuse. I have an attention deficit disorder." She took another sip of coffee. "Will transition into immortality cure me of that?"

"First of all, it's not a disease. They call it a disorder, but I call it a special set of tools that should be utilized accordingly. You function well under pressure, while others don't. I bet many firefighters, commandos, and trauma surgeons will test positive on that scale. And secondly, I doubt that the transition will have any effect on it. I don't think our special genetics can do anything about brain chemistry. We have people with obsessive-compulsive disorder, some with lingering post-traumatic stress disorder, and others that I don't know the name of or have forgotten it."

"Any idea why?"

He shrugged. "I'm a Guardian, not a scientist. Next time Julian comes in, you should ask him." He handed her a wrapped pastry. "He didn't say anything about not allowing you food."

Cassandra shook her head. "I'd rather not. I don't want to get nauseous."

Onegus didn't argue. Instead, he unwrapped the pastry. "What were you dreaming about that caused the surge in energy?" He took a bite out of it.

She let out a breath. "It's not something that I like talking about or even thinking about, but you are my mate, and you should know who you are stuck with."

"I'm not stuck." Rising to his feet, he leaned over and kissed her forehead. "I'm blessed."

"Really? I'm an ADHD, argument-seeking, high-maintenance lady. I bet your friends pity you for the mate the Fates have saddled you with."

He pinned her with a stern look. "I don't care what anyone thinks, but I assure you that no one pities me. If anything, they are jealous of me for snagging such an incredible mate. You're smart, accomplished, successful, and you are gorgeous. You are also loyal, devoted, and you fight hard for the ones you love. I have nothing but love and admiration for you, and I wouldn't change even one thing about you."

That was the sweetest thing anyone had ever told her, but it wasn't true. Cassandra wished she could be less difficult, and she promised herself to work on it after her transition. It was a new beginning and an opportunity to improve.

"I bet you would love for me to at least argue less."

"Actually, I wouldn't. It makes you who you are, and that's who I fell in love with." Onegus leaned closer. "There's always a tradeoff. A mellow and accommodating person will not be a go-getter, and a success-driven person will not slow down or stop to smell the flowers. You have to choose the traits you love and realize that you can't expect to also get the flip side of the coin. That's like demanding your mate to develop a split personality."

"Thank you." She cupped his cheek. "You are more accepting of me than I am, and that makes me love you even more." She hoped he would still feel that way after she told him her darkest secret. "But you might change your mind when I tell you what my nightmares are about."

"Not going to happen. Just spit it out and get it off your chest."

She nodded. "I might have killed a guy."

Onegus didn't recoil like she'd expected. In fact, his expression remained blasé. "So what? I've killed many."

She should have realized that Onegus was no stranger to killing. It was easy to forget that under his veneer of charm, sophistication, and eloquence, Onegus was a battle-hardened warrior.

"That's different. You're a soldier, a defender. That's your job. I just got angry and discharged my energy on a guy. He probably had a pacemaker because he collapsed and was taken to the hospital. I don't know if he died or lived because I was too much of a coward to find out."

"Just give me his name, and I will find out for you."

"I don't know his name. He was just a random older guy who copped a feel in an elevator."

"He did what?" The question came out sounding like one long growl.

"Copped a feel. He touched my breast. We were the only two in a mall's elevator. I was just standing there, waiting for the thing to get down to the parking garage, and as the doors opened, and I was about to step out, he grabbed my breast. Instinctively, I zapped him without even thinking about it, and he collapsed on the floor outside the elevator. I called 911, and they told me to start CPR on him. I didn't know how, but in the meantime, another elevator arrived, and one of the people coming out of it knew how to do it. I waited until the paramedics arrived, told them that he'd just collapsed for no apparent reason, and that was it. I don't know if he survived, and the guilt has been eating at me for years. If I told them that he'd been zapped with an electric discharge, they might have known how to treat him, and they might have saved his life."

"You acted in self-defense, and you shouldn't concern yourself with his fate. The pervert got what he deserved."

"Copping a feel doesn't deserve the death penalty. A punch to the face, a couple of broken teeth, that's appropriate, but not death."

"First of all, you will never know if that would have been the end of it if you hadn't zapped him. He could have raped you or attempted to. Secondly, even if he did die, you didn't kill him on purpose. You reacted to what he did."

"He was an older guy who probably had a pacemaker, who maybe was mentally challenged. I don't think he could have raped me even if he wanted to." She sighed. "Let's put it this way. If I could undo what I did, I would."

As tears started trickling down her cheeks, Onegus wrapped her in his arms. "I wouldn't. Your safety is my first priority, and that perverted human can rot in hell for all I care. Just think about all the girls he probably groped and traumatized before you. If he survived, he most likely went back to doing that."

"I hadn't thought of it from that angle, but you're right. I probably wasn't the first."

"Or the last."

Talk about a new perspective.

Now she regretted not finishing the job. "Perhaps we should find out whether he survived or not, and if he did, zap him again, but this time make sure that it's fatal."

Leaning back, Onegus grinned. "That's my girl."

50

GERALDINE

$\mathcal{A}$s Geraldine's phone buzzed on the coffee table, her gut clenched with worry, but then she remembered Onegus's promise to text her about small changes and call her if something big had happened.

Nevertheless, she snatched it up and read the text. Relief washing over her, she looked up at Shai, once again catching him staring at her lips. "Cassandra is awake. Onegus even brought her coffee."

He'd been doing it a lot over the four hours or so they'd been talking, but he'd never made a move to even sit closer to her on the couch.

"That's good." Shai shifted his gaze to her eyes. "Is Cassandra already out of danger? When did she start feeling symptoms?"

"After the party, when we went to Onegus's house, I noticed that she was sweating, but the symptoms might have started long before that. My Cassy is the type who powers through even if she's so sick she can barely open her eyes. Thankfully, she rarely gets sick."

"Do you think it's because she's a Dormant?"

Geraldine shrugged noncommittally.

It was funny that he was asking her that, a clueless immortal who hadn't known she was one until only a few days ago. Was Shai confused because he was preoccupied with her lips?

It was obvious that he wanted to kiss her, but it seemed like he was misreading her cues.

She'd smiled coyly, had laughed at all his jokes, and had even put her hand on his arm a couple of times. For most men, that was enough to get the hint that she was interested, but maybe her worry for Cassandra had skewed her signals.

Geraldine looked at her phone and debated whether it would be okay to call Cassandra. Perhaps it would be better to text Onegus and have him ask Cassy to call her.

A moment after she'd sent the text, her phone rang.

"What are you still doing awake?" Cassandra asked. "I told you not to worry and to get some sleep."

Bossy girl.

"Shai was telling me more about the clan's history, and it was so fascinating that I didn't notice it was so late. Then Onegus texted me that you were awake, and I wanted to talk to you. Is that a crime?"

"No, of course not." Cassandra chuckled. "I'm just surprised that you are still awake. I thought you went to bed a long time ago." Her daughter's words were innocent, but her tone was far from it.

"Well, I'm awake. Can I come over to see you? Are you out of the danger zone?"

"Julian thinks that the worst is over. He measured my blood pressure again just a few minutes ago. It's still high, but lower than it was when I got to the clinic, which is a good sign. It seems that the energy I discharged while asleep helped lower it."

Geraldine tensed. "That rarely happens to you during sleep. It hasn't since you were going through puberty. Was it because of the transition?"

"Maybe. But I've never discharged a blast that strong during sleep, not even when I was a hormonal teenager with a bad temper. The surge was so powerful that it disrupted the monitoring equipment, which was why Julian had to measure my blood pressure the old-fashioned way. I'm surprised he even had the manually operated monitor on hand."

Oh, dear. Would Cassandra be charged for damages? Those machines looked expensive.

"Is the equipment still operable?"

"Thankfully, it is." She chuckled again. "All the machines are plugged into surge protectors, but they were ineffective against my blast. I should be registered as a lethal weapon."

It was surprising to hear Cassy joke about it. Ever since she'd zapped a guy with a heart problem, and he'd been taken to the hospital, she'd never talked about her energy as a weapon.

Geraldine wondered what had changed.

"Can I come to see you?"

"Don't. I want to get some more sleep. Julian says that I need to preserve my strength for the transition my body is going through."

Cassandra didn't sound like someone who was tired and wanted to sleep. She sounded fully awake, but maybe she wanted to be alone with Onegus.

"Please ask Onegus to keep me informed."

"I will. Now stop worrying and go to sleep."

"I'll try. Good night, Cassy."

"Good night, Mom. I love you."

"I love you too, sweetie."

As Cassandra ended the call, Geraldine blew out a breath. "I think that I can finally relax. I just hope that Cassy was telling me the truth, and that she's really out of danger."

Shai frowned. "Why would she lie to you?"

"So I wouldn't worry." Geraldine rose to her feet. "Perhaps I should get a few hours of sleep."

He followed her up. "I can give you a T-shirt of mine to sleep in."

"That would be much appreciated." She smiled at him brightly and took his hand.

"The clothes Sylvia lent me are comfy, but there is nothing better than an old T-shirt that has been washed a thousand times." Especially if it retained his scent.

Given how bad her memory was, it was surprising how well Geraldine remembered smells. Sometimes a familiar scent would even trigger forgotten memories, or at least fragments of them. It wasn't much, but it was better than the nearly complete loss of them.

She wondered whether it was possible for a particular scent she'd smelled before the head trauma to bring back vestiges of the memories she'd lost as a result.

51

SHAI

*S*hai loved the idea of Geraldine wearing one of his shirts to bed. Imagining her small, feminine body encased in his clothing had his mind go all kinds of places it shouldn't.

Despite the good news about Cassandra, Geraldine was still worried and probably not in the mood for seduction. For him to make a move at a time like this would be inappropriate and might even turn her off him for good.

She was alone with him in the house, which must make her at least a little uncomfortable. He'd promised to be a gentleman, and he wasn't about to break his promise just because he craved her as much as he craved his next breath.

All good things were worth waiting for, right? Reining in his libido tonight would give him a better chance with Geraldine another day.

"I don't have any T-shirts that have been washed a thousand times."

He took her hand and led her through his bedroom into the walk-in closet. "I have, however, a pack of new ones. Wouldn't you prefer a T-shirt that hasn't been worn?" He opened a drawer and pulled out a pack of Hanes that had not been opened.

Knowing that she was sleeping in the room across the hallway wearing nothing but a cotton T-shirt and a pair of panties would be torturous enough. He didn't need to imagine the fabric that had touched his body touching hers, his scent intermingling with hers—

Geraldine leaned over his arm, reached into the drawer, pulled out one of his used T-shirts, and brought it up to her nose. "It smells like you." She sniffed loudly and then rubbed her cheek over the fabric. "And it's so soft." She clutched the shirt to her chest and smiled coyly. "Wearing it will be comforting for me."

Damn.

Shai tried to cover the groan rising up in his throat by faking a cough. "As you wish." He turned around to hide what had popped up behind his zipper. "You can

148

change in Thomas's room. But first, I need to find you a new toothbrush." He started toward the door.

"Shai." She said his name with a huskiness in her tone that had his shaft swell even further.

"Yes?" Slowly, he turned his head to look at her over his shoulder.

Eyeing him from under lowered lashes, his T-shirt still clutched to her chest, Geraldine smiled shyly. Or was it coyly? "Would you mind if I slept here with you? I don't want to be alone tonight."

Damn and double damn.

How could he refuse that?

And why would he? But what if all she wanted was to sleep in his bed?

Could he just hold her in his arms and not initiate a thing?

Perhaps he wouldn't have to. The way Geraldine was looking at him was far from innocent, so unless he was misreading her completely, sleeping was the furthest thing from her mind.

Except, he couldn't scent her arousal, which given her coquettish expression, he should have.

Was she playing games with him?

How could she act so seductive while experiencing no arousal?

Sadly, he'd encountered human females who, in their desperation for companionship, had pretended to want sex. The thing they'd really been after was to be held, comforted, and not sleep alone.

The thing was, Geraldine didn't fit the profile of a desperate female. She was confident in her own way, her fragility more an expression of her femininity than any real weakness.

She might not remember her past, but she was still a product of her generation. Young women in the fifties had been taught to act feminine and ladylike, and to let men feel as if they were in charge. Knowingly or unknowingly, Geraldine still behaved according to those expectations.

Shai was a product of the same generation, but as a male who'd been raised in a clan where females had always been held in the highest regard, he hadn't succumbed to the male attitudes of the time. He'd always been well aware that men overestimated their own importance and underestimated female strength, endurance, tenacity, and ability to lead.

"Are you sure?" He didn't want to assume anything or take something that was offered for the wrong reasons. "I'm a gentleman, and I'll do my best to behave accordingly, but certain things are beyond my control." He turned fully around, giving her an unmistakable frontal view.

As Geraldine's eyes traveled down, she lifted her hand to her mouth.

"Oh, dear." She giggled softly. "Perhaps I don't want you to be a gentleman." She walked over to him and put her arms around his neck. "You've been staring at my lips all night like you were dying to kiss me, and I was waiting patiently, or rather impatiently, for you to do it. I'm a lady, but certain things are beyond my control as well." She pulled him down to her, bringing their mouths almost together but waiting for him to close the last of the distance.

Done with second-guessing Geraldine's motives, he wrapped his arms around her waist and crushed her soft body against his chest. "I'm going to kiss you now," he murmured against her lips. "You have two seconds to change your mind."

"Why would I?" She closed the rest of the distance and fused their mouths.

GERALDINE

*S*hai's lips were soft against Geraldine's, but his fangs weren't, and neither was his body.

He was gentle with her, careful not to nick her with what she was sure was sharp enough to draw blood. Surprisingly, she found the idea of his bite erotic rather than scary.

Perhaps the vampire romances she'd read had mentally prepared her for tonight, or perhaps it was the subconscious memory of another time and another bite.

After all, to turn immortal, she must have been bitten by an immortal male.

When he deepened the kiss, Geraldine's thoughts returned to the here and now, her body melting against his, her breasts against his chest, her thighs against his.

For a personal assistant who self-confessedly stayed away from the gym, he was surprisingly muscular, not as in bulging biceps and pectorals, but as in lean and athletic.

As her hand lowered to travel down his back, Shai was emboldened to do some exploring of his own, his hands roving over her waist, her hips, and then cupping her bottom.

She pressed herself to him, seeking closer contact, wanting their clothes to magically disappear so they would be skin to skin.

As if reading her mind, Shai lifted her and laid her down on his bed.

For a long moment, he just stood there, gazing at her, waiting, and she realized that he was seeking her permission to continue.

"I want you." She held her arms out.

Accepting her invitation, he lowered himself over her, propping himself up on his elbows.

They were both still fully dressed, but she could feel his hard length pressing into her through the thin fabric of her borrowed leggings.

Looking up at his handsome face, she thought that his fangs didn't do anything to detract from his masculine beauty or even the gentleness of his expression. They were just part of who he was, an immortal male who was as beautiful on the inside as he was on the outside.

"You are overdressed for the occasion," she teased.

"So are you."

"That can be easily remedied." She reached between their bodies and gripped the bottom of her borrowed T-shirt.

He lifted on his elbows, giving her just enough room to whip the shirt over her head and toss it on the floor.

At the sight of her bra-covered breasts, his breath hitched. "I knew you were gorgeous, but I didn't know how absolutely perfect." He dipped his head and pressed a soft kiss to the top of one breast and then the other.

She wasn't big-breasted, just a modest C cup, but she was a small-boned woman, and their size was proportionate to her build.

When he lifted his head, the glow in his eyes provided enough illumination to cast her entire upper body in soft light. For long moments, he just gazed at her with admiration as if she was a work of art instead of a woman who was aching for him to make love to her.

She gave him another moment before asking, "Aren't you going to take it off me?"

He shook his head as if waking from a trance. "May I?"

"Please."

What happened next was a blur of motion, and at the end of it, she was completely naked, and so was he.

Talk about gorgeous.

There wasn't an ounce of fat on him. He was all lean muscles and hairless, with smooth skin, and the velvety arousal nestled between her thighs was long and hard.

"You're some kind of perfect yourself."

As she reached between their bodies and took hold of him, they both groaned. Stroking him lightly, she lifted her head and kissed him.

He took over, somehow deepening the kiss without involving his fangs, and then he was sliding down her body, and she had to let go of his shaft.

Knowing where he was heading made her ache in all new places. The first contact between his lips and her nipple was like an electrical jolt, making her arch up, and when he sucked it into his mouth, her eyes rolled back in her head.

For long moments, he licked and rolled, kissed and nipped, tormenting her nipples one at a time. She'd been so starved for him that it didn't take long for a sweet climax to wash over her, and that was even before he touched her achy center.

The growling was what had done it for her. It was in such stark contrast to the gentleness with which he handled her.

Geraldine loved it that he responded to her with such fervor, as if she was special, as if he had never been with a woman as marvelous as her—thankful for the privilege of pleasuring her.

She wanted to give back as much as she was being given, but with him being so much taller than her, she couldn't reach his arousal.

"Shai." She threaded her fingers through his hair. She had to pull to get his attention. "I want you in me."

He shook his head. "Not yet. I didn't feast my fill yet."

She let go of his hair to cup his gorgeous face. "If you are worried about me not being ready, don't."

When he looked skeptical, she let go of his face, took his hand, and placed it over her heated, moist center.

"I'm ready."

53

SHAI

*G*eraldine was soaking wet, and yet Shai still couldn't scent her arousal.

How was she so different from any female he'd ever been with? Was it because she was immortal and he wasn't familiar with the scent of an aroused immortal female?

A closer sniff of the unique bouquet might help solve the mystery, but that wasn't his main motivation for craving a taste of her nectar.

Penetration was the culmination of the sexual act, but Shai loved the prelude even more. For someone whose intimacy with females had been limited to sex, satisfying a woman orally was the closest to an emotional connection he could get.

He loved slowing down and appreciating a woman's body with his hands, his lips, his tongue. The incredible intimacy, the undivided attention he could give her without getting distracted by the intensity of his own pleasure, the satisfaction of bringing her over the edge, possibly several times—it all made the whole experience more special, more memorable.

"I need to get a little taste." Slowly, he slid down her body, kissing a path to her bellybutton.

When he pressed a soft kiss to the top of her sex, she threaded her fingers through his hair and let out a moan that was all about pleasure and acceptance—a sweet surrender that tugged at his heart in a most unexpected way.

Geraldine was unlike any other woman he'd been with. She was passionate and uninhibited, which led him to believe that she'd been quite active sexually, and yet there was an innocence to her. It was a sense of wonder and discovery, a soft femininity, which by contrast made him feel more male. And even though Geraldine hadn't been a wallflower who'd spent her life waiting for Prince Charming to appear and wake her with a kiss, Shai selfishly hoped that all the men she'd had before him had been garden-variety, warty frogs.

He wanted to be her one and only prince.

Except, he was more like the one from *Beauty and the Beast*, and right now, the less civilized side of him was fighting for supremacy.

Barely able to stifle an animalistic growl and attack her core like a ravenous beast, he gently parted her folds with his tongue.

"Shai." She arched up, her fingers tightening on his scalp.

The sexy, breathy way she'd said his name felt like a caress on the most sensitive part of him, and when she tugged on his hair, the erotic jolt went straight to his groin. No longer able to contain the growling animal inside of him, Shai attacked her femininity with all the pent-up ferocity of his hunger, sucking, licking, nipping, kissing. When he added his fingers to the play, Geraldine exploded, her spine arching and her pelvis shooting up.

He kept going, worshiping her with his mouth and wringing two more orgasms out of her. He only stopped when she cupped his cheeks and pulled him up and away from her core.

By some miracle, he hadn't climaxed all over the bed sheets, and as she tugged on his cheeks, urging him to come up, he was on her between one blink of an eye and the next.

Going slow was impossible, and as he surged into her scorching heat, he didn't wait for her to get accustomed to the penetration, joining them in one swift thrust.

Geraldine's groan was all about pleasure. Wrapping her slender legs around his hips and her arms around his torso, she pressed her small feet into his butt and her mouth to his lips.

As she kissed him, he wasn't sure who was devouring whom, but what he was certain of was that her ferocity matched his and then some.

Geraldine's dainty appearance was misleading. She was strong, wild, and demanding, and he rewarded her by giving her exactly what she asked for. He didn't have to hold back, he didn't have to be mindful of her fragility.

She could take everything he had and probably ask for more.

Their lovemaking wasn't gentle. It was a mutual claiming that had the bed rattling, the sheets tearing, and the plaster peeling off the wall as the headboard kept banging into it.

Lasting longer than a couple of minutes was not happening, but since he could go for seconds and thirds with her, it wasn't a problem.

She must have realized that as well because she was spurring him on as if he was a racehorse, her feet digging into his flanks, her nails digging into his back muscles, and her hips lifting to meet his thrust for thrust.

No longer able to keep the seal on her lips, he let go of her mouth, and as she immediately turned her head to expose her neck, his seed exploded from him like a geyser.

She climaxed even before he struck the pearly column of her neck, moaning in pleasure even though his venom hadn't entered her system yet, and when it did, she climaxed again, and again.

5 4

GERALDINE

*G*eraldine awakened before the sun was up, which was surprising given the marathon sex with Shai that had lasted until the early morning hours.

She should be exhausted, but instead, she felt invigorated.

Talk about earth-shattering orgasms.

For some reason, she doubted it was only about the incredible stamina, although she had to admit it was incredible, allowing Shai to go four rounds with her with no recuperating time needed between them. He'd bitten her only once, though, and the effects of the venom had been the stuff of legends.

There was no way she'd been bitten before and forgotten it, unless it had happened before the head trauma that had caused her amnesia.

It must have occurred sometime after she'd been released from the rehab facility. She still had lingering memory issues, but she would have remembered something as monumental as that bite. Perhaps the details would have become foggy, and she might even have thought that she dreamt it, but she would have remembered something. As it was, she had absolutely no memory of experiencing anything even remotely as extraordinary.

Was it like that with all immortal males? Or was Shai special?

Well, of course he was.

There was an unexpected emotional connection between them that had no right to be there after such a short acquaintance. But then, she'd never been with an immortal male, or at least with none that she remembered, so the connection could arguably be on the level of like recognizing like.

But she knew it wasn't.

Geraldine had never felt anything like that with the human males she'd been with, and she was quite sure that she would have remembered an emotional connection that powerful.

Her memory lapses were curiously uneven. Some things she remembered vividly, others only vaguely, and some not at all. She remembered feelings of fondness, or conversely disappointment, but not names or what they had done together or when. Her imagination filled in the details.

With Shai, however, she was convinced that she wouldn't forget a single thing—his handsome face, his lean body, the things he told her about himself, the gentle way he handled her, and then the wild abandon when he could no longer hold back.

Wow, what a ride.

Perhaps she should write it down just in case, to make sure she wouldn't forget any of it.

Planting a soft kiss on Shai's cheek, she extracted herself from his arms, got out of bed, and padded to the bathroom.

Everything in there smelled like him—the towels, the bathrobe, even the drawer where he kept a stash of new toothbrushes.

Stepping into the shower, Geraldine didn't feel as if she was intruding. She felt as if she was home.

That feeling lingered even after she'd left the house and headed toward the clinic. Surprisingly, there were more people on the walkways this early in the morning than at any other time she'd walked along the winding paths before. Some were jogging, others were fast-walking, and everyone she passed waved and smiled. People were friendly in the village, and she could see herself joining their community.

Perhaps she could start a book club or join an existing one if they had it. It was a great way to meet people and make friends. But what about her old friends? She could probably still meet with them, but what was she going to tell them? They would ask where she moved to, would want to visit her, have meetings at her place.

She didn't have a car or even a valid driver's license, but those were solvable problems. What wasn't as easily fixed was the gut feeling that she shouldn't move until something she couldn't articulate signaled that it was okay. The feeling was so strong and so peculiar that while trying to analyze it Geraldine lost her bearings and stopped to look around.

Wasn't Shai's house right off the village square?

Realizing that she'd gone in the opposite direction, she slapped a hand over her forehead.

A jogger slowed down next to her and kept running in place. "Are you lost?"

"Yes." Geraldine smiled at the girl. "Can you point me in the direction of the clinic?"

"I can do better than that. I can walk with you there." She extended her hand. "I'm Ella, Julian's mate."

"Geraldine. I've met the young doctor. He's taking care of my daughter." As she shook the girl's hand, she realized that neither Ella nor Julian was probably as young as they looked. "I might have been mistaken referring to your mate as young. Looks are misleading in this place. He could be hundreds of years old, right?"

"Actually, Julian is as young as he looks." Ella motioned for Geraldine to turn around. "And so am I. By the way, I heard the good news. Congratulations."

"On what?"

"Cassandra's transition, of course. Is there cause for congratulations about something else? An engagement, perhaps?"

Geraldine shook her head. "Not as far as I know. I keep hoping for Cassandra and Onegus to announce their engagement, but they are in no rush. Did Doctor Julian tell you anything about Cassandra's progress this morning? I didn't call Onegus because I figured he might be sleeping. I thought I would just show up at the clinic and see for myself."

"Julian said that she was doing well. He also told me that both Cassandra and Onegus were sleeping." Ella smiled. "In the same hospital bed. He wasn't happy about it, but he didn't want to wake them up."

CASSANDRA

assandra scratched at her arms. "Why am I still so itchy?"

Next to her, Onegus opened his eyes and smiled. "Good morning to you too, sunshine." He kissed her cheek. "How are you feeling?"

"Itchy."

"Other than that?"

"I feel good." The corners of her lips lifted in a small smile. "I need to use the bathroom."

"Let me help you." He swung his legs over the side of the bed.

They'd done the maneuver before, with him giving her a hand and rolling the IV contraption to the bathroom.

Thankfully, Cassandra hadn't lost consciousness. Her blood pressure had remained steadily high, but it hadn't increased, which was why Julian had agreed not to up the relaxant dosage. The downside was that the itchiness had gotten worse. Not that she knew the reason for its return. She must have been asleep when Julian had checked on her last, so she couldn't ask him.

Taking Onegus's hand, she lifted to her feet and adjusted the hospital gown, which had become undone during the night. "Is it my imagination, or did the gown shrink? When I put it on, it reached to the middle of my knees, and now the hem is above them."

"It's the wrinkles." Onegus kept her steady as she shuffled to the bathroom. "That's why it seems shorter."

"I guess so."

Bridget had said that some of the transitioning male Dormants had grown an inch or two, but it hadn't happened to any of the females, which she hoped would be the case with her as well. At five feet and eleven inches, she was tall enough.

"I'm good from here." She shooed Onegus out of the bathroom.

He didn't like it but knew better than to argue.

When she was done and opened the door, Bridget was in the room, waiting for her.

She must have arrived sometime during the morning to relieve Julian, or maybe she just wanted to check on Cassandra.

"How are you this morning?" Bridget asked.

"Good." Cassandra pulled the IV with her. "I'm still itchy, though. What's the deal with that?"

"You're probably growing, and your skin is stretching." Bridget pulled a tape measure from her coat pocket.

"Great." Cassandra grimaced. "I didn't need to get any taller." She sat on the bed and swung her legs up. "Wouldn't it hurt if I did, though?"

"The painkillers made the process as comfortable as possible for you, so you didn't feel the pain associated with such rapid growth." Bridget unrolled her tape and started taking measurements.

She'd taken many when Cassandra had been admitted to the clinic, so she would have a baseline to compare to.

"As I suspected, you gained an inch. You are six feet even now."

"Ugh." Cassandra pulled the sheet over her exposed legs. "I can no longer wear four-inch heels. I'll be taller than Onegus."

He grinned. "I don't mind."

"But I do. I'll have to get rid of them and get new ones."

"And that's a problem?" He leaned over her and kissed her forehead. "Think of all the fun you are going to have shopping for new shoes."

Bridget nodded in agreement. "Shoe shopping is a weakness of mine. I have way too many."

Her mood improved, Cassandra laughed. "My mother and I love to shop for shoes together." She turned to Onegus. "Is she here?"

"I don't know."

Bridget shook her head. "She wasn't there when I came in. It's still early. She might be sleeping."

Or having wild monkey sex with Shai. Otherwise, she would have already been camped out in the waiting room.

He was a fine man, and if things heated up between her mother and Kian's assistant, persuading Geraldine to move into the village might get much easier.

Stifling a smirk, Cassandra readjusted the blanket over her middle and turned to Onegus. "Perhaps you should text her and tell her that I'm awake. She will want to see me."

"Sure thing." Onegus pulled out his phone and typed it up.

A moment later, the device pinged with a return text.

"Your mother is out in the waiting room. Do you want me to call her in?"

"Yes, please. I want to talk to her." Cassandra grinned and added, "About the shoe shopping."

"Naturally."

As Onegus opened the door and stepped out of the room, Bridget folded her measuring tape and tucked it away in her pocket. "I'll leave you to talk to your mother and see what I can do about breakfast."

Cassandra's mouth watered. "I'd sell a kidney for a cup of coffee and a pile of scrambled eggs."

"I don't know about the kidney or the eggs, but I can probably get you a sandwich and a cup of coffee."

Cassandra steepled her hands and bowed her head over them. "You'll have my eternal gratitude."

"Easily earned." Bridget headed for the open door. "After breakfast, I'll conduct the test." She left the room before Cassandra had a chance to react.

It was all good news. Julian had said that she might be ready for the test today, but she'd expected it to happen later, perhaps in the afternoon or the evening. She'd also expected Julian and not his mother to perform it.

Cassandra wondered why the plan had changed.

It wasn't about seniority because her transition had been so easy, but maybe Bridget was more worried about the high blood pressure than she'd let on.

As her mother entered the room and closed the door behind her, Cassandra spread her arms. One was never too old for a hug from one's mother to make everything seem better somehow.

"Did you hear the news?" Cassandra asked.

Geraldine frowned. "About what?"

"I got taller by a whole inch. We need to go shoe shopping because I'm donating all of my four-inch heels. Onegus is six feet and three inches tall, and although he doesn't mind, I don't want to be taller than him in heels."

Her mother leaned against her hospital bed. "It's a shame that we aren't the same size. I could have taken them off your hands. Shai is so tall that even with four-inch heels, the top of my head will only reach his shoulder."

Cassandra couldn't contain her happy grin. "So you are an item now?"

Geraldine shrugged, but a sheepish smile bloomed on her face. "I guess we are. I like him a lot."

Asking her mother whether they'd done the deed wasn't something Cassandra was comfortable doing, but she could ask other things. "Do you like Shai enough to move into the village to be with him?"

"That's an unfair question. I like him a lot, but we've just met, and I don't know where it will lead. Shai promised to come to visit me at our house and to take me out on dates in the city." She pushed a strand of hair behind her ear. "I guess I will need to start driving again. Do you know how much those special self-driving cars cost?"

"I don't. But I can ask Onegus."

"When you do, can you also ask him if he can get me a new fake driver's license? The last one I had expired, and I didn't know where to get a new one."

"Where did you get the other ones?"

Geraldine's hand flew to her temple the way it always did when she couldn't remember something. "I don't know. I must have forgotten."

56

ONEGUS

*O*utside Cassandra's room, Onegus expected to find Shai, but the guy was gone.

Pulling out his phone, he started typing up a text to Roni to inform him about Cassandra's progress when Bridget walked up to him.

"If Cassandra agrees, I would like to conduct the test on her."

"Do we need it? There is no doubt that she's transitioning."

If he could spare Cassandra pain, he'd rather avoid the unnecessary test, and he'd told Julian as much. Not that Cassandra minded. When Julian had mentioned performing it today, she hadn't objected.

"The test will determine whether she's over the critical stage of the transition. It will give us all peace of mind."

That was an important piece of information that was worth a little pain.

"Isn't it too early?"

She shrugged. "If it is, we will just conduct another one tomorrow."

As if he would allow it. If Cassandra didn't pass the first stage and her body couldn't heal fast yet, she would suffer from the damn cut for hours.

"Then let's wait until tomorrow. I don't want Cassandra to endure pain needlessly."

"I believe that she's ready, and if the result is positive, I can get out of here. I have a pile of work waiting on my desk, and I need to get to it if we want to resume the rescue missions. With you unavailable, the entire thing falls on me."

That was true. He'd been so preoccupied with Cassandra that he'd forgotten that it was Monday and he needed to get to his office as well. The rescue missions needed to resume as soon as possible, and with him and Bridget being busy with Cassandra, that wasn't going to happen. Julian could replace Bridget after he'd gotten a few hours of sleep, but those would still be hours lost.

His conscience was heavy enough because of the week-long halt in rescue missions during the clan celebrations.

"I'm sorry. You're right, and I need to get back to work as well."

"That's okay." Bridget put her hand on his arm. "I'll gladly shoulder the entire operation for a couple of days until you are ready to resume your job."

"You're the best, Bridget, and I owe you. Next time you and Turner go on vacation, I'll take over your part of the job as well."

She smiled. "I'm counting on it. Talk it over with Cassandra and let me know what she decides." She opened the door to her office. "Shai texted me that he's getting breakfast for Cassandra, you, and Geraldine. He'll probably need help carrying it."

"I'm on it." Onegus walked out of the clinic door.

He intercepted Shai midway and took the cardboard tray with coffees from him. "Good morning."

"Good morning to you too. How is Cassandra doing?"

"Very well."

Thankfully, the clinic was only a few steps away, so the awkward silence between them didn't last long.

The door to Cassandra's room was open, and as Onegus poked his head inside, both mother and daughter beckoned him in.

"Coffee!" Cassandra waved him over. "You're my angel."

He chuckled. "You need to thank Shai for that."

"Where is he?"

"Outside in the waiting room, holding two large bags stuffed with everything the café has to offer." He handed one cup to Cassandra and the other one to Geraldine.

"Tell him to come in," Cassandra said. "So I can thank him in person."

"Good morning." Shai entered the room. "How are you doing?"

Cassandra eyed the bags in his hands. "Starving. Thank you for getting us breakfast."

"My pleasure." He pulled out an assortment of sandwiches and pastries and put them on the rolling table.

As Cassandra unwrapped a sandwich, Onegus reached for the remaining paper cup. "Bridget wants to conduct the fast-healing test today. It's not necessary to determine whether you are transitioning because that's a given, but it can tell us whether you are past the critical stage. Once the body can heal at an immortal speed, the worst is over. On the other hand, if you are not there yet, she will have to do it again tomorrow, and the cut she inflicts today will take a long time to heal. So, it's up to you whether you want to go for it today or wait until tomorrow or not at all."

"Of course, I want to do it." Cassandra wiped her mouth with a napkin and handed her mother the empty wrapper to toss away. "You said that all Dormants go through it, so even though it's not necessary in my case, I don't want to deviate from tradition and skip the ritual. In fact, I want someone to video record it so I'll have a souvenir."

"We can invite Roni and Sylvia to witness it," Geraldine suggested.

"Great idea, Mom."

Onegus pulled out his phone. "When do you want them to come over?"

"An hour from now is good." Cassandra lifted a pastry and started unwrapping it. "But you need to check with Bridget if it works for her."

The doctor would have preferred to be done with it sooner, but she wouldn't object to waiting one more hour.

"Do you want me to invite Connor too?"

Cassandra nodded. "I would have liked to invite all of my new friends, but I don't think this room is big enough." She tilted her head. "Is it okay to invite anyone at all, though? I don't know what the tradition is."

"Usually, it's just the transitioning Dormant, their partner, and the doctor." Onegus leaned and kissed her cheek. "But I'll gladly share the experience with your nephew, his mate, and my roommate. It warms my heart that, after knowing them for only a short time, you already think of them as your family."

5 7

CASSANDRA

*B*ridget didn't like the idea of so many people congregating in Cassandra's small patient room. "You need to choose who you want to witness the test. I can allow no more than two people in here."

It was good that Onegus and her mother had cleaned up after breakfast, eliminating all evidence of the little feast they'd shared in the room. Bridget would have been livid if she'd walked in when all the mess was still there.

"We will wait outside." Sylvia tugged on Roni's hand.

"I can come out to the waiting room," Cassandra offered. "I feel fine. Even the itchiness has subsided."

Bridget shook her head.

"I suggest a compromise." Onegus turned to the doctor. "Can you tolerate three people in here with Cassandra? Geraldine, Roni, and me. Sylvia, Shai, and Connor can watch through the open door."

Letting out a breath, Bridget nodded. "Fine. Let's do it."

As the doctor assembled the necessary tools, everyone got in position. Onegus, her mother and Roni stood on the left side of her bed, with Roni holding up his phone, ready to record the event.

The doctor took position on the right side of the hospital bed. "Give me your hand."

Smiling broadly for the camera, Cassandra did as Bridget asked. The doctor swiped her palm with an antiseptic, then lifted a small surgical knife and made a tiny cut in Cassandra's palm.

It hurt, but she kept smiling. When showing the recording to her future children, Cassandra didn't want them to think that their mother was a wuss.

It took longer for the small wound to close than it had taken Geraldine, but it was definitely faster than anything Cassandra had expected. She could actually see the skin knitting back together, and thirty seconds later no sign of the injury remained.

"Welcome to immortality." Bridget smiled broadly. "Since you are out of danger,

I'll leave you in the capable hands of Hildegard. The office building is next door, so if needed, I can be back here in under a minute."

"Thank you, doctor." Cassandra clasped Bridget's hand. "I truly appreciate the fantastic care you and Julian have provided me with. But can I go home now? I need to get back to work."

The doctor shook her head. "I want you to stay in the clinic for a few more hours, and then you can go to Onegus's house and take it easy for the rest of the week, but you can't leave the village. I need to keep an eye on you."

If she took a week off, Kevin would have a stroke.

"How long?"

"You can probably go back to work next Monday. I'll come to check up on you in a few hours."

Damn, Cassandra had planned on sneaking out while Bridget was away.

"Thank you," she said again as the doctor headed for the door.

"You're welcome."

As the doctor left, Roni leaned down and kissed her cheek. "Congratulations, Auntie Cassandra. Welcome to immortality."

"Thank you. And just so you know, I love it when you call me auntie."

He chuckled. "I'll do some light editing on the recording and send it to you, Auntie."

Next, Connor, Sylvia, and Shai entered the room and congratulated her as well, and when everyone other than Onegus and her mother left, Cassandra finally stopped smiling.

"I can't take a week-long vacation." She flung the blanket off and swung her legs over the side of the bed, remembering too late that she was still hooked up to the monitoring equipment and the IV drip. "Can you check if Bridget is still here? She forgot to unhook me."

"I'll check." Her mother rushed out of the room and came back a moment later. "The nurse said that she will do that once Bridget approves your discharge. She said it will be at least four more hours."

"Damn." Cassandra swung her legs back up on the bed. "I thought I could take a shower and get dressed." She looked at Onegus. "I need to call Kevin and tell him that I'm not coming in to work today, but I don't know what else to tell him. Is it possible to convince Bridget to shorten my sentence?"

Onegus sat on the bed and took her hand. "You can tell him that you are sick but that you will work from home."

"I don't have anything with me."

"Once Bridget discharges you, we can swing by your house and collect your art supplies as well as a few changes of clothes."

Huffing, she crossed her arms over her chest. "And where am I going to work? Your house doesn't have a spare bedroom that I could use as a studio, and I can't work on the kitchen counter or on your dining room table. I need peace and quiet to concentrate." She uncrossed her arms to tap her temple. "ADHD brain here, remember?"

Her mini tantrum had no effect on Onegus. "I can find you an unoccupied office next to mine in the underground," he suggested.

She shook her head. "I need natural light, at least for the artsy part of my work. I don't want to be difficult, but I really can't work exclusively with artificial light. It will mess up my perception of colors. Maybe there is a vacant space in the office building? It has large windows that I'm sure allow in plenty of sunshine."

Onegus's eyes brightened. "The gallery. Amanda's mate is an artist, and he created such a spectacular portrait of Annani that Kian decided to dedicate a room to display it permanently. I'm sure he'll be okay with you putting a small desk in there and making it your impromptu studio."

58

GERALDINE

*B*ridget returned to the clinic at precisely eleven o'clock, checked on Cassandra, and approved her discharge.

Then the nurse kicked Geraldine and Onegus out to give herself room to work while she disconnected Cassandra from all the things that were nourishing and monitoring her.

Out in the waiting room, Geraldine pulled out her phone and texted Shai. *I need to get my things from your house. Onegus is taking Cassy home to pick up a few things, and he's going to drop me off there.* She looked at the text and added, *We also didn't get the chance to say goodbye.*

After Cassy's test, Shai had gone to the office, probably expecting Geraldine to remain in the village for as long as Cassandra stayed, which was a whole week, but Geraldine couldn't do that.

Something was tugging at her subconscious, or her gut, or her intuition that she couldn't leave the house for so long. Who was going to pick up the mail? And what about opening the windows in the morning to air it out? If it stayed locked up for long, it would start smelling funny, and she couldn't allow that.

Glancing at her phone, she expected a text back, but instead the clinic door opened and Shai walked in.

"You're leaving?"

Onegus looked at her with surprise in his eyes. She hadn't told him her plan to go home with him and Cassy and stay there.

"Yes." She offered him a tentative smile. "Someone needs to hold the fort while Cassandra is gone. She called her boss and told him that she's sick. What if he calls the house and no one answers?"

"That's what call forwarding is for," Onegus said. "If you're worried about not having a place to stay, I assure you that I can find you an entire house. In fact, I should have thought of it sooner. You and Cassandra can get a place of your own, and she can have her studio set up there." He rubbed a hand over his stubbled chin. "Naturally, I would prefer for Cassandra to stay with me, but if that bothers you, I won't."

Geraldine rolled her eyes. "Don't be silly. We don't live in Victorian times, and you and Cassy are a couple. But not having a place to stay is not the reason I want to go home. I just need to go back to my place. I have friends I want to visit and go out to lunch with, I have book club meetings that I need to attend, and I want to sleep in my own bed." She turned to Shai. "You could come to visit me if you want. I can make us dinner, we can watch a movie on Netflix, or we can go on a walk around our neighborhood. It's not as big or as green as the village, but it's really nice."

"I would like that." Shai looked uncomfortable when he turned to Onegus. "When are you leaving?"

"Not for another hour or so. Cassandra wants to take a shower and get dressed, and then I need to stop by my house and do the same. I've been wearing these clothes for two days straight."

"Good, then it gives us some time." He took Geraldine's hand. "I took an early lunch break so I could spend some time with you. We can go to my place, collect your things, and then grab something to eat at the café."

"Sounds lovely." She looked at Onegus. "Would you let Cassy know that I'm with Shai?" When he nodded, she added, "Just please don't leave without me."

"I wouldn't dream of it."

As she and Shai walked out of the clinic hand in hand, people glanced in their direction, nodded their greetings, and smiled. She wondered whether they were being polite or were they happy for Shai and her and their nascent relationship.

"Why don't you stay here for at least a couple of days?" Shai asked. "I can take you home whenever you wish. That way, we can spend more time together while you won't miss any of your book club meetings or lunches with your friends."

"It's a lovely offer, but I really can't. Maybe I just need to get used to the idea." She looked up at him. "I don't have a car, but Onegus said that he can get me one of those the clan uses, so I can come and go as I please. He's also arranging for a new fake driver's license for me. It's not such a long drive, so I can keep my old house and come to the village every day." She smiled coyly. "Or every night."

"But until that happens, you could stay here," Shai said as they climbed the stairs to his front porch.

Struggling to come up with a convincing argument, Geraldine remembered that Shai didn't live alone.

"You said that your roommate is coming back home tomorrow. We'll no longer have privacy."

"He's a nice guy, and he has his own room." Shai opened his front door that hadn't been locked. "If you haven't noticed, we have excellent soundproofing in our houses. We can be as loud as we want in my room and he's not going to hear a thing."

"That's convenient." She walked into the house. "For my nightly visits." She turned to him and wrapped her arms around his neck. "But I really need to be in my own house. Can you accept me with my limitations?"

"Always." He dipped his head and kissed her.

When they came up for air, Geraldine smiled at him. "How hungry are you?"

"It depends on what hunger you are referring to?"

She looked at him from under lowered lashes. "An hour is plenty of time, and if you are willing to skip lunch, we can make good use of it."

When he grinned, his fangs were already elongated. "I like the way you think."

59

KIAN

*I*n his office, Kian stood next to the window overlooking the café and debated whether to go down and grab something to eat before his meeting with Stella.

Syssi and Allegra were home, but both were asleep, and Kian didn't feel like making small talk with his in-laws. He liked Adam and Anita, but he wasn't a people person, and having them in the house was tiring through no fault of their own.

He just needed his peace and quiet, but his needs were secondary to Syssi's, and her mother and father were a great help with the baby.

Despite Okidu proving to be as loyal and as devoted as always, Kian still didn't feel comfortable with the Odu holding Allegra even for a moment. Perhaps it was paranoia, but Kian felt as if he was already taking a chance by having the Odu in the house.

For now, that was as far as he was willing to go.

Perhaps he could ask Shai to bring him something from the café. The guy had taken an early lunch break and was atypically late.

Kian smiled. Shai had planned to invite Cassandra's mother to lunch, but he'd never made it to the café. In all likelihood, his assistant hadn't eaten either.

Pulling out his phone, he texted him, *Can you get me a sandwich and a cup of coffee on your way back? And get yourself one as well.*

Kian put the phone on his desk, sat down, and opened the fourth file Shai had put on his desk that morning. The briefs his assistant prepared for him were big time-savers, for which Kian was grateful. Now that he was a father, working fifteen-hour days was not happening. His plan was to start his day at six in the morning and be back home at four, so he could spend time with his daughter.

Whether he would be able to stick to that schedule remained to be seen, but he'd already made the mental adjustment and had even changed plans accordingly.

The week of celebrations and family gatherings had left him with a big backlog of work. He was going to concentrate on catching up, and everything else could wait.

He'd asked Turner to go over all the information they had on the Kra-ell and provide him with a risk assessment. The guy was extremely busy with his own projects, so his analysis was superficial, but when he'd said that finding the Kra-ell wasn't urgent, it was good enough for Kian, and he decided to push the China mission to next month.

There was also the issue of the trafficking victims rescue operation. New intel needed to be collected, plans needed to be changed accordingly, and in order to catch up, they needed to dedicate every available Guardian to the task.

Not to mention that Onegus was unavailable for the next couple of days, and Kian didn't expect the guy to return to working twelve-hour days even after Cassandra recuperated from her transition. As a newly mated male, Onegus would want to spend as much time as possible with his beloved.

That was another reason to postpone the China mission. Also, it would give Mey and Jin more time to make progress with the languages they were rushing to learn.

There were plenty of reasons why it was a good decision, but knowing that didn't make it any easier for him.

Kian didn't like postponing things. His natural preference was to have things done as soon as possible, but he had to work on curbing that.

He was immortal, which meant an abundance of time to achieve whatever goals he set for himself. Time became a precious commodity only when applied to his daughter. She wouldn't be a baby and child forever, and he wanted to savor as much of her during those formative years as he could.

That didn't mean that he would neglect the clan's needs until Allegra became an adult, but he'd make a serious effort to better balance his professional and personal life.

As the door to his office opened, and his assistant rushed in, Kian lifted his head. "Hello, Shai."

The guy's expression was sheepish as he put what he'd gotten in the café on the conference table. "I apologize for the longer than usual break I took. Geraldine needed to collect her things from my place. Onegus is taking her home."

It wasn't like Bridget to allow a newly transitioned immortal to go where she couldn't monitor her. "Is Cassandra going home already?"

"Bridget wants her to stay in the village until next Monday, but Cassandra needs to collect her laptop and art supplies so she can work from here. Geraldine insisted that they take her home." Shai pulled a sandwich out of the café's paper bag and handed it to Kian. "Kalugal's compulsion still holds, so you have nothing to worry about. She can't even say immortal. The word wouldn't leave her mouth no matter how hard she tried." He pulled the other sandwich out and removed the wrapper. "Besides, Geraldine has a reputation for telling tall tales, so no one is going to take her seriously anyway."

Kian removed the wrapper from his eggplant and bell peppers sandwich. "The best way to discredit a witness is to make them appear unreliable. Humans have been employing that tactic successfully for years."

Shai nodded. "Regrettably, that doesn't apply to Geraldine. She says that sometimes she has a difficult time distinguishing between events that happened only in her dreams and real ones. But an even simpler explanation is that she makes up stories to compensate for the gaps in her memories."

60

SHAI

*A*s a knock sounded on Kian's office door, Shai tossed the remnants of his and Kian's lunch into the trash and walked over to open the way.

"Thank you for coming." He offered Stella his hand and then shook Richard's.

"Good afternoon, Kian." Looking nervous, Stella moved her satchel to her other shoulder. "You didn't say what this is about."

"The China mission." Kian motioned for them to take a seat at the conference table. When they were seated, he turned to Stella. "Since you are fluent in Chinese, and you are much more personable than Morris, we thought that you might be a valuable asset to the team."

She didn't look enthusiastic. "I thought that Mey and Jin were learning the language."

"They are." Kian pulled out a chair and sat down. "But their progress is slow. Perhaps in a month they will get better, but they are not going to be fluent."

Richard shifted in his chair. "Weren't they supposed to leave next week?"

Kian nodded. "They were, but I decided to give Mey and Jin more time to prepare. Besides, I can't spare any Guardians at the moment. The intel we had for the rescue missions that got canceled during the week of celebrations needs to be updated, and then we need to double down to make up for the lost time. I can't in good conscience give the Kra-ell investigation priority over the trafficking victims who have no one else to help them."

For a long moment, no one said a thing, Stella and Richard probably mulling over Kian's somber words.

It was like a splash of cold water, cooling Shai's excitement about his own newfound happiness that had followed a week of celebrations. Having been caught up in their own happy times, it had been easy to forget the incredible suffering happening practically in their backyard, figuratively speaking, not to mention the world at large.

As was usually the case, after a short period of progress and prosperity in which things had seemed to be improving, the unraveling had started once more, and entire nations were succumbing to the darkness.

Except, this time Shai doubted that the Brotherhood had an active hand in it. The seeds of the evil ideology, though, of treating women as enslaved possessions and the complete disregard for the most basic human rights—those had been planted by the devout followers of Mortdh over the millennia.

"What's the danger level the team is expected to face?" Richard asked.

"Very low," Kian asserted. "It's just a recon mission. Even if the team discovers a thread we can follow, it will not be your job to pursue it. Stella's part ends there."

"I accept," Stella said. "Theater productions are still at an all-time low, and I don't have any new costume orders. The designs for Mey and Jin are done, and since they are going, they won't have anything new for me to do." She smiled at Richard. "Other than the virtual adventure we shared, I haven't had any in many years. How about it? Are you up for going on another one with me?"

Richard took her hand and lifted it to his lips. "Always. Wherever you go, I go." He looked at Kian. "I hope that's clear."

"Of course." Kian leaned forward. "I spoke with Kalugal to check if I could steal you from him, and he graciously agreed for me to offer you a position. I could use an experienced supervisor for our building project here in the village and also for other projects the clan is developing all over the US and abroad. We can negotiate your salary at another time."

Crossing his arms over his chest, Richard pretended to think it over, but his excitement showed in his eyes. "I'll be happy with what Kalugal paid me."

"I'll raise whatever he did by fifteen percent. After all, you are more experienced now, and you have a glowing recommendation from your previous employer."

"When do I start?"

"How about next Monday?"

"It depends on Kalugal. I need to speak with him first."

"Naturally."

"What about Emmett Haderech?" Stella asked. "I was under the impression that following confirmation of the information he provided, you'd allow him into the village. If the mission is postponed by a month, so is his release from prison."

Shai was surprised that she cared, but she wasn't wrong. Keeping Emmett prisoner was a drain on their resources. The Guardians monitoring him were needed elsewhere.

"I'm aware of that." Kian drummed his fingers on the conference table. "Perhaps I'll free him on probation before confirmation. If the information he provided proves false, I'll lock him up again."

This was news to Shai. "Has he bonded with Eleanor?"

Kian shook his head. "Not as far as I know, but I can't keep him locked up forever. Peter called, saying that Emmett is not doing well. Eleanor noticed it first and brought it to his attention, and Peter confirmed her assessment. Evidently, the Kraell need sunlight to thrive just as humans do. In that respect, they differ from the gods, who are perfectly comfortable living underground. Emmett also needs physical activity. Peter suggested taking him up to my old penthouse once a day to soak up the sun, and to be allowed to use the Keep's gym and swimming pool. I can either do that or allow him in the village. I haven't decided yet which I'm more comfortable with."

"He could wear a cuff like I did," Richard said. "You mentioned that you can't spare any Guardians at the moment, so why waste two on Emmett? Allow him in the village and give him a job. Let him earn his keep."

"Good thinking," Kian said. "Perhaps he could be your assistant."

Richard blanched. "I'm allergic to snobs."

Kian laughed. "After working for Kalugal, you should have developed a tolerance."

"That's different. I can tolerate a snobbish boss, but not an underling."

"Maybe he could work in the sanctuary," Stella suggested. "After all, he's a wellness guru. Perhaps he could design a special program to help the victims."

Shai shook his head. "I wouldn't risk it. Emmett is a strong compeller, and even though the Clan Mother mitigated his ability, I suspect that he's clever enough to circumvent it."

"I like the sanctuary idea," Kian told Stella. "I just need to find a way to ensure Emmett's good behavior. If needed, the Clan Mother can do another session with him to secure his full cooperation."

61

RONJA

*M*erlin walked out of the department store's dressing room and turned in a circle with his arms spread wide. "What do you think?"

Ronja got up from the chair and walked up to him. "Everything fits beautifully, but it's just not you." With the gray slacks and a light blue button-down, he looked like an office clerk. Without the bright colors and the crazy hair, he just wasn't Merlin.

"I kind of like the slacks. Maybe a different shirt? Something with more pizazz?" He winked.

"Yes. I liked the purple paisley shirt you tried before." It was the only bold shirt in the entire men's clothing section of the department store. "Perhaps we should shop someplace else."

He made a pouty face. "I thought that you wanted me to look distinguished. Like a real doctor should."

She chuckled. "What would be the fun in that? You will end up boring yourself."

"True." He started unbuttoning his shirt.

"Not here." She gave him a playful shove. "Go back inside and change. I know just the place we need to check out."

He arched a brow. "You do? Was Frank a fancy dresser?"

As usual, the mention of Frank's name evoked a pang of sadness, but it wasn't as painful as it had been in the beginning. She could talk about him now without choking.

Her second husband hadn't been the big love of her life like her first, but he was Lisa's father, and Ronja had loved him, just in a different way.

She still missed him.

"Frank was as far from a fancy dresser as a man could get. The only reason I know that place is because of Lisa. She liked window shopping there. It's on the pricy side, so we couldn't afford it unless it was for a special occasion, but she had fun trying stuff on. She said it was hip and chic."

"It sounds like a store I would like to visit." Merlin leaned and kissed her cheek. "I'll be out in a jiffy." He ducked back into the dressing room.

The guy was difficult to resist, and he acted as if it was a forgone conclusion that they were a couple.

To the people around them, they must look like mother and son. But even if she was willing to ignore the looks, Ronja wasn't ready to start seriously dating yet. It was disrespectful to Frank's memory to start a new relationship so soon after his death.

Merlin was moving too fast.

Ronja had just wanted to flirt a little, so she could feel alive again. She hadn't planned on starting anything. That being said, she could go for a long, platonic courtship. That way, she could enjoy Merlin's company without disrespecting Frank.

Heck, who was she kidding?

A human male wouldn't have tolerated that, let alone an immortal. They were such highly sexual beings. Merlin probably expected her to jump into bed with him after dinner tonight. He would be very disappointed when she turned him down.

Maybe she shouldn't?

Frank was gone, and unless he was watching her from the great beyond, he no longer cared what she did. But Lisa cared, and she would be upset if her mother didn't honor her father's memory.

God, she hated being alone.

Lisa was growing up so fast, and she had her own life that didn't include her mother. She spent most of her time either studying in her room or spending time with Parker, and that was fine. That was the way it should be.

Maybe it painted Ronja as a weak female, but she needed a man in her life. She used to think that it was because she felt safer with a man in the house, but that wasn't a concern in the village. She just needed company, someone to take care of, someone who appreciated her, shared her life, someone who saw her.

Pathetic.

As Merlin emerged from the dressing room in his old colorful clothes, she forced a smile. "That's more like it."

He threaded his arm through hers. "I'm starting to think that I shouldn't have chopped off my beard and mustache. I think that you liked me better with them."

"You looked older."

"I am older." He leaned closer to whisper in her ear. "Much older than you. In fact, you're a baby compared to me."

"I know. It just feels weird knowing that people think I'm your mother."

"Screw what everyone thinks." He led her out of the department store. "So, where is that fancy hip and chic place?"

"On the lower level."

62

KIAN

On his way home, Kian made a detour to visit William in his lab. Despite his insistence that it wasn't urgent, William had probably been working nonstop on Okidu's journals and only taking catnaps at his desk instead of going home.

As Kian had suspected, he found William in his office in the lab, looking more disheveled than he'd ever seen him before.

The guy hadn't shaved or combed his hair in days, and Kian suspected that he hadn't showered either.

Pulling out a chair, he sat down. "What's going on, William?"

As the guy lifted his head, the surprised look on his face indicated that he hadn't even noticed Kian walking into his office.

"I'm dumbfounded. That is what's going on." He let out a long breath and sagged his shoulders. "This is so beyond anything we know that I feel like a caveman trying to understand quantum physics."

That was most likely a gross exaggeration. Except, William wasn't prone to making bombastic claims. "Is it that much more advanced than what's on Ekin's tablet?"

Leaning back, William pushed his glasses up his nose. "Compared to what I'm starting to glimpse from Okidu's journals, the information contained in Ekin's tablet is like Newtonian physics to quantum mechanics." He flipped through the journal pages in front of him. "This is based on genetics, which as you know is not my field of expertise, but I need to master it if I want to understand this. I've read about advances in gene sequencing and the curative potential they introduced, but I didn't delve into it, thinking that it was Bridget's field. Boy, was I wrong. Somehow it didn't dawn on me that genetic coding can be used like any other computer language. The potential is just staggering, and what I'm talking about is humans gaining immortality in the near future and much more than that. Talk about god-like power." He tapped the journal. "This is the key to creation."

178

Kian frowned. "Are you saying that these journals contain the information to alter human genes to become like us?"

William rubbed his temples. "Possibly, but I doubt they contain everything. The human genome is composed of 3.2 billion letters, which is approximately a million pages, so it's not possible for the journals to contain it all, but it's enough if they provide the code for the specific enhancements we enjoy. But that's just the tip of the iceberg. With gene-editing technology, which has made huge strides in the last couple of years, we can create new materials, like the ones used to create indestructible Odus." He put his hand on the closed journal. "That's what I expect to find in these." He chuckled. "But Okidu's gift is much more than just a way to build more Odus. I believe that it will usher a quantum leap into the future."

That wasn't what Kian had expected to hear when he walked into William's office. What the clan's genius suspected was both exciting and terrifying.

"I find it serendipitous that Okidu's accident coincided with breakthroughs in gene-editing capabilities." Kian crossed his arms over his chest. "Correct me if I'm wrong, but several years ago, even you wouldn't have understood the significance of what's in them."

William nodded. "The technology has existed for at least a decade, but it was far from mainstream and only used in research. It didn't make headlines until last year when two scientists received a Nobel Prize for developing the CRISPR-Cas9, a gene-editing tool that allows precise edits to the genome." William shifted in his chair. "After I realized what the journals were talking about, I did some reading on the subject. The advancements in the field of gene sequencing are such that we can now purchase a sequencer for a reasonable price and perhaps finally figure out what makes us different. Perhaps we can use the CRISPR device to produce synthetic venom and use it to induce Dormants. Lisa wouldn't have to wait until she's old enough to fall in love and have sex to transition."

It all seemed too good to be true.

In Kian's experience, discoveries that had been hailed as miraculous, promising the moon, had usually ended up under-delivering. Besides, a synthetic venom would undermine the Fates' matchmaking game, which meant that they wouldn't allow it. That wasn't how they worked.

There was something else in those journals that they had deemed necessary for the clan.

Superstitious much?

Maybe.

But he was old enough and experienced enough to realize that more than pure science and natural forces animated the universe.

"I'm surprised that Bridget is not on top of all this hoopla about genetic manipulation."

"It's not her field of expertise either." William sighed. "She should have encouraged Julian to study biochemistry instead of becoming a doctor. As it is, we don't have anyone in the clan who's studied the field, let alone an expert."

"That's a shame." Kian pushed to his feet. "I will offer an incentive to anyone who's interested in pursuing the field, and in a few years, we will have as many experts as we need. After all, we are not in a rush. The mystery of our origins has waited to be solved for thousands of years, it can wait for a few more."

63

CASSANDRA

*a*fter collecting her art supplies, Cassandra put them in a box that went inside her art bag. Her laptop and tablet went inside her spinner carry-on.

Turning toward the closet, she stopped, startled to see her reflection in the mirrored wardrobe doors. The inch she'd grown overnight shouldn't make that much of a difference, but for some reason, it did. She felt huge and awkward like she had in high school after her growth spurt. She'd always been tall, but at tenth grade she'd grown two additional inches, which made her the tallest girl in the school, and taller than most of the boys.

It would seem that her mother had gotten it all wrong about who her father was. Perhaps she should look at NBA stars' pictures and see if she looked like any of them. Those men were notorious for their womanizing ways, and Geraldine had a thing for tall guys. NBA players also came with other benefits, like hefty bank accounts and fame.

Some were very handsome despite their gangly limbs. Cassandra had even had a celebrity crush on a couple of them when she was a teenager. That was until she'd read about their shenanigans, which had been enough to cure her of her infatuation.

Taking a closer look at her face, she had to admit that other than the extra inch, the changes she noticed were subtle and welcome.

Her skin was tauter, which might be the result of the sudden growth, her eyes were more open and had a sparkle to them that hadn't been there before, but her hair was still a little too sparse for her liking. Until she'd smartened up and let her curly hair be, she'd ruined it with too many straightening products and treatments over the years. Hopefully, the transition would heal it, and over time, some volume would return to her curls.

Overall, Cassandra was happy with the change. It was still her in the mirror, only fresher and younger.

Bridget claimed that she would keep changing over the next six months, and that she might look even younger, which could be difficult to explain to people at the office.

She could claim plastic surgery or some other cosmetic procedure, or maybe just having found love with an incredible man, but the height difference would be harder to explain away. The doctor suggested spine manipulation as a possible explanation. She said that it had worked for one of the transitioned male Dormants who'd grown even more than Cassandra had.

Still, that wasn't a huge problem. Leaving her mother at home alone was.

Heaving a sigh, Cassandra pulled a suitcase from the closet's top shelf and started dropping outfits inside. She needed stuff that would last her a week, and since she wouldn't be going to the office, she could pack mostly casual stuff. Still, a couple of nice outfits found their way into the suitcase, along with some lower-heeled shoes than what she usually wore to work. When everything—including makeup, jewelry, and her hairdryer—was packed, she closed the suitcase and lifted it to a standing position.

It hadn't been effortless, but she had a feeling that it had been a little easier. Supposedly, she was still weak from her transition, and her immortal strength would take time to develop, but she didn't feel weak.

As she rolled the carry-on and the suitcase out into the hallway, Onegus came up the stairs and lifted both pieces of luggage as if they weighed nothing. "Is there more?"

"No, that's it." Holding her art bag, she followed him down the stairs.

Her mother was waiting for them in the living room.

Geraldine had changed out of her borrowed clothes and was wearing one of her summer dresses, a yellow sheath with big white flowers printed all over it and a thin black belt.

Was she planning on going out?

"Are you sure about staying here all by yourself?" Cassandra asked for the tenth time.

"I'm sure." Geraldine straightened to her full height of five feet and four and a half inches. "I'm the guardian of the house."

"The house doesn't need guarding, Mom. We can lock it up, and you can spend a nice week in the village with me. Think of it as a vacation."

Geraldine shook her head. "Don't pressure me, Cassy. You know that I need time to adjust to new things. Besides, I have a book club meeting this afternoon, and Veronica is picking me up."

So that was why she was all dressed up.

"I'm curious," Onegus said. "Who attends those book club meetings? What's the demographic?"

"Oh, it varies from book club to book club." Her mother smiled. "Most members are ladies in their thirties, forties, and fifties, but we have the occasional husband or boyfriend join from time to time. They don't last long, though."

"Why is that?" Onegus asked.

"Because we love reading romance novels, and not many guys are comfortable sharing their impressions about reading them with a bunch of women." She shrugged. "They think it's not manly. But in my opinion, if more men read romances, there would be fewer divorces. After reading some, it's very easy to figure out what women want. And it could also be beneficial for bachelors. It would give them a leg up on the competition."

Onegus laughed. "Someone should have told me about them years ago."

Cassandra patted his arm. "You don't need any help. You're perfect the way you are."

64

MERLIN

"Close your eyes." Merlin put down his shopping and takeout bags and took Ronja's hand.

She eyed him suspiciously. "Why? Did you plan a surprise party for me? It's not my birthday, no matter how many times you try to convince me that it is."

He'd wanted to buy her things, and she'd kept refusing. So he'd used silliness as a weapon to dissolve her defenses, but the woman was much more stubborn than she looked, and she hadn't allowed him to buy her even one thing as an advance birthday gift.

"It's not a party. Just humor me and close your eyes for a moment."

"Fine."

He threw the door open and walked her inside. "You can look now."

She gasped. "Wow, Merlin. Everything is clean and well organized. When did you have time to do this?"

"Lisa and Parker helped. That was the secret project I needed their help with."

"Unbelievable." She walked around his living room, touching the books neatly arranged on the shelves in the bookcases. "Lisa did all this?"

"She and Parker worked really hard. They deserve much more than what I've paid them, but other than a dip into my stash of chocolates, they refused to accept a tip for a job well done." He took her hand and lifted it to his lips. "When you came over the other day, I was deeply embarrassed, and I knew that it was time for me to change my messy ways."

"Oh, Merlin." She regarded him with soft eyes. "That's so sweet. But will you be able to keep it like this?"

He smiled sheepishly. "Probably not. But now I know that I can hire help." He led her to the couch. "I know that you're tired after all this shopping. Sit down, rest for a bit, and in the meantime, I'll set the table."

"I'm not going to argue." She sat down and crossed her legs. "Shopping is exhausting. And to think that I used to love it."

183

"Can I get you something to drink?" Merlin asked as he walked out to the front porch to bring in the bags he'd left there. "Maybe wine?"

"Sure, but I'll have it with dinner."

He'd done his best to amuse and entertain her, but despite all his efforts, Ronja had been tense throughout their day on the town.

Was he moving too fast?

Perhaps she wasn't ready?

The other day on the swing, the sweet scent of her arousal had hinted that she was, but maybe she needed more time.

Once the table was set, he walked over to her. "Dinner is served, my lady." He offered her a hand up.

"Thank you."

He pulled out a chair for her, and when she sat down, he poured her a glass of wine.

"To a wonderful day together." He raised his glass. "May there be many more."

Smiling nervously, she clinked her glass with his. "Thank you. I've enjoyed spending the day with you."

"I should be the one thanking you. You helped me select a whole new wardrobe. That was a lot of work."

"It was my pleasure."

Merlin opened one of the takeout boxes and ladled out the orange chicken onto her plate. "What's bothering you, Ronja? You've been uneasy the entire time we were out." He ladled the rest onto his own.

With a sigh, she unfurled a napkin and draped it over her lap. "I like you, Merlin. A lot. But I'm not ready for anything other than friendship at the moment, and with you making all these changes for me, I feel pressured."

Not really expecting her to answer honestly, he was surprised that she had. "Don't. If all you want for now is friendship, you've got it. I'm not good at courtship, so I might seem overzealous. But all I wanted to do is to show you that I like you, and that I want to get to know you better."

That was a lie. He wanted her in every possible way, and waiting would be torture, but that was what she needed to hear him say to feel at ease.

"Are you sure? I know that immortals have stronger needs than humans, and I don't want you to wait around for me. If you need to see others, that's perfectly understandable."

He almost choked on the piece of chicken he was chewing on.

Talk about honesty. He hadn't been expecting that. Not that she was being really honest. Ronja was doing the same thing he had done. Saying what she thought he wanted to hear.

"I'm not like other immortal males. I'm too consumed by my work and my research to obsess about sex. I'll wait for you for as long as it takes, and I don't want you to feel pressured by it. Even if you weren't here and hadn't caught my fancy, I wouldn't be out on the town. I would be right here, poring over ancient texts and obsessing about potions."

65

RONJA

*R*onja could hardly admit it to herself, but she was glad that Merlin was willing to wait.

Had he been honest, though?

Was it really not a big deal for him to abstain for a few months?

How long was long enough?

"Thank you for being so understanding. But I really don't know why you are interested in me." When he opened his mouth to protest, she lifted her hand to stop him. "It's not that I suffer from lack of self-esteem. I know that I'm still attractive, and a human man in his sixties might consider me quite a catch. But you are an immortal, and there could be nothing lasting between us. Sadly, I don't have long."

He reached for her hand and clasped it in his. "Whatever time you have, I'll be honored to share it with you. But if you are just being polite and it's really about you not being interested in me, don't hesitate to let me know. I have a thick skin, and I'm not easily offended."

"Oh, I'm interested alright. But I have a daughter who is my first priority, and she wouldn't want her mother to jump into a new relationship so soon after her father's death."

He arched a brow. "Have you talked with Lisa about it? Because to me, it seemed like she was all for it. The girl is smart, and she figured out right away why I was suddenly concerned with my appearance and the state of my house. She was very happy to assist me on both fronts."

That was surprising to say the least.

"I guess you are right. I need to talk to her. But even if she's okay with me seeing you, I need a little more time."

"Perfectly understandable." He let go of her hand and picked up his fork. "Friends?"

"The best." She lifted her own utensil and speared a piece of chicken.

When they were done eating, Ronja dabbed at her lips with the napkin and leaned back. "Thank you for a wonderful dinner."

Merlin grinned. "My pleasure."

"I have an idea," she blurted before she had a chance to lose her nerve. "Before I got married, I used to volunteer in a hospital. I wanted to become a nurse, but then I got pregnant with the twins, got married, and those dreams never materialized. Do you need an assistant? I'm not completely clueless about medicine. After all, I was married to a doctor for many years." She looked around the neatly organized living room. "I can help you keep this from slipping into disarray again, and I can also cook for you, so you don't have to live on sandwiches from the café."

That was probably one of her stupidest ideas, but she was bored and alone, and Merlin was fun, and he definitely needed help. Taking care of him would give her something to do.

"I would be overjoyed. But I'll accept only on two conditions."

Her heart leapt with hope. "What are they?"

"That you will let me teach you."

"I would love that."

"And that I pay you."

She shook her head. "I don't need to be paid. Kian gave me an allowance that is more than Lisa and I need. And with the clan also providing lodging for us and paying for Lisa's school, I really don't have anything I can spend it on."

Merlin folded his arms over his chest. "No pay, no work."

"But I really don't have any use for the money. What am I going to do with it?"

He shrugged. "Buy diamonds or donate it to charity. I really don't care what you do with it. I just can't accept free labor."

"It's not free. It's a bartering agreement, or an apprenticeship. I help you in exchange for your teaching."

"No go. If I don't pay you, I can't boss you around."

She chuckled. "Then I definitely don't want to get paid because I'm probably going to boss you around. You need to learn better habits. What are you going to do once I'm gone?"

That sobered Merlin's good mood. "Please, don't talk like that. I'll find a way to prolong your life."

"That's sweet, but I doubt that even a genius like you could do that."

That brought the smile back to his handsome face. "You think that I'm a genius?"

"Naturally. I don't date guys with average intelligence."

He leaned on his elbows and smiled. "Does that mean that we are dating?"

"Not yet. But we will."

"That's good enough for me."

66

ONEGUS

"Watch the railing." Connor hoisted the desk higher.

"I am." Walking backward up the stairs, Onegus looked over his shoulder at Cassandra, who was standing in the doorway and eyeing the desk. "We will probably need to turn it sideways to fit it through the door."

"You won't." Cassandra stepped back and held it open. "It will fit."

Naturally, she was right, and the desk made it through with merely half an inch to spare.

Maneuvering it through the bedroom, however, was not that easy.

"I should have taken measurements." Onegus lowered the thing to the floor. "There isn't enough room for it between the bed and the window. Perhaps you would reconsider working in the display room in the office building?"

She shook her head. "I can't work with Annani's portrait looming above me. It's too distracting. Besides, the light from this window is perfect." A hand on her hip, she looked at the bed. "If we get rid of the nightstand, we can push the bed closer to the wall, and then there will be enough space for the desk and the chair."

The truth was that Onegus loved the idea of her working from the house, but he wasn't sure the bedroom was the best place for it. The living room had plenty of space for the desk. It was the smallest one he and Connor had found in the underground classrooms, but it was still too big for where she wanted it.

Except, Cassandra wasn't happy with the natural light coming through the living room's windows, and she was concerned about being distracted by Connor's piano playing.

"I'm on it." Connor grabbed the nightstand and carried it out to the corridor.

Once the furniture was rearranged to Cassandra's liking, she put her art bag on the table, sat down on the chair, and smiled.

"Thank you. This is perfect. And now, if you don't mind, I need to work."

Onegus would have liked her to take it easy for at least one day, but her boss had freaked out when she'd told him she was ill and wouldn't be coming in to work for a week. Something about major changes to an advertising campaign that was scheduled to launch next week, and Cassandra being the only one who could handle it.

Was the entire operation of Fifty Shades of Beauty dependent on Cassandra? If so, she should get paid even more than she already was, and Kevin needed to hire more people for her department.

In fact, Onegus had wanted to take the phone from her and tell Kevin to go screw himself, but when Cassandra had cast him a glare and glasses started rattling on the kitchen counter, he'd reconsidered.

Besides, Cassy loved what she did, and working was a creative outlet for her. She would probably be calmer when creating than idling.

"I love Cassandra, but she is even bossier than you," Connor murmured under his breath.

Onegus had said the same thing on more than one occasion, but for some reason, it irked him to hear someone else talk about her like that.

"She knows what she wants and how she wants it," Onegus corrected.

"Isn't that the same thing?"

"It's a different nuance of meaning."

Onegus loved Cassandra's assertiveness, and the way he'd phrased it conveyed it better than calling her bossy.

"I meant no disrespect." Connor walked over to the piano and lifted the lid. "You know that I adore her."

"The feeling is mutual. She likes you too." Onegus put his laptop on the dining table and pulled out a chair. "I might as well get to work too."

Connor arched a brow. "Do you want to use my bedroom? It's not like I can move the piano over there, and I need to work too."

"Your playing doesn't bother me. I can hyper-focus no matter what's going on around me."

His Guardians had been collecting new intel that he had to go over before making new plans and rescheduling rescue missions. Bhathian was filling in for him, but the guy wasn't experienced in planning missions, and Bridget had enough on her plate as it was.

Thank the merciful Fates that Kian had decided to postpone the China team deployment, giving them more time to reorganize and get those rescue missions going.

Less than an hour later, Onegus's phone buzzed with an incoming message. He pulled it out, replied, and then walked into the bedroom.

For a long moment, he just stood in the doorway and looked at Cassandra's graceful back. Fully focused on her work, she hadn't felt him standing there, admiring the elegant movement of her wrist, her slender fingers holding the pencil.

He walked up to her and peered over her shoulder at the drawing. "I don't know what you're selling, but I'm buying."

Turning to look up at him, she smiled. "Nail polish or lipstick? What's your pleasure?"

"Both, if you are wearing them." He dipped his head and kissed her lips. "Roni is on his way."

"Did he find out anything new?"

"Probably. He sent me a message that he's stopping by on his way home. I replied that it was okay."

Cassandra rolled her chair back and stood up. "I'm peckish. Is there anything to eat?"

They'd eaten a couple of hours ago, but apparently, Cassandra's appetite was still ravenous after her transition.

"We have plenty of leftovers from dinner."

"Is there enough to feed the four of us?"

He wrapped his arm around her slim waist. "Connor and I are still full, and Roni will want to go home and eat dinner with Sylvia."

She scrunched her nose. "I can't eat while the three of you just look at me."

"Fine. We will join you. Just don't complain when I get fat."

"That's not possible." She leaned on his arm.

"Which one? Me getting fat or you complaining about it?"

"Both."

67

GERALDINE

Geraldine checked that the polenta was tender and creamy, removed it from heat, and whisked in the mascarpone cheese until the mixture was smooth. With that done, she pulled a large skillet out of the drawer, put it over medium heat, and added olive oil.

While it was heating, she chopped a large yellow onion and a full bulb of garlic, and when the oil was heated through, she added the onion, garlic, and some red pepper to the skillet.

Trying out a new recipe for a dinner date was risky, but Veronica had sworn that there was no way to mess up her tomato-braised baccalà with olives and polenta dish, and that it was guaranteed to come up perfect even on the first try.

After Shai had called and told her that he was coming over, her book club friends agreed to continue discussing the book during their next meeting, so she would have time to prepare dinner, and had even volunteered recipes that were sure to please any palate.

Geraldine was a decent cook, and if she managed not to get distracted and forget something on the burner for too long, chances were it would come out as tasty as it had for Veronica.

Wooden spoon in hand, Geraldine stirred the onions and garlic around, then leaned back and watched it sizzle. The recipe said six minutes or until soft and translucent.

Six minutes to think about how empty the house felt without Cassandra.

It was a silly thought.

Her daughter had dropped her off earlier today, and soon after that, Geraldine had gone to the book club meeting, so it wasn't as if she'd had time to feel lonely, but knowing that Cassy wasn't coming back tonight, or tomorrow, or the day after made her sad.

It shouldn't, though. Shai was coming for dinner, and he was probably going to stay the night, something Geraldine hadn't let any man do before.

For the first time since becoming a mother, she would have a guy in her home and in her bed.

Well, after becoming Cassandra's mother.

If what Roni had said was true and she was indeed his grandmother, then she had been married, had a child with her husband, raised that child until she was twelve, and then faked her own death for some reason.

That scenario still felt completely foreign to her, and the hypothesis of an identical twin sister seemed to make much more sense. The only hitch in that theory was the quilting, but it wasn't big enough of a deal to invalidate it. Identical twins also had identical genes, so they were bound to have similar talents and gravitate toward similar hobbies.

When the onions looked ready, Geraldine added a cup of dry white wine, stirred the mixture, and leaned back again. It was supposed to take about eight minutes for the wine to evaporate, and she needed to stay and watch it lest she got distracted and let the mixture burn.

Over the years, she'd learned to live with her faulty memory, her distractibility, her vague and often inexplicable urges that were like an odd sixth sense that compelled her to do or not to do certain things.

Like the need to stay in the house. It would be so much easier on Cassandra and on her if she moved into the village. She could be near her daughter, near Shai, near other people who were like her.

Immortals.

Was it fear of change? Or was it something else?

As a dull headache started behind her temples, her first impulse was to shift her thoughts to another subject, to forget that something about the situation bothered her, but unlike other times, Geraldine tried to power through it.

There was a vague impression of a man, someone she could trust, someone who had helped her before, someone who needed to know where she was—

When the headache became intolerable, and the pan started to smoke at the same time, Geraldine was forced to abandon that thought and refocus on the dish she was making for Shai.

She added the crushed tomatoes she'd prepared beforehand, the olives, the oregano, and after checking the recipe once more, the bay leaves and another quarter of a cup of olive oil. Stirring slowly, she realized that her headache was gone.

What had she been thinking about when it had started?

Something about Cassy not coming back home tonight and about Shai being the first man Geraldine had invited to her home since becoming a mother.

She'd never felt the need to invite any of the guys she'd met to her home before. None of them had been special enough to bend the rules for. But Cassy was all grown, and the rules hadn't been applicable for a long time. And yet Geraldine hadn't invited any guy to dinner, let alone to spend the night.

Would she have bent the rules if she'd met Shai when Cassy was growing up?

Probably.

Shai was special. He was a keeper, and not just because he was an immortal like her. She felt a connection to him like she'd never felt to any man before.

Or maybe she had?

Perhaps she just didn't remember having feelings for Emanuel? For Luis?

Except, Geraldine had proof that she hadn't. If she had, she would have invited them home, and Cassy would have remembered them.

When the sauce thickened, she added the four pieces of cod to the pan and covered them with sauce. It was only her and Shai tonight, so it should be more than enough. She would probably have leftovers for tomorrow and eat them alone in front of the TV.

6 8

CASSANDRA

*a*s Cassandra used a piece of bread to scoop up the rest of the sauce from her plate, she ignored the amused expressions on her dinner companions' faces. They had indulged her by nibbling a little, while she'd devoured every last morsel of food.

The transition must have super-charged her metabolism because no matter how much food she stuffed down into her belly, less than an hour later it felt empty again. While working she hadn't noticed the gnawing hunger, but the moment Onegus had distracted her, her stomach had refused to wait for even a moment longer.

Poor Roni was probably impatient to go home to his mate, but he had waited with his news until she was done and wiped her mouth with a napkin.

"So, my mother has ordered the 23andMe genetic test," Roni announced as she put the napkin over her plate. "Darlene opted into the DNA relatives feature, which means that she'll get notified of matches. It also means that her information is visible to those matches. I can plant fake results for you and Geraldine in their database that will match hers enough to prove that you are closely related. The question is whether you want to wait for her to get notified of the match or to contact her beforehand."

"She will be less suspicious if she contacts us." Cassandra turned to Onegus. "What do you think?"

"I think that you're right. And if she doesn't, you can contact her."

Roni rubbed the back of his neck. "I was thinking that maybe I should plant fake information about myself as well, and then you could claim that you found me through the registry. That way we can meet them together." He chuckled nervously. "Maybe I could use amnesia as an excuse for why I haven't contacted them in four years."

Onegus shook his head. "I don't think it's safe for you to see them even after all this time. They might still be monitored." He cast Roni an apologetic glance. "Their phones, internet, and social media are watched for sure."

Cassandra reached for another piece of bread. "What if the test was bait to flush Roni out?"

"Not likely." Onegus moved the breadbasket closer to her. "They don't need to bait Roni because he knows where to find his parents. They haven't moved since he disappeared."

"There must be a way around it. I could ask them to meet Geraldine and me at a restaurant somewhere in town. You could check if they are being followed, and if they are not, Roni can join us."

"They might be carrying location trackers and listening devices, knowingly or unknowingly." Onegus rose to his feet and walked over to the bar cabinet. "Right now, I can't spare any Guardians, but if we schedule the meeting for a couple of weeks from now, I can assign Guardians to follow Roni's parents as they leave their house to make sure that they are not being followed. Another team can check their place for listening devices and hidden cameras. And as for the trackers, I can ask William for one of his portable signal disrupters."

Roni turned to him. "Will all that be needed if Cassandra and Geraldine meet them without me?"

"To a lesser extent. I will still need to make sure that no one is following either of them in the hopes of finding you."

Roni let out a breath. "Good. I want to meet my parents, but not if that means a major security issue. I like my freedom much more than I miss them." He waved a dismissive hand. "I don't miss them at all, but I'm curious to see if the fuckers miss me."

The vulgarity was a defense mechanism.

Cassandra hadn't missed the hurt in Roni's voice. Naturally, the kid wanted his parents' love, and his prickly attitude was just bravado meant to disguise his insecurity and longing.

She had no doubt that her sister loved her only son and missed him. How could she not? Wasn't it hardwired into every mother's psyche to love her children?

The only instance in which Cassandra could conceive of a mother rejecting her child was if he was a monster—a murderer or a rapist. But despite his prickly attitude, Roni was a good kid, and he deserved his mother's love.

Onegus pulled out a bottle of whiskey. "Can I interest anyone in a shot?"

Connor shook his head, but Roni nodded. "With pleasure."

"What can I get you, love?" Onegus asked her.

"I think I'll stick to water for the next seven days." She smiled. "After all, I'm a growing girl, so I shouldn't drink alcohol."

Roni arched a brow. "Are you?"

"Other than the inch that I grew overnight, I hope not. I'm referring to the other changes I'm undergoing. Judging by how hungry I am all the time, a lot is still happening on the inside."

Her nephew grimaced. "I got taller as well, and my shoulder span increased. But I hoped to get bulkier and got skinnier instead." He ran his hands over his cheeks. "But at least the acne is gone, along with the acne scars I had. I'm much more pleasant to look at now."

"I think that you are very handsome."

He cast her a doubtful look. "You're my aunt, but that doesn't mean that you have to say that. I have a mirror."

She put her hand on his shoulder. "What we see in the mirror is not how others perceive us. The reflection you see is colored by your perception of yourself. I'm an artist, and I have an artist's eye for symmetry and beauty. And as many can attest, I'm not polite or politically correct either. So when I tell you that you're handsome, you can take it to the bank."

69

GERALDINE

*E*verything was ready for Geraldine's dinner date with Shai.

The tomato-braised baccalà with olives and polenta had come out delicious and was in the warming drawer next to the chickpeas and kale in spicy pomodoro sauce. The table was set for a romantic dinner for two, including a vase with fresh white roses from her garden and the finest bottle of wine she found in the pantry. She was showered, her hair and makeup were done, and she was dressed in a pull-on skirt and loose blouse that were all about subtle chic and comfort.

So why was she so nervous?

Shai knew all of her secrets, or at least the ones she knew herself, they'd already made love, and he still wanted to see her again, so he obviously liked her.

Perhaps her nervousness was more about the novelty of the situation than about Shai. She was so used to playing the part of the mysterious woman who didn't talk much about herself that having it all bared before a man felt odd.

Maybe it was about the stakes being higher.

She'd connected with Shai in a way she hadn't connected with any of her previous lovers, and the prospect of making a mistake and losing his affection was terrifying.

How was she supposed to act? What was she supposed to say?

It was all new territory to her.

Perhaps she should stick to what she knew how to do best, which was a quick seduction.

When the guard called to let her know that Shai was there, she opened the front door and leaned against the frame. Her heart racing, her lips stretched in a smile, she watched him pull up to the curb and turn the engine off.

When he got out of the car, holding a bouquet of flowers and a wrapped box, her heartbeat doubled.

He was so handsome in his neatly pressed dark gray slacks, his tight fitting white button-down, his body moving with the fluidity of a dancer.

"Hello, beautiful." He kissed her cheek and handed her the flowers and the box. "I was told that chocolate paves the way to a woman's heart."

She could think of several things that paved it much faster, but flowers and chocolates were always welcome.

"Thank you." Geraldine smiled sweetly and stepped inside, waiting for him to follow. "I need to find a vase for these." She put the flowers and the box on the entry table.

Turning around, she gasped as she found herself a scant inch away from his chest. He moved as soundlessly as an assassin, not something she'd expected from an executive assistant, and neither was the hungry expression in his glowing eyes.

He was a predator, and she was his very willing prey.

Nevertheless, his touch was infinitely gentle as he took her face in his hands and lowered his head. "I missed you." He smashed his lips over hers.

With a moan, she wrapped her arms around his shoulders and hoisted herself up. Her breasts pressing against his chest, she kissed him back. Lips playing, tongues dueling, it wasn't elegant, but the passion was all-consuming.

When he put her down, she felt the loss of him down to her core, but as she made a move to come to him again, he took a step back. "Something smells divine." He walked to the dining table. "This looks beautiful."

Rooted to the spot where he'd left her, Geraldine was torn between continuing with the small talk while serving dinner or tearing Shai's clothes off and having her way with him on the living room couch.

He must have felt her eyes on him and turned around.

The bulge in his slacks tipped the scales toward the second option.

Putting on a coy smile, Geraldine sauntered toward him, reached up, and touched his face. "How hungry are you?" She traced her fingertips over his jaw, his chin, his lips.

His eyes blazed with blue light. "Ravenous."

She knew he wasn't talking about food. "Should I serve dinner?" she teased.

His answer was to pick her up, smash her against his body, and kiss her while he carried her to the couch.

Yes! That was exactly where she wanted to be—on her back, with him on top of her, his weight pressing her into the cushions.

"Is it okay if we skip dinner?" he breathed into her neck.

"Dinner can wait." She slipped her arm around his neck and parted her thighs.

Settling between them, he rubbed his erection against her core, the thin, stretchy fabric of her skirt yielding to the pressure.

As she rolled her hips and lifted to kiss him, their mouths somehow fused despite his elongated fangs.

When she licked around one, he shuddered, and when she licked around the other, he groaned and pressed his hard shaft into her.

Pulling back, he looked at her with those glowing eyes of his. "I don't think I can make it to the bedroom."

She smiled. "Nothing wrong with the couch."

SHAI

*I*nsatiable.
Both of them.

After making love in the afternoon, Shai had been sure that he could manage to be a gentleman and have a nice dinner with Geraldine, but as soon as he'd laid eyes on her, he'd wanted her again.

Thank the merciful Fates, she was just as hungry for him as he was for her, and not shy about it.

Reaching for the hem of her blouse, she jerked it over her head and tossed it over his.

The lacy red bra covering her breasts was the stuff of wet dreams, and its front clasp was made for snapping it off without much hassle. In the next instant, his mouth was on her nipple, his tongue teasing the turgid peak as his arms went around her to lift her to him.

The sweet sounds she was making went straight to his shaft, evaporating his resolve to take it slow and worship her with his hands and his lips and his tongue.

He needed to be inside her, and given the way her hips were churning under him, she was fully on board with that plan.

Hooking his fingers in the waistband of her skirt, he pulled it down over her long, shapely legs, leaving her covered only by a tiny triangle of red lace.

"Gorgeous." He breathed over the scrap, and then his tongue darted out as if of its own accord and licked at her through the soaked fabric.

As the flavor of her hit his senses, his eyes rolled back in his head. "Delicious." He caught the fabric with his teeth and pulled it down.

Geraldine giggled. "These panties are not edible."

"But you are." He shook his head like a dog with a bone and was about to throw the red lace on the floor but changed his mind. "I'm going to keep these." He balled them up and tucked them in his pocket.

"Pervert." She laughed.

"Only with you." And that was the honest truth. Shai had never collected souvenirs from ladies before.

Lying naked before him, her legs slightly parted, and her perky breasts proudly displayed, Geraldine regarded him with hooded eyes. "Should I help you undress?"

That was an offer he couldn't refuse, even if it was bound to slow things down.

"Yes, please." He pulled back to give her room to maneuver.

So far, he hadn't seen Geraldine do anything to betray her immortality, but the speed with which she undressed him was not human. Her deft fingers blurred over his dress shirt as she undid the buttons, and a moment later, she parted the two halves, slowing down for a moment to gaze at his chest with hunger in her expressive eyes.

"I love it that you have no hair on your chest. Are all immortal males like that?"

He didn't want her to talk about other males, especially not while she was naked.

"No," he growled.

She laughed. "Okay. No more talking."

The rest of his clothes were off in seconds, and then she was on her back again and pulling him on top of her. "I need you inside of me."

The moment the tip of his shaft nudged her entrance, she pushed up, her slickness engulfing him as she joined them.

Petite, gentle Geraldine was much more assertive than she let on, and he found the dichotomy sexy as hell.

Gripping her leg, he lifted it to open her more fully to him, and then he was moving inside of her with long hard strokes that had her moaning and calling out his name.

The harder he took her, the rougher he was with her, the wilder she got, and when she climaxed, screaming his name at the top of her lungs, he struck her vein again even though he'd already bitten her twice in less than twenty-four hours.

As Geraldine orgasmed again, his own climax barreled out of him, emptying into her as he kept pumping venom into her vein.

She blacked out, but only for a moment, her eyes popping open as he licked the puncture wounds closed.

The smile she rewarded him with could have lit up a city block, and then she closed her eyes again and nuzzled his neck.

For long moments, they lay in each other's arms, still joined, neither making a move. Realizing that his weight must be crushing Geraldine, Shai shifted to the side and pulled her with him.

They must have dozed off because the next time he opened his eyes, his stomach was making a growling sound, reminding him that they hadn't had dinner.

"What time is it?" Geraldine murmured.

He lifted his arm to look at his watch. "It's quarter after ten. We fell asleep."

She sighed contentedly. "I like sleeping with you." She kissed his jaw. "Let's hit the shower and check whether my baccalà is still edible. It's been sitting in the warming drawer this whole time."

"I'm sorry." He caressed her bare back.

"What for?"

"Ruining dinner."

She smiled. "I'm not. It was worth it."

CASSANDRA

"*L*eaving so soon?" Kevin stopped Cassandra at the door.

She pretended to glance at her watch. "It's five o'clock. Do you need me for anything?"

"I'm just surprised. You've never left the office this early before. Especially after a week of absence." He smirked. "Actually, you've never taken that much time off before. Eager to get home to your guy?"

She smiled. "Absolutely."

"Say hello to Onegus for me."

"I will." She leaned and kissed his cheek. "Give my regards to Josie."

"The four of us should plan an evening together. Josie is dying to meet your new boyfriend."

"Great idea. But I need to run. Can we talk about it tomorrow?"

"Sure thing."

As Cassandra got into her new car, she didn't turn the engine on right away. Instead, she leaned back and closed her eyes, needing a moment to pause and reflect on her first day back at the office.

It had gone better than expected.

It seemed that the transition into immortality had changed more than just her physiology. She was calmer, more patient, and since she didn't need as much sleep, she wasn't operating on fumes like she used to before the change.

Then again, it might have been Onegus's positive influence. While with him, she was happy, but it wasn't just about that.

Seeing him interact with his Guardians had taught her more about leadership than the numerous books she'd read on the subject. His people liked him and respected him, and they were willing to go above and beyond for him, and after watching him interact with them, it had finally dawned on her why.

Onegus treated all of them as family. He not only knew everyone's personal situation, their likes and dislikes, their struggles and achievements, but he also genuinely cared about their lives outside of work. In his case, his team members actually were his family by blood, but that didn't mean that she couldn't pretend that her team at Fifty Shades of Beauty was hers and treat them accordingly.

Today, she'd put that philosophy into practice, and the results had exceeded her expectations. Apparently, carrots were much better motivators than sticks. It helped that she wasn't behind on anything. She'd actually managed to keep up with her workload better from Onegus's home than when she'd worked in the office.

Overall, Cassandra felt happy and content, the energy usually swirling under her skin feeling more like a pleasant hum than an explosion waiting to happen.

Only three issues infringed on her newly achieved harmony, one minor and two major ones.

The minor one was the new clan car she was now driving. The self-driving portion of the route unnerved her, especially when the windows turned opaque. She hated ceding control to the onboard computer. Those things were known to glitch from time to time, which was infuriating when it happened while she was sitting at her desk, but would be absolutely terrifying when she was sitting behind the wheel.

It was the only so-called perk she'd agreed to accept as a new member of the clan. Since that was the only way she could commute to and from work, she hadn't had much choice. But she'd refused the share in the clan profits that Kian had offered her. She wasn't Annani's descendant, and it wasn't hers to take even though she was considered officially mated to Onegus.

Cassandra was making good money and didn't plan to stop working anytime soon. Not even if by some miracle she got pregnant right away. Having a baby would be wonderful, and it would force her mother to move into the village to babysit while she was at work, solving one of the two major issues casting shadows on her happiness.

Geraldine still refused to move into the village, giving all kinds of excuses that didn't make sense. Shai had been spending every evening and night with her, so at least she wasn't lonely, but that was a temporary solution, especially since the two seemed very serious about each other.

He was a good man, and he seemed to care deeply for her mother, but he was Kian's personal assistant, and there was no way he could live with Geraldine in her home. At some point, she would have to move into the village.

The other big issue was Geraldine's past.

Roni had planted fake genetic profiles for her and her mother, but so far, Darlene hadn't called them. It was time to initiate the first contact, and that made Cassandra apprehensive.

Today, she was going to call her sister and talk with her for the first time, pretending to be her cousin.

The call would be placed from her house, with Geraldine, Onegus, and Shai listening in.

Shai was there to provide moral support to her mother, but given his eidetic memory, he would also serve as a live voice recording of the phone meeting.

She would probably be too nervous to remember all the details.

The meeting place Onegus had suggested was a café owned by one of the clan members and operated by Sylvia's mother. She would make sure that they had the privacy they needed, while Onegus's Guardians would secure the coffee shop and its surrounding area.

GERALDINE

"*L*et's eat first." Geraldine walked into the kitchen and opened the warming drawer.

She was only postponing the inevitable.

Onegus and Cassandra hadn't come over to have dinner with her and Shai. They'd come to make the phone call to Darlene.

During the week that had passed since Cassandra's transition, Geraldine had thought of it often, hoping that Darlene wouldn't take the bait, and that they would decide to drop the idea of initiating a meeting with her.

Things were going so well for Geraldine, she'd been so happy, and she dreaded the emotional upheaval that was sure to follow.

Cassandra had visited only twice during the time she'd been recuperating from her transition at Onegus's place, but it had still been magical.

Shai had spent every night with her, leaving early in the morning so the neighbors wouldn't see him. Geraldine had told him not to bother, that was an adult woman and that it was nobody's business who was staying at her house, but he'd insisted nonetheless.

It was a good thing that immortals didn't need much sleep, or he would have been exhausted. They had been going at each other like cats in heat.

She'd always had a healthy libido but with Shai it had gone into overdrive and refused to slow down.

Smiling, Geraldine pulled out the curry dish and carried it to the table. "Dig in, everyone."

"It smells delicious." Shai loaded rice on his plate and then topped it with the curry.

"I'll get the sodas." Cassandra walked over to the fridge and pulled out a six-pack.

Once everyone was seated, Onegus unfurled a napkin and put it over his slacks. "Let's go over the details." He turned to Cassandra. "How are you going to present yourself to Darlene?"

She put her fork down. "The story is that my sister and I did the genetic test to find out whether we had any family on our mother's side. Our mother was adopted, and she never bothered to find out who her birth parents were. After she died, my sister Geraldine and I did the test in the hopes of finding more relatives. Darlene came out as such a close match that she could have been our sister. Which led us to believe that our mother had a twin sister and that Darlene was our cousin."

"There is one problem with that story," Shai said. "You both look much younger than Darlene. In reality, Geraldine is seventy-two years old. To have a daughter who looks thirty at most and another one who looks even younger, your so-called mother would have needed to have Cassandra at forty-two, and Geraldine even later. It's possible, but you need a good cover story for why she waited to have children so late in life."

"Infertility," Cassandra offered. "Or maybe she just didn't find the right guy to settle down with. Once she despaired of ever finding Mr. Right, she decided to use a sperm donor. Twice."

They all turned to Onegus, who shrugged. "A sperm donor is a bit much. I would go for two flaky boyfriends who didn't stick around once their daughters were born." He looked at Geraldine. "Unless you want Cassandra to tell a different story. It's your call."

Onegus's suggestion was closer to the truth, but Geraldine didn't want Darlene to think that she was a loser who didn't know how to attract quality men. Then again, Darlene wouldn't think that of Geraldine but of the mother she'd lost. She wouldn't know that Geraldine and her mother were supposedly the same person. Still, Geraldine wasn't comfortable with that either.

"We need to come up with a name for our supposed mother. I think Monica sounds nice. Monica was married to a soldier called Jerome Beaumont, and she couldn't conceive for many years. She went through some fertility treatments and had Cassandra. Their happiness was short-lived. Jerome was stationed overseas, where he died in the line of duty. A few years later, she met another fine man, let's call him Roger Warner. It was a second relationship for both of them, and they never married but they lived happily together for many years. Roger died two years ago of complications after surgery, and Monica was so devastated that she died shortly thereafter."

Cassandra shook her head. "You should write stories, Mom. When you were done, I wanted to know more about your fictional characters."

Shai nodded enthusiastically. "That's a wonderful idea."

It appealed to her, but her memory issues were an impediment.

"To write a story, I need to remember what I wrote before. With my faulty memory, I would be doing more rereading than writing."

Shai took her hand. "I can serve as your external memory. I'll read whatever you write, and whenever you are not sure about something, you can ask me. We can work on your stories together."

"That's so sweet of you." She patted his hand. "I'll give it some thought."

"Just don't use Beaumont as your pretend father's last name," Onegus reminded Cassandra. "The name Roni planted was Bogler."

"What about our first names?" Geraldine asked.

"They stay the same."

Cassandra cleared her throat. "Let's finish dinner and then make that call. The sooner I'm done with it, the better. I don't like dragging things out."

73

ONEGUS

"What if she's not home?" Geraldine asked as Onegus handed Cassandra the special phone William had given him.

The call was going to be rerouted through an apartment building the clan owned in Glendale, so if the government was still monitoring Roni's parents' communications, that's where the signal would appear to come from.

The Guardians he'd sent to check out their house hadn't discovered any listening devices, but then the government didn't need that. It had access to the landlines and cellular connection.

"I have Darlene's cell phone number," Cassandra said. "So unless she's in a no reception area, she'll answer."

"Or not," Shai said. "She will not recognize the number and might assume that it's a spam call."

"Right." Cassandra looked at Onegus. "What are we going to do then?"

He stifled a chuckle. The younger generation was so used to immediate connectivity that they'd forgotten that up until not too long ago, snail-mail used to be the main conduit for formal and informal communications.

"You could always send her a letter."

"True." Cassandra nodded. "I didn't think of that."

"Put the call on speakerphone," Geraldine said. "I want to hear Darlene's voice."

"That was the plan." Cassandra punched in the number.

Onegus found it curious that Geraldine appeared to have human limitations she shouldn't. Like the rest of them, she should have been able to hear whoever was on the other line without the amplification. Most likely, her limitations were mental rather than physical, and he wondered whether they stemmed from the same trauma that had caused her amnesia and subsequent memory issues.

"Hello?" came the hesitant reply.

"Darlene?" Cassandra assumed an excited tone.

"Yes. Who is this?"

"My name is Cassandra, and you don't know me, but we are related. My sister and I did the 23andMe genetic test, and you were flagged as a very close match. So close that we might be sisters. Of course, we are not, but we are cousins for sure."

There was a brief moment of silence, and then a huff. "You must be from my father's side. He comes from a family of twelve siblings, and I have hordes of cousins. I can't believe that any of those hillbillies are the types who explore their genetics. Who are your parents?"

Cassandra and Onegus exchanged perplexed looks. Roni had never mentioned having a large family on his grandfather's side.

"We are not your father's relatives. We are your mother's."

"My mother died many years ago." Darlene's voice turned cold. "And she had no family. Did your parents get tested as well? Because that's the only way to find out on which side we are connected."

They'd figured the question might come up and had a contingency for it.

"Our mother did, but she opted not to have her information public. Regrettably, our mother is no longer with us either. That's why my sister and I made our test results public. We wanted to find out whether we had any blood relatives on our mother's side. She was adopted as a baby."

"So was mine." Darlene's voice warmed up a shade. "Maybe several siblings were put up for adoption. In those days, they still separated kids."

That was a surprise, and it added credence to Geraldine's twin hypothesis.

Go figure. She might have been right.

"Our thoughts exactly," Cassandra said. "We would love to meet you and compare notes. After all, you are the only family we have."

"What about your father and his side of the family?"

"My father died in the line of duty many years ago, and my sister's father died recently. Neither had large families."

"I'm so sorry to hear that."

"Yes, well..." Cassandra sighed. "It is what it is. So, when can we meet?"

Darlene hesitated for a brief moment. "It will have to be sometime after the fifteenth of next month. My husband and I are about to leave on vacation, and we won't be back until then."

Onegus wondered whether that was true or an excuse that Darlene had made up on the spot.

"No problem." Cassandra affected a nonchalant tone. "Let's set a date for after you come back. We can meet up at a coffee shop. I know this great place in Glendale that serves the best pastries. How is seven o'clock in the evening, Monday, three weeks from now?"

"The location is perfect, but it's a bit late. Can you make it earlier?"

Seven was chosen for a reason. Ruth usually closed the café by then, but she was going to keep it open for them so they would have privacy.

"I wish I could," Cassandra said in what was an attempt to sound apologetic. "Regrettably, I don't get off work until six-thirty."

"Seven it is, then. I'll bring my husband along. Are you and your sister married?"

"Marriage is such an old-fashioned term. My sister and I will be accompanied by our significant others."

"I'm looking forward to meeting you all. Is the number you called from a good one to reach you?"

"Yes. When we hang up, I'll text you the name and address of the café."

"I almost forgot. What's your sister's name?"

"It's Geraldine."

74

SHAI

*A*fter Cassandra and Onegus had left, Geraldine collapsed into the couch cushions. "I'm so relieved. I have three weeks to mentally prepare for the meeting."

Sitting down next to her, Shai wrapped his arm around her shoulders. "How was it to hear your daughter's voice?"

She turned wide eyes to him. "Like hearing a stranger. I didn't feel anything. I really believe that I had a twin sister who was Darlene's mother."

Obviously, Geraldine wanted to believe that.

Shai understood guilt all too well. He'd been carrying his around for nearly twenty years.

Keeping it a secret had become so ingrained in his psyche that he couldn't bring himself to tell Geraldine about it. Except, there should be no secrets between mates, and even though he'd known her for only a little over a week, he was pretty sure that she was his one and only.

"Guilt is a difficult burden to carry," he said. "But in your case, it wasn't your fault. You suffered head trauma and lost your memories. You didn't abandon your daughter willingly."

"What if I did? What if the memory loss came later?" She lifted a hand to her temple and rubbed it. "The doctor said that there was nothing wrong with me physically. The scan showed no traces of damage. What if my memory issues are mental? What if they are rooted in guilt?"

"I know what Bridget said, and no one was surprised by it. Whatever damage you might have suffered would have been fixed by your immortal body. The original trauma might have been physical. Bridget told you that."

Geraldine sighed. "I know, but I can't help thinking that there might be a different explanation. It's terrible to know absolutely nothing about my past. I don't know who I was before, or when I was turned immortal or by whom. Even the memories I have of events that happened after the recovery are hazy."

208

Tightening his arm around her, he kissed the top of her head. "Sometimes I think that not remembering is a blessing. You can imagine whatever you want about your past. You can make it fantastic."

Turning to look up at him, she smiled. "That's precisely what I've been doing. I treated my dreams as if they were reality. I just hope that you are not a dream as well. I would be very unhappy to wake up and realize that you were just another figment of my imagination."

"I'm real." He hooked a finger under her chin and kissed her lightly on the lips. "And as long as you don't kick me out, I'm not going anywhere."

"I would never do that."

The conviction in her voice was reassuring.

Perhaps she wouldn't judge him too harshly.

Well, she probably wouldn't judge him at all. His so-called transgression was against clan law, but he hadn't broken any human ones.

"I need to tell you something about me, a secret that I've kept from everyone, and I need you to swear not to reveal it to anyone. Not even Cassandra."

Especially not to Cassandra, who was mated to the chief.

"I promise," she whispered.

"I have a son," he blurted.

Geraldine blew out a breath. "That's your big secret? I was afraid that it was something terrible. I have two daughters. And I can't remember one of them."

"That's different. Immortal males are not supposed to father children with humans, and if we do, we are forbidden from having contact with them."

"That's awful. Why?"

"Because those children are human, and keeping in touch with them risks our exposure."

"Because you don't age."

"Precisely. We can help financially, but we are not allowed to have a relationship with the mother or the child."

"How old is your son?"

"He's nineteen. When he was growing up, I didn't stay away. I was always there for him. Not every day, but at least twice or three times a week. He's a college student now, and I'm still in touch with him."

"How do you explain your unchanging looks to him?"

He shrugged. "So far, that hasn't been a problem. When I met his mother, I told her that I was twenty." He smoothed his hand over his short beard. "With this facial hair, I can pass for a forty-year-old who takes good care of himself."

"Are you in touch with the mother?" Geraldine's tone carried a shade of jealousy.

"Not romantically. She lives with her boyfriend, who has two daughters from a previous marriage. I'm the ex-boyfriend who she tolerates for the sake of our son." He sighed. "I dread the day I will have to fake my own death and stop seeing Rhett."

"Rhett? Like Rhett Butler from *Gone with the Wind*?"

"Yeah. I once told Jennifer that she looked like Vivian Leigh. After that, she watched all of her movies and got obsessed with *Gone with the Wind*. Hence the name."

"You have a type then. I also look a little like her."

"You look more like Elizabeth Taylor." He lifted her onto his lap. "Not only in looks but also in style and mannerisms."

"What do you mean?" She shifted in his lap, angling her beautiful face to give him a better view.

"Are you fishing for compliments?"

Geraldine's reaction to his revelation had been better than he'd expected. She didn't mind that he had a son. Her only concern was whether he still had feelings for Jennifer.

He and the mother of his son were on friendly terms, but they were far from close.

Geraldine leaned her head on his chest. "Elizabeth Taylor was called the most beautiful woman in the world, and being told that I look like her is a great compliment. But I want to hear why you think that."

"Ms. Taylor was a lavish beauty, just like you, with a cascading mane of dark hair and unique colored eyes."

"My eyes are not violet."

"No, but they are a unique shade of blue. Like her, you also have an hour-glass shaped figure, but yours is prettier, tighter, more compact." He cupped her breast. "These are pure perfection."

"What else?" She breathed.

He smoothed a finger over her chin. "The small, pointy chin and these sensuous lips." He dipped his head and kissed them. "You are also classy yet coquettish, demure yet coy, sweet yet spicy. You're perfect in every way."

She frowned. "Except for a faulty mind."

"Don't say that. You are intelligent and resourceful, and you found a way to navigate around your memory issues. You are remarkable."

"You're blinded by an infatuation." She kissed his lips. "But thank you. It means a lot to me to hear you say these things."

"They are all true. Besides, I have a feeling that at least some of your lost memories will be retrieved soon."

"Because of the meeting with Darlene?"

He nodded. "She might not know the entire story, but she might provide us with a thread that we could follow."

"I don't know whether I want to find out what happened."

"Why not?"

She lifted her hand and cupped his cheek. "Because I'm happy, and I don't want anything to ruin it."

He tightened his arms around her. "It won't because I won't let it. I'll keep you safe."

DARK MEMORIES EMERGE

THE CHILDREN OF THE GODS BOOK 54

1

GERALDINE

The day Geraldine had been anxiously awaiting had arrived. She was about to meet Darlene, the daughter she didn't remember giving birth to forty-nine years ago. She also had no memories of Darlene's father, of being a wife and a mother, or of raising Darlene for the first twelve years of her life.

After awakening from a coma thirty-seven years ago, Geraldine couldn't remember a single thing about her life before the catastrophic injury, or how it had happened, or the injury itself. Her first memories were of the rehab center. In those, she'd been recovering mentally, but physically she had already been completely healed.

Geraldine had been told that she'd suffered a severe head trauma, which she had to believe was true because she'd had to relearn everything, including speech.

And yet, no physical evidence of the injury remained.

The staff at the rehabilitation center hadn't known how the injury had happened either. Then again, Geraldine might have forgotten what she'd been told.

Her memory was still spotty, with some things forgotten almost immediately and some things remembered vividly, which probably depended on their importance.

Geraldine could forget where she'd been the day before, but she remembered every moment of her second daughter's birth thirty-four years ago. She also remembered each important milestone in Cassandra's life, from her first words as a baby to her incredible achievements as an adult.

Then again, other events that were almost as important were missing—like getting bitten by a male with fangs and injected with venom, and like transitioning into immortality—but those might have been intentionally erased from her memory, so she couldn't blame the accident for that.

Nevertheless, Geraldine found it unfathomable that she'd forgotten her firstborn child, even given the fickle and random nature of her memory loss. That was why she clung so hopefully to her hypothesis about having an identical twin.

They had found out from Roni that Darlene's mother had been adopted as a baby,

213

so it was entirely possible that Sabina Bral had been Geraldine's twin sister. The name had never belonged to her, which could explain why it hadn't evoked any emotion in her—no recognition whatsoever.

Sabina Bral had been reported missing and assumed dead when the girl was twelve, but since no body had ever been found, the others assumed that the drowning had been staged by Geraldine to hide the fact that she was immortal and so she could start a new life as someone else.

All things considered, Geraldine's theory made much more sense to her. If Darlene were her daughter, something about the child she'd given birth to and raised surely would have been retained, like snippets of memories, or dreams, or the muscle memory of knowing how to hold a baby while feeding her and how to change a diaper.

And yet, when Cassandra was born, Geraldine had felt like a complete novice, stumbling clumsily and learning as she went along.

Regrettably, Cassandra didn't put much stock in the identical twin theory, and neither did Onegus, but they were using it as their cover story for meeting Darlene nonetheless, so it couldn't be entirely unbelievable, could it?

Cassandra had come up with the idea of planting fake DNA test results in the database of one of the companies that offered the service.

Fortunately, or maybe serendipitously, Roni had found out that his mother had done one of those DNA tests, and he'd planted fake results for Cassandra and Geraldine in the company's database as well. Geraldine's grandson, or perhaps the grandson of her deceased twin sister, was a gifted hacker.

After that had been done, Cassandra called Darlene, claiming to be the daughter of her mother's twin sister.

Who knew? Maybe after the meeting, the others would realize that Geraldine's hunch about having a twin was right, and that she hadn't made it up just to assuage her guilt for abandoning her daughter.

They had hoped that Darlene would see the test results flagging them as close relatives and contact them, but when that hadn't happened, Cassandra had called her instead and scheduled a meeting.

That had been three weeks ago, which at the time seemed like long enough for Geraldine to emotionally prepare for facing her presumed firstborn daughter, but time had moved much faster than she would have liked.

She should have used those three weeks to learn as much as she could about Darlene from Roni, but Geraldine had been happy to leave that to Cassandra, who seemed to get along well with him.

It had been easier to hear secondhand bits and pieces about Darlene's life from Cassandra. It had felt less personal.

Another thing that she should have figured out was how to make herself look different than the mother Darlene remembered. Since they were posing as the daughters of Geraldine's identical twin sister, some familial resemblance would be expected, but not a carbon copy.

Luckily for them, Darlene had acknowledged that her mother had been adopted and had agreed that a twin could have existed and been adopted by another couple.

It also added credence to Geraldine's hypothesis and had eased some of her anxiety, but not enough.

If only she could be like Cassandra, who didn't seem anxious about meeting her half-sister for the first time.

Perhaps she'd been too busy to overthink it. Cassandra was still adjusting to her newly transformed immortal body, her new boyfriend, and her new life living among immortals in their hidden village.

The truth was that Geraldine had been busy as well. She'd been spending her nights with her new immortal boyfriend, her days meeting up with friends, and her evenings preparing fancy dinners for herself and Shai.

Perhaps pushing the upcoming meeting out of her mind had been her way of coping with the stress of facing Darlene for the first time and the possible memories that it might bring forth, but now she regretted the lack of planning.

A different hair color could have dramatically changed her appearance, or perhaps a pair of colored contact lenses. But she'd wasted those weeks having fun, and now she was out of time.

It was three o'clock in the afternoon, and only four hours remained until the meeting.

Standing inside her closet, Geraldine debated what to wear. For many years, her main objective had been to look like a woman who could have a daughter Cassandra's age, so nearly all of her outfits were meant to make her look older. Today, though, she needed something that would make her look young enough to be Cassandra's younger sister.

Ironically, Geraldine always had to pose as someone she was not. Well, at least during the part of her life she remembered. Perhaps later today she would learn a thing or two about who she was before the amnesia, provided that she was indeed Darlene's mother and not her aunt. Since that was still the leading assumption, she should mentally prepare for it.

Hopefully, she hadn't been a terrible person, and her older daughter would remember her fondly. But how would Darlene react to seeing her, a so-called cousin who looked exactly like the mother she had lost to the sea all those years ago?

It would be like seeing a ghost.

The poor woman might faint from shock before hearing Cassandra repeat the identical twin story, which would explain why Geraldine was a carbon copy of Sabina.

Onegus had made a valid point saying that Darlene would never suspect the truth because to her it would be inconceivable that her mother, who was supposed to be dead, was alive and looked exactly the same thirty-seven years later.

Knowing how emotional she could get, Geraldine feared that she might break down and sob, overwhelmed by guilt and sorrow upon seeing her daughter, but that wouldn't be too big of a disaster. Darlene would just think that her cousin was an overemotional nutcase who cried at the drop of a hat.

Ugh, if only the twin hypothesis were true, and Darlene was indeed her niece and not her daughter, Geraldine could at least get rid of the damn guilt. The sorrow would still be there because it would mean that she'd had a sister who had died when she could have been turned immortal, but it wouldn't be as bad as knowing that she'd abandoned her own child and didn't remember ever having her.

Regrettably, there was no way to prove or disprove the theory.

Adoption records from seventy-something years ago were sealed, and even Roni with all his hacking magic couldn't find anything about Sabina except a marriage certificate that listed her maiden name as Smith.

Not a big help there.

Geraldine shook her head. How could she have been Sabina, first Smith and then Bral, if the names didn't evoke even a smidgen of emotion from her?

With a sigh, she regarded her old-fashioned wardrobe and wished that she had a pair of jeans, the kind that had multiple rips in them, not from use but as a fashion statement. The younger she managed to look, the less she would remind Darlene of the mother she'd lost.

The only outfit that fit that bill was what she used for her morning walks around the neighborhood—a pair of yoga pants, a loose T-shirt, and a pair of white sneakers. But even if Darlene wasn't her daughter, that kind of outfit would imply that Geraldine didn't assign much importance to meeting her cousin, and that wasn't the impression that she wished to impart.

2

KIAN

*A*s Kian entered his office, the Kra-ell investigative team he'd assembled was seated around the conference table.

"Good afternoon, ladies and gentlemen." He took his place at the head of the table.

Four Guardians—two of them senior, four civilians, and one pilot should be enough for what he needed done, but given the ratio of civilians to Guardians, three of the civilians being female, perhaps he should err on the side of caution and add two more men.

But making the team any larger would be counterproductive, especially if he increased the ratio of males to females. Six of the team members were posing as rich American parents who had come to tour the international school now occupying the Kra-ell former compound, and it would be difficult to explain the additional three males. On top of that, Yamanu, Mey, and Jin were too strikingly good-looking to be forgettable. Perhaps Yamanu could cast a shroud around himself to change his distinctive appearance, and maybe that of some of the other members of the team as well. Jin and Mey might have the right facial features, but their beauty and height would attract a lot of attention.

Then again, perhaps it was a good thing. If the locals would focus their attention on the beautiful females, they wouldn't notice the inquisitive nature of the team.

Opening his laptop, Kian scanned the notes Turner's local subcontractor had sent over. He'd already read them twice, but it had been a few days ago, and he needed to refresh his memory.

"The boarding school has a decent number of international students, so the administration won't view mixed couples suspiciously." Kian shifted his eyes to Yamanu. "That being said, it might be a good idea for you to shroud yourself. Your looks are too distinctive and memorable."

The Guardian nodded. "Not a problem. Do you want me to shroud anyone else?"

"The ladies are fine. Their beauty will distract the locals from paying attention to what the team is up to." Kian glanced at Jay and Alfred. "Maybe you should shroud these two and Morris. They don't have female counterparts, so it will be difficult for them to pose as prospective parents. Either make them invisible, or just make them look more average, forgettable."

"That won't be necessary," Arwel said. "While the couples go to the meeting, the others will stay behind. Yamanu and I can ensure the ladies' safety. After all, we are visiting a school, not a military installation."

Pursing her lips, Stella leaned back in her chair. "Since everyone is going to be staying in one hotel, the only one in the area, that won't solve the problem of three additional men. Jay and Alfie could pose as our bodyguards, but it would be even better if we find clan females to pose as their wives. Couples are always less suspicious than single men. It would be easier to pretend to be a group of tourists." She shifted her eyes to Morris. "You can be our tour guide and interpreter, so we don't need a fake wife for you."

Kian shook his head. "I was thinking about adding more Guardians because I don't like the ratio of civilians to warriors. I don't want to add even more civilians."

"What about Kri and Eleanor?" Mey asked.

"Wherever Kri goes, Michael goes as well, and I need Eleanor to stay in the village to keep an eye on Emmett." Kian had released the guy from the dungeon two weeks ago and had tasked Eleanor with keeping him out of trouble.

Unbeknownst to either of them, they had been placed under tight surveillance. Tiny cameras had been installed all over the house they'd been given, including bedrooms, bathrooms, and even the laundry room and backyard.

It was an invasion of privacy, but no one was actually watching the footage twenty-four-seven. An AI software that was designed to flag certain words and phrases was monitoring the recordings, and only if it detected something suspicious and sent an alert would someone take a look. As long as neither of them were plotting against the clan, no one was going to invade their privacy.

"You need more female Guardians," Richard said. "Single ones."

"I know." Kian grimaced. "But I don't see a lineup of females in front of Onegus's office asking to join the training program."

Frankly, he was thankful for that.

He couldn't ask Onegus to turn females away if they wanted to join, but he didn't like the idea of them ever having to face Doomers in battle.

That was just an excuse, though, and he was well aware of that. Kri wasn't allowed to join any missions involving Doomers, and Kian could easily do the same with any future female Guardians.

He just didn't like the idea of putting females in danger. It went against every immortal male instinct he had, and he knew that he wasn't the only immortal who felt that way. The Kra-ell, on the other hand, seemed to have a very different attitude toward female warriors.

"If our fashion line fails, I might join," Jin said.

Arwel cast her a glare. "Over my dead body."

Kian stifled a smile. Arwel had just proved he was right.

The look Jin pinned him with would have petrified a lesser man. "You don't tell me what to do, Arwel. If I want to become a Guardian, I will."

As Arwel opened his mouth to retort, Kian lifted his hand to stop the banter from turning the meeting into a fighting arena. "Save the arguments for later. This is not the time or place."

Her lips forming a thin line, Jin leaned back in her chair and folded her arms over her chest.

"Let's hope that our business endeavor doesn't fail," Mey said. "On a more pleasant note, I'm happy to report that since Jin and I decided to split the Chinese and Kra-ell languages between us, we've made good progress. I can understand some Kra-ell, but my Chinese is much better than Jin's."

"I can't speak Kra-ell either because it's just impossible to pronounce," Jin said. "But I understand most of it. Unless Emmett talks very fast or uses sophisticated words, I understand everything he says. My Chinese is not as good as Mey's, but it's good enough to understand basic things."

"That's great." Stella switched to Chinese. "Can you understand what I'm saying?"

Kian's knowledge of the language was rudimentary, but he'd understood that.

Jin nodded and then replied in Chinese, "I can. How is my accent?"

Stella scrunched her nose. "It needs work."

"Yeah," Jin agreed. "But at least I can communicate, which is a huge improvement." She smiled at Morris. "Thank you for teaching me. I couldn't have done it without you."

The pilot grinned. "Perhaps I should change professions. If I can teach you, I can teach anyone."

Kian lifted his hand to get their attention. He wanted to go home, make silly faces at Allegra, and have her smile at him her sweet toothless smile.

"What if the echoes you hear are in Kra-ell?" he asked Mey. "Can you understand enough of it?"

She nodded. "Jin is going to attach a tether to me, and if I don't understand what I'm hearing, I'll repeat it out loud for her to translate."

It wasn't perfect, but it was better than where they'd been a month ago when both sisters could barely communicate in either language.

"It will have to do." Kian glanced at his laptop. "Shai prepared each of you a file with all the intel Turner's guy has collected, including the schematics for the school building, the dormitories, the other structures on the property, and a map of the surrounding area. Has everyone gone over it?"

When they nodded, he asked, "Is everything clear, or do you have any questions before we adjourn?"

"No questions," Yamanu said. "Shai answered even those I didn't know I had. Best brief I've ever gotten. My fake dossier is so elaborate that I read it like a romance novel." He turned to Mey. "Shai has a good imagination, but our real story is even better than his imagined one." He leaned in and pushed a strand of her long hair behind her ear. "His story is not nearly as exciting."

Kian smiled.

Ever since Shai had become his assistant some twenty years ago, he'd always known that the guy was capable of more, but Shai had resisted Kian's attempts to transfer some of his responsibilities to him. Now that Kian was a father and had made the decision to limit his time in the office, Shai had no choice but to pick up the slack.

To his credit, his assistant did that without complaining even though he had a new love interest with whom he wanted to spend more time. He was working his ass off in his usual calm and methodical manner.

Later today, Shai was accompanying Geraldine to a meeting with the daughter she'd had in her previous life as Sabina Bral, which was why he wasn't present at the briefing.

It would be interesting to hear how that went.

Kian pushed to his feet. "If no one has any further questions, I'll see you all Wednesday morning before your departure."

3

SHAI

"*Move* out of the way!" Shai honked his horn.

When the car in front of him slowed down even further, he struggled to curb the urge to ram into it.

Shai had never succumbed to road rage before, but he was getting close to losing it today. He should have left the village an hour ago, when traffic was still tolerable, but with Kian assigning more and more responsibilities to him, his workload had doubled.

Most days, he had no problem with that. Kian wanted to spend time with his newborn daughter, and Shai didn't mind picking up the slack to make it possible for him. Kian had worked hard for many centuries, building a business empire for the clan from the ground up. He deserved his slice of happiness—spending time with his little princess.

Today, though, was the meeting with Darlene, and Geraldine was probably freaking out from stress. If Shai didn't calm her down, she would be in no state to attend it.

Over the month they'd been together, he'd learned that Geraldine escaped into her fantasy world when stressed, either making up new stories on the spot, or retelling old ones from her repertoire of fantasies. She was very imaginative, he had to give her credit for that.

Perhaps one day he could use her stories as ideas for his screenplays.

Right. He would have to quit his job first.

With the long hours he was working, most days he didn't make it to Geraldine's place before ten at night, which made her anxious, which in turn meant more stories.

Cassandra's advice was to ride it out and not confront Geraldine about their veracity, but Shai wasn't sure that was the right approach. He had planned on getting professional advice, but so far Geraldine had refused to see the therapist, coming up with one excuse after another.

In fact, she was coming up with every excuse under the sun to avoid visiting the village. He'd barely managed to convince her to see Bridget, who had confirmed what they had all suspected.

If Geraldine had ever suffered from a head injury, no trace of it remained. Her brain scan hadn't revealed any abnormalities.

Thankfully, when Shai finally got off the freeway, he found the surface streets not nearly as congested, and less than ten minutes later he parked in front of Geraldine's house.

She opened the door wearing an exercise outfit. "I'm so glad that you made it early."

He was late, but she must have forgotten that he'd promised to be there much earlier.

"You look adorable." He pulled her into his arms. "Were you on your way out for a walk?"

Just like him, Geraldine wasn't into exercising, but she liked to take walks around the neighborhood.

"No." She pushed out of his arms, took his hand, and led him inside. "This is what I plan on wearing to the meeting. It makes me look younger."

"It does. But why do you want to do that?" He followed her into the kitchen.

"Darlene remembers me just the way I am. I need to look different, and this outfit is the only thing I could come up with."

"We could go shopping for something else. We still have a couple of hours, and we can do it fast."

In fact, that was a great idea. Shopping would distract her from obsessing about Darlene, and they could go to the meeting straight from the mall.

"Is this so bad?" She looked down at herself. "People wear sneakers for more than just walks."

"People do, but you are not people. You are you, and you enjoy dressing up. You won't be comfortable wearing gym clothes to an evening meeting. We can go to the mall, get you a nice, youthful-looking outfit, and go to Nathalie's café straight from there."

Chewing on her lower lip, Geraldine looked at her outfit again and sighed. "You're right. I don't feel comfortable showing up like this." She looked at her watch. "It will have to be quick, though. What about Cassandra and Onegus? We were supposed to meet here and drive to the café together."

"They can meet us there."

"Can you call Onegus and check with him? What if he planned on giving us some last-minute instructions?"

Treating the meeting as if it was a military recon mission, the chief had already supplied them all with briefs that they had to memorize. He'd also grilled them last Wednesday to make sure that they had.

Naturally, Shai could recite the brief word for word, but Geraldine kept getting confused. He planned on going over it again with her in the car, but he wasn't worried. If she forgot her made-up background story, Geraldine had no problem improvising on the spot.

"I doubt Onegus needs to see us before the meeting, but I'll check." Shai typed up a quick text to the chief.

When the response came a moment later, he read it aloud. "No problem. Be there at quarter to seven. Cassandra and I will meet you there."

4

EMMETT

"*H*ello, everyone." Amanda stopped by Emmett's table. "Holding court in the café again?"

Despite her pregnant belly, she was a spectacular female—gorgeous, well-educated, elegant, and sophisticated—the kind of female a male like him deserved. She was taken, though, and so was Emmett, but unlike his mate, hers was far below her on the totem pole of desirability.

Emmett had seen the former Doomer only once, and what the male lacked in all the things he appreciated in a man, he compensated for in size and brute strength. Amanda's mate was the tallest and scariest male in the village.

Perhaps that was his appeal?

After reading the numerous romance novels Eleanor had insisted he needed to read, Emmett had come to the conclusion that women, no matter how sophisticated and educated, loved brutes. Well, most of them did.

Eleanor claimed that fantasizing about sex with a brute was not the same as living with one, and since she'd chosen him—a sophisticated non-brutish male—she wasn't saying that just to make herself sound better and smarter than those females who fell for thugs.

Smiling brightly, Emmett pushed to his feet and offered Amanda his hand. "Would you like to join our discussion?"

She glanced at the females seated around his table. "I would love to, but it seems like there are no more seats left at your round table this afternoon."

Emmett loved the King Arthur reference, and he adored being compared to the mythical figure.

"My table won't be full until it seats one hundred and fifty knights, and as you can see, I still have a long way to go." He grabbed a chair from an adjoining table and motioned for Marla to scoot hers sideways. "Please, we would be honored by your presence."

"Thank you." Amanda lowered herself gracefully onto the chair despite her pregnant belly. "So, Emmett, what is it that you are preaching?"

"Personal growth and how to achieve it one step at a time." He cast a sidelong glance at Eleanor.

Thankfully, she didn't roll her eyes.

Per Kian's instructions, Eleanor was to keep an eye on him at all times, so she had no choice but to sit and listen to what she'd already heard at Safe Haven, which she most regrettably hadn't found as helpful as he would have hoped.

In many aspects, Eleanor reminded Emmett of the Kra-ell females. She wasn't cruel like them, or indifferent to the suffering of others, but she was just as stubborn and unwilling to learn new things.

Thankfully, the other immortal clan females weren't like that. In the two weeks since his release from the clan's dungeon, he'd managed to accumulate a small following.

It wasn't Safe Haven, and his disciples didn't contribute their money or labor to his wealth, but Emmett needed something to do, and he enjoyed having a group of women gazing at him in admiration and hanging on every word leaving his mouth.

So far, no one influential had joined his discussion group, but if he could manage to pique Amanda's curiosity and have her come to his impromptu gatherings, it would be a major achievement.

If he gained her friendship, it would be an even greater one.

After Kian, Amanda was the most influential immortal in the village. Their mother, the goddess Annani, was naturally more influential than either of her children, but she was just visiting and would be going home soon. Besides, he knew better than to hope she would join his group of followers even though his message didn't contradict hers.

They were both interested in improving lives, but the way they went about it was different.

Annani's goal was to improve human society at large, while Emmett was more interested in the personal improvement each individual could attain with the proper guidance, and his teachings applied not only to humans but also to immortals. Perhaps even the Kra-ell could gain some insight from him if Kian ever found them and brought them to the village.

Not that Emmett was eager for that to happen.

Humans and immortals were much easier to deal with than the Kra-ell. His people were rooted in their traditions, combative, aggressive, and unwilling to listen to reason.

The only thing they respected was might.

He'd told Kian so, but he didn't know whether the guy had internalized the message. If the team investigating the Kra-ell former compound found clues about their new location, they shouldn't follow them. Showing up with a strong Guardian force was Kian's only hope of getting the Kra-ell leader to the negotiations table. To reach an agreement with her, he would have to make her fear him.

Jade, if she was still the one in power, would not respect anything less.

In fact, Emmett was quite certain that if she could get away with it, she wouldn't hesitate to kill Kian's peace-seeking delegation and then move to a new location, never to be found again.

5

ANNANI

*A*s Annani, Alena, and their regular entourage of Guardians turned the corner, Ronja opened the door and stepped out onto her front porch.

When Annani smiled and waved at her friend, Ronja smiled and waved back, but her shoulders looked tense, and her smile looked forced.

Ronja's young daughter looked anxious as well.

Were they nervous about a goddess visiting their home for the first time? Or was it the sight of the Guardians accompanying her?

Before Kalugal and his men had moved into the village, Annani had not been assigned guards and could take her early morning walks without a couple of them trailing her. Nowadays, Kian insisted on her having Guardians follow her everywhere even though she had nothing to fear from Kalugal or his men. Her son had refused to listen to reason, and Annani had decided the issue was not important enough for her to upset him, especially since her visit was so long this time. She did not want to agitate him when he needed to be calm around Allegra.

Children, even tiny ones like Allegra, were very sensitive to their parents' moods, and it was important to project love and tranquility in their formative years. It had a big impact on the kind of people they grew up to be.

"Good afternoon, Clan Mother." Ronja bowed her head. "Alena." Next to her, Lisa did the same.

"Oh, Ronja." Annani walked up the steps and pulled her friend into her arms. "How many times do I need to tell you to call me Annani?"

"You're not alone," Ronja whispered. "In front of other people, I need to address you formally."

Annani glanced at the two Guardians who had taken up position at the foot of the stairs. "The Guardians assigned to me know that they need to pretend that they hear nothing other than what they perceive as a threat to me." She leveled her eyes at the Guardian standing to the right of the stairs. "Am I right, Brodie?"

He turned around and dipped his head. "Always, Clan Mother."

"Thank you, Brodie." She sighed. "I would invite you two to come in, but you always refuse, so I am not going to bother this time."

Callum turned to cast her a smile. "Our job is to keep you safe, Clan Mother, and we can't do that while sipping tea and nibbling on biscuits."

Despite his comment bordering on the impudent, Annani liked the young Guardian. She preferred to be regarded as a benevolent grandmother rather than a scary matriarch, and that meant allowing comments with a touch of cheeky humor.

Alena chuckled. "Aren't you the comedian."

He winked at her and turned his gaze back to the pathway.

"Please, come in," Ronja said.

Stepping inside, Annani looked around, noting the many individual touches Ronja had added to the professionally decorated interior. It transformed the place from a house into a home, giving it a cozy feel that the beautifully coordinated everything could not achieve.

"I love what you have done with the place." Annani sat down on the couch and motioned for Ronja to sit next to her.

Alena and Lisa each sat in one of the armchairs.

"Thank you." Ronja dipped her head. "Can I offer you both some tea?"

"Yes, please," Alena said.

"I would love some." Annani shifted her eyes to the delicate porcelain tea set arranged on a silver tray on the coffee table. "This set is gorgeous. Where did you get it?"

Lifting the teapot, Ronja smiled. "I bought it in Vienna. When I was still married to David and Jonah's father, we traveled abroad a lot, and I bought many pretty things. When we got divorced, he allowed me to keep all those mementoes." She poured tea into Annani's cup. "He let me keep my jewelry as well." She smiled sadly. "When we got married, Michael was wealthy, and I had nothing. I signed a prenuptial agreement, thinking naively that we would never part."

"How did you manage after the divorce?" Alena asked.

"I did get alimony, just not much." She poured tea into Alena's cup and then Lisa's. "It was enough for what I needed at the time." She poured the last teacup and sat down.

"And then you met Frank?" Annani took a sip. "Did you fall in love with him right away?"

Ronja cast a sidelong glance at Lisa. "Michael was a tough act to follow, but Frank was patient and persistent. He won me over time. You know the saying about still waters. They run deep."

That was the opening Annani needed to shift the conversation to Merlin, which was the real reason for her visit and what kept her from going home.

She wanted her friend to attempt transition, and at Ronja's age, the only way that could be possible was with the help of Annani's 'blessing,' in other words, her blood, and hefty doses of it at that.

Ronja had found an immortal love interest, which brought her closer to where Annani needed her to be to facilitate her transition. The problem was that the two had not consummated their relationship yet, and until that happened, there was little Annani could do.

First, though, Ronja needed to consent to induction. If she did, the next step would be several of Merlin's venom bites along with Annani's secret injections.

"I heard that you are assisting Merlin these days." Annani put her teacup down. "How are the two of you getting along?"

"Very well." Ronja's face brightened. "Merlin is so much fun to be around, and I learn a lot from him, but keeping him organized is a daily struggle."

Lisa snorted and then covered her mouth with her hand. "I'm sorry, Clan Mother."

Annani waved a dismissive hand. "Do not fret, child, and feel free to be yourself. The only thing I cannot stand is vulgar language."

"Thank you. It's just that my mother is being polite. By keeping Merlin organized, she means keeping his house from looking like a dump. I love Merlin, but he's the quintessential disorganized, messy genius."

Hmm, that was interesting. If the child was fond of Merlin, it would be much easier to push the mother toward ending her mourning period and embracing new love with the fun-loving doctor.

6

RONJA

*A*nnani smiled. "I have never visited Merlin's home or one of his clinics, but his reputation precedes him in more ways than one. He is quite the colorful character, and he is also brilliant."

"Or crazy," Alena grumbled. "I still think that his fertility potions are just a hoax, and he relies on their placebo effect. So far, only Syssi and Kian have gotten pregnant with his help, but none of the other couples undergoing the so-called treatment have."

Ronja felt insulted on Merlin's behalf. "He's not crazy, and his potions are based on a lot of research. Gertrude grows many of the herbs he uses in her garden, and she swears by their effectiveness on humans. She's been prescribing the same herbs to mothers wishing to conceive and has seen their effectiveness. Merlin tweaked them to be suitable for immortals, and Syssi and Kian were the first to try. I bet that it didn't work right away on humans either. The other couples just need to give it more time."

Leaning over, Annani patted her knee. "No need to get so upset, Ronja. I'm sure it is only a matter of time before we see more pregnancies."

Ronja let out a breath and cast Alena an apologetic glance. "I'm sorry for my outburst. It's just that over the past couple of weeks, I've gotten to know Merlin better, and there is nothing crazy about him. His wild hair and colorful clothing were meant to confuse the humans he was helping in his clinics. It seems counterintuitive, but the more eccentric he looked, the more he could get away with moving from place to place and claiming to be his own son or nephew who'd adopted his style. People used to murmur that he was a wizard who had found a way to cheat death, but nowadays such rumors are dismissed as ignorant nonsense. I'm just glad he didn't do that during the witch hunts."

Alena shuddered. "Don't remind me. It was one of the worst periods in human history. My mother was so upset that she was ready to give up on humanity."

"I was not," Annani protested. "It was just a low point. We saved as many as we

228

could, but we could not get to everyone. It was such a tragedy." Annani's usually vibrant eyes dimmed with sorrow. "There are so many wrongs I wish I could prevent or undo. It is so frustrating. It reminds me that I am just flesh and blood and that my power is limited." She shook her head. "But enough about things we cannot change. I want to talk about happy things, like love and family." She took Ronja's hand. "We need to grasp every moment of joy we can squeeze out of life and not waste any of it because joy is so rare. That is why I believe it is time for you, my dear, to stop mourning and embrace love."

Ronja's throat constricted. "It has only been three months." She shifted her eyes to Lisa. "It's too early."

As a tear slid down her daughter's cheek, she pulled her hand out of Annani's, pushed to her feet, and walked over to Lisa. "I loved your father." She leaned in and hugged her tightly. "Never doubt that."

"I don't." Lisa pushed out of her arms. "It just feels as if much more time has passed. I can't believe it has only been three months."

Alena put her teacup on the coffee table and reached over to pat Lisa's arm. "The perception of time is influenced by how much is happening during a certain period. Time intervals associated with many changes are perceived as longer than those with fewer changes."

"That makes sense." Lisa wiped her cheeks with the back of her hand. "So much has happened to me since then." She pushed to her feet. "Can I offer you some cut fruit?"

Obviously, Lisa needed a few moments to herself. Normally, she would have just escaped to her room, but that wasn't possible with a goddess sitting in her living room.

"I would love some," Ronja said. "We have watermelon, cantaloupe, and fresh strawberries."

As Lisa ducked into the kitchen, Ronja returned to her spot next to Annani. "It's still difficult for her." She sighed. "It's difficult for me too."

"I understand," Annani said. "Believe me, I do. I mourned my Khiann for many years. But I am immortal, and my time is limitless. Yours is not. In fact, your time is running out, my dear."

The lump in Ronja's throat swelled, blocking the passage of air. Gasping, she clutched her neck. "Why?" she managed to croak. "Am I dying? What do you sense?"

Annani's eyes widened. "Oh, no. That was not what I meant." She put her hand on Ronja's thigh. "As far as I can sense, you are perfectly healthy. It is just that you are mortal, and the older you get, the more difficult it will be for you to transition."

This time around, it was Ronja's eyes' turn to widen. "Isn't it too late for me already? The oldest guy to transition was forty-six, more than a decade younger than me, and he barely made it."

"That is true. But since then, we have learned a few things. Medicine has made big strides just in the past two years. I keep reading about discoveries and innovations that make my head spin. Furthermore, we have not lost a single Dormant yet, so maybe Bridget is wrong about the increased risk to older Dormants. It is true that older Dormants have a more difficult time transitioning, but it has not been easy for some of the young ones either. And let us not forget Merlin, who has a vested interest in your transition. I am sure that he can concoct some potions to strengthen your body and make it biologically younger."

Hope surged in Ronja's chest.

She hadn't allowed herself to think about the lost opportunity to turn immortal, had even convinced herself that she didn't want immortality, but if there was even a slight chance to live forever, shouldn't she take it?

Lisa came back and put a platter of fruit on the table. "Isn't it too risky?"

"It is risky," Annani admitted. "But I have a gut feeling that it will work, and my gut is never wrong." The goddess said it with so much conviction in her voice that there was no way she didn't believe it wholeheartedly.

Annani had lived for over five thousand years, and if her gut hadn't been wrong in all that time, then Ronja could probably trust it.

But what if Annani was exaggerating? Or what if her gut had just remained silent on the outcome of issues that she hadn't been sure about?

And why was it so important to the goddess that Ronja transition?

Was it because Annani cared for her so much and didn't want to lose a friend?

"I need to think about it." Ronja shifted her gaze to Lisa. "And I also need to discuss it with my daughter." She turned back to Annani. "She's only fifteen, and she still needs me. If I die, who is going to take care of her?"

"Don't talk like that," Lisa said. "The Clan Mother is right. For obvious reasons, your induction can't wait until I'm eighteen and can finally have sex so I can transition too." She rolled her eyes. "Besides, I will always need you, even when I'm married with children."

Ronja's heart melted. "I'd rather live out the rest of my mortal life and see that happen than attempt immortality and chance losing it."

Lisa closed her eyes for a moment, and when she opened them to look at Ronja, they were misted with tears. "Don't count on me making the decision for you. I won't tell you to do it, and I won't tell you not to do it. It has to be your choice. But you need to think it through. Remaining mortal doesn't guarantee that you'll get to see my children, or that I'll have any to start with. Jonah was so young when his heart gave out, and I bet that he thought he had many decades left to live, to find a wife and to have children, but he didn't. Sadly, the outcome of long-term plans is not entirely up to mortals. Besides, after I transition, it might take centuries until I get pregnant. If you stay mortal, you'll be long gone by then."

It was a morbid thought, but Lisa was right.

"You do not have to decide anything today," Annani said. "Talk it over with Merlin and Lisa."

Ronja's cheeks flushed. Talking it over with Merlin was like inviting him to her bed, and she really wasn't ready for that. "You are both right, but I need more time to make up my mind."

7

GERALDINE

As Shai looked for a place to park, Geraldine opened the car window and waved at Cassandra and Onegus, who were waiting outside the café's front door. Thankfully, Shai found a spot only a few doors down, so she didn't have to walk a long distance in the crazy high heels she'd bought earlier.

"Mom." Cassandra gave her a thorough look over. "You look hot. I didn't know you owned a single pair of jeans, let alone a pair so fancy."

"I didn't. Shai took me shopping for some younger-looking attire."

The skinny jeans with small decorative rips and slashes looked good on her, especially when paired with four-inch heels and a form-fitting white T-shirt. The little shirt had been insanely pricey, even compared to the jeans, which had given Geraldine her first sticker shock, but Shai had insisted on paying for everything.

"You should dress like this more often." Cassandra threaded her arm through hers. "It makes you look twenty years younger."

"Which is why I don't. Who is going to believe that I'm your mother?"

"From now on, we can pretend to be sisters. You no longer need to keep making yourself look older."

That was true, but given that all of her friends knew that Cassandra was her daughter, it was irrelevant. Geraldine didn't want to move once more and make new friends all over again.

As Onegus pushed the café's door open, the bells hanging on its other side jingled, startling her.

"Welcome." Sylvia's mother smiled. "Let me show you to your table." She led them to the last one in the row of booths and then motioned with her chin at the only couple sitting in the first one. "They are about done. Soon, you will have the place to yourself."

"We are fifteen minutes early," Onegus said. "By the time Darlene and her husband get here, your other customers will have left."

She nodded. "Can I get you something? Coffee? Tea? Pastries?"

"I would love some coffee," Cassandra said. "Geraldine probably wants tea. Right, Mom?"

"I do. But you'd better stop calling me Mom. From now on, I'm Geraldine, your sister."

"Right." Cassandra grinned. "My hot younger sister."

"What's the husband's name?" Onegus asked, probably to test them.

"It's Leo, but we are not supposed to know it," Shai said. "Darlene hasn't told Cassandra his name."

Onegus nodded his approval and looked at Geraldine. "Don't forget that."

"I won't."

Shai wrapped his arm around her shoulders. "How are you holding up?"

She sucked in a breath. "I'm okay." And she would keep telling herself that until her daughter arrived.

When the café's last customers had left, Onegus pulled a small green box from his jacket pocket, flicked a switch on, and attached it to the table's underside. "This is the signal disrupter," he explained. "If either Darlene or her husband have bugs on them, this box will scramble their transmission. It will also scramble cellular signals, so if any of you need to make a phone call, you should step outside and walk about twenty feet away from the restaurant."

As they waited, time slowed to a crawl.

Ruth served them coffee and tea, brought out a cheese platter with crackers to munch on, and yet the hands of the clock on the wall seemed stuck in place.

When the bells hanging on the coffee shop's door jingled, Geraldine's fingers tightened on her teacup. She knew what Darlene looked like, she'd seen pictures of her, but it wasn't the same as seeing her in person.

Forcing her head up, she looked at her supposed daughter and her husband and didn't know whether she should smile or cry. Her emotions were all over the place.

Cassandra rose to her feet and turned to greet her sister. "Darlene." She smiled and offered Darlene her hand. "I'm Cassandra."

Darlene looked confused as she shook Cassandra's hand, probably not expecting her cousin's ethnic appearance, but she got over it quickly. "I've seen you before. I mean not you in person, but your picture. It was in a gossip magazine. You wore a beautiful gown, it was very unique, dark purple with sheer panels. I remember wondering if you wore a skin-colored bra under it or none at all."

"I didn't wear a bra," Cassandra admitted.

They hadn't taken into account that Cassandra and Onegus would be recognizable from the articles published following the gala event they'd met at, but since they were using their real names, that wasn't a problem.

Besides, Onegus or Shai could thrall Darlene and Leo to forget that piece of information.

"Oh my gosh." Darlene's hand flew to her mouth. "My cousin is a famous person."

Cassandra chuckled. "I'm not famous. Let me introduce you to my sister." She moved aside, giving Darlene a clear view of Geraldine.

Darlene gasped. "No way." She took a step back. "You are the spitting image of my mother. I thought that the twin story was far-fetched, but you are proof of it."

As Geraldine tried to stand but stumbled back, Shai helped her up.

"I'm so glad to see you." Her voice came out on a sob, and a moment later, she was crushing Darlene to her chest.

They were about the same height, but Darlene was plumper. She was still very pretty at forty-nine, much prettier than she looked in her pictures, but even holding her close didn't bring back any memories.

After a long moment in each other's arms, Darlene untangled herself from Geraldine's hold and looked her over. "You are so beautiful, just like she was." She wiped her teary eyes. "The same hair, the same eyes." She sniffled. "You look skinnier, though. She was a bit heavier."

"Let me introduce you to our partners," Cassandra interrupted, motioning to the men, who had risen to their feet as well. "This is my fiancé, Onegus. And this is Shai, Geraldine's boyfriend."

8

CASSANDRA

*W*ith the introductions out of the way and the refreshments served, it was time to get down to business.

Cassandra put her coffee cup down and assumed her most charming smile as she asked Darlene, "Do you want to go first?"

Her sister cast a quick glance at her husband before answering. "I was only twelve when I lost my mother, so I don't have many memories of her. You two had yours for much longer. Why don't you start?"

Cassandra put her hand on Geraldine's thigh. "As you've probably noticed, my sister tends to get overemotional, especially when talking about our mother. They were very close." She gave Geraldine's thigh a light squeeze. "Our mother was very sweet, but she was absentminded. My sister took it upon herself to watch over her, while I made sure that the bills were paid, and the fridge wasn't empty. Was your mother forgetful?"

Darlene shook her head. "Not that I noticed." She chuckled. "My mother had her quirks, though. She was very secretive."

"About what?" Geraldine asked.

"She didn't like talking about her past. I knew that she was adopted, but I never got to meet my adoptive grandparents. When I asked her why we never visited them, she said that they weren't on good terms but refused to say why. I asked my father if he knew. He told me that her adoptive parents had sent her away when she was sixteen to stay with their relatives on a farm, and those relatives hadn't treated her very well. She hadn't got to finish high school, and she had worked long days to earn her keep."

Cassandra's heart clenched with sympathy for her mother. Geraldine liked to believe that she'd been well-educated before her memory loss, perhaps even had a college degree. Finding out that she hadn't even finished high school would be a blow to her self-esteem. She was an immortal, so she could still get the education she craved, but with her memory issues, it might be difficult for her to attend classes and actually retain anything.

Perhaps she could go to art school. There weren't as many facts to remember, and since Geraldine had a good eye for colors and patterns, it shouldn't be too difficult for her.

"That was where my parents met," Darlene added. "My father was a farm boy as well."

That was a good opportunity to switch the conversation to the grandfather, who was the number one suspect on Cassandra's list.

Actually, he was her only suspect.

"It must have been difficult for your father to raise a daughter alone."

"He didn't." Darlene lifted her teacup and took a sip.

"What do you mean?" Geraldine asked.

"After my mother died, my father was devastated and in no shape to take care of himself, let alone a child who'd just lost her mother. We moved back to Oklahoma to be near his family. My grandparents took care of me, and being surrounded by my many aunts and uncles and their kids was just the medicine I needed." She smiled. "At twelve, it didn't bother me that they were a bunch of rowdy hillbillies. I loved them." She turned to glance at her husband. "I still do, but Leo can't stand them. He doesn't like my father either, and I can't really blame him for that. He's not an easy guy to get along with."

"You hate his new wife, and you hate how they live." Other than 'hello' and 'nice to meet you,' those were Leo's first words of the evening. "So don't you put the blame on me."

"That's true." Darlene grimaced. "He married a bimbo eighteen years younger than him, and they are both nuts." She huffed out a breath. "She infected him with the survivalist bug. They live in the middle of nowhere and use an outhouse for crying out loud."

That didn't sound like a place Cassandra wanted to visit, but she would have to get to the bottom of her mother's history.

She needed to find out more about the kind of relationship Geraldine and her husband had, but she couldn't ask directly without making Darlene suspicious. "Your father must have loved your mother very much to be so heartbroken after her death."

Darlene nodded. "He did."

That wasn't the answer Cassandra had been waiting for, and it seemed like Darlene wasn't going to elaborate, at least not until Shai thralled her cooperation.

Regrettably, Onegus was too straitlaced to thrall a human for anything other than clan security.

"Did your mother have an artistic talent?" Geraldine asked. "Our mother was a talented quilter."

Darlene's eyes widened. "No way. My mother quilted too. Her quilts won many competitions."

"Did your father support her hobby?" Cassandra asked.

"Why wouldn't he? She loved doing it."

"It's very time-consuming," Geraldine said quietly. "My father wasn't happy about the many hours our mother spent quilting."

Cassandra nudged Onegus's foot, reminding him of what they'd agreed on before.

If the conversation reached a point where thralling was required, he would excuse himself and go outside to allow Shai to do that.

If he stayed, he was obligated by clan law to stop Shai from thralling humans for non-essential reasons.

Not missing her meaning, he pulled out his phone and pretended to check his messages. "If you'll excuse me, there is a phone call I have to make." He rose to his feet. "It won't take long. I promise to be back in no more than ten minutes."

Hopefully, that would be enough time for what they needed.

9

SHAI

Onegus leaving was Shai's cue that it was time to thrall Darlene.

But first, he had to take care of Leo. If they grilled the wife for too long, her husband might intervene.

Turning to Leo, he sighed. "Geraldine and Cassandra have so many questions for Darlene about her mother. I hope you don't mind."

Thankfully, the guy was easy to thrall. He wasn't suspicious, only bored, and he wanted to be done and go home.

"I don't," Leo said.

"Thank you." Shai turned to Darlene and looked into her eyes. "Tell me the truth, Darlene. Did your father approve of your mother's time-consuming hobby?"

The emphasis was on her telling him the truth. The second part of the question was just an opening for what he needed to ask her next.

She shrugged. "He might not have liked the production side of it, but he sure loved the prize money she won. He complained about how messy the house was, about the pieces of fabric and loose threads everywhere, about the unwashed dishes in the sink, the clothes piling high in the laundry hamper, and so on. But what he hated most was her attending those competitions. He was the jealous type, and he imagined her meeting men there, which was absurd since there were no male partic-ipants. Quilting is a predominantly female thing."

"I bet your mother didn't like those accusations," Cassandra said.

Darlene huffed out a breath. "Of course she didn't. They fought endlessly about that and many other things." She looked at Geraldine and smiled. "Just like you, my mother was a beautiful woman, so naturally men looked at her. That was enough for him to get mad and imagine things. But she was also a little flirtatious. It wasn't intentional, it was just part of how she was, and it drove him nuts."

"It sounds like they didn't have a good marriage," Geraldine said.

"It wasn't any better or worse than what I saw in my friends' houses. No marriage is perfect, and couples fight about many things. Money usually being the biggest issue, followed by whose responsibility it was to do what, and in some cases, infidelity. My parents fought about all three, but I think that they loved each other nonetheless. I know for sure that my father loved my mother. He mourned her for many years."

"When did he remarry?" Cassandra asked.

"When I went to college. I guess he felt lonely, or maybe he felt like I betrayed him too. He didn't want me to go because we didn't have the money to pay for it, but then I got a full-ride scholarship to USC." She shook her head. "Don't ask me how. I was a good student, but I wasn't good enough for that kind of scholarship." She looked at her husband. "That was where I met Leo."

"Didn't your mother have a life insurance policy?" Cassandra asked. "That could have paid for your education."

Darlene shook her head. "Not as far as I know, and if she did, the amount must have been negligible. My father was a carpenter, and he never lacked work, but money was always tight. I don't remember it getting less so after she died."

Shai stifled a relieved breath. With no financial motivation, it was less likely that Geraldine's husband had tried to kill her.

"What about your mother's other peculiarities?" Shai asked. "When you mentioned it before, it sounded like there was more to it than just her secretiveness about her past."

When Darlene didn't answer right away, he leaned forward and looked into her eyes. "We are family. Whatever you tell us is not going to leave this table."

"It's not that." She glanced at her husband. "It's just that the things I remember are too strange to be real. I was twelve, and I suffered a terrible loss. My memories of her might have become part fantasy over time."

"That's okay," Geraldine said. "My memories are funky as well. Sometimes I think that things I dreamt about really happened, and other times I think the reverse. We are not going to judge you."

Taking a deep breath, Darlene filled her lungs with air and then released it through her mouth. "What I remember is that my mother was never sick, never got hurt, and was incredibly strong for a woman. I was five or six when she forgot a pan full of onions on the burner. When they started smoking, she rushed to the kitchen and grabbed the handle with her bare hand. She hissed in pain, dropped the pan in the sink, turned on the faucet, and put her hand under the stream. I was crying because she was hurt and I was scared for her, but then she showed me her hand and said that she was fine." Darlene took another breath. "I expected a red welt on the palm of her hand, but the skin wasn't even marked. It was like magic."

Given Darlene's surprising recollections, Geraldine had to have been turned immortal before her injury. That didn't make sense because if she hadn't been particularly forgetful before, then her memory issues resulted from the injury and should have cleared as soon as her body had repaired the damage. The only explanation Shai could think of was that the injury had been of catastrophic proportions, the kind that even an immortal body couldn't repair. But if that was the case, she wouldn't have survived.

"Maybe the handle wasn't as hot as you thought it was?" Cassandra suggested.

"I remember the smell of singed flesh." Darlene shuddered. "It was terrible."

"You might have expected to smell it," Shai said. "Sometimes, when we expect something, our minds fill in the blanks."

Darlene waved a hand. "I told you that my memories of her are too fantastic to be real. I don't know why I remember these strange things. Maybe Geraldine is right, and I dreamt them, later thinking that they actually happened."

Geraldine smiled reassuringly. "My imagined memories are more fun than that." She winked. "What other strange things do you remember?"

Taking a deep breath, Darlene leaned back. "My mother's sewing machine was this big clunky thing that weighed a ton. My father grunted every time she asked him to move it so she could sweep underneath it, and he was a strong man who'd worked with his hands. I once saw her lifting it and moving it to the other side of the room as if it weighed no more than a stack of towels."

"Impossible," Geraldine whispered.

Darlene huffed out a breath. "I missed her so much that I must have turned her into a superhero in my mind."

1 0

ONEGUS

*a*fter getting an update from Bhathian, Onegus spent a few more minutes scrolling through his emails. He answered a couple and then headed back to the café.

His conscience wasn't clear. In the ten minutes he'd been gone, Shai might have broken the clan law by thralling Darlene. Not being there to witness the transgression was not the same as not knowing it had happened, but it was plausible deniability. Intentions were not a crime, and Shai might not have done it after all. As long as Onegus didn't ask, he could pretend not to know.

Edna would probably have a different take on this, but even though morally he was guilty, the law was on his side. Suspecting that a crime had been committed wasn't proof admissible in court.

As he walked over to the booth, the vibe he felt was a slight excitement, but mostly the mood seemed neutral. Darlene was anxious, but she seemed fine, so he had to assume that she hadn't revealed anything incriminating about her father.

"What did I miss?" He slid into the booth next to Cassandra.

"Stories of marital bliss or rather the lack thereof." Cassandra shifted closer to him. "And about some children regarding their parents as superheroes." She turned to Darlene. "I remember thinking that my mother was the most beautiful woman and the kindest person, but I didn't think of her as omnipotent, not even when I was still very young. Because of her forgetfulness, I knew that she was fragile and needed my help. But my experience was probably different than most. Onegus and I hope to have kids someday, and I wonder if what you thought about your mother is common. Do your children look upon you and Leo as infallible and all-knowing?"

It was a clever way to bring up Roni without actually mentioning him by name. The idea was to get a sense of Darlene and Leo's feelings toward their son. Also, if Cassandra was shifting the conversation to Roni, it meant that she'd gotten all the information she needed from Darlene to continue her investigation into her mother's past. Or at least all that Darlene knew.

The woman snorted. "We only have one child, and he never thought much of us. Roni is a genius, and to him, we seem like a couple of simpletons." She sighed. "We haven't seen him in years."

"Why is that?" Geraldine asked, her question sounding genuinely innocent.

Onegus wondered whether she was such a superb actress, or she'd forgotten why Roni couldn't have kept in touch with his parents. The latter was more likely.

"It's a long story," Leo said. "Roni is very good with computers, and we think that he was hired by some secret organization, maybe he even moved abroad."

The father was obviously trying to avoid mentioning Roni's crime, sentencing, and subsequent escape.

Cassandra leaned forward. "What if I told you that I can get you a meeting with your son?"

Darlene's eyes widened. "Do you know Roni?"

Cassandra nodded. "He found us through the genetic testing company. He also had his genes tested, but for obvious reasons, he kept his profile confidential. We've made ours public, and he contacted me. We talked, and he explained about the delicate situation he was in, and why he couldn't contact you. I told him about our meeting, and he asked me to find out whether you would want to meet him somewhere. He's concerned about you still being watched, which means that he can't just walk up to your front door and ring the bell, or even give you a call."

"I would like to see those test results," Leo snapped, and a bitter scent hit Onegus's nostrils. "Maybe they can tell us where he got his smarts from."

Did Leo question Roni's paternity?

Darlene's chin started to wobble, and a moment later, tears appeared in her eyes. "I didn't know if he was even alive. As long as the agents kept watching our house, I believed that he was fine and just hiding somewhere. But when they stopped, I feared the worst."

"Where is he?" Leo asked.

"I don't know," Cassandra lied. "But he's going to call me tomorrow. What do you want me to tell him?"

"That we miss him terribly and want to see him." Darlene wiped her eyes. "Can he meet us here? Is it safe?"

"It is," Onegus said. "I work in security, and we checked this place thoroughly before the meeting."

"Are you free on Wednesday at the same time?" Cassandra asked.

"Of course." Darlene looked at Leo. "We are also free tomorrow."

Cassandra shook her head. "Roni told me that he can meet you on Wednesday, and he might not call me tomorrow. So let's keep it the way he wants it."

Darlene pulled a paper napkin from the dispenser and dabbed it at her eyes. "What did Roni tell you? Is he okay? Is he living in hiding?"

"Yes to both." Cassandra reached over the table and took Darlene's hand. "He told me about the trouble he had with the government, and about his escape. He figured out that he was too valuable, and even when his sentence was served, they would never let him go. So when the opportunity to run presented itself, he took it. The people he works for now helped him escape from the hospital."

11

GERALDINE

"*D*o you have Roni's phone number?" Darlene asked. "I would love to at least talk to him."

Geraldine could understand her so well. Darlene hadn't seen her son in four years, hadn't even been sure that he was still alive, and now that she knew he could be reached, she couldn't wait until a meeting could be arranged.

"I'm sorry," Cassandra said. "But given that Roni is still a fugitive, he can't even call you. The government can tap any phone conversation, and they are probably still monitoring your calls. You will have to wait for the face-to-face meeting."

"Don't even mention his name after leaving this place." Onegus pulled the signal disrupter from under the table. "You might have tiny recorders on you and not even realize it. This jumbles the signal, but it's only effective in close proximity."

Leo eyed the device curiously but didn't say anything.

"I understand." Darlene closed her eyes. "I just can't wait to see him."

"He's eager to see you too." Cassandra patted her hand. "He would also like to visit his grandfather. With him living off the grid, there is very little chance that he's watched. Is there a way to contact him?"

Darlene nodded. "He doesn't have a phone, but you can call one of my cousins. He visits my father twice a month to bring him mail and other things he and his wife need. His name is Edgar." She pulled out her phone and scrolled through her contact information. "I can share the contact with you."

"Edgar Bral," Cassandra read the name. "What's your father's name?"

"Rudolf Bral. And his wife's name is Niki." Darlene's eyes shifted to Geraldine. "I don't know if it's wise for you to visit him, though. You look so much like my mother that he might have a stroke when he sees you."

Geraldine had no wish to see her supposed ex-husband. After seeing Darlene and having no visceral reaction to her, she believed more than ever in her identical twin theory. Geraldine had never been married to Rudolf Bral. He'd been her sister's husband.

"I don't think I will." She turned to look at Cassandra. "We are not related to him, so I don't see any reason to upset an old man. Roni can go by himself."

"True." Cassandra rapped her fingers on the table. "But I'm curious to see how the survivalists live. Besides, he might know something about our mother's family. Perhaps her sister told him things that she didn't tell Darlene." She patted Geraldine's arm. "We will talk about this later."

"We should go." Leo glanced at his watch. "It's getting late." He rose to his feet and offered a hand up to Darlene.

She took it and let him pull her up. "Are you going to come over with Roni on Wednesday?"

Geraldine wasn't sure and glanced at Cassandra, who nodded.

She had to wait for her and Onegus to get up before she could slide out of the booth, and when she did, she pulled Darlene into her arms. "This should be the first time of many. I don't want us to drift apart."

"Definitely." Darlene squeezed her tight. "I want to keep in touch."

Now that Geraldine was convinced that Darlene wasn't her daughter, it was much easier to say goodbye.

After the couple left the café, Cassandra regarded her with concern in her eyes. "Are you okay?"

She nodded. "I know in my gut that Darlene isn't my daughter. She's my twin's."

Cassandra shook her head. "You're in denial, Mom. Didn't you hear her talk about her mother's super strength? The time she grabbed the hot handle of a pan, and her hand showed no burn marks? You were already immortal when you suffered the head trauma and lost your memory. What are the chances of your twin sister also encountering an immortal male who induced her?"

Geraldine's heart sank.

Apparently, her selective memory had decided to ignore what didn't fit into the narrative she'd created, and she'd forgotten Darlene's comments about her mother's super abilities. Then again, it was just more circumstantial evidence that proved nothing.

"I trust my gut instinct more than I trust a young girl's impressions of a mother she's lost and idealized. Besides, I probably couldn't lift that sewing machine because I didn't gain super strength with my transition. I still stand behind my conviction that Darlene couldn't be my daughter."

Even if she had actually tested her DNA and compared the results to Darlene's, it would prove nothing because identical twins had identical genetics. Just as Geraldine couldn't prove her theory, Cassandra couldn't disprove it.

As Onegus and Cassandra gave her simultaneous pitying looks, Shai wrapped his arm around her shoulders. "Let's leave it as a possibility but operate under the assumption that you are Darlene's mother. We've learned a few things this evening that we didn't know before, and we might learn more after visiting Rudolf Bral. When are we going?"

"I don't want to go," Geraldine protested. "He's not my husband and never was. The shock of seeing what he'll assume is the ghost of his dead wife might kill him."

"We will change your looks." Cassandra reached for a lock of her hair. "We can turn you into a redhead and straighten your hair, and I can have the makeup artist who preps our models for photoshoots change your appearance so dramatically that you won't recognize yourself in the mirror."

"We have someone like that in the clan," Onegus said. "You've met Eva, right?"

Cassandra nodded. "Nathalie's mother. The one with the detective agency."

"She's a master of disguises. She uses prosthetics to change everything. When disguised, even her own daughter didn't recognize her, and the only thing that gave Eva away was the smell of latex."

"Why did she want to disguise herself from her daughter?" Geraldine asked.

"It's a fascinating story." Shai tightened his arm around her. "I can tell you all about it on the way." He turned to Onegus. "When are we going to pay Rudolf a visit? And are you going to come with us?"

"Of course I am."

"Perhaps you shouldn't," Cassandra said.

"There is no way I'm letting you go into a damn survivalist community without me. Those people are nuts."

12

SHAI

$\mathcal{O}$n the way to Geraldine's house, Shai scanned his memories for all the lapses in her recollections that he'd noticed since they'd met.

The pattern, or rather lack thereof, hinted more at a faulty brain function than the effect of thralling or compulsion, but he wasn't ready to discard that possibility yet.

First of all, only a super powerful immortal would have been able to compel or thrall Geraldine because she was an immortal, and apparently had been one before her amnesia. That immortal would have to be of Kalugal's caliber or higher, and that was highly unlikely. The only known immortal who met that criterion was Navuh, and it couldn't have been him. He never left the island, and even if he had done so in secret, he would have never bothered with Geraldine for any reason. For all his insanity and his many faults, Navuh was bonded to Areana and wouldn't have dallied with another.

Besides, her memory issues were evident in everyday life, especially when she was excited or anxious. He'd witnessed several incidents for which no one was responsible.

Even if some unknown powerful immortal had messed with her long-term memories, that immortal couldn't have been responsible for the small lapses that Shai had noticed.

Unless said immortal had done a hatchet job, thralled her too many times, and caused her irreversible damage, but that seemed unlikely as well. Shai had seen the poor humans who'd been thralled into a near-zombie state by Doomers. More than their memory had been affected. Their cognitive and executive faculties had been drastically reduced as well.

Geraldine's were intact.

Other than her haphazard memory, her mind functioned not only well but at a high level. She was intelligent, resourceful, and had no problem asserting her will.

All of that brought him back to the one explanation that could possibly account for the plethora of Geraldine's symptoms. The head injury she'd suffered must have been so severe that even her immortal body couldn't heal all the damage in time to preserve the memories she'd accumulated prior to the accident. It was also possible that it hadn't healed right, messing up some of the synapses as it fixed itself.

Shai wasn't a doctor, but he assumed that it was similar to what happened when an immortal broke a bone and didn't have it set correctly. Often, it fused the wrong way, and Bridget had to re-break it to set it properly.

Except, a brain wasn't a broken bone, and if the injury had been that severe, it was a miracle that Geraldine had survived.

A massive injury to the brain or the heart was one of the few things that could kill an immortal. Geraldine had probably survived thanks to her strong godly genes. Her healing rate was spectacular even in immortal terms.

"I'm still waiting," she said.

Startled out of his contemplation, Shai arched a brow. "For what?"

She chuckled. "You are supposed to possess an eidetic memory, and yet you've already forgotten that you promised me Eva's story."

"You are right. But I didn't forget. I was just preoccupied with other thoughts."

He was glad to see that her mood had improved. After Cassandra had shattered her illusions about having a twin, Geraldine had seemed despondent.

Perhaps she'd forgotten that already?

He had a feeling that some of the things she didn't remember she had chosen to forget.

Tilting her head, Geraldine regarded him with a coquettish smile. "Perhaps I can use your excuse as well. I'm often preoccupied with all kinds of thoughts when I need to remember something that has just happened." She tapped her temple. "I have a very creative and busy mind."

That might explain how she'd forgotten Darlene's story about her mother's superpowers mere minutes after she'd heard it.

He hated to do it, but he needed to keep her at least partially grounded in reality. "That wouldn't explain the loss of your long-term memories."

"I was just teasing. Now, I want you to tell me Eva's story. I want to hear all of it before we get home, and we are almost there."

He cast her a sidelong glance. "Am I not invited to finish it inside?"

She chuckled. "You are definitely invited, and you are most definitely going to finish inside, hopefully more than once, just not your story-telling."

Instantly, his shaft hardened, and his venom glands swelled. "What do you have in mind?"

"The kinds of things that are show and not tell." She kicked her shoes off, turned toward him, and pulled a leg under her bottom. "So, how did Eva earn the title of master of disguise?"

He shifted to accommodate the discomfort in his pants, but it didn't help much. "Just like you, Eva was accidentally turned immortal. By an incredible chance, she and Kalugal hooked up many years ago when she was still in college. He didn't know she was a Dormant, and after he erased himself from her memories, she didn't remember ever getting bitten. She was young and healthy, and her transition was so uneventful that she thought it was just the flu and had no idea that she'd turned immortal."

Geraldine nodded. "I didn't know either. Has she also lacked immortal super skills like me?"

"Perhaps she wasn't aware of them. Fast forward several years, she became a DEA agent, which is how she acquired her detective skills. Decades later, she met another immortal on one of her assignments, where she was posing as a flight attendant. Miraculously, that one night with him resulted in a pregnancy."

"That's truly incredible." Geraldine huffed out a breath. "What are the chances of one woman meeting two different immortal males by chance?"

"Almost nonexistent."

"So maybe my twin sister and I both turning immortal is not as inconceivable as you think. Is it?"

"You have a point. Do you want to hear the rest of the story or not?"

She waved a hand. "Please, continue."

"Eva was forty-five at the time, and she had given up on ever conceiving. Bhathian, the immortal who fathered her daughter, followed clan guidelines and offered to help her financially but told her that he couldn't be involved, even suggesting that she terminate the pregnancy. Naturally, Eva refused. She left the DEA, found a man whom she deemed a suitable father for her daughter, and married him. When the years passed, and she still wasn't aging, she became frightened. She imagined that her genes had been tampered with during her time with the DEA, and that those who had done it would come searching for her and her daughter. When Nathalie went to college, Eva divorced her husband and fled. She opened a detective agency and used the skills she'd learned. That's how she became the master of disguise."

It wasn't the end of the story, but since they reached the gate to Geraldine's community, it was time to shift gears into something more fun.

"And?" Geraldine asked. "How did she reunite with Nathalie? How did they both end up with the clan?"

"I thought that you wanted me to be done with the story by the time we got to your house." He parked the car. "We are here."

"Finish the story, please. Otherwise, I'll keep speculating and won't be able to concentrate on having fun."

He would have preferred to tell her the rest over breakfast, but she seemed adamant about hearing it now.

"I'll make it short. Bhathian never forgot about Eva and about the child they'd created. He lived with terrible guilt. He searched for her, but she was very good at covering her tracks. When Syssi's brother joined the clan, Bhathian learned that Andrew had access to confidential government data and asked for his help. In turn Andrew asked Roni, who worked in the same building, to help him track Eva's government pension money."

"So that's how you found Roni."

Shai nodded. "First they found Nathalie, father and daughter met for the first time, and Nathalie and Andrew fell in love. Then Bhathian followed the money trail to an orphanage in Brazil, where Eva donated her pension. He was told that she came to visit the place from time to time, so he left her a note, telling her about Nathalie's upcoming wedding. Eva got the note and decided to come snooping around her ex-husband's café, but she suspected that it might be a trap, so she used a very convincing disguise. It was actually in the café we'd just left. The place used to belong to Nathalie's adoptive father, but now it belongs to her. She hired a young immortal to work there, and when Eva came to snoop disguised as an old lady and asked a lot of questions, the guy smelled the latex and figured out that she was wearing prosthetics. He called Nathalie, and that's how mother and daughter were reunited. End of story."

"Wait. What about Bhathian?"

"They were reunited as well, and they had another child together. It was an all-round happy ending." Shai opened the driver's side door before Geraldine had a chance to ask more questions, moved with immortal speed to the passenger side, and opened her door. "Story-time is over. It's show time."

13

GERALDINE

*G*eraldine took Shai's hand and let him haul her to her feet. He didn't crush her against his chest as she'd expected though, probably because it was still early enough for her nosey neighbors to be peeking from behind the curtains to see who was parked in front of her house.

Shai was a gentleman, so he didn't want to give them a show. Instead, he led her to the front door and waited patiently for her to find the key in her purse.

When she did, she handed him the keychain and waited for him to open the way. Focusing on the breadth of his shoulders, the shiny sweep of his blond hair, and the elegant long fingers that would in a few minutes play her body like a musical instrument, she tried to empty her mind of all other thoughts.

She could use the distraction. Eva's story had temporarily slowed down the turmoil in her head, but it was back now, and she wanted it gone.

Geraldine wanted to forget about the daughter she felt as much for as she did for Roni, the grandson she'd just learned about. She liked them both, but it was a faint echo compared to what she felt for Cassandra.

If Darlene was indeed her daughter, though, she needed to fight for her, and that was why her mind had been going in circles during the car ride back home.

Darlene was a Dormant, but Leo wasn't, so if she turned immortal, what would happen to him? The two hadn't seemed like a couple in love, but they'd been married for a long time, so she couldn't expect them to be all lovey-dovey with each other.

Besides, Darlene was forty-nine, which was considered too old to transition safely. But shouldn't it be her call to make?

And even if Darlene wasn't her daughter, she was still family, so shouldn't she fight for her anyway? Her mother wasn't around to do that, and the job fell to Geraldine.

Perhaps that was the answer to her inner turmoil. Regardless of whether Darlene had come out of her womb or her sister's, she should get over the guilt and treat her as if she was her daughter.

249

With that settled, relief washed over Geraldine, and she smiled brightly at Shai. "It has been a long day, and I need a shower." She tossed her purse on the entryway table and started toward the stairs.

He followed behind her. "Am I invited?"

"Of course."

"Your ass looks spectacular in these jeans. And these heels, damn. I want you to leave them on while I drive into you."

There was no way she would leave the new shoes on in the shower, but she might put them back on after.

"You're such a naughty boy." Gripping the bottom of her shirt, she pulled it over her head and tossed it behind her.

"Only with you." He caught it as she'd known he would.

Her bra went flying next, and as she'd also expected, it was a tease Shai couldn't ignore.

In a split second, he was at her back, his hands closing over her bare breasts.

At the contact, her eyes rolled back in her head, and she leaned against him, trusting that he wouldn't let them both tumble down the stairs.

"Why did you stop climbing?" he whispered against her ear and then nipped the soft earlobe.

The slight hurt went straight to her core, and as a moan left her throat, she dropped her head on his shoulder. "Because I can't concentrate on putting one foot in front of the other."

Before the last word left her mouth, she was in his strong arms, gasping at the incredible speed and strength.

"I love how responsive you are to me. So much passion." Dipping his head, he licked her nipple and then nipped it lightly with his blunt front teeth, all while climbing the rest of the stairs and walking with her into the master bathroom.

A pleased smile crossed his handsome face as he sat down on the bench inside the shower, and a moment later, his lips closed over her other nipple.

As he sucked and nipped, she had a feeling that her body would not touch water anytime soon.

Still feasting on her nipples, Shai let his hand reach between her legs and rubbed her needy center over the jeans she was still wearing.

"Take them off me," she husked.

14

SHAI

"Compliance." Shai lifted Geraldine with one arm while pulling her jeans down with the other.

Regrettably, she'd kicked her shoes off when he'd lifted her into his arms on the stairs. While he'd carried her to the bathroom, Shai had conjured a scene in his mind of Geraldine standing in the shower with nothing on but those fuck-me heels, her small hands braced on the marble wall, and her rounded bottom sticking out as he drove into her from behind.

Heck, that scene might work without the shoes. She was nearly a foot shorter than him, but her legs were long, and she could stand on the tips of her toes.

When she was in his arms without a stitch of clothing on, he returned his fingers to her center, gently tracing them over her wet petals.

She moaned, and as the sound echoed in the glass enclosure, it reminded him that the water wasn't on and that he was still fully dressed.

"Do you want to skip the shower?"

Geraldine opened her eyes, a lazy smile lifting the corners of her full, red lips. "I want you to soap me all over." She cupped her breasts, lifting them and playing with her own nipples. "I want your hands to glide all over my soap-slicked body."

Damn, her imagination was even better than his, and the erotic picture her words painted in his head had his fangs punch out over his lower lip.

With a groan, Shai lifted Geraldine off his lap, set her down on the bench, and got rid of his clothes. That maneuver had taken no more than two seconds, and another fraction of one was wasted on throwing their clothing out and closing the shower door.

Geraldine chuckled. "Oh, my goodness, you're fast."

"Not where it counts." He winked.

Turning all three faucets on, Shai winced when the cold spray pelted him from above and from the front. It took much too long for the water to warm up, and when it was finally the right temperature, he reached for the soap bar and offered Geraldine a hand up. "Let's get you wet first."

Taking his hand, she batted her eyelashes at him. "There is more than one way to go about that."

"Naughty girl." He playfully smacked her bottom.

"Oh, you have no idea." Geraldine winked as she stepped under the spray.

Tipping her head back, she let the water sluice over her hair, her face, her breasts—her hands roaming over her curves, tempting him to replace them with his own.

He didn't.

For a long moment, Shai just watched, drinking in her perfect beauty.

"I always wash my hair first," she murmured.

Glancing at the bar of soap still clutched in his hand, he put it back, lifted the shampoo bottle, and squirted a generous amount into the palm of his hand.

She stepped back and tilted her head, so it was not directly under the overhead spray.

As Shai gently massaged the shampoo into her hair, Geraldine moaned as if he was touching her intimately, and as his shaft reacted in a predictable way, he pulled her against his chest and pressed his hardness into her soft behind.

"Oh, dear. Someone is ready for action."

"And then some." He moved them both to get her under the water and rinse her hair out.

Then it was shampoo and rinse again, and then conditioner.

It was slow and excruciating torture, but he loved every moment of it.

While the conditioner did its thing, Shai took the soap and worked it into a lather.

As his hands slid over her arms, her sides, her stomach, and her breasts, her head fell back against his chest, and as his fingers closed around her nipples, she moaned and pressed her bottom into his erection.

Letting go of one breast, he slid his hand down and cupped her center.

She lifted on her toes and widened her stance in a clear invitation that he was loath to deny even temporarily, but he wasn't done teasing them both into an erotic frenzy.

Pressing the heel of his palm into the apex of her thighs, he rubbed it gently in sync with the gyrating of her hips.

Geraldine was beyond ready, but Shai wasn't done cleaning her. She still had conditioner in her hair, and he hadn't soaped every inch of her yet.

Guiding her to the wall, he turned her around and had her lean against it before dropping to his knees.

"Lift your foot for me."

She opened her eyes and looked down at him. "I think that I'm clean enough."

"Not even close." He wrapped his hand around her ankle and lifted her foot for her, placing it over his shoulder.

Her glistening sex was right where he wanted it, and as he extended his tongue and flicked it, she shuddered.

"Is that how you're going to clean me? With your tongue?"

He licked at her again. "Is that a problem?"

"Not at all." She let her head fall back against the tiled wall. "It's my favorite method of going about it."

15

GERALDINE

*G*eraldine had thought that she knew where things were going, but Shai had other ideas.

The foray with his tongue wasn't a prelude to things to come, but rather a short tease, a taste, and then he was back to soaping her calves, her feet, her toes.

It could have been pleasant if she wasn't so desperate for relief.

"Please," she murmured.

"Turn around."

She did as he asked, placing her palms on the shower wall and sticking her bottom out in a blatant invitation.

"Impatient girl." He slapped her bottom and then kissed the spot. "I need to rinse the conditioner out of your hair."

"Leave it," she hissed. "The longer it stays on, the better my hair will look."

He chuckled. "Fine. Let's pretend that's the reason you want to leave it on."

Rising up behind her, he put his palms on the wall above hers and kissed her shoulder. "Lift up on your toes."

She'd forgotten about their height difference.

Was it even going to work?

Evidently it did because as soon as she lifted up, the velvety head of him nudged at her entrance, and as she wiggled on the tip, trying to get it inside her, Shai dropped his arms, gripped her hips, and pushed up, joining them in one swift thrust.

They groaned in unison.

His arm wrapping around her middle, he started moving. As his hips slammed into her from behind, his lips closed on her shoulder, sucking on the spot he would later sink his fangs into.

The thought of that made her sheath spasm around his shaft, sending him into a frenzy of thrusts that would have caused her to lose her footing if not for the arm wrapped around her middle and holding her in place.

The tension growing tighter with each hard surge, she gritted her teeth, trying to stave off the release, to hold on for a few seconds longer, but it was no use. It exploded out of her with a shout that echoed off the shower walls.

Geraldine was barely coherent when Shai sank his fangs into the spot he'd prepared. The sharp pain was sobering, but only for a split second. When the sensation of his venom entering her system registered, another climax ripped through her like an F5 tornado, sucking her into its vortex and spitting her out on a cloud of euphoria.

She didn't know how long she'd floated, or what had happened in the time span between losing her grasp on reality and regaining it, but when Geraldine opened her eyes, she found herself wrapped in a thick towel and cradled in Shai's arms.

"Hello." He smiled down at her.

"Did I black out?"

"For a little bit."

"Oh, wow." She lifted her hand and touched her hair. "You even washed out the conditioner."

"I did." He lifted off the bench with her in his arms and carried her to the bedroom. "Do you want me to comb it out for you?"

"Yes, please."

No one had ever done that for her. Cassandra used to braid her hair when she was little, but combing out wet hair was something only mothers did for their children, or lovers did for their beloveds.

Had her adoptive mother ever done that for her?

From what Darlene had told them, that didn't seem likely. Sabina's adoptive parents had sounded terrible, and it made her sad to think that either she or her twin sister hadn't been loved as children.

There was no twin sister—she had to accept that.

As Cassandra had pointed out, the likelihood of both of them turning immortal was dismal. The only shard of hope she could cling to was that the strange things Darlene had said about her mother hadn't happened the way she remembered them, and what her father had told her about her mother's childhood hadn't been true.

The emerging picture was just too sad.

According to Darlene, Geraldine had had a lousy childhood and a tremulous marriage. Was it any wonder that her mind had conjured all those wonderful men who might or might not have been her lovers?

When Shai returned to the bed with a comb, wearing nothing but a goofy grin, she forced a smile and tightened the soft towel around her.

"What's the matter?" He sat on the bed behind her. "You look sad, which is really bad for my ego."

"Oh, sweetheart." She turned around and kissed his chin. "You are wonderful. I just remembered what Darlene said about my adoptive parents and about my marriage. It would seem that despite all the difficulties I faced, my life after the amnesia was better than it was before."

16

KIAN

"Good luck." Kian clapped Arwel on the back.

"Thank you." The Guardian climbed into the van where the rest of the Kra-ell investigative team was seated. Morris had headed to the airstrip earlier to prep the clan's jet for departure.

Kian waited until Okidu pulled out of the parking spot, waved his last goodbye, and turned around to head back to his office.

Glancing at his watch, he figured that he had about fifteen minutes until his next meeting, which was just enough for a quick smoke on the roof of the office building.

Lately his cigarillo consumption had dropped significantly. It had started with Anita giving him the stink eye every time he went outside to smoke, partially because Adam had joined him on several occasions, and partially because she just didn't approve. Syssi, in her usual diplomatic manner, had waited until her parents had gone back home to point out that Kian shouldn't hold his daughter close to his chest because his clothes smelled of tobacco and the baby inhaled it.

That comment had been enough for him to overhaul his entire routine.

Now, he only smoked during work hours, and he showered and changed as soon as he got home from the office. It wasn't a hard rule, and sometimes he'd been tempted to light up in the backyard, but given that another shower and another change of clothing had to follow, he rarely succumbed to the urge.

"I'll be up on the roof," he told Shai as he passed by his office. "Call me if anyone arrives before I get back."

"Enjoy." His assistant didn't even lift his head from the file he was reading.

Perhaps it was time to hire an assistant for his assistant, and on that note, maybe he should change Shai's job title as well. Kian had hired him about twenty years ago when Shai had graduated college, and back then even the assistant title had been generous. Shai had majored in English literature, and Kian had needed him mostly for typing up correspondence.

Over the years, though, Shai had become so much more.

Thanks to his intelligence and his eidetic memory, the guy was like a sponge for information. He was privy to everything that crossed Kian's desk and could recall every detail, email, and document he handled. Shai could probably run the clan's conglomerate on his own.

Except, he lacked Kian's business instincts.

Or so he claimed.

Perhaps it was a question of the ability to handle risk, which was an integral part of running a successful business. Shai wasn't a risk-taker, and it terrified him to make decisions that could potentially result in significant financial losses.

Lighting up his cigarillo, Kian sat on the lounger and tried to come up with an appropriate job title for the guy but came up with nothing. Vice President implied a decision-making position, which didn't fit, but maybe the title would encourage him to level up and fit the bill?

Then there was the question of who to hire to assist him. Maybe it was best to leave it to Shai. Since there was no more vacant office space in the building, the assistant would have to share Shai's office, so the person needed to be someone Shai got along with.

When Kian's phone rang, he lifted it, and as he saw it was Onegus, he checked the time. Their meeting wasn't for another ten minutes, and the chief knew better than to arrive early.

"Are you in my office?" Kian asked.

"I'm on my way, but I got a phone call from Kalugal's guy in West Virginia and thought that you would want to know right away. Roberts had a stroke, and it doesn't look good."

"Explain."

"He's alive, but he's been taken to the hospital, and they called his wife. Kalugal's guy offered to sneak him some blood."

"Let me check with Bridget, and I'll call you back."

"I'm in the building. Are you in your office?"

"I'm on the roof."

"I'll join you there."

After ending the call, Kian called Bridget.

"The blood is not going to help him," the doctor said. "The damage to the brain has already been done, and strengthening Roberts' body, which is all our blood can do for him, will not help him regrow brain cells. It's not worth the risk of exposure."

"Thanks, Bridget." Kian ended the call.

This wasn't good. Roberts was their link to the Echelon system, and without him, they wouldn't have access to what the system flagged as suspected paranormals. Not that it had helped them find even one Dormant so far, but it might in the future.

Then there was the issue of the trainees.

As the rooftop door opened and Onegus stepped through, Kian pulled a fresh cigarillo out of the box and lit it.

The chief sat down on the other lounger. "We need a plan."

Kian lifted a brow. "For installing a new director or for getting the trainees out?"

"Whichever is more manageable." Onegus leaned his elbows on his knees and steepled his fingers. "The problems with getting the trainees out are mostly still the same as before. Spencer has just turned eighteen, so there is only one kid left who we can't approach directly. And as to the adults, we know that some of them want to be there. The money is good, and their prospects on the outside are not. Are you willing to offer them a better deal than what they have now? Not that I think you should. After the changes we forced Roberts to implement, they are no longer being exploited, and they don't really need rescuing."

17

ONEGUS

*K*ian chuckled. "I would say that immortality and membership in the clan is a much better deal, but I can't promise them that. Not all of them are Dormants. In fact, we don't know if any are. Roberts kept them in the program instead of sending them on missions, and with all that was going on, we didn't have the manpower to get to them during their sporadic vacation time."

"True," Onegus agreed. "But we are back on track with the rescue missions, and I can spare a couple of guardians for that. The question is whether that's the best approach. I don't like the idea of losing access to the Echelon system. Not because I believe it will lead us to Dormants, but because it could be the only warning we have that the government is onto us. We need someone we trust with access to the lists Echelon spits out."

Kian sighed. "This is something Turner should be involved in, but he has his hands full with rescue missions in Central Asia. I doubt he can spare any time."

"This is no less important than what he does over there." Onegus crossed his feet at the ankles. "Maintaining our access to the Echelon system is a safety issue."

"I'm aware of that. But I can't just order Turner to do it, and he has contracts that he needs to fulfill. I'm open to ideas if you have any to offer."

The boss wasn't going to like the idea Onegus had come up with, but he'd thought it through on his way over, and with all of her shortcomings, Eleanor was the best person for the job.

"With Roberts out of the way, Eleanor can get herself reinstated."

Kian shook his head. "I still don't trust her completely. I put her in charge of keeping an eye on Emmett, but as you know, we have eyes on both of them."

On a visceral level Onegus didn't trust her completely either, but it had more to do with her abrasive personality than with her conduct. So far, Eleanor had proven herself capable and trustworthy.

Folding his arms over his chest, Onegus leaned back. "She has no motive to betray us, and she's perfect for taking over the program."

"She doesn't have a doctorate, which seems to be a requirement for the job. As far as I know, she has a college degree, but I don't know in what."

That wasn't a real concern, and Kian knew it.

"We can get her a fake PhD in whatever. It's not that it's really needed to run the paranormal program. With Eleanor's compulsion ability, and with some help from our in-house hacker, she will appear as the best candidate they could possibly find."

Kian stubbed out his cigarillo in the ashtray and pushed to his feet. "She probably won't agree to do it. Why would she leave the village and her new love interest to live in a godforsaken underground nuclear fallout shelter?"

"Let's ask her." Onegus followed Kian up.

"Even if she agrees, we'll still need Turner to devise a plan for getting her instated as the director. She was only the recruiter when Robert's fired her."

Onegus schooled his features not to show how Kian's words had wounded him.

He was a damn good strategist, and until Turner had shown up, Kian had trusted him to plan the clan's missions. His plans might not have been as elaborate and as fancy as Turner's, but they had worked just fine.

He opened the rooftop door for Kian. "I can make a plan and then run it by Turner."

"I need you to also devise a plan for getting the trainees out." Kian took the stairs down to his office. "If we can't get Eleanor to take over, we can compel the new director to give us the relevant information Echelon produces. That notwithstanding, we need to start pulling out the trainees who wish to leave."

"I hope that some want to stay. If we take out all of them, there will be no reason to keep the program going." Onegus followed Kian into his office. "And if the program closes, we will have no access to Echelon."

"True." Kian sat behind his desk. "But if the paranormal program is no more, the government will have no need for the system to flag conversations about paranormal abilities. It might be in our best interest to have the program shut down."

"We hope that they will do that." Onegus pulled out a chair and sat down. "But if we don't have anyone on the inside to report to us, we won't know that for sure. I, for one, prefer to have eyes in the system."

"I'll talk to Eleanor tomorrow." Kian put his hands on his desk. "How did it go with Roni's parents yesterday?"

"We learned a few things. The most important piece of information is that Geraldine was turned immortal before losing her memory. Darlene remembered a couple of episodes about her mother that implied fast healing and abnormal strength. The other thing is that Geraldine and her husband had a turbulent marriage, which reinforces Cassandra's suspicion of him having something to do with Geraldine's head trauma and memory loss."

"Did he kill her for the life insurance money?"

"That's what Cassandra thought, but Darlene said that their financial situation didn't improve after her mother's death. They moved to Oklahoma to be near her father's relatives, who helped him take care of her. Geraldine's ex is still living there with his second wife. Apparently, he turned survivalist at some point."

"I assume that you plan on visiting him?"

Onegus nodded. "If it's okay with you, I thought about using the small jet to fly over to Oklahoma Friday evening and return Saturday."

"Of course, you can take it." Kian waved a hand. "You don't need to ask my permission."

Normally he wouldn't have, but since the Kra-ell team had flown to China on the big jet, Kian would be left with none for the weekend.

"I asked in case you had plans for a weekend getaway."

Kian snorted. "Since when do I take weekends off? And now with the baby, I'm certainly not going anywhere."

"Still, I needed to make sure, and I also don't like the idea of you not having a jet at your disposal in case of an emergency."

"If something comes up, I can use the helicopter, and if it's too far for the chopper, I can borrow Kalugal's jet or even Annani's. She's not going home yet."

18

RONJA

*R*onja had been obsessing about the idea of immortality ever since Annani had planted it in her head.

Should she? Or shouldn't she?

Lisa had refused to talk about it, saying that she didn't want to influence Ronja's decision one way or another, but Ronja had a feeling that her daughter wanted her to do it.

If so, she was a braver soul than her mother.

Yesterday and today, Merlin had been casting Ronja curious looks, probably wondering what was going on with her and why she was less talkative than usual, but he was a patient man, and he hadn't pressured her with questions, which she appreciated.

But Ronja needed to talk with someone, even if that someone was Merlin, who might jump to conclusions and assume she was hinting that she was ready to take their relationship to the next level.

Boy, was she ready.

If not for the overwhelming guilt assailing her each time her thoughts wandered places they shouldn't, she wouldn't have waited another moment.

But it had been only three months, for heaven's sake.

She'd waited longer to start a new relationship after mourning the end of her marriage to Michael, where no one other than their marriage had died. The cheating bastard certainly hadn't deserved it, but she'd been too heartbroken to even look at another man, let alone go out on dates.

Frank deserved better. He'd been as loyal as they came, a rock of stability, a devoted husband and father, and he deserved to be mourned properly, which in most people's opinions meant no less than a year.

But she might not have that long.

What if a year was what made all the difference between her making it through the transition or not?

Was it worth the risk?

Would the transition rewind the clock and make her look young again?

It was silly to think about such frivolous things when her life was on the line, but Ronja would be lying if she claimed that wasn't one of the most tempting perks of gaining immortality.

She used to be the kind of woman men turned their heads after to get a second look. It still happened, but rarely, and only with those much older than her.

Not that looking young and beautiful guaranteed happiness. She was proof that it didn't. Ronja missed her youthful good looks, but she didn't miss her youthful naïveté. Even if the transition shaved thirty years off her face and body, it wouldn't erase thirty years of wisdom.

She would never again fall for a man like Michael—brilliant, successful, and totally self-absorbed. She would never again be a decoration on the arm of a powerful man.

The kind of man she would pick now would be as smart and as exciting as Michael, but loyal and devoted like Frank.

Merlin was that and much more.

She loved his playful character, his inner joy, his boyish carefree manner. Being around him was like getting hooked up to an energy generator. He made her feel alive.

Michael had been a mood dampener because of his critical and uncompromising nature, and Frank had been, well, Frank. She hated to admit it, but he'd been boring.

Damn, was she in love with Merlin?

"Ronja, dear. If you keep washing that Erlenmeyer flask, you're going to rub the markings off."

Startled, she nearly dropped the thing into the soapy water. "I'm sorry. My head was somewhere else." She rinsed the flask and put it on the rack to dry.

"So it would seem." Merlin walked over to the refrigerator and pulled out the cheesecake she'd baked that morning. "How about we take a little break? I've been thinking about this cake and salivating over it since you walked in with it and filled the house with its irresistible aroma."

The glint in his eyes suggested that he'd been salivating after more than the cake.

"Sure." She dried her hands with a dishrag. "Do you want me to make tea to go with it?"

"That would be most welcome. Thank you." Merlin carried the cake to the dining table which, thanks to her, was free of clutter and dust and ready to serve its purpose.

Ronja filled the electric kettle with water from the filter and put it on its base. "I'll bring the plates."

If she didn't announce her intentions, Merlin might just stick a fork in the cake and eat it straight from the pan. The man was a work in progress, but he was making an effort, which was all she could ask for.

"I'll get them," he offered.

Merlin had been a bachelor for centuries, so Ronja didn't expect him to change his ways overnight, and she appreciated every little thing he did because he knew it would please her. Every time she noticed him doing something like that, Ronja's heart warmed a little. Not even Frank had cared about her little quirks and tried to please her as much as Merlin did.

When the tea was ready, she brought the two mugs to the table and sat down.

Merlin waited for her to cut him a piece and one for herself as well. He only took his first bite after she'd taken hers. "Delicious." He licked his lips. "With all the amazing cakes you're baking, I'm going to get fat."

She chuckled. "I also cook you nutritious meals, so that's not going to happen."

"You're the best." The heated look he cast her didn't leave room for misinterpretation. "Can I keep you?"

A lump formed in her throat. "I'm not going anywhere. We have a deal."

"You know what I mean."

Of course she did.

Should she tell him about her conversation with Annani?

"The Clan Mother visited me the day before yesterday," she said quickly before having a chance to chicken out.

He arched a brow. "What does that have to do with me keeping you? Did she offer you a better deal? Because I'll double whatever she offered."

Ronja chuckled nervously. "What she offered me involved you."

"Oh?" He licked a crumb of cake from his upper lip. "Do tell."

"She thinks that I should attempt the transition."

19

MERLIN

*L*uckily, Merlin had nothing in his mouth, or he would have ejected it. "She does?"

He'd been thinking a lot about ways to prolong Ronja's life, but he hadn't considered inducing her.

It could kill her.

Was Annani out of her mind?

"She says that the clan hasn't lost a transitioning Dormant yet, and she thinks that Bridget might be wrong about the increased danger to older Dormants. She also says that medicine has made big strides in the last couple of years, and also that you might be able to brew some potions to strengthen my body, so it will be as healthy as that of a much younger person."

He opened his mouth to say that the Clan Mother didn't know what she was talking about but then clamped it shut.

Hadn't he been thinking along the same lines?

He'd been brewing potions meant to strengthen the human body, reading up on ways to reverse the aging of organs and arteries, all in the hopes of finding ways to prolong Ronja's lifespan. He just hadn't taken it all the way like Annani had. After he did all that was possible to improve Ronja's biological markers to the level of a person twenty years younger, she might be able to go through the transition.

Ronja regarded him with amusement in her eyes. "In all the ways I imagined you'd respond, speechless wasn't one of them. You look dumbfounded."

"I am. Over the past month, I've been researching ways to turn the biological clock back, to make you as healthy as possible in hopes of prolonging your life. I just lacked the courage to take that line of thought to its inescapable conclusion that you should be attempting transition. If I can get your biological markers to match those of a healthy thirty-something woman, you might have a chance."

"You really believe that's possible?" She looked at him with hope in her eyes.

Excitement bubbling in his gut, he reached for her hand and lifted it to his lips.

264

"We should start right away." He smacked a loud kiss on the back of it.

"Not so fast." Ronja pulled her hand out of his grasp and leaned back. "I'm not ready."

He frowned. "Hardly anyone likes to exercise, Ronja. I don't like it either, but it's the best way to fool the body into thinking that it's younger. And my potions might taste bad, but you can chase them with a piece of chocolate to improve the aftertaste."

She seemed relieved. "I thought that you meant we should start working on the transition, and I haven't made up my mind about that yet." Her pale cheeks reddening, she cleared her throat. "I need to think of Lisa. I can't take such a dangerous step when I have a young daughter who needs me."

He reached for her hand again. "First, we will take care of your mortal body. When we get it to operate in peak condition, and both Bridget and I agree that all your biological markers are adequate for transition, you will need to make up your mind. But even if you decide against it, you will still be in much better health than you were before. So it's a win-win either way."

Ronja nodded. "Okay. What do we do first?"

"Do you own a good pair of sneakers?"

"I don't know if they're good, but I have a pair stashed somewhere. Just don't expect me to jog. I'm not in great shape, and even a brisk walk leaves me gasping for air."

"No worries. Tomorrow morning, we will go for an easy walk. Every day we will increase the duration of our walk by a few minutes, and when we reach an hour and a half, we will work on increasing the speed. Some weightlifting would be good for you too, but we will need to get light weights. What they have down in the gym is too heavy for you to lift even once." He smiled. "I don't want you to get injured. Slow progress is the name of the game."

She eyed him from under lowered lashes. "You keep saying we. Does that mean that you will train with me?"

"Of course."

"Well." She folded her arms over her chest. "Then it's a triple win. It will get you out of the house and some fresh air into your lungs."

"There you go." He lifted the knife she'd used before and cut them each another piece of the cake. "Since we are going to start eating super healthy, no more cakes. But let's enjoy this one until it's gone." He put a forkful in his mouth.

The taste was heavenly, and Merlin was going to miss all the wonderful cakes Ronja baked, but he was more than willing to sacrifice many things to give Ronja a chance at immortality.

Hell, if there were any dragons around who granted wishes to knights who defeated them, he would have challenged one to a duel even though he'd never held a sword in his hand.

"You don't have to suffer because of me, Merlin. You can eat whatever you want. Besides, Lisa will be very disappointed if I stop baking."

"I'm sure she wouldn't mind once we explain the plan to her. Maybe she'll even join us on our morning walks."

Ronja laughed. "That's not going to happen. I can barely drag her out of bed in time for school. There is no way she'll get up even earlier to go on a walk with us."

"It never hurts to ask. She might surprise you."

20

RONI

*U*nease churned in Roni's gut as Sylvia's car exited the tunnel. He rarely left the village, and it always made him anxious. If not for Sylvia insisting that he needed to get out from time to time, he probably would have never ventured out.

Public places like restaurants, supermarkets, and shopping malls were all peppered with surveillance cameras, and even though he wore specialty glasses that prevented facial recognition, he still feared discovery.

The only place he had no problem going to was the beach.

Together with Sylvia he'd learned to surf and parasail, and since they usually went with their group of friends, it was lots of fun.

Today though, the anxiety had little to do with fear of discovery. He was about to meet his parents after not seeing them for nearly four years.

Roni had changed a lot during that time. He was no longer the prickly teenager with a sour attitude, and he no longer felt as if it was him against the world. Having a wonderful mate and an entire clan in his corner had changed his perspective on life, even more so than turning immortal had.

He was no longer the odd man out. The outsider looking in. He not only belonged to the clan, but he was also a respected and valuable member of the community.

Roni had never felt like that with his parents. Could things be different now that he was an adult?

Secretly, he'd yearned for a better connection with them, for the kind of loving relationship that Sylvia had with her mother. The two teased each other constantly, and there had been a time when Ruth was a little too clingy with her daughter, but since she'd mated Nick, she'd eased up on that. Nick was also a great guy, and the four of them often met either for family dinners or just to hang around the café.

It would have been nice to have the same kind of easygoing relationship with his parents, but Roni doubted that it would ever be possible. They were just too different, and not all of their shitty parenting had been in his head.

Only some of it.

Perhaps they weren't that bad, but they weren't the cool kind of parents he would have loved to hang out with. It was just not meant to be.

When his phone rang, he instinctively reached for it, forgetting that it was synced with the car's speaker system.

A moment later, Onegus's voice came through. "There's been a change of plans. We are not meeting in Nathalie's café."

The churning in Roni's gut intensified. "What happened? Did my parents cancel?"

"One of the Guardians I assigned to watch the café spotted suspicious activity. It might be nothing, but I'm not taking any chances with your safety. I moved the meeting to another location. I'll text you the address after we end the call."

"What about my parents? If they are being tracked, changing the location will not solve our problem."

"I have it covered. Cassandra called them and arranged a meeting in a mall's food court. One of my guys is following your parents there to make sure that they have no physical tail. If they don't, I'm going to pick them up from there and drive them to the place. But first, I'll stop somewhere and search them for bugs."

"What will you do if you find any?" Sylvia asked.

"I'll have to activate the signal disrupter, which is a pain in the ass because I will have to turn off the car's onboard computer."

Roni frowned. "Is that even possible without taking the car apart?"

"On mine it is."

It made sense for the chief's vehicle to be equipped differently than those the clan's civilians drove.

Sylvia's forehead furrowed. "Can't your guy in the café get ahold of the spook and find out why he's there?"

"I'd rather not. I tread lightly where the government is involved. It's better to avoid the agent than to mess with him. I'll see you in about an hour at the new address." The chief ended the call.

Sylvia cast Roni a sidelong glance. "Onegus said that there was no one watching your parents' house, and he had a signal disrupter on during their meeting with Cassandra and Geraldine. Why would anyone be sent to watch Nathalie's place? Cassandra and Geraldine are of no interest to the government agents."

"My parents might not have followed Onegus's instructions and talked about me either on their way home or in their house. They are not technologically savvy, and they don't know or understand all the ways in which they can be monitored. I bet they have Alexa in their house and that it's on at all times."

"What about the signal disrupter? If your parents are carrying bugs, maybe the loss of transmission has raised the spooks' suspicion?"

"A lot of things can disrupt a radio signal, so I doubt they were alarmed by that. It's quite common."

CASSANDRA

*T*he place Onegus had chosen for the meeting was an Italian restaurant that offered private rooms for small parties and was across town from Nathalie's café.

As Shai opened the door for her and Geraldine, the smell of garlic that wafted out would have been strong enough to kill a horde of vampires, and it also aroused Cassandra's appetite.

"Good evening." The hostess smiled at them. "Do you have reservations?"

"Yes. Party of eight, under Cassandra Beaumont."

"Two of your party are already here." The woman smiled and picked up three menus. "Please, follow me."

The main room of the restaurant was packed with diners, and Cassandra wondered how Onegus had managed to secure a private room on such short notice. Was it another one of the clan's secret meeting places?

Shai would know, but she couldn't ask him until after the hostess left and they were alone.

As the woman opened the glass door to the private room, Roni rose to his feet to greet them. Sylvia just smiled and waved.

He looked so tense that the moment the hostess left, Cassandra pulled him into a fierce hug and kissed his cheek. "Whatever happens with your parents, remember that we are here for you. We've just met, but we are a family."

It was good to hear herself say that.

After so many years of thinking that she and Geraldine were alone in the world, it was nice to know that they weren't. It was also good that they were both immortal, so she no longer needed to worry about who would take care of her mother if anything should happen to her.

Roni tightened his arms around her. "I like having a kick-ass aunt who can blow things up."

"And I like having a nephew who can hack into anything."

"Not anything, but most things."

"Good enough for me." She sat down and glanced at the half-empty breadbasket. "I'm starving. What do you say about ordering a few appetizers?"

"I'm all for it," Roni said. "Even if it will make my mouth stink of garlic."

"It might take Onegus a while to get here with your parents," Shai said.

"I know. He's taking them on one of Turner's loops."

"What's that?" Geraldine asked.

As Shai was about to start explaining, the waiter came in to check on them, and they ordered a bunch of appetizers to tide them over until the rest of their party arrived.

Over appetizers and drinks, Shai entertained them with stories about Turner's ingenious missions, while Roni alternated between relaxing and tensing up again.

When more than an hour later the door finally opened, and Onegus walked in with Darlene and Leo, two things happened at once—Roni rose to his feet so quickly that his chair toppled to the floor, and Darlene burst out in tears.

As he rushed to her and the two embraced, his father stood a couple of feet away and watched the display with a detached expression on his face that gave Cassandra pause.

It was okay for Leo to act manly and not cry hysterically like his wife, but he should have shown more emotion upon seeing his son for the first time in four years.

Something was off about that.

"You look so grown up," Darlene said after releasing Roni from her arms. "You look good."

"I'm great, Mom." He turned to Sylvia, who'd been waiting patiently for mother and son to acknowledge her while dabbing at her teary eyes with a cloth napkin. "This is my fiancée, Sylvia. I owe my freedom and my new life to her."

Without hesitation, Darlene reached for Sylvia's hand and pulled her into her arms. "Thank you."

Sylvia sniffled. "I'm the one who should thank you. Without you, Roni wouldn't be here."

Cassandra smiled at the emotional display and then cast a sidelong glance at Roni's father. The guy was smiling, but the smile didn't reach his eyes. He was either a cold fish, or there was a story there that Roni wasn't aware of.

Was it possible that Leo wasn't Roni's biological father?

Roni and Leo had similar coloring, but Roni looked more like his grandfather than his father. That didn't mean much, though. To the casual observer, Cassandra didn't look anything like her mother either. A closer examination revealed the slight familial similarities.

Darlene let go of Sylvia, wiped her tears away, and took Roni's hand. "I want to hear about everything that happened to you during the four years of your life that I've missed."

2 2

GERALDINE

*G*eraldine listened to Roni tell his parents a highly edited version of how he'd met Sylvia, her part in his daring escape from the hospital, and what he did for the new company he worked for.

She didn't know the full story herself, but Roni had done a great job of spinning a tale that was almost as fascinating as what had really happened. Had he inherited his story-telling ability from her?

Thinking that made Geraldine feel all warm and fuzzy.

Cassandra and Roni were both highly intelligent and very talented in their respective fields, and given what Geraldine had learned about her ex-husband, Roni hadn't inherited his smarts from him.

So even though she hadn't graduated from high school, she must be intelligent enough to produce such a smart and talented daughter and grandson.

Cassandra's father might have been a smart and creative man, though. It was a pity she wasn't sure which one of her dream lovers had been the one who'd given her Cassy.

What about Darlene, though?

Compared to her half-sister and son, Darlene seemed to be of only average intelligence. Then again, she'd gotten a full-ride scholarship to a prestigious university, which implied that she was much more capable than her achievements suggested.

Keeping in line with the story of finding Cassandra and Geraldine through the DNA testing company, Roni had omitted mentioning Onegus's or Shai's involvement with the company he worked for, treating them as if they'd just met.

That seemed to make Leo suspicious. His expression doubtful, he turned to Onegus. "I'm surprised that a billionaire like you is willing to aid a fugitive. You've taken Darlene and me on quite a ride to get here."

Onegus shrugged. "My family has many enemies. I'm used to taking precautions."

"You said that you work in security," Leo said.

"I do. I manage that aspect of the family business."

That seemed to shut him up, but Geraldine didn't like his attitude. Onegus was helping Roni, and Leo should appreciate it instead of questioning his motives.

Darlene's husband shook his head. "It still doesn't explain why you are willing to put your neck on the line for our son, and why you are doing it yourself instead of assigning the task to one of your goons."

Onegus regarded him with a frosty look that should have turned Leo into an icicle. "Cassandra is my soon-to-be wife, and Roni is her cousin. I will do anything for my family."

"That's incredibly sweet of you," Darlene said. "And you have my gratitude. I'm so glad that my cousin is marrying an upstanding man like you."

"Thank you." Onegus gifted her with one of his beautiful smiles. "But there is no need to thank me. I consider it a duty and an honor."

As the main course was served and the conversation shifted to Sylvia and her current graduate studies, Geraldine made it a point to observe Leo carefully. The more she got to know him, the less she liked him, and it seemed that Cassandra shared her opinion.

"We need to have a girls' day out." Cassandra looked at Darlene. "Since you didn't get to experience having a sibling, Geraldine and I invite you to be our honorary sister." She cast Geraldine a sidelong glance. "We can go shoe shopping, which is the best way for sisters to bond. Then we can have lunch, and after that more shopping." She leaned forward. "Are you busy this Sunday?"

They were flying out to Oklahoma Friday afternoon and coming back Saturday evening. It was going to be an exhausting weekend, but Geraldine had a feeling that they could learn a lot more from Darlene about herself and her father without her husband present.

Before answering, Darlene cast a quick glance at Leo, but even though he didn't indicate his agreement, she turned back to Cassandra and nodded. "I have nothing planned. Where would you like to shop?"

"I love the Glendale Galleria, and it's not far from where you live, right?"

"It's fifteen minutes away." Darlene cast another look at Leo. "Is that okay with you?"

He shrugged. "You can do whatever you want."

That didn't sound encouraging. In fact, Geraldine thought that it sounded like a threat. She was liking Leo less and less by the minute. Not that she had liked him at all to start with.

He turned to his son. "While your mother hangs out with her cousins, how about you and I meet up somewhere for a drink?"

When Roni opened his mouth to answer, Onegus put his hand on his shoulder. "Roni can't go anywhere without taking proper precautions, and unless I'm there to provide those precautions, he needs to give his employers a two-week heads up to arrange it. Regrettably, I'm not available this Sunday. Next Sunday will work better for me, and then his mother can join you two as well."

Geraldine knew that the two-week heads up was nonsense, and she also suspected that Onegus's reasons for objecting were not about Roni's security needs. Just like her, he must have sensed something was off about Darlene's husband.

23

ONEGUS

*O*nce dinner was over, Onegus called an Uber for Darlene and her husband to take them back to their car. Naturally, it wasn't really an Uber driver but a Guardian who drove them to the parking lot in the mall, and he was going to report to Onegus everything they said on the way.

When the two left, everyone around the table, including Onegus, let out a relieved breath.

"Is it me?" Cassandra looked at Roni. "Or is your father acting strange?"

Wincing, Roni rubbed a hand over the back of his neck. "He's just as *loving and supportive* as I remember him—meaning, he's the same cold and jealous asshole he's always been. Looking at him and my mother from an adult's perspective, I see things that I didn't as a kid, and I think I understand the dynamic better. She seems completely dependent on him and follows his cues. She's different now and dares to assert herself a little because she feels that she has a second chance with me and doesn't want to blow it again."

"Why would he be jealous of you?" Geraldine asked.

"I guess because I'm smarter, and because he blames me for losing his job. When I got caught hacking, he got fired and couldn't find another job. He blamed me for that even though I had nothing to do with it. My so-called crime didn't make the news or anything, and no one knew about it. The government kept the entire thing quiet because if news got out that a fifteen-year-old kid had hacked into their most secure servers, it would have been embarrassing, to say the least. And they certainly didn't want anyone to know that they hired me to work for them."

Sylvia put her hand on his arm. "Is that why they took the money you earned instead of putting it in a savings account for you?"

"That was the excuse."

"What does he do now?" Shai asked.

"A few months after I escaped, he somehow got a cushy job managing an antiques store. He majored in world history, which is why he didn't have any marketable skills, but that didn't qualify him as an antiques expert. I have no idea how he managed to get that job."

"Maybe a family member of his owns the store," Geraldine suggested. "Do you know your father's family?"

"Not very well. They are from the East Coast, and I don't think I met them more than once or twice when I was little. From what I remember, they were typical wealthy snobs who probably didn't approve of my mother—a working man's daughter. A hick from Oklahoma."

"By the way." Cassandra looked at Onegus. "Did you find any bugs on Darlene or Leo?"

He shook his head. "They were clean. I checked them with William's device twice. I also asked them to turn their phones off and leave them in their car, which I didn't do the first time we met them. Since that meeting had been arranged over the phone, whoever monitored their phones had known about it, so I didn't think it was necessary. Besides, they would have bolted if I had done it before we talked with them."

"What about the snoop outside Nathalie's café?" Cassandra asked.

"Gone. He must have left after realizing that the second meeting was not taking place there."

"Well, we will find out more from Darlene on Sunday." Cassandra lifted her coffee cup. "I have a feeling that she will be much more talkative without Leo breathing down her neck." She took a sip and put the cup down.

"Don't count on her showing up," Roni said. "If my father is not happy about her going, she won't. She's too afraid of him."

Cassandra narrowed her eyes at her nephew. "Why? Is he abusive?"

"Not physically, but whenever he's displeased with her, he gives her the silent treatment for weeks. She has to apologize and grovel at his feet, so to speak, to get back into his good graces."

"That's disgusting." Cassandra crossed her arms over her chest. "Why does she put up with that? Doesn't she have any backbone?"

Roni shook his head. "That's what I used to think, but I've gained a little more understanding over the years." He smiled at Sylvia. "My mother doesn't have anyone apart from him. She can't afford to lose him."

"What about her father's side of the family?" Cassandra asked. "All those cousins she grew up with?"

"She hasn't seen them in years."

"I don't like Leo." Geraldine's lips twisted into a grimace. "Maybe we need to tell Darlene the truth and invite her to join the clan. If she says no, someone can thrall her to forget what we told her." She glanced at Roni. "Do you think it's a good idea?"

Onegus shook his head. "Darlene is too old to transition. It wouldn't be kind to tell her that she missed her chance."

"I feel guilty," Roni said. "Four years ago, she was the same age Turner was when he transitioned. She might have made it."

"Or not." Onegus put his hand on Roni's shoulder. "Turner knew about us, and he deduced that Andrew went through a change. He demanded to be induced despite the risk because he had cancer and thought that he was dying anyway."

"Wasn't his cancer healed first?" Roni asked.

"It had to be in order for him to transition, and he underwent chemotherapy. But the thing about cancer is that there is always a chance of it coming back, and Turner didn't want to live with its shadow looming over him."

24

ELEANOR

*E*leanor pushed to her feet and leaned to kiss Emmett smack on his lips. His following was growing, with more females showing up to join his round table at the café, and she felt the need to stake her claim publicly so none of them would get any ideas.

He reached for her hand. "Do you know what Kian wants to talk to you about?"

She shrugged. "Maybe it's about this." She waved a hand at the eight females crowding the small café table. "Maybe he's not happy about your proselytizing on his turf."

"That's not what I'm doing."

"I know. But he might think that." She patted Emmett's shoulder. "I'll find out soon."

Turning around, she headed for the office building. It was only several steps away from the café, and Kian could probably see Emmett and his geese through his office window. Secretly, she hoped Kian was upset about it and wanted it to stop. She wouldn't have minded if some of Emmett's followers were male, but so far, he'd attracted only female followers, and she had a feeling that what he had to say was much less appealing to them than the man himself.

If only the damn bond had formed already, it wouldn't have been a problem. The females would have known that he was taken and would have stayed away. But with no bond, he was fair game.

Perhaps she should insist on a marriage ceremony. It wasn't as good as an unbreakable mate bond, but it would set proper boundaries for the horny vultures.

Stopping in front of Kian's door, she tugged her T-shirt down, smoothed a hand over her hair, and then knocked.

"Come in." His gruff voice didn't fail to unnerve her even though she'd been prepared for it and knew that it didn't mean that he was angry.

Taking a deep breath, Eleanor opened the door and walked in. "Good afternoon." She cast a glance at Onegus.

What was he doing there?

Kian didn't need him around to tell her that he didn't like Emmett getting too popular too fast.

"Good afternoon, Eleanor." Kian pointed to the other chair in front of his desk. "Please, take a seat."

As Onegus moved his long legs to make room for her, she sat down and faced Kian. "To what do I owe this invitation?"

"There are new developments with the government's paranormal program," Onegus said. "Roberts might be out of the way. He has suffered a massive stroke and is on his death bed."

This hadn't been even remotely on the list of things she'd thought Kian might have wanted to talk to her about. "Is that a good thing or bad? I was under the impression that you used him to get information on potential Dormants."

"We did, and although so far none of the names turned out to be good suspects, having access to the information is valuable." Kian pulled his rolling chair closer to the desk. "We also think that it's time to make an offer to some of the trainees and see who is willing to leave."

"About time." She crossed her arms over her chest. "What do I have to do with it?"

Leaning his elbows on the desk, Kian pinned her with his intense blue eyes. "How would you like to become the program's new director?"

Talk about unexpected, and also impossible. There were so many reasons why it couldn't work.

"Roberts destroyed my reputation. My security clearance was revoked, and I can't even get into the facility. I'm also not qualified for the position. I'm not a psychologist, or a medical doctor, or a geneticist, or anything else that could be even remotely applicable."

Onegus chuckled. "We can get you any diploma you want. As for what Roberts did to you, you can claim that he harassed you sexually, and when you refused to capitulate, he took revenge by destroying your reputation. You'll get reinstated with profound apologies and maybe even some monetary compensation for wages lost."

Eleanor's lips twisted in distaste. "The bastard wasn't as active as his best buddy, but he was far from virtuous, and I would have no qualms about destroying his reputation like he did to me. But I would hate to do it to his soon-to-be widow. She's about to lose her husband, and I don't want to add a sex scandal on top of her grieving."

Kian smiled for the first time since she'd entered his office. "I'm surprised that you care."

She shrugged. "I have a soft spot for women married to cheating bastards. Roberts hadn't cheated in many years, but he'd done his share of philandering when he was younger. You can read all about it in Simmons's journals."

"They are not going to make it public," Onegus said. "In fact, your best strategy is to threaten going to the press. They don't want a sex scandal shining a spotlight on whatever they are doing in that underground city."

That was true, and she wasn't too scared about the spooks trying to off her instead of reinstating her and compensating her for the wrongs done to her. She was an immortal, which meant that she was very hard to kill, and she would also have Guardians watching her back.

Perhaps taking Roberts' position was not such a bad idea.

Uncrossing her arms, Eleanor leaned forward. "What is it that you want me to do?"

25

KIAN

When Eleanor hadn't rejected the idea as Kian had expected her to do, he wondered whether she was already plotting how to use the new assignment to her best advantage.

Perhaps he was being unfair to her, but he couldn't help being suspicious of her motives.

"We don't want you to use compulsion on the trainees," Onegus said. "That's for sure. But you can start feeling around for discontent. We don't want to approach those who want to be there or those who are underage. We only want to lure out those who are unhappy about being there but see no way to get out."

She nodded. "I'll check with the kids as well. If they are unhappy, I can convince their families to let them go."

Onegus shook his head. "What if those families are depending on the income those kids generate?"

She turned to look at Kian. "If they are Dormants, perhaps it would be worthwhile for you to pay the parents off."

Kian grimaced. "I'm not keen on paying for people, even if it's for their own good."

She tilted her head. "If the only way to free trafficking victims was for you to buy them, wouldn't you have done it?"

"No, I wouldn't have. It would have saved those I paid for, but it would also propagate the trade. In the long term, it would have done more damage than good."

Letting out a breath, she leaned back and folded her arms over her chest. "What if the victim was someone you knew? Someone you cared about?"

"Then I would kill the perpetrators and free the victims. Where are you going with this, Eleanor?"

She shrugged. "Nowhere. I just wanted to make sure that we are on the same page. There is only one underage kid left in the program. Spencer should have turned eighteen by now, so it leaves only Andy, who is fourteen. I know that his

278

parents need the money, and Andy volunteered to go. I didn't need to compel him. He's an empath, so he's not very valuable to the program for anything other than breeding, and he's too young for that. I can get him out easily, and since he's a boy, he can be induced right away. But if he turns, he can't go back, and that leaves his family in a bad situation."

As both Eleanor and Onegus looked at him expectantly, Kian debated his options. A male immortal wasn't as valuable as a female, but he wouldn't turn the kid away just because of his gender. On the other hand, Andy had time. They could wait many years before approaching him, and by then, his parents' situation might no longer be relevant.

"If he's miserable in the program, we will give him a shot, and if he turns, I'll pay the family. But if he's fine, I see no reason to rush. Andy has plenty of time to transition."

"I will need an excuse for getting people out of the program for a couple of weeks, so we can find out whether they are Dormants or not. A seminar or a convention could allow us to do that in one shot and save us time."

"Perhaps we could stage a paranormal convention," Onegus suggested. "Like the one Julian found Vivian at."

Kian lifted his hand. "We will cross that bridge when we come to it. First, we need to figure out a plan for installing Eleanor as the program's director."

"I haven't agreed yet." She pushed a strand of hair behind her ear. "I was just playing around with the idea. I can't move to West Virginia and leave Emmett behind. I can go for a couple of weeks, maybe even a month, and work on getting the trainees out, but I don't want to stay on as the director."

Kian had been afraid of that. "Let's put this aside for now. If you were to start the process of getting back inside, how would you go about it?"

"I can start by going to Roberts' funeral. His superiors will be there, and maybe even the trainees. I can approach one of the big honchos and compel him to reinstate me."

It sounded too easy, but maybe that was all it would take.

"If you are not willing to stay on as the director," Onegus said, "would you at least stay long enough for the new director to be assigned? You could compel him to provide us with the same lists Roberts had."

Her eyes sparkling, Eleanor straightened in her chair. "Or, I can find out who works in the Echelon system and compel that person to provide us the lists of names. Direct access is better. If they decide to shut down the program, there would be no new director."

"Do you think you can do that?" Kian asked.

She smirked. "There is a lot a strong compeller like me can do when she puts her mind to it."

Eleanor's comment started the gears in Kian's head spinning. If she could compel a key person in the Echelon system to leak information to them, it didn't need to be limited to paranormals. The system collected information from all over the globe, and being able to harness its power for the clan's benefit could be one hell of a strategic advantage.

Kian could even use it to find the Kra-ell. With Emmett's help, they could program the system to flag communications in the Kra-ell language. Then again, if they were indeed the people who'd founded one of the largest communication networks in the world, they had their own means of communicating like the clan did. On the other hand, if there were several groups of Kra-ell scattered over the planet, not all of them might have access to private satellites.

In any case, it was an interesting idea to pursue at a later date. First, they had to get Eleanor back into the program, and then see if she could gain access to someone inside the Echelon system.

26

ELEANOR

*E*leanor loved the idea of going back to the program and getting whomever she could out. The government had betrayed her, and payback was always sweet.

Well, it had been Roberts who'd done that, but he couldn't have thrown her out on her ass without getting approval from the higher-ups. They deserved everything she could unleash on them, and what Kian wanted her to do wasn't even the half of it.

The problem was Emmett.

She couldn't leave him behind with all those clan females throwing themselves at him. Without the bond, he would have to be a saint to refuse their aggressive advances, and Fates knew that he was no saint. He claimed to love her, and she loved him back, but would that be enough to keep him loyal?

Probably not if she was gone for a long period of time. Perhaps she should give him the benefit of the doubt, and maybe it was a good way to test him, but she wasn't brave enough for it.

Was there a way to convince Kian to let Emmett accompany her?

Probably not a chance in hell, but she had to try. If Emmett went with her, she would even be willing to take on the director's position. Between the two of them, they could compel the entire underground city to work for the clan.

Except, Emmett might use the opportunity to run, and even if he didn't, Kian would fear that. But what if they had a Guardian escort?

No, that wouldn't work. They would have to wear earplugs at all times.

What if the Clan Mother used her compulsion power to ensure Emmett's cooperation? She'd already done that, but she could reinforce it with another dose of compulsion.

Lifting her head, Eleanor leveled her gaze at Kian. "I have an interesting proposition for you."

"Let's hear it."

She swallowed. "If you let Emmett come with me, I will take the position of the program's director. If you want, the Clan Mother can do another round of compulsion on him to make sure that he doesn't run, and you can send Guardians with us to keep an eye on him."

When Kian huffed his incredulity, she pressed on. "Imagine what the two of us could do. We can make everything that they work on in that facility available to the clan. You could put your hands on breakthrough military technologies that can make this village even safer from the Doomers."

When Kian started shaking his head, Onegus lifted his hand. "Before you dismiss it out of hand, let's think this through. Eleanor is onto something."

"Emmett can't leave the village," Kian said. "We won't be able to contain him in that underground city because we have no access to it, and we can't send Guardians with him."

With Onegus in her court, Eleanor felt more confident about pressing forward. "What if I manage to move the program out of the fallout shelter?"

"Where to?" Onegus asked.

"Safe Haven. It's isolated and easily defendable. I can have the government purchase it from Emmett and use it for training paranormals. I can convince them that paranormals can't function properly underground, and that they need the serenity of nature for their senses to flourish. It's not going to be a difficult sale even without resorting to compulsion. It sounds logical."

In addition, she knew that Emmett would not do well in an underground facility. He'd been wilting in the dungeon despite having comfortable accommodations and his nutritional needs met. Which reminded her that it would be damn difficult to get him fresh blood in there. They would need to raid the facility's hospital for blood bags.

Kian shook his head, but the dismissively mocking expression was gone from his handsome face. "What about the Safe Haven community? Where would they go?"

"They can stay." Eleanor leaned forward. "We can segregate the lodge from the community building. In fact, the government can rent the lodge from Emmett. Corporations do that all the time. They rent a retreat for their employees. The government can do the same. This will make our job of testing the trainees so much easier."

Kian chuckled. "The Safe Haven idea actually has merit, but it nullifies your other idea of stealing all the military technological breakthroughs the government is developing in the underground city. Also, I liked your idea of gaining access to those working inside the Echelon system and compelling them to give us any information we want." He leaned forward and pinned her with a hard look. "What is your real objective, Eleanor?"

He'd busted her bluster.

Defeated, she slumped in her chair. "My objective is to keep an eye on Emmett. I don't want to leave him behind in the village with all those females flocking to him like vultures to carrion."

Kian grimaced. "Your analogies need some work, but I get it."

"So, which way are we going?" Onegus asked. "Moving the paranormal program to Safe Haven and leaving Eleanor and Emmett in charge of it, or just getting as many of the trainees as we can out of there and calling it a day?"

"I need to think it through." Kian leaned back in his chair and crossed his arms over his chest. "It depends on what the Kra-ell team uncovers. If Emmett's people are gone and never received his email, I'll feel better about using Safe Haven and letting Emmett go back there. Frankly, I like the idea of a remote and secluded place where we can test potential Dormants without a rush and without fear of discovery. We can assign several Guardians to the place, having them pose as community members, and when new Dormants come along, we can have them brought to the retreat instead of the village. This will probably require some reorganization of Safe Haven, maybe even adding a new building, but it can work."

"Do you want to buy it from Emmett?" Onegus asked.

"That's not a bad idea. The government can then rent it from us. But I need to give it more thought."

27

STELLA

*S*tella gathered up her unruly hair, twisted it into a loose bun on top of her head, and turned to Richard. "How do I look?"

"Gorgeous as always." He pulled her into his arms.

Smiling, she pushed on his chest with her other hand. "The question is not if I look good, but if I fit the fake social media profile Roni made for me."

She was supposed to be a successful fashion designer, Richard was her entrepreneur husband, and they had a fifteen-year-old son whom they wanted to learn the Chinese language and culture so he could one day expand their business into the Asian market. They worked with Mey and Jin's modeling agency and shared the same social circle, which was why the three couples were touring the school together.

Bottom line, they both needed to look rich, with all the status symbols that went with that. She wore a borrowed pair of diamond earrings that were a carat and a half each, a four-carat engagement ring, and Jimmy Choo three-inch pumps. When the mission was over, she would get to keep the shoes, but the expensive jewelry would go back to Amanda.

Stella would be glad to see it go back to its owner. She wasn't a fan of diamonds, and she didn't like the responsibility of wearing expensive stuff that didn't belong to her. Not that she had anything to worry about with four Guardians for companions, but still.

When she and Richard were ready, they headed to the hotel's tiny lobby to meet the two other couples. Yamanu, whose fake profile made him into a music label founder and owner, was sporting a big pair of sunglasses to hide his unique eyes, and his long hair was braided into dreadlocks.

Kian had suggested that Yamanu should shroud himself and some of the others to look less distinctive and draw less attention, but Arwel had decided that the Guardian should opt for more mundane methods of disguise and conserve his energy for their nightly mission.

The rest of them had done the same, matching their looks to their social media profiles.

Mey, who was supposed to head a modeling agency, looked like a supermodel despite the conservative cream-colored suit she wore, and Jin, who was posing as her sister's VP, was dressed in an elegant white dress. Arwel, their pretend business manager, had his hair tied back from his face and wore a pricy suit.

Jay was there as well, looking suave in an inexpensive department store number and wearing a somber expression, both befitting his bodyguard role.

For the meeting with the principal they would arrive in a limo driven by Alfie, but for their night mission, which was when the real investigation was going to take place, they would use a nondescript van that Morris would bring around when it was time.

Since Mey needed complete quiet and absolute concentration when she listened to the walls, she wouldn't be able to do anything during the meeting with the principal, and they didn't really expect to learn much from the man. But the school was located outside a small town with just one hotel and no tourist attractions, so their visit couldn't go unnoticed.

They had to do it for the sake of keeping appearances, and later, they might even drive around the countryside and take a lot of photos, so the entire thing would look legit.

"Is everyone ready?" Arwel took Jin's hand, and when everyone nodded, headed for the front door.

Outside the hotel Alfie waited with the limo, posing as their chauffeur.

He opened the door for Mey with a bow worthy of Okidu. "Madam."

"Thank you, Alfred." She winked at him before entering.

They had to assume that there were eyes everywhere, and appearances had to be kept up in all public spaces.

When they were all seated in the limo, and Alfie closed the door, Yamanu took off his glasses. "I feel like an idiot wearing these inside."

Mey leaned her head on his shoulder. "You could use a shroud like Kian suggested. It was your choice not to."

"It would have been too exhausting to maintain it everywhere we went. I need to conserve my energy for tonight. The compound houses over three hundred students and nearly a hundred faculty and staff. That's a lot of people to keep dreaming with a thrall."

"What if some of them are immune?" Richard asked.

"We have a contingency plan for that," Arwel said. "Merlin prepared a concoction that will knock people out just from the smell but has no effect on immortals. He claims that it's harmless and can be safely used on kids. The youngest students are fourteen, so that shouldn't be a problem."

Stella didn't trust Merlin as much as she trusted Bridget and Julian. In her opinion, he was slightly unhinged, and it had nothing to do with his choice of apparel. The guy practiced unconventional medicine, and his potions didn't go through the same rigorous testing as the human medications that Bridget and Julian used.

"I don't like the idea of drugging kids." She crossed her arms over her chest. "And with Merlin, we don't know how safe that stuff is."

"Don't worry." Arwel leaned back and crossed his leg over his knee. "Merlin would never take chances with the lives of children. Besides, the chances that we will need it are very low."

"The alternative was much less appealing," Yamanu said. "Julian suggested a tranq gun."

That was even worse, but Stella was still worried about using Merlin's untested potions on children.

"I don't know." She uncrossed her arms. "I say that we test it on ourselves first and make sure that it doesn't put us to sleep. If the smelling potion passes that test, we should then test it on some random human adult before we use it on kids."

"Merlin has already done that," Arwel said. "Stop stressing, Stella. It's not our first rodeo. We know what we're doing."

Uttering an indignant huff, Stella leaned against Richard's side and looked out the window. She didn't like admitting it, but Arwel was right. Her only so-called mission had occurred inside a virtual adventure, and although it had felt real to her, it hadn't been. She was a civilian with no military training or skills, and she shouldn't doubt experienced Guardians.

The thing was, everyone made mistakes, and when kids were concerned, she wasn't taking any chances. She would rather offend Arwel's Guardian pride than saying nothing and then regret it.

28

ARWEL

"Good morning." The principal greeted them with a big smile, a gracious dip of his head, and an extended hand to Mey.

Arwel stifled a smirk. The guy had obviously read their fake social media profiles and figured that Mey was the most successful person in their group.

She dipped her head in a polite bow and took his hand. *"Zao shang hao*, Doctor Wáng."

"Oh." He smiled broadly. *"Zao shang hao*, Mrs. Williams."

"Please, call me Mey."

"Then you must call me James."

He was either a super friendly dude or a good salesman. Americans preferred informality, and the more comfortable he made them feel, the more likely they were to send their imaginary children to his school and put up the small fortune of over a hundred thousand dollars in tuition and board.

Once the introductions were done, and the principal had shaken everyone's hand, he motioned to the six chairs that no doubt had been brought into his office especially for their visit.

Next, a twenty-minute-long sales pitch followed. The principal went on and on about the high quality education their pretend children would receive, emphasizing the valuable social network the students would form. The sales pitch closed with several examples of school graduates and how both the education and connections had greatly benefited their success.

Arwel's companions pretended to hang on his every word, nodding and asking questions when appropriate.

"Naturally, to ensure optimal results, we only admit the highest caliber of students." Dr. Wáng smiled apologetically. "The application process is lengthy, I'm afraid, and it is done in several stages. First, the student's parents or legal guardians need to fill out an application and schedule a future appointment for their child to be tested. The test can be done online via a teleconferencing application, but since it's a

287

verbal face-to-face test with one of our teachers, you shouldn't worry about some students and their parents attempting to get an unfair advantage."

"You mean cheat," Yamanu said.

The principal nodded. "Regrettably, it is part of human nature, but as I said, you have nothing to worry about. If your children answer a minimum of seventy-five percent of the questions correctly, they will continue to the next step, which is a personal interview with me that can also be done via teleconferencing. After those steps are successfully completed, the administration will evaluate each application and recommend the best candidates to the head of school. The last step is an in-person interview with Mr. Wu, who has the final say. But since he hardly ever turns a student down, that's more of a formality than a roadblock. When you receive the invitation to see the head of school, your student's acceptance is practically guaranteed."

"That's good to know," Yamanu said. "It would be a shame to drag Junior out here only to be rejected."

None of that had been spelled out in the school's advertising material, but since the entire thing was a charade, it was inconsequential. Still, Arwel didn't remember seeing anything about a head of school named Mr. Wu. He'd been under the impression that the school was run by a board of directors.

Doctor Wáng pulled three glossy folders from his desk drawer. "Would you be filling in the applications today?"

"We will take them with us," Mey said. "We plan on touring several other schools, and we will apply only after we decide which one we like best."

Arwel nodded his approval. Mey had fed the guy some of his own medicine. The school wasn't the only game in town, and the principal didn't have a monopoly on snobbism.

"We would like to see the grounds," Richard said. "Our son is an athlete, and outdoor activities are important to us."

"I'm interested in seeing the dormitories," Stella said. "I'm more concerned with the living conditions." She smiled haughtily. "Our son is used to luxury. I don't expect the school to provide him with the same level of accommodations as he's enjoying now, but I don't want him to spend the next three years in boot camp-like conditions."

The principal gasped. "I assure you, Mrs. Furman, that our students enjoy every convenience and amenity. The main school building is relatively new, and the dormitories were completely remodeled to bring them to the standards our discriminating parents and students expect. These new buildings were designed by one of the top architectural firms in Beijing according to Mr. Wu's exact specifications."

He rose to his feet. "Let's go on a tour so you can see for yourselves. Our classrooms are spacious, well-ventilated, and equipped with the latest and best educational tools. No other school on your list will come even close to ours."

That was an unexpected twist. If the dorms had been completely renovated and the other buildings had been built after the Kra-ell had left, there would be no echoes of them embedded in the walls for Mey to collect.

2 9

MEY

*M*ey stifled a groan. All those months of preparation, and for what? She would be lucky if she could collect faint echoes from the dormitories.

"What was done to the dorms?" Stella asked, no doubt thinking the same thing.

"Everything." The principal led them out of the administration building. "Let's start there. The students are in the classrooms now, so it's a good time."

They followed him across a large, well-maintained grassy central area. It had freshly painted green benches and rose bushes arranged in an alternating pattern around its perimeter. The school buildings surrounding the court were only one-story high, allowing for plenty of sunlight and fresh air.

Mey imagined the place during breaks and after school hours, with students sprawled on the grass, doing their homework or eating their lunches, but those images were taken from her own memories of school life that were probably very different. For starters, this was a boarding school, so the students ate in the dining hall, and it was possible that homework was done in classrooms and supervised.

During their walk to the dorms, they passed several other open green areas that were all as meticulously groomed and clean as the central one.

Richard fell in step with the principal. "When the school was founded, were the dormitories the only buildings on the property?"

Doctor Wáng shook his head. "I was hired after everything was completed, but I was told that there was a large central building that burned to the ground. It was located where the central lawn is now. The new classrooms and offices were built around it."

Mey wondered if she could pick up echoes by sitting on that lawn.

"Do you know what happened to cause the fire?" Richard asked.

"I don't. But you have nothing to worry about. The school is built to the highest standards and there are fire extinguishers located every few feet." He pushed the double doors open and pointed to the fire extinguisher housed in a glass enclosure to its right. "Every dormitory has its own common area." He waved at the couches and armchairs. "As you can see, we don't have televisions anywhere. We encourage our students to engage each other in conversation or to entertain themselves with music or reading." Dr. Wáng pointed at the grand piano, the cello, and the harp tucked into a corner of the room. On the walls, an array of brass and string instruments hung from hooks, and in another corner, an impressive drum set rested on an elevated podium.

"Who did the property belong to before the board of directors acquired it?" Jin asked.

"I don't know." The principal smiled apologetically. "You will need to ask Mr. Wu. He's the founder of our school as well as its head."

"Is it possible for us to meet him today?" Jin asked. "I'm curious about the history of the place." She glanced at Mey. "My sister and I believe that places get imbued in either positive or negative vibes, depending on who occupied them and what happened to them. I know that sounds superstitious, but if people died in that fire, we need to know that."

That was a good cover story, and Mey smiled at Jin over the principal's head.

"I'm afraid that it won't be possible." He assumed an apologetic expression. "Mr. Wu travels abroad extensively on behalf of our school. Many Chinese families who live in other countries are interested in a school like ours, and Mr. Wu spreads the word."

"That's a shame," Jin said. "I guess we will have to go to the library and dig through old newspapers to find out what happened here."

That might have been possible in the US, but not in rural China. Jin probably knew that and was putting on an act.

Opting to ignore her comment, Doctor Wáng led them down the wide hallway and opened the door to a bedroom. "As you can see, there is plenty of room for two students." He walked over and opened a bathroom door. "Every two rooms share a bathroom, so it's only four students per washroom. Also, it is the students' responsibility to keep their dormitories clean." He opened a utility cabinet. "We inspect the rooms without notice, and if we find a mess, those students lose certain privileges for a week."

"Don't you have a cleaning crew?" Richard asked.

"We do, but the school believes that giving students chores and holding them to certain standards builds good habits and strong characters."

Mey couldn't care less about the school's philosophy. "When will Mr. Wu be back?"

"On Monday, but I'm afraid that he doesn't meet with touring parents." The damn fake apologetic smile was back. "Since we get so many applicants, it would be a waste of his time to entertain everyone who shows interest. He only meets with the students and their parents for the final interview."

They would have to find a way to see him, even if it meant thralling the fake-smiling principal and every other member of the school staff.

"What happens on weekends?" Richard asked. "Does anyone go home?"

Dr. Wáng shook his head. "Since most of our students live either abroad or too far for a day's travel, they only go home for major holidays. That's when maintenance is done." He put his hand on the wall. "We take pride in our school. You won't find peeling paint or smudged walls anywhere. Even the furniture gets polished."

"What about the teachers?" Yamanu asked. "Do they live on the premises together with their families?"

The principal nodded. "The staff lives here, but not with their families. They get to visit them on holidays."

It was like a prison sentence for the kids and the teachers. Mey would never send her children to a boarding school, and it had nothing to do with them being immortal. She wanted to enjoy them every day, not just on holidays.

"Does Mr. Wu live in the teachers' quarters?" Jin asked.

"Yes, he does." The principal ushered them out of the dorm room and closed the door. "Naturally, his apartment is more lavish than the standard rooms the others get, but why do you ask?"

Jin shrugged. "I'm just curious. My husband and I would really like to meet with him face to face. Can you arrange a meeting? I'm sure he wouldn't mind making a one-time exception. After all, we have three prospective students between us, so it's not going to be a waste of his time."

He dipped his head. "I'll see what I can do."

Mey was sure that without a thrall, the principal wouldn't even call the head of school, but that was fine. After tonight, she would either get the answers they sought or know if they needed to have a talk with the mysterious Mr. Wu.

30

ANNANI

"I hope you do not mind." Annani put her hand on Dalhu's arm. "I invited Ronja over, but we are going to sit in the backyard, so we will not disturb you."

He froze, the contact stunning him.

Annani rarely touched Dalhu, but after staying for so long at his and Amanda's house, she felt that he deserved to be treated with the same familiarity as Syssi, whom she regarded as a daughter and embraced as frequently as her own children.

After a long moment, he seemed to shake it off. "Not at all, Clan Mother." He dipped his head. "My home is your home." He bowed again and then ducked back into his studio.

Amanda was still at work, and Dalhu had been holed up in his studio all day, venturing out only to eat or grab a fresh bottle of water out of the fridge. The poor man was uncomfortable having her and Alena take over his peaceful house, but Amanda refused to hear of them moving into one of the vacant residences, of which there were many now that the guests had left and Kalugal's men had started moving into his part of the village.

It was time for them to go home.

She should have left at the same time Syssi's parents had gone back to the Congo, or even before, but Annani had hoped Ronja would fall in love with Merlin and consent to inducement. For that, she was willing to stay even longer and help Ronja through with her *blessings*.

But Ronja was not ready, and she would not be in the foreseeable future. When she finally made up her mind, Annani could come back.

The problem was Amanda, who wanted her to stay longer, and as always, Annani felt powerless to refuse her youngest child anything she wished for. Nevertheless, tonight she was going to inform Amanda that she and Alena were leaving on Monday. That would give her a few days to get used to the idea.

Naturally, even if nothing changed about Ronja and Merlin's relationship, Annani would come back a week or two before Amanda's due date, which was approaching fast.

Hopefully, Ronja would make up her mind by then, but it was not likely. Amanda had only eleven weeks to go, and Annani doubted that Ronja would be willing to shorten the customary year of mourning by nearly six months.

As the doorbell chimed, Onidu rushed to open the door. "Mistress Ronja." He bowed. "Please, come in."

"Thank you." Ronja walked into the living room, and the smile she gave Annani was full of sweet secrets.

"Well." Annani rose to her feet and walked over to her friend. "You look lovelier than ever." She kissed Ronja's cheek and then the other. "I smell love," she whispered in her friend's ear.

Ronja's eyes widened. "You do?"

Annani laughed. "It is just an expression, my dear. All I smelled was your perfume." She took Ronja's hand and led her out to the backyard. "But you are glowing, and I do not think the culprit is hot flashes." She sat down next to the small bistro table.

"Oh, I'm way past those." Ronja took the other chair. "And I don't miss them."

Annani waited for Onidu to come out with the lemonade he had prepared in advance.

When he was gone, she leaned closer to her friend. "So, what is the secret behind the glow? Does it have to do with a certain handsome doctor?"

A pretty pink hue bloomed on Ronja's pale cheeks. "It does. I told Merlin about your idea."

Annani's heart leaped with renewed hope. "And? I am sure he was overjoyed."

"He was speechless. Apparently, he's been thinking of ways to prolong my life, but he didn't venture as far as to consider my induction. But Merlin is a quick thinker, and after getting over the initial shock, he realized that his plan was a precursor to yours. He will help me to get younger on the inside, and once my body is as healthy as he can get it, I will decide whether I want to take the final step and start working on transitioning."

Annani's heart sank. It seemed that Ronja was not any closer to making up her mind than she was two days ago.

"So, what is Merlin's plan?"

"Good nutrition, strengthening potions, and lots of physical activity."

"That is a good plan." Annani smirked. "Is the physical activity he suggests the kind that would really get your blood pumping?"

"Not yet." Ronja lowered her eyes. "One small step at a time. That's all I can do for now."

"I understand." Annani patted her knee. "Just do not take too long to go through all those steps. The clock is ticking."

31

SHAI

*I*t was seven in the evening when Shai parked his car in front of Geraldine's home and reached for the flowers he'd put on the passenger seat.

He hoped she wouldn't be too upset about him being nearly an hour late. He could have been there fifteen minutes earlier, but he'd stopped to get the bouquet and a bottle of wine. Since dinner would have to be reheated anyway, he figured that the additional delay wouldn't matter, and the flowers and wine would go a long way toward gaining her forgiveness.

The truth was that Geraldine had never given him grief over being late. It had happened so many times that it had become a joke between them. Nevertheless, he felt bad about disappointing her once again.

Geraldine opened the door, wearing the beautiful polka-dot dress that she'd worn the first time he'd seen her and a sweet smile on her lovely face.

She reached for the bouquet. "You shouldn't have, but thank you." Lifting on her toes, she kissed him lightly on the lips.

That wasn't nearly enough.

Wrapping his arm around her narrow waist, Shai lifted Geraldine and crushed her to him, so her breasts were pressed to his chest. "I'm glad that you're not mad at me."

"Why would I be mad? You would have been here on time if you could. I bet your boss dropped a last-minute assignment on your desk, and it was urgent and couldn't wait until tomorrow."

Geraldine was so accepting and accommodating. Was he a lucky guy or what?

He let her down and followed her inside. "You are very understanding. Most people wouldn't have reacted so rationally. They would have been mad about having to reheat a meal that they had worked hard on and wouldn't have cared what the excuse was."

Geraldine turned her head and smiled at him over her shoulder. "No one has ever accused me of being rational before." She motioned for him to take a seat at the table.

"My friends call me fanciful, and they are being polite. They probably think that I'm a little nuts, but they like me nonetheless." She sauntered into the kitchen, her billowing skirt swaying from side to side. "I'm entertaining."

"You are also friendly and sweet, not to mention gorgeous."

"Still, all those nice things have nothing to do with being a rational person." She pulled a casserole dish from the oven and placed it on the trivet next to the salad bowl. "I'm well aware that some of my memories are not real, and that they only happened in my dreams, but I can't tell them apart. My sense of reality is iffy."

Shai couldn't imagine living like that—not knowing what was real and what was a dream—and he admired her even more for managing to have a relatively normal life in spite of the challenges she had to deal with.

"You have a bad memory and a great imagination, so sometimes you plug the holes in your recollections with stuff from your dreams, or maybe from something that you've read or seen, but your stories are cohesive, and they make sense. That indicates a rational mind." He smiled. "And I'm not saying that because I'm biased."

"You're so sweet." Geraldine leaned over him and kissed his cheek. "But you're definitely biased." She sat across from him and removed the lid from the casserole. "Enjoy."

"Thank you." He ladled some of the stew onto her plate and then his. "I meant what I said. You are very intelligent."

Smiling, she tilted her head. "I would like to know what you are basing your opinion on, and not because I'm fishing for compliments. I know that I'm not stupid, but it's really hard to feel smart when I forget to pay the bills or return phone calls, or when I can't remember where I was, or what I did the day before."

He reached across the table and clasped her hand. "Forgetfulness doesn't indicate lack of intelligence. Merlin, our fertility doctor, forgets to comb his hair in the morning, or launder his clothing, but he's brilliant, and he doesn't have a medical reason for his forgetfulness like you do. What I find even more amazing is that you manage to work around your issues. You raised a successful and confident daughter on your own without any help, and you supported yourself and her despite the challenges you had to deal with. You also knew how to stay under the radar and get fake identities every so often. In addition, you don't need things explained to you twice and you grasp new concepts with ease."

"I guess." She pulled her hand out of his and scooped a piece of potato with her fork. "I still can't understand how I retained the memory of quilting but not of my daughter. I can even understand forgetting a husband with whom I didn't have the best of relationships, but not forgetting my own child."

That was progress.

"Does that mean that you've given up on the identical twin idea?"

Geraldine nodded. "If what Darlene remembers about her mother is not a fantasy, then her mother was an immortal before the drowning incident, and that makes it nearly impossible that she really drowned. But even if she survived and is hiding somewhere, it's also highly unlikely that we both were accidentally turned immortal."

Smiling, Shai reached for her hand again. "As I said, that's a very rational and astute conclusion."

She let out a breath. "Oh, well. I didn't have much choice. By tomorrow, I'll probably forget the reasons for why it's not possible and go back to talking about my imaginary twin. You'll have to remind me why I can't have one."

"You can, but it's unlikely."

Geraldine giggled. "The only way that's possible is if the same immortal bumped into my sister and me at about the same time and shagged both of us. Maybe he thought that we were the same person."

He frowned. "I don't like to think about you shagging anyone."

She tilted her head and cast him an amused look. "I hate to break it to you, but Cassandra wasn't the result of an immaculate conception, and neither was Darlene."

"I know, but I'd rather not think about it."

He wondered, though, whether Darlene had been born before Geraldine had turned immortal or after. If it had happened after, then Geraldine was uniquely fertile for an immortal.

It was one more thing that made her different from most other immortal females but oddly similar to Eva. Perhaps Bridget should check whether they were related.

32

GERALDINE

*S*hai put his fork down and wiped his mouth with a napkin. "I have a theory that I want to run by you."

"Can it wait for coffee?" Geraldine pushed to her feet and collected their plates.

He'd seemed preoccupied during dinner, and she'd wondered whether he was still stuck thinking about her former lovers. She didn't like to think about Shai being intimate with anyone either, but in her case, she had no problem forgetting that he'd had a full life before meeting her.

Shai didn't have the same luxury. He remembered everything.

"I can tell you all about it while loading the coffeemaker." Taking the casserole dish with him, Shai got up and walked over to the sink.

"What's your theory?"

"Here is what I think happened to you. You went on a swim and collided with a boat, which resulted in a massive injury that destroyed a large portion of your brain. The reason I think it was a collision is that hitting your head on a rock would not have caused a head trauma destructive enough to cause such catastrophic damage. Your incredibly fast healing capability probably saved your life, allowing you to regrow those regions, or at least enough of them, before death could occur. But since that brain mass was new, there could have been nothing stored in it. You had to relearn everything like a newborn baby."

Feeling faint, Geraldine sank onto a barstool. "Could I have died even though I was already immortal?"

Shai nodded. "When an injury to the heart or the brain is too massive for our bodies to repair fast enough, we die."

"So how could I have remembered quilting?"

"Perhaps muscle memory is stored in a different region of the brain, but I'm not a doctor, so I can't say that for sure. We will have to ask Bridget. We also need to ask her whether your subsequent memory issues are the result of your brain not rebuilding itself correctly. When immortals break a leg or an arm, it's crucial to get them to Bridget as soon as possible so the bone doesn't fuse itself the wrong way. Often, she has to re-break the bone to reset it correctly."

Geraldine lifted her hand to her head, her fingers brushing over the phantom injury. "I don't know much about medicine either, but what you said makes sense." She let out a breath. "I hope that you're right about the collision. Thinking that I staged my own death for some reason made me feel so guilty. I couldn't understand how I was able to leave my child behind. It's just not the kind of person I am." She lifted her eyes to Shai. "But then, if I regrew a large portion of my brain, maybe I'm a completely different person now than the one I was before."

Shai walked over to her and put his arms around her. "I can schedule a meeting with Bridget for tomorrow, and we can ask her all these questions."

"I can't do it tomorrow. Cassandra is taking me to see the detective lady. Cassy spoke with her about giving me a makeover before the trip to Oklahoma. If I don't want to scare Darlene's father to death, I need to look different, and a pair of jeans with slashes is not going to cut it. I need a proper disguise."

"You can see Bridget before going to Eva's place. If Cassandra can't pick you up earlier, I will. I can also schedule an appointment with Vanessa, the clan's therapist. Bridget can only help us understand the physical implications of a massive brain injury that healed itself, but Vanessa has other tools she can use to find out more about what happened to you. She also might be able to help you with your current memory issues."

Shai was such a man, seeking to solve every problem as expediently as possible. But Geraldine didn't cope well with being rushed. She needed time to prepare mentally for things she considered difficult, and seeing a therapist was near the top of that list. As long as no one had diagnosed her mental state, she could believe that she was mostly normal.

"I can deal with my memory lapses. Right now, I'm more interested in finding out what happened to me and what kind of person I was before the accident."

"Maybe Vanessa can help you with that too."

"How can she help me with memories that were destroyed along with half of my brain?"

Shai winced. "I have one more possible scenario. The boat collision is not the only theory I have."

"What else could have happened to me?"

Avoiding her eyes, Shai shifted his gaze to the kitchen window. "The immortal who induced your transition might have been more than a one-time hookup. He could have thralled you repeatedly, which could have caused irreparable damage to your brain that not even transition could fix. If he was inexperienced and didn't know what he was doing, he could have done a hatchet job."

That was an even worse scenario than the one about re-growing a new brain. "Why would he do that? Why would he thrall me repeatedly?"

"You were a married woman, and you had an affair. He might have thought that he was protecting you, or he just didn't know that what he was doing caused damage."

Geraldine shook her head. "I'm not the kind of woman who would have cheated on her husband, not even if the marriage was unhappy. I would have divorced Rudolf first. I must have met the immortal when I was still single."

"We don't know who that immortal was, and he might not have sought your consent beforehand. He might have thralled you to have sex with him, and then thralled you to forget him."

A cold shudder slithered down her spine. That was the worst possibility yet. "Are you suggesting that he raped me?"

"It's possible, especially if he was one of our enemies. The Doomers don't concern themselves with consent. For many of them, women are just objects to be used."

Shivering, Geraldine leaned her head on Shai's chest. "I like the boating accident scenario much better." She shook herself. "But if I wasn't aware of being unfaithful, why would I fake my own death? And how did I lose all of my memories from before? Your first theory makes much more sense."

"It's possible that both happened. Maybe you had no choice but to fake your own death. Your husband was suspicious, you thought that he was insane because you didn't remember being unfaithful, and you tried to leave him. He might have refused to let you go. What if he threatened your life or Darlene's? Perhaps you were scared and thought that the only way out was to make him believe you were dead?"

"You're confusing me, Shai."

"I'm confusing myself, and I'm also talking out of my ass. I'm not qualified to make any of those assumptions. We really should talk to Bridget and also Vanessa."

As the coffeemaker beeped, announcing that it was done brewing, Geraldine pushed on Shai's chest. "One thing at a time. I can talk to Bridget, but the therapist will have to wait for some other day. Just thinking about talking to a shrink makes me anxious, and I'm already stressed enough about seeing my ex-husband."

"It doesn't have to be tomorrow." Shai walked over to the coffeemaker and poured the brew into two cups. "I just thought of one more thing we could try. In case your inducer was also a compeller, Kalugal might be helpful. He's a powerful compeller and he might be able to release you from the compulsion."

Kalugal was a charming guy, but what he had done to her was scary. Geraldine had needed to see him again just so he would modify his initial compulsion, which prohibited her from saying certain words, so she would be able to talk freely with Shai, Cassandra, and the others from the village. She wasn't letting him get into her head unless it was a question of life or death.

"I don't want Kalugal messing with my head again. The only thing I'll allow him to do is to release me from his own compulsion."

33

EMMETT

"*K*ian can't be serious." Emmett rose to his feet and started pacing. "It must be a test."

There was no way Kian would reinstate him as the leader of Safe Haven, not even if the team he'd sent to China confirmed every word he'd told the guy.

"He sounded serious to me." Eleanor folded her arms behind her head, which resulted in her beautiful breasts thrusting forward.

Damn. She wasn't wearing a bra, and he could see her nipples through the thin cotton, not just the shape, but also the color.

He couldn't let himself get distracted.

Forcing his eyes from the mouth-watering display, he kept on pacing. "What's the catch?"

"I don't know, and I don't know whether Kian will do it. He might have been just thinking out loud."

Emmett stopped and leveled his eyes on hers. "Is he known to do that?"

"Not really. He's a get-it-done kind of guy. But I'm sure he will think of something. He's not going to let you do whatever you want in there." She lowered her arms and leaned forward. "If I were Kian, I would have also offered to buy Safe Haven from you. It provides the perfect solution for several of his problems. He needs a secluded place to test new Dormants, but the problem is that those are few and far between. He will probably realize that it's not worth spending so much money for that alone. If we can find another use for the place that's beneficial to the clan, it will be easier for me to sell him on the idea."

"I thought that he already was."

"Kian said that he needs to think it through. I want to help him arrive at the right decision." She smiled. "Right for us as well as for him."

"What about the trafficking victims the clan is rehabilitating? The Safe Haven community would love to undertake such a noble cause. After all, it is a sanctuary for lost souls."

Eleanor rolled her eyes. "Right, as if a free-love community is the right place for sexually exploited people to recover in." She cast him a withering look. "And don't think for even one moment that I'll let you go back to enjoying that. You belong to me."

He smirked. "I love it when you get jealous, but you have nothing to worry about. Why would I want to drink diluted cheap wine when I have the best vintage in the world?"

Given Eleanor's satisfied expression, she liked what he'd said. "Can you sell your community on the idea of celibacy?"

"I don't think so. One of the fundamental principles of the community was the elimination of the pressure of finding a permanent partner and the need for one. The people who joined my Safe Haven were all deficient in what it takes to form lasting relationships. The community offered them a solution they couldn't find anywhere else. I can't take that away from them."

She eyed him suspiciously, but he was sincere. Safe Haven had been a goldmine for him in more ways than one, but it hadn't been a total con. Emmett truly believed that he'd created a shelter for lost souls, the rejects of human society, and had given a purpose to their empty lives.

"Then it can't serve as a sanctuary for victims of sexual abuse. What else can we do with it?"

"How many people are there in that paranormal program of yours?"

"It's not mine, but currently there are only nine people in it."

"What if we bring in more? I can easily add a paranormal element to the retreat's menu of courses."

A big smile spread over Eleanor's pretty face. "Emmett, you are a genius. With Safe Haven's New Age bullshit curriculum, no one will think anything of it. We can start an advertising campaign promoting the expansion of perception, of opening oneself to the universe, and all that crap. We might attract some real talent, meaning Dormants." She rose to her feet, walked over to him, and wrapped her arms around him. "This is going to be such an easy sell, both to the government and to Kian. I can even get the government to finance the advertising, and the clan can pluck the Dormants while making money out of it. I love it."

As she kissed him, the scent of her arousal filled his nostrils, and his fangs punched out.

"Ouch." She wiped a drop of blood off her lips. "Careful with those."

He licked the blood off and smiled. "I didn't know that making money was such a turn-on for you. Especially since it's not going to line our pockets. The clan would be the one profiting from our combined genius."

"First of all, what gets me turned on is coming up with a brilliant scheme. Secondly, I'm sure I can negotiate something with Kian. He's a businessman, and he knows that in order for people to do their best, they need to be motivated by more than just a job well done. We should get at least half of whatever is left from what we get from the government after all the expenses are paid."

"I like the way you think, but before we get all excited, there are several things that have to happen. First, you need to become the program's new director, and then you need to convince the upstairs guys to let you relocate it to Safe Haven, and then you need them to agree to your new recruiting scheme. Are you up to it?"

Eleanor's lips twisted in a wicked smile. "With the proper motivation, I certainly am."

34

KIAN

"Good morning, Turner." Kian clapped the guy on his back. "What a nice surprise. "What brings you to my office?"

Kian had scheduled a meeting with Bridget and William to discuss Okidu's journals, and having Turner show up together with his mate was an unexpected bonus.

"Curiosity," Turner admitted. "Bridget kept me updated on all the highlights, but when she said that William needed her help to decipher the journals, I just couldn't stay away."

"You are more than welcome to join in." Kian motioned for him to take a seat at the conference table and pulled out a chair for Bridget. "Are you still super busy?"

"My roster is full, and I have several new missions planed, but due to personnel shortages, I can't start them until the current ones are completed. I also need to incorporate lessons from the field before deploying the teams again. So until they are done, my only job is to sit back and wait for their reports, and I have a couple of people in the office on top of that."

"I'm glad that you came. I need your input on a few things, but I didn't want to bother you. You have enough on your plate."

"I do, and that's another reason for my visit today." Turner smoothed a hand over his blond hair. "I have to pull my subcontractor out of China. I need his team."

That wasn't good.

"I was counting on his team being on standby in case we need them. If you are pulling them out, I need to send more Guardians to safeguard my investigative team."

"What did they find so far?"

"I don't know. They were supposed to meet with the principal in the morning and then go snooping at night. I expect a report from Arwel in the afternoon."

"Let me know if they discover anything interesting."

As a knock sounded on the door, Kian rose to his feet and opened the way for William.

"Good morning." The guy walked in with his laptop clutched under his arm. "Turner, I didn't expect to see you here."

"I was curious to hear what you found in the journals."

"One journal." William pulled out a chair and sat down. "I barely managed to get through one-third of the first journal in a month." He turned to look at Bridget. "How good are you at genetics?"

"Pretty good, but I'm a doctor, not a biologist, so I might not be as much help to you as a geneticist."

William opened his laptop, brought up a photo of a page, and turned it toward Bridget. "I get that this is a genetic sequence, but it's only a snippet. How do I know where it goes on the chain?"

Bridget narrowed her eyes at what looked like scribbles to Kian. "You need a bioinformatician, which is a computational biologist."

"Can you tell anything from looking at this?" Kian asked. "My knowledge of genetics is less than rudimentary, so I'd appreciate it if you'd dumb down your explanation for me."

She cast him an amused look. "Humility doesn't suit you, Kian."

"Trust me, I'm not being humble."

"As you wish." She leaned back in her chair. "The human genome is composed of a sequence of about three billion base pairs, bonded chemicals that we mark as A, C, G and T—adenine, cytosine, guanine, and thymine. Those chemicals are grouped together on our chromosomes in strings. There are about thirty thousand of them. I assume that these markings are the equivalent of our A, C, G, and T, but that's all I can tell you. I can get William a file of the human genome and he can run the snippet against it to compare, but since the Odus are not human, I don't know if it will do him any good."

Slumping in his chair, William took his glasses off and put them on the table. "Where can I get a couple of bioinformaticians?"

"We don't have any," Bridget said. "You can hire humans and then erase their memories."

"I know that we don't have any. I've already checked. Where do I get good human bioinformaticians? I need people with a lot of experience. People who will look at those damn journals and know what they are seeing."

"I can make you a list of the top research facilities." She looked at Kian. "Are you okay with that?"

"I'm not crazy about the idea of using humans, but it seems like that's our only option. I suggest that you hire people from another country, though. Lure them with a promise of excellent pay for a secret project. In order to minimize thralling, we will need to lock them up until they are done with the project."

"That might take years," Bridget said. "We can't do that."

"What if we rotate them?" Turner suggested. "Keep one team for a few months, let them crack some of it, and then replace it with another team. It's not as efficient as letting one team tackle it from start to finish, but it's doable."

"How many of those bioinformaticians are out there?" William asked. "If they are scarce, we might have to reuse teams."

"They are in high demand, and there aren't many who are qualified for what you need. They need to be PhD level biologists who are also computer scientists."

William picked up his glasses and started cleaning the lenses with his shirt. "Where are we going to put them? The keep?"

"That's one option." Kian leaned back in his chair. "Or we can acquire a new place."

"What about Kalugal's bunker?" Turner asked. "Did he sell the property?"

"I don't know," Kian admitted. "But even if he didn't, I don't like that it's in the middle of a residential neighborhood. We need a secluded place that is not underground. Humans don't do well without natural sunlight and fresh air, especially when it's a prolonged project."

"What do you have in mind?" Turner asked.

"Eleanor came up with an interesting idea. We were discussing the paranormal program, and she suggested moving it from the government's underground facility to Safe Haven. She said that she can convince them to buy the property from Emmett. Then Onegus said that we should purchase it instead and rent it out to the government. That would allow us to use it for several purposes."

Bridget shook her head, but Turner seemed to like the idea.

"There is a clear advantage to using a place that has an established reputation of a commune that runs self-help retreats. That's a very good cover, and no one would look too closely at what's going on in there. But you need to decide what you want to do with it, and how to make it work. Can you use it for testing the paranormals and for the work William needs done?"

"I need to take a look at the place." Kian folded his arms over his chest. "If the grounds are big enough, I can add structures and segregate the facilities. In order for the cover to work, the community needs to stay, but it needs to be separated from the other activities."

"I wish I could help you plan it." Turner sighed. "But it will take months until this tornado of trouble I'm dealing with passes. Can you wait that long?"

"Not with the paranormal program. With Roberts on his death bed, we need to move quickly on that. As far as I'm concerned, the journal deciphering can wait, but I know that William doesn't agree with me."

3 5

ARWEL

"Stella, what the heck?" Jin looked the woman over. "You look like a ninja."

She wore all black—leggings, T-shirt, sneakers, and even a scarf that was wrapped around her head and covered half of her face.

They were all wearing black, including Mey and Jin, but no one else had gone to such lengths. Mey had her hair in a braid, Jin in a ponytail.

Richard pulled a black hat over his hair, which was also overkill.

"A very curvy and sexy ninja." Richard ran a hand over his mouth. "How am I supposed to concentrate on anything with you wearing a Catwoman outfit." He shook his head. "That ass should be declared illegal for anyone under seventeen to look at. Scrap that. Any male of any age."

Arwel cleared his throat. "You don't have to come. Jin's tether works just as well from here."

Stella glared at him. "Yeah, but Jin is not staying, and she might need me to translate what she can't understand Mey saying in Chinese. And you need me if someone stumbles upon us and we need to communicate with them. None of you speak the language."

"We have Morris," he reminded her. "But I didn't say that you can't come, just that you don't have to."

The truth was that Arwel would have preferred for Jin to stay in the hotel, but he couldn't order her to do that without incurring her wrath. She would have agreed to stay behind if he weren't going, but he had to keep Mey safe while Yamanu thralled the entire school to dream sweet dreams.

And if Stella was going, so was Richard.

"I just want to remind you that we are going to park the van far from the school and cover the rest of the distance on foot. It's an hour's brisk walk. Are you sure that you want to come?" He looked at Jin, whose stubborn expression was all the answer she was going to give him.

"I'm sure." Stella tightened the scarf around the lower part of her face. "I didn't go to all this trouble to stay in the hotel. Let's go."

"Morris is not here yet." Arwel glanced at his watch.

"What's keeping him?" Richard asked.

"The van he bought is a piece of crap," Arwel grumbled. "It's good that the guy knows his way around an old engine and could fix it, but he had to get parts." He sat on the bed next to Jin and wrapped his arm around her shoulders.

While waiting for Morris, they were all crammed in his and Jin's hotel room, and he contemplated sending them back to their rooms until the pilot arrived with the van.

He didn't want one of the other hotel guests to bump into ninja Stella and wonder whether they were being robbed. His and Jin's room was on the ground level, and there were several trees in front of their window that made it the perfect exit point. It was easier than having Yamanu shroud them so they could pass through the lobby, disabling the security camera, erasing a portion of the recording, and Fates knew what else. Yamanu needed to preserve his energy for the compound.

"Did any of you find anything about that Mr. Wu?" Mey asked. "I only found mention of a board of directors, but since the school is privately owned, there were no names."

"I don't think the board even exists," Arwel said. "It just sounds fancier and more official than a guy named Wu heading the entire thing."

"It's a shame Roni can't hack for information in China." Richard leaned against the dresser and crossed his arms over his chest. "We are flying blind in more ways than one."

"I think that going about it the old-fashioned way makes the mission more exciting," Jin said. "It's like the adventure books I read as a kid."

Mey snorted. "I know which books you are talking about, and even they weren't imaginative enough to make one character able to listen to echoes in the walls and another to tether a string of her consciousness to other people. There is nothing old-fashioned about the way we are investigating this compound." She sighed. "Just to let you know in advance, I plan to sit on the central lawn for a while. Maybe I'll get echoes of what happened there." She looked at her sister. "Although to be frank, I'm afraid of what I'm going to hear."

When Arwel's phone pinged with an incoming message, he gave it a quick glance and pushed to his feet. "Morris is here." He slung his backpack over his shoulder and offered Jin a hand up.

Yamanu, Jay, and Alfie checked their weapons, while Richard looked on.

"I wish I knew how to use a gun," he murmured.

Arwel ignored him and turned to Yamanu. "Can you provide us with a little shroud? Or do you need to conserve your energy?"

"I can spare some for this."

Arwel walked up to the window and opened it. "Who's first?"

"I am." Stella hoisted herself up on the sill, swung her legs over, and jumped out.

She was really into playing it out like Catwoman.

Richard followed with much less elegance, and then Alfie. Mey accepted Arwel's helping hand to do the same, and so did Jin. It left him and Yamanu.

"I'm going out. Give me thirty seconds before dropping the shroud."

Yamanu smiled. "I can walk and shroud at the same time. I don't need to drop it."

36

MEY

*M*ey sat on the central lawn for five minutes before giving up. Evidently, the echoes had been burned together with the walls that had housed them, and not even ashes of them remained.

With a sigh, she pushed herself up. "Let's go to the dorms."

Arwel nodded, and he and Alfie followed.

The others hid behind the administration building, keeping Yamanu company. When casting such a massive thrall, he needed to be watched because he was unaware of his surroundings and vulnerable. Jay was watching over him, and so was Richard. Morris stayed with the van in case they needed a quick evacuation.

She cast a quick glance at the new buildings they were passing by. They might provide some clues about the school's founder and possible owner, but that wasn't what they were there for. They needed clues about the Kra-ell, and the only place she might still find echoes of them was in the dorms.

Yamanu's magic ensured that the kids were sleeping soundly and wouldn't wake when she entered their rooms, but the question was whether she could concentrate while they were there. The sounds of them breathing or snoring was not conducive to concentration.

She wondered whether noise-canceling headphones would have worked. The echoes she heard didn't travel through her ear canals. They traveled straight to her mind, so headphones shouldn't have interfered, but she hadn't thought of the idea until now.

If they returned the next night, she would come better equipped.

The dorms were coed, which she found surprising for a traditional society like the Chinese. In the first room she entered, Mey found two boys whose breathing was too loud for her to concentrate. The next room belonged to two girls who slept peacefully and hardly made any sounds.

Sitting on the floor, Mey closed her eyes, slowed her breathing, and reached deeper inside herself, focusing on her mind's eye and ear.

Echoes of a fight between two girls boomed loudly in her mind, but the visuals were faint. They were fourteen or fifteen, one was a plump blonde and the other a skinny brunette. They were speaking French, of which Mey knew only a few words, but the accusing tones and the crying that followed didn't need translation. Once that echo played out, Mey dug deeper, and another started playing. A bespectacled boy accusing his brawny roommate of copying his homework and the other denying it vehemently, both speaking English. She had no choice but to let the teenage drama play itself out before another echo could start.

One after the other those mini-dramas played out, draining Mey, but there was no point in switching rooms only to go through the same thing again. The most recent echoes always played out first, and if she had hope of reaching the Kra-ell time in the compound, she might need to spend the night in that room.

Her friends were probably worried about her, but she couldn't interrupt the connection to tell them what was going on. If she did, the echoes might start from the beginning again, or rather from the end, and her time would be wasted.

Only strong emotions left echoes in the walls, but the problem was that teenagers felt everything strongly, and every trivial thing turned into a drama. So she sat, listening with half an ear to arguments and triumphs in every imaginable language, male and female voices, some loud, some subtle, and a lot of sobbing.

The school certainly lived up to its promise of providing high-achieving students from all around the world with a place to not only gain a good education but also form networks that would serve them well in the world of big business and international politics.

Several hours must have passed before she gave up and severed the connection.

Out in the hallway, Arwel pushed away from the wall. "Anything?"

She shook her head. "I had no idea how much drama happens in dorm rooms. I need a room that is not occupied by students. The custodian's place, or a storage room that might have been used for something else back then."

Arwel nodded, and the three of them continued down the long corridor until they reached a door that looked different from the others. It was locked, but Alfie had it open in no time using a burglar's tool.

"It's an office," Arwel said.

"Perfect." Mey walked in, closed the door, and made herself comfortable on the floor.

The first echoes were of arguments in Chinese, the two women speaking so fast that she only understood every third or fourth word. More echoes followed, mostly of students getting reprimanded about some wrongdoing or another, and Mey had to listen to the apologies, some accompanied by sobbing, some sincere, most not so much.

When the next round of echoes started with a faint sobbing, she was barely listening, but then the visuals revealed two young Chinese women, and the conversation that started made it obvious that they weren't part of the school staff.

The one with the short bob was trying to comfort the one with the braid, a woman named Fang, and even though Mey was far from fluent in Chinese, she could easily understand the simple exchange between them.

Fang was crying her eyes out because she was pregnant and knew that her child would be taken away and given up for adoption. The other, whose name was Tao, was comforting her.

"How do you know that the baby is Krag's?" Tao asked.

"He knew right away. You know how they can smell everything."

"He was supposed to use protection," Tao said.

"He did. Or at least I think he did. You know how it is with them. They mess with our minds."

"It's forbidden for the half-breeds to impregnate humans. He's going to get in trouble."

"I know." Fang started crying again. "What if she kills him? She has no mercy."

Tao huffed. "I don't know why you like him. He's just as much of a monster as the rest of them."

"He's not. Krag is kind."

"He's a bloodsucker."

"So? It's not his fault that he was born like that." Fang wiped her eyes with her sleeve. "The pureblooded ones treat him just a little better than they treat us. I don't know why they bother breeding more of them."

"There is strength in numbers. They need the half-breeds for protection."

"From whom?"

"Us." Tao pointed to her own chest. "Humans. If they are found, the soldiers will kill them."

"But why do they forbid the half-breeds to have children with humans?"

"Maybe there is a good reason for that."

"How can you say that?"

"Think about it. They only take away the children that the half-breeds father. They let us keep the children we have with human men. Maybe these children grow up to be monsters?"

"Then they wouldn't be giving them up for adoption and risking someone tracking them back here. These children are human. They only do that to punish the half-breeds and to keep them in line. I wish Krag and I could escape and be together like a normal couple."

"There is no escape," Tao bit out. "They will find you both, kill him, and make your fate worse than death."

"I know." Fang started sobbing again. "Maybe I should take my own life and be done with this world."

"Don't talk like that. If the queen bitch doesn't kill Krag, you can still be with him. You just need to be careful and use protection."

"Shh, don't say that."

"She can't hear me all the way from her throne room."

"I don't know. Sometimes I think that she hears and knows everything." The woman sighed. "We are slaves here. We have no freedom, and we are used by the pureblooded ones like breeding cows."

Tao snorted. "You talk as if life is so much better on the outside. It's not. They feed us and clothe us and keep us healthy."

Healthy?

"I don't believe that. It's just what they tell us, so we won't fight them when they take our blood. The old people die just like they do on the outside."

"They don't need to tell us stories because they can do whatever they want with us. We can't fight them because they control our minds and are so much stronger. But have you seen anyone getting sick? I've been here five years, and I haven't. It must be what they secrete to numb the pain when they bite. It's like an immunization shot, only it hurts less." Tao shuddered. "I still remember how hard I cried and how long it took for my arm to heal after the nurse that came to our school stabbed me with that dull needle."

"I remember when I got mine." Fang shuddered as well. "And you're right. It was worse than the monsters' bites, and it was followed by misery, not pleasure. Still, what's the point of being healthy and living longer as a slave?"

"Don't be stupid, Fang. We are slaves no matter where we live, just to different masters. The point is to live, to survive, and to find joy wherever we can."

37

STELLA

"My butt is numb," Jin complained. "We should have stayed in the hotel."

Stella snorted. "Don't let Arwel hear you say that. You'll never hear the end of I-told-you-so."

"I thought that it would be more exciting, but Mey has been at it for hours, and no one tells us anything."

"Didn't you tether her?" Stella asked. "Can't you see what she's seeing?"

"It doesn't work like that. I can only see what Mey sees with her eyes and hear what she hears with her ears. I can't access what she hears and sees in her head. She needs to repeat what she hears out loud, and she hasn't done that."

"Then it might be a good sign that she's taking so long," Richard said. "Perhaps she's getting something."

"I hope so." Jin closed her eyes and let her head drop against the wall.

Another hour passed before Mey, Arwel, and Alfie finally showed up.

"How did it go?" Jin pushed to her feet and rubbed her bottom.

"I'll tell you what I learned when we get back to the hotel. Yamanu is exhausted after keeping up the thrall for so long."

Mey didn't look any better than her mate, but she refused to let Arwel prop him up and lent Yamanu her shoulder to start the trek back to the van.

When they were about a mile away from the school, he dropped the thrall and sighed in relief. "That was one of the longest thralls I've ever had to hold."

The sun was rising on the horizon, and Stella was worried that soon they would run out of the cover of darkness. "Perhaps Morris should bring the van closer. We won't make it to him before the sun is up."

Nodding in agreement, Arwel called the pilot. "Come get us. We will meet you on the road."

"Find a place to hide until I get there," Morris said on the other side of the line.

"We will."

312

They cut a path to the road but stayed crouched in the tall bushes until the old van rolled up.

When Arwel rose to his feet and waved, the van came to a full stop, and they all rushed inside, making it in the nick of time before a truck loaded with produce trundled by.

"Do you have any juice left?" Arwel asked Yamanu. "We will need a cover to get back into the hotel. If you don't, that's okay. I can shroud one person at a time."

"You'll have to do that," Yamanu said. "I have nothing left."

It was another hour before they got to the hotel, and the last vestiges of darkness were gone as Arwel, Jay, and Alfie each shrouded a person and helped them through the window into Arwel and Jin's room.

"I'm so thirsty." Mey opened the small fridge and pulled out a bottle of water.

The others had to make do with whatever was left, which wasn't much.

"I'll get more bottles from the vending machine in the hallway," Arwel volunteered.

When he came back, and everyone had a bottle in their hands, Mey told them what she'd heard. "I didn't get anything about what happened to them and where they went, but at least we have confirmation that the Kra-ell were here, and we know that Emmett didn't feed us wrong information."

Arwel nodded. "What you heard confirmed other parts of the story he told us as well. What I don't understand is how your mother got to have two girls before you were taken away from her."

Stella had been thinking the same thing, and she had a theory. "Mey and Jin's mother probably didn't live on the compound. From my own experience and from what Mey heard, it seems that the half-breeds were also half-decent people, and one of them might have had a long-term relationship with a woman outside the compound. Perhaps Jade discovered it at some point and forced them to give their children up for adoption."

Jin plopped on the bed beside her sister. "I wonder if there is a chance we might find our mother. She must have lived somewhere close to here. Maybe she is still around."

"Or maybe something happened to her," Mey said. "And that's why we were given away. There was no one to take care of us."

"It's worth looking into," Jin pressed on. "Now that we know that we weren't given up because we were not wanted, I feel like we owe it to our mother to at least try to find her."

"I wouldn't know where to begin," Mey said. "Besides, if we go looking for her, it will have to be some other time. We have a mission to complete." She looked at Arwel. "I need to go back tomorrow and search for more echoes, preferably newer ones that will tell us what happened to those humans and where they went after most of the compound burned down, if the two events were even connected. They might have left long before the fire."

"After the one with the pregnant lady, did you hear any other echoes?" Stella asked.

Mey shook her head. "I'm sure there were more, but I was exhausted, and there was no point because they would have been even older echoes. It always goes from the most recent ones back. Besides, the dawn was coming, and we had to get out of there."

"We can go again tomorrow," Arwel said. "During the day, we will tour some attractions to explain why we are still here, and on Monday, we will ask to have a meeting with Mr. Wu."

38

KIAN

*K*ian closed the file he'd been working on, swiveled his chair around, and looked out the floor-to-ceiling windows of his office.

Down in the café, Emmett was holding his second session of the day, and the number of females sitting at the two tables he'd commandeered was even larger than during his morning session.

It was Friday afternoon, so it was no wonder that his crowd was larger. People were winding down for the weekend, and sitting through one of Emmett's motivational speeches put people in a good mood.

As with everything else Emmett was doing in the village, those meetings were secretly recorded, and Kian had listened to one of them. His impression was that most of it was hyped-up New Age nonsense, but here and there Emmett provided nuggets of sound advice, so it wasn't a total waste of time. Kian didn't care how clan members spent their leisure time, but he wanted to make sure that Emmett wasn't sowing feelings of dissent or causing other kinds of trouble. Even without using compulsion, the guy was charismatic enough to draw people to him and gain followers.

Maybe it would be better to have him reinstated in Safe Haven, just without the full autonomy he'd enjoyed before, and with one of William's cuffs permanently attached to his wrist so he couldn't run.

Although now that he'd gotten to know Emmett better, the best way to keep him from running was to lock down his bank accounts.

The guy valued his money, which raised another concern.

Kian would have to ensure that there would be no more emptying of community members' bank accounts, and everyone working at the retreat would get paid according to what their job was worth.

Could he trust Eleanor to do that?

Probably not.

Kian believed that her intentions were good and that she'd turned over a new leaf, but her character was what it was. She was ambitious and opportunistic, and putting her in charge of safeguarding a goldmine like Safe Haven would be too much of a temptation.

He needed to put another person in charge of keeping an eye on her and on Emmett. Peter seemed like a good choice. Eleanor and Peter got along well, but they weren't romantically involved, and Peter wouldn't let her and Emmett do things that they were not supposed to. In addition, a team of auditors would have to go over the books to make sure that neither Emmett nor Eleanor was swindling the community.

Kian really liked the idea of having another location for testing potential Dormants. Safe Haven was isolated, the community members were easily controlled, and the guise of a spiritual retreat could serve many purposes. Except, Emmett was one hell of a wild card, and to some extent Eleanor was as well. But putting others in charge of the place didn't make sense either. Emmett was the face on the advertising brochures, and having him as the figurehead was the best cover-up he could think of.

When Kian's phone rang, he swiveled his chair back and picked it up from the desk.

"Good morning, Arwel. How did last night go?"

"Do you want the good news first or the bad?"

"Let's start with the good."

"Mey heard an echo of a conversation that confirmed that the Kra-ell had used the compound. Some of the details also matched what Emmett had told us about them."

"Is she around? I would like to have a transcript of that conversation."

"She is sleeping now, but when she wakes up, I'll ask her to type up the conversation as best as she remembers it."

"That would work. What's the bad news?

"The conversation she heard was between two human occupants of the compound, and that's probably all we are going to get. We've learned that most of the place had burned down over twenty years ago, which included the Kra-ell quarters. All that remained from the original compound were the dormitories, which had been probably used to house humans and animals in the past. They had been completely remodeled, so it's fortunate that Mey managed to hear anything at all. The buildings that house the classrooms, the administrative offices, and the staff quarters are all new. Mey sat on the grass where the main structure used to be, but she didn't pick up anything."

"Turner's guy messed up. I assume that the schematics he sent us of the place are of the new structures."

"Correct. He might not have been aware of the fire that happened over two decades ago. Tomorrow night, Mey will try again, but to hope that she'll find clues about what happened to the Kra-ell is optimistic. She would probably need weeks of nightly sessions to get something, and it's possible that no walls that contain echoes of the Kra-ell remain."

"Does anyone in the school administration know what caused the fire?"

"The principal we've spoken to didn't, but he hinted that the head of school and its founder, a guy named Wu, might know. He's out of the country at the moment, but he's supposed to come back on Monday. I plan on getting a face-to-face with him, and if he doesn't tell us what we want to know, I will sift through his memories to make sure that he isn't hiding anything."

"I don't remember reading about a head of school in their brochure, and Turner's people didn't mention him either." Kian rolled his chair closer to the desk and woke up his computer. "I'm looking at it right now."

"We did the same thing. I think that whenever it says board of directors, it actually means that guy. A board of directors sounds fancier."

"I wonder if that's all there is to it."

"Yeah. Same here. We will know more on Monday, and in the meantime, Mey is going to try to collect more echoes."

"Good deal. Keep me posted."

"I will."

When he ended the call, Kian turned back to the window and looked down at Emmett. The guy was in his element, practically glowing with excitement and good humor.

Had Eleanor shared with him the news of his possible reinstatement?

Obviously, which was most likely why he looked so happy.

Kian hadn't made up his mind about it yet, and he might still scrap the whole idea, but it was good to get confirmation of Emmett's story and know that the guy hadn't lied. It certainly tipped the scales in his favor.

39

SHAI

"*J*'m nervous." Geraldine leaned her head on Shai's shoulder.

"You have nothing to be nervous about." Cassandra opened the clinic door. "We are just going to talk to Bridget, and she's not going to run any tests on you today."

"She might," Shai said. "She mentioned something about running a few more cognitive tests, but that's just her asking questions and you answering them."

"That's what I'm nervous about," Geraldine admitted. "What if my cognition is impaired?" She cast him a worried look. "If I really lost a big chunk of my brain and then regrew it incorrectly, that's possible."

"So far, I haven't noticed you struggling to understand anything." Shai knocked on Bridget's office door. "You're fine."

The doctor opened the way. "Good afternoon. Please come in." She cast Cassandra a questioning look. "Shai didn't say anything about you joining the consultation."

He hadn't counted on Cassandra wanting to be there. He'd assumed that she would drop Geraldine off and go home. But he should have known better. Cassandra was very protective of her mother.

"Is that a problem?" Cassandra leveled her eyes at Bridget's.

"Not for me." The doctor rounded her desk and sat on her chair. "But it might be for Geraldine."

"I'm okay with Cassandra being here," Geraldine said. "My daughter and I have no secrets from each other." She closed her eyes. "Perhaps it is more accurate to say that I don't have any secrets from my younger daughter. I sure have many that my older daughter is not aware of."

Shai cleared his throat to get Bridget's attention. "You said that you will give some thought to my theory about Geraldine's brain injury."

"I did." The doctor steepled her fingers. "Normally, a massive injury like that would have killed even an immortal, but according to your testimony, Geraldine heals incredibly fast." She turned to look at her. "Would you mind if I repeated the experiment and timed your rate of recovery?"

Geraldine shifted in her chair. "Is it going to be like before? Just a scratch?"

"I need the injury to be a little more substantial than that, but not by much. A small cut to the palm of your hand should be enough."

"After Martha scratched me and there was no sign of it when I looked at my hand, I went to the bathroom and used a pair of nail scissors to make a deeper cut. I watched it heal in seconds, perhaps not even that."

"That's why I would like to time it," Bridget said. "Re-growing brain mass is much more difficult than fixing broken skin and several small blood vessels, but it will give me a better idea of what your body is capable of."

Geraldine extended her hand. "Let's do it."

"I need a few moments to assemble my tools." Bridget rose to her feet. "With no new patients in the clinic, I can't justify having my nurses here, which means that I have to do it myself." She opened the door and stepped out.

Geraldine huffed out a breath. "I wasn't expecting this, and frankly, I don't think it's necessary."

"It's not a big deal, Mom." Cassandra patted Geraldine's thigh. "You were there when I was tested. You saw how small the cut was and how quickly it was all over."

A moment later, Bridget returned with a tray. "Since we know that you'll heal rapidly, I don't need to get you into a patient room. We can just do it over my desk." She returned to her seat. "Shai, use your phone to time it. Geraldine, give me your hand."

As Geraldine once more extended her hand, Shai put his on her thigh and gave it a gentle squeeze.

Moving with practiced speed, Bridget gripped her hand, and without bothering to disinfect it or give her time to change her mind, she made the cut.

Geraldine hissed and tried to pull her hand back, but Bridget held on. "Look at this," she murmured. "I made a deeper cut than usual, and it's already closing."

It took a second and a half for the wound to close and another second for the pale line to disappear. In two and a half seconds, the wound was gone as if it had never happened.

"I don't think that even Annani's children heal that fast." She wiped the little drop of blood on Geraldine's hand with a piece of gauze. "I'll have to ask Kian to volunteer for a test so I can time his healing rate."

"What does it mean?" Geraldine cradled her hand as if she could still feel the pain from the wound Bridget had inflicted.

"Your mother must have been the child of a god or a goddess."

"Maybe my grandmother was a goddess herself?" Cassandra suggested.

"That's unlikely. Other than Annani and Areana, no gods have survived. Their immortal children, though, might have. Perhaps your grandmother was saved the same way as Wonder. Possibly, your mother doesn't even know what she is."

"We've considered that scenario," Cassandra said. "But it's just speculation that we can't prove or disprove. Could my mother be an anomaly? Because I don't heal nearly as fast."

"That's possible." Bridget regarded Geraldine with a frown. "Let's talk about Shai's hypothesis for a moment. With what I've just witnessed, I believe that you could have regrown brain tissue fast enough to defeat death. And that would explain why your memories from before the accident are lost. Though that doesn't explain your current issues."

"What about the brain not rebuilding itself correctly?" Shai asked.

"A brain is not a bone. Neurons have the ability to modify the strength and efficacy of synaptic transmission through activity-dependent mechanics. It's called synaptic plasticity. If your body was able to regrow what was lost and your brain was exposed to enough stimuli, it would have gone back to optimal functioning. That being said, we are not machines, and emotions have a big impact on physiology. If you believe that your brain is incapable of retaining memories, you will manifest it."

40

GERALDINE

*G*eraldine shook her head. What Bridget had said implied that she was physically fine but not mentally, and that her memory lapses were imagined rather than real.

That was absurd.

"There must be another explanation. It wasn't easy for me to raise a child while living in constant fear that I would forget to feed her or pick her up from school. Why would I convince myself of something that wasn't real if it was causing me so much trouble?"

Bridget lifted her hands. "That's a question that should be addressed to Vanessa."

"Can those issues result from frequent thralling?" Shai asked. "I know that our bodies don't heal mental problems, and we know that excessive thralling can cause irreversible damage."

"In humans." Bridget leaned back in her chair. "Although, to be fair, I don't know what effect it would have on an immortal. Only a god or a goddess can thrall other immortals, and since Annani has never abused her ability, we don't have experience with that."

Shai shook his head. "We also thought that only gods and goddesses could compel other immortals, but we know now that's not true. Navuh and Kalugal can do that. What if the immortal who induced Geraldine's transition continued to thrall her after her accident?"

Geraldine's head snapped to Shai. "Are you suggesting that the immortal who induced me had something to do with my accident and then continued thralling me after I recovered? That sounds absurd."

"I agree that it's far-fetched, but it's possible." He smoothed his hand over the back of his neck. "I thought of this scenario last night. What if he wanted to get you away from your husband and daughter? What if he was in love with you, but you refused to leave your family? He might have decided to erase them from your

321

memory and stage your drowning accident so they wouldn't look for you. He could have been inexperienced or overzealous and caused irreparable damage."

"That's an even less likely scenario than the boating accident," Bridget said. "But if a powerful immortal is responsible for your memory problems, Annani might be able to look into your head and find out whether you've been thralled too many times."

As the phantom pain of her head injury started throbbing, Geraldine's hand flew to her temple. "I was injured. I'm sure of that, and I'm terrified of anyone messing up my brain even more than it is now. I allowed Kalugal to compel me because I had no choice. But I'm not sure about the goddess getting inside my brain. She is much more powerful than Kalugal."

"Annani won't hurt you." Shai took her hand and clasped it between his two. "She's very conscientious about using her abilities on immortals. If she encounters resistance, she won't push. She would pull back."

"Are you sure?"

"I'm certain. We will also explain the situation to her so she would know to be extra careful."

Geraldine's head was throbbing so badly that she could barely concentrate. Perhaps Bridget had been right, and it was all in her head, but not physically. She shouldn't get headaches, and yet it happened every time she got stressed or anxious.

Was she imagining the pain? Or was she inflicting it upon herself?

It was all so confusing.

Shai's creative mind had come up with too many scenarios, and perhaps he could keep all of them straight in his head, but they were a big jumble in Geraldine's.

"If the goddess agrees to help me, I will be grateful. But I don't see why she would. I'm not one of her descendants."

"That's a good point," Bridget said. "Annani might not want to get involved."

"Why not?" Cassandra asked. "Because my mother is not a clan member yet?"

As Bridget nodded, Shai lifted Geraldine's hand to his lips and kissed her fingers. "Don't worry. The Clan Mother will see you. As my mate, you automatically became a clan member. In addition, I'm Kian's assistant, and he owes me. If I have to, I will play that card."

Geraldine had stopped listening after Shai had called her his mate. By now, she knew what that meant, and it was a big deal.

A mate was much more than a wife.

Had he meant it? Or was it just something he was going to use to get the Clan Mother to help her?

"You called me your mate," she whispered.

He frowned. "Do you have a problem with that?"

"No, it's just that you've never called me that before."

Chuckling, Cassandra put her hand on Geraldine's shoulder. "Perhaps you two should continue this conversation later in private. I'm sure that Bridget has more important things to do than to listen to you lovebirds talk about your mated bond."

Mated bond?

When had that happened?

They hadn't even declared their love for each other yet. The feelings were there, but neither of them had said the words. They were both pretending as if their relationship was casual and as if they were just having fun with each other. But the truth was that it had pretty quickly turned into much more.

Geraldine couldn't imagine her life without Shai in it, and apparently, he felt the same way.

But why had he waited for this moment to tell her that he thought of her as his mate? His one and only?

As Cassandra had said, they needed to talk, but Eva was expecting her, and she was probably already running late.

As she glanced at the clock hanging on the wall behind the doctor, heat rose in Geraldine's cheeks. "Oh, dear. I was supposed to be at Eva's fifteen minutes ago."

"I'll text her that you are running late," Cassandra offered.

"We should go." Geraldine pushed to her feet. "Thank you, doctor. I'm sorry for taking so much of your time."

"Nonsense." Bridget got up and rounded her desk. "You can come to me or call me with whatever questions you might have, and I'll do my best to answer them. I wish I could have been more helpful to you, but you are a very unique case, and I don't have experience in forensic medicine."

41

SHAI

*O*utside the clinic, Cassandra read the return text from Eva. "She says that there is no rush. Her son and granddaughter are taking a bath after a finger-painting incident." She put the phone back in her purse. "Do you need me to come with you?"

Shai put his arm around Geraldine's waist. "I'll escort your mother to Eva's place."

Cassandra's lips curved in a knowing smile. "Good. I still have to pack." She glanced at her watch. "We need to be at the airstrip at five, so you have about an hour to spend with Eva. Are you going to stop by Onegus's, or are we meeting at the parking garage?"

"We will stop by your place," Shai said.

"Good." Cassandra leaned to kiss Geraldine's cheek. "I need to drag Onegus out of his office. He hasn't packed yet either."

"Bye, sweetie," Geraldine said in a faint voice.

Cassandra cast her a worried glance, kissed her other cheek, and then turned on her heel and headed toward the pavilion.

"What's wrong?" Shai stroked Geraldine's back. "Did what Bridget said stress you out?"

"A little," she admitted. "And then you called me your mate, and just now you told Cassandra that we would meet her at her place. Not Onegus's, but hers. It makes it sound so permanent."

"Does any of this surprise you?"

"Not really. I just thought it would take more time. Everything is happening so fast."

Shai couldn't fault Geraldine for feeling overwhelmed.

He'd taken his time, letting her get used to his presence in her life, and he had refrained from making any claims on her or pressuring her into admitting her feelings for him. Geraldine was skittish, and she still didn't trust him completely. Or maybe she didn't trust herself and her own feelings, which was understandable given her tendency to remember things that had never happened. She probably second-guessed everything.

He shouldn't have slipped and called her his mate. It was too soon, and she wasn't ready to commit to him. Besides, the bond wasn't there yet.

"Don't worry about things happening too fast with us. I'm not in a rush, and it's entirely up to you how fast or how slow you want to go."

She lifted her eyes to him. "You can't help the way you feel, Shai. And keeping it bottled up inside of you because you're afraid of how I will react is not doing either of us any good. Just be honest with me."

The opening Geraldine had provided was impossible to resist. Turning to her, all the pent-up emotions he'd been keeping locked in burst out in a flood. "I love you." He looked into her eyes, searching them for signs of withdrawal or stress, but when she just smiled, Shai continued. "I fell in love with you the first time I laid eyes on you. I love everything about you—your passion, your flirtatiousness, your intelligence, your easygoing, sweet character, your perfect hour-glass figure, your lush lips, your gorgeous, expressive eyes. I could go on and on about all the things I love about you."

Lifting on her toes, she kissed him softly, and as he closed his arms around her and kissed her back, she melted into him.

If they weren't out in the open, he would have stripped her bare and made love to her right then and there.

"I love you too," she whispered against his lips. "I don't know why it has taken me so long to tell you."

If they were being honest with each other, he should tell her what he suspected. "You didn't trust your feelings, that's why you were afraid to admit it even to yourself."

She nodded, but then shook her head. "I knew from the very start that you were different than any man I've been with, or rather remembered being with. I knew that you were a keeper, and I could see myself spending my life with you. I don't remember feeling that toward anyone else, but I can't trust my memories, so there is that."

"Vanessa might be able to help you. I don't know why you are resisting seeing her so much. I understand about avoiding human shrinks, but fearing discovery is not an issue with her."

"I know." As Geraldine pulled out of his arms, he regretted bringing up the subject of Vanessa. "It's not what you think." She resumed walking. "Vanessa is going to ask me questions about what I remember, and I can't answer those questions honestly. I know that some of my memories are not real, but I don't know which ones are and which ones are not. The only memories I feel confident about are those that Cassandra can verify."

"Then you can start with those. But your confused memories are not the only thing Vanessa can help you with."

Geraldine arched a brow. "I don't have any other issues."

"What about your phobia of leaving the house for more than a couple of days?"

"I don't have a phobia. I just love the house Cassandra bought for us. We both put our souls into that house, decorating every corner of it. I'm attached to it."

"It's just a house. You can decorate your new house in the village any way you like. And if you want, we can load up your furniture on a truck and bring everything here. You'll feel right at home."

She shook her head. "It's not just about the furniture. I have friends out in the human world. I don't want to lose them."

They'd had the same discussion so many times before that Shai had realized it was futile to argue the point that Geraldine could still visit her friends whenever she wanted to.

"I think it's more than that, and you should talk about your excessive attachment to the house with Vanessa."

She loosed a breath. "If it's so important to you, I'll talk to her."

"When?"

"After the investigation into my past is over." She shivered and leaned into him. "I'm not looking forward to meeting my former husband. I'm afraid of what my reaction to him will be." She sighed. "I'll probably feel nothing, which will confirm your theory about the massive brain injury. But if I do feel something, then my guilt over feeling nothing for Darlene would grow exponentially."

Smoothing his hand over her arm, he kissed the top of her head. "I'm pretty sure that you will respond to Rudolf the same way you responded to Darlene. It will be like meeting a stranger. What I'm more curious about is seeing his reaction to you."

42

GERALDINE

"I've never flown on a private jet." Geraldine looked at Eva through the mirror. "Have you?"

"A number of times." The woman adjusted the short bob wig on Geraldine's head. "Although frankly, I prefer flying on commercial jetliners."

"I like flying on the clan's jets," Nathalie said. "But not on any other small planes. I don't trust that they are as well maintained as the big airliners."

"I want to go flying on a plane, Mommy." Her adorable little daughter bounced up and down on her grandmother's bed.

"You did, sweetie. We went to visit Grandma and Grandpa in the Congo, but you were too little to remember."

"Then let's go again." The bouncing resumed.

"We will." Nathalie lifted the girl off the bed and put her down on the floor. "Go check on Ethan."

"Okay." Phoenix trotted to the master bedroom's sitting area, where Ethan was playing with blocks.

"They seem to be getting along wonderfully." Geraldine turned sideways to examine her reflection in the mirror.

"Phoenix thinks that she's his mommy." Eva took the wig off and pulled another one from her trunk.

Geraldine turned to look at Nathalie. "You said that you visited Phoenix's grandparents in the Congo. I thought that clan members lived either here or in Scotland."

"Andrew's parents are not immortal," Eva said as she put a shoulder-length light brown wig on Geraldine's head. "When Kian met Syssi, who is Andrew's sister, her mother was already too old to go through the transition. Besides, I don't think she would have done it anyway. It's a difficult decision for someone who is happily married to a human."

Geraldine sighed. "I have a daughter who is too old to transition as well, but I don't think she's happily married. It's so unfair that she's missed her chance."

327

"How old is she?" Nathalie asked.

"Darlene is forty-nine. I can't even tell her about it. Do Andrew's parents know about him turning immortal?"

Eva nodded. "The Clan Mother compelled them to keep the existence of immortals a secret."

"I was compelled to keep it a secret too." Geraldine looked up at Eva. "By Kalugal." The same guy who'd induced Eva without her knowledge.

Had she forgiven him? Did she feel anything at all toward him?

And what about her husband? How could she have reconciled with him after he'd suggested that she abort their child?

Except, those weren't the kind of questions Geraldine could ask a woman she'd just met. Maybe once she moved into the village, they could become best friends, and then she could ask Eva such personal questions.

The moment the thought passed through her head, the anxiety about moving out of her house gripped Geraldine by the throat.

Perhaps Shai was right, and she had a phobia about leaving her house.

Eva rummaged through her trunk and pulled out a deep-red shoulder-length wig. "I should have started with this one." She put it on Geraldine's head. "What do you think?"

"It looks good, but it doesn't make me look different enough. Do you have a blond wig? That would be a major change."

"I do, but it would look too fake on you." Eva pulled a pair of dark-rimmed glasses out of the trunk and handed them to Geraldine. "Put them on."

"That's better," she admitted. "I look like a sexy librarian."

"Hmm." Eva put a hand on her hip and regarded Geraldine's reflection in the mirror. "You just gave me an idea."

She took the wig off and unpinned the net covering Geraldine's hair. "I'm going to spray your hair with color that washes out." She pulled a spray can out of her box of wonders. "It will make your hair look duller." She sprayed just a little, waited for it to dry, and then twisted Geraldine's hair into a tight bun at her nape.

"Ugh, I look ugly."

Eva chuckled. "You are still beautiful, just a little toned down. After I'm done with your makeup, you'll look worse." She put a hand on Geraldine's shoulder. "This is not a beauty makeover. The goal is to make you look less like you."

"I know." She waved a hand. "Do your best. I mean worst."

"Close your eyes."

"Yes, ma'am."

The woman had a commanding personality, but Geraldine was comfortable with her. They were about the same age, and Eva had also been induced without her consent or even knowledge. That was where their similarities ended, though. When Eva had run, she'd also left her daughter behind, but she'd done it after Nathalie was an adult and had gone to college. She hadn't abandoned a young girl and made her believe that she was an orphan.

Eva had just disappeared.

As guilt threatened to dampen Geraldine's spirits, she shifted her mind to more pleasant thoughts. Shai had told her that he loved her, that he'd been in love with her from the first moment they'd met. She'd been intrigued and infatuated from the first moment as well, but love had come a little later. Not by much, though.

She'd fallen in love with him slowly, and with each passing day, she was falling even deeper in love.

Still, she didn't feel the bond that Cassandra and Onegus had. Cassandra had described it as snapping into place, but nothing had snapped for Geraldine. Maybe she and Shai were different, and their bond would weave itself over time.

"Open your eyes." Eva planted the fake glasses on Geraldine's nose. "Do you think that you look sufficiently different?"

"Wow. I look like a boring librarian now, but it's still my face, more or less."

Nathalie walked over and peered at her reflection. "You don't look the same. I think that you look different enough to pass as your cousin."

"That's good enough, I guess." Geraldine huffed out a breath. "Can we try the red wig again? It will work better with this makeup."

"Sure." Eva pulled it out of the trunk and put it on Geraldine's head.

"I like it." She turned to look at Eva. "Can I take it? I'll bring it back, I promise."

"Of course, you can." Eva took the wig off and lifted the net. "But you need to learn how to wear it properly, so it will look more natural."

43

SYSSI

"*Y*ou are so precious, my little one," Annani cooed at Allegra. Watching the goddess making funny faces to get the baby to smile at her warmed Syssi's heart.

"Should I serve coffee, tea, and dessert, mistress?" Okidu bowed from the waist as usual.

"In a little bit." Syssi smiled up at him. "Everyone needs time to digest the wonderful meal you prepared for us."

He grinned happily. "It pleases me to hear that everyone enjoyed it."

Okidu was getting better and better at expressing emotions, surprising her time and again with how quickly he was learning.

Then again, she shouldn't be surprised. He had a computer for a brain. Up until his accident, the program responsible for allowing him to learn to express feelings had been locked, but once it had been opened, Okidu had been absorbing every emotion he witnessed like a sponge.

Syssi had to admit that it was a bit unnerving, but nevertheless, she was incredibly grateful to have him around. Now that she had Allegra, the Friday family dinners she cherished would not have been possible without him. Okidu prepared the food, served it, and cleaned up after the meal. All she had to do was go over the menu with him.

"Give her up, Mother." Amanda extended her arms. "You've been hogging her up for ten minutes straight. It's my turn."

"Oh, Mindy." Annani let her take the baby from her arms. "I am going to miss her so much when I go home. I cannot get enough of those adorable smiles."

"Then don't go home." Amanda took Allegra with her and sat on an armchair.

Syssi loved the way her mother-in-law adored her granddaughter. The goddess didn't worry about looking or sounding undignified as she made funny faces at the baby and uttered sounds that no human could make.

"I have been away from my people for too long." Annani adjusted the skirt of her long gown. "It is time Alena and I went home."

"What's the rush?" Amanda asked. "It's not like they can't manage without you."

Amanda was right. Besides, Syssi wanted the goddess to spend as much time with Allegra as possible. When she'd asked how long a baby girl had to be exposed to the goddess to transition, no one had given her a straight answer.

Alena had murmured something about three months, Kian had said that he didn't know, and Annani's answer had been that it depended on the child and that it was different for every girl.

"It is not that my people cannot manage without me. It is just not right for me to be gone for so long, especially since Alena is with me. No one is in charge."

"Then appoint someone," Amanda suggested. "I don't understand why you didn't do that yet. If you don't have anyone you deem capable enough, you can appoint a committee or a board of directors."

Responding to Amanda's irate tone, Allegra made a displeased sound that Syssi knew would soon turn into a crying fit. But as she rose to her feet to take her from Amanda, her sister-in-law cuddled the baby close to her chest and softened her tone.

"I'm not angry, sweetie. I love you so much." She kissed her soft cheek. "I just want my mommy and my sister to stay a little bit longer. They never stayed at my new house before, and I'm having so much fun with them." She kissed Allegra's other cheek and was rewarded with a cute smile and a tug on her long bangs.

"You can talk to her in a normal voice," Syssi said. "She'll think that all adults talk funny."

"That's how everyone talked to Phoenix." Nathalie cast a loving glance at her daughter, who was sitting on the floor with Ethan and pretending to read him a baby book. "She turned out just fine. In fact, she has the vocabulary of a much older child. Sometimes she sounds so grown up that it's startling."

"How did it go with Cassandra's mother?" Amanda changed the subject. "Did Eva find a good disguise for her?"

"Just a wig and a few tips on how to change her looks with makeup and accessories. Geraldine didn't want anything that would be too difficult to do herself. They left today, but they're going to meet up with her ex tomorrow."

"Will a wig and some makeup be enough to disguise her features?" Annani asked.

"Her disguise doesn't need to be elaborate." Nathalie crossed her legs and brushed a few crumbs off her shirt. "She only needs it to be convincing enough to make her ex-husband believe that she's his dead wife's niece."

Syssi couldn't imagine how difficult it would be for Geraldine to face a husband who she didn't remember. It would probably be less difficult than facing the daughter she'd forgotten, but then no one suspected the daughter of foul play.

The husband, on the other hand, was the number one suspect.

4 4

SHAI

*A*ll throughout the flight and the drive to the hotel, Shai was in a state of heightened arousal that was difficult to hide from his immortal companions. At first, Onegus and Cassandra had hidden their amusement, and then they'd forgotten all about him and Geraldine, launching into a heated political discussion that normally he would have loved to take part in. But he was too preoccupied with his rioting body and what it wanted to do.

The only one who seemed oblivious to his distress was the one causing it.

Was it the damn red wig?

Geraldine had decided to leave it on until they got to their hotel room so she could get used to the feeling of wearing it. She'd thought that the makeup and wig made her look drab, but Shai disagreed.

She looked sexy, sophisticated, and he couldn't wait for them to be alone so he could show her how she was affecting him.

As soon as they entered their hotel room, he dropped their suitcases on the floor, wrapped his arms around her, and pinned her to the door.

"I've been dreaming of doing this for hours." He kissed her, pouring into the kiss everything he'd told her on the way to Eva's place.

Geraldine responded as she always did with him, throwing herself into the passion with an abandon that equaled his.

When they had to break the seal of their mouths to suck in a breath, she smiled at him. "I've been dreaming of doing something to you too."

She wiggled out of his arms and turned him around, so his back was pressed against the door.

"What do you have in mind?"

"You'll find out." She leaned into him, her hands roving over his shirt as she kissed his neck and then nipped it.

He hissed. "Careful."

"Or what?" She drew her hands down his chest.

332

"Or I'll pick you up, throw you on the bed, and be inside of you in two seconds flat."

"Easy, big guy," she purred as she sank to her knees in front of him. "I think you are going to like this."

Like it?

He was going to love every fucking moment of it. The image of her red painted lips around his shaft was nearly enough for him to climax before she even put her soft small hands on him.

Geraldine unhooked his belt and lowered the zipper maddeningly slowly, then leaned in and inhaled. "I love the way you smell." She looked up at him as she reached into his boxers and freed him. "Like clean man and sex." Her soft palm wrapped around his shaft.

He shuddered, and as a groan left his throat, his head banged against the door. "Fates, Geraldine. That's what I want to do to you."

"I know." She kissed the tip softly. "But today, it's my turn, and you are going to let me do this."

"You can do anything you want to me, anytime you want." He lifted his head and looked down at her. "But this, Fates, I don't know how long I'll be able to last."

"Let's see." Her hand glided down his length and then up again.

And then her tongue was on him, lapping at the drop that accumulated at the tip.

"Fuck," he hissed.

She chuckled, the sound reverberating through his shaft and squeezing his balls. "We will. After I'm done." She took him into her mouth.

He jerked his hips, threading his fingers into her hair and then pulling them out as they touched the inner net of the wig. The guy who'd never forgotten anything had forgotten that she was wearing a wig.

Instead, he threaded his hand under the hair and cupped the back of her neck while his other hand cupped her chin. He held her as gently as he could, needing to take over but not succumbing to the urge.

This play was hers to direct, and he was there just to enjoy the ride.

Easier said than done.

As she worked his length with her mouth and her hands, he couldn't stop his hips from moving and his shaft from thrusting into her mouth. He could control the intensity, though, and he made sure that his thrusts were gentle and shallow and that she never felt overwhelmed.

45

GERALDINE

*S*hai cupped the back of Geraldine's neck, but it wasn't meant to hold her in place so he could thrust deeper. Not that she would have minded if he did. Pleasuring a man orally wasn't something she did often or well, but she was determined to give Shai as much pleasure as she could.

He'd been so generous with her, always taking care of her pleasure first, and she wanted to reciprocate. She needed to do it.

As his fingers on her neck gently massaged her muscles, his entire body shook with effort not to deepen his thrusts.

Should she let him take over?

What would he enjoy more? The slow torture of letting her dictate the pace, or going as deep and as fast as he could?

Even though it obviously cost him, Geraldine had a feeling that he preferred her to be in control. That way, it was a gift from her to him, and not him taking what he wanted and needed from her.

But she could do it for him, make her gift more pleasing, or at least try to.

Taking him deeper down her throat than she'd thought possible, she fought the gag reflex and increased the tempo of her head bobbing up and down his length.

"Geraldine," he breathed her name as if it was a prayer. "I can't—" His entire body stiffened, and when his fingers tightened around her neck, and his seed shot down her throat, he shouted her name.

She'd never gone that far into pleasuring a man like that, and her first instinct was to withdraw, but she didn't. Instead, she swallowed everything, and when he was fully depleted, she even licked him clean.

"Fates, Geraldine." Shai dropped to his knees in front of her, wrapped his arms around her, and kissed her.

The kiss lasted forever, and only when it ended did she suddenly remember that they were in a hotel room and that the entire floor had probably heard Shai shouting her name.

Her cheeks heating with embarrassment, she rested her forehead on his chest. "I forgot."

"What did you forget?"

He sounded so worried that she had to laugh. "That we are not in the village where buildings are soundproofed for immortal ears. Everyone on this floor must have heard us."

"You mean that they heard me." He hooked a finger under her chin. "Do I look like I care?"

Given how his eyes were glowing and his fangs were protruding over his lower lip, Shai wasn't nearly done, and what he had in store for her made her core tighten in anticipation.

She shook her head. "You look like the appetizer wasn't enough, and you can't wait for the main dish."

"Right on."

In an impressive display of strength, he lifted her with him as he rose from a kneeling position to his feet. "Let's make some more noise for the other guests to enjoy." He carried her to the bed, which was an even more impressive display since his pants were still all the way down around his calves.

Geraldine giggled. "Are you going to get even and make me shout your name?"

"You bet." He kicked his shoes off.

The pants and boxers followed the shoes, and when he pulled his dress shirt over his head, she heard a couple of buttons hitting the floor.

Not wanting to delay things any longer, she took off the belt cinching her waist and started on the row of small buttons on the front of her dress.

When Shai pushed her hands away and attacked the buttons himself, she was afraid they would meet the same fate as the ones on his dress shirt, but he took his time, making sure none were lost as he opened enough of them for the dress to come off.

Left with only a lacy bra and matching panties on, Geraldine sprawled on the bed, enjoying Shai's heated gaze. "Do you want me to take off the rest? Or do you want to do it?"

"Mine," he hissed through his protruding fangs.

Had he meant that it was his job to get her naked, or had he meant that she was his?

Geraldine was fine with both, but she needed to know.

"Am I yours?"

"Forever." He hooked his fingers in the elastic of her panties and pulled them down. "If you'll have me," he added.

She smiled. "Are you being politically correct, love?"

He crawled over her and reached under her to unclasp her bra. "I don't want to sound like a caveman."

When he removed it, she wrapped her arms around him. "I have no problem with being a cavewoman, and I claim you as mine, Shai."

He lifted his head and gazed down at her. "I'm yours. Now and always."

46

MEY

"We are almost there." Yamanu tugged on Mey's hand, helping her up the steep outcropping their group had to surmount on the way to the school.

"I'm okay. You don't have to fuss over me."

He grinned, his teeth gleaming in the moonlight. "That's my job, my love."

"I took a nap in the limo on the way back from the city. I'm more worried about you. How are you going to keep the thrall all night?"

"With no problem whatsoever." He leaned closer to whisper in her ear. "No sex for two days left me with plenty of energy reserves."

"Poor baby," she whispered back. "We'll make up for lost time when we get home."

"I can't wait."

Neither could she. Because of the mission, they had paused their potion-taking regimen, which meant that they would have to start from the beginning when they got back. Merlin had said that it was actually good to take a break and let the body rest for a while.

Hopefully, the next round would result in conception. Lifting her eyes heavenward, Mey offered a silent prayer to the Fates, beseeching them for their help.

"I'm glad that Stella and Jin had decided to stay in the hotel for tonight's mission," Yamanu said. "The men will have less to worry about."

Mey nodded her agreement. "Me too."

After a day of sightseeing, which had turned out to be quite interesting despite being just a cover for their stay in the area, Jin had surprised Mey, saying that she was too tired for the long trek on foot to the school. Since she stayed behind, Stella had been forced to do so as well. Naturally, Richard didn't want to leave Stella unprotected and volunteered to sit the mission out too. Jin had objected to that vehemently, saying that she had more fighting experience than he had, which was true.

Mey would have felt better if Jay or Alfie had stayed to guard her sister and Stella, but they were needed to keep her and Yamanu safe while they did their thing.

Both Mey's and Yamanu's tasks required full concentration, leaving them exposed, and someone had to watch over them while they were at it.

The truth was that Mey was tired as well, but she had a job to do, and there was no one who could do it for her.

When they reached the school, Yamanu left her side and went to the same spot he'd stayed hidden in the night before and cast his thrall.

They waited a few more minutes, leaving only when Yamanu's nod confirmed that they were okay to go.

"Let's try the other dorm building this time," Arwel suggested. "Maybe you'll have better luck there."

"Sure," Mey agreed readily, "If the other dorm was used for something else, I might hear some of the Kra-ell interacting with the humans."

Arwel huffed out a breath. "According to Emmett, the purebloods barely interacted with the half-breeds. They probably didn't deign to speak to the humans."

"They had to. How else were they breeding with the females?" It sounded so wrong, but there was no nice way to phrase it.

Arwel grimaced. "With mind control, no talking is necessary."

"True."

When they entered the second dormitory building, Mey cast a quick look at the common room, which had a very similar arrangement of furniture and musical instruments to the first. There were two more floors in the building, but those might have been added later. The first floor was a safer bet.

Going down the hallway, she went to the last room, hoping that it was also an office like in the other building.

The door wasn't locked, and when she entered, she was disappointed that it was a bedroom. Only one boy was sleeping there, though, and she wondered whether his parents were super rich and had paid for him to have a room of his own. It was smaller than the others, so maybe he'd been made an outcast for some reason.

Perhaps it hadn't always been used as a bedroom, and she wouldn't have to suffer through hours of teenage drama.

The boy was a peaceful sleeper, and as she sat down on the floor and closed her eyes, the echoes started playing in her head almost immediately.

For a long while, she listened to the echoes of kids lamenting their separation from their parents, the insane workload, the cliques that refused to admit them, the power games.

Thankfully, she reached the old echoes much faster this time, but regrettably, they didn't tell any interesting stories.

"It's your turn to clean the muck in the pigsty," one man bit out. "I did that yesterday."

"So what? I didn't sit on my ass all day doing nothing. I was tending to the sheep."

When the argument escalated to a fistfight, another man with an authoritative tone threatened to report them to the supervisor, and that was how that echo ended. Then there was another fight between the same two men about a woman, with one accusing the other of always going after the ones he liked, and a third one telling them both that they were idiots. The women belonged to the monsters.

Mey found it interesting that none of the humans referred to the Kra-ell by name, not a collective name or the name of an individual. Except for the half-breed named Krag, they called them either monsters or masters. Perhaps they hadn't been told what to call their captors?

When she started feeling dizzy, Mey severed the connection with the echoes and got up.

Out in the hallway, Arwel and Jay greeted her with expectant looks.

"Anything?" Arwel asked.

Mey shook her head. "More of the same, just from a male perspective this time."

As they walked back to where Yamanu was keeping up the thrall, Mey looked at the large grassy center. "I wonder if the humans did that, I mean set the building on fire. They all referred to their captors as monsters or masters."

"What would they have gained by it?" Arwel asked. "The Kra-ell would have broken out of there."

Mey shrugged. "Humans are ingenious, and they don't appreciate being kept as slaves. They might have found out a way to knock the Kra-ell out, maybe by poisoning the animals they drank blood from, and then finished them off with the fire."

Arwel looked intrigued. "We need to question people in the area. If the humans killed their captors and escaped, people would know about it. Twenty years is not so long ago. I didn't think of the possibility before because I assumed that the Kra-ell had left and had taken the humans with them, but you might be onto something."

47

CASSANDRA

*E*dgar Bral and his wife stared at Geraldine as if they'd seen a ghost, and that was despite the red wig, the glasses, and the elaborate makeup that Cassandra had helped her mother with this morning.

"You are the spitting image of Sabina," Edgar said. "The old man will have a stroke when he sees you."

Edgar wasn't a youngster himself. The man was in his early to mid-sixties, and given the size of his belly, Cassandra couldn't picture him still working his farm. Except farmers, like other small business owners, didn't get to retire. Very few had enough saved up to be able to do that, and looking at Edgar's worn-out jeans and old truck, he wasn't one of them. Nevertheless, he and his wife were helping his uncle, which was very kind of them.

They seemed like good people.

Geraldine smoothed a hand over her wig. "Darlene told me that I looked a lot like her mother. That's how we figured out that our mothers must have been identical twins."

"That's one hell of a story." Edgar bent to lift the two grocery bags that he'd put down on the ground to shake their hands. "I knew Sabina was adopted, but I doubt even she knew that she had a twin sister. She never mentioned her."

"Our mother didn't know either. They were probably separated as babies."

"Must be." The guy's eyes shifted to Cassandra. "I assume that you two had different fathers."

"We did," Cassandra confirmed the obvious. "Shouldn't we get going?"

"Yes, we should." The guy opened the passenger door of an old pickup truck for his wife. "Maddie and I visit Rudolf every other Saturday about the same time, so he expects us. We bring him his mail and the things that he and Niki, that's his wife, ask us to get for them. But he's not expecting you."

Cassandra frowned. "I thought that you spoke with him."

"How? He doesn't have a phone. But that's okay. Niki will love seeing some fresh faces, and if she's happy, Rudolf is not going to come out with a shotgun."

"Is he militant?" Onegus asked.

"What do you mean by that?" Edgar handed his wife the two bags and closed the passenger door.

"Is he the type that shoots first and asks questions later?"

Edgar chuckled. "He's not that bad. Some of the others in their community might be less welcoming to unannounced strangers, but since you are with me, they are not going to pull out their shotguns."

Geraldine's eyes widened. "Do they really shoot at people?"

Edgar opened the driver's side door. "Not if you come in peace."

"Does he live in a bunker?" Geraldine asked.

"He has a bunker, but most of the time he lives in a cabin on top." Edgar climbed into the driver's seat. "The bunker is for an end-of-days-type of catastrophe." He winked at her. "Follow me or you'll get lost in these mountains."

"Come on." Cassandra took her mother's elbow and led her to the rented Suburban. "We don't want to get lost."

"Definitely not." Geraldine got in the back with Shai. "They shoot at strangers out here."

Shai wrapped his arm around her shoulders. "I think that Edgar was teasing."

"I wouldn't bet on it," Onegus said.

"Don't tease my mother." Cassandra elbowed him. "She's anxious enough as it is."

"Survivalists aren't that bad." Onegus smiled reassuringly at Geraldine through the rearview mirror. "They have weapons, but unless there is a real danger and they need to protect their stockpiles of supplies, they are not going to shoot at people. They also use shotguns for hunting."

"How do they support themselves?" Cassandra asked. "Do they grow their own food and make their own clothes and stuff like that?"

"Frankly, they are not so different from the clan." Onegus cast her an amused sidelong glance. "We are just much more sophisticated. The clan has an underground facility we can relocate to in case of a catastrophe, we also have stockpiles of supplies, and we generate our own electricity and provide our own water. We don't grow our own food, though, and we don't make money off tourists who want to experience the survivalist lifestyle."

"Do they rent out their bunkers to tourists?" Geraldine sounded incredulous.

"They don't live underground year-round," Onegus said. "I assume that they have cabins that they rent out as well."

Throughout their discussion, Shai hadn't said a word, which wasn't like him. With his incredible memory, the guy was like a walking, talking Wikipedia. He probably knew more about survivalists than all three of them combined.

Was he worried about meeting Geraldine's former husband?

It wouldn't be a pleasant experience for him, that was for sure, especially if their suspicions were confirmed, and Rudolf was guilty of trying to kill Geraldine.

Shai had shared with her and Onegus his theory about Geraldine's massive brain injury and how it could have explained her total amnesia, but a boating accident wasn't the only possible explanation. If Rudolf had bashed Geraldine over the head with a heavy object, he could have cracked her skull.

As a shiver ran down her spine, Cassandra wrapped her arms around herself.

"Are you cold?" Onegus asked.

"A little." Not wanting to worry her mother, she reinforced the pretense of being cold by leaning forward and closing one of the air conditioning vents. "That's better."

"I'm worried about showing up unannounced," Geraldine said. "Rudolf isn't expecting visitors and seeing me might give him quite a shock. I don't want to be responsible for his heart failing." She sighed. "Given how stunned Edgar and his wife were when they saw me, I don't look different enough."

Her mother's comment reminded Cassandra of her own culpability in a man's possible death. What would happen if her suspicions got confirmed? Would she be able to refrain from zapping Rudolf? Should she even try?

"Easy, love." Onegus reached over the console and clasped her hand. "Do we need to stop on the way for you to discharge your energy?"

She chuckled. "That would be an interesting conversation with Edgar. Hey, buddy, we need to take a pee break, and Cassandra needs to blow up some things."

"I'm serious. I don't want you going up there fully loaded."

"I'm fine." She cast him a reassuring smile. "Who knows? If we get shot at, my superpower might come in handy."

GERALDINE

*A*s Onegus parked the Suburban behind Edgar, Geraldine's heart started hammering against her rib cage.

The drive up the narrow winding road had made her anxious, her stress increasing the higher up they climbed. Normally, her coping mechanism was to bring up pleasant memories, real or imagined, but since Shai had entered her life, she couldn't do that.

The need to escape into fantasy had rarely arisen since they'd become a couple. There was no reason to rely on good memories to self-medicate when her reality was better than any of those fantasy scenarios.

Right now, though, she needed a temporary reprieve from the storm brewing in her mind, and she had nothing to latch on to.

"Breathe." Shai wrapped a supporting arm around her back. "He's a stranger, the former husband of a different woman. I'm your mate, your one and only, and I won't let anyone hurt you."

His words were like warm sunlight, chasing off the storm's dark clouds and calming the waves below.

"Thank you." She kissed the underside of his jaw. "I needed that."

"Anytime." He opened the door and got out. "Are you ready?" He offered her his hand.

Cassandra and Onegus had already gotten out and were standing next to Edgar and his wife.

Nodding, Geraldine took Shai's hand, slid over, and stepped out of the car.

The cabin's door opened, and a plump blonde squealed happily and rushed down to embrace Edgar's wife and then Edgar himself.

"Hi." She smiled at their group. "I'm Niki. Are you Edgar and Madeleine's friends come to see the crazy folks living in a bunker?"

Niki seemed like a fun person, and Geraldine liked the woman immediately, wondering why Darlene didn't. It wasn't as if Niki had taken away her father's love or had anything to do with her mother's drowning. Rudolf had married her after Darlene had gone to college.

"They want to talk to Rudolf." Edgar turned to look at Geraldine. "These two ladies are the daughters of Sabina's twin sister." He motioned for Geraldine to come forward. "One look at this lovely young woman was enough to convince me that they weren't making it up."

Niki lifted her hand to shade her eyes from the sun and gasped. "Oh, my Lord. You look exactly like her. I've never met your aunt, but I've seen pictures."

"I'm Geraldine." She offered Niki her hand. "And this is my sister, Cassandra."

"A pleasure to make your acquaintance." Niki shook their hands. "Rudolf is on the back porch." She took a quick glance behind her at the cabin. "I hope you don't mind going straight out back." She smiled apologetically. "I've just swept the floor."

"Perhaps I should go first and warn him." Edgar handed Niki the two shopping bags. "He might get a fright when he sees Geraldine here. I'll come get you when he's ready."

"Good idea." Niki nodded. "You and Maddie go ahead."

As the two went around the cabin, Niki excused herself to go put away the things Edgar and Maddie had brought her, and to make fresh lemonade.

While they waited for Edgar to return, Shai kept running soothing circles on Geraldine's back. "Remember what I told you in the car."

"I remember." She leaned her head on his arm. "You are my one and only, and you'll always have my back."

"Close enough."

"Okay." Edgar waved them over. "He's ready for you."

Geraldine smoothed her hand over her red wig, pushed her fake glasses up her nose, tugged on the hem of her plain black T-shirt, and took Shai's hand.

The pair of khaki pants she had on were loose and not flattering, making her bottom look twice as large. She didn't like looking less than her best, especially in company, and even more so with Shai, but she wasn't there to impress anyone with her good looks. Her outfit was meant to make her look as different from Sabina as possible.

But what if Sabina had been a bad dresser?

As they rounded the back corner of the house, and she got her first look at her former husband, Geraldine's jumbled thoughts screeched to a halt.

Rudolf looked well for a man in his mid-seventies. He still had a full head of hair, although it was all white, and as he rose to his feet to greet them, his posture was straight. He was in good shape for his age.

But just as it had been with Darlene, seeing him in person was like seeing a stranger. Other than curiosity, he evoked no feelings in her. Then again, he looked very different from the young man who'd stood next to her on their wedding day. Nearly four decades had passed since she'd been with him. Even if her memory loss hadn't been as catastrophic, she might have felt nothing upon seeing him.

As Rudolf's eyes met hers, they widened and then narrowed. "Edgar warned me that you look a lot like Sabina. He didn't exaggerate." Rudolf's eyes lingered on her face for a moment longer and then shifted to Cassandra. "You look familiar. Have we met before?"

49

CASSANDRA

*C*assandra had never met the old man, and she doubted that he'd read gossip magazines. But Niki seemed like the type who would. Perhaps the necessities Edgar's wife was bringing her every other Saturday included reading material of the trashy tabloid kind.

"You might have seen my picture in a magazine." She threaded her arm through Onegus. "My fiancé and I attended a charity gala and were photographed dancing together."

Rudolf shifted a calculating gaze to Onegus. "So, who's the famous one? You or your girlfriend?"

"Neither of us. Those publications probably just wanted to adorn their pages with a gorgeous woman wearing a beautiful dress. Many of the other attendees were photographed as well, but my Cassandra outshined them all. She's so striking that she's impossible to forget."

"You're making me blush." She leaned on his arm.

That got a giggle out of Niki, who'd arrived with a pitcher of lemonade and six glasses. "You are such a handsome couple." She put her tray down on the table. "No wonder they put your pictures in magazines, but we don't get any up here. So that wasn't where Rudolf could have seen you. Were you also on TV? We have that." She pointed to the tall antenna sticking out from the cabin's roof. "We know what's going on in the world." She shook her head. "But I don't like watching the news. It's all so sad."

Cassandra wasn't sure which world affairs Niki found upsetting, but they weren't there to discuss the state of the world at large. Instead, she nodded sagely and said, "Indeed," covering all possibilities.

"Please, sit down." Rudolf motioned to the wooden Adirondack chairs and matching loveseat. "I'll get more chairs from the house."

"I'll help you," Edgar offered.

As the two stepped inside, Niki sat down in the one he'd vacated and poured lemonade into their glasses. "Rudy made these chairs himself. He's so talented."

Cassandra remembered either Darlene or Roni mentioning that the guy was a carpenter. "What made you choose the survivalist lifestyle, Niki?"

"It's freedom." The woman passed the glasses around. "We need so little to live on that we can be comfortable on Rudolf's social security income. And if God forbid the unthinkable happens, we will survive. We have food stored to last us a couple of years."

If Rudolf had attempted to kill his wife for insurance money, it must have been long gone. Being a carpenter, he could have built the cabin with his own two hands, but building materials still cost money, and an underground bunker wasn't cheap to build either.

"Doesn't it get lonely?" Geraldine asked.

"Not at all. We have a large community of like-minded people up here. And if we get the itch to get out, we can drive down to one of the nearby towns, but we rarely do. Rudy doesn't like leaving the mountain."

"I don't." Rudolf put down a straight-back chair and sat down. "I have everything I need right here."

Edgar came out with two more chairs.

Cassandra put her half-empty lemonade glass on the table and turned to Rudolf. "Do you know anything about Sabina's real parents? My sister and I would love to find out whether we have more family out there."

He shook his head. "I don't."

"Did Sabina ever try to find out who they were?"

"If she did, she didn't tell me."

"How old was she when she was adopted?" Cassandra knew that there had been no twin, but she had to keep up the pretense for a little longer. "Did she remember having a sister?"

"She was a baby." Rudolf took a sip from the lemonade and then put the glass back down. "Her adoptive parents told her that her birth mother was unwed and that she had no means to raise a baby on her own. They never mentioned that there had been another baby up for adoption."

"They might not have told her the truth," Geraldine said. "Maybe they wanted to protect her feelings."

It was a good save, especially since Geraldine had sounded so sincere. But then, she might have still believed it.

"What did your mother tell you?" Niki asked. "Did her parents tell her about her twin?"

"They didn't," Cassandra rushed to answer. "They told her a similar story. Maybe that's what the adoption agency told both couples."

Niki nodded. "That makes sense. The rules were different seventy-some years ago." She snorted. "But not so different. Heck, people are being lied to by the government to this day, just about different things. There is really nothing new under the sun."

"Amen to that." Rudolf lifted his lemonade glass. "Like all those damn UFO sightings. They can't be all fake. The government has been lying to us about it for decades." He put his arm around Niki's shoulders. "When the aliens come, we will be prepared to fight for our freedom."

Cassandra had a feeling that the guy's brain was not running on all cylinders, which could be a problem when the time to thrall the truth out of him arrived. If he believed in the wild scenarios in his head, like an impending alien invasion, thralling wouldn't help because they were true to him.

In fact, the time for thralling had already arrived. Rudolf didn't have any helpful information about Sabina's birth parents, and they needed to shift the questioning to what he knew about his wife's unfortunate accident, and to find out whether he'd had a hand in it. Since Rudolf might not volunteer the information, a thrall was needed to get him to talk.

Casting a sidelong glance at Onegus, she waited until he felt her eyes on him and turned to look at her.

"It's time," she mouthed.

He nodded in agreement.

They'd discussed the legalities beforehand and had agreed that this time, Onegus would stay around and witness Shai thralling the human. He'd explained how it was possible for him to legally get away with it without attempting to stop the violation, but she hadn't followed the convoluted logic of his explanation.

The important thing was that he was going to be present in case they needed his expertise. Out of the four of them, Onegus was the only experienced interrogator.

This might be their only shot at questioning Rudolf, so it was important to get it right the first time.

In her opinion, it would have been even better if Onegus did the thralling himself, but he'd assured her that Shai was a competent thraller and that he would do the job just as well as Onegus would have.

50

SHAI

*W*hen Cassandra gave Shai the cue he'd been waiting impatiently for, he leaned forward and waited until Geraldine's ex felt his gaze and turned to look at him.

Eye contact wasn't always necessary for thralling, but it was helpful, especially if the subject was the suspicious type. Mistrustful people were more resistant to thralling, and survivalists were the definition of mistrustful and suspicious.

Not that they were wrong about the general population being overly gullible, but the measures they took to safeguard themselves against the deceit and its potential consequences were extreme. There was a difference between intelligent skepticism combined with rigorous fact-checking and living as if the end-of-days was eminent and everyone was out to get them.

Holding Rudolf's gaze, Shai smiled reassuringly, putting the man at ease. "Before coming over here, we met your daughter, Darlene. She told us that your relationship with her mother was stormy. Is that true?"

"Stormy? I wouldn't call it that." Rudolf leaned back in his chair.

"What would you call it then?" Shai asked.

"Sabina wasn't the combative type. She rarely raised her voice, and she tried to avoid confrontations at all costs."

"What kind of confrontations?" Shai increased the pressure just a smidgen.

Rudolf sighed. "She lied to cover up her indiscretions."

"Meaning?" Geraldine asked, even though she'd been told that she shouldn't while Shai held Rudolf in a thrall.

She probably couldn't help herself.

The old man's eyes shifted to her. "She was beautiful, just like you. Naturally, men found her desirable and pursued her even though she was a married woman and a mother."

The wave of guilt emanating from the guy was a red flag. Hell, it was a neon sign the size of an aircraft carrier, but Shai wasn't ready to pronounce him guilty without hearing the rest of the story.

As Geraldine leaned forward, Shai put a hand on her knee to stop her from asking more questions. He needed Rudolf to look into his eyes.

"Did an indiscretion actually happen? Or did you assume that it had because men found Sabina desirable?"

"I caught her meeting up with a man."

As Shai felt Geraldine tense, he squeezed her knee reassuringly. "Meeting as in having coffee with someone, or was it more?"

"Why are you asking him all these questions?" Niki glared at him. "Don't you see that he's hurting? Even after all these years, Sabina's betrayal still pains him. She died before he could reconcile with her, and it eats at him to this day."

Shifting his eyes from Rudolf to his wife, Shai smiled again and pushed a light thrall. "I'm only interested in finding out the truth. Besides, it's good for Rudolf to get it off his chest. He will feel lighter after sharing it with us." He turned to Edgar and his wife and silently pushed the thrall at them as well.

Staring at him with round eyes, Niki nodded. "He will feel lighter after sharing his pain with you."

"Go on, Rudolf," Shai prompted using a gentle tone. "Get it off your chest. Tell us what happened."

The man closed his eyes for a moment, then sighed. "Sabina and I, we lived modestly, but I tried to give her all the things a woman might want. She got her hair done in a fancy hair salon once a week on Fridays, and she usually went together with our neighbor Suzy." He rubbed a hand over the back of his neck. "We only had one car. It was a truck that I used for work. One of those Fridays, I happened to be in town because I needed to pick up a tool from the hardware store, and I decided to surprise her at the hair salon and take her out for lunch. The hairdresser said that she'd just left and that she'd seen her walking over to the diner across the street. I thought nothing of it and headed there thinking that she and Suzy were having lunch together. But it wasn't our neighbor sitting with my wife at the table. It was a man I'd never seen before."

Rudolf pulled out a handkerchief from his pocket and wiped the sweat off the back of his neck. "He was the most strikingly handsome guy I've ever seen in my life, better looking than any of the movie stars of the time. David Hasselhoff and Brad Pitt couldn't hold a candle to him. I was stunned, but I didn't want to jump to conclusions. I thought that maybe he was the brother or cousin of one of her friends, so I didn't storm into the place and demand explanations. I went into the barbershop next to the ladies' hair salon, and I sat in a chair that was facing the front window. I could see Sabina and the guy clearly. They were talking and smiling, but then the man got up and pulled her into his arms. They kissed each other on the cheek as if they were old lovers reunited, and I lost my shit. I tore the barber's apron off and was about to rush over there. But then they parted ways. Sabina walked down the street to the bus station, and the guy got into a fancy car and drove away."

"What did you do?" Cassandra asked.

"I decided to cool off and went back to work. I reasoned with myself that if they were lovers, he would have at least driven her home instead of letting her take the bus. When I came home that evening, I asked her who was the guy she met for lunch.

I expected her to say he was an old acquaintance or invent some other lie, but I didn't expect her to deny it completely. She said that I must have been hallucinating because she'd had lunch alone."

51

GERALDINE

*G*eraldine tried to make sense of Rudolf's story.

The man he'd described was probably the immortal who'd induced her transition, and she hadn't lied to her husband because that immortal had thralled her to forget their meeting.

But why had he invited her to lunch? Had he known that she'd transitioned and wanted to check up on her?

Things didn't add up, and for once, it wasn't because she couldn't remember all the details. Her conversation with Bridget was still fresh in her mind, as were Shai's theories. The immortal must have taken a fancy to her, and he'd wanted to enjoy her more than once.

Had he fallen in love with her?

How could he have taken her without her consent, thralling her into sharing his bed, and love her at the same time?

Maybe he was twisted.

Perhaps he was one of those Doomers who thought that there was nothing wrong with using a woman for his enjoyment, whether she was a willing participant or thralled to think that she was.

"What did you do when Sabina denied it?" Shai asked.

Rudolf rubbed his hands over his knees. "I started to doubt myself. The next day, I went to that diner and asked the waitresses if they'd seen an incredibly handsome young man having lunch with a beautiful brunette. They had no idea who I was talking about. They remembered a pretty brunette, but she had lunch alone. I thought that I was losing my mind."

The immortal must have thralled everyone at that diner to forget him. Was it even possible to thrall that many people at once?

"So that was it?" Shai asked. "You imagined her meeting up with a guy and convinced yourself that she'd been unfaithful?"

"I wish." Rudolf reached for the lemonade and gulped it down. "Over the following week, I came home unexpectedly at different times to check on her, but there was no fancy car parked in front of our home, and Sabina was there, quilting or cooking, or doing whatever else. She only left the house to get Darlene from school or to go to the grocery store. On Friday, when she went to the hair salon again, I followed my gut feeling and waited to see whether she would go straight home or meet that guy again."

As he paused to refill his glass, Geraldine couldn't help herself. "Did she?"

Rudolf nodded. "It was the same as the week before. She went into the diner where he was waiting for her, they had lunch, kissed each other on the cheek good-bye, and parted ways. The next week it was the same thing, but this time I decided to follow the guy. I parked my truck a few blocks away so Sabina wouldn't see it, and as that fancy Aston Martin of his passed me by, I followed him."

"Where did he go?" Cassandra asked.

"To the airport." Rudolf put his glass down. "I said to myself good riddance, and I decided to get the truth out of my wife. She denied it again, and that guy must have paid off every damn person working in that diner because they all swore that Sabina had been coming in every Friday and eating alone."

"And that was it?" Shai asked.

"I went to that hair salon to check on her for several weeks after that, but the guy never came back. To this day, I don't know who he was and what he and Sabina had done together."

"Maybe he was someone she'd been involved with before she met you?" Cassandra offered.

Rudolf shook his head. "He couldn't have been a lover from before we got married because she was seventeen when I met her and a virgin. That means that she was unfaithful to me during our marriage. She must have met him in one of her damn quilting competitions and had an affair with him there. She never went anywhere else without me, so that was the only place she had an opportunity to do that."

"Did she go alone to those competitions?" Onegus asked.

"I went with her when I could, but mostly she went alone. I needed to work, and I didn't mind her going because I thought they were all women there, but I was wrong. What I can't understand is why would a rich dude like him go somewhere like that."

"Maybe he was a quilt collector," Cassandra said. "And maybe there was nothing romantic between them. Those could have been business meetings, but since you were the jealous type, Sabina lied about it."

Geraldine would have liked to believe that, and if not for the induction and transition, Cassandra's theory might have been right. But someone had to induce her, and the most likely someone was that rich and good-looking guy.

"How soon after those events took place did Sabina drown?" Onegus asked.

"Five months," Rudolf said in a broken voice. "Five months of endless arguments. She was so angry at me for accusing her. But I needed to know the truth. I even told her that I would forgive her if she admitted it. She asked me if I wanted her to lie and invent a lover just so we could put the entire thing to rest and go on with our lives."

Rudolf sounded so despondent, so broken that Geraldine felt sorry for him.

From the way he'd told it, that dreadful immortal had ruined a good marriage. But according to Darlene, the strife between her parents had been part of their marriage for much longer than those turbulent months that preceded her so-called accident. Rudolf was either romanticizing the past or trying to paint himself in more favorable colors.

Nevertheless, even though she was certain that she'd been coerced into the affair because there was no way she'd willingly have cheated on her husband, Geraldine still felt guilty.

5 2

SHAI

*R*udolf was either a superb actor or had convinced himself that he'd done everything right over the years.

Shai couldn't find fault with any of Rudolf's actions. If he were in the guy's shoes, he would have been much less understanding. He would have marched into that diner and demanded explanations. Perhaps he would have been polite about it the first time, but after the denial and the repeated meetings, he would have been much less so.

Especially since he knew much more than Rudolf about what had been going on. The immortal had to have thralled Sabina and everyone else in that diner to forget him, and he had probably thralled her during one of those quilting competitions she'd attended to have sex with him as well.

Or maybe not.

If Sabina had been anything like Geraldine, then she'd been a passionate and flirtatious woman. Still, he couldn't imagine her being unfaithful. She just wasn't that kind of person.

However, what happened with that immortal and how it had happened was a different investigation. Right now, he wanted to find out whether Rudolf had a hand in Geraldine's accident, and if he had, how he was going to end him as painfully as possible.

"Did you kill Sabina?" he asked point-blank.

Niki gasped, and Rudolf looked as if he'd been punched in the gut.

"I loved Sabina. I would have never hurt her."

Shai increased the pressure to where it was reaching a dangerous level, but he needed that one question answered truthfully. "And yet she drowned five months after you caught her meeting with the guy."

"It was my fault." Tears glistened in Rudolf's eyes. "It was a Sunday, and we took Darlene to the beach. I thought that a family outing would be nice, but somehow the conversation in the car went from civil to ugly, and by the time we got to the beach,

Sabina was fuming." He let out a shuddering breath. "As soon as we put the blanket down on the sand, she went for a swim. She was a good swimmer, so I didn't worry too much when she didn't return right away. But when an hour passed and then another, I started panicking and sounded the alarm. The lifeguard radioed the coast-guard, and they searched for her the rest of the day. By nightfall, I knew that she was gone even though her body was never found. What I can't forgive myself for is that our last words to each other were angry."

There was no way Rudolf could have lied with such a heavy thrall forcing him to tell the truth, but there was always a small chance that he'd rewritten history in his mind.

Reaching in, Shai almost choked on the intensity of the guy's anguish. With the memory freshly retrieved, he could see Rudolf trying to comfort the twelve-year-old Darlene while he himself had been barely holding it together.

The scene was so emotionally charged that Shai couldn't stand being in the guy's mind for any longer than absolutely necessary. As soon as he was convinced that what he'd seen were the actual events of that day, he pulled out and released Rudolf from the thrall.

The guy sagged in his chair. "I don't know why I told you all of that. I've never even told Niki the whole story."

"It's therapeutic to get things off your chest," Geraldine said softly. "Even though it was a sad story, I'm glad that you told it."

Maddie wiped tears from her eyes, and Edgar looked like he would rather be anywhere but there.

Geraldine pushed to her feet first. "We should go. This has been an emotional day, and Rudolf looks like he needs some peace and quiet."

The rest of them followed her up, and after handshakes and hugs, they parted from the couple and headed to the front of the house.

"That was intense," Edgar said. "How could you have asked Rudolf if he killed his wife?"

Shai shrugged. "Don't tell me that the thought never crossed your mind."

"It didn't. I know my uncle. He might be rough and gruff, but he's a good man."

"Crimes of passion are often committed by people you would never have expected to harm a fly. I'm just glad that Rudolf didn't do it."

"Did you believe him?" Maddie asked hesitantly.

"I did. It happened exactly as he told it."

"How can you be sure?"

Shai tapped the side of his nose. "I can sniff out lies, and Rudolf wasn't lying."

That seemed to satisfy Madeleine even though it shouldn't have.

She let out a breath. "Good to know. It would have been awful if Edgar and I had been helping a murderer for all these years."

53

CASSANDRA

*C*assandra waited for Onegus to pull the Suburban out of its impromptu parking spot and follow Edgar's truck before turning to look at Shai. "You were in his head. Was he telling the truth?"

"He was. I took a look at his memories from that day, and the guy was frantic, barely holding it together for Darlene's sake. Given how macho he tries to look, I don't think those could have been fabricated memories. A guy like him would have liked to think that he'd handled the situation better."

Cassandra nodded. "I thought so too." She shifted her eyes to her mother, who looked perturbed. "What's your take, Mom? Was he telling the truth?"

"I think so." Geraldine's eyes were slightly unfocused. "If you are wondering whether seeing Rudolf evoked any emotions in me, the answer is no. Logically, I knew that he used to be my husband, but I didn't feel it in my heart. It was like looking at and listening to a stranger."

"Then why do you look so troubled?"

Geraldine sighed. "I learned nothing today that could make me feel good about myself, and witnessing the pain Rudolf still carries with him after all these years was heart-wrenching."

Cassandra wasn't as soft-hearted as her mother, and throughout most of the interrogation, she'd still suspected Rudolf of arranging Geraldine's accident. At the end, though, she'd felt sorry for him as well. His wife's presumed death had traumatized him, and nearly four decades later, he still hadn't fully recovered.

"At least now, we know for sure that you were induced before your memory loss."

"We kind of knew that before." Geraldine looked out the window, and for a moment, Cassandra thought that she was done, but then she continued. "There are only two possible explanations for what happened with that immortal, and both of them are bad. In one, I was an unfaithful wife having an affair with an attractive immortal and lying about it to my husband's face. In the other, I was basically violated because thralling an unwilling woman to have sex is the same as drugging her or coercing her, and those are all different forms of rape."

Onegus tipped his head up and looked at Geraldine through the rearview mirror. "If he was a Doomer, the second option is more likely. But if he was an unaffiliated immortal who didn't follow the clan's rules of conduct and safety protocol, the first one is possible. He fell in love, wanted to keep seeing his beloved, and he didn't know that repeated thralling is dangerous to humans."

"Maybe he was the one who tried to kill me," Geraldine murmured. "Because it wasn't Rudolf."

Shai arched a brow. "Why do you think anyone tried to kill you? It might have happened exactly as I theorized. You were angry at Rudolf, went for a long swim, and were hit by a speedboat. The driver either didn't see you at all, or did see you and left you for dead."

Looking depressed, Geraldine shrugged. "It's possible."

Knowing her mother, Cassandra feared that she was about to spiral into one of her moods. It hadn't happened since Shai had entered her life, but it had happened enough times before for her to recognize the signs.

Geraldine wasn't always full of smiles and sunshine.

Onegus lifted his eyes to the rearview mirror again to look at the passengers in the backseat. "Did you see the immortal when you entered Rudolf's mind?"

Shai shook his head. "When I dove in, his mind was full of memories from the day his wife drowned. They were so saturated with anguish that I didn't want to linger any longer than I had to. All I wanted was to find out whether he tried to kill my mate. I'm glad that he didn't because I would have hated to make Niki a widow. Despite Darlene's opinion of her, she seems like a nice person."

"That's a shame," Onegus said. "I wondered how vividly Rudolf remembered the guy after so long. If he can still see the immortal clearly in his mind, we can have Tim draw the guy from Rudolf's memory. If it's good enough, we might be able to run it through the facial recognition software."

In the back seat, Shai groaned. "You know Tim. He will demand your firstborn as payment."

Onegus chuckled. "Not mine. Yours. You're paying for him."

"Who's Tim?" Geraldine asked.

"He's a forensic artist that works in Andrew's office," Shai said. "Roni knows him too. We used him before, and the portraits he produces from people's descriptions are phenomenally accurate. It's like he has a paranormal talent for that."

"Maybe he does?" Cassandra turned in her chair so she wouldn't have to crane her neck looking at Shai and her mother. "Did anyone test him? He might be a Dormant."

Both Shai and Onegus chuckled.

"It was suggested before," Onegus said. "But given the guy's personality, no one is in a rush to offer him membership in our exclusive club."

Cassandra folded her arms over her chest. "I didn't know that a Dormant needed to be likable to get induced. Is there a committee that decides who gets invited and who doesn't?"

"Not really." Onegus took her hand in his. "Let's revisit this topic after you have spent some time with Tim. You might come to see things differently."

54

ONEGUS

"Are we going to ask the forensic artist to come here and give it a try?" Geraldine asked. "I think that Rudolf remembers the immortal quite vividly. I just don't know if, after thirty-six years, the image didn't get distorted in his mind."

Cassandra turned to look at her mother. "The better question to ask is how are we going to convince Rudolf to work with Tim." She chuckled. "We can't just show up on his doorstep with Tim."

"We will have to use Edgar again," Onegus said. "And you can leave the convincing to me."

"Are you going to thrall him?" Geraldine asked. "I thought that you are not allowed."

"An unaffiliated immortal on the loose is a security issue, which means that I can thrall him. But I hope it won't be necessary." He smiled at Geraldine through the rearview mirror. "I doubt he would be able to resist a request from you."

Given her expression, Cassandra didn't seem to share his opinion. "We will probably need to come back in two weeks when Edgar visits Rudolf and Niki again. You need to talk to the forensic artist and find out if he's available that Saturday."

"Not necessary." Onegus cast her a sidelong glance. "Perhaps I can get him here this weekend. I don't want to wait two weeks. Onegus activated his phone's virtual assistant. "Call Andrew Spivak."

"Calling Andrew Spivak," the Scottish-sounding artificial female voice confirmed.

Cassandra arched a brow. "Your automated voice lady sounds sexy."

"She does, doesn't she?" He winked at her.

She opened her mouth to say something when Andrew answered the phone. "Onegus, what can I do for you?"

"I need Tim." Onegus went straight to the point. "Can you ask him how soon he can get here?"

"By here, I assume that you mean Tulsa International Airport?"

"Correct. I can pick him up from the airport, so there is no need to give him more details."

"It's the weekend, so he should be free, but he'll demand an arm and a leg."

"We know," Shai said from the back seat. "I'll pay for it."

"Let me check with him first and see how much he wants to charge for the service. How many portraits are we talking about?"

"Just one," Onegus said. "But it's a long drive to Geraldine's ex's place. Tim needs to dedicate at least half a day to this project."

"I'll call you right back." Andrew ended the call.

It was a pleasure to work with the guy. He was a professional, and he didn't waste time by asking whose portrait Tim was about to draw or why. It wasn't a secret, and Onegus would gladly share the story with Kian's brother-in-law, but it could wait.

Cassandra shifted in her seat, tucking one long leg under her bottom. "If that Tim guy is so good, you should have his phone number in your contacts list."

"I do, but since Tim is a government employee, and we know him through Andrew, it wouldn't feel right calling him directly."

His phone rang a few moments later.

"Tim will happily hop on the first flight he can catch to Tulsa in exchange for twenty-five thousand dollars and all expenses paid, including a business-class ticket so he can sleep on the plane on his way back."

A gasp escaped Geraldine's throat. "No way."

"Tell him it's a deal," Shai said.

"I'll call him right now." Andrew ended the call.

Cassandra turned to look at Shai. "That's an obscene amount for one day's work. You shouldn't agree to it."

"Tim knows that he's one of a kind and can ask any price," Onegus said. "No one can do what he does."

"Still." Cassandra crossed her arms over her chest. "You should negotiate. I'm sure Tim expects it. Besides, I don't know what good that portrait is going to do us."

"I admit that I'm curious to see the portrait," Geraldine said. "I wonder if it will evoke any reaction in me, but I don't want you wasting so much money on it. You have better things to spend it on."

Onegus wondered what those things might be. Shai had been Kian's assistant for the past twenty years or so, and he wasn't a big spender. He should have more than enough saved up.

"We don't have any other clues," Shai said. "We've exhausted everything Darlene and Rudolf know, but we aren't any closer to solving this mystery. If we can gain some additional insight from that portrait, it would be money well spent."

Onegus had a feeling that Shai wanted to see what his potential rival looked like.

Someone had been buying Geraldine's quilts for much more than they were worth, and that same someone had probably also helped her in other ways, like the fake IDs she'd needed.

The prime suspect was that immortal, and the guy probably wasn't a Doomer. It seemed like he cared for Geraldine and had stayed in touch with her over the years, which was not typical Doomer behavior. She didn't remember him because he'd thralled away her memories of him, but Annani might be able to retrieve them, especially if Geraldine had seen him recently.

As the call from Andrew came in, Onegus answered using the car's speakers. "What do you have for me?"

"Tim booked the first American Airlines flight leaving Los Angeles at six o'clock tomorrow morning and landing the same morning at Tulsa at eleven o'clock local time."

"Perfect. We will pick him up from the airport."

"Is there anything else you need from me?" Andrew asked.

"That's all. I appreciate your help with getting Tim out here. Thank you."

"Anytime. Good luck."

"Thanks." Onegus ended the call.

"How are we going to let Rudolf know that we are coming back?" Cassandra asked. "If we come back without Edgar, he might start shooting before you have a chance to thrall him."

"Then we get Edgar to escort us back." Onegus turned on the blinker and flashed the SUV's lights to signal for Edgar to pull over.

"What about Darlene?" Geraldine asked. "We were supposed to be back tonight and meet her tomorrow in the afternoon. We won't be able to make it."

"I'll call her and cancel." Cassandra pulled out her phone. "This is far more important."

55

GERALDINE

*E*dgar hadn't been happy about turning around and driving all the way back to Rudolf's place, but Onegus had somehow charmed him into agreeing. Geraldine had heard him promise Edgar and his wife a fancy dinner in town the following day, so maybe he'd managed to do so without even thralling the guy.

This time around, she was much less nervous when Onegus parked the SUV behind Edgar's truck. If Rudolf refused to have the forensic artist come to his cabin, Shai would have to thrall him into agreeing, but hopefully her charm alone would do the trick, and that wouldn't be necessary.

Shai had admitted to using a strong thrall to get Rudolf talking, and doing that again so soon after the first time could damage his mind.

Rudolf opened the door and stepped out. "Did you folks forget something?"

Geraldine walked up to him and smiled sweetly. "I need to ask you for a favor, and it would mean a great deal to me if you agree."

He regarded her for a long moment before nodding. "Come on out back, and I'll hear you out, but I can't promise to agree before I know what it's about."

"Of course. That's all I ask."

As they walked back to the other side of the house, they found Niki still sitting in the same spot they'd left her.

"Well, hello there." She smiled. "When I heard the cars pull up, I told Rudy that you must have forgotten something. I didn't see anything, so it must be something small. An earring, perhaps?"

"We didn't forget anything." Geraldine sat next to her. "We just thought about something on the way."

"I'll explain," Onegus said. "We talked about the guy Sabina was meeting, and from what Rudolf told us the two didn't behave like lovers. They acted more like old acquaintances, or maybe even relatives."

That wasn't at all what they'd been saying, but apparently lying wasn't against clan law, and Onegus had no problem with weaving a fake story.

"What of it?" Rudolf asked.

"We thought that he might have been another sibling neither of the sisters knew about. You said that he was good-looking, and so were Sabina and her sister. He might have found out who their birth parents were and tracked down Sabina."

Rudolf frowned. "Why would she lie about it?"

"Maybe he was a wanted man?" Niki suggested. "She might not have wanted to be associated with him, or maybe he asked her not to mention him to anyone and paid off the people working in that diner."

Onegus nodded in agreement. "That could be a possible explanation. You said that the guy looked rich and drove a very expensive car. He might have been a drug or weapons dealer. Those people make shitloads of money. But all we can do is guess. The thing is, we would like to find the guy, and you might be able to help us with that."

Rudolf narrowed his eyes at Onegus. "How?"

"Do you know what a forensic artist is?"

"I think so."

"It's someone who can draw a portrait from a verbal description. I know a guy who is exceptionally talented at that. In fact, he is so talented that he can draw a portrait accurate enough to run through facial recognition software. If you remember the man Sabina was meeting with vividly and can describe him to my friend, we might be able to find the guy."

Rudolf waved a dismissive hand. "It was thirty-six years ago. He won't look the same now. He might even be dead."

"True," Onegus agreed. "But Tim can age the portrait." He leaned forward. "Wouldn't it be a huge relief for you to find out that the man your wife was meeting with was her brother and not her lover?"

Yes, it would.

For one silly moment, Geraldine felt hope flare in her heart. If only that was true, and she hadn't been an unfaithful wife.

But there was no brother, and there was no twin sister. It was just a story Onegus was inventing for Rudolf's benefit.

"When can your friend get here?" Niki asked.

"Tomorrow after lunch, if that's okay with you two."

Rudolf nodded. "I doubt you'd be able to find the guy just by having a portrait of him done that shows how he looked decades ago, but if you do, and he turns out to be Sabina's brother, or even a cousin, it would be a great relief. I would finally be able to put her memory to rest and stop obsessing about whether she'd cheated on me or not. The not knowing is the worst part." He lifted his eyes to Geraldine. "Seeing you reminded me how much I loved Sabina. You look so much like her."

"I'm sorry if it causes you pain."

He shook his head. "It doesn't. Darlene looks more like me than her mother. She's a good-looking woman, but she is not Sabina. I'm glad that her beauty was preserved in her niece."

When he said things like that, Geraldine could understand why her young self had fallen in love with him, or rather why Sabina had. There was a soft heart under the roughness, and the dichotomy made Rudolf interesting.

5 6

ARWEL

*J*in slung the strap of her purse over her shoulder and followed Arwel out the door. "Are you leaving anyone behind to guard Mey and Yamanu?"

The two were exhausted after their night's work and needed the sleep.

"Alfie is going to stay with them." He walked over to Richard and Stella's room and knocked on the door. "Normally, I wouldn't have offended Yamanu by leaving a guy to guard him while he slept, but with the amount of energy he and Mey have used up over the past two nights, I figured he wouldn't be as alert as he usually is, even when asleep."

"My thoughts exactly. Is Alfie going to stand by their door?"

"It's enough that he leaves his open. Theirs is only two doors down from his and Jay's room."

Richard opened the door. "Stella is almost ready. We will meet you in the lobby."

Arwel waited until they were all inside the limo before explaining Mey's theory. "If the humans killed off the Kra-ell, they escaped with their memories intact, and since it happened only a little over two decades ago, some of the town folks should remember that."

Stella shook her head. "If I was one of those humans, I wouldn't have stayed in the area. I would have run as far away as I could, and since China is huge, that would have been really far."

"The thought has occurred to me, but there is no harm in asking."

"Except for the thralling," Jay murmured. "Is it authorized in this context?"

"Of course, it is. The Kra-ell are a potential threat to the clan, and everything we do here is related to finding out as much as we can about them."

Jay shrugged. "I have no problem with that. There are many gray areas in the directive of not thralling humans for advantage, and sometimes I'm not sure when it's okay and when it's not."

That was why civilians could get away with thralling unless they grossly misused it and were caught. Guardians were held to higher standards.

"Where to, boss?" Morris asked.

Arwel and Jin had already done a short walkabout of the town's center and had talked with several people, but no one remembered anything about the compound before it had become a school.

There was another town nearby that was closer to the compound, but since it didn't have a hotel, they had to stay farther away.

He pulled out his phone and showed the map to Morris. "Ginje is closer to the compound. Maybe someone over there remembers the fire."

Less than an hour later, when Morris parked the limo on the main road cutting through the small town, people gawked at it as if it were an alien craft.

From his prior experience in the other town, Arwel knew that just asking wasn't going to yield any results. People were wary of strangers, and almost nobody spoke English. Picking into their memories hadn't been helpful either. Jin had asked if they remembered seeing a fire, but all he'd gotten were memories of burning wood in the winter months. Then again, Jin's command of the language might not have been good enough, and Arwel preferred having Stella and Morris ask the questions and also peek into the people's memories.

"Do you mind staying in the limo?" Stella asked. "I need a few minutes alone in the grocery store. People will be less guarded with just me there."

"Go ahead." Arwel opened the door for her. "Take as long as you need."

"She's right," Jin said as Stella walked into the store. "There are too many of us. Maybe I should have gone alone before too." She smiled at Arwel. "I blend in."

As if he would have let her roam the streets alone. "You're too beautiful to blend in."

She chuckled. "Too tall as well. Shandong is where all the tall Chinese live."

"Where is that?" Jay asked.

"It's a coastal province in the east."

A full twenty minutes passed before Stella exited the grocery store with two canvas bags filled with produce.

"The more I bought, the chattier the old lady got." Stella put the bags on the floor between the seats. "She told me an interesting story. She remembered a fire on a nearby farm twenty-some years ago. She lives on the edge of town, and she woke up in the middle of the night because she heard a sheep baying and looked out the window. She saw a distant fire and a bunch of sheep trotting down the street. The next day, she asked around if anyone had seen anything, and someone told her that a barn had caught fire on one of the neighboring farms, and the animals had been set loose. She asked about the people, but no one knew what happened to them. Someone said that he saw several migrant workers passing through the town in the early morning hours."

"Did you reach into her memories?" Arwel asked.

"I did. She told me all that she knew. There was nothing else in there."

"She might have been thralled," Jin said. "If the Kra-ell weren't killed by the humans like I hypothesized before, and the fire was a way to destroy evidence of them being here, they might have thralled people to forget them before leaving the area."

Arwel nodded. "It's possible, but after so long, there is no way to retrieve those memories. Besides, despite what Emmett said about their leader, I doubt that she was able to thrall the entire town at once. Her power might have worked on the animals, but not on so many humans."

"What do you mean?" Jin frowned. "Why would she thrall animals? I wasn't aware that it was even possible."

"According to Emmett, the Kra-ell use something that is part thrall and part compulsion to hunt. The strong ones can control entire herds. Humans are not herd animals, though."

She chuckled. "I'm not sure about that."

5 7

S H A I

*S*hai hadn't liked the way Geraldine had embraced Rudolf before leaving him the second time that day. He hadn't liked the fond smile she'd given her former husband either.

It was irrational, Shai was well aware of that, but then there was nothing rational about jealousy. It was an unpleasant feeling that he didn't know how to process or get rid of, and he also didn't know how to pretend that everything was okay.

"What's bugging you?" Geraldine asked as they entered their hotel room. "You've been brooding the entire drive back here."

"I wasn't brooding. I was just thinking." He sat down on the bed and took his shoes off.

I'm such a miserable liar.

"What were you thinking about?" She plopped into his lap and wrapped her arms around his neck.

"About Tim drawing the portrait tomorrow. I wonder what the guy looked like."

"Yeah, me too." She leaned her head on his chest. "What if he kept seeing me after I recovered from the accident and thralling me to remember him as other men?" She lifted her head and looked at him with worried eyes. "What if he's Cassandra's father?"

"He couldn't have been Cassandra's father. Rudolf compared the guy to David Hasselhoff and Brad Pitt, not Denzel Washington."

"Right." Geraldine let out a breath. "My mind is not working right." She then smiled coquettishly. "I'm a big fan of Denzel. He's such a sexy man. I wouldn't have minded if he were Cassandra's dad. I also liked Harry Belafonte and Sidney Poitier."

Shai grimaced. "Denzel is no longer as good-looking as he used to be. The other two were sixty when Cassandra was born. How come you had crushes on such old movie stars? You shouldn't remember them as young and handsome."

Was that proof that not all of her memories were gone?

Geraldine cupped his cheek. "I like watching old movies. Is that a crime?"

365

He was going insane.

"It's not." Shai let out a breath. "I didn't like it when you hugged Rudolf," he admitted. "Has he evoked any feelings in you the second time around?"

"Oh, sweetie." She cupped his other cheek as well. "Is that what got you so upset? What I felt for Rudolf was not the kind of feelings that would make you jealous. It was pity. He carries so much guilt around because he's still angry at Sabina for betraying him, and he hates himself for his inability to forgive her. I wish that handsome man he saw with me was my brother or cousin or uncle. Anyone except for a lover. But I know he had to be, or I wouldn't have transitioned into immortality."

"It might not have been your fault. You might have been thralled."

Geraldine let go of his cheeks and slumped against his chest. "I thought about that, and it's not likely. If he was that type of man, he wouldn't have hung around to be with me. And since I was a virgin when I met Rudolf, that immortal couldn't have induced me before I started dating my future husband." She sighed. "I could keep wishing that it's not true, that I had a twin sister who married Rudolf and then cheated on him, but I have to accept that I'm not the same person I was before the accident. Re-growing a big chunk of my brain apparently came with a change in personality because Sabina was capable of things Geraldine would never have done."

Shai wished he could believe that as wholeheartedly as she did, but Geraldine wasn't as different from Sabina as she thought she was.

The woman who called herself Geraldine had never been married. She'd had a child with a casual lover, one among many, and given her swiss cheese memory, she could have been seeing more than one man at a time without even being aware of doing that or remembering it.

But all of that shouldn't matter to him. What Geraldine had done before meeting him had no bearing on their relationship, and he shouldn't dwell on her past transgressions, real or imagined. That made him no better than Rudolf, who nearly forty years later was still obsessing about his wife's betrayal.

Regrettably though, Shai was just as bad, and he didn't like discovering that about himself. The truth was that he would have felt better if Geraldine moved into the village, where no other male would approach her knowing that she was his, but she kept refusing.

Was that why she refused to move in with him?

Was she seeing other men during the day when she knew he was at work?

Fates, he was just as psychotic as that old man—an old man who was actually the same age as Shai.

Perhaps they were both a product of their generation, the movies and novels that had portrayed women as fickle and unreliable. Except Shai was raised in the clan, which should have made him immune to the influences of films and books of that era.

Then again, Geraldine had a history of disloyalty...

Damn, he really needed to talk to Vanessa and have her help him get rid of the gut-clenching, ugly feelings of suspicion and jealousy.

Geraldine frowned. "Why are you shaking your head?"

He couldn't tell her why. Not only would he offend her, but he would also lose her respect. Confident people didn't entertain doubts like that about their partners unless they had concrete and irrefutable proof. Jealousy was a sign of insecurity, of thinking that they weren't good enough, that they weren't worth their partners' love and devotion, that they hadn't earned it.

Instead, Shai did the only thing that could give him reprieve from the storm swirling in his head.

He cupped the back of her neck and smashed his lips over hers.

58

GERALDINE

*S*hai's kiss wasn't about passion, it was about possession, and Geraldine was perfectly fine with that.

They were both troubled by the day's discoveries, and there was no better way to put the demons of jealousy and guilt to rest than having hot, mindless sex to reaffirm their connection.

In a matter of seconds, the kiss morphed into uncontrollable lust that burned hot in her veins, and sometime during that whirlwind of passion, Shai had gotten rid of her clothes.

Caging her between his arms, he scraped a fang down the side of her neck, then licked the slight ache he'd left behind, soothing it. He wasn't going to be gentle with her, and that was fine as well.

As Geraldine closed her eyes and surrendered to the slow torment, one of Shai's hands closed over her breast while the other skimmed over her stomach and then slid between her legs. She held her breath as she waited for him to touch the pulsating bundle of nerves that was starving for his touch, but when he reached it, he only brushed the pads of his fingers against it.

The slight touch didn't provide the relief she needed, but it was enough to send a shiver up her spine and wrestle a throaty moan out of her.

As he lightly stroked between her legs, his fingers curled around her nipple, pinching it while nipping her neck.

With what Shai's erotic torment was doing to her, with how wet she was and how restlessly her bottom churned over his groin, Geraldine was sure that his fine slacks wouldn't survive, but even though he must have felt the wetness, he didn't seem to care. She was hovering on the edge of a climax, but he was very adept at keeping her close to the edge without allowing her to tumble over.

He slipped a finger inside her and commanded, "Open your eyes. Watch what I do to you." He added another finger and pumped both in and out of her.

It was both erotic and embarrassing to watch. As she lifted her eyes to his face, his smile was absolutely wicked and he brushed his thumb over that most sensitive spot. When she uttered a needy mewl, the smile tuned into a grin.

"You want more of this?" He traced slow circles around that spot while avoiding touching it directly.

"Please," she breathed.

"How can I refuse such a heartfelt request?" He kept circling her bud with those maddening feather-light fingertips.

"Shai," she panted.

"Yes, my love?" The maddening circles continued.

He was taunting her, and she'd been waiting patiently, but her patience ran out. Geraldine wasn't assertive in bed, she rather liked it when Shai took control, but she'd had enough.

Twisting in his lap, she pushed on his chest until his back hit the mattress, and then she attacked his belt buckle and the zipper of his slacks, her restless fingers doing a quick job of opening things up.

As he smiled and stretched his arms over his head, his eyes blazed with inner light and his fangs flashed white in his mouth. "I was wondering when you'd snap."

"You're evil." She pulled the slacks down his thighs and then did the same to his boxer briefs.

His erection sprang out from its confinement, standing up like a flagpole from his hips.

The things she could do with that. But right now there was only one thing that would satisfy the hungry ache, and she intended to get it without further delay.

Placing a knee on each side of his hips, she took hold of the velvety mast and lowered herself slowly until the tip breached her entrance. Then she let go, braced her hands on his chest, and sank all the way down.

They both groaned, and Geraldine's eyes rolled back in her head. Shai's might have done the same, but she was too overwhelmed with the sensation of their joining to check.

"You are mine," he hissed as he curled his hand around her neck and brought her head down to crush his lips onto hers.

"Yes," she murmured into his mouth as she lifted and sank onto him again.

As he let go of her mouth and neck so she could move faster, she clutched his shoulders for purchase and got into the rhythm of lifting and lowering herself on his magnificent erection.

Geraldine's thighs burned from the effort, and she was glad when Shai gripped her hips and took over. Lifting her as if she weighed nothing and lowering her onto his length, his hips came up on a roll, hitting the right spot with each powerful upward thrust.

As the coil inside her tightened, she readied for the climax, but then he gripped her bottom, lifted to a sitting position, and kissed her. With the thrusting momentarily halted, the momentum was lost, and she was no longer on the edge of the precipice.

Not that she minded.

The way Shai was kissing her was better than any orgasm he could give her. He was pouring his soul into the kiss, and as his fingers fisted her hair, she was sure he was about to bite her. Instead, he held her to him as though he would never let her go and then tugged on her hair, forcing her to look into his glowing eyes.

"Tell me that you're mine, Geraldine."

"I'm yours," she whispered. "Forever."

59

SHAI

"*A*gain," Shai demanded.

"I'm yours." Geraldine rocked on top of his shaft. "And you are mine."

"You'd better believe it." He lifted her off his lap and flipped her down on her belly. "And this is all mine too." He lightly slapped her ass.

Not missing a beat, she lifted her bottom, and as he gripped her hips and surged into her from behind, slamming home with one powerful thrust, she threw her head back and groaned.

She was so beautiful from every angle, passionate and uninhibited, his perfect match that no computer could have chosen for him.

The Fates had brought them together, and he needed to remember that when doubt and jealousy reared their ugly heads. Geraldine was his, and he was hers, and nothing was going to change that—not a former husband, and not her former lovers.

From the moment their eyes had met at the café, their fate had been sealed.

His hips grinding into her rear, he folded his body on top of hers and snaked an arm under her. "I love you." He held her tightly to him and kissed her neck.

Turning her head, she caught his lips, kissing him hungrily until neither of them had another breath left in their lungs, and she had to let go. "I love you too, but I need you to move."

"Your wish is my command." He started a punishing tempo.

Pounding into her with the kind of abandon he could have never allowed himself with a human, Shai felt liberated, relieved, and lighthearted.

As he and Geraldine moved in perfect synchronization, their bodies and souls entwined in the most beautiful way, the reasons for his bad mood seemed so silly.

The only thing still missing was the bond, but he wasn't going to dwell on it while he was making love to his mate. She was his, with or without the bond.

"Now, Shai." She turned her head, elongating her neck.

As venom drops slithered down his fangs, her sheath rippled around his shaft, triggering his own climax. When he sank them into her welcoming flesh, she hissed in pain, but a split second later another climax rippled through her, and then another, and another, until they both collapsed exhausted on their sides.

Some of the euphoria she felt must have infiltrated his senses, or maybe he'd swallowed some of his own venom, but Shai was floating on a cloud as if he'd been bitten and not the other way around. Still joined, they both drifted away.

When sometime later a knock sounded at their door, he didn't know whether minutes or hours had passed.

"We are going to the hotel's restaurant for dinner and then to the bar," Onegus said. "Are you going to join us?"

Geraldine stirred in Shai's arms. "I'm hungry, but I also need to shower."

"We will be there in half an hour." Shai pulled out gently, soaking the sheet under them.

He would have to call housekeeping and have them change the bedding.

"See you there," Onegus called out.

Turning toward him, Geraldine smiled sheepishly. "Do you think that they heard us?"

He cupped her bottom. "I'm sure of it, but I don't care."

"I do." Geraldine raked her fingers over the sparse hairs on his chest. "Cassandra shouldn't hear her mother making love."

"What do you think people did when entire families shared one room?"

She scrunched her nose. "Keep very quiet?"

"I doubt that it was possible every time. I'm sure that children were used to hearing their parents making love."

"Maybe people did it outside? Under the stars?"

"Or on the roof?" He tapped her bottom. "Let's continue this fascinating discussion in the shower."

The corners of Geraldine's lips lifted in a small smile. "If we shower together, there is no way we will make it in time to have dinner with Onegus and Cassandra."

"Then they will have to dine without us."

Her expression turning serious, she regarded him with worry in her eyes. "Are you feeling better now?"

There was no point in denying that he hadn't felt okay before. "I am. Whatever happened before should stay in the past. We need to focus on the future."

"Then why are we bothering with this investigation? Why is it so important to find out how I lost my memory and who my inducer was?"

"Aside from needing to know what happened to you, and whether I need to kill anyone to avenge you, we also need to find the immortal who induced you. An unaffiliated immortal might be part of a community we don't know exists. He could be a friend or a foe to the clan, and we need to find out everything we can about him."

60

MEY

*A*fter she had slept for most of the day, Mey's energy was replenished, and the need to uncover the story behind what had happened at the compound more than twenty years ago had her marching toward the dorm buildings with a determined stride. Tonight, she was getting some answers.

What Stella had found out from the lady in the grocery store had only deepened the mystery. Arwel and the others had interviewed several others, and a couple had remembered a farm being abandoned a long time ago and later the place being rebuilt as a school.

Since farmland didn't belong to the farmers in China and was only leased, it wasn't that uncommon for people to abandon a farm that wasn't profitable, especially after it had suffered major damage. Most didn't have the means to pay for the repairs.

So far, none of what Stella and the others had learned seemed extraordinary, or inexplicable. The locals didn't even remember the fire as a big deal, but rather as an anecdote.

She followed Arwel into the third dorm building and held the door open for Jay. "I have a feeling that tonight I'm going to find out something useful."

"Let's hope so," Arwel said. "Tomorrow, the mysterious Mr. Wu returns, and I would like to have some information before I approach him."

The common area was different in this one. Instead of couches and musical instruments, this one had long tables and chairs, which meant that it was used as the students' dining room. The adjacent commercial kitchen was sparkling clean, and Mey wondered whether it was in the same location as its predecessor, the kitchen that served the human inhabitants of the building during the Kra-ell rule. If so, she might be able to pick up something in its walls from before the renovation.

"I'm going to start here." She sat on the floor and crossed her legs. "Can you guys wait for me in the dining hall?"

"Of course." Arwel smiled. "We know the drill."

After the door swung shut behind them, Mey closed her eyes, took several deep breaths, and emptied her mind as best as she could.

The first echoes were kitchen accidents that made her wince. Someone cut her finger and was screaming her head off. Then there was a pot of boiling soup that had tipped over and scalded two assistant cooks. Then there were the kitchen squabbles over this and that, which went on for what seemed endless hours. It was fortunate that only the most emotional moments got embedded in the walls, and Mey only had to listen to the highlights. Otherwise, she would probably have had to spend years listening to the episodes from start to finish.

"Listen up!" A commanding voice startled her.

It was so strong that her eyes popped open, expecting to see someone standing over her. The moment her eyes opened though, the voice disappeared, and she panicked, thinking she'd lost the connection with the echo. But as soon as she closed them, the man appeared before her mind's eye.

He wasn't a Kra-ell, or at least he didn't look the way she imagined them. He could have been a hybrid though, because he looked like a mix between an Asian and a European and was very tall.

But then what she was seeing was not the man's real image but rather a reflection of how he saw himself, or the way the people looking at him saw him. The echoes were not machine recordings. They were what people projected, and if he'd been shrouding himself, that was what she was seeing.

"Listen up," he repeated, and this time she detected a foreign accent in his standard Mandarin dialect. It wasn't guttural like the Kra-ell language. It was softer, like Russian, but since she wasn't familiar with all the different dialects spoken throughout China, she couldn't be sure. It was obvious, though, that he wasn't native to the area. "I'm only going to say this once. Gather your children and your belongings and run as far as you can. It's not safe for you here. You are going to forget everything about what happened to you in this place. You worked on a farm, a fire destroyed it, and you had to flee. That's what you are going to remember, and that's what you are going to tell anyone who asks. Now go! There is no time!"

The six people working in the kitchen obeyed without uttering a single word, which made it obvious that the man had used either a thrall or a compulsion on them.

Once the kitchen emptied, Mey opened her eyes and pushed to her feet. She had to find out if a similar thing had happened in the dining hall.

"What's wrong?" Arwel asked as she stepped out through the door.

"I'll tell you later. I need to listen to the walls in here. Can you and Jay wait outside?"

Arwel nodded, and when he and Jay left, Mey sat on the floor, closed her eyes, and tried to relax.

Easier said than done. She was so shaken up after what she'd witnessed in the kitchen that it took her almost half an hour of meditation to get into the proper state. Thankfully, not many dramatic events had happened in the dining hall over the years, and soon the commanding man reappeared. He repeated the same short speech he'd given in the kitchen, only this time to a much larger crowd.

61

ARWEL

"Good night." Arwel parted ways with Mey and Yamanu at the door to their hotel room.

When he entered his and Jin's room, he found her awake. "How is Mey?"

"She's well." He leaned and kissed her lips. "Tonight wasn't as exhausting for her as the two previous ones. She got to the interesting parts quickly."

"I know. I heard her telling you what she'd learned. I was just worried that she might be upset."

"Why would she be?"

Jin shrugged. "I heard it in her tone. Something bad happened in that compound. She felt it, but she didn't say anything because she had no proof."

He frowned. "What she heard was actually good. The humans were released. After we learned that the main structure was destroyed in a fire, I feared that they didn't survive." He rubbed a hand over the back of his neck. "From what Emmett has told us and the other tidbits Mey heard, we know that the Kra-ell are not what you would call compassionate humanitarians. When they decided to move, I assumed that they didn't want to drag a bunch of humans with them, and I'm relieved that they released them instead of slaughtering them all."

"You're right." She pulled the blanket up to her chin. "It could have been worse. Are you coming to bed?"

"I have to call Kian first and give him an update. Will it bother you if I do it here?"

"Not at all." She patted the spot next to her.

He shook his head. "My clothes are dirty. I need to shower and change before getting in bed."

Jin's expression turned sultry. "Just shower. Don't put anything on."

"Yes, ma'am." He flashed her a smile with a hint of fangs.

Pulling out a chair, he glanced at his watch before placing the call. It was four-fifteen in the morning local time, which meant that it was one-fifteen in the afternoon in California.

375

Kian answered on the second ring. "What's up, Arwel?"

"The echoes revealed a little more of the story tonight." He repeated what Mey had told him.

Kian let out a breath. "I'm glad that at least some of the humans made it out of there. I was afraid that none had."

"Yeah. I feared the same thing. Tomorrow, I plan on getting an appointment with the head of the school, and hopefully, we will learn more."

"Take Jin with you. I want her to tether him. If there is a board of directors, and he reports to them, I would like to know who they are."

"Do you think the Kra-ell have anything to do with the school?"

"It's possible. They attract students from all over the world, and those kids' parents are rich and influential people. It might be a good way to gain access to some of the movers and shakers who have connections to China."

"That would be more in line with the Chinese government's tactics. I don't see what the Kra-ell could gain from that."

"That's because you don't think like a businessman. Connections are everything, and insider information is gold. The Kra-ell can pick and choose whose mind they want to enter, and they don't even have to bother seeking these people out. They can ask them to come for a face-to-face instead of teleconferencing for the semi-annual meetings to discuss their students' progress with their teachers. It's in the brochure."

"I've read it." Arwel pushed his hair out of his face. "I think this is a far-fetched possibility, but just in case you are right, I'll take Jin with me."

Across the room, his mate pumped her fist in the air.

"Let me know how it goes."

"I will." Arwel ended the call.

"Finally." Jin bolted out of bed and did a victory dance in her tiny nightgown that rode up her hips when she lifted her arms, exposing her lack of underwear. "I get to do something useful." She plopped in his lap and wrapped her arms around his neck. "Are we taking Stella with us to see Mr. Wu? She was complaining today about having nothing important to do."

With her bare bottom in his lap, the last thing Arwel wanted to do was talk about Stella. "I haven't decided yet." He smoothed his hand over her thigh, hiking the nightgown up and cupping her butt. "How about you join me in the shower?" He dipped his head and sucked her nipple into his mouth through the satin.

Throwing her head back, she tightened her hold on his neck. "I don't think we are going to make it to the shower."

Reluctantly, he let go of her nipple and pushed up to his feet with her in his arms. "We definitely are, and I know precisely what we are going to do in there."

"Oh, yeah? What?"

"You are going to clean me from head to toe."

She smirked. "Giving most of the attention to the middle."

"You've got it."

62

ONEGUS

Onegus clicked open the trunk and offered to take Tim's bag, but the guy shook his head.

"No one touches my art portfolio case." Tim regarded the suitcases and carry-ons already taking up most of the trunk space. "I'm going to hold on to it."

Thankfully, the rented Suburban was a seven-passenger vehicle, so there was plenty of room for Tim and his large canvas tote.

"As you wish." Onegus closed the trunk. "Let me introduce you to my friends." He opened the back passenger door.

Tim lifted his hand. "Hello. I hope everyone is hungry because breakfast is the first order of business." He turned to Onegus. "And I don't mean one from a drive-through. I don't eat junk."

"Of course not." Onegus motioned for him to get in. "We will find a restaurant on the way."

Shai got out and folded his seat forward for Tim to get in the back. "Let me help you with that." He reached for the tote.

"I've got it." Holding the bag under his arm, Tim climbed in. When he was seated, his gaze zeroed in on Geraldine. "Well, hello, pretty lady." He offered her his hand. "My name is Timothy, but my friends call me Tim."

"I'm Geraldine." She offered him a bright smile as she shook his hand. "It's a pleasure to meet you. I heard that you're extraordinarily talented."

"I am." He leaned back with a satisfied smirk on his rotund face.

Cassandra turned to look at him and waved. "Hello, Tim. I'm Cassandra."

Tim's smile grew even broader. "I must stop somewhere and buy a lottery ticket. Meeting two gorgeous ladies in one day makes me feel lucky."

Onegus pulled into the road. "If you don't mind breakfast from 7-Eleven, I'll get you a lottery ticket to go with your burrito."

That erased the smirk from the guy's face. "I don't eat junk, but I'm hungry, so you'd better find a good place fast. They don't serve food on domestic flights these days, not even in business class."

"Don't expect gourmet," Onegus said. "There's nothing fancy in the area."

Ten minutes later, Onegus pulled into the parking lot of a diner calling itself the Smoke Shack.

Tim made a face but followed them inside nonetheless. "I'm too hungry to be picky." He pulled out a chair for himself and sat down.

A gentleman, he was not.

Once everyone was seated, and the orders were placed, Tim leaned back in his chair and regarded Cassandra and Geraldine with an intensity that bordered on rude.

"You two are sisters or cousins?" He pulled out a pencil from his shirt pocket and a white napkin from the dispenser.

"Sisters," Geraldine said. "You have an artist's eye for detail. Most people don't notice the resemblance."

"I'm not most people." Tim started sketching.

By the time their meal arrived, he'd sketched both Geraldine and Cassandra and handed them the napkins. "That's just to whet your appetites."

As Tim devoured an enormous beef brisket sandwich with a side of potato salad, Cassandra admired the two small portraits he'd made in as little as ten minutes.

"Tim emphasized the features we have in common." She handed Geraldine the two napkins.

The guy lifted his coke glass, slurped it down, and then wiped his mouth with another napkin he'd pulled out of the dispenser. "So, which one of you is going to describe the suspect?"

Apparently, Andrew hadn't told the guy much.

"Neither." Onegus put down his fork. "The man you are going to work with is their uncle, and the subject of the drawing is a man who might be their mother's brother." He leaned forward. "Geraldine and Cassandra's mother was adopted as a baby, and they just now discovered that she had a twin sister, who was put up for adoption as well. The sister died many years ago, but her widower remembers seeing a man who we think was the sisters' older brother who was also put up for adoption. Geraldine and Cassandra want to know what he looked like."

Looking skeptical, Tim arched a brow. "I find it doubtful that anyone would spend that kind of money to satisfy their curiosity. What's the story?"

Tim was an arrogant, greedy bastard, but he wasn't stupid.

"Other than one cousin, we don't have any family left." Geraldine's voice quivered as she pulled out a napkin and dabbed at her eyes. "This portrait might help us find more of our relatives." She looked at Tim and smiled sadly. "We were told that you are so good that your portraits can be run through facial recognition software."

"It has been done before." Tim's tone softened, and his expression turned from suspicious to empathic.

Geraldine was a superb actress, and Onegus knew it was an act because she'd remembered not to mention having a nephew.

He was surprised, though, that she had paid attention while they'd talked about it on the way to the airport. She'd seemed distracted, and he'd been sure that she hadn't listened to his conversation with Shai about thralling Rudolf and Niki before allowing Tim anywhere near them. It was important that neither mentioned

Darlene, especially not together with her last name, and that Rudolf didn't mention his grandson.

Tim wasn't immune to thralling, so they had debated the need to thrall the old man and his wife again, but in the end, they decided that it was safer that way. Tim was suspicious by nature, and since he'd worked with Roni and had known him well, he might make the connection and react strongly, which would make him resistant to thralling.

63

CASSANDRA

*O*n the way to Rudolf's cabin, Cassandra listened to Geraldine charm Tim the way she charmed most men. Shai didn't seem to care, which Cassandra marked as a point in his favor.

Then again, he might have been good at hiding his frustration.

If she were acting like her mother, Onegus would have been fuming by now. Her guy wasn't prone to displays of machismo, but Cassandra had learned to recognize his subtle tells of irritation or displeasure.

Perhaps Geraldine thought nothing of it because Tim couldn't hold a candle to Shai, but he had a certain charm despite his crusty and greedy attitude.

Tim was sharp, knew how to hold a witty conversation, and he had a good sense of humor.

"I want to draw your portrait," Tim told her mother. "Cassandra's too. You are both beautiful in an unconventional way."

"If we agree," Cassandra turned to look at him, "what are you going to do with them?"

His smirk was lascivious. "Don't worry. I won't hang them in my bedroom and use them for inspiration."

Ugh, gross. It hadn't even crossed her mind, and now that he'd said it, Cassandra liked him a lot less.

Onegus growled. "If you value your life, you'll never do that."

Tim chuckled. "Calm down, big guy. I've already said that I wouldn't. I'm collecting portraits of beauties for my portfolio. When I have enough, I'll approach a gallery about exhibiting my art. I don't want to do forensic work for the rest of my life."

Cassandra could understand that. Tim's creative talent was stifled by the work he did. No wonder he was looking for a way out, which could also explain the amounts he was charging. Although his overinflated ego might have something to do with that as well.

Nevertheless, she could use his aspirations to her advantage.

"I'll make you a deal." Cassandra held Tim's gaze. "My sister and I will pose for you if you cut your fee for this project in half."

His eyes sparkled with interest. "When?"

"Not today because there is no time, but we can come for a sitting sometime during next weekend if you are free, that is."

"He might be, but you might not be," Onegus said, his tone indicating that he didn't approve.

She lifted a hand. "We will figure something out. What do you say, Tim? Half off in exchange for Geraldine and me posing for you?"

When a smirk joined the gleam in his eyes, she shook her head. "Fully clothed and with either Onegus or Shai keeping an eye on you."

The smirk wilted and the sparkle dimmed. "That's a shame, but I'll still do it. Not for half off, though. I'm willing to shave a quarter off the price."

"A third," Cassandra countered. "And we will give you an hour each. No more. I have no patience for sitting still even for that long."

Tim groaned but nodded. "You are a tough negotiator, lady."

Onegus chuckled. "You don't know the half of it."

The rest of the drive passed with Tim bragging about the cases he'd helped solve. He couldn't provide details because most of those cases were classified, but his stories were interesting enough to keep them entertained.

When they arrived at the cabin, Niki came out to greet them. "I hope you all are hungry. I made clam chowder for lunch."

Onegus took her elbow. "We ate breakfast not too long ago. I need to talk to you and Rudolf for a moment about something I forgot to mention the other day." He led her to the back of the house.

Tim got out of the SUV last and regarded the cabin. "What is this place?"

"It's a survivalist community." Shai pointed at the entrance to the couple's bunker. "Rudolf and Nikki are ready for the end of days."

That sparked Tim's interest. "Can I see it? I've heard about those bunkers, and some of them are as big as apartments."

"I doubt this one is." Cassandra walked over to the door that looked as massive as the ones at the clan's dungeon in the keep. "They live off social security."

Once again, a thread of insidious doubt flitted through her mind. It cost a lot to build one of those bunkers, and Shai had been busy asking other questions the day before. He'd been so convinced that Rudolf hadn't tried to kill Sabina that none of them thought to question where the money to build the bunker had come from.

A few moments later, Onegus returned with Niki. "Rudolf is out back." He looked at Tim. "Do you want to check whether the light is good for what you need?"

The guy tucked his art portfolio bag under his arm. "Lead the way."

64

GERALDINE

*O*negus returned to the front of the cabin alone. "Tim doesn't want anyone disturbing him and Rudolf while they work. Can we go inside?"

"Of course." Niki smiled nervously. "But it's a little stifling in there. We don't have air conditioning. Instead, I can give you a tour of the area. Wouldn't that be nicer?"

Geraldine had a feeling that the poor woman was embarrassed to bring guests into her modest cabin.

"It would." She threaded her arm through Niki's. "It's a lovely day to meet some of your neighbors."

It felt surreal to walk arm in arm with the woman who was married to her former husband, but since she had absolutely no feelings toward Rudolf, it was like getting to know a new friend, which Geraldine enjoyed doing.

"I'm curious," Cassandra said. "How much does it cost to build a bunker like the one you have?"

Niki waved a dismissive hand. "Not much. We got it done for under forty thousand. The founder of the community is a structural engineer, and he let everyone use the plans he made for his own place. We just had to provide the materials and the equipment, and the neighbors helped Rudy build the place. Rudy helped plenty of the others build their own. That's how the community works. Folks help each other."

"Forty thousand is still a lot of money," Cassandra said. "Where did you get it?"

It was a rude question to ask, and Geraldine felt uncomfortable that Cassandra had done so, especially since she knew why her daughter wanted to know where the money had come from.

Rudolf hadn't tried to kill Sabina. Shai had established that the day before. There was no reason for Cassandra to keep pursuing that line of investigation.

"Rudy sold his house, the one he and his wife shared. He couldn't keep living there because it was too painful for him. That's why he came back here."

Geraldine cast Cassandra a reproachful sidelong glance. "I bet there was plenty left over from the house sale."

"I wish," Niki said. "The house had a mortgage that needed to be paid off. While Rudy still worked, he made good money, and we managed to save up enough to supplement his social security income when needed."

"Do you have any children of your own?" Geraldine asked to change the subject.

Niki shook her head. "I couldn't have children," she admitted. "It's a long story why, and I don't like talking about it." She forced a smile and turned to Onegus. "How long do you think the artist needs?"

He glanced at his watch. "Let's give him a couple of hours."

They continued walking around the sprawling community, meeting some of Niki's neighbors, who were mostly older couples like her and Rudolf. The cabins and bunkers weren't clustered together. There were big swaths of wilderness between them, and some of the paths were so overgrown that Geraldine wondered if those people ever ventured out of their hideouts. She also wondered about all the critters hiding in the bushes, the snakes, and the bugs, but with Shai and Onegus at her side, she knew that she had nothing to worry about.

When Onegus finally agreed that it was time to turn back, Geraldine's gut clenched. She kept on smiling and talking with Niki, but by the time they returned to the couple's cabin, she couldn't remember what they'd talked about.

Her nerves were stretched to their limit, and she felt faint.

"Can I bother you for a glass of water?" she asked Niki.

"Of course." The woman rushed up the stairs to her home. "You go on around back, and I'll bring it to you. I'll also heat up the chowder. After such a long walk in the fresh air, you must have regained your appetites."

Geraldine nodded even though she couldn't even think about putting food in her dry mouth. All she wanted was a glass of water to wet her parched throat.

"A chowder would be lovely," Cassandra said.

Shai wrapped his arm around Geraldine's shoulders. "Breathe, love. It's just a portrait. It can't do anything to you."

"I know." She leaned against his side. "I'm afraid of my own reaction to it."

"Understandable." He kissed the top of her head. "I just want you to know that I'm here for you no matter what."

Geraldine wondered what Shai meant by that, but as they rounded the corner and she saw Tim's portable easel, she could barely concentrate on putting one leg in front of the other.

"You have perfect timing." Tim pulled out a spray can from his bag and started spraying the portrait. "This will protect it from smudging. Give it a few minutes to dry."

"Can I take a look?" Geraldine managed to ask through her constricted throat.

"Sure. Just don't touch it."

"I won't."

The easel was positioned at such an angle that where Geraldine stood with Shai, all she could see were the face's general contours. She held her breath as Shai led her in front of the portrait, letting it out in a whoosh upon getting her first look.

Rudolf had only described her inducer as good-looking, but he hadn't given any details aside from comparing him to Brad Pitt and David Hasselhoff, two very different-looking male actors.

The young man in the picture was beyond gorgeous. The sculpted cheekbones, the kind blue eyes, dark longish hair, and full lips stirred something in her, a sense of familiarity, of fondness, of longing. She missed him, but she didn't know why.

Had she been in love with him?

As she swayed on her feet, Shai's arm tightened around her. "What's the matter? Do you recognize him?"

Thinking quickly, Geraldine lifted a trembling hand to her lips. "He looks like someone who could be my brother. We have the same hair, dark and wavy, and his eyes are a light shade of blue like mine."

65

SHAI

*S*hai didn't see the resemblance—not while the portrait had still been on the easel, not while Geraldine had stared at it on the way to the airport, and not when they had boarded the clan's jet, and she'd unrolled the portrait to stare at it again.

The only one who'd bought the story was Rudolf, who'd been relieved to hear that both Geraldine and Cassandra thought the guy was their uncle—their mother's other missing sibling.

Not that Cassandra had believed it either. It had been a fiction constructed for Rudolf's benefit, but Geraldine was using it as an excuse to drool over the portrait as if the guy was the lost love of her life.

Obviously it was the immortal who'd induced her, and Rudolf's suspicions had been spot on. He just hadn't caught them in the act.

What didn't make sense, though, was that the immortal had kept in touch with her after she'd transitioned and hadn't taken her as his mate. Perhaps the bastard had a shred of decency left in him, and he hadn't stooped so low as to take a mother away from her daughter.

Or maybe he had?

He could have been the one who'd staged the drowning.

But then why hadn't he stayed with Geraldine? Maybe something had happened to him? Perhaps Geraldine had survived the boating accident, but he hadn't?

Someone else might have been helping her over the years, purchasing her quilts and arranging fake identities. Perhaps it was another immortal, a friend or a relative of the one who'd perished, one who already had a mate.

If Geraldine's lover was gone for good, that would be great news for Shai, but sad news for her.

Except, it was all speculation. He'd constructed a script in his mind that might be completely wrong.

And to think that he'd paid for the damn thing.

But Shai had never expected Geraldine to react to it so strongly.

Hell, he'd hoped she wouldn't react to it at all.

"Perhaps I should take a nap," Geraldine murmured. "Now that my memory has been jogged, and I've looked at this portrait for so long, I might dream about him." She looked at Shai. "You said that thralling doesn't really erase memories, only pushes them into the subconscious, and that they might come up in dreams."

He wanted to take the damn portrait out of her hands and shred it to pieces, but instead he schooled his features and kept his tone even. "What you should do is see Vanessa. She might help you retrieve your memories."

Thankfully, Geraldine didn't have the ability to smell emotions like other immortals, so she didn't detect his bitterness.

He didn't want her to remember that she'd been in love with another immortal. What if the guy was still alive and she somehow knew where to find him?

Without a bond, there was nothing stopping her from choosing another. Perhaps the area of her brain that was responsible for smelling emotions had been damaged along with the one that was responsible for bonding, and neither could be regrown.

What if he and Geraldine never bonded?

Shai could live with that provided she chose him and stayed loyal to him. According to Annani, most of the gods hadn't been each other's fated mates, and yet some of those couples had long-lasting loving relationships without it.

"I'll take the portrait to Roni," Onegus said. "He'll run it through facial recognition software, and maybe we will get lucky and find this guy."

Geraldine shifted a pair of pleading eyes to the chief. "Can you make a copy of it? I don't want to part with it. I'm afraid that if I stop looking at it, I'll forget him again."

Cassandra eyed her mother with worry in her eyes. "You don't remember him. All you have is a sense that you've met him before. It might be wishful thinking, or he might resemble someone famous."

Geraldine shook her head. "It's more than that. I can feel it."

Shai's gut clenched.

"I'll make a copy," Onegus said. "When we get to the village, instead of going straight home, you can come with me to the underground office complex. We have a big copier that can handle a page this size."

She loosened a breath. "That would be wonderful. Thank you. Do I get to keep the original?"

"Of course. A copy is good enough for what Roni and I need."

Geraldine tilted her head. "I thought that you only needed it for Roni. What else are you going to do with it?"

"I want to show the portrait to some of the former Doomers. Perhaps they will recognize him as one of theirs."

"I'm tired of calling him a guy," Cassandra said. "We need to make up a name. How about we call him Mr. X?"

Shai cast Geraldine a sidelong glance, checking her reaction to Cassandra's suggestion. "What do you think?"

She lifted her eyes to him. "About what?"

"About naming your guy Mr. X."

"I guess that's okay. I don't have anything better."

That was a small comfort.

Despite how possessive Geraldine acted toward the damn portrait, she hadn't named its subject yet, so she might not have felt that he belonged to her.

66

ONEGUS

*O*negus pulled out his phone. "I need to call Kian and let him know that we have another unaffiliated immortal on the loose." He rose to his feet. "I'll do it from the cockpit."

Cassandra nodded in understanding, which he was grateful for. Some of the things Kian might want to talk about were not meant for civilian ears. Charlie was technically a civilian, but he'd been trained to keep his mouth shut about what he heard while flying Kian and Onegus to and from meetings, as well as shuttling Guardians on missions.

"Hello, boss." The pilot greeted him as he opened the door to the cockpit. "To what do I owe the pleasure?" He lifted his headphones to hear Onegus's response.

"I need to call Kian." Onegus slid into the copilot's seat.

"No problem." Charlie put the headphones back on.

Onegus placed the call, and when Kian answered, he gave him a quick summary of what they'd discovered on the trip and what they suspected.

"He might be a Doomer," Onegus said. "I want to show the portrait to Dalhu and Kalugal. Maybe they will recognize him."

"Make another copy and bring it to Amanda's place. She and Dalhu are hosting the family for dinner later this evening, and Kalugal is going to be there."

"Perfect. It will save me time chasing him and Dalhu down. I'll make one more copy and give it to Kalugal to show to his men."

"I don't think Geraldine's inducer is a member of the Brotherhood. Navuh wasn't sending them to the US back then, and even if he did, it would have been for a limited time. The guy couldn't have stayed around for weeks. Also, he wouldn't have driven a fancy car. Navuh didn't give his men those kinds of budgets."

"I know it's a long shot, but we would be remiss not to investigate the possibility."

"I'm not saying that we shouldn't, only that Dalhu is not likely to recognize the guy. Kalugal might, though. It could have been one of his men who'd left his team. There were several of them. It would explain how the guy had money to throw around on fancy cars, and why he didn't know that excessive thralling could cause brain damage. The Doomers are not told any of that because Navuh doesn't care what happens to humans. But on the other hand, Kalugal would have known if one of his men was powerful enough to thrall other immortals, and he's never mentioned that."

Onegus switched the phone to his other ear. "Kalugal might have known that one of his could do that but failed to tell us."

"True. It's not like he tells me everything. I still haven't figured out how he knew about Okidu's journal, or what scheme he's working on."

Onegus chuckled. "Taking over the world, of course. Your cousin has big ambitions."

"That he does. But we've digressed. Let's get back to the issue of Geraldine's mysterious inducer. If he's not a Doomer, and he's not one of Kalugal's men, then we have an unaffiliated immortal on the loose."

"Correct. And he must be ancient to be able to thrall other immortals, and he's probably a descendant of a powerful god. The question is how to find him, and if we do, what to do with him."

Kian huffed out a breath. "One step at a time, Onegus. Let's find him first and then worry about what to do with him."

"Yeah, you're right. I almost wish that we never find him."

"Why's that?"

"Geraldine's reaction to the portrait rattled Shai badly. He loves her, and it messes with his head when she looks at the portrait like she's in love with the memory of that immortal. She keeps staring at it as if her gaze could bring him to life."

"Then perhaps I shouldn't ask my mother to help Geraldine retrieve her memories."

"I don't think even the Clan Mother can do that. If Geraldine lost a big chunk of her brain like Shai theorizes, her memories of the affair with the immortal are gone forever. Then again, he must have kept in touch with her after she recovered from her injury for her to remember him. It's also possible that more than one immortal was involved. Shai came up with several theories, some more believable than others, but they are all just speculation."

"What's your take on this?"

"In most cases, the simplest explanation is the correct one. In my opinion, the most likely scenario is that the immortal didn't know what he was doing and caused irreversible damage to Geraldine's brain. That's why she can't remember anything from her life as Rudolf's wife and Darlene's mother, and also why she has trouble remembering things that happened a few hours or several days before."

"He might have done it on purpose."

Onegus frowned. "What do you mean?"

"You assume that the immortal caused the damage because he didn't know how to do it correctly. But what if he was in love with Geraldine and wanted to take her away from her family? A very powerful thrall would have been needed to make her abandon her child."

"Then why did he leave her after staging her death? He would have stayed around."

"Shai thinks that he did, and he's the closest to Geraldine. We shouldn't dismiss his gut instinct."

"Shai is not objective, and his thinking is clouded by his feelings for Geraldine. Personally, I don't think that the immortal stayed around. Cassandra would have noticed something. Besides, Geraldine has had many lovers over the years, including Cassandra's father. Do you think the immortal would have been okay with that if he loved her?"

"They didn't bond. Otherwise, he would have stayed with her or taken her with him. And without the bond or even a memory of the guy's existence, she had no problem being intimate with others. On his part, he might have fallen out of love with her, but still cared enough to come around once in a while to check on her."

"What you're saying makes sense. Seeing the portrait has greatly shaken Geraldine. She remembers him on a visceral level, which implies that she had strong feelings for him. Now that her memories of him have been jogged, I wouldn't be surprised if more of them start to emerge."

67

KIAN

ian's phone buzzed with an incoming message just as dinner was winding down. He pulled it out, took a quick look at the message, typed an answer, and put it back in his pocket.

"Was it something important?" Syssi asked.

"It was from Onegus. He's on his way to the village and asked if it was still okay for him to stop over. I answered him that it was." Kian had told Syssi about the portrait and who it was of, but he hadn't told the others about it yet." He wants to show Dalhu and Kalugal the portrait that Tim drew from Rudolf's memory."

"Whose portrait is it?" Annani asked. "Tim did such an amazing job recreating Areana's face just from my description of her. He has unparalleled talent."

Andrew chuckled. "What a shame that his talent is also coupled with unparalleled attitude."

Annani smiled indulgently. "Great artists are known for their eccentric and often demanding attitudes." She turned to look at Dalhu. "Except for you, my dear son-in-law. You are overly modest."

He dipped his head. "I'm not a great artist. I'm just a guy who draws pleasant landscapes and passable portraits."

"Speaking of portraits," Kalugal said. "Jacki and I are still waiting for you to complete ours. We reserved the spot over the living room fireplace for it, and the room looks unfinished with that empty expanse of stone. When do you think it will be done?"

"Soon," Dalhu said. "I'm still working on some of the details."

"Take your time." Jacki scowled at her mate. "You don't rush art, Kalugal. It will be ready when it's ready."

When they were done with their banter, Annani returned her gaze to Kian. "I am still waiting to hear who the subject of Tim's latest masterpiece is."

"I was about to answer that." He told them an abbreviated version of Geraldine's memory loss and her former husband's suspicions of the immortal he'd seen spending time with his wife.

Amanda shook her head. "That idiot deserves a proper whipping for damaging that poor woman's mind."

"Whipping is not enough." Andrew wrapped his arm around Nathalie's shoulders. "I say we put him in stasis for a couple of decades. That should do a number on his memory. An eye for an eye and all that."

"It wasn't one of my men," Kalugal said. "None of them can thrall immortals."

"What about those who left over the years?" Kian asked.

Kalugal shook his head. "Most of my men can barely thrall a human woman to forget their bite."

"What I don't understand," Nathalie said, "Is how come Geraldine's body didn't heal the brain damage from the thralling? Doesn't the transition fix everything?"

"The brain is not like the rest of the body." Amanda assumed her lecturer tone. "I don't think the transition affects it at all. I believe that's the reason older transitioned Dormants have a hard time thralling." She turned to Andrew and Nathalie. "Can either of you thrall at all?"

Andrew grimaced. "I tried, but it was no use. I gave up."

"I didn't even try," Nathalie admitted. "But my mother learned how to do it. She's not great at it, though."

"Can Turner thrall?" Annani asked. "He is such a brilliant man. If anyone can teach himself how to thrall it would be him."

"I don't think he can," Kian said. "It seems like Eva is the only one. Eleanor could compel even before her transition, but she couldn't thrall, and she still can't. I used to think that older transitioned Dormants just lacked enough practice and motivation, but perhaps only those who transition at a young age can learn to thrall because their brains are still malleable."

Annani nodded. "It is possible, and it is worth investigating." She leaned over to Amanda and patted her hand. "You could make it your next project."

"I might." Amanda rubbed a hand over her pregnant belly. "But it will have to wait until after I have my baby. Lately, my energy level is so low that I don't feel motivated to start anything new."

Syssi smiled. "I understand that all too well."

Turning to Kian, Annani put her napkin over her plate. "I still did not have a chance to have a chat with Cassandra and her mother. Perhaps Onegus could bring them along? We could invite them to have coffee and dessert with us." She glanced at Amanda and then at Dalhu. "If that is agreeable to you."

"Of course," Amanda said. "Let's invite Shai too. He's Geraldine's mate."

Annani's eyes sparkled. "How exciting."

Amanda arched a brow. "You didn't know? That's old news."

"Oh, I knew that they were enjoying each other's company, but I did not know that it was serious." She waved a hand. "I was busy poking my nose into another love story."

"They might be tired from their trip," Kian said. "Perhaps now is not the best time for formal introductions. I'm sure that both Cassandra and her mother would want to be rested and refreshed when meeting you for the first time."

Surprisingly, his mother accepted his suggestion. "Very well. I will issue a formal invitation to see them tomorrow."

"Cassandra works during the day," Amanda said. "But you can invite them to dinner."

"I will do that." Annani glanced at Dalhu and offered him an apologetic smile. "I hope you do not mind."

"Not at all."

"Thank you. I truly appreciate your hospitality, and I would like to reciprocate. I invite you to be my guests when Amanda's time nears. It would give me great pleasure to have my newest granddaughter born in my sanctuary."

68

ANNANI

*B*y the time Onegus arrived with the portrait, the dining table had been cleared, and Onidu was serving coffee, tea, and dessert.

Annani was a little disappointed that he had arrived without his mate, but Kian had been right to point out that Cassandra and her mother would want to be better prepared for meeting her face-to-face for the first time.

She was glad to see how much Kian had grown emotionally, and she knew that Syssi deserved credit for that.

Her son was a wonderful man, a dedicated leader, a devoted husband and father, but his emotional intelligence was not on the same level as his other exceptional qualities.

Syssi was doing a great job teaching him to be more compassionate.

"Good evening, Clan Mother." Onegus dipped his head. "I hope I'm not interrupting." He cast her one of his charming smiles.

"Good evening. Please join us." She motioned to the chair Okidu had pulled out for him.

"Thank you." He pulled the rolled-up cylinder from under his arm and placed it on the table. "I hope you don't mind me showing this to Dalhu and Kalugal, Clan Mother. We need to find out who the man in the portrait is. Perhaps they will recognize him."

"Go ahead." She waved a hand. "Kian told us what this was about."

"Yeah." Amanda glared at the chief. "And when you find the jerk, he should stand trial for his crimes."

Onegus smiled. "As your brother has aptly stated, we need to take this one step at a time. First, we need to find him." He unrolled the portrait and handed it to Dalhu first. "Anything?"

Dalhu shook his head. "I would have remembered a male who looks like that. He bears a slight resemblance to you." He passed the portrait to Kalugal, who arched his brow.

"I don't recognize him, and he doesn't look anything like me. I'm much better looking." He passed the portrait to his wife. "What do you think?"

"He's handsome, but not as handsome as you."

Kalugal smirked. "Of course not. He's not a three-quarter god."

Amanda rolled her eyes. "Don't you ever get tired of mentioning that at every opportunity?"

"Nope." Kalugal folded his arms over his chest.

"You're hopeless." She extended a hand toward Jacki. "I want to take a look."

"Here you go." Jacki passed her the sketch.

"He's gorgeous." Amanda cast a reassuring smile at Dalhu. "But compared to you, he looks almost feminine. He's not my type."

As the portrait was passed from one person to the next, each giving his or her opinion of the male's attractiveness, Annani waited patiently for her turn.

"Do you want to take a look, Mother?" Kian asked.

Apparently, Kian's emotional intelligence still needed a lot of work. She could barely contain her curiosity and he was asking her if she wanted to take a look?

"I might as well." She extended her hand. "Everyone seems to have an opinion." As her eyes shifted to the portrait, Annani's breath lodged in her throat.

Frowning, Kian leaned toward her. "Do you recognize him?"

Speechless, she nodded.

It could not be. That was not him. It was someone who looked a lot like him, but not precisely. Perhaps he was a descendant, but even that was impossible. As far as she knew, he had not fathered any children.

The room fell deathly quiet.

"Do you know who he is?" Kian sounded alarmed, while everyone else around the table held their breath as they waited for her answer.

"I do not know this male, but I am pretty certain about whose descendent he is." She paused and looked at the portrait again. "He is the spitting image of Toven, Mortdh's brother. Except, Toven was lost along with all the other gods, and as far as I know, he had not fathered any children, gods or immortals." She leaned back and lifted the portrait to view it from a different angle. "He looks so much like Toven that at first glance I thought it was him, but there are small differences."

"Don't forget that this was taken from Rudolf's memory," Kian said. "That memory is four decades old and might not be accurate. Not that I think that it's Toven. We would have known if another god was roaming free. Toven wasn't as weak as Areana, and he would have left his mark on the world."

Hope flared in Annani's chest. Toven had been a good guy, a brilliant scientist like his father, but lacking Ekin's charm. On the other hand, Toven had not been a womanizer like his father either. But most importantly, he had been nothing like his power-hungry older brother. Could he have somehow survived?

"Perhaps he did?" Annani passed the portrait to Syssi. "He could have chosen to establish his seat of influence somewhere else on the planet. I was focused on Europe and later on the United States. He might have chosen Africa, or South America, or the Orient. Toven also might have decided to not interfere in human affairs."

6 9

ONEGUS

*O*negus had come over hoping that someone might recognize Geraldine's inducer as a former Doomer. Instead, it turned out he might have been a god.

"How well did you know Toven?" Syssi asked. "He might have fathered immortal children and kept it a secret."

"I knew Toven well." Pausing, Annani lifted her coffee cup and took a couple of sips, while everyone sitting around the table anxiously waited for her to continue.

The Clan Mother was known for her theatrical inclinations, and today was no exception. She was making the most out of the situation and basking in the spotlight.

"In many ways he was like his father." Annani put her cup down. "He was a champion of humanity and a brilliant researcher in his own right. Ekin was a gifted scientist and engineer, but Toven's areas of interest were different. Today, those would be called the humanities—morality, philosophy, literature. The humans called him the god of wisdom and knowledge and nicknamed him *Good*." She smiled. "Not surprisingly, Mortdh's nickname was *Bad*. Toven's only vice was his snobbishness. He understood the gods' need to take human partners, but he chose not to do so himself. He mated a goddess who was in no way his match, intellectually or otherwise, but even though she was not his fated one and did not give him a child, he did not indulge himself with other bed partners like the rest of his brethren."

"How do you know that she wasn't his one and only?" Syssi asked. "According to your descriptions of the gods, they weren't known for fidelity. Only those who were fated mates were faithful to each other."

"There were exceptions. Khiann's parents were not fated mates, but they loved each other dearly and were faithful to each other. The reason I know that they were not fated mates and that Toven and his mate were not either, is that both males traveled extensively and were often gone for months at a time. They would not have been able to tolerate being away from a fated mate."

"I remember you saying that he wasn't as gorgeous as some of the other gods," Amanda said. "Given what I see in this portrait, that wasn't true."

The Clan Mother sighed. "You not have seen the other gods, Mindy. Compared to some of them, Toven was average-looking."

Onegus could believe that. As beautiful as Amanda and Sari were, they couldn't approach Annani's otherworldly beauty. The gods had been engineered to perfection.

"Were Toven's father and half-brother even better looking than him?" Syssi asked.

"Ekin was not as handsome as his younger son, but he had charm and charisma that attracted females to him like flies to honey, which worked well for him because he wanted to bed every female he met. Mortdh was Ekin's older son from a different mother than Toven—a goddess who was known as one of the most beautiful, so he was exceptionally handsome. But his beauty was marred by his evil soul and crazy eyes. Mortdh was also obsessed with producing a male heir, bedding scores of goddesses, immortals, and humans, but to his great disappointment, he only managed to have one immortal son." She looked at Kalugal. "Your father."

"I have a feeling I would have liked Toven." Kalugal accepted the portrait from Jacki. "He sounds a lot like me. Handsome, brilliant, and faithful." He leaned toward her and kissed her cheek.

"Now that I look at this portrait again—" Jacki held it up for both of them to see "—I notice the familial resemblance."

"Naturally. He's my uncle." Kalugal took another look. "Provided that this is indeed Toven, and not a lookalike immortal descendant of his."

Jacki pursed her lips. "If the original is even more gorgeous than this sketch, then I can understand why Geraldine was tempted to cheat on her husband." She lifted the portrait and moved it from side to side so everyone around the table could get another look. "What mortal woman could say no to this?"

Amanda crossed her arms over her chest. "If Geraldine was induced by a god, it's one hell of a dubious honor given the hatchet job he did on her poor mind." She turned to her mother. "If Toven is as smart and as good as you claim, he should have handled Geraldine with more care."

"That is not Toven," Annani said. "This man must be a descendant of his. Toven would have never done that to a human or an immortal." She lifted her chin. "After all, he wrote the first book on morality."

Amanda's expression was dubious. "That doesn't mean anything. Some people do not practice what they preach. You said that he didn't take human lovers, so he might not have known how to handle their minds."

The goddess looked down her nose at her daughter. "I know that you are trying to play devil's advocate, Amanda, but you are entirely off the mark. Besides, the more I look at the portrait of Geraldine's inducer, the less he looks like Toven to me."

"The last time you saw Toven was over five thousand years ago, Mother. You might not remember him as well as you think you do."

"That might be true." The Clan Mother shifted her eyes to Onegus. "I need to take a look at Geraldine's mind. The answers might be in her submerged memories. Please arrange for her and Cassandra to come to Kian's office tomorrow at ten in the morning."

"Why do you need Cassandra to be there?" Kian asked. "She'll have to miss work."

"I do not need Cassandra to be present, but her mother might." She turned to

Onegus. "I understand that your mate works during the week, so if she prefers, I can see both her and her mother tonight. I am not a patient woman, Onegus, and I want to do this as soon as possible."

Given the power surge the goddess had just emitted, Annani was not in the mood to negotiate a meeting time other than the two time options she'd given. Cassandra would have to either convince Geraldine to come tonight or take a day off and come with her tomorrow morning.

"I'll check with Cassandra and Geraldine right away." Onegus typed up a long message to Cassandra, explaining the urgency and asking her to check with her mother.

CASSANDRA

"*D*amn." Plopping down on the couch with the phone clutched in her hand, Cassandra reread Onegus's text to make sure she understood it correctly.

Apparently, the goddess recognized the man from Geraldine's past as one of the gods or a close descendant of his, and she wanted to see her mother as soon as possible to probe Geraldine's mind.

Onegus hadn't used the word probe, but that was what the Clan Mother was going to do, and given how powerful Annani was, she might fry what remained of Geraldine's functioning synapses.

Could she say no?

She texted Onegus. *How safe is it for my mother?*

He answered right back. *It's safe. Annani is very gentle, and she knows what she's doing.*

Was he telling her the truth? If he wasn't, and her mother ended up worse after Annani's probe than she was before, Cassandra was going to zap Onegus so hard that his hair would stick out for days.

Not that he had much choice in the matter either. No one could refuse Annani's directive.

Her heart hammering in her chest, Cassandra placed a call to her mother's phone, but there was no answer, and after several rings, Geraldine's new automated message came up. "I'm not available to take your call at the moment, but if you leave me a message, I'll call you back as soon as I can."

"Call me," Cassandra said after the beep. "It's urgent."

Next, she tried Shai's number but got the same result. If they hadn't heard their phones ringing, the two must be busy doing things Cassandra wished she and Onegus were doing instead of jumping to obey the goddess's commands.

What was she going to do? Drive over there?

The Clan Mother was waiting for an answer, and making her wait longer than necessary was not a good idea.

Damn and double damn.

Maybe she should give Onegus an answer on behalf of her mother and make an appointment with the goddess for the next day. Kevin would be angry at her for taking yet another day off, but he'd live.

What Geraldine and Shai were probably busy doing right now would do wonders to smooth over the rough patch in their relationship that the trip to Oklahoma and the portrait had caused.

Cassandra snorted.

Calling it a rough patch was a gross understatement. It was more like a Grand Canyon, and she wondered whether a love-making session would be enough to fix that chasm.

Geraldine had stared at that damn portrait like a woman in love, and poor Shai had looked like he wanted to tear the thing into pieces and then burn them.

Staring at her phone, she started typing up a message to Onegus about scheduling the meeting for the next day when the thing rang.

"What's so urgent?" Geraldine sounded irate. "I was in the shower, and I didn't hear the phone ringing."

Cassandra debated whether to tell Geraldine about her inducer possibly being a god. Perhaps it was better to just tell her about Annani's invitation and leave the god thing for later.

With how fragile her mother's mind was, it might be better to pace things to avoid overwhelming her. When the pressure became too much, Geraldine's solution was to dive into her dream world and check out.

"The goddess wants to meet both of us. She can do it either later this evening or tomorrow morning. I'd prefer to do it today, so I won't have to miss work tomorrow."

The truth was that Cassandra wanted to do it sooner rather than later because she was burning up with curiosity. Did having a god as an inducer influence the results of the transition? She knew from Roni's story that the purer the inducer's blood, the better the chances of a Dormant going through a successful transition, even those with very weak godly genes. Her mother might have transitioned effortlessly because of the potency of a god's venom.

But did it affect anything else?

As the silence on the other side of the line stretched beyond what was reasonable, Cassandra prompted, "Are you there, Mom?"

"Yeah. I'm here." Geraldine's reply sounded shaky. "I just don't know what to say. Do you know why she suddenly wants to meet us? Does it have anything to do with the portrait?"

Damn. She hadn't counted on her mother figuring it out right away.

"Yeah. It does." Cassandra had no choice but to reveal a little more. "The Clan Mother wants to take a look at your memories. Being a goddess, she is the only one who can enter the minds of immortals to either thrall them or release them from a thrall."

"I know that. I just didn't expect the goddess to invite me so soon. Shai thought that he would need Kian to ask on his behalf."

Good, so she'd been ready for it.

"I'm glad that you're not freaking out."

There was another long moment of silence. "Who said that I'm not?" Geraldine sighed. "But it's not like I can decline an invitation from the Clan Mother. How soon do we need to be there? I just got out of the shower, and my hair is wet."

"Onegus is waiting for my answer. If you need a little more time to get ready, I can tell him that you've just stepped out of the shower and that it will take you about half an hour to leave the house."

That should give Geraldine enough time to choose a nice outfit and do her hair and makeup.

"What does one wear to a meeting with a goddess?"

"It's an impromptu meeting, and the goddess doesn't expect us to show up in evening gowns. Almost every one of your outfits will do. They are all pretty and elegant without being too fancy."

"Are you sure that's good enough? Meeting the Clan Mother is like meeting a queen. I can't show up in an outfit I wear to my book club meetings."

It was good that Geraldine's focus was on what to wear and how to look. That would keep her from going into panic mode.

"The blue dress with white polka dots will do just fine. But if you want to look a little more formal, you can put on the purple midi dress with the wide black belt."

"It's too dreary. Shai loves the polka dots. I'll wear that."

"Good choice. Tell Shai to stop by Onegus's place so we can walk together to Amanda's house. That's where the goddess is staying during her visit and where she expects us."

"Is Amanda going to be there?"

"It's her house, so it's safe to assume that she will."

Geraldine let out a breath. "I'm glad. I like her."

71

GERALDINE

On the way to the village, Geraldine held on to Shai's hand as if it was her lifeline. It might have been dangerous for him to drive with only one hand on the wheel, but she trusted his quick immortal responses to compensate.

When the car windows turned opaque, and the vehicle switched to self-driving mode, the anxious energy swirling inside her reached fever pitch.

"I'm scared and excited at the same time," she admitted. "Perhaps we will finally get some answers."

"There is nothing to be scared of. Annani is goodness personified. She is not going to harm you."

"I hope you are right." Geraldine lifted her other hand to her temple. "Things are pretty messed up in there. I hope the Clan Mother is not going to make it worse." She smiled sadly. "I'm barely functioning with what I have now."

"It's going to be okay." He gave her hand a reassuring squeeze.

As they neared Onegus's house, Cassandra opened the door, wearing black wide-leg trousers and a cream-colored silk blouse. It was one of her work outfits, but it was a little more elegant than the rest, and she usually wore it to board meetings and other important work-related events. She also had heels on, which made her as tall as Shai or perhaps even taller by an inch or so.

Was that smart?

The goddess was tiny, even shorter than Geraldine. What if she didn't appreciate people towering over her?

Then again, Annani's children were all tall, so maybe she didn't mind.

"How are you holding up, Mom?" Cassandra closed the door behind her and joined them on the path.

"I'm okay. I think." Geraldine cast her daughter an uncertain smile. "There is a whirlwind of jumbled thoughts in my mind, but I hope to get some answers tonight."

Cassandra eyed her with a frown. "Are you scared?"

"I'm anxious, which is not the same as feeling fearful. Shai reassured me that the goddess is a good person and that she would not harm me intentionally. I'm only a little scared of her doing so unintentionally."

"Annani is very skilled," Shai said.

"Has she ever probed you?" Cassandra asked.

"Probed?" He lifted a brow. "That's not what she does. Edna probes. Annani will only take a peek."

"What's the difference?" Geraldine asked.

"Edna goes deep, searching for intentions, feelings, hidden hurts, guilt, those sorts of things. Annani just takes a peek at recent memories, and if there is a thrall keeping them submerged, she might be able to release them."

"Only the recent ones?" Geraldine asked.

She was not interested in those. If she'd forgotten things lately, Cassandra and Shai were there to remind her of them. What she needed was to find out what had happened to her decades ago.

"I misspoke," Shai said. "From my experience and that of other immortals, we can thrall away or retrieve only recent memories or those that have been brought up to the forefront of a human's mind. Sometimes, it is possible to retrieve memories that had a great impact. People remember more vividly important events in their lives, even those that happened decades ago. In addition, the Clan Mother is a very powerful goddess and she might be able to do more than any of us. I don't really know what her limits are."

He turned into the walkway of a house that was no different than many of the others they'd passed, walked up the stairs, and knocked on the door.

A butler opened up. "Good evening." He bowed. "The Clan Mother is awaiting you in the living room."

There were other people there as well, and Onegus came over to stand next to Cassandra, but Geraldine's eyes were glued to the small glowing woman sitting in an armchair and holding Kian's baby daughter in her arms.

"Good evening, Clan Mother." Shai dipped his head. "Let me introduce my mate and her daughter." He motioned for Geraldine to step forward. "This is my mate, Geraldine."

"Clan Mother." Geraldine curtsied and kept her head bowed.

"And this is my mate," Onegus introduced Cassandra. "Geraldine's daughter."

The goddess pushed to her feet and handed the sleeping baby to Kian, whom Geraldine hadn't noticed before. "I'm so glad to finally meet you both." Smiling broadly, she glided over to Geraldine. "You can rise, child." She turned to look at Cassandra. "You too."

No one had ever called Geraldine a child, not that she could remember anyway, and she wondered if it was just an expression, the way pastors referred to members of their congregations—or did the goddess regard everyone as children because she was ancient?

When Shai nudged her elbow, she offered another quick curtsy. "It is a great honor to meet you in person, Clan Mother."

The goddess reached for her hand, clasped it, and then turned to Cassandra and took hers as well. "Come sit with me." As she walked over to the couch, those who were sitting there jumped to their feet to make room for the three of them.

ANNANI

*G*eraldine was nervous—it was evident from her facial expression and the way her energy was humming just under the surface, and it was also understandable. The thing that puzzled Annani, though, was how little of that inner turmoil manifested in the female's scent.

She was one of those rare individuals who did not advertise their feelings in scent form. Turner was like that, but probably for different reasons than Geraldine.

From what Annani had learned about her so far, the woman was fairly intelligent but in no way brilliant. She was a talented quilter, which meant that she was artistically inclined like her daughter, and artists were usually very open with their feelings. Even Dalhu, who showed very little outward emotion, emitted plenty of scents for Annani to figure out exactly what he was feeling at any given time.

"I have heard a lot about you both." Annani put on a charming smile. "I understand that both of you are artists."

Perhaps talking about the things Geraldine was passionate about would help her relax. To reach into her mind and dig out old memories, Annani needed the woman to lower her shields and let her in without resistance.

"Cassandra is the talented one," Geraldine said. "She can draw beautifully, and she combines a good sense of esthetics with a good nose for business. That's why she's such an asset to the firm she works for. I'm just a quilter with a good eye for colors and patterns."

Annani liked that Geraldine was not boastful and that she held her daughter's achievements in higher regard than her own, but there was no reason for her to be so modest.

"I heard that your quilts won competitions and fetched impressive amounts. Do not sell yourself short." Annani leaned closer. "A woman should never be modest about her achievements. Fates know that it is difficult enough for females to make a name for themselves in what is still mostly a patriarchal world."

Geraldine tilted her head as if she did not understand. "There are very few men who quilt. It is mostly a female occupation."

It seemed that Geraldine was not the kind of woman who was interested in the big picture, or maybe she was just too nervous to discuss big issues like gender equality and the painstakingly slow progress humanity had made so far in that aspect.

"Indeed. Although I was led to believe that you might have met your inducer in one of those competitions."

Geraldine looked doubtful. "That's what my former husband thinks, mostly because I had no other opportunities to have an affair. But if I was thralled into having sex with a stranger, it could have happened anywhere and at any time. He could have met me in the supermarket, or at my daughter's school, or he could have been one of our neighbors." She lifted her hand to her temple. "Until my memories are retrieved, it's all just guesswork."

Annani nodded. "You are correct, and you are also very brave for giving me access to your submerged memories. Is it okay if I reach into your mind now?"

The woman looked around the room that had been vacated while they had talked. "Where is everyone?"

"They are giving us privacy. I asked them to wait out in the backyard so no one would distract us. Do you need anyone other than Cassandra for support while we do this?"

"Do you even need me here?" Cassandra asked her mother. "Or should I join the others out in the backyard? I assume that the fewer distractions there are, the easier this will go."

Annani nodded to confirm Cassandra's astute assumption. What she needed to do required her complete and undivided attention. According to what Onegus had told her about Geraldine's condition, the woman's mind and emotional state were fragile, and she needed to be handled with extra care.

For a long moment, Geraldine looked undecided, but then she nodded. "You can go, Cassy. Once the Clan Mother releases my submerged memories, you and Shai can come back inside." She looked at Annani with pleading eyes. "I don't know what is in there for you to retrieve, but some of it might be very personal. I don't want to make a spectacle of myself and have my story told to everyone. Can it be just Cassandra, Shai, and Onegus?"

"Of course." Annani squeezed her hand and turned to Cassandra. "Syssi and Kian probably have already left with Allegra, but knowing my curious nephew, Kalugal and Jacki are still out there waiting to hear Geraldine's story. You can tell them to go home. Amanda and Dalhu can retire to their bedroom."

Cassandra cleared her throat. "Is it appropriate for me to deliver that kind of message?"

"You are just the messenger, child. But if you are uncomfortable doing so, have Onegus do it."

"Good idea." Cassandra rose to her feet and bowed her head. "I shall deliver your instructions, Clan Mother."

"Thank you." Annani waited for the sliding door to close behind Cassandra before turning her attention to Geraldine. "Are you ready?"

She swallowed. "As ready as I will ever be."

405

"First, I want you to think of the most pleasant memory you have."

Geraldine smiled. "Does it have to be real? Because many of my pleasant memories are imagined."

"It does not matter. I just need you to go to a good place in your mind."

73

SHAI

*A*s Cassandra stepped out through the patio doors, all eyes turned to her.

Only a few minutes had passed since Shai and the others had left the living room to give the goddess and Geraldine privacy. It hadn't been long enough for Annani to do her thing.

"Did my mother kick you out?" Amanda asked Cassandra.

"No, my mother did." She smiled apologetically at Shai. "She doesn't want anyone to distract her, and she also wants to discuss what will be revealed in private, with just Shai, Onegus, and me present."

That's how it should have been from the start, and Shai couldn't understand why anyone other than Annani, Amanda, and Dalhu had been waiting for them. The family dinner had been over a long time ago.

It was probably Kalugal's fault. The guy was a busybody, and since he hadn't left with his wife, Kian had felt that he and Syssi had to stay as well.

"Bummer." Kalugal rose to his feet and offered Jacki a hand up. "I'll have to wait until tomorrow to hear all the juicy details."

"Oh, well." Syssi got up and handed Kian their sleeping daughter. "We can move the party to our place. You are all invited for drinks and coffee." She glanced at Amanda. "Otherwise, you and Dalhu will have to wait out here or hole up in your bedroom until Annani is done."

"Thanks." Amanda glanced at Dalhu. "What say you?"

He nodded. "Sounds like a plan."

"I think we will go home," Jacki said. "I'm tired."

Kalugal didn't look too happy about it, probably hoping to hear updates about Geraldine and her mystery inducer when Annani was done, but Jacki's suggestive smile was enough of an incentive for him to say his goodbyes and follow his wife out the side gate.

When the other two couples left the same way, Onegus sprawled on a lounger and pulled out his phone. "If you don't mind, I have several emails I need to answer."

Cassandra waved a hand. "Go ahead." She looked at Shai. "How are you holding up?"

"I'm fine."

He was worried about what Annani might find in Geraldine's memories and the impact it might have on their relationship, but he wasn't about to share that with Cassandra and Onegus.

"Are you sure? You've been pacing since we've gotten out here."

"Leave him be," Onegus said. "He has every right to be nervous."

"So do I." She glared at her mate. "My mother is in there at the mercy of a powerful goddess, and I don't know whether she'll still have a functioning brain after that probe is done."

Shai shook his head. "Geraldine will be fine."

"So why are you pacing?"

He stopped and looked her in the eyes. "I'm not worried about the goddess causing additional damage to Geraldine's brain. I'm worried about what she'll find in there, and what impact it will have on all of our lives."

Cassandra's expression softened. "Even if she loved him, it was in the past. You are her future."

"Am I? What if she remembers still loving him? What am I supposed to do then?"

"Fight for her." The conviction in Cassandra's tone was absolute. "Whoever he is, he doesn't deserve her love. He might have helped her over the years, but he hasn't been there for her. He doesn't love her." She shifted her eyes away from him. "If he left her because of me, the guy is an asshole. He thralled himself out of her memories and left her alone. What did he expect? That she would live like a nun?"

Shai pinched the bridge of his nose. "It wasn't your fault, Cassandra. They didn't bond, or she wouldn't have been able to look at another male even if she didn't remember her inducer."

"There you go." Cassandra waved a hand. "He wasn't the one for her. You are."

"Thank you." Shai dipped his head.

Except, he and Geraldine hadn't bonded either, so there was that.

Still, Cassandra knew her mother better than anyone, and her belief that he was the one for Geraldine was not only appreciated but also encouraging.

Shai had hated thinking that the right thing to do would be to step aside and let Geraldine reunite with the one she loved. He couldn't do that and had felt selfish for wanting to fight for her. But if Cassandra thought that he should, then perhaps he'd been wrong, and his gut had been right.

She'd just given him the green light.

He would do whatever it took to win, including fighting dirty. He'd done it before, breaking clan law to take an active role in his son's life, and he was still doing that.

No one suspected Kian's straitlaced, good-natured assistant of being a lawbreaker.

That didn't mean that Shai wasn't a moral man, though. On the contrary, he believed himself to be morally right. He just had a different view on what was right and what was wrong, and he didn't agree with the clan's policy regarding the mortal children of immortal males.

74

GERALDINE

*G*eraldine closed her eyes and tried to float away on the wings of one of her favorite fantasies, but now that she had Shai, hazy memories of walking on the beach with Emanuel were no competition for her new reality. So she tried to think of Shai, but all she got was the worried, pinched expression he'd adopted since Tim had created the portrait that had such a big emotional impact on her.

"You are still tense," the goddess said softly. "Where is your safe place, Geraldine?"

Cassandra.

She had been Geraldine's safe harbor since the day she was born. Thinking of Cassy as a toddler, then as a little girl, and later as a gangly teenager brought a smile to her face. Her daughter was the joy of her life, and the woman Cassandra had become was Geraldine's greatest source of pride.

"There you go." The goddess stroked the back of her hand. "Keep thinking about your daughter for a little longer and then let your mind wander."

The Clan Mother's hypnotic voice was like a balm on Geraldine's agitated synapses, and the more the goddess talked, the more relaxed Geraldine became.

So far, she hadn't felt the rush of returning memories Shai had warned her about, but maybe that would come later when the goddess reached the hidden place in her subconscious where her memories were submerged and locked away.

At some point, Geraldine's mind wandered so much that she lost track of her thoughts, and when a gentle squeeze on her hand brought her back, she had a difficult time opening her eyes.

"Wake up, Geraldine." The Clan Mother's angelic voice was like a gentle command that had her eyelids rising as if the goddess was in control of them, not her.

"Is it over?" she asked.

The goddess nodded. "Do you remember anything?"

As Geraldine focused inward, she found fragments of memories floating at the

409

border between her consciousness and subconscious. Most were of the man from the portrait. In one, they were sitting at a coffee shop and sharing a cake. In another they were walking around a mall, and in yet another, he handed her a brown envelope with documents.

"I remember him. But it's still hazy." She lifted her eyes to Annani. "What did you see?"

"Would you like the others to be here when I tell you? It would save me the trouble of repeating the story."

Not if the goddess had seen intimate moments that Geraldine couldn't access yet for some reason.

"It depends on what you saw."

The Clan Mother smiled and patted her hand. "I did not see anything that you might consider embarrassing or would not want your mate or your daughter to hear about."

That was a relief.

Then again, the immortals had different ideas about what was embarrassing and what was not. The goddess might not consider an illicit affair as something to be embarrassed about.

"Was the man from the portrait my lover?"

"He was not."

That was surprising.

"Did you see any of my other lovers?"

Smiling, the goddess nodded. "They are irrelevant to what we want to find out, so I am not even going to mention them."

That was a relief, but there was one lover she needed to find out more about. "Did you see who Cassandra's father was?"

The Clan Mother nodded. "You remember him quite well. His name was Emanuel, and he was an aide to the Ethiopian ambassador."

Oh dear. The goddess had seen her fantasies. "That memory might not be real," Geraldine admitted. "I might have made him up."

"You did not. He was one of the memories that were suppressed by the man in the portrait. But since it was dear to you, it came back in your dreams. The other men you have dreamt about were real too, but they were not Cassandra's father. They were just fond memories."

Geraldine frowned. "If the man from the portrait was not romantically involved with me, why did he submerge my memories of my lovers?"

"Since they could not be part of your life, he probably thought that he was protecting you by submerging your memories of them. But that is a guess. His motives might have been different."

Geraldine didn't want to inconvenience the goddess unnecessarily, but she still had questions she needed answers to before the others were called in. "Shai said that once you release my memories, they would come rushing in, and I would remember everything. Why is it not happening?"

The goddess smiled benevolently. "I was very gentle with you, and instead of releasing everything at once, I looked at each memory separately and tucked it back near the surface of your consciousness. That way, these memories will bubble up to the surface sometime over the next few days instead of overwhelming you all at once. You might not have been able to process everything flooding in suddenly."

"Thank you. I think." Geraldine lifted a hand to her throbbing temple. "Did you see what happened to me?"

The goddess shook her head. "I saw you recovering from the accident, and I have a good idea of what happened to you, but regrettably, your memories of the event itself and your life before it are lost forever."

She'd suspected as much, but having it confirmed brought tears to her eyes. She would never remember giving birth to Darlene, would never have memories of her daughter growing up like she had of Cassandra, and knowing that the loss was irreversible felt devastating.

"So Shai was right. There was an accident. My drowning wasn't faked."

"I do not think that it was staged, but it is still possible that it was, and things went terribly wrong." The Clan Mother squeezed her hand. "It's a miracle that you survived. You should be thankful to the Fates for sparing your life."

When Geraldine nodded and more tears escaped her eyes, the goddess took her other hand in hers as well. "The Fates looked out for you for a reason. If you had perished that day, you would not have had Cassandra, you would have never met Shai, and you would not be sitting here with me today." The goddess let go of her hand to pick up a napkin from the table and handed it to her. "Wipe your tears and let us call the others back in."

The Clan Mother was right. Geraldine might have lost memories of a big chunk of her life, but she'd survived, had another child, and had met the love of her life. She should count her blessings instead of bemoaning what could not be changed.

Wiping her tears with the napkin, Geraldine forced a smile. "I'm ready."

The goddess lifted her hand, and a moment later, Amanda's butler emerged.

Had he been listening in from the kitchen?

Frankly, Geraldine didn't care. Nothing of what she and the goddess had discussed was shameful. It was just sad.

The butler bowed from the waist. "Can I be of service, Clan Mother?"

"Yes, Onidu. Please tell the others to come in."

7 5

SHAI

*A*s Shai heard the patio door slide open, he turned around so fast that he almost lost his footing, but it wasn't Geraldine who'd opened the door.

Onidu bowed. "The Clan Mother and Mistress Geraldine would like you to join them."

Shai squeezed his eyes shut and then took a long breath before following the Odu inside.

Seeing Geraldine's eyes sparkling not with excitement but with tears, he rushed to her side and sat on the couch without getting the Clan Mother's permission first.

She'd forgive him this one-time transgression.

He took Geraldine's hands. "What happened?"

"You were right. I had a terrible accident, and the memories from before it happened are lost forever." She turned to look at the goddess and then back at him. "The Clan Mother didn't release my memories." Her hand rose to her temple. "My mind might be too fragile for the sudden release. They will bubble up over the next several days."

That wasn't what he'd expected. Annani was supposed to bring Geraldine's memories to the surface. Why the hell had she pushed them back down?

Leaning forward, Shai looked at Annani. "Forgive me, Clan Mother. But may I ask what made you do that?"

Annani gave him a motherly smile. "Onegus warned me that Geraldine might not be able to process the onslaught of years of memories released all at once, so I took a look and then put them back just below the surface, ready to percolate over time. But I can tell you what I saw."

"Please do." Cassandra shook out her hands. "The stress is making my energy crackle."

"I will start with Geraldine's oldest memories." The goddess leaned back against the couch cushions. "She was in a small coastal cabin, recovering from a head injury. The man who took care of her was the one from the portrait, but there was another

412

man there, a human fisherman who I believe found Geraldine when she had been washed to shore. A lot of those old memories are hazy and only in picture form because of Geraldine's injury. She lost her language skills, so I could not follow what was said between the immortal and the human. I could only see things the way she did."

Onegus leaned forward. "Was the fisherman's face clear? Perhaps we can find him and question him."

The goddess shook her head. "Geraldine's accident happened nearly four decades ago, and the human I saw in her memories was not young. I doubt that he is still around."

"I remembered a fisherman. He was an older guy." Geraldine rubbed her temple. "But I didn't remember the immortal."

The goddess patted her hand. "It will come back to you."

Shai had no patience left. He needed to know who the guy was and whether he was still a threat.

"Who was he?" Shai asked. "Was he in love with her?"

"He cared for you," Annani said to Geraldine. "But he was not your lover. He said that you and he were family, and that was why he was helping you." She smiled. "Of course, that did not happen in the fisherman's cabin because you would not have remembered a verbal communication. That happened much later, after you were released from the rehabilitation center. He helped you rent your first apartment, and he arranged your first fake identity. He also gave you money."

"Does he have a name?" Cassandra said.

The Clan Mother sighed. "He does, but I do not think he gave your mother his real name. He called himself Orion."

"Figures," Onegus grumbled. "A hunter and also a rapist."

As a growl escaped Shai's throat, Onegus lifted a hand. "Not many know about the rapist part. I doubt the guy would have named himself Orion if he knew that. He probably only heard about Orion, the great huntsman, the handsome prince, etc."

"The name he chose for himself might also be meaningless," Cassandra said. "Let's not get hung up on that." She turned to the goddess. "Did you see how often he met with my mother?"

"Not very often, but since he has been in Geraldine's life for many years, those visits accumulated. Sometimes he would show up once every two or three months, and sometimes many months passed between visits, but he always came back to check on you both. Those memories are old, and most are uneventful, so I did not get to see much. They were more of an impression than actual memories, and I cannot tell you what happened during those visits, or what you talked about. But I can reassure you that your feelings for him were not romantic, and they were not sexual in nature either."

"Did I meet him?" Cassandra asked.

The goddess nodded. "Not every time he came, but I saw you with him and your mother on several occasions when you were younger. Not recently, though."

Cassandra pushed a strand of hair behind her ear. "Is there a way to retrieve my memories of him?"

"Of course." The Clan Mother smiled. "But since you are an immortal now, only I can do that, and at this time, I do not think it is warranted. Also, since those memories are old and uneventful, I will not be able to tell much from them."

Cassandra didn't look happy. "But what if I remember something that might prove useful?"

Given the goddess's stiffening posture, Cassandra was pushing her luck by arguing. Thankfully, Onegus knew the Clan Mother well enough to know when enough was enough.

"Let's focus on your mother." He rose to his feet and walked over to Cassandra's chair. "I'm sure the Clan Mother still has a lot to tell us." He put his hand on her shoulder.

"Yes, of course." Cassandra dipped her head. "Forgive me for the interruption, Clan Mother."

GERALDINE

*W*hile Cassandra argued with the goddess, Geraldine tried to make sense of what she'd learned so far, but it seemed like crucial pieces of the puzzle were still missing.

"How is it possible that Orion wasn't my lover? He must have been at some point for me to transition."

The goddess turned her attention back to her. "That would be a logical assumption, but in the interactions that I have seen, he treated you like a sister or a cousin. It was not just about the things he said, but also about how he regarded you. There was no passion in his eyes, only concern."

Geraldine shook her head. "If it wasn't him, then who? Someone must have induced me."

"There is also the issue of how powerful Orion is," Onegus said. "He obviously thralled Geraldine when she was already an immortal." He rubbed a hand over his jaw. "To be that powerful, Orion must be the son of a god or a goddess." He looked at the Clan Mother. "Given how much he resembles Toven, he was probably his son. Perhaps he somehow survived the bombing, and he wasn't the only one. He might have been away with a group of immortals, and someone from his group induced Geraldine."

The Clan Mother didn't respond right away. Her hands tucked between the folds of her long silk gown, she gazed at the wall for a long moment. "Toven traveled a lot. He had his own flying vehicle as I had, and he made good use of it. Perhaps he dallied with a human on one of those long journeys of his and produced an immortal son. But to create a group of immortals like I did, he had to have a daughter as well. His son could not have created more immortals."

"Perhaps I'm his descendant as well?" Geraldine suggested. "That would explain why Orion referred to me as family, but if I was born to one of his sister's daughters, why would I end up in an orphanage? Wouldn't they cherish every child born to them as the clan does?"

The goddess smiled sadly. "Who knows? Navuh does not even bother to induce the dormant females and uses them as breeders. Perhaps Toven's son is just as bad as his cousin."

Geraldine shook her head. "Then why would he help me?"

"Maybe Orion is not Toven's son," Cassandra said. "He might be Toven's grandson who happens to be very powerful. He could have escaped his father's tyranny, just as Kalugal escaped Navuh's, and he might have been hunting for the discarded females and trying to correct the wrongs of his father. Is it possible that he found a way to induce Dormants that does not involve sex?"

The Clan Mother's expression was sad as she shrugged. "Everything is possible. But what I cannot fathom is Toven's son growing up to be a tyrant like Navuh. Toven was the polar opposite of Mortdh."

"But he might not have been there to raise his son properly," Onegus said. "A son who carried the same genes as his grandfather—the power, the brilliance, and the megalomania. We know that nature and nurture are equally important, and without proper nurture, nature was predominant in solidifying a character like Navuh's."

"Then again," Shai said. "All of those theories might be completely wrong. All we can safely assume is that Orion is related to Toven and that he helped Geraldine over the years. Everything else is guesswork. We need to run his portrait through the facial recognition software and find him. That's the only way to uncover the true story."

Onegus sat on the arm of Cassandra's chair. "If there is another group of immortals out there, it is imperative that we find them."

"What if the facial recognition software doesn't work?" Cassandra asked. "How are we going to find him then?"

"We don't have to look for him," Geraldine said softly. "He will come back." She lifted her eyes to Shai. "He always does. That's why I couldn't leave the house without letting him know where I was going. He probably planted that in my mind."

77

SHAI

"We can definitely do that," Onegus said. "Hopefully, Orion will show up soon." He looked at Shai. "It seems that you will have to continue to make the trek between the village and Geraldine's place for a while longer. We also need to install cameras all over her place."

"Obviously." Shai pinched the bridge of his nose.

He had a feeling that the goddess and everyone else in the room, including Geraldine, were trying to convince themselves that Orion hadn't been Geraldine's lover to spare his feelings.

It was absurd.

Naturally, he was jealous, but his only real concern was Geraldine's feelings for the guy at present time, not what had happened years ago.

Annani hadn't seen any intimate moments between them, but she hadn't had access to Geraldine's memories prior to the accident.

Orion might have induced Geraldine, had formed some sort of attachment to her that hadn't been permanent like the bond between fated mates, and after the accident, he kept helping her either because he was a good guy or because he needed to make sure that no one found out about her immortality.

In fact, that was the most logical explanation, and the others needed to hear it.

Shai took in a long, deep breath and then cleared his throat to get everyone's attention. "There is another thing that we might safely assume. Given that Orion's visits were so infrequent, his thralling couldn't have caused Geraldine's memory issues. We can also safely assume that those issues were somehow the result of the accident and that Orion was aware of them."

"Where are you going with this?" Cassandra asked.

"The guy might have kept an eye on Geraldine not out of the goodness of his heart but because he feared she would reveal her immortality. He needed to ensure that she didn't do anything to expose what she was. He must be not only extremely powerful but also very skilled to be able to do what he did." He looked at Geraldine.

"Somehow, he managed to suppress your immortal abilities, so you wouldn't inadvertently reveal yourself."

Annani nodded sagely. "That could only be achieved with a powerful compulsion, not thralling. It would seem that Orion can thrall and compel immortals, which is truly remarkable. Only a handful of gods could do that. Compulsion was a rare trait even among the gods."

Cassandra groaned. "If Orion is that powerful, we might not be able to hold on to him for long enough to question him."

Grinning, Onegus put a hand on her shoulder. "We know how to deal with compellers. It's nothing a good pair of earplugs cannot solve. As opposed to thralling that works on some kind of mysterious mind waves, compulsion hitches a ride on sound waves. No sound, no compulsion."

Geraldine regarded him with round eyes. "I don't understand. Are you suggesting that from now on Shai and I wear earplugs twenty-four-seven?"

He chuckled. "That won't be necessary. We will have surveillance equipment all over your house and in your purse. We will know when he shows up, and I will send Guardians to apprehend him. Your job will be to keep him entertained long enough for us to arrive."

"Are you going to hurt him?" Geraldine asked.

"We will try not to. We will use tranquilizers."

"And do what?" Cassandra asked. "Take him to your dungeon?"

"A dungeon?" Geraldine squeaked. "You can't do that to Orion. He didn't do anything to you."

"We will only keep him for questioning." Onegus leaned forward. "And who knows? Maybe he will want to join the clan?"

Annani sighed. "I would like that. I hope that Orion is as caring and as brilliant as Toven was. After my beloved Khiann and my parents, I miss Ekin and Toven the most." She chuckled. "Is it not ironic? Three members of the same family—a father and his two sons. One son's name is a synonym for death and destruction, the other's is a synonym for all that is good. Perhaps that is a manifestation of universal truth—balance must be preserved."

VOLUME THREE

1

MR. WU

"Mr. Wu. It's so good to have you back." Doctor Wang dipped his head. "How was your trip?"

"Uneventful." Wu put his briefcase on the desk. "How did the meeting with the three prospective families go? Did they fill out the applications?"

"Not yet." The principal smiled apologetically. "They are very superstitious for Westerners. I wanted to reassure them that the school buildings are either new or completely renovated, so I made the mistake of telling them about the fire that destroyed most of the original structures on the property. When they heard that there was a fire, two of the mothers became concerned and wanted more details before making their decision."

"What kind of details?"

"Mainly, they wanted to know whether anyone died." The principal winced. "They are concerned about bad vibes imparted by the spirits of those who might have lost their lives in such a horrible way."

Superstitions were very common in the Chinese culture. If those ladies were of Chinese descent, they might have been influenced by their parents' or grandparents' beliefs.

Wu rounded his desk and pulled out his chair. "What did you tell them?"

He didn't invite the principal to sit down. If he wanted Wang to leave anytime soon, it was better to leave him standing. Doctor Wang was a charming guy and a great salesman, which made him perfect for the job he'd been hired for, but it also meant that he was overly talkative.

"I told them that I didn't know. They asked if it was possible to speak with the founder of the school."

The principal wasn't supposed to mention him to the parents of prospective students until it was time for the final interview. Regrettably, the man's excessive talkativeness was as much of a hindrance as it was an asset.

Wu stifled a groan. "I hope you told them that I don't meet with the parents or the students until after they pass the tests."

"I did, sir." The principal bowed. "But perhaps you'll be willing to make an exception for these families. They are planning on visiting other schools, and we might lose three potential students." The principal's lips lifted in a small smile. "I promise that it will not be a waste of your time. The three ladies are exceptionally beautiful. Mrs. Williams runs a modeling agency, and she looks the part. She's very tall." He held a hand over his head to indicate her height. "Her sister is just as good-looking and perhaps even taller—a gorgeous woman who looks much too young to have a teenage son. The designer they work with is shorter and curvier, but she's also very alluring and seems feisty." He smiled lasciviously. "Naturally, they are all married, but it is not a crime to look and admire such fine ladies."

Wu pretended that he was not at all curious. "I will take your word for it, Doctor Wang."

"What should I tell them, sir?"

Three new potential students meant a lot of money for the school, and it would be a shame to lose them.

"Tell them that I can see them first thing tomorrow morning. Today, I want to rest from my trip."

"Of course." The principal inclined his head, his disappointed expression indicating that he'd hoped to secure an interview for the families for today. "I hope they won't mind prolonging their visit. I called their hotel, and the clerk told me that they were scheduled to check out later today."

Calling the hotel was sneaky of the guy, but smart.

"If they decide to stay another day to meet with me, it means that they are serious about the school, and if they don't, it means that they are not, and I will save myself the hassle of meeting with them."

The principal nodded. "Very astute, Mr. Wu. I will inform them of your decision."

"Make a big deal out of it." Wu waved a hand. "Tell them I had important meetings scheduled for tomorrow, which I had to reschedule in order to accommodate them. Hopefully, that will make them feel indebted, and they will not only stay, but also complete the applications."

"Very true, sir. I will call them right away."

"Hurry up before they check out of the hotel."

"Yes, sir." The principal dipped his head and pivoted on his heel.

When the door closed behind him, Wu pulled his laptop out of his briefcase, turned it on, and connected it with a wire to the school's network. Entering his ten-digit passcode, he accessed the school's surveillance network and searched for footage of the visitors.

Wang's comments about the three women piqued his curiosity. They most likely weren't the ones he'd been awaiting, but he was curious to see if they were indeed as impressive as the principal claimed. After all, he was a male, and not everything he did in life was about duty and honor.

Viewing the feed from Wang's office at ten times the normal speed, Wu didn't have to wait long before he found the relevant footage.

As the three couples entered the room, the incredibly tall guy with dreadlocks caught his attention first. He was wearing sunglasses indoors, which was strange, but since he was supposed to be a famous former star athlete, which made him a sort of celebrity, perhaps the shades were part of his image.

Wu had read the short profiles Doctor Wang had prepared about the prospective students and their parents, but he'd skimmed over most of it. To him, what mattered most was whether they had the means to pay the substantial tuition and board, and that the students had the minimum required academic qualifications and weren't troublemakers.

The athlete's statuesque wife was no doubt the model agency owner, and she was indeed magnificent. Tall for a woman, but elegant and graceful nonetheless. Her sister looked a lot like her, younger, less refined, but just as impressive.

The third one was partially obscured by her husband's broad back. From what Wu could see, she was much shorter than the other two and not of Chinese descent, as evidenced by her unruly hair. Even though it was gathered in a loose bun, it looked curly, and its ends were colored blond.

There was only one camera in Doctor Wang's office, and the way it was positioned, Wu couldn't see the woman clearly even when the couples sat down. The husband was still obscuring his view.

He could've switched to an earlier recording from the entrance camera but, curiosity aside, it wasn't necessary. Wu was more interested in the principal's sales presentation and the parents' responses to it than in the third woman's reported good looks.

During the presentation, the guy with the sunglasses made some disparaging comments about students cheating on their entrance exams, to which the principal's answer was perfectly worded. It was polite and yet encouraging.

"That's good to know," the guy with the glasses said. "It would be a shame to drag Junior out here only to get rejected."

The names of the three visiting couples had been included in the brief Doctor Wang had prepared for him, but Wu had glossed over them as well.

Williams.

That was the last name of the modeling agency owner and her husband, but he'd forgotten their given names. He should learn them before the meeting tomorrow.

Wang pulled out three folders and put them on his desk. "Would you be filling out the applications today?"

"We will take them with us," the modeling agency owner said. "We plan on touring several other schools, and we will only apply after we decide which one we like best."

"We would like to see the grounds," said the husband of the woman Wu was still waiting to see. "Our son is an athlete, and outdoor activities are important to us."

"I'm interested in seeing the dormitories," his wife said. "I'm more concerned with the living conditions."

Her voice sounded vaguely familiar, and Wu increased the volume to hear her better.

"Our son is used to luxury," she said. "I don't expect the school to provide him with the same level of accommodations as he's enjoying now, but I don't want him to spend the next three years in boot camp conditions either."

Wu had heard that voice before, the slightly nasal inflection grating on his nerves for some reason.

The principal gasped dramatically. "I assure you, Mrs. Furman, that our students enjoy every convenience and amenity. The main school building is relatively new. The dormitories have been completely remodeled to bring them up to the highest standards, and the new buildings were designed by one of the top architectural firms in Beijing according to Mr. Wu's exact specifications." He got up from behind his desk. "It's best, though, for you to see for yourself. Let me give you a tour of the school. Our classrooms are spacious, well-ventilated, and equipped with the latest and best educational tools. No other school on your list will come even close to ours."

When the parents rose to their feet, the shorter lady's husband finally got out of the way, and as she lifted her head and looked straight at the surveillance camera, the sight of her face was like a punch to his gut.

A growl started low in his throat. "You fucking bitch. Did you come to finish the job?" Baring his teeth, he banged his fist on the desk. "Not this time around, sweetheart."

2

KIAN

"*I* apologize for my mother." Kian poured Dalhu a shot of whiskey. "She shouldn't have commandeered your house like that."

To give Geraldine the privacy she'd requested during the retrieval of her memories, Annani had taken over Amanda and Dalhu's place, practically throwing everyone out, including its rightful owners.

"It's fine." Dalhu offered him a rare smile. "I can understand why Geraldine needed to be alone with the Clan Mother. If it were me, I wouldn't have wanted a bunch of people whom I hardly know to hear my life's dirty details or even the not so dirty ones."

"We could have stayed in your backyard until it was done."

Dalhu lifted the whiskey glass in a salute. "Then I would have missed an opportunity to share a drink with you. I've grown fond of your whiskey and cigars."

Kian grinned. "I'm glad to have you as a partner in crime, but I bet Amanda isn't happy about it." He cast his sister a sidelong glance. "You hate the smell of cigars."

"Not true." Amanda rubbed a hand over her belly. "I hate the smell of cigarettes. I can tolerate cigars."

"Good to know." Kian saluted her with his glass.

She gave him a small smile. "I'm dying of curiosity. I can't wait to hear what Mother finds out."

"Me too." Syssi handed Amanda the cappuccino she'd made for her and sat on the couch. "I'm also worried for Geraldine. I know that Annani will handle her with the utmost care, but still. Geraldine's mind is fragile." She sighed. "Poor woman. I can imagine how frightening it must be for her to have a goddess prowling around inside her head."

Amanda lifted the cup to her lips, took a sip, and leaned back. "Do you remember how it felt when Kian released your memories?"

"How could I forget? I thought that my head was going to explode. That's why I'm so worried for Geraldine. When Kian released mine, I had only accumulated several days' worth of memories. She has a lifetime of them, and she won't be able to handle the onslaught."

"My mother is aware of that." Amanda sipped her coffee. "While we waited for Geraldine and Cassandra to arrive, she had time to think it through, and for a change, she asked my opinion." Amanda chuckled. "After all, I am a neuroscientist, so she figured I would know a thing or two about what the brain can handle. I advised her not to release Geraldine's memories all at once. Annani is going to bring them close to the surface so they can bubble up over time. But while she's at it, she'll take a look at them to find out what really happened with that immortal."

"I'm happy that she consulted with you." Kian walked over to the living room's sliding door. "I just hope that she'll actually follow your advice." He pulled the door open. "Dalhu and I are going out to the backyard for a smoke. If you hear from Annani or from Geraldine, let us know."

"Sure thing," Syssi said. "But I doubt we will hear anything anytime soon. Annani has years of memories to sift through."

Dalhu followed Kian outside. "I know the Clan Mother is powerful, but how can she access memories that are so old?"

"She can't, which is a good thing." Kian closed the sliding door behind Dalhu. "Otherwise, she would need to spend years inside Geraldine's head. She can only access recent memories and those that have left a lasting impression." He lifted the box of cigarillos off the patio table and offered one to his brother-in-law.

"Can you do that?" Dalhu asked as he pulled one out. "I mean with a human. Can you see old memories that left an impact?"

Kian shrugged. "Perhaps, but I don't have my mother's patience. I've only ever attempted to access recent memories." He lit Dalhu's cigarillo and then his own.

For a few blissful moments, he and Dalhu puffed on their cigarillos and sipped their whiskey in silence.

When Kian's phone rang, disturbing the quiet, Dalhu sat up. "That was faster than I expected."

Kian pulled the phone out of his pocket, but it wasn't Syssi's or Onegus's number on the screen. It was Arwel's.

"It's not about Geraldine," he told Dalhu before answering the call. "Good morning, Arwel. Or is it afternoon? What time is it over there?"

"It's eleven o'clock in the morning. I wanted to let you know that we are staying one more day."

"Why? Did Mey decide to give the echoes another try?"

"Since we are spending another night here anyway, that's the plan. We got an appointment with the head of school, but he could only see us tomorrow. The principal told me some crap story about meetings that had to be rearranged so Wu could see us, emphasizing over and over again how fortunate we were that he'd agreed to meet with us at all."

"Couldn't you just thrall him to schedule the meeting for today?"

"It won't help to thrall Wang when it's Wu that we need to talk to. Besides, Mey likes the idea of listening to more echoes. She learned a lot during the two previous nights."

They were perpetually short on Guardians, so pulling four of them for the investigation in China meant one less rescue mission each day that they were there. But finding out more about the Kra-ell was important. That being said, saving victims of trafficking was as important if not more so, and Kian hated to have to choose between investigating a potential threat to the clan and the trafficking victims.

The worst part of being the leader was making those kinds of calls.

"If you and the rest of the team don't mind staying another day, then I don't have a problem with that either. This investigation is important, and it's not like there is an emergency you need to take care of elsewhere. The trafficking cells, regrettably, will still be out there when you come back."

"I know." Arwel loosed a breath. "But I'm grateful that there are no emergencies. I tried to call Onegus earlier, and when his voicemail answered, it got me worried because he always answers his phone."

"He probably turned it off. He's dealing with family drama."

"Oh, yeah? What's going on?"

Kian didn't like gossip, but since all the Guardians would soon learn about the immortal's portrait and Annani's suspicion as to who Geraldine had to descend from, there was no harm in telling Arwel the news now.

"I'll give you the highlights. Before Geraldine lost her memories in what we believe was a boating accident, her former husband saw her with a guy that Onegus suspected was the immortal who'd induced her. Onegus got Tim to draw his portrait from the ex-husband's memory, and he brought it over earlier today for Dalhu and Kalugal to take a look at. They didn't recognize him as one of the Doomers, but Annani knew right away who he was, or rather who he was a descendant of. According to her, the guy is the spitting image of the god Toven, Mortdh's younger half-brother. She summoned Geraldine and Cassandra and offered to retrieve Geraldine's memories of the guy. She's doing it as we speak, and Onegus is waiting with Cassandra to hear the results."

"That's big news, especially if Geraldine's guy is not alone. What if there is a community of Toven's descendants out there?"

"My thoughts exactly."

3

SHAI

A steaming mug of coffee in hand, Shai walked into his and Geraldine's bedroom. She looked so peaceful, and after all the excitement of the previous day, she needed the rest. He would have liked to let her sleep a little longer, but William's guys were on their way, so he had little choice in the matter.

When they'd gotten home last night, Geraldine had been exhausted. The summons from the Clan Mother right after they'd returned from Oklahoma had been stressful enough. Then the emotional upheaval of the goddess's revelations sapped the rest of Geraldine's energy.

For the first time since they'd started spending their nights together, they'd gotten in bed but not to have sex. Shai had held Geraldine in his arms until she'd fallen asleep, but with thoughts and speculations about Orion swirling through his head, he couldn't even close his eyes, let alone relax enough to sleep.

"Wake up, love." He put the mug on the nightstand, sat on the bed next to her, and kissed her on the lips.

Murmuring something incomprehensible, she pulled the blanket up to her chin and turned on her side.

He tugged on the blanket. "The guys are going to be here in less than half an hour."

She opened her eyes. "Which guys?"

"William's crew is coming over to install the surveillance cameras and listening devices in the house. You need to get up and get dressed."

"So soon?" She reached for the coffee mug. "We only talked about it last night, and it's already happening?"

"After we left Amanda's place, Onegus made the calls and texted me to expect the crew today. I didn't know that they would be arriving so early, though. One of the guys called me half an hour ago to let me know they are coming."

Usually, Shai left for the village around that time, so it was good that they'd caught him home. Otherwise, he would have had to turn back to make sure that Geraldine was up and ready.

"What time is it?" she asked.

"Six-thirty in the morning."

"That's early." She took a sip from her coffee. "Can you stay until they are done? I don't want to be alone in the house with men I don't know."

It warmed Shai's heart that Geraldine considered him her protector, but she had nothing to worry about from William's crew, and he needed to get to work.

"You are perfectly safe with them, but I'll stay until they get here and make the introductions." He took her hand and lifted it to his lips. "If you want, you can leave them to do their work and come with me to the village."

"What am I going to do there while you are at work?"

"What did you plan to do here?"

"Think." She took another sip of coffee. "The Clan Mother said that the submerged memories she'd placed closer to the barrier between my conscious and subconscious mind would start to percolate, but I didn't dream of Orion last night."

Shai stifled a relieved breath. He would never tell Geraldine so, but he didn't want her dreaming of the immortal. He hadn't bought the story the guy had told her about them being related to each other—a family. He was convinced that Orion had been the one who'd induced her, and after the accident, he'd wiped out her memories of him because he'd decided to change the story and pose as her benefactor.

What Shai couldn't understand, though, was why.

Geraldine was beautiful, intelligent, and passionate, and that immortal would have been hard-pressed to find any female her equal, human or immortal. Why hadn't he wanted to continue their romantic relationship, but had still wanted to check in on her from time to time and take care of her?

So far, Shai had come up with three possible explanations, two of which painted Orion as a prick who deserved to be beaten into a pulp, and one that didn't.

The first one was that the immortal had something to do with Geraldine's near-fatal accident and stayed around out of guilt.

The second one was that Orion hadn't been involved in her accident, but upon finding out that she'd suffered irreparable brain damage, he considered her damaged goods.

And the third and least likely one was that he had never been romantically involved with her, and that he was a friend or relative of her inducer, and that for some reason, her inducer couldn't keep an eye on her and had tasked Orion with her care.

Geraldine lifted her hand to her temple, a reflexive move that usually signaled that she was nervous or that she'd forgotten something and was trying to remember it. "Perhaps I did dream about him and forgot?"

"It's possible." Shai rose to his feet and affected a neutral tone. "Dreams are difficult to remember, and I don't recall most of mine." He pulled the blanket off her. "Time to get up, my love."

The smile she gave him was enough to melt the thorny icicles around his heart. "I love it when you call me that." She took his offered hand and let him pull her against his chest but didn't let him kiss her. "I need to brush my teeth first."

"Fine." He turned her around and smacked her bottom to get her going. "Hurry up. I'm not moving from this spot until you come back and give me a proper kiss."

Turning to look at him over her shoulder, she cast him a sultry smile. "Do we have time for more?"

The answer was probably no, but he didn't care. The installation crew could wait outside the door until he let them in.

"We'll make time." He prowled after her into the bathroom.

4

WU

*C*loaked in darkness, Wu crouched behind a rocky outcropping and lifted the binoculars to his eyes. It was still early, only a little past eleven at night, and Stella and her companions didn't seem to be winding down for sleep anytime soon.

He didn't mind the wait. In fact, he'd arrived early to watch the way they interacted with each other. It was important to figure out who was the leader of the team, who was the second-in-command, and whether any of the couples were real romantic partners or just pretending for the sake of the recon mission.

It made a difference.

Love was a foreign concept to the Kra-ell for a reason. It caused people to make stupid mistakes, and knowing whom it affected improved his chances of success.

With the room's window facing the back of the hotel, they didn't expect anyone to be watching them. The window looked out onto a large open field that was sparsely wooded but still provided privacy. What they hadn't accounted for, though, was that it just as easily provided a watcher with the perfect hiding place. Perhaps they weren't professional spies, just murderers come to finish the job they'd started twenty-two years ago—an execution team.

Spies would have closed the opaque set of curtains and not just the sheers.

From Wu's vantage point, he could see them clearly, and with the help of his binoculars, it was like he was in the room with them.

He counted eight people, recognizing the three couples from the surveillance tape, and two additional men he hadn't seen before. Four of the males looked like they could give him trouble. Their muscled bodies and postures betrayed their military training. The fifth one seemed a little softer, a civilian perhaps.

The question was whether they were armed and whether they were as strong as the Kra-ell.

The females weren't, he knew that, but if any one of the males was his equal in brute strength, he couldn't take them on all at once. His best option was to wait for an opportunity to catch Stella alone or just with the one pretending to be her husband. Fortunately, that guy seemed to be the weak link in the chain, and Wu had no doubt that he could overpower him, provided the male was unarmed.

The only weapon Wu had with him was a hunting knife, and even that was considered dishonorable for a Kra-ell male to carry.

The Kra-ell were traditionalists for whom knives and swords were the females' weapons of choice. Males were expected to fight with their fangs and claws. Wu's nails were not nearly as hard and effective in battle as those of the purebloods, but his fangs worked just fine, and he didn't regret bringing the hunting knife.

He wasn't about to repeat the same mistake that had gotten the others killed.

Their stubborn adherence to tradition had cost them dearly.

When they'd been attacked, having firearms on hand might have saved them. But perhaps tradition hadn't been the real reason for the compound's lack of proper weapons. Jade's reasons for refusing to purchase contemporary weaponry might not have been about old-fashioned beliefs but about her continuous hold on power. She might have feared that the simmering internal unrest would eventually reach a boiling point and her tribe would turn against her.

Throughout the years, Wu had often wondered if the attackers had been his own tribesmen. Many of the hybrids hadn't been happy about the way they'd been treated —their second-rate status, their lack of access to Kra-ell females, and Jade's prohibition on them fathering children with humans.

They might have rebelled.

They might have gotten the weapons without Jade's knowledge.

Having guns and ammunition might have given them the edge they needed to overcome the superior strength of the pureblooded males and claim the females for themselves.

If not for the fire and the abandonment of the compound, that would have been the most logical assumption. But if the hybrids won, why would they leave?

Sitting back, Wu leaned against a smooth boulder and stretched his long legs in front of him.

Twenty-two years.

He'd been waiting twenty-two years for Jade and the other females to return, hoping against hope that they would escape their abductors, that he hadn't gotten all of them killed, and that he wasn't going to spend the rest of his long life alone, surrounded by humans who had no idea what and who he was.

It had been so long that he hardly ever thought of himself as Vrog anymore—a hybrid Kra-ell who was part of a tribe, who had a father and a mother, who had friends and cousins.

All gone, and it was probably his fault.

Since the rebellion theory had too many holes to be valid, only one suspect remained—Stella.

If he had never met her, had never revealed to her who he was, no one would have known his people even existed, and no one would have come to eliminate the supposed threat they posed.

A couple of months after his affair with Stella, Vrog had started suspecting that something was amiss, becoming concerned when his emails, phone calls, and voice messages hadn't been answered.

Even though he'd told no one about her, he'd assumed that Jade had somehow found out and feared that she'd decided to cut him off instead of giving him the whipping he deserved.

Hell, he had even been willing to redeem himself the old-fashioned way—dueling to the death with a pureblooded male. But when all his communication attempts had been unsuccessful, it had seemed as if the door had been slammed shut in his face and he could no longer return to his tribe.

Normally, Vrog wouldn't have dared to abandon his assignment in Singapure without Jade's permission, but after a week of utter silence, he could no longer stand the uncertainty. He had to find out for sure.

Incurring Jade's wrath was better than not knowing where he stood with her.

He'd booked a flight back home.

What he found was much worse than he'd expected.

Everything apart from the human living quarters, the barns, and some storage shacks had been burned down to the ground. His people, the humans, and even the livestock had all gone.

At first, he'd assumed that they'd left without him as punishment for Stella, his offense coinciding with the move, but not the cause of it. When relocating, it was a common practice for the tribe to eliminate all traces of themselves from the former location. However, after thinking it through and digging around for clues, he'd realized that something much more nefarious had taken place.

His first clue was finding the fireproof safes buried under the rubble, still locked, and given their weight, still full.

Using explosives to break in, Vrog had found gold, precious stones, money, and business files. Jade wouldn't have left those behind if the move had been voluntary.

Further inquiry into the tribe's bank accounts revealed that they had been emptied.

Only Jade and her second-in-command had access to the tribe's accounts, so either they had survived the attack and decided to cooperate with their abductors, or the information had been tortured out of them.

He'd even suspected a government raid, but no one in the adjacent towns and villages had seen soldiers passing through.

Searching for more clues, Vrog had kept on digging in the rubble for weeks, and what he'd found out painted a gruesome picture that he still didn't fully understand.

Lifting his hand, he looked at his father's ring.

Just like the other rings he'd found in the rubble, it was intact despite the fire that had turned his father's body into ash.

Vrog had found twenty-one rings, one for each of the pureblooded males they'd belonged to, each engraved with its owner's name and position in the tribe.

The males' rings were made from a dark blue stone that he suspected had originated on the Kra-ell's home planet, while those worn by the pureblooded females were made from a similar stone that was green. They too were engraved with their names and positions, but he'd found none of those.

His findings had led Vrog to believe that the pureblooded males had been slaughtered, while the females had either been taken or had escaped.

The males would have fought to the death to save the females, to give them a chance to escape, which was why Vrog still harbored hope that they would one day return to claim what had been left in the safes.

The hybrids didn't get the special stone rings, so he didn't know what fate had befallen them. The males had probably perished together with their pureblooded fathers. The females had either escaped or had been taken along with the pureblooded females.

The big question that he needed an answer to was who had done that and why.

After he had given it a lot of thought, Stella and her clan had become the prime suspects.

It couldn't have been a coincidence that the compound had been attacked mere months after he'd met her, and in his infinite stupidity, had let her walk away with the knowledge of his people's existence and the child he'd unwittingly planted in her womb.

5

STELLA

*S*tella plopped down on the small couch in Arwel and Jin's room. "It was a fun day, but I'm exhausted, and I'm happy to stay here tonight and veg in front of the TV." She cast a suggestive glance at Richard. "Or take a long bath and go to sleep early."

To keep up the pretense of curious American parents who wanted their children to learn the Chinese language and culture, they'd spent the day sightseeing and doing touristy things.

Before Vlad was born, Stella had traveled extensively throughout the east, but she'd been more interested in visiting the big cities, not rural communities. It was a different type of experience, which she found surprisingly enjoyable.

Jin's mouth twisted in a grimace. "I'm tired as well, but I'm going anyway. I don't understand half of what they are saying on those Chinese soap operas you like, and watching Netflix on my satellite phone is just depressing."

"You can watch it on my tablet," Arwel offered.

Jin shook her head. "I'm coming with you, and there is nothing you can say to make me stay behind tonight. I can't sleep without you, and I end up waiting awake, anxious, and bored."

Being the smart man that he was, Arwel didn't argue.

"Watching Chinese television is a great way to learn the language," Stella said. "It's not for someone who doesn't know the basics, but you do, and it will improve your skills."

"I'll take your word for it." Jin opened the closet door and pulled out a pair of black yoga pants. "I just hate being useless."

"You're not useless." Arwel put down his tablet. "Tomorrow, we need you to tether the head of school so we can learn who he reports to, and you're the only one who can do that."

"You can learn all you need to know by thralling him. I'd rather not tether anyone unless there is no other way. You know how I hate the feeling of being weighed down by the consciousnesses of those I tether."

Mey turned to look at her sister. "Do you hate being tethered to me?"

"No, of course not. I know when to follow the string to you and when not to, so I don't catch you in embarrassing moments."

"I'm glad." Mey shoved a bottle of water into her backpack. "There is no reason for you to schlep with me tonight, though. I realized that I can't listen to the echoes and talk at the same time because it breaks my concentration."

It would have been a helpful piece of information to know before they'd invited Jin to join the team. The girl was a whiner, and sometimes she got on Stella's nerves. Then again, with Arwel as their team leader, they were stuck with Jin regardless of her usefulness.

Besides, she could still be helpful in some way. The head of school might be resistant to thralling, or he might be under someone else's thrall, and in both cases, Jin's unique talent would be invaluable.

Holding the pair of yoga pants in her hand, Jin sighed. "I know that you don't need me for that, but I want to come along nonetheless." She cast a sidelong glance at Arwel. "I can keep you company while you wait for Mey to be done. I know that if I stay, you'll insist on Jay or Alfie staying behind to guard me, which means less protection for Mey and Yamanu, who actually need it."

He nodded. "I can't argue with that logic. But since Stella and Richard are staying, I'm going to leave Jay to keep an eye on them anyway."

Richard shook his head. "Stella and I don't need a Guardian to keep us safe. This is a sleepy little town, and aside from the Kra-ell's compound burning down two decades ago, nothing happens here. In addition, the compound is located more than sixty miles away." His eyes lowered to where Arwel's holster was peeking out from under his windbreaker. "That being said, I wouldn't mind having a firearm under my pillow if you could spare one."

Stella chuckled. "Do you even know how to use it?"

Her mate looked offended. "I wouldn't have asked if I didn't. We got weapons training in the government paranormal program. I know my way around guns and rifles and even a rocket launcher."

She'd forgotten about that, and also about Richard and Jin being a couple during their time in the program. Maybe that was why she didn't like Jin as much as she liked her older sister?

Jealousy wasn't a pleasant feeling, especially when it was totally uncalled for. Richard and Jin hadn't been in love, and they had never become intimate. If not for Eleanor compelling them to start dating, they wouldn't have been together at all.

"What else did you learn in the program?" Arwel asked.

"Hand-to-hand combat, how to disarm an opponent, and a bunch of other stuff that I will probably never use. I don't regret getting the training, though. It might come in handy one day."

"True," Jin said. "I hated the self-defense class because the instructor was brutal, but I'm in great shape thanks to it, and I also feel more confident." She sat on the bed next to Arwel. "In retrospect, though, I don't think Simmons and Roberts were training us to become good spies. They just wanted to test our resilience so they would know what to expect from the super babies they wanted us to breed." She shivered. "I forgave Eleanor for everything else she compelled me to do, but not for pushing Richard and me to procreate." She cast an apologetic glance at Stella. "I'm so glad that my instincts fought so hard against it. On a subconscious level, I must have known that we were not meant to be together."

Looking like he would rather be anywhere but there, Richard pushed away from the wall which he'd been leaning against. "Let's go to our room." He offered Stella a hand up.

She turned to Arwel. "Are you sure that we can't be of help out there tonight?"

For a long moment, he didn't answer, looking as if he needed to think it through. "Frankly, I prefer not to split the team and to have everyone together, but it's not fair to drag you out there when there is nothing for you to do."

"We'll be fine," Richard said. "What about that gun, though? Can I have one?"

"I don't have one to spare, but I can give you a tranquilizer gun with some darts. I have two, and it doesn't seem like we will need any."

"That would be greatly appreciated." Richard looked relieved. "Do you have it here?"

"Morris has them in the van. When he gets here, you can come out and get it."

"Text me when he does."

"No problem."

"Good luck to you all," Stella said as they headed for the door.

Jin glanced at her watch. "What's your rush? We have at least two hours until we need to go."

Wrapping her arm around Richard's toned midsection, Stella gave Jin a conspirator's smile. "You said that you didn't like watching Chinese dramas with me, but if you don't mind, Richard and I can stay and watch them with you."

"Go." Smirking, Jin waved them off. "Let's pretend that watching television is what you have in mind."

6

GERALDINE

*G*eraldine tried to stay out of Tyler and Aiden's way as they installed the cameras around her house. It seemed that the devices didn't even require wiring, but given how tiny they were, she wondered where the batteries went.

"Can I offer you something to drink?" she asked Aiden.

"Water would be nice." He came down the ladder.

"Can I ask you a question?"

"Shoot." He fell into step with her as she headed toward the kitchen.

"How do those cameras get their power supply?"

"They will be connected to your home's electrical wiring. But don't worry about power outages. We are putting a backup battery in your garage."

"I didn't see you installing wires."

"First, we wanted to find strategic spots for maximum visibility on the receiving side and minimum visibility on the recording side. After the cameras are all in place, we will run the wires."

"I see." Geraldine opened the fridge and pulled out two bottles of water. "So the big mess is still to come." She handed them to Aiden.

He nodded. "We will need to drill holes and patch them up, but we will clean up after ourselves. When we are done, you won't be able to tell where the cameras are or that anything was done in the house."

"Can you show me where you put them?" She smiled sheepishly. "So I will know where not to walk naked."

A blush creeping up his cheeks, he walked out of the kitchen. "I'll show you where they are. We didn't put cameras inside the bedrooms or bathrooms. We put them outside in the hallways pointing toward the doors, and outside on the windows and balconies." He chuckled. "Provided that Orion can't walk through walls, that should do."

"Got it." She smiled up at him. "So all I have to do is make sure I close the door and the curtains before getting undressed and remember not to leave the bedroom with no clothes on."

"Precisely." He started up the stairs where Tyler was working.

"Are there cameras on every window?" She followed him up.

"Not all of them, but on most. We wanted to cover all entry points. There are also several cameras monitoring the street outside and the backyard." He pointed to where Tyler was mounting a camera across from the master bedroom doors. "Do you want to see the one on your balcony?"

"No, that's okay. How long do you think everything will take?"

Tyler looked down from his perch on top of the ladder. "Hopefully, we will be done by the end of the day."

"I hope so too." She smiled up at him. "I should get out of your way and let you work."

That was much longer than she'd expected. Perhaps she should go out, call up one of her friends and see who was in the mood for shopping.

Shai had said that it was okay to leave the guys alone in the house, and even if he hadn't, she wouldn't have hesitated to do so. They were clan members, looking out for her and making her house safe, and they wouldn't touch anything they shouldn't.

Or so she hoped. Geraldine still remembered the house painters Cassandra had hired, whom she'd caught rummaging through her underwear drawer.

Some men were such creeps.

Were immortal males more respectful?

She wouldn't know unless she caught them, but Geraldine had no intention of wasting time or energy on that. If Tyler or Aiden wanted to look at her panties, let them. She hoped they enjoyed it.

Downstairs, Geraldine took the cordless off the cradle and sat on the couch to call Gail. It started ringing before she had a chance to dial the number.

"Hi, Mom," Cassandra said. "I tried both your cellphones. Did you forget them in your purse again?"

"Oh dear." Geraldine bolted up. "I did. What if Shai tried to call me?"

"Relax. He would have called the home number like I did."

"Oh, right." She plopped back down.

"How is the work progressing in the house?"

"They won't be done until the end of the day. I was just about to call Gail and ask her if she wanted to go shopping."

"Good idea. You need to get out of the house more."

"I know. But what if you-know-who shows up?"

Cassandra cleared her throat, reminding Geraldine that she shouldn't mention Orion's name on an unsecured line. "Don't worry about it. Anyway, I spoke with Darlene, and we made plans for tomorrow. We are going out to dinner, just you, me, and her."

"What about Leo?"

"He's out of town. Something about getting antiques for the gallery he works for, and he'll be gone until Friday."

Geraldine twined a lock of her hair around her finger. "What are we going to tell her about Rudolf?"

"Can you get your cellphone and call me in a minute? Someone just walked into my office."

"Sure." Geraldine disconnected the call.

Wisely, Cassandra didn't want to discuss Rudolf and what they'd discovered over the landline.

Geraldine's purse was upstairs in her bedroom, and as she took the stairs, she hoped that Aiden was done installing the camera pointing at the master suite's door.

Thankfully, he'd moved his ladder to the other end of the hallway, and the coast was clear.

When Geraldine pulled both phones out of her purse, her old one and the one Shai had given her, she first checked for calls she might have missed. Other than Cassandra, though, no one had called her. Then she looked at the little bar indicating how much charge she had left and was relieved that there was still plenty.

The clan phone that Shai had given her was so much better than her old one. That thing needed to be recharged nightly regardless of whether she'd used it or not.

Everything the clan did was done better. The houses in the village were better insulated and soundproofed, the cars they used were a technological marvel, and the village was so cleverly hidden even though it was only a short distance from downtown Los Angeles, Beverly Hills, and Hollywood.

Sitting on the bed, Geraldine called Cassandra.

"Did someone really walk into your office?"

"No, I was just being careful. So back to Rudolf. We will tell Darlene the same story we told him about the brother our mothers supposedly had."

"What if she wants to see his picture?"

"I have it on my phone. Who knows? Maybe Orion is keeping tabs on her as well, and she'll recognize him."

"I haven't thought of that, but you're right. If he's been taking care of me throughout the years, he might have been helping Darlene too." Geraldine sighed. "I want to tell her the truth so badly. She deserves a chance at immortality, or at least to have the choice to attempt it or not."

"I want it for her as well. But we need to get to know her better first, and we need Shai to be there when we tell her, so he can thrall the memory of what we told her."

Geraldine switched the phone to her other ear. "What's the point of telling her if we make her forget right away?"

"So she can decide. She would have to leave Leo and hook up with an immortal male. That's not an easy decision to make."

"And yet you don't want to give her time to think it through. You want her to decide on the spot."

"That's why I said that we need to get to know her better and gently inquire about her true feelings toward Leo. The guy is a jerk, but he's been her husband for a long time, and she might really love him."

Geraldine leaned her elbow on her knee. "I don't think she loves him enough to give up immortality for him."

"I don't think so either, but we can't assume. We'll find out more tomorrow."

7

VROG

hen Vrog saw Stella and her partner leave their teammates in the hotel room, he stuffed his binoculars into his backpack and jogged the short distance from his hiding place to the hotel lobby.

Recognizing him, the clerk bowed her head. "Good evening, Mr. Wu. How can I be of service?"

He looked into her eyes, bending her will to his. "I need to know the room numbers for the Americans staying here. I'm particularly interested in the woman with the curly hair."

Her eyes glazing over, the woman opened her ledger. "Mrs. Furman and her husband are staying in room number six. Mr. and Mrs. Williams are in room number two."

As she continued listing the names of the American guests and who was in which room, he committed the information to memory. According to the clerk, the two single men shared a room adjacent to Stella's, which complicated things.

He'd counted on her partner being the weak link, but with two fighters sleeping in the next room over, that advantage might not be enough.

Vrog hadn't been trained as a warrior. His hybrid features and ability to eat human food allowed him to pass for a human, and since he was also fairly intelligent, Jade had groomed him for business instead of fighting. He might be physically stronger than the males guarding Stella, but he wasn't sure of that. These long-lived males could be even stronger than him, and they were probably better trained fighters.

If they were anything like the pureblooded Kra-ell males, he had no chance of overpowering them despite the hundreds of pushups and pull-ups he did every day.

His innate Kra-ell aggression wasn't nearly as explosive as that of the purebloods, but he still had to work hard to curb it while living among humans, and the only way he found effective was to exhaust his body with physical exertion.

441

Being fit and strong wasn't the same as being militarily trained, though, and those males looked like they were warriors.

Nevertheless, Vrog had no choice but to proceed. He needed answers, and that meant getting to Stella and forcing those answers out of her. He just needed to figure out how to get her alone. He couldn't thrall her partner, who was no doubt long-lived like her, so he needed to knock him out before either he or Stella could raise the alarm. Or maybe he should just put a knife to the guy's throat and scare her into talking by threatening to kill him.

Perhaps if he had more time, he could have planned it better, but it had to be done tonight. Tomorrow would be too late.

As soon as Stella walked into his office, she would recognize him, and if he canceled the meeting and refused to see her and her companions, she and the others might go home without him learning anything.

How would she react when she saw him?

Perhaps she'd come for answers as well?

If her people were responsible for what had happened to his tribe twenty-two years ago, then what did she hope to achieve by coming back and investigating the school?

His initial reaction to her had been fueled by anger and his assumption that she'd come to finish the job and murder whoever had survived.

But why wait so long to do that?

None of it made sense.

"Thank you." Vrog smiled at the clerk. "Forget that I was ever here and that I asked you anything."

Her eyes losing even more of their focus, she nodded.

The term his people had for what he had done had no equivalent in English or Chinese, but the literal translation was strong influence. Humans called it hypnotism or compulsion, while Stella had called it thralling, and he supposed that it was a combination of both skills.

Back in his hiding place behind the outcropping, Vrog pulled out the binoculars. He didn't need them to see who was in the room, but they were useful to detect details he might have otherwise missed, like the sidearm holster one of the males wore under his jacket.

If one was armed, it was safe to assume the others were armed as well, and that reinforced his belief that Stella had come to finish the job and eliminate the last of his people.

How had she found out that he'd survived?

And how had she found the location of his tribe in the first place?

He hadn't told her anything other than admitting that he was long-lived like her and that he was part of a group. She couldn't have followed him to the compound either, because he hadn't gone home until after the attack.

The only thing she or her people could have done was to find out the firm he'd been overseeing for the tribe and follow the money trail back to Jade. Supposedly, it was next to impossible to do, but Stella's people must have found a way.

Why kill the males and take the females, though?

Stella had seemed genuinely angry at the way Jade treated the males of his tribe, and she'd said that her clan's leader was a much more pleasant female.

It must have been all lies.

Her clan was probably just as short on females as his was, and if it was as small as his tribe, they were just as desperate for genetic variety to save themselves from extinction.

Perhaps after she'd told her people about his group's existence, they'd decided to fortify their numbers with the Kra-ell females. After all, five females were more precious than all the money and gold they'd left behind in those safes.

Hopefully, he would have his answers tonight.

Stella and her guy had gone to their room, but he needed everyone to be asleep before making his move, and the two couples he was watching weren't showing signs of retiring to their beds anytime soon. In fact, they looked as if they were waiting for someone to arrive or something to happen.

8

RICHARD

$\mathcal{U}$sually after making love, Richard slept like the dead until morning, but this time he hadn't allowed himself to doze off. Instead, he spent the time waiting for Arwel's text, gazing with satisfaction at the blissed-out expression on Stella's beautiful face.

His ears, though, were trained on any noise coming from the street. He had plenty of time until Morris arrived with the van at two o'clock in the morning, but in case he made it there earlier, Richard would hear the old van's noisy engine and its rattling parts from a mile away.

So far, though, all he'd heard was nature in its nightly glory—rustling leaves, small nocturnal animals going about their hunt for food and mates, and the occasional hooting of an owl.

He should get dressed.

Taking one last look at Stella's rosy cheeks and puffed-up lips, he smiled and kissed her softly.

She sighed contentedly, but she stayed sleeping even after he gently extracted himself from her arms and got out of bed.

In the bathroom, Richard emptied his bladder, cleaned himself in the sink, brushed his teeth, and wetted a couple of washcloths with warm water.

When he walked back into the room, a slight noise outside the door froze him in place, but as a couple of moments passed with no other suspicious sounds, he figured it must have been a mouse scurrying down the hallway.

After cleaning Stella as best he could without waking her up, he went back to the bathroom and tossed the washcloths in the corner. Back in the room, he snatched his cargo pants and T-shirt off the back of a chair, got dressed, pushed his feet into a pair of shoes, and stuffed his wallet into one of his pants' many pockets.

Since he hadn't fallen asleep as was usually the case after a rigorous lovemaking session, Richard was experiencing the other kind of side effects, which were thirst and hunger. The fridge in their room was mostly empty by now, but there was a vending machine at the end of the hallway where he could get bottled water, some Chinese-made soft drinks, and snacks.

The vending machine accepted his credit card, which was good, but his luck was short-lived. The damn thing got stuck, the mechanical arm pushing the bottle out of its slot but not releasing its claws to let it drop. A bit of shaking solved the problem, but it made too much noise. Fortunately, his team members were the only guests in the hotel tonight, and other than Stella, none were asleep. When no one came rushing to check out what was causing the ruckus, he repeated the operation three more times, getting another bottle of water and two bags of chips.

He stuffed the chips in his cargo pants pockets, tucked the bottles under his arm, and headed back to the room.

His phone buzzed with an incoming message at the same time he heard the van's engine.

Good timing.

He left the bottles by the door and jogged down the hallway.

When he reached Arwel and Jin's room, the team was already gone, but the door had been left open for him, and he left the same way they had—out the window.

The van was parked a hundred feet or so from the hotel, and as he jogged the rest of the way, it occurred to him that they weren't being very stealthy about their departure.

Then again, the town was more than an hour's drive away from the school, so the precautions weren't really necessary. The only reason for using the window as their exit point was the surveillance camera mounted in the hotel's lobby.

When he climbed into the back of the van, Morris handed him the tranquilizer gun. "Did you ever use one of these?"

Richard turned the thing in his hands. It looked like something from a Wild West movie or a Halloween prop and nothing like the autoloaders he'd trained with.

"What is this thing? It looks like a museum exhibit."

Jin smirked. "I thought that you were a weapons expert."

"I'm as much of an expert as you are. We took the same training."

"I should show you how to use it," Arwel said. "Close the door."

"Why?"

"Because I can't do it inside the van, and I can't demonstrate using a tranq gun on the sidewalk." He turned to Morris. "Drive to that wooded area at the end of the street."

Richard paused with his hand on the door's handle. "I don't want to leave Stella alone for too long."

Arwel shrugged. "It's up to you. You can leave now, but if you want the gun, you need to learn how to use it, which will take no more than five minutes including the time we are wasting talking about it."

"Fine." Richard closed the van's sliding door. "Let's do it."

9

VROG

*A*s Vrog heard a vehicle stop somewhere nearby at two o'clock in the morning, he wondered if that was what the two couples had been waiting for.

When a moment later the two single men entered the hotel room and then everyone left through the window, his suspicions were confirmed.

It seemed that Stella and her partner weren't joining them, which would be a tremendous stroke of luck for him, but he needed to make sure before making his move.

Running on stealthy feet, Vrog made it in time to see the six climb into an old beat-up van.

Where were they going?

Perhaps they were planning to attack the school again?

No, that was a stupid thought. They had no reason to go after the kids or the faculty. They were probably just after him.

Vrog smiled.

They wouldn't find him in his apartment in the staff quarters, and the joke would be on them because they were leaving Stella with only her partner for protection, and the guy didn't look like he would pose a challenge.

Vrog thought that his luck couldn't get any better when Stella's partner jogged to the waiting vehicle and climbed in.

Were they leaving her utterly alone?

That didn't make sense. If they suspected that there were more Kra-ell in the compound, they wouldn't do that. The van was just idling though, so perhaps not everyone on board was going, and someone would take his place guarding Stella.

If one of the fighters went back, Vrog's best option was to intercept him and cut his throat before he had a chance to make it back to the hotel.

Bile rose in his throat.

He wasn't a cold-blooded killer, and until he knew for sure that Stella and her people were responsible for his tribe's annihilation, he wasn't entitled to revenge.

446

The Mother of all Life would not look kindly upon him killing without provocation and without giving his opponent a fighting chance.

Perhaps he could knock the male out instead.

No, that wouldn't work. The male wouldn't stay down long enough for Vrog to interrogate Stella. He would have to eliminate him permanently, which could damn him forever if he had no right to the kill.

The Kra-ell were brutal and unforgiving people, but they lived by a code of honor imposed upon them by The Mother of all Life and her earthly embodiment—their tribe's leader. Vrog had broken the code only once, and even that had been unwittingly.

Jade had forbidden the hybrid males to impregnate human females, and as the goddess's mouthpiece, she was the law. But Vrog had no way of knowing that Stella's body did not work like that of human females—she didn't need to be in her fertile cycle to conceive.

When he'd hooked up with her, he'd assumed she couldn't get pregnant because she hadn't been ovulating. If she had been, he would have detected it. Too late, he'd learned that with the right male, the females of her kind conceived on demand.

Why her body had decided that he was the most compatible male it had ever encountered was beyond him, though.

Perhaps it hadn't been what Jade had wanted, but it might have been the wish of a higher authority—The Mother of All Life.

It had occurred to him even then that The Mother's hand might have guided his encounter with Stella, and that the son they'd created together was destined for something great—something The Mother needed him to do.

That was why Vrog had let Stella go with his child growing in her womb.

Had it been the biggest mistake of his life?

When the van's door closed and it drove away with Stella's partner, Vrog lifted his head heavenward and thanked The Mother.

She must be smiling upon him tonight, guiding his steps.

He'd come with no plan and no weapons other than a hunting knife, his brute strength, and his fangs, and yet he would succeed.

He had to move fast, though.

As the van neared his hiding spot, Vrog sprinted away, using the shadows to cover his retreat.

When the van stopped right where he'd been a moment ago, shameful fear gripped Vrog, and he ran even faster while keeping his footfalls as silent as he could.

They had guns, and he couldn't outrun a bullet. His only hope was that they hadn't seen him.

Reaching the back of the hotel with no sound of pursuit, Vrog climbed inside through the window that Stella's people had left open, and then rushed out of the room.

Not knowing how long they would be gone, he sprinted to the end of the hallway, careful not to make any noise.

It didn't matter whether Stella was awake or asleep. He had the element of surprise on his side, and she was no match for him. But if she heard him coming, she might call her people back, and he had to get to her before she had a chance to do that.

1 0

RICHARD

*A*fter the explanation and demonstration Richard had gotten, he doubted the usefulness of the dart gun, or rather of the darts themselves.

The tranquilizer just didn't work as fast as a bullet to incapacitate a perpetrator.

Morris had assured him that William's tinkering with the gun mechanism and Merlin's magic touch with the paralytic inside the ballistic syringe made the thing a highly effective non-lethal weapon. But the tranquilizer needed a few seconds to work, and if a perpetrator had a gun, he could kill him and Stella in the time it took for the chemical to enter his bloodstream.

Arwel had shown him how to load the syringe and had given him one more to put in his pocket. Apparently, Charlie, the other pilot, had gotten one into Emmett's neck without the help of a gun just by throwing it.

Richard had a decent aim with darts and a strong throwing arm, so if push came to shove, he could use that option. But since anyone attacking him or Stella in the little sleepy town was such an unlikely scenario, Richard carefully tucked the gun into one of his pockets, the extra syringe into another, and headed back to the hotel.

His pockets were so overstuffed with the potato chips he'd bought, his wallet, the vials with the sleeping potion that he'd forgotten to take out, and now the gun and the additional syringe, that they were stretched to bursting and uncomfortable to run or even walk fast in, but he did anyway, a sense of foreboding urging him to get back to Stella as soon as possible.

It was probably nothing. All that thinking about potential perpetrators must have gotten his adrenaline pumping.

When he found the door to their room slightly ajar, his anxiety increased tenfold, the adrenaline rush swelling his muscles, readying them for a fight.

With his mate sleeping in the nude, it was unlikely that he'd forgotten to close the door, but he tried to reason with himself that the lock might have not latched properly. He'd been careful not to wake her, so he might have closed the door too softly for it to lock.

Except, glancing at the two bottles of water he'd left on the floor, he knew that he would have noticed the door not being closed when he'd put them down.

Richard pulled out the tranquilizer gun.

Softly nudging the door open with his foot, he thanked the merciful Fates when it didn't make any sound and entered.

What awaited him was a scene from his worst nightmares.

A tall man held the terrified and naked Stella in front of him, an arm wrapped around her middle, right under her breasts, pressing a knife to her neck with the other.

"Don't move or I'll slash her throat," he bit out. "Put the gun down."

"Please, don't hurt her. What do you want? Do you want money?" Richard put the gun on the dresser. "I'm going to take out my wallet. You can have it all." He reached into his pocket.

The guy hissed, revealing a pair of razor-sharp fangs. "Not another move, or I make her bleed."

A Kra-ell male.

Richard's blood froze in his veins. He was no match for the male's strength, and the guy was holding a knife to Stella's neck.

The gun was useless and so was the extra tranquilizer dart.

Other than that, all Richard had were his wits, the wallet in his left pocket, two bags of chips, and the useless sleeping potion vials...

Or perhaps not so useless.

Could he use the sleeping potion to distract the guy? Perhaps the Kra-ell weren't immune to the chemicals?

It was worth a try.

One vial was enough to put a couple of teenagers to sleep, two vials were enough to knock out an adult male. He didn't need to knock the guy out. He just needed to disorient him while not making one single threatening move.

Feigning terror, which wasn't hard, his hand closed on the bag of chips and the two vials in his left pocket.

"Why?" Stella whispered.

"Why?" The male dipped his head to look at the side of her face. "You slaughtered my people, and you are asking me why?"

The guy was insane. What the hell was he talking about?

As a small trickle of blood started where the knife was pressed against Stella's carotid, Richard's hands started shaking. "Don't hurt her, please." He made his voice tremble and his teeth rattle while crushing what he held in his hand.

The crunching noise of the chips covered the sound of breaking glass, and Richard stifled a wince as the glass shards cut into his fingers, focusing instead on the wet liquid sliding down his leg.

The male's head snapped to him. "What did you do?"

"I'm sorry." Shaking violently, Richard looked down at the stain forming on his sweatpants.

The male sneered. "Did you wet yourself?"

Richard didn't have to work hard to force blood up into his face and feign embarrassment. The rage inside him was boiling the blood in his veins and painting his vision red.

"I've never even met your people," Stella whispered, tears sliding down her cheeks. "Don't do this. We have a son, Vrog. His name is Vlad, and he looks just like you."

This was Vrog? Vlad's father? He looked nothing like Vlad, but Stella was smart to say that.

Talk about a shocker.

He would think about the implications later. Right now, Richard's entire focus was on the hand holding a hunting knife to Stella's throat.

Something passed over the guy's eyes, something that looked like uncertainty and remorse, and he lowered the knife but didn't let go of Stella.

Regrettably, it seemed like the sleeping potion had no effect on him, but at least he was no longer holding Stella at knifepoint.

He still had the knife in his hand, though. He could still change his mind and kill her.

The guy sniffed. "What's that smell?" He swayed just a little, enough for Richard to realize that the potion was working after all.

Stella must have realized the same thing, or perhaps she just took advantage of the guy's arm around her slackening a fraction. Dropping to the floor, she slipped out of his hold, exposing him to Richard.

There was no time to grab the gun.

As Vrog bent down to grab Stella, Richard delivered a powerful kick to the guy's head, sending him flying backward, pulled the syringe out of his pocket, jumped on top of him, and stabbed him in the neck.

That wasn't enough, though. Despite the sleeping potion, the kick to the head, and the tranquilizer dart, the guy wasn't out and managed to deliver a punch to Richard's face that would have knocked him out if he were still a human.

Hell, it might have knocked an immortal out as well, but Richard's rage and need to protect his mate gave him the boost of power he needed.

Ignoring his broken cheekbone, he returned the favor, delivering one punch after the other to Vrog's face until the combined effort of his fists and the tranquilizer finally weakened the guy and then knocked him out.

In case Vrog was just feigning unconsciousness, Richard kept punching. He might not be able to kill the Kra-ell with his bare fists, but he was going to smash his ugly puss into a pulp.

"Stop!" Stella caught his arm. "He's already out. Let's tie him up before he regains consciousness."

Richard freed his arm from Stella's hold and delivered one last punch to the guy's bloodied face. "He's not going to wake up anytime soon."

"If he's like us, he will."

11

ARWEL

*A*s Arwel's phone rang, everyone's eyes turned to him. They'd left the hotel no more than fifteen minutes ago, and people back home knew that he was on a mission and wouldn't be calling him.

Arwel pulled the device out of his pocket. "Richard. What's up?"

"You need to turn around. We have a Kra-ell male tied up in our room. He's out cold, but I need something better to tie him up with than my belt, and I need to get more of those sleeping potion vials. I stabbed him with the tranquilizer, but I don't know how long the effect will last and if it's safe to stab him so soon with the other. Stella doesn't want me to accidentally kill him."

"The sleeping potions will probably not work on him."

"They do to some degree. I used the two I had on me to disorient him."

Arwel had so many questions, but he didn't want to keep Richard from doing everything he could to secure the guy before they got back. "I have more vials in my room. They are in the backpack inside the closet. But be careful. He might not be alone."

Morris slowed down and looked at him through the rearview mirror for approval.

Arwel nodded and made a circling motion with his finger.

"He is. The mysterious Wu, the head of the school who we were supposed to meet tomorrow, is actually Vrog, Stella's old flame. Just get here as soon as you can and bring handcuffs or a strong rope. The guy is a damn gorilla."

"We will be there in less than ten minutes."

"Good. I need to hang up. I'll tell you the rest when you get here."

Shaking his head, Arwel put his phone back in his pocket. He'd had a number of surprises during his life, some good and some bad, but Stella's old boyfriend showing up at their hotel made it to the top of the list.

"So instead of us finding the Kra-ell, one has found us," Jin said. "And not just any random Kra-ell, but Stella's Vrog."

451

"Do we have jumper cables in the van?" Yamanu asked. "We don't have reinforced handcuffs, and a regular rope won't be enough to hold him if he's as strong as Emmett. The jumper cables might do the job, though."

Arwel had never used those cables to do anything other than jump-start his car, and he doubted they were flexible enough to tie up a prisoner. "Our best option is to tranq him all the way to the airport and get him to the jet as soon as possible."

"We don't have jumper cables," Morris said. "And even if we did, I don't think we could use them for tying up a prisoner, but a good rope might be enough to hold even a gorilla."

"We can't leave yet." Mey twirled the end of her braid over her finger. "I need to listen to more echoes."

Arwel gave her a smile. "We captured a Kra-ell male, and he can tell us all we need to know. You no longer need to listen to echoes."

"I think that's a mistake, but you're the boss, Arwel."

She hadn't said it angrily, only factually, and she might be right. "If necessary, we can come here again. The walls are not going anywhere."

Jin snorted. "Unless someone sets them on fire."

With Morris pushing the old clunker to its limit speeding down the road toward the hotel, they made it back in much less than ten minutes.

Arwel didn't bother with stealth as he jogged through the lobby to Stella and Richard's room. With Yamanu no longer needing to preserve his energy, he could cast a shroud around them, hiding them from the woman at the front desk.

Later, they would tamper with the surveillance feed from the lone camera in the lobby. Thankfully, it was the old kind that wasn't connected to an outside server.

Richard waited for them with the door open. "Remind me to thank Merlin for his potions."

His face had taken a beating, but Arwel knew that it looked worse than it was, and it was already on the mend.

Mey winced. "Is your cheek broken?"

"It was." Richard put his hand over the side of his face. "I hope I pushed it back in place correctly. I don't want to have it re-broken to fix it."

"It must have hurt like hell," Yamanu said.

"It did, but the other guy looks worse."

Inside, Stella sat on the floor next to the unconscious male, her eyes red-rimmed as if she'd been crying for hours.

The Kra-ell was on his belly, hands tied behind his back with a leather belt. It was a good makeshift restraint, but anyone with minimal training and a bit of muscle strength could break free from that.

"Oh, sweetie." Jin rushed to Stella's side and wrapped her arms around her. "Were you frightened?"

Stella nodded.

"Did he hurt you?"

As Stella shook her head, Arwel released a relieved breath.

"Then why are you crying?" Jin asked.

"He hates me."

Mey frowned. "Who hates you?"

"Vrog." Stella's chin wobbled. "He thinks I'm responsible for slaughtering his people."

For a long, shocked moment, no one spoke.

"The Kra-ell were slaughtered?" Yamanu asked.

She nodded. "That's what he said. And he thinks I did it."

"Why would he think that?" Jin helped Stella up.

"I don't know." More tears slid down Stella's cheeks.

"I think I can explain," Richard said. "As some of you know, Vrog and Stella have a history. He's Vlad's father. He's also Mr. Wu." He tossed a wallet to Arwel. "I found this in his pocket."

Arwel flipped the thing open and looked at the identification card. "This is written in Chinese. I can't read it."

"Neither can I," Richard said. "But Stella can, and it says that his name is James Wu."

Arwel closed the wallet, put it in his pocket, and looked at Stella. "Can you think of any reason for why he blames you for his people's demise?"

Looking distraught, she shook her head.

"Maybe because he told Stella about them," Richard said. "The fire happened about the same time they hooked up. So, he might have assumed that there was a connection."

As the guy on the floor groaned, Richard pulled out a vial from his pocket and snapped it open over the male's head. "I was lucky to have two in my pocket." He looked at Arwel. "They were enough to distract him a little, but even after I stabbed him with the tranquilizer and beat the hell out of him, he still wouldn't stay down. By the way, when I went to get more vials from your room, I didn't want to waste time going in through the window, so I forced the door open. We will have to cover the cost of the repairs."

"That's fine. You did very well." Arwel patted Richard's shoulder and then crouched next to the prone Kra-ell male.

Richard jingled the vials he still had in his pocket. "We have five left, which doesn't give us much time. We also have more darts, but I'm not sure how many we can use on him safely. We still need to interrogate him, and I don't mind knocking him out the old-fashioned way." Richard shook out his hand. "Now that I heal so fast, the bruising is not a big deal."

The guy was obviously enjoying it, but Stella wasn't.

"I'd rather use as few as possible of the tranquilizer darts, but I will if the sleeping potion is too weak to hold him down." Arwel checked Vrog's pulse. "We need to get him out of here."

Holding a rope in his hands, Morris walked in through the open door. "I found this in the hotel's storage room."

"Good. Tie him up." Arwel rose to his feet. "We are all leaving. Jay and I will load him into the van and head to the airport. The rest of you pack up and take the limo." He turned to Yamanu. "Before you leave, take care of the surveillance footage and leave money on the front desk to compensate them for the broken door and for cleaning up the mess in here."

"I'll clean up the blood." Stella lifted her gaze to him. "Just try not to hurt Vrog. He's not a bad guy. He's angry because he thinks that I had something to do with his people's fate." She shook her head. "It's so sad. All this time we thought that they'd just moved on."

12

STELLA

*S*tella squirted hand sanitizer on the bloodstained carpet and attacked it with the spare toothbrush she'd sacrificed for the task. "You were amazing, Richard. But did you really need to beat him up so badly?"

She still couldn't believe that the two of them had managed to overpower a Kra-ell male. Richard had been magnificent—cool-headed, fast, strong.

While they'd been waiting for the team to arrive, Stella had told him as much, and since then he'd been strutting around like a peacock, wearing his bruised cheek like a badge of honor.

Nevertheless, she was so proud of him. He was entitled to a little strutting. What she didn't like, though, was his attitude toward Vrog.

Vrog wouldn't have hurt her, she was sure of that, but he'd held her at knifepoint while she was naked, and her mate would never forgive and forget that.

Richard closed his suitcase. "I didn't hit him hard enough, and you should leave that bloodstain alone." He lifted his suitcase off the bed and set it down next to hers. "We need to get going."

"It's not coming out." She scrubbed even harder.

"And it's not going to. Arwel said to leave money for the repair and for the cleanup. We don't have time for this."

Leaning back on her haunches, she looked up at him. "It's not a coffee stain, Richard. It's Kra-ell blood, and it can be analyzed. This place looks like a crime scene. What if someone calls the authorities?"

"You're right, and I have an idea how we can solve it. I'll be back in a minute." He strode out of the room.

When more scrubbing only diluted the brownish red splotches and spread the stains further, Stella let out a sigh and sat back. It seemed that the only way to get rid of the evidence was to cut out the affected area, and maybe she should do that. Who knew what could be found in Vrog's blood. The last thing they needed was for someone to analyze the stain and find abnormalities.

454

A few moments later, Richard returned with a bottle of bleach. "This should take care of it."

"Smart. Where did you find it?"

"In the hotel laundry room. Step aside so I don't get any of it on you."

She pushed to her feet and moved away from the spot. "The bleach is going to ruin the carpet."

"That's less of a problem than leaving traces of Vrog's blood behind." He removed the cap from the bottle.

"Careful. If you pour from up high, the bleach will splatter all over your clothes."

Richard looked down at the cargo pants he'd been wearing for four days straight. "Not a big loss." Nevertheless, he crouched next to the stain and poured the bleach directly over it.

She'd given him so much grief about wearing the same pair of cargo pants since the start of the investigation, but he'd insisted on roughing it, and in the end, those damn pants might have saved their lives.

The first night they'd gone to the compound, Arwel had given each of them two vials of Merlin's sleeping potion in case Yamanu's thrall didn't work on some of the students or faculty, but they hadn't used any. If Richard wasn't such a slob, he would've given the vials back to Arwel instead of keeping them in his pocket.

Lifting a trembling hand to her neck, Stella ran her fingers over the spot Vrog had nicked with his knife. What if she was wrong about him? What if he would have killed her if Richard hadn't stopped him?

Was Vrog capable of murdering the mother of his son?

Fates, what a mess.

Stella had spent long years feeling sorry for Vrog, wondering what other hardships his bitch of a leader had forced upon him, and during all that time Vrog had been fanning the embers of hate and plotting revenge for a crime she hadn't committed.

"What smells so bad?" Mey walked into the room.

"Bleach." Stella looked at the carpet that had turned white and yellow. At least the bloodstains were gone.

"We are ready to go," Mey said.

"So are we." Richard hefted both of their suitcases.

"I need to wash my hands and dispose of the last bit of evidence." Stella took the nearly empty bottle of bleach, tossed in the toothbrush she'd been using, put the cap back on, and gave it a vigorous shake.

That should take care of any traces of Vrog's blood.

After washing her hands, she lifted her purse off the nightstand, took one last look around the room to make sure they hadn't left anything behind, and followed Richard out.

Mey, Jin, and Alfie were already waiting for them in the limo, but Yamanu wasn't there.

"Where is your mate?" Richard asked Mey.

"He had to wait for you to be out before tampering with the surveillance footage. He also needs to thrall the front desk clerk."

Thankfully they hadn't thralled her too often, so hopefully the poor woman wouldn't suffer irreparable damage.

"I can't believe that they were all slaughtered," Jin said softly. "Why spare the humans and kill the Kra-ell?"

Stella had been pondering the same thing. "Maybe they are not dead. I didn't have a chance to ask Vrog why he thought they were."

It was wishful thinking, and Stella was well aware of that. Vrog wouldn't have been so filled with hate if he hadn't had a good reason to believe his people had been killed.

"He probably found their bodies," Alfie said.

Stella shook her head. "Whoever did that burned them to destroy the evidence. They wouldn't have left bodies of aliens lying around." She lifted her eyes to him. " That's why Richard and I bleached the carpet in our room. We had to destroy all traces of Vrog's blood." She cast Richard an accusing glance. "Richard broke his nose and he bled all over the place."

"Who could have attacked them?" Mey murmured, looking out the window. "And what is taking Yamanu so long?"

"Perhaps it was the Chinese government," Jin suggested. "They could have discovered the Kra-ell and eliminated them, or rather most of them. I bet they took a few to interrogate."

A shiver rocked Stella's body. "I'm glad that we are leaving. I don't feel safe here."

Richard wrapped his arm around her shoulders. "I'm glad to be out of here as well, and I can't wait to interrogate that son of a bitch."

"Don't insult his mother," Mey admonished. "She might have been a good woman."

"She must have been." Stella leaned her head on Richard's arm. "Despite what he did tonight, Vrog isn't a bad guy, and given what Emmett told us about Kra-ell fathers, it wasn't his father's doing."

"I disagree." Richard tightened his hand on her shoulder. "A good guy doesn't attack a defenseless woman while she's sleeping naked in her bed. Whatever he imagined you did to his people is no justification."

"He lost his mother and father," Stella whispered. "His friends and relatives are all gone and probably dead. Would you have been as forgiving if you thought some ex-lover of yours was responsible for your people's annihilation?"

When Richard didn't respond, she let loose a sigh. "That's what I thought."

13

ANNANI

"*M*erlin." Annani opened her arms and embraced the lanky doctor. "I love your new look."

"Thank you." He straightened, but not to his full height, remaining in a slightly hunched position, probably not wanting to tower over her. "I was delighted to receive an invitation from you. It has been ages since we had tea together."

"Indeed." She sat back down and motioned for him to join her on the couch. "I enjoyed our talks very much." She smiled. "But you have been busy lately."

He dipped his head and sat next to her. "I'm never too busy for you, Clan Mother."

"That is so nice of you to say." She tucked her legs to the side and smoothed her skirt. "How many couples have joined your conception expediting experiment?"

"Since Kian and Syssi, only four more are participating in my program." He sighed. "I wish more would join, but even if all of the mated couples participated, my sample would still be too small to qualify as a scientific study."

Annani waved a hand in dismissal. "What you are doing is part science and part magic. In the end, it is up to the Fates to decide who will be blessed with a child and when."

As Merlin nodded in agreement, Onidu arrived with their tea.

"Tea is ready, Clan Mother." Bowing, the Odu put the tray down on the coffee table.

"Thank you."

"Should I pour for you, Clan Mother?"

"Yes, please."

Annani waited for Onidu to pour the tea into both cups, lifted hers, and turned to Merlin. "You are probably wondering why I invited you here today."

Merlin's eyes sparkled with mischief. "I guessed it has something to do with Ronja and her acquiescence to consider attempting transition."

"You guessed it. Am I correct in assuming that despite her acquiescence, things have not progressed much in the romantic department?"

His smile wilted. "Ronja needs time. In her mind, it would be disrespectful to her husband's memory to get romantically involved so soon after his death."

"Yes, I am aware of that." Annani took a sip of her tea. "The reason I wanted to talk to you is that I am going home, and I do not want you and Ronja to start anything without me here. My blessing is absolutely crucial to the success of her transition. I will return to the village in one month to be with Amanda when she nears full term, but in case Ronja relents sooner, you do not have to wait with romantic activities, but you will need to use precautions until I arrive."

Annani had expected Merlin to be dismissive of her so-called blessing, but his expression was somber as he nodded. "I will wait for your return, Clan Mother. Ronja needs time not only to mourn her husband but also to strengthen her body, and that cannot be done overnight."

Did he suspect what her *blessing* really was?

Merlin was very bright, and he might have guessed, but as long as he did not know for sure and did not mention it to anyone, there was no harm in him speculating.

Annani refilled her cup from the carafe and lifted it to her lips. "Ronja told me about the exercise program you suggested. What else is included in the rejuvenation regimen you put her on?"

"Some dietary changes, mainly the elimination of sugar and the inclusion of large quantities of greens and herbs, including medicinal herbs from Gertrude's garden." He smiled sheepishly. "I do miss Ronja's amazing cakes, but I can't expect her to bake them and not eat them. Once she transitions, though, I hope she'll bake me a new cake every day." He smacked his lips.

That sounded like a good healthy approach, but it did not sound like a miracle in the making. "Is that all it would take to make her younger from the inside out?"

"I also remind her to drink plenty of water, and I'm dialing in a perfect combination of substances for her potion. Every person is different, and what works for one might not work for another."

"That is very true." She put her cup down. "Geraldine's older daughter is forty-nine, which up until recently was considered too old to transition. So far, she has not been told about us or her special genes, but I believe that at some point in the near future her mother and sister will tell her everything and offer her the option to attempt transition. You might have one more person in your biological health experiment. It would be interesting to see what things work on both women and what will work on one, but not the other."

Merlin reached for the carafe and refilled his own cup. "I will do whatever I can for Geraldine's daughter. Is there any news with the facial recognition program finding Orion?"

Annani laughed. "How did you hear about that so soon?"

"I saw Amanda in the café this morning. She told me about the mysterious Orion. Was it supposed to be a secret? I told Ronja, but I can ask her not to tell anyone else."

That was how rumors spread so fast through the clan.

"By now, Onegus has probably shown the pictures to so many people that it no longer matters."

"Maybe Kian should call a village meeting and let everyone know about Orion,"

Merlin suggested. "Instead of people having to rely on rumors, which have a tendency to distort the original story, they would get it without all the embellishments."

"That is a good idea." Annani sighed. "William ran the portrait through his facial recognition software, but it did not flag anyone. It seems that Orion knows how to effectively obscure his features."

Merlin nodded. "Another option is that he is limiting his travels now that the technology makes it difficult to hide. He might reside in another country that doesn't have cameras on every corner."

Annani lifted a brow. "Where would that be?"

"Many places in the world are still safe in that regard. Most of South America, Africa, part of the Middle East, and even some of the Far East, the Caribbean and other islands. There is no shortage of places to hide." He smiled. "For now."

1 4

ARWEL

*A*rwel sat in the back of the van, watching the Kra-ell male sleep. He would have liked to wake the bastard up and find out what he'd hoped to gain by attacking Stella, but he couldn't risk it.

Pointing a gun to his head might keep him in line, but Arwel didn't know enough about Vrog to risk it. The guy might decide that committing suicide via Arwel's gun was better than getting captured and later interrogated.

Arwel had seen his share of misplaced heroics. For all he knew, the guy could have a poisoned tooth ready to deploy.

"How are we going to get him to the jet?" Morris asked.

"Good question." Arwel's lips twitched with a suppressed smile. "Do you think we could stuff him inside a suitcase?"

Vrog was at least six feet four inches tall, but he was slim. If he was flexible, they could stuff him in a crate and carry it into the jet, but it wouldn't be necessary. Arwel wasn't a great shrouder, but he could probably manage the twenty-minute walk with the guy slung over Jay's shoulder.

"He's too tall," Morris said as if Arwel's comment had been serious. "We will have to wait for Yamanu to arrive and shroud us. It's better to wait another half an hour than risk dragging the dude through the airport with his bloody face on display."

"He already looks better. Besides, Jay can carry him while I shroud the three of us, but you'll have to thrall the officials on the way."

"No problem. But I still think that we should wait for Yamanu to make it as smooth as possible. It's a busy airport, and Chinese officials are suspicious bastards. We might get delayed, and you'll run out of shrouding juice. If you're worried about pretty boy waking up too soon, I have more tranquilizer darts back in the jet, and I can bring them back to the van."

"That's an option." Arwel pulled out his phone and called Yamanu.

"Hello, boss," the Guardian answered. "Cleanup is complete, and we are on our way."

"Good. Tell Alfie to put pedal to the metal. We might need you to shroud Vrog as we carry him through the airport, and I don't like waiting while we don't have him properly secured."

"No problem. With the piece of junk Morris is driving, we will catch up to you in no time."

"How is everyone doing?" And by everyone, Arwel meant Stella.

Understandably, she had looked shell-shocked when he'd left. The woman was tough, but she was a civilian, and waking up to a crazed guy holding a knife to her neck must have been traumatic.

"Everyone is fine. We are brainstorming ideas about what might have happened to the Kra-ell. Do you think that the Chinese government did it?"

"It has crossed my mind, but I'd rather wait for our guest to wake up and give us more information to work with."

"Mey says that she should go back and listen for more echoes. Now more than ever, it's crucial to learn what happened to them."

"Right now, we are going home. I can't risk detaining Vrog in China. We might come back, though. I'm going to call Kian, give him an update, and check what he wants to do."

"Good deal. See you later, boss."

It was nearly four o'clock in the morning Beijing time, but given the time difference it was only about one o'clock in the afternoon in Los Angeles.

Kian answered on the second ring. "Trouble?"

"Yes and no. We've gotten ourselves a Kra-ell male, and we are taking him to the jet. Hopefully, no one will try to stop us." Arwel continued with the rest of the story, which didn't take long since he didn't know much.

Kian let out a long breath. "Talk about a twist. So let me get this straight. Vrog met Stella and fathered Vlad in Singapore twenty-two years ago. When he returned home and found that the compound was deserted and most of it burned down, he assumed that Stella had something to do with it because of the timing."

"That seems to be it. We will know more once he wakes up. If I had reinforced handcuffs, I would have interrogated him on the way to the airport, but without them, I don't want to risk waking him up before we get him on the jet."

"How strong is he?"

"Strong. He fought Richard even after getting hit with a tranquilizing dart. Richard kept beating him up until the drug took effect, but after that, he kept the guy down with Merlin's sleeping potion. Frankly, I'm surprised that it worked on Vrog, even if the effect is short-lived. It has no effect whatsoever on us, and we are supposed to be distant relatives of theirs."

"Perhaps we are not related to the Kra-ell after all."

"We certainly share a common ancestor." Arwel pushed his fingers through his hair. "The Kra-ell seem to be an older version though, less enhanced than the gods. Perhaps whoever created all of us kept improving the design."

Kian chuckled. "I hate to think that there is an even more enhanced humanoid version than the gods out there, but I wouldn't be surprised if there were. Hundreds of thousands of years have probably passed since the gods created humans, and probably millions of years since the gods themselves were created. That's a lot of time to experiment and improve on the model."

461

15

STELLA

$\mathcal{A}$s the limo hit yet another pothole, Richard gripped the handle above the window. "I'm glad that we are immortal." His arm around Stella's shoulders tightened.

Alfie was driving the thing like a bat out of hell and grinning like a kid who'd gotten permission to go wild.

"Relax." Yamanu crossed his massive arms over his chest and smiled at Richard. "Guardians get race car driving lessons, and with our enhanced senses and faster response times, we can handle speeds that even professional race car drivers would be hard pressed to surpass." He leaned closer. "You're no longer human. Stop thinking like one."

"I can't help it. These country roads are not meant for speeding limousines."

That was true.

Stella didn't doubt Alfie's driving skills, but they couldn't compensate for the road condition. At the speed he was going, a deep pothole could send the limousine tumbling into a ditch.

Thankfully, the limo's seats were incredibly cushy. As they kept hitting one pothole after the other and getting jostled from side to side and up and down, their backsides didn't suffer too badly.

The one good thing about the rollercoaster ride was that it helped take her mind off Vrog and the rabid hatred she'd seen in his eyes.

"Here is the van," Alfie said. "I told you that I would catch up to it in no time."

"You're insane." Richard huffed. "We left almost an hour after them, it should have been impossible for you to catch up. I didn't even know that a limo could go that fast."

"Live and learn, buddy. Live and learn." Alfie flashed his headlights to alert Morris that he was right behind him. "You can relax. It's going to be a slow ride from now on."

Stella's heart started hammering in her chest.

Soon, they would board the plane, Arwel would let Vrog wake up, and she would have a chance to talk to him, tell him about the son they shared, and what a wonderful man Vlad was.

Reaching into her purse, she pulled out her phone and searched for pictures of Vlad. There were so many, and those she had stored in her phone were just the recent ones. Vlad with Wendy, Vlad and Wendy together with Richard and Stella, Vlad and Richard—

The pictures told a story—a story of a family. How would that make Vrog feel?

Angry, most likely.

He'd lost his family and had been alone for the past twenty-two years, while she'd had a son, had been surrounded by her clan, and had found her true-love mate.

Perhaps she shouldn't show him the pictures.

"I like this one," Richard said. "Wendy is making a goofy duck face and Vlad is laughing. He doesn't laugh often enough."

She turned to look at him. "It's not that he's unhappy. Vlad is just shy and introverted."

"I know. I just wish he'd let loose a bit."

The quintessential extrovert, Richard was the opposite of reserved. He was easy to laugh, easy to befriend, and easy to love.

She smiled. "You want him to be more like you."

"Is that a bad thing?"

"Not at all." She kissed his cheek. "You are wonderful, but Vlad can't be you. He has a different personality."

"Like his father's?" There was a distinct note of jealousy in Richard's tone.

"I don't know Vrog well enough to answer that. From what I remember, he was somewhat reserved, but that was probably because he was hiding who he really was."

"He's insane." Richard's fingers dug into her shoulder. "Living alone and hiding for all these years must have messed with his head. You've heard what Emmett said about the Kra-ell males. They revere their females. It should have been impossible for him to attack you, and yet he did."

That was only partially true. Given what Emmett had told them about the Kra-ell sexual practices, a male had to fight the female, and if he wasn't able to subdue her, she wouldn't grant him the right to father her child. But what was sanctioned during sex was not tolerated at any other time.

Vrog might have been her lover at one time, but nothing about their encounter tonight had been sexual. Perhaps his Kra-ell half was less dominant than his human half.

"I'm not Kra-ell, and Vrog is half human. He might have absorbed human attitudes toward women."

That was a poor excuse, and she knew it. Just a small percentage of human males mistreated women, and it wasn't fair to condemn the entire male gender because of the misdeeds of the few. The immortals and the Kra-ell might have had it hardwired into their psyche, but humans had a choice, and Vrog had chosen poorly.

"Don't excuse his behavior," Richard bit out. "I just want you to be careful, and I don't want you to take to heart the unfounded accusations he'll no doubt throw at you."

"I'll try." She sighed. "You know me. I'm not as fragile as I might seem, and I don't give up easily. By the time we land in Los Angeles, I'll have it all sorted out."

16

SHAI

*W*hen Shai pulled up in front of Geraldine's house, William's guys were loading their equipment into their van and blocking the driveway, where he usually parked.

For some reason, he still didn't use the garage even though there was enough space next to Cassandra's old car. Geraldine joked that he wanted the neighbors to know she had a boyfriend so no one would get ideas. But the truth was that he still treated her place as a temporary arrangement even though he'd de facto moved in. His clothes were hanging in her closet, his shaver was on her bathroom counter, and the only reason he still stopped by his house from time to time was to pick up more things to take to her place.

Shai would have preferred for things to be the other way around, but he wasn't complaining. He was with the female he loved, so it was all good.

For now.

One day, Orion would show up, and everything might go to hell.

With a sigh, Shai killed the engine, stepped out of the car, and walked over to the van. "All done?"

Aiden nodded. "Do you want me to show you where the cameras are?"

"Good idea."

Aiden laughed. "Your lady wanted to know where they were so she wouldn't walk by one in the nude. Is that what you are worried about?"

Shai stifled a growl. Geraldine's flirtatiousness was frustrating even though it was harmless. Such a remark would have given human males ideas.

Hell, it could have given Aiden and Tyler ideas as well.

Without the bond, Geraldine was theoretically fair game, and immortal males were desperate enough for mates to try to seduce a female who was already in a relationship with another.

To keep his anger down and his expression neutral, Shai had to remind himself that many couples stayed loyal to each other without being forced by a chemical or hormonal bond.

"It hadn't even crossed my mind." He affected a smile. "How many feeds are going out?"

"Eighteen. I don't envy the Guardians monitoring all that. They'll have long hours of boredom staring at nothing."

Shai cringed. "How many walls did you have to patch up after the wiring was done?"

"Not many. Since the cameras are installed at ceiling level, we ran the upstairs wires through the attic. Downstairs we needed to get a little more creative, but we managed with very few holes to patch up."

"I'm glad." Shai opened the front door.

As the cooking smells from the kitchen filled his nostrils, his belly rumbled, reminding him that he hadn't had lunch.

"Shai." Geraldine's smile was radiant as she took the apron off and walked toward him. "You're early."

"I couldn't stay away." He pulled her into his arms and kissed her on the lips despite Aiden watching, or perhaps because of it. "What are you making, love?"

"Butternut squash soup and curry." She looked at Aiden and smiled. "Are you sure that you guys can't stay for dinner? I cooked enough for four."

"Thank you, but we need to get going." Aiden looked at Shai expectantly.

If he was waiting for an invitation, he would be disappointed.

"You probably have plans for later this evening," he told the guy.

"Oh, I'm sure they do." Geraldine smirked. "Two handsome men like you would not be spending your evenings alone in front of the TV." She winked, making Aiden blush.

He needed to have a talk with her about that flirting. She might not mean anything by it, but others might, and it was grating on his nerves.

"Show me where the cameras are," he told Aiden.

Less than ten minutes later, they were done with the short tour.

"Thank you for doing this for us." He walked them out. "And thank William for me."

"It was our pleasure," Tyler said.

When the van pulled out of the driveway, Shai let loose a breath and thanked the merciful Fates that they were finally gone.

Schooling his expression, he walked back into the house. "I'm starving." He leaned against the kitchen counter and crossed his arms over his chest. "Is dinner ready?"

"Almost. But we can start with the soup, and by the time we are done, the curry will be ready."

"I'll ladle it." Shai filled two bowls to the brim and brought them to the table.

"Did you see how well they hid those cameras?" Geraldine asked.

He nodded. "That was the easy part. The tricky part was the wiring and making as few holes in the walls as possible. That was what impressed me the most."

Now that they were gone, Shai had calmed down enough to appreciate the incredible job they'd done.

He took another couple of spoonfuls. "William's squad is the best. If Rhett were an immortal, I bet he would have wanted to join them." Thinking of his son, Shai smiled. "Unlike his father, the kid is good at math and he finds programming fascinating."

Geraldine got up to check on the curry. "Is that what he's studying?"

"He studies computer engineering at Berkeley," Shai said with no small amount of pride.

It was one of the toughest computer programs in the entire nation to get into.

She brought the dish to the table and put it on a trivet. "That's not far from Los Angeles. Do you visit him a lot?"

"Not lately," he admitted.

"Is it because of me?"

Shai could lie and say that it wasn't, but he didn't like doing that, even to spare her feelings. Instead, he said, "Would you like to come with me to visit him? We could drive up there this weekend."

Her eyes widened. "I would love to."

"Great. We can take Pacific Coast Highway and stop for lunch in Monterey. It'll be like a mini vacation."

"How long is the drive?"

"With the stop for lunch, probably eight hours."

Her excitement dwindled. "That's way too long. We won't be able to make it there and back the same day, and I can't be away from the house for so long. Can we fly to Berkeley?"

"If we take a commercial flight, it will take almost as long to fly as to drive there. We will need to get to the airport at least an hour before the flight, and the drive there will take about an hour. The flight itself will take about two hours, and we will need to rent a car when we get there and drive to Berkeley. We won't be saving much time if at all, and the trip would be much less fun."

She put a generous heaping of curry onto his plate and then on hers. "I assume that you can't ask Kian for the clan's jet. He would want to know why you're flying to Berkeley, and you can't tell him."

"I could say that I want to take you on a romantic vacation, but that wouldn't justify borrowing the jet and it would be an outright lie. If I'm forced to lie about Rhett, I prefer to lie by omission."

17

GERALDINE

$\mathcal{G}$ eraldine felt guilty. Shai hadn't visited his son since they'd become a couple, and now she was keeping him from going because of Orion.

"Let's take a red-eye flight to Berkeley. We can leave Friday night, get there early in the morning, and then fly back in the evening."

Shai smiled. "We could also drive there Friday night and drive back Saturday evening. If we don't stop on the way, it'll take almost the same time, and our schedule would be much more flexible."

"Sounds good to me." She leaned over and took his hand. "I can't wait to meet Rhett."

Shai had shown her pictures of the boy, and they looked a lot alike. Same blond hair, same vivid blue eyes, and they were about the same height. In fact, if someone who knew Shai met Rhett, they would wonder about the resemblance.

"I don't think it's fair of Kian to issue such draconian rules. I understand that the human children of the males can't be told about immortals, but to prohibit contact with them is just cruel."

Shai smoothed a hand over his hair. "It's the smart thing to do. I'm risking a lot by having close contact with Rhett, but I just couldn't turn my back on Jennifer when she got pregnant. I wasn't in love with her, but she needed financial and emotional support, and it was important to her that my name was on the birth certificate." He chuckled. "Naturally, it was a fake name, so I didn't object. I planned to leave after the baby was born, but the moment they placed him in my arms, I fell in love. So I told myself that I would stay around for his first year of life and then disappear, but I just couldn't do that."

"Of course not." She pushed to her feet, walked over to him and sat in his lap. "You're a good man." She cupped his cheeks and kissed him softly.

"I strive to be," he murmured against her lips.

Leaning away, she looked into his eyes. "You are. Never doubt that."

He sighed. "Sometimes the line between good and bad isn't clear. I'm breaking clan rules to follow my heart, which some might regard as bad and others as good. Some would view a man staying away from his child as a shitty person, while others would appreciate his sacrifice. Clan rules allow for financial support, but for me that wasn't enough. I love my son."

"Of course, you do. As you should." She rested her cheek on his chest. "Immortality is a blessing and a curse." She sighed. "A memory of Orion surfaced while William's guys worked on the electrical wiring, and it was so sad."

The muscles in Shai's arms and chest contracted. "What was it about?"

"Every time Orion came to visit me, he released some of the memories he suppressed so I would recognize him. One of those times he told me about a woman he loved. He told me that he was grateful that she was barren and hadn't given him offspring. He said that it had been difficult enough outliving her, and he couldn't imagine outliving his children."

"He shouldn't have gotten involved with a human female. That's asking for heartache."

"Maybe he didn't know that he was immortal yet?"

Shai frowned. "That's impossible. I mean for a male, it's quite obvious. Where did he think his fangs came from?"

Geraldine rubbed a hand over her temple, willing more of that memory to surface. Orion had told her how he'd discovered that he was immortal, but he hadn't given her a time frame. Was it before or after he'd met the woman?

Could that memory be false?

It was possible that she was mixing up real memories with fantasy.

"I'm not sure when he was turned, and he didn't tell me how." She smiled sadly. "Although even if he was immortal when he fell in love with her, leaving her might have been impossible for him. As you know, the heart doesn't always listen to logic."

Shai nodded. "Indeed. Perhaps he knew, but with no guidance, it would have been difficult for him to hide what he was from his sex partners. Thralling needs to be learned and practiced, but then we know that he can also compel, and I believe that's an inborn skill. I know four compellers, and all of them became aware of their ability at a young age. I just wonder what Orion thought he was, and who induced him." He rubbed his hand over the back of his neck. "Inducing a male also requires biting, and that's something he should have remembered. The other option is that he was fathered by Toven, who as a pureblooded god could sire an immortal child with a human female. The mother most likely didn't know who the father was."

Geraldine chuckled. "Maybe he thought that he was a vampire. Back then, it was a very popular myth."

"When was back then?"

She chewed on her lower lip, debating whether she should tell him what she thought she remembered but wasn't sure that it hadn't been a dream. "I might be making some of his story up, but I can't tell which parts he really told me and which I imagined. It could be that he told me none of that."

Shai's eyes softened. "That's okay. Just tell me what you think Orion said."

"He discovered that he was immortal on the battlefield, when he sustained an injury that should have killed him. He talked about swords and shields, so it must have happened a long time ago." She lifted her eyes to him. "Do you think the Clan Mother would agree to take another look at my memories? I think she can tell which ones are real and which are not."

Shai shook his head. "Annani is leaving today, and she won't be back for another month. But you can talk to Vanessa. She might be able to help you figure out what's real and what's not."

The idea of talking with a shrink still terrified her, but not as much as it had before Annani verified some of her memories. Perhaps the clan therapist would be okay.

"Will you come with me?"

"Of course. I can schedule an appointment for tomorrow."

She winced. "Damn my stupid memory. I forgot to tell you that Cassandra and I are meeting Darlene for lunch and then we are going shopping, and after that we're having dinner together as well. It was supposed to be just dinner, but Cassandra thought that we would need more time with Darlene to get her to open up to us, so she added lunch and shopping. Thankfully, Darlene doesn't work, so she had no problem with the change of plans."

He arched a brow. "Can I at least join you for dinner?"

"I'm so sorry, but it's girls only. Cassandra and I want to get Darlene talking about her relationship with Leo. She won't do that with you and Onegus around. That's why Cassandra is taking half a day off. It's that important." She kissed his cheek. "You know that I would have preferred for you to be there. I hate being apart from you."

"Same here." He let out a breath. "But that's fine. It's a good opportunity for me to stay late in the office and catch up on work."

"Tomorrow morning, I'll pack lunch and dinner for you so you don't go hungry." She gave him a mock stern look. "I know that you don't take breaks for food so you can finish earlier and come home to me."

Shai smiled. "Are you worried about me?"

"Of course. I love you."

"I love you too." He kissed the tip of her nose. "Back to Vanessa. Is Wednesday okay?"

"I guess. But maybe we should wait until we come back from Berkeley."

"There is no reason to wait. I'll give her a call tomorrow and check when she's available."

18

VROG

*V*rog came to with a pounding headache, a vile taste in his mouth, and a rough rope tied around his wrists and ankles.

He'd been captured, and he was no longer in Stella's hotel room.

Keeping his breathing even and his eyes closed, he let his other senses assess his environment. Given the steady engine noise, he was on an aircraft, a private jet most likely. They couldn't have transported him hog-tied and bloodied on a commercial flight. Surprisingly, though, he hadn't been dumped on the floor or in the cargo bay. He was lying in a comfortable, reclining seat, and other than the beating he'd gotten from Stella's partner, he hadn't incurred new injuries.

His mistake had been to underestimate the guy.

Stella's partner might not be a trained fighter, but he performed well under pressure and was a damn good actor. The act he'd put on had been so convincing that Vrog had ignored what should have been an obvious warning sign.

He remembered hearing a crunching noise and wondering why the guy was squashing a bag of chips in his pocket while shaking in fear and wetting his pants.

Now he knew.

The wet stain hadn't been urine. The guy had crunched a bag of potato chips to cover the sound of him breaking a container with an anesthetizing liquid that had turned into a gas. Somehow, Stella and her partner hadn't been affected by the fumes, but he surely had been.

Had they formulated it to work only on the Kra-ell and their hybrid offspring?

They must have experimented on the females they'd taken twenty-two years ago and found a way to incapacitate his kind without harming themselves.

The fumes hadn't rendered him unconscious though, so the formula must have been off. But it had been enough to disorient him and weaken his muscle control. Then the guy had kicked him in the head with much more force than Vrog had thought him capable of. That one kick had nearly finished the job, sending him flying away from Stella.

When he'd landed on the floor, the guy had pounced on him and stabbed him in the neck with something stronger, a tranquilizer of some sort. Vrog had kept fighting for as long as he could, but eventually the drugs and the beating had knocked him out.

Given the taste of his own blood in his mouth and the tingling in his nose, Stella's partner hadn't stopped once Vrog was out and had gone to town on his face.

"I know that you're awake," a woman said softly.

Stella.

For her to detect that he was conscious despite his efforts to appear the opposite, her senses must be just as sharp as his.

A vile curse at the ready, he opened his eyes and cast her a baleful look.

She lifted her hand to stop him. "Before you say things that you are going to regret later, I want you to know that I had nothing to do with what happened to your people. My team and I thought that they'd moved to a different location, and we have no idea what happened to them. I hope that you can help us figure it out."

Her lies were not convincing.

As the guy sitting next to him activated the seat's mechanism, lifting Vrog to a sitting position, a wave of nausea hit him so hard that he struggled to keep the contents of his stomach down. Except, with how empty it was, all that would come up was bile.

Perhaps he shouldn't have. Covering the bitch with vomit would serve her right.

"Are you okay?" She sounded concerned. "You look like you are about to barf."

"I'm fine," he bit out, refusing to show weakness.

"Perhaps you should put the blanket up as a shield," the team's leader said without looking up from his tablet.

He was sitting across the aisle from Vrog, next to the sister of the modeling agency owner, who Vrog assumed was sitting behind him. His bindings didn't allow for much maneuvering, but he could smell a woman's perfume and a man's cologne coming from that direction.

Between what he could see and what he could hear and smell, only the eight team members from the hotel were with him on the jet. Naturally, there was also a pilot and possibly a copilot.

"I'm sure Vrog can hold it down," Stella said. "Some water might be helpful, though." She turned to her partner. "Can you get him a bottle?"

"He didn't ask." Glaring at Vrog, the guy crossed his arms over his chest.

At least he was honest and not faking concern like Stella. Were they playing the good cop/bad cop game with him?

Ignoring the guy's glare, Vrog trained his gaze on Stella. "How did you know where to look for my people?"

She glanced at the team's leader for approval, but the guy was still reading on his tablet as if the conversation was of no interest to him.

Vrog doubted that was the case.

Shifting in her seat, Stella adjusted her skirt over her knees. "A hybrid Kra-ell who'd left your tribe thirty-some years ago joined our clan recently. He told us where his old compound used to be."

Vrog had never heard about a hybrid deserting their tribe, but that didn't mean that there had been none. It wasn't something that Jade would have wanted to be known, and she would have compelled everyone's silence on that so the others wouldn't get similar rebellious ideas. What gave Stella's story credence, though, was that Vrog had never told her how old he was. She could have perhaps guessed, but if she wasn't sure, she would have just said that the hybrid had left a long time ago instead of providing a narrow and easily challenged time frame.

Not giving anything away, he said, "I don't know of anyone who has ever left the tribe—hybrid, human, or pureblood."

"You were probably a young boy when he left, so you don't remember him."

The hybrid children had stayed with their human mothers, and they had been pretty much ignored by the purebloods as well as the adult hybrids. The guy wouldn't have remembered him, but he should have known the hybrid.

There hadn't been that many of them.

"What's the guy's name?"

Stella winced. "He calls himself Emmett Haderech. He hasn't told us his Kra-ell name."

On the one hand, knowing what his people called themselves added more credence to her story, but on the other hand, if she'd been involved in abducting the females of his tribe, she could have gotten the information out of them. She could also have learned how old he was, and that he'd been away from the compound when her clan had sacked it.

"Did you ask him if he remembers me?"

"He doesn't."

Vrog pinned Stella with a hard stare. "How convenient."

"You don't believe me."

"Why should I?"

"Because she's telling you the truth, moron." Her partner leaned over and slapped him over the head, but since there had been no force behind it, the slap was meant as an insult.

Vrog stifled the growl rising up his throat. To a Kra-ell, that was an invitation to a duel, but even if he weren't bound like a hog, responding with aggression would have done him no good. His damn Kra-ell instincts had to be subdued or they would get him in trouble.

"Don't hit him," she admonished. "Can you get Vrog a bottle of water, please? He really doesn't look good."

In his anger, Vrog had forgotten to eat, and with how fast his hybrid metabolism worked, he was probably anemic by now. Blood wasn't necessary for his sustenance like it was for the purebloods and some of the hybrids, but he needed to eat plenty of meat to compensate for its lack.

The guy frowned. "If you barf on my mate, the beating I gave you before will seem like gentle patting."

Despite the threat, he opened the side compartment next to him, pulled out a bottle, and tossed it to the male sitting next to Vrog. "I'm not helping him drink."

The male removed the cap and held the bottle to Vrog's lips. "I'll give you just enough to wet your lips. Too much and you will barf for sure."

"It must be a side effect of the sleeping potion," Stella said. "Didn't Merlin test it on humans before assuring us that it was safe?"

"He did," the leader of the team said. "Maybe it has that effect only on the Kra-ell." He pushed to his feet. "I'll check the first-aid kit for anti-nausea medication."

Vrog turned his face, signaling that he was done drinking. "Don't bother. I'm not going to take any medication from you."

The guy shrugged and sat back down. "You're wasting your energy on hating the wrong people, Vrog. We are not your enemy."

"I don't have enemies. No one else had anything to gain from slaughtering the males of my tribe."

Stella's eyes widened. "Just the males were killed? Not everyone?"

As if she didn't know.

"I can't be sure of that," he admitted. "But the evidence I found suggests that the females were spared." He narrowed his eyes at Stella. "What did you do with them? Are your people using them as breeders?"

19

STELLA

To convince Vrog that the clan had nothing to do with what had happened to his tribe was going to be much harder than Stella had expected.

The 'introduction' he'd gotten probably didn't help matters.

Richard had broken his nose and probably one of his cheekbones as well. Vrog was fast-healing, but not as fast as an immortal. His face was no longer swollen, and the cut on his upper lip was almost fully healed, but the bones were probably still knitting themselves back together. He had dried blood on his cheeks and on his black T-shirt.

He looked exhausted, physically and mentally.

Vrog needed someone to blame, and it would be hard for him to accept that his own people had done the unthinkable.

Now that she knew that only the males had been killed, the Chinese government seemed like a less likely suspect, but it was still possible that they'd killed the males and taken the females to interrogate or to experiment on. The other suspects were the hybrid males. Tired of being denied access to Kra-ell females and not allowed to father children with humans, they'd had good cause to rebel.

From Emmett's descriptions and from what she remembered Vrog telling her, the Kra-ell females didn't sound like such a coveted prize, but they were the only ones who could provide the hybrid males with long-lived offspring.

Jin chuckled. "From what we know about your females, we wouldn't take them even if they begged us. They are vicious."

One side of Vrog's mouth twitched in a barely-there smile. "That might be true, but when your people face extinction, five extra breeders with new genetic material are welcome no matter what their attitudes are."

"We are not facing extinction," Stella said.

They had faced it up until not too long ago, but then the merciful Fates had taken pity on them, and suddenly after thousands of years of nothing, Dormants had started popping up left and right. It was only a matter of time before the next generation arrived—a generation that would not suffer from the same limitations as their clan mothers and fathers. With the new matrilineal genes introduced into the genetic pool, their numbers would soon start increasing more rapidly.

Hopefully, the trend of incoming Dormants wouldn't end anytime soon, not until every clan member was blessed with a mate, preferably a true-love match, but any love match would do.

There was something to be said about free will and choosing to stay with a partner instead of being compelled to do so by the mate bond. There was nothing wrong with loving a mate without the mystical bond to tie them together for eternity.

Trying to come up with a succinct way to explain it to Vrog, Stella started to lean forward, but Richard pulled her back. "Don't get too close to him."

With how tightly Vrog was bound, he couldn't do much, and even if he tried, Jay would stop him. But he was supposedly super strong and could possibly snap the bindings. Not that she believed he would do that. It would be extremely stupid to attempt anything on board a jet flying at thirty thousand feet, and with five males who would overpower him in seconds. But she didn't want to worry Richard.

As it was, her mate was having a difficult time with the situation.

She leaned back in her seat. "We don't have the same problem the Kra-ell have. We have nearly an equal number of males and females."

"I have no choice but to take your word for it." Vrog released a resigned breath and closed his eyes.

Obviously, he didn't believe her, and the truth was that given Kalugal's men tipping the gender balance, what she'd told him wasn't entirely true. But the clan had other problems that the Kra-ell didn't have or had to a lesser extent. The clan might be made of a nearly equal number of males and females, but since they were forbidden to each other, it didn't matter as far as producing the next generation went. They were on the right track, but it would take a long time.

Nevertheless, the Kra-ell females wouldn't be helpful in that capacity because they couldn't produce Dormants. The pureblooded females could produce hybrids, but the longevity ended with them. A hybrid female's offspring was human no matter who the father was. Or so they assumed.

Emmett had left the community a long time ago, and during that time, they might have found out that the hybrid females could have hybrid children with humans as well as the pureblooded males. It was also possible that pureblooded Kra-ell females with immortal males and immortal females with pureblooded Kra-ell males could produce a whole new breed of offspring.

Vlad, Mey, and Jin were the offspring of hybrid Kra-ell males, and they were definitely different from other immortals. What would their lifespans be?

Since they'd inherited the godly gene of immortality from their mothers, they would most likely be immortal.

Or so she hoped.

Stella pulled out her phone. "Don't you want me to tell you about our son? I can show you pictures."

Vrog's eyes snapped open. "Show me."

As she tried to lean forward again, Richard snatched the phone from her hands and handed it to Jay. "You can do that."

She cast him a reproachful sidelong glance. "What can he possibly do to me?"

"I don't know. But if you care enough for him not to see him beaten to a pulp again, he'd better not touch you."

She wondered whether Richard was motivated by concern for her or by jealousy, but this was not the time to have a talk with him.

"Fine."

Jay lifted the phone to Vrog's face. "This is Vlad. Handsome fellow, isn't he?"

Vrog tried to keep his expression impassive but failed. His eyes softened and he leaned toward the small screen as much as his bindings allowed. "He does look like me. I thought that you were just saying that to get me to release you. Who is that pretty girl next to him?"

"That's Wendy," Stella said. "His fiancée."

Vrog lifted his head. "He's about to get married? He's too young even in human terms."

"They are in love, and they want to get married. The wedding is scheduled for a couple of months from now." She cast him a bright smile. "Vlad would be thrilled to have his father attend his wedding."

Next to her, Richard stiffened. "Vrog is not Vlad's father. He's only the sperm donor." He glared at Vrog. "A father is the man who raises a child, or at least contributes financially to their upbringing. You planted the seed and then ran like a coward back to your mistress."

"You're not helping," Stella hissed at him. "Vrog didn't plan on getting me pregnant. It was just a fling, and it's not his fault that he wasn't part of Vlad's life. He could not have been there for Vlad even if he wanted to."

"Why not?" Vrog asked. "My mistress was gone. I could have acknowledged my son."

"How was I supposed to know that?" Her eyes misted with tears as she shifted her gaze to him. "Remember the vow you made me take? I didn't tell anyone who fathered my child. Everyone assumed that Vlad had been sired by a random human."

20

VROG

*V*rog had forgotten about the vow. Even when he made Stella take it, he hadn't believed she would keep it, and the truth was that he'd just used it as a loophole to sidestep his own oath to Jade.

The Mother of all Life demanded the most from her chosen children—the Kra-ell. Stella was a non-believer, and as such, she wasn't expected to uphold the code of honor the Kra-ell lived by. She wouldn't have been punished as severely for breaking her promise, if at all.

He, on the other hand, was still bound by that damn oath of loyalty to Jade, awaiting her return, making the most of the money left in those safes, and accumulating profits on her behalf.

Only her death would release him, but until he had proof that Jade was gone, he wouldn't dare break it. His own mother was probably dead, so he no longer had to uphold the vow to protect her life, but he still needed to do so for the sake of his son —the only remaining blood relative Vrog cared for.

The Mother of All Life could punish him for breaking his vow by hurting Vlad.

Had Vlad inherited Stella's longevity?

He prayed to The Mother that he had.

"How long have you kept the secret?" he asked.

"I kept it until a few months ago when we discovered your tribesman running a cult in Oregon. Then other things started surfacing, and I knew that I could no longer keep the secret." She turned to her partner. "I didn't break the vow even then, though. Richard connected the dots and figured out that Vlad must have been fathered by a Kra-ell. Technically, that doesn't count as breaking my oath."

Vrog ignored the comment about his tribesman running a cult. He was curious, but he was even more curious about how Richard had figured out that Vlad hadn't been sired by a human. Was he clairvoyant?

"How did you know?" He addressed the male directly.

Richard shrugged. "It's a long story and one that you need to earn the right to hear. Right now, I'm not in the mood to indulge you."

"Fair enough."

Vrog could understand why the male was still enraged. It seemed that Stella and her kin followed human traditions of couples' exclusivity, and Richard regarded her body as his property.

She'd been naked when Vrog had attacked her, and even though his intent hadn't been sexual, it might have been interpreted that way.

"I apologize, Stella." Vrog bowed his head as much as his bindings permitted. "Once I realized that you were naked under the blanket, it was too late to retreat. I wanted to force answers out of you, not to violate you. That's not the Kra-ell way."

Richard snorted. "You think that's what I'm angry about? You held the woman I love at knifepoint, threatening to cut a major artery that could potentially kill even an immortal. You made her bleed. You're lucky my fangs are not fully developed yet, or I would have torn your throat out."

Vrog frowned. "What's wrong with your fangs? You are a fully grown male."

The guy grimaced. "I transitioned only about three months ago, and it will take another three for them to become fully functional."

What the hell was he talking about?

"Transitioned from what?"

Stella put a hand on Richard's arm. "He doesn't know what transition is."

"Right." Richard sent him a pitying look. "I forgot that they don't have Dormants."

"What are Dormants?"

Stella turned to look at the team leader. "Can I tell him?"

"Not yet."

"I'm sorry." She smiled apologetically. "That's privileged information. If you join our clan, you will become privy to it."

He sneered. "Is that an invitation?"

"It's not up to me to invite you. The head of our clan needs to decide what to do with you."

Vrog swallowed. She would probably order him to be tortured. That was what Jade would have done. But Stella had told him that her leader was a kind female.

Besides, what could she want from him?

"Let's assume for a moment that I believe you, and that your people had nothing to do with the slaughter of my tribe's males or with the fire. If not you, then who?"

"I hoped that you would know more and help us solve the mystery." She glanced at those sitting behind him. "So far, we've come up with two possible theories. Mey thinks that the Chinese government discovered your people and decided to eliminate them. Perhaps they spared the females thinking that they would be easier to interrogate." She closed her eyes and sighed. "It's also possible that they took them to experiment on. Even though your females sound vicious, I wouldn't wish that on anyone." Her eyes popped open. "Were there any children in the compound?"

He winced. "Human, hybrid, and pureblooded. I hope that whoever did that at least spared the children."

"They let the humans go," said the woman sitting behind him.

"How do you know that?"

"Mey has a special paranormal ability," Stella said. "She can listen to echoes of conversations that were imbedded in walls, but only the highly emotional ones leave echoes. That's how we were searching for clues. She listened to the old walls, but since only the human quarters were left still standing, she only heard echoes from emotional events involving them."

That was a paranormal talent Vrog had never heard of, but as someone who could enter human minds and manipulate them, he was not as skeptical as those with no paranormal abilities would have been upon hearing of such an outlandish ability.

He strained his neck, trying to look behind his shoulder. "What did you learn from the echoes?"

Taking pity on him, the woman got up, took a couple of steps, and then sat on the armrest of their leader's seat. "I hope you don't mind." She smiled at him.

"Not at all." The guy just scooted sideways, giving her more room.

Apparently, these people didn't believe in formalities. Jade would have snapped the neck of anyone daring such disrespect. Then again, maybe Mey was the leader, and he was just the military commander who took his orders from her.

"I don't only hear echoes, I also see them." She crossed her legs at the ankles. "What I see is not the actual people speaking but the way others see them, so it's far from accurate." She pushed a strand of her long hair behind her ear. "A male, who might have been a hybrid Kra-ell, walked into the humans' kitchen and told them to pack their things and leave as soon as they could. That's why I think the humans were spared."

The relief Vrog felt was tremendous, but then the guilt came. He'd assumed that his mother had been killed along with her Kra-ell masters, but if the humans were spared, she might still be alive. He'd wasted twenty-two years during which he should have been looking for her.

But why hadn't she stayed around?

She'd known that he was in Singapore at the time, and that he survived.

Perhaps the human females had been taken along with the Kra-ell?

If his theory about the hybrids rebelling was true, they might have taken some of the human females with them. They wouldn't have killed the humans, only the pure-bloods whom some of the hybrids hated with a passion even though their hatred had been misdirected.

The pureblooded males obeyed Jade and the other pureblooded females. If the hybrids had needed someone to hate, they should have directed their hate at the females, and especially at Jade.

Except, the vows of loyalty tied them all to her. No one would have dared to harm her and risk the lives of everyone they cared for.

Still, he could understand the hybrids wanting the females for themselves, but why leave the compound?

Who had they run from?

As far as he knew, he'd been the only one absent from the compound when the place burned down, and the hybrids wouldn't have feared him. There had been enough of them to overpower him even if he decided to avenge his father and the others they'd slaughtered.

"What did the male look like?" Vrog asked the woman who heard and saw echoes in addition to supposedly running a modeling agency. Even though she looked the part, that was probably just a cover story.

"He was a tall and slim Eurasian. His looks weren't particularly distinctive. He had a commanding attitude, though." She folded her arms over her chest. "He spoke good Chinese, but he had a slight accent that I thought sounded Russian, but I'm not sure of that. It could have been some other Slavic accent. He didn't talk for long enough for me to get a better grasp on it."

A chill ran down Vrog's spine. "None of the hybrids had foreign accents. Our first language was Chinese because that was what our mothers spoke. And later we learned the Kra-ell language and some of the Western ones, but none of us spoke Chinese with a foreign accent."

21

RICHARD

*I*t seemed that Stella had achieved what she'd set out to do.

She'd sorted things out, albeit partially, but she'd made a lot of progress in a short time.

Vrog no longer looked at her with hatred in his eyes, and now Mey had offered him a new suspect to ponder.

Richard didn't like where Stella's head was going. Did she really expect Kian to welcome Vrog into their village with open arms?

The problem was that Kian might do just that. The guy was an unknown, so there was a risk in that, but he was without a community, and Kian might take pity on him. The big boss seemed gruff, but he had a soft heart.

Richard didn't want Vrog in the village.

He finally had a family to call his own, and he wasn't going to share it with a guy who hadn't done anything for Stella or for Vlad aside from reluctantly contributing his sperm.

Richard hadn't done much either, but that was only because he hadn't been in their lives for long enough. Still, he had been there for Stella when she needed him, and he'd been there for Vlad when the kid needed to face Wendy's jerk of a father. He'd earned his position as the honorary dad in their small family.

Vrog didn't deserve even the title of an honorary uncle.

A small vicious voice in Richard's head whispered that Vrog was a temporary nuisance. He was long-lived but not immortal, so Richard wouldn't have to tolerate him for eternity.

"How do I know that you are telling me the truth about what you've heard?" Vrog asked Mey. "You could have made it up."

"Why would I?" She leaned close enough to breathe in the guy's face. "We have no interest in your females. And we don't go around slaughtering people. That's not what and who we are. I can spend hours telling you about all the good the clan has done for humanity, while your people treated humans as breeding stock and free labor, keeping them as slaves. And don't get me started on all the babies your people had gotten rid of, the ones fathered by hybrid males and born to human females before your leader forbade it."

Richard stifled the urge to applaud Mey's bold words. Everything she said was true, and as one of those babies who had gotten discarded, she had every right to rain on Vrog's holier-than-thou parade.

"Did the hybrid who joined your clan tell you about that?" Vrog asked.

"Some of it," Mey said. "The rest my sister and I experienced ourselves." She smiled, revealing her tiny fangs. "We were two of those discarded babies."

Vrog seemed stunned, looking at Mey as if she had grown a pair of horns.

"You are Kra-ell?"

She shook her head. "My father might have been a hybrid and my mother a human. My sister and I were given up for adoption and were lucky enough to be adopted by a wonderful couple."

"So you are both human," Vrog stated. "Not immortal."

"No, we are both immortal."

"How?"

Mey smiled, but it was a cold smile. "That information is on a need-to-know basis, and right now, you don't need to know." She stood up and returned to her seat.

Vrog shifted his gaze to Stella. "Did your clan find a way to turn regular humans into immortals?"

She shook her head. "No, and I can't say any more on the subject."

He let out a breath. "Is there a chance you can unbind me? I really need to use the bathroom."

Jay pushed to his feet. "I'll take you." He glanced at Arwel. "Can I untie his legs?"

Arwel leveled his eyes on Vrog's. "If you vow on your honor that you will not try anything stupid, I'll let Jay untie you."

Richard arched a brow but didn't say anything. Arwel was the boss, and to question his authority was bad form even for a civilian.

"I vow it," Vrog said. "We are on a plane. Where would I go?"

"Nowhere but down," Arwel said. "But there is no limit to people's stupidity. I want to make sure that you are thinking with your head and not your heart."

Vrog let out a breath. "Frankly, I don't know where my heart is right now. Everything Mey said was true, and it shames me to admit it. Not that I could have done anything about it. As a hybrid, I had no say in how things were done. But they were still my people, and now I have no one. I don't know what to do or think anymore."

"What did you think before we showed up?" Jay started on the knot at Vrog's ankles.

"I hoped Jade and the other females would come back to get what they'd left behind. I thought that I was holding the fort for them, so to speak."

"Twenty-two years is a long time to wait." Jay removed the rope from Vrog's ankles and pushed up to his feet. "If it were me, I would have given up hope after a year." He motioned for Vrog to lean forward so he could untie his hands.

"It's not like I spent that time idly, just waiting. I founded the school with the money Jade left behind in a safe, and I've been actively involved in managing it throughout the years. I only used a small portion of the profits for what I needed to live on. The rest was deposited for Jade to claim when she returned."

Such loyalty to the queen bitch.

Richard wondered what she'd done to earn it. Perhaps she had used some alien supernatural talent of persuasion, or maybe tethering of a different sort than Jin's. Who knew what powers these Kra-ell had.

When Jay freed Vrog's hands, the guy pulled his arms forward and rubbed at his chafed wrists. "Thank you." Pushing up to his feet, he looked at Stella. "Once again, I apologize for attacking you."

"So do you believe me now that I had nothing to do with what happened to your people?"

He nodded, but Richard could tell that the guy wasn't convinced. There was doubt in his eyes, but it wasn't as strong as it had been before.

Perhaps Stella was right, and by the time they landed in California, they would have everything sorted out.

"The bathroom is in the back." Jay took Vrog's elbow. "You can go in by yourself, but leave the door open so I can see you. I'll close the curtain to give you privacy."

Vrog nodded. "I understand."

22

KIAN

*K*ian couldn't remember ever having so many people in his office since he'd moved into the village. Onegus, Turner, Bridget, Shai, and the eight-person Kra-ell investigative team had taken up all of the twelve chairs surrounding the conference table. Shai had to roll over Kian's desk chair so he would have a place to sit.

The team had returned from China early in the morning, depositing the Kra-ell male in the keep's dungeon before heading to the village.

"Who did you put in charge of guarding Vrog?" Kian asked Onegus.

"Alec and Vernon." The chief shifted his gaze to Alfie and Jay. "These two will take over after they get some sleep. They have experience taking care of a Kra-ell."

Alfie's lips twisted in a grimace. "I'm not looking forward to being cooped up in the keep again or getting blood for the leech from the Chinese market."

"Did you check with Vrog if he drinks blood?" Stella asked.

The Guardian shrugged. "I didn't, but I assume that his nutritional needs are the same as Emmett's."

"Not necessarily," Bridget said. "It is true that both Vrog and Emmett are half human and half Kra-ell, but one's metabolism might have taken after his human mother, while the other might have taken after his Kra-ell father."

Onegus pulled out his phone. "I'm sure that Alec and Vernon will sort it out with Vrog." He started typing on the screen. "But I'm texting them just in case."

Richard huffed. "The bastard is getting the royal treatment as if he were an honored guest and not a prisoner awaiting trial." He folded his arms over his chest. "I hope Edna sentences him to a whipping."

"Stop it," Stella hissed. "Revenge is stupid, and it will achieve nothing."

Kian lifted a hand to stop the argument from escalating. "Vrog is a guest. Other than his attack on Stella, for which he got pummeled by you, he hasn't done anything to us. We are actually the ones in the wrong in this situation—we had no right to abduct him, and we have no right to keep him imprisoned—but we need to interrogate him, and that couldn't have been done in China."

"The same can be said of Emmett." Richard unfolded his arms and braced his elbows on the table. "He hadn't done anything to us either, and you kept him in the dungeon for months."

Kian cast him an incredulous look. "Emmett abducted Eleanor and then Peter. He planned to take Peter to his leader to be used as a breeder and an inducer. I think that justified his imprisonment."

Refusing to back down, Richard held Kian's gaze. "I don't see the difference. If the clan hadn't sent a team to investigate Safe Haven, Emmett wouldn't have done anything to threaten or harm the clan. It could be said that we were in the wrong in his case as well."

It seemed that Richard was no longer intimidated by him, and Kian wondered whether he'd lost his edge after Allegra's birth and had become too soft. More likely, though, Richard's anger over Vrog's attack on Stella had obliterated his healthy self-preservation instincts.

"Emmett is dangerous. I don't get the sense that Vrog is." Kian signaled that he was done with the discussion by turning toward Arwel. "Is there anything you would like to add to what you've told me about him so far?"

Arwel nodded. "During the flight, Stella successfully engaged Vrog in conversation, and we learned a few more details, but perhaps I should start from the top for the benefit of those who haven't heard my previous report yet."

Kian nodded. "Go ahead."

Those present who hadn't been part of the team had been given a brief summary of what Arwel had told him, but it was likely that Kian had omitted details that Turner might find important. Having the guy attend the meeting without giving him all the relevant information would be counterproductive.

Throughout Arwel's retelling of Vrog's attack, capture, and what the team had learned from him, Turner scribbled on his yellow pad and asked the other team members to elaborate on a few points.

When all was said and done, Turner put his pen down and leaned back in his chair. "Frankly, based on what I've heard from you all, I don't think the coup was perpetrated by the Chinese government or by rebelling hybrids. In my opinion, Vrog's tribe was attacked by another group of Kra-ell who were after their females. But I admit that we don't have enough information for me to conclude that with any level of certainty."

The same thing had occurred to Kian. The hybrids would have stayed in the compound or at least taken the money Vrog had mentioned his leader leaving behind. A Chinese task force wouldn't have left the money either, and they would have taken the humans instead of telling them to leave.

"We need to brainstorm this with Vrog." Kian let out a sigh. "I just hope that he's cooperative."

"Let me know when you plan to interrogate him," Turner said. "I would like to be there. I want to know what he's basing his assumptions on, and why he thinks the males were killed while the females were taken."

"The Russian accent Mey detected in the echoes is a clue," Kian said. "I assume that you remember David's theory regarding the Tunguska event?" He glanced at Shai. "If you don't, I'm sure Shai can refresh your memory."

Jin pursed her lips. "I don't remember hearing anything about it, but my memory leaves a lot to be desired, so I might have been told and forgotten."

Shai smiled. "I can summarize it for you in under one minute. The Tunguska event was a massive explosion that occurred at the beginning of the twentieth century over a sparsely populated Eastern Siberian Taiga. It was attributed to a shock wave produced by an air burst of a large stony meteoroid entering the atmosphere. But even though the shockwave flattened about eighty million trees, there was no impact crater, suggesting that whatever had exploded had disintegrated at an altitude of several miles above ground. Since then, hundreds of scholarly papers have been written about the event. A recent one published in 2013 included an analysis of micro-samples taken from the area, which showed fragments that might be of extraterrestrial origin."

"Okay..." Jin cast a sidelong glance at Kian. "What does this have to do with the Kra-ell?"

"According to Emmett's best educated guess, the Kra-ell arrived on earth at about the time of the event. Their mothership might have malfunctioned and entered the atmosphere, which a craft that big had no business doing. It was destroyed over Siberia, but smaller landing crafts or perhaps escape pods might have been deployed before the explosion or there would have been no Kra-ell survivors. Some pods could have landed in China, while others could have landed in Russia."

Jin nodded. "If that's what happened, why did it take those who landed in Russia nearly a century to find those who landed in China?"

Turner tapped his pen on his yellow pad. "The landing crafts or escape pods might have lost communication between them when the mothership exploded."

"Then how did they find them twenty-two years ago?" Stella asked. "Vrog's tribe kept a very low profile. We didn't know that they even existed, and we've been actively monitoring every bit of news about alien sightings and the like."

"We might not have known what to look for." Kian leaned back in his chair. "Perhaps the Kra-ell have a tell."

"Yeah," Richard snorted. "Their tell is humans disappearing in the vicinity of their compounds, especially young, attractive females."

Bridget sighed. "Regrettably, the Kra-ell are not the only ones who prey on young women and girls. As we know, there are enough human predators who contribute to that abhorrent phenomenon."

When a long moment of silence stretched across the table, Stella lifted her hand. "If it's okay with you, Kian, I would like Vlad to meet his father."

"Not yet. I need to question Vrog first."

Stella wasn't happy to hear that. "He's not going to attack his own son."

"I don't think he would either." Kian crossed his arms over his chest. "In fact, I'm counting on Vrog desperately wanting to meet Vlad. Withholding visitation rights might motivate him to talk."

"Good luck with that," Richard spat. "The guy is as stubborn and as suspicious as they come."

"What do you plan to do with him?" Stella asked Kian. "Are you going to invite him to join the clan like you did with Emmett?"

Kian nodded. "Possibly. He's all alone."

Richard huffed out a breath. "I knew that you would feel sorry for him."

Kian arched a brow. "Shouldn't I?"

"He attacked Stella and held a knife to her throat. He should be punished, not rewarded with an invitation to the most exclusive club on the planet."

"I forgave Vrog," Stella said. "And so should you. Try to walk a mile in his shoes. He was distraught, thinking that I was responsible for his people's fate, which made him feel guilty for letting me go all those years ago. He wanted answers, but he was outnumbered and desperate, so when he thought that I was alone, he made his move. He wouldn't have hurt me. He just wanted to get the truth out of me."

"You're naive and softhearted."

Kian lifted his hand to stop the argument between the two from taking over the meeting. "I'm not inviting him yet, and he will probably spend as long in the dungeon as Emmett did, which is punishment enough."

"Right." Richard snorted. "As if staying in that fancy apartment is such a hardship."

Kian was in no mood to go down that path again.

"Enough," he snapped. "I suggest that all of you get some rest." Leveling a hard stare at Richard, he added, "You are tired and irritated."

Richard was smart enough to clamp his mouth shut, and as the team left the room, Kian let out a breath. "I can't blame him. If someone attacked Syssi, I would have done much worse. There would have been nothing left of Vrog to scrape off the rug."

Onegus chuckled. "It reminds me of Amanda and Dalhu in that cabin, and your heroic rescue attempt. You thought that he was hurting her, when what he'd been doing was the exact opposite of that."

Kian rolled his eyes. "I'd rather forget it ever happened." He shifted his gaze to Turner. "I'm planning on visiting Vrog around four in the afternoon today. Does that work for you?"

"I'll make it work. I'll meet you at the keep."

23

ONEGUS

*O*negus left Kian's office and took the stairs down to the lobby. Pulling out his phone, he checked the two messages he'd received during the meeting. Since they had been at least half an hour apart, he'd assumed that they weren't urgent, and he'd been right.

One was from Bhathian, asking for authorization to reorganize two of the Guardian teams that needed shoring up, and the other was from Andrew, asking Onegus to text him when he was free to receive phone calls.

He typed his responses to both messages while walking toward the pavilion.

Andrew wouldn't call him from inside the government building where he worked. There were cameras everywhere, and every word said was being recorded. If he had information that he thought Onegus needed to hear, he would drive out of the building and call from one of the nearby coffee shops.

Onegus was back at his office when Andrew finally called back. "Do you have a moment?"

"For you, I have all the time you need." Onegus pushed the chair back and propped his legs on the desk. "What's up?"

"I did what you asked and checked who was still monitoring Roni's parents. Just as I thought, up until Cassandra told Darlene and Leo about Roni contacting her, the only surveillance remaining was a tap on their phones. The landline and both their cellphones. My next suspicion was that one of them had said something over the phone that had raised a red flag, so I pretended to compile data about potential hackers in connection to a case I'm working on. When I looked into Roni's, I found out that his damn father had called in and reported that Roni had resurfaced."

"I'm going to kill that asshole." The rage rising in Onegus's chest refused to obey his command to stand down. "Slowly."

"Do you need help?"

Onegus's smile was vicious. "Actually, I do. Since I can't actually murder him, I will have to be satisfied with making his life hell. From what I hear, you're the perfect man for the job."

Andrew could access the government database and flag Leo as a suspected terrorist, have his credit cards canceled and his bank accounts frozen.

"I have a few tricks up my sleeve, but Roni can do the same. I think it should be his decision what to do about his father."

"True." Onegus put his feet down. "Why did he do that? Is there a big prize on Roni's head?"

"You've got it. Half a million dollars if the information leads to his capture. Roni was a very precious asset that our government did not like losing, especially if he crossed over to our nation's enemies."

"Bastard. Selling out his own son is lower than low."

"I know. He's either a sociopath or he hates Roni."

Remembering the guy's comment during their meeting, Onegus uttered a vile curse. "I think Leo suspects that he's not Roni's father."

"Suspects or knows?"

"I'm not sure. Cassandra and Geraldine are meeting Darlene today without her husband. They might be able to get her to talk."

"You can do that with a little thrall. Why leave it to chance?"

"When the clan's security is not on the line, I prefer not to resort to thralling."

"Roni is an important asset to the clan and to its security. It may be argued that any information you collect in connection with him is a security matter."

Onegus chuckled. "I don't think Edna would be impressed with that argument."

"If you want, I can help. What I do is not thralling and it's not against clan rules. You can ask Darlene questions and I will tell you if her answers are truth or lie."

"Thank you. If all other methods fail, I might ask you to do that. We could also get into their house, collect a few hairs from Leo's comb, run it through a DNA testing machine, and compare the results to Roni's."

"True. But before you do anything, I suggest that you talk to Roni."

"I will right now. Thank you, Andrew."

"Anytime."

Onegus ended the call and rose to his feet. Roni's lab was two minutes' walk from his office, and what he needed to tell the kid required face-to-face.

With a heavy heart, he made the short walk to the lab and entered through the open door.

As usual, Roni sat in his enormous black swivel chair that dwarfed his slim frame, the side wings making it look like a bat mobile.

"Onegus." He swiveled the monstrosity around. "What brings you to my lab?"

"I have upsetting news."

When Roni's eyes flared with alarm, Onegus raised his hand. "No one got hurt. The news is upsetting on an emotional level." There was no gentle way to say it. "Your father betrayed you to the government."

Roni frowned. "What do you mean? How?"

"I couldn't understand why and how the snoops showed up, so I asked Andrew to dig around if he could. He found out that your father called the office to tell them that you've resurfaced. Apparently, there is a big prize for any information that will lead to your capture."

"Bastard," Roni spat out. "I knew that he was a piece of crap, but I didn't know how pestiferous."

"Do you want to deal with him yourself? Or do you want Andrew to make his life hell?"

Roni closed his eyes. "I need to think about it. If I destroy him, my mother will suffer too, and I don't want that."

Onegus put his hand on Roni's shoulder. "It's up to you. Whatever you decide, just know that Andrew and I are ready and willing to help in any way we can."

Roni nodded. "Thank you."

24

STELLA

*I*t was almost noon when Stella left Richard sleeping at home and headed out to the café. In half an hour or so, Vlad would be back from his shift at the bakery, and he would stop by the café to have lunch with Wendy.

There was no perfect time or place to tell him about Vrog, but this was as good as any, and the sooner she did it, the better. The news about Vrog's capture and what he had done leading up to it would soon spread throughout the village, and Stella didn't want Vlad to hear what had happened from anyone but her.

She'd texted him on the way from the airstrip, telling him that they were back and that she and Richard were having a meeting with Kian and then going home to catch up on sleep. But telling him about Vrog in a text message or even a phone conversation seemed wrong.

Fates, how was she going to break it to him? Perhaps she shouldn't tell him about the attack. Or maybe she should tell Wendy first?

Or should she tell them together?

Wendy might be a calming influence on Vlad.

Or maybe the right thing to do was to tell just Vlad and let him decide if he wanted to share the news with Wendy.

What was she thinking? Of course, he would want to tell his mate.

She was overthinking it. Vlad was a resilient young man, and he could handle the news. Then again, given Richard's response, Vlad might be enraged by what Vrog had done to her. She could tone it down, but he would hear about it from Richard anyway.

When she entered the café's enclosure, Wendy waved at her. "Welcome back, Stella. How was your trip?"

"Interesting." She walked up to the counter and leaned over it to kiss the girl's cheek. "How were things here while we were gone?"

"Busy as usual. Can I get you a cappuccino?"

"Yes, thank you. I haven't had a decent cup of coffee in days."

491

"Awesome. I'll make myself one as well, and you'll tell me all about China. Did you enjoy your trip?"

Had she? More than anything, it had been stressful.

"It was full of surprises." Stella sat on the only barstool available and glanced around the crowded café.

Perhaps it hadn't been such a good idea to tell Vlad about Vrog in a public place. Not every member of the clan knew about the Kra-ell, and perhaps she shouldn't be telling Wendy about it where she could be overheard.

"Did you get to do any sightseeing?" Wendy put a cup of cappuccino on the counter in front of her. "Or was it all work and no play?"

"We did some touristy things, but that was only to support our cover of being parents searching for a good international school for their kids." She leaned closer to Wendy. "I'd rather we talked somewhere private. I have interesting news."

The girl's eyes sparkled with excitement. "Oh, yeah? We can talk behind the café. I just need to wait for Wonder to come back from her break."

"How long?"

She lifted a hand with splayed fingers. "She should be back in less than five minutes."

When Wonder returned, they took their cappuccinos with them to a neat little hiding spot tucked between the back wall of the café and the tall hedge forming the café's enclosure. There were no more than five feet of space between the two, but it was shaded, and there were even two bar stools to sit on.

"That's Wonder's and my makeshift break room." Wendy sat on one of the stools. "When we need a break, we hide back here."

Perching on the edge of the seat, Stella took a sip from her cappuccino. "So here is the big news." She was just going to pull the Band-Aid off. "We brought Vlad's father back with us. He's in the keep."

Wendy's arm froze with the cup midway to her mouth. "What do you mean, you brought Vlad's father? From where? How did you find him?"

Stella told her most of the story, omitting only the gruesome details of how badly Richard had beaten up Vrog. "I didn't tell Vlad yet. I'll tell him when he gets here."

"Oh, wow." Wendy finished the rest of her cappuccino in one gulp. "Is Vrog excited about meeting his son for the first time?"

"Very. He tried to play it cool, but I know he cares. Regrettably, Kian isn't allowing Vrog to have visitors yet. He wants to interrogate him first."

Wendy tilted her head. "It has just occurred to me that the names Vrog and Vlad both have four letters and start with the same one. Was that why you chose the name Vlad for your son?"

Stella nodded. "I couldn't tell Vlad about his father, but I wanted him to have something of Vrog. People thought that I was nuts, calling my child after the most psychotic immortal ever born, but it had nothing to do with the Prince of Darkness."

Wendy had heard the stories about the infamous Vlad and who he'd really been, so she wasn't shocked to hear that.

Lifting her hand, she looked at her watch. "Vlad should be here any minute now. Do you want to wait here? I can send him over."

Stella nodded. "Do you think Wonder would mind if you took a longer break? It might be a good idea for you to stick around."

"She won't mind at all."

"Here you are." Vlad strode toward them. "Wonder told me that you were both here." He kissed Wendy's cheek and then Stella's. "Is this a secret meeting or can I join?"

"It's not a secret from you." Stella got up and motioned for him to take her seat. "Actually, what Wendy and I were talking about has to do with you. There is something I need to tell you."

His smile turned into a frown. "How bad is it that you want me to sit down for it?"

"It's not bad, but it might come as a bit of a shock. Your father is in the keep."

He looked confused. "Do you mean Richard? And why is he in the keep?"

A warmth spread through her. "I'm thrilled that you think of Richard as a father figure, but I meant your biological dad. We brought Vrog back with us from China."

For a moment, Vlad just stared at her with his mouth gaping. "How did you find him? Or did he find you?"

"He found us." She repeated the story, omitting the same details she'd chosen not to tell Wendy.

Threading his fingers through his long bangs, Vlad pushed them back. "I don't know if I want to see him. It's not like he wanted me. He asked you to abort me."

"He wants to see you. I showed him your pictures, and he got very emotional when he saw you with Wendy."

Vlad arched a brow. "Are you trying to make him sound better than he is? From what you've told me about him, I don't think Vrog is the kind of guy who gets emotional."

"Oh, he is. He tries to hide it behind a veneer of machismo, but I see right through it. Vrog is a good man who's been dealt a bad hand in life. Cut him a little slack."

Vlad shook his head. "What does Richard think about all this?"

Stella sighed. "He's not happy. I think he's a little jealous, not so much about me as about you. He doesn't want Vrog to become a father figure to you."

"There is no chance of that. Richard had my back when I needed him." Vlad put a hand over his chest. "He might be too young to play the role of my father, and I don't think of him in those terms, but he's been doing his best to support me whenever I needed it. I'm not going to forget that anytime soon, or ever."

25

GERALDINE

"*A* Brazilian grill." Geraldine read the sign embossed on the restaurant's window. "I've never had it. Is it the same as Argentinian?"

Cassandra pulled the door open for her. "They use a different breed of beef, but frankly, I can't taste the difference. I've never dined in this one, but the place was highly rated, so it should be good."

Nothing Cassandra had said was upsetting, not now and not on the way to the mall, but Geraldine knew her daughter well and she could detect the sharp edge in Cassandra's tone, which she'd been trying to soften without much success.

Perhaps someone at the office had upset Cassy. It wouldn't be the first time her daughter's explosive temper had gotten the better of her. But when she'd asked, Cassandra had said that she was fine and to stop bugging her.

Geraldine had no intentions of doing that. After lunch, when Cassy was more relaxed with a full belly, she might fess up to whatever was bothering her.

"Two for lunch?" The hostess pulled out two menus.

"Three," Cassandra said. "My sister is joining us."

"Maybe she's already here." Geraldine craned her neck to look over the tables. "I don't see her."

"I hope she doesn't bail on us." Cassandra followed the hostess. "I took half a day off to spend time with her, so she'd better be here."

The place didn't accept reservations, but it was conveniently located inside the galleria, where they planned to go shoe shopping after lunch.

Geraldine was looking over the menu selection when Cassandra got up and waved. "Over here."

Darlene rushed over, a big shopping bag swinging from her arm. "I'm sorry I'm late." She huffed as if she'd been running. "There is a big sale at Bloomingdales." She hugged Cassandra and then leaned over to hug Geraldine. "I got here earlier to catch the bargains before they were all gone. I found two gorgeous outfits at fifty percent off." She put the bag on the floor, pulled out a chair and plopped down.

494

Perhaps it was the excitement of getting new clothes, or maybe the freedom to be herself without the oppressing presence of her husband, but Darlene looked like a different woman. There was a sparkle in her eyes, and even her skin looked more radiant.

"You look lovely," Cassandra said. "Did you lose weight since the last time we met?"

Darlene beamed happily. "It's the outfit. Black is slimming." She winked at her sister.

As the waitress came to take their orders, Geraldine kept staring at her older daughter. Without the worried and pinched expression, Darlene was beautiful. It was astounding the kind of transformation a simple mood change could achieve.

Once the waitress left, Cassandra leaned back and regarded her sister from under lowered lashes. "Forgive me for saying it, but you look much happier without your hubby around. What's the deal with that?"

Geraldine nearly choked on a piece of bread. That had been the least diplomatic way to phrase the question.

Darlene winced, her good mood vanishing as if a dark fairy had waved a nasty-smelling magic wand over her face. "I can finally breathe. There is no pleasing that man, and I'm tired of trying and walking on eggshells when he's around."

"That's not a healthy way to live," Cassandra said. "Why do you put up with him?"

"Leo is not that bad." Darlene sighed. "And I'm too old to look for a new adventure. The devil you know and all that."

Cassandra cast a sidelong glance to Geraldine. "What do you think? Should Darlene stick with what she knows, or should she strive for something better?"

"The second one. Definitely."

As the waitress came back with their drinks, Darlene reached for the glass of wine with a hand that trembled slightly and drank it in one gulp.

"It's easy for you to say." She waited until the waitress left. "You are both young and beautiful. I'm an overweight, forty-nine-year-old woman who doesn't have a job or friends. If I leave Leo, I would be alone, and I'd rather suffer his mood swings than have no one to talk to. Besides, we've been together for so long that I wouldn't even know what to do with another guy."

"Were you always like that?" Cassandra leaned toward her. "Or were you a wild party girl in college?"

A small smile lifted Darlene's lips. "I wouldn't call myself wild, but I partied a little." She chuckled. "Coming to Los Angeles after growing up in Oklahoma, I had to let loose, right?"

"Of course." Geraldine sipped on her wine. "I never went to college. Was it fun?"

"For me it was. How come you didn't go?"

"Life happened." Geraldine put her glass down. "I just didn't get the chance. But maybe I still will. It's never too late to learn, right?"

"What do you do now?"

She couldn't tell Darlene that she was retired, and if she said she was quilting and selling her creations, Darlene might ask her where and how, and she wouldn't have an answer for that. What else could she claim to do?

"Geraldine works for me," Cassandra said. "She's my assistant."

That was a quick save.

The answer seemed to satisfy Darlene, and what was even better, it had shifted her focus to Cassandra. "You work for Fifty Shades of Beauty, right?"

"I'm their marketing director."

"That's an impressive job for a woman as young as you."

"I'm not that young." Cassandra lifted her wine glass. "I'm thirty-four."

Darlene scrunched her nose. "You don't look it."

"You don't look forty-nine either," Cassandra returned the compliment.

"Thank you." Darlene tucked a strand of hair behind her ear. "Even if it's not true, it's nice of you to say."

As the waitress put the plate in front of her, Geraldine leaned back. "That smells delicious, but how am I going to eat ribs smothered in barbecue sauce without getting it on my blouse?"

"Like this." Cassandra lifted a napkin and tucked it in her décolletage. "Dig in, ladies, and forget about all those good manners. Ribs are meant to be eaten with hands." She grabbed a rib from both sides and bit down.

"Well, when in Rome..." Darlene tucked a napkin the same way Cassandra had and lifted the rib. "*Bon appétit*, my lovely cousins."

26

CASSANDRA

*A*fter Cassandra had demolished the two ribs that came with her combo plate, she attacked the steak on her platter with an unprecedented enthusiasm, imagining that it was Leo she was cutting into little pieces.

Damn, she needed to calm down or things would start blowing up.

With Sylvia's help, Cassandra had been practicing controlling her power, and she was getting better at focusing it, using it like a well-honed weapon. But sometimes it still boiled over.

Hopefully, concentrating on the food she was consuming would distract her enough to diffuse the buildup.

How the hell was she going to tell Darlene what her husband had done?

And what if Darlene knew about that and hadn't warned Roni? Or worse, what if she was just as guilty as Leo? Selling out her son because of greed or fear or a combination of both?

Regrettably, neither she nor Geraldine could thrall the truth out of Darlene, but once Cassandra told her sister what Leo had done, her response should be telling. Would Darlene look shocked? Angry? Or guilty?

The problem was that Cassandra couldn't say anything without implicating Andrew. Onegus had warned her against sharing what they'd learned from him.

Geraldine would have been too upset to keep quiet, or she might have forgotten why she shouldn't tell Darlene about Leo's treachery.

Perhaps the best way was to approach the subject from another angle, to find out whether Roni's father was a sociopath who didn't care for his son, or whether he resented Roni because he wasn't really his.

Putting down her fork and knife, Cassandra lifted a corner of the napkin she'd tucked into the neckline of her blouse. "What's the deal with Leo wanting to see Roni's DNA test? Does he suspect that Roni is not his?"

Darlene nearly choked on a piece of shrimp. Going red in the cheeks, she coughed and reached for her glass of water.

Cassandra didn't relent, waiting patiently for her sister to regain her composure while not taking her eyes off her.

"You're awfully blunt, Cassandra."

"I know. But I'm not going to apologize for it. We are your family, Darlene, and if you need to get something off your chest, we are here for you, and we are never going to betray your trust. And if you want to leave Leo, Geraldine and I are also going to help you in any way we can, which is quite a lot. You are not going to be alone. I can promise you that."

Darlene regarded her with wide eyes and a slightly gaping mouth. "Why are you pushing so hard for me to divorce Leo? Did my father say anything to you about him?"

Geraldine put a hand on Cassandra's arm. "Stop pestering your cousin. Not everyone is as assertive and as independent as you."

Cassandra let out a breath. "You are right." She looked at Darlene. "I'm sorry. It's just that Leo got on my nerves the last time we met. But then I don't have to like your husband, right? It's enough that I like you and your son. I even like your father, and I didn't expect that after what you told us about him."

"I even liked Niki," Geraldine said. "I don't know why you don't like her."

Darlene grimaced. "She's a loser who found herself a sugar daddy. But whatever. If he's happy with her, who am I to object."

"He seemed contented," Geraldine said. "He's still hurting, though. He loved your mother very much."

As a tear slid down Darlene's cheek, she wiped it away angrily. "I don't know why I still get upset when I talk about it. I guess one never gets over the death of their mother, no matter how many years have passed, or how old they are." Darlene smiled apologetically through her teary eyes. "I'm not telling you anything you don't know, though. You lost your mother as well."

Under the table, Cassandra gripped Geraldine's hand for support. "We might have an uncle who's still alive," she told Darlene, to cheer her up.

"We do?"

As Cassandra and Geraldine took turns weaving the story about the uncle who was meeting with Sabina in secret, Darlene listened intently. When they got to the part about the forensic artist drawing his picture from her father's memory, her eyes widened.

"Do you have it?" Darlene asked.

"I do." Cassandra pulled her phone out of her purse and scrolled through her photos. "He looks a lot like Geraldine, so I assume he also looks a lot like Sabina and our mother." She handed Darlene the phone.

The truth was that the resemblance was superficial, but she wanted to plant the suggestion in Darlene's mind.

"He's gorgeous." Darlene stared at the picture. "Am I the only ugly duckling of the family?" She handed the phone back to Cassandra. "Our mothers were beautiful, you two are stunning, our uncle looked like he belonged on the cover of a men's fashion magazine, and I'm just a plain Jane."

"You are not plain." Geraldine reached for her hand. "You are beautiful. When you smile, you light up the room. You just don't smile enough."

27

VROG

"I can eat regular food." Vrog took the cup of blood the guard handed him. "And by that I mean meat that is not overcooked." He removed the lid and took a sniff. The blood was fresh. "But thank you. I'm not averse to blood either."

The guy let out a relieved breath. "I would gladly skip the butcher shop and get you hamburgers from now on."

"Steaks would be better, but sure. Hamburgers are fine."

To his great surprise, Vrog was being treated like a visiting dignitary. The apartment they'd put him in was much fancier than the one he had in the school compound, and the guards assigned to him served him like a couple of fussy butlers, bringing him a fresh change of clothes and making sure that he approved of their selection. They'd also gotten raw meat and blood for him, which they believed was what he preferred to eat.

If that was how they treated their enemies, he wondered how they treated their friends.

It could all have been an act, but why go to so much effort to convince him that they were the good guys?

He had nothing to give them. Perhaps they thought that he did?

Or maybe Stella hadn't lied about her leader being a kind female, and maybe she also hadn't lied about anything else.

Would she come to visit him?

Richard would probably try to prevent her from doing so, and if he allowed it, he would most likely tag along.

Sometime during the flight, Stella had told Vrog that they weren't married, but that they were mated, which supposedly was a bigger deal than human marriage. According to her, the bond between immortal mates was so strong that no official ceremony was needed to ensure their eternal commitment to each other.

That was taking human attitudes toward sex and reproduction to a whole new level, and Vrog wondered whether it was the result of a belief system or something biological that was unique to this particular breed of long-lived people.

Stella had kept referring to herself and the others as immortals, though, not long-lived, so perhaps their lifespans were even longer than that of the Kra-ell.

He'd tried to ask the guards about it, but they'd refused to answer, saying that he would need to save his questions for the big boss's visit.

The time of that visit was approaching fast, and with it Vrog's apprehension.

What did they want with him? Why did they bring him here?

He knew that he was somewhere in Southern California, but not precisely where. As soon as he'd been seated in the bus that had picked them up from the airstrip, Arwel, the team's leader, apologized and then tranquilized him once again.

The next time Vrog opened his eyes, he found himself in this lavish underground apartment, with a metal cuff around each of his wrists and two new guards who explained what the cuff was for.

They contained trackers and were impossible to remove, but that wasn't the only thing they did. They also contained explosives that would blow his wrists up if he crossed the threshold of his apartment or tried anything stupid.

His guards could activate the explosives remotely.

But that hadn't been the most shocking thing Vrog had learned. When he'd asked if the cuffs could malfunction and blow his wrists up for no reason, the guard named Vernon told him that it wasn't likely, but even if it happened, it would be painful, but he shouldn't worry because he could regrow new hands.

Apparently, Stella's people could regrow limbs. The Kra-ell healed much faster than humans, but Vrog didn't know whether they could do that. He had never lost a limb, and as far as he knew, neither had any of the purebloods or the hybrids.

The lack of information about their origins had been one of the major reasons for the hybrids' discontent. It hadn't been as critical as being denied access to pure-blooded females and the chance of producing long-lived offspring, or any for that matter. They weren't allowed to father children with humans either. But it had been one more way the purebloods lorded over them and reminded them of their lowly status.

Vrog didn't even know how long he was expected to live. A few centuries? A thousand years? Perhaps he was immortal like Stella but didn't know that?

When the door mechanism activated with a whizzing sound, Vrog pushed to his feet and mentally readied himself for the clan leader's visit.

He would show her the proper respect, but if she expected him to grovel at her feet, she would be disappointed. He'd obeyed Jade, but he hadn't groveled to her, and he wouldn't grovel to Stella's leader either.

28

KIAN

"It will only take a moment," Vernon said as he opened the door to Vrog's cell.

The Guardian insisted on following protocol and securing the prisoner before letting Kian and Turner walk inside.

It wasn't necessary because he had Anandur and Brundar with him and also because Vrog wasn't a threat. For some reason, Kian wasn't as worried about Vrog stepping out of line as he'd been about Emmett when they'd first brought him to the dungeon.

From what he'd heard so far about the guy, Vrog didn't seem dangerous. Richard, who wasn't a Guardian and had gotten only minimal combat training, had managed to overpower him with relative ease.

On the other hand, Kian might have been underestimating Richard, and Vrog could be as dangerous as he'd believed Emmett to be at the time.

Emmett had grown on him, though. The guy was selfish and opportunistic, but he also had redeeming qualities. He genuinely believed that he could help people, especially those who had trouble fitting into mainstream society, and it wasn't total crap. Some people didn't do well in one-on-one relationships or were just too awkward to secure a partner, and for those, Safe Haven's free-love philosophy was a good match. It was a place they could call home, a community of like-minded people who accepted them for who they were.

There was something to be said for that.

There had also been some lines that Emmett hadn't allowed himself to cross, which meant that most of what he had done couldn't be regarded as criminal activity, or at least no more criminal than what clan males did to hide their venomous bites.

The problem was that Kian still wasn't a hundred percent sure that Emmett hadn't used compulsion and drugs to seduce his partners. The guy claimed that he'd never needed to resort to unsavory methods to secure bed partners, and that he'd used those methods only to hide who he was.

Margaret had confirmed his claims, but she might have been protecting him. The guy had taken her in when she'd had nowhere else to go, and in his own twisted way, he'd protected her from her deranged husband.

She probably felt indebted to him.

When Alec stepped out and gave them the all-clear sign, Kian motioned for Turner to go ahead. "After you."

Holding his Mulberry black leather briefcase in one hand and his thermos in the other, Turner followed the two Guardians into the dungeon apartment.

Kian entered last. "Good afternoon, Vrog." He walked up to the guy and offered him his hand.

"Good afternoon." The Kra-ell gave him a tight smile and looked at the door as if he was expecting another person to come in.

"Please, sit down." Kian motioned to the couch.

Vrog glanced at the door again. "She isn't coming?"

"Who? Stella?" Kian sat in the armchair closest to the door.

Gingerly, the guy lowered himself to the couch. "Your leader. I thought the meeting was with her."

Did he mean Annani? Why would he expect her to come?

"What gave you that impression?" Turner asked.

Vrog shifted his eyes to Alec and Vernon, who were sitting at the small dining table together with the brothers. "They said that I would be visited by the big boss. I assumed they meant your clan's leader."

Understanding dawning, Kian smiled. "The head of our clan is my mother, but she leaves the day-to-day management to my sister and me."

He doubted anyone had told Vrog about Annani being a goddess, but given the way Vrog's society was structured, it was natural for him to assume that the big boss was a female.

In a way, it was refreshing. Human society was still largely patriarchal, and when someone said 'boss' and didn't clarify by saying 'lady boss,' people usually expected a man.

"I see." Vrog still looked as if someone had pulled the rug from under his feet. "Stella told me that the head of your clan was a kind female."

"My mother is indeed very kind, and so is my sister." Kian crossed his legs at the ankles. "I'm not as nice, but I'm a reasonable male. If you cooperate, you'll find me a very generous host. But if you don't, you'll see a side of me that you won't like."

It was a very vague threat, but Kian didn't want to scare Vrog. After all, the guy was Vlad's father, and Stella insisted that he was a good male despite his attack on her.

"What do you want with me?" Vrog asked.

"We just want information. You had time to investigate the crime scene so to speak, and we want to know what you found out."

"Why?"

Richard had been right. The guy was stubborn and suspicious.

"Let's start with introductions. My name is Kian, and this is my advisor, Victor Turner."

As Vrog dipped his head, Turner opened his briefcase and pulled out a yellow pad and a pen. "If you don't mind, Kian, I would like to ask Vrog a few questions first."

"Go ahead."

Turner clicked his pen open. "Do you know about any Kra-ell communities outside of yours?"

Vrog frowned. "There are no other tribes."

"You mean to say that you don't know of any other Kra-ell. You might not have been told."

Vrog cast Kian a questioning look. "Do you know of any?"

"We know even less than you do," Kian admitted. "But our leading theory is that your compound was sacked by a different group of Kra-ell. We are basing this assumption on what Mey heard and saw in the echoes."

Vrog lifted his hand and pinched his temples between his forefinger and thumb. "The hybrids weren't told much by the purebloods. I thought that the precautions they were taking were meant to defend against discovery by humans, but perhaps they feared their own people."

Kian nodded. "Emmett said the same thing."

"Stella told me about the Kra-ell hybrid who joined your community. I would like to meet him. Perhaps we could compare notes."

"That can be arranged at a later time," Turner said. "I understand that you believe only the pureblooded males were killed and the females were taken. Did you find their bodies when you returned?"

Shaking his head, Vrog took in a deep breath. "The fire destroyed the evidence. All I found were the rings." He lifted his hand. "This was my father's." He took off the dark stone circle and held it up between his thumb and forefinger. "Each of the pure-blooded males had one, engraved with their names and their rank. I found all twenty-one of them. The pureblooded females had different-colored rings, a dark shade of green instead of blue, and I found none of those. The hybrid males and females didn't get rings, but given what happened to the purebloods, the hybrid males were most likely killed as well, and the hybrid females were taken."

"Who did you think did that?" Turner asked.

"I didn't know what to think, but Stella was a prime suspect."

"Why did you think that she had anything to do with that when you never told her the location of your tribe?"

"I assumed she or her people followed me and found the businesses I was over-seeing for Jade. I thought that they might have found some correspondence, or that they followed the money trail and that's how they found my tribe."

"Makes sense," Kian admitted. "But it wasn't us. The way I see it, those who did that are a threat to us as much as they are to you. They might be Kra-ell, but that doesn't make them your friends. They are still your enemy. They are our enemy as well, or at least a threat that we need to protect ourselves from."

29

VROG

$\mathcal{V}$rog had often wondered whether there were more Kra-ell out there. When he asked his father, the answer he'd gotten had been cryptic.

"We are all that's left of our people, at least in this corner of the universe," his father had said. "I don't know about other worlds. There might be more out there."

There had been pain in his father's eyes when he said it, and when Vrog opened his mouth to ask more questions, his father stopped him by lifting his hand. "That is all I'm going to say. Don't ask me any more questions."

At the time, Vrog had had a feeling that his father had already said more than he'd been allowed to. Out of all the pureblooded males, his father had been the least dismissive of his hybrid offspring, but the rare displays of affection he'd shown Vrog had always been done in private where no one could see them.

Jade would have frowned upon that, would have called it coddling, and would have made it her mission to make Vrog's life miserable. The hybrids needed to know their place, which was serving their superior masters.

Not that the few pureblooded children had it any easier. They trained twice as hard as the hybrids to satisfy Jade and their mothers' demands.

There had been no room for weaklings in the Kra-ell society.

"There is one more option that we need to consider," Victor Turner said. "Perhaps the pureblooded males rebelled against your leader, and they tossed the rings aside as a symbolic gesture."

Vrog shook his head. "That's not possible. They were bound by oath and honor to protect Jade, the other pureblooded females, and the children." When the guy looked doubtful, Vrog added. "The Kra-ell take their vows very seriously. Without his honor, a male is no better than an animal, and to break a vow is nearly the most dishonorable act possible, second only to killing a female."

"What about the hybrid males?" Kian asked. "Could they have rebelled? Weren't they also bound to your leader by oaths of loyalty?"

"They were bound by the same vows." Vrog shifted his gaze from Kian to the four guards sitting at the dining table and listening to every word. "But as hybrids, perhaps honor was not as essential to the self-perception of some of them. It wasn't such an integral part of who they were." He looked down at the cuffs on his wrists. "We were regarded as second-tier members of the tribe, and some of the purebloods treated us with derision."

Victor Turner leaned forward and braced his elbows on his thighs. "So do you agree that it was possible for the hybrids to rebel?"

Vrog nodded. "Personally, I would have never done that. I took my vows seriously. But perhaps the others didn't feel the same way."

Kian pinned him with his intense gaze. "Did you keep your vows out of loyalty or out of fear?"

"Both," Vrog admitted. "Not fear for myself, but for those I loved. They would have been punished by The Mother of All Life for my crime."

"Do you still believe that?" Turner asked softly.

Vrog swallowed and then nodded. "Mey said that the humans were spared, so my mother might still be alive. I also have a son who I need to protect."

Kian let out a sigh. "It's just superstition, Vrog. You seem like an intelligent guy. Why would you believe in such utter nonsense?"

"Because the stakes are too high to risk testing the belief."

"I understand that," Kian said. "But if another hybrid broke his vows and nothing happened to his loved ones, would that shake your belief?"

"Maybe."

"The other Kra-ell hybrid who joined our clan had left your tribe, which I understand meant breaking his vow. Did his loved ones suffer as a consequence?"

"I wouldn't know," Vrog said. "No one ever spoke of a hybrid who deserted. Perhaps he was excommunicated and just claims to have left of his own accord."

"Have you heard of such a hybrid?" Turner asked.

"I have not," Vrog admitted. "But Jade threatened it often enough. That was why I at first thought that they left without me. I thought that Jade had somehow learned about Stella and the baby I put in her womb, and my punishment was excommunication." He rubbed a hand over the back of his neck. "Although I should have known better. Jade would have made a spectacle out of it. She wouldn't have missed an opportunity to make an example out of me."

Kian smiled. "And yet, even though you broke your oath, none of your loved ones suffered for it."

Vrog winced. "I thought that I found a loophole, but shortly after that my entire tribe vanished. Maybe that was my punishment."

Kian regarded him with pity in his eyes. "It was just a coincidence. You need to talk to Emmett and get his take on this. I'm sure he had loved ones who he cared about when he left your tribe."

"Do you know how old he is?" Vrog asked.

"Over seventy. Why?"

"And when did he leave?"

"Thirty-some years ago."

"If his mother was no longer alive and his father was one of the meaner purebloods, he might not have cared who suffered because of his actions."

"Gentlemen." Victor Turner lifted his hand. "Arguing about religion is futile. Beliefs are not rational, and they cannot be changed with rational arguments. We need to concentrate on the investigation. What else did you find in the rubble?"

As Vrog listed all the things he had found and then all the important things that had been missing, like money in the tribe's bank accounts, Victor Turner wrote everything down on his yellow pad.

"I assume that you kept the files, correct?"

Vrog nodded.

"I would like to take a look," Turner said. "Maybe we will find clues that you missed. Were the files written in Chinese or in the Kra-ell language?"

"Both."

The guy turned to Kian. "We will need Emmett's help going over those."

Vrog lifted his hand. "I didn't agree to hand them over yet. What are you looking for?"

"Other Kra-ell," Kian said without hesitation. "The bastards who killed your males and took your females." His blue eyes blazed with inner fire. "Don't you want to find them and avenge your people?"

"I do."

"Then work with us, not against us."

"When can I see my son?"

Kian smiled. "When you tell us where we can find those damn files."

Vrog crossed his arms over his chest. "You claim to be on the same side as I am, and yet you treat me as a prisoner. If you want me to hand the files over, you will let me see my son first."

For a long moment, the two of them played chicken, staring each other down and waiting to see who would blink first.

"You can see your son whenever you want," Victor Turner said. "But if you renege on your promise, it will be a long time before you see him again."

"I can live with that." Vrog released Kian's gaze. "When can I see Vlad and Stella?"

Kian leveled his eyes at him. "You know that she's mated, right?"

"I'm not interested in her that way. I just want to hear more about Vlad growing up. She promised to show me more pictures of him as a baby and a little boy."

Kian's eyes softened. "I'll tell Stella that she can see you whenever she wants, but it's up to her and Vlad to actually show up."

Vrog nodded. "Are you going to send someone to collect the files from China?"

"Not yet." The guy rose to his feet. "It's not urgent. These fuckers murdered your people twenty-two years ago. Another week or two will not make any difference."

That was a strange reversal.

A moment ago, the guy wanted those files badly enough to deny him seeing his son, and now he was in no hurry?

"Why the change of heart?" he asked.

Kian shrugged. "Since you don't know much, Mey needs to go back and listen to more echoes, but the team needs to rest for a few days. When they are ready to go, I'll have you call the principal and ask him to make the files and the facility available to my team."

"Which brings the next issue I wanted to discuss." Turner put the yellow pad in his briefcase. "You need to send an email to your principal, explaining why you had to leave suddenly." The blond pushed to his feet. "We wouldn't want the esteemed

Doctor Wang to think that you met an untimely demise." The guy made a step toward the door, stopped and turned around. "By the way. How did you explain your youthful looks?"

"Good genetics and good nutrition." Vrog smoothed a hand over his cropped hair. "The age listed on my passport is my true age. People just assume that I'm lucky."

30

GERALDINE

"*A*re you coming in?" Geraldine asked as Cassandra stopped in front of their house.

Cassandra glanced at Shai's car that was parked in the driveway. "I'd better go home."

It still hurt a little to hear her daughter refer to Onegus's place as her home. Cassy still had a closet full of clothes in the house, and she hadn't taken the quilt hanging in her bedroom to her and Onegus's place yet, but it was quite obvious that it was only a matter of time before she loaded all her belongings into her car and made the move final.

Geraldine offered Cassandra a tentative smile. "Help me at least get the shopping bags inside?"

Letting out an exasperated breath, her daughter turned the engine off. "You don't need my help to carry four bags, but fine. If it's that important to you, I can stay for a cup of coffee."

Geraldine gave her a bright smile. "Wonderful. You hardly ever come by the house anymore. I feel like you no longer live here." She stepped out of the car and closed the passenger door behind her.

"Because I don't." Cassandra opened the trunk and pulled out Geraldine's purchases.

Ouch.

Cassy never beat around the bush, which on the one hand was a blessing because Geraldine never had to wonder what she was really feeling, but on the other hand, her bluntness was a little abrasive, alienating some people.

But her directness didn't mean that she shared everything with her mother, and today had been a perfect example of that. Her angry power had been simmering during the entire afternoon and evening, but she'd refused to tell Geraldine what or who had gotten under her skin.

"Your stuff is still here," Geraldine murmured as they headed toward the front door.

"I know." Cassandra followed her inside. "We still share the house with Onegus's roommate, and I don't want to have to move everything twice. I'll do that once we get our own place." She put the bags by the door.

"When is that?" Geraldine headed to the kitchen.

Shai was probably upstairs, taking a shower.

Cassandra pulled out a chair next to the breakfast table and sat down. "As soon as I give it the green light. I should have done it already."

"Why haven't you?" Geraldine loaded the coffeemaker.

"I didn't know how you'd take it."

She rolled her eyes. "I don't need to be coddled, Cassandra. I'm not as fragile as I seem."

A door opened on the second floor, and a moment later Shai's light footfalls sounded on the stairs.

"Hi." He walked into the kitchen and pulled her into his arms and kissed her cheek. "Did you two have fun today?"

"I did." She glanced at her daughter. "But Cassandra was moody the entire time and refused to say why."

Shai threw her a glance. "Is it because of what Andrew found out?"

She arched a brow. "You heard?"

"Of course." He let go of Geraldine. "Being Kian's assistant there isn't much I don't hear." He pulled out a chair and sat down.

Geraldine had had enough. "What are you two talking about?"

"You didn't tell her?" Shai asked Cassandra.

"I didn't want to upset her."

Geraldine pulled out a chair next to Shai. "You'd better start talking and don't leave out any details."

Shai took her hand and gave it a light squeeze. "Leo was the one who told the agents about Roni. That was why they were snooping around Nathalie's café. Turns out, there is a hefty reward for anyone supplying information leading to Roni's capture."

"What a jerk." Geraldine pinned Cassandra with a hard look. "Why didn't you say anything about it to Darlene?"

"Because telling her about it would have meant revealing how I knew, and that would have cast suspicion on Andrew. Besides, I wasn't sure that she didn't know about it, and frankly, I was too much of a chicken to find out. If she knew and didn't warn Roni, I want nothing more to do with her. And if she knew and encouraged Leo to go for the prize money, I shouldn't be around her at all, or I might do something I'll regret."

"Fair enough." Geraldine rose to her feet. "But you should have told me."

"I was afraid to do that before we met her and then have you blurt something out."

Geraldine hated when Cassy treated her like a child, but it wasn't entirely unwarranted. With her memory issues, it was sometimes better not to tell her things that needed to remain a secret.

"We need to arrange another meeting with Darlene." Geraldine poured coffee into three cups. "But this time it will be just Shai and me." She brought them to the table.

"I'll thrall the truth out of her." Shai got up and brought the cream and sugar. "Did she act guilty today?"

"Not at all." Geraldine dropped a sugar cube into her coffee. "In fact, she was in an exceptionally good mood, and that was even before we told her about Orion."

Shai froze. "You did what?"

"Relax." Cassandra chuckled. "We told her the same story we told Rudolf. She was excited about having an uncle who might still be alive."

Shai let out a breath and then eyed Geraldine from under lowered lashes. "Did you do that on purpose?"

She cast him a grin. "It was payback for the two of you keeping me out of the loop as if I was a child."

"It wasn't my fault." Shai lifted his coffee cup. "I thought that Cassandra told you."

"I bet Roni is furious," Geraldine said. "What does he want to do?"

"I don't know." Shai put his cup down. "But whatever it is, Roni has Kian's full support and Andrew's standing offer to exact revenge on his behalf."

31

SHAI

*I*t started raining when Geraldine walked Cassandra to the front door. "Drive carefully."

"I will." Cassandra kissed her cheek and then leaned over to peck Shai on his. "Goodnight, you two."

"Goodnight, sweetheart."

As Geraldine closed the door, Shai lifted the shopping bags Cassandra had left on the floor. "Ready for bed?"

She gave him a seductive smile. "It has been a long day."

It was only ten at night, but he wanted her, and with the cameras watching them from nearly every corner, the bedroom was the only place they felt free to play.

It was strange to live in a house that was monitored twenty-four-seven. Shai felt like he was on one of those reality shows, and given Geraldine's reserved behavior throughout the evening, she felt the same. They were both aware that they were being watched and acted accordingly—their vocabulary a little too formal, their laughter a little subdued, and their usual sexual banter reduced to what was accepted in polite company.

When he closed the bedroom door behind them, Geraldine let out a breath and walked over to the balcony doors. "I love the smell of rain." She opened them and walked outside.

"You'll get wet." Shai dropped her shopping bags on the floor and walked up behind her. Wrapping his arms around her middle, he dipped his head to kiss the spot where her neck met her shoulder.

"It's only drizzle." Leaning against his chest, she let her head drop back.

As if to prove her wrong, a faraway lighting streak was followed by a loud boom. It elicited a soft gasp from her. "That was scary."

"It seems that the drizzle is about to become a deluge." Shai brushed a finger over her soft cheek. "Let's get inside."

Turning in his arms, she lifted on her toes and kissed one corner of his mouth, then the other, her lips soft and teasing.

He tightened his arms around her, carried her inside, and closed the balcony door with his foot. "We haven't made love in the rain yet."

She laughed. "We can go back out and make love on the balcony. With the rain, the neighbors won't be outside to see us."

"Did you forget about the camera? William's guys installed one out there as well." He sat on the bed with her in his lap. "This is our only safe space. Well, this and the bathroom, the closet, and Cassandra's old room."

She pouted. "I can put a Band-Aid over the camera."

"You're creative, I'll give you that, but I'm not giving anyone a show, not even the night owls."

Loosening a disappointed sigh, she cuddled closer and lifted her lips to his. "Kiss me."

He slanted his mouth over hers, and with lazy strokes teased her until her hand closed over the nape of his neck, and she deepened the kiss.

When long minutes later she came up for air, Geraldine regarded him with a seductive smirk and hooded eyes. "Since you are such a dork, we can make love in the shower and pretend that we are standing in the rain."

"A dork, eh?" He laid her down on the bed and straddled her hips. "Let's see what name you will call me once I get you naked." He started on the row of annoyingly small buttons holding her blouse together.

In response, she gave him a lazy smile, her hands roaming over the sides of his arms as he unbuttoned her blouse and pushed the two halves aside, exposing a sexy, red bra. "Is this new?" He flicked the front clasp open.

"Do you like it?" she purred.

"I love it." He parted the cups and dipped his head to kiss one stiff nipple. "But I love naked skin more." He kissed the other.

Her fingers threading into his hair, she moaned softly. "Wait until you see the panties."

The woman was such a tease, but she'd gotten his attention and then some. His imagination going wild with possibilities, he lowered the zipper on her tight skirt and gently pulled it down her hips, exposing the aforementioned matching panties.

"You're killing me." He ran his finger down the center where the lace gave way to a sheer panel that covered nothing.

Finding the fabric soaked through, he debated whether to eat her with the hot panties on or without.

She lifted a hand to his chest, her fingers tugging on his T-shirt. "Take it off first."

He was naked in two seconds flat, flinging away his clothes along with the last of hers, including that scrap of red lace.

When he prowled on top of her, she palmed his erection, running her soft palm up and down in lazy strokes that were more of a hello than a tease.

Shai kissed her again, letting her stroke him for as long as he could stand it without taking over.

"I love you," she murmured against his lips, her hand abandoning his shaft so she could wrap her arms around his torso.

He lifted on his forearms and looked down at her beautiful face. "Always and forever."

Bond or no bond, she was his mate, and he was going to love her to the end of their days, whenever that might be.

Smiling, she arched in a silent demand, her soft petals perfectly aligned with his hardness.

It would have been so easy to slam home into that welcoming heat, but the unique sweet scent of her made his mouth water.

"I need to taste you."

"Okay," she breathed. "I will never say no to such an offer."

"Good." He pulled away and ran a hand down her belly to that throbbing heat between her thighs. "This is mine." He cupped her center.

She didn't argue as he slid down her body and spread her legs, baring her for him.

His woman wasn't bashful, and as he flicked his tongue over that most sensitive spot on her body, she groaned and arched up. "Prove it."

Stifling a laugh, he thrust his tongue into her once, twice, and then looked at her from between her spread thighs. "You're on, love."

3 2

GERALDINE

$\mathcal{A}$s Shai tasted and teased, his strokes featherlight, his kisses soft and sweet, Geraldine's hips churned until he clamped his hands on her bottom and kept her anchored to the bed.

When she mewled and pleaded for more, the evil male laughed against her petals.

Leaning up, she looked at his blond head between her spread thighs, his wicked tongue darting in and out of her.

Oh, goodness. It was too much.

"Please, Shai, please..."

He lifted his glowing eyes to her, lust and mischief dancing in their depths. "Please what?"

"I need you inside me."

"Patience, my love." He slid a finger into her, pulling a ragged groan from her throat.

It was so lewd to see that digit disappear between her folds, making a wet sound as it pumped in and out of her, but it only made her hungrier, needier. When he flicked his talented tongue over her sensitive nubbin, she cried out his name, but the edge still eluded her.

He added another finger, but even that wasn't enough.

Tonight, Geraldine needed the real thing.

She needed his magnificent erection filling her, the weight of his slim body pressing her into the mattress, and his glowing eyes gazing at her with a mixture of hunger and love.

"Shai," she whimpered. "I need you."

Pressing one last soft kiss to her petals, he rose over her and looked into her eyes. "I need you too." He braced a hand on the pillow beside her head, dipped his head, and kissed her.

Tasting herself on his tongue was so wickedly erotic, bringing her closer to the cliff's edge she'd been hovering over. And then he was nudging her entrance, the heat of him amplifying her own.

Geraldine arched up, getting the tip inside of her, but even though Shai was trembling with restraint, he pushed inside of her slowly, gently.

By now they had made love countless times, and yet, even when he was wild for her and more male animal than man, he was always careful, always considerate, showing his love for her with every action, every move.

They both groaned when he completed their joining. She lifted her hands to his face and cupped his cheeks, pulling him down for another kiss and pouring all of her feelings for him into it—the love, the gratitude.

The tenderness was precious, but the gnawing need for more had her end the kiss, dig her fingers into his back, and push her heels into his muscular backside.

Shai went wild, his thrusts going deeper, faster, his back and arm muscles bunching, his forehead beading with sweat. And as his shafting became frenzied, she turned her head, exposing her neck to him.

Growling, he licked the spot in the crook of her neck, and as he hissed, she climaxed even before his razor-sharp fangs pierced her skin.

She knew the venom would soon send her soaring to the clouds, but she forced herself to hang on long enough to feel Shai's own release barrel through him, savoring the feeling of him filling her with his essence.

Fates willing, one day, perhaps even tonight, their lovemaking would result in conception, gifting Cassandra, Darlene, and Rhett with a little brother or sister.

33

KIAN

*S*hai closed his laptop and pushed to his feet. "Anything else, boss?"

Kian nodded. "Call Eleanor and ask her to come to my office."

"What time?"

"At her earliest convenience. I want to discuss Safe Haven with her."

Shai raised a brow. "Did you make up your mind about buying the place?"

"I want to inspect it first and go over the financials. I want to see how much it's bringing in before making an offer. I have no experience with that sort of business, and it would be foolish of me to buy a cat in a bag just because it seems like a good idea." Kian leaned back. "Perhaps we should lease it instead of buying it outright."

"Right." Shai nodded. "I will never argue with your business instincts. When do you want to go?"

"The sooner the better. We can fly over on Monday two weeks from now and come back the following day. I want to stay the night and experience the place as a guest. Besides, you and I probably will need more than one day to go over the financials."

Normally, Kian didn't need Shai to accompany him on business trips, but this time he wanted the guy's help with sorting through the financial information in a speedy manner. Besides, Shai's incredible eidetic memory would come in handy, noting details that Kian might gloss over or forget.

His assistant looked surprised. "I assume that you want to take Syssi and Allegra with you."

"Of course."

"Did you discuss it with Syssi?"

"Not yet, but I'm sure she'll want to come."

Syssi loved being a mother, but being cooped up at the house for so long was getting to her. She'd even mentioned going back to work and arranging for a babysitter at the university to watch over Allegra. He wasn't enthusiastic about the idea of his daughter leaving the village, where she was the safest, especially before transitioning into immortality, but if that was what Syssi wanted, he wasn't going to say no.

"Can I bring Geraldine along?" Shai asked.

"Of course. The big jet is back from China, so we have plenty of seats, and Syssi would love Geraldine's company." Kian rapped his fingers on the top of his desk. "Naturally, I need Emmett to come with me, which means that Eleanor might be joining us provided that Roberts doesn't die by then. If he does, she will be in West Virginia. That still leaves plenty of seats in the jet. Perhaps I should ask Amanda and Dalhu if they want to come along. We can treat it as a mini-vacation."

Shai shook his head. "I don't think Safe Haven provides the kind of accommodations Amanda will find suitable. From what I've heard, the guest rooms are quite spartan."

Kian hadn't considered that. "Are there any fine hotels in the area?"

Shai shook his head again. "It's in the middle of nowhere, which is why Safe Haven is suitable for our needs."

"Right. I don't mind roughing it out for one night, but Syssi might not be comfortable there with the baby. I'll check with her."

"And I'll check with Geraldine. I'll also call Safe Haven to make sure that they have rooms for us. They might be full."

"What about Emmett's place? Peter said that the bunker under the cottage had several bedrooms."

Shai winced. "They might not be appropriate. From the way Eleanor and Peter described the bunker, it sounded like a shag pad. Perhaps you should ask Emmett if the rooms are suitable for Syssi's sensibilities."

"I'll do that."

As his assistant walked out of the office and closed the door behind him, Kian turned his swivel chair around to face the window and put his feet up on its low sill.

He'd delayed making a decision about Safe Haven until the Kra-ell investigative team reported their findings. Now that he had their report and also Vrog's testimony, it was time to get off the fence and make a decision.

The problem was that he still wasn't a hundred percent sure that the Kra-ell's leader hadn't gotten Emmett's email, informing her of the existence of immortals other than the Kra-ell, and offering her Peter as an inducer for their Dormants.

Emmett hadn't told her about Safe Haven, so as long as she and the other Kra-ell didn't know about the clan, it should be fine.

Kian was no longer wary about working with Emmett, but despite what the team had reported, he was still worried about the Kra-ell.

All they had was circumstantial evidence, mostly supplied by Vrog but given credence by what Mey had heard in the echoes.

Vrog believed that the males were dead because he'd found their rings, and he believed that the females had been taken because he hadn't found theirs.

That was not conclusive evidence.

The males might have been forced to remove the rings by the attacking force. Or they might have been punished by Jade and told to discard them as a form of humiliation. They could have also done so as a protest. The two pieces of evidence supporting Vrog's conclusions were the contents of the safes that had been left behind, and what Mey had heard from the echoes left in the walls.

Then there were the emptied bank accounts and the abandoned tribe's businesses that could also support Vrog's conclusions but in a more circumstantial way.

Kian needed to get his hands on those files Vrog had mentioned and have them translated. A lot could be gleaned about a society from examining their financial ledgers—everything from what they'd spent their money on to how much they'd invested in those businesses that they'd left behind, and how much they'd kept in liquid assets.

Perhaps it had made sense for the Kra-ell to just walk away from those businesses. They might have been losing money, and abandoning them had been done to avoid paying their debts.

Hopefully, he would find some clues in those files, and the rest was up to Mey. She would need to go in again, perhaps with Vrog this time, so she would have free access to the entire school.

Kian had no real reason to keep holding the guy in the dungeon. It seemed that Vrog hadn't been doing anything unsavory with his thralling powers, however weak or strong they were, and he'd laid low for the past couple of decades, pretending to be human.

If the guy wanted to wait around for his mistress to return, it was his prerogative. Naturally, Kian would keep an eye on him in some fashion, probably with advanced surveillance gadgets rather than boots on the ground.

There was no reason to waste resources on the guy either, or so he hoped. Kian was a good judge of character, but no one was infallible, and Vrog might be a superb actor, feigning his strong sense of honor and unwavering loyalty.

It would be interesting to see how things went between him and Vlad. Vrog seemed excited about meeting his son, and if he extended the same feelings of loyalty and devotion to the kid, maybe that would be enough to ensure his cooperation.

After all, unless Vrog abandoned his post at the compound, joined the clan, and mated an immortal female, he would never have any other long-lived children. Vlad would be the only one who would carry on his legacy.

That must mean something to Vrog even if he was as emotionally distant as the other Kra-ell.

Still, only time would tell if Kian's gut feelings about the guy had been right.

The one thing Kian had no more doubts about was that Emmett had told him the truth about his people. So far, there wasn't even one piece of information he'd provided that Vrog hadn't confirmed.

Vrog had added a few details from his own experience, and his view of his people was somewhat less critical than Emmett's. Perhaps Vrog was more of a follower, while Emmett was more of a leader, and that's why Vrog had been more accepting of the totalitarian rule of his mistress.

Other than safety considerations, which Kian was confident were not an issue, the Kra-ell business had little to do with his decision regarding Safe Haven. His instincts were telling him that he should go for it and buy the place, but he needed more information for his mind to agree with his gut.

3 4

ELEANOR

S hai hadn't told Eleanor what Kian wanted to see her about, but she assumed it had something to do with the Kra-ell investigative team returning from China and bringing with them Vlad's father.

She'd heard about it from Kri, and when she'd told Emmett, his reaction was part excitement and part worry. She just hoped the worry wasn't about the male disputing what Emmett had told Kian.

If Emmett lost credibility, all her plans would go to the crapper.

Hopefully, that wasn't the case. If it was, no doubt Kian would have summoned Emmett to his office, either alone or with her, but not just her.

Maybe Roberts had died?

That would be a good reason for the summons.

So far, the old bastard had refused to die, but he hadn't woken up either. The males stationed there hadn't heard anything about a new director being nominated, but then their only access to information was gone.

She knocked on Kian's door, waited for his gruff *come in*, and entered.

"You wanted to see me?"

"Yes." He waved at the chair in front of his desk. "Take a seat."

She lowered herself to the chair, leaned back, and crossed her legs in a show of confidence that she actually felt. Kian still intimidated her, but not as much as he had at the beginning.

"How is Roberts doing? Do you have any news on him?"

"Still clinging to life, but it's a matter of days before he gives up the fight."

"What if he doesn't? If he doesn't die, I can't go to his funeral. I will need another way in." She uncrossed her legs. "We could do him a favor and help end him. Even if he regains consciousness, he will be severely disabled. If it were left up to me, I would prefer to end it."

His eyes shot daggers at her. "We are not in the business of ending lives."

She grimaced. "Yeah, I didn't think you had the stomach for it. I just don't like it

519

that we have no access to information. They could have shipped everyone in the paranormal program to another state, and we wouldn't even know."

He regarded her with his intense gaze, but his anger had subsided. "If I didn't know you better, I would think that you really cared about these people."

Ouch. That was uncalled for. She was assertive and ambitious, but she wasn't an evil, cold bitch, especially when there was nothing for her to gain by it.

Then again, she'd implied that he was a softy, which was true despite all his bluster, but he didn't like being called soft, so he'd paid her back with an insult of his own.

"I care."

He arched a brow.

"Fine. I don't care for all of them, but I care about some. I also care about the safety of this village, and I want us to have access to the Echelon system."

She half expected him to refute her claim or accuse her of lying to make herself look good, but he didn't do that.

"Same here," Kian said. "That's what I wanted to discuss with you. I like your idea about Safe Haven, and now that I've gotten verification for the information Emmett provided me, that's still on the table for you both. But I want you to go to West Virginia first, find a couple of people who work in the Echelon system, and compel them to cooperate with us. The more senior the better. Only after that is done, can you start working on moving the paranormal program to Safe Haven."

That would take time, but the prize was worth it. Running the paranormal program and helping Emmett manage Safe Haven would be a huge step up in status for her. She would be the boss, the head honcho—a role she was born for.

"Are you going to buy it from Emmett?"

"I need to see the place first and go over its financials. If the numbers don't justify a purchase, I might lease it from him."

She snorted. "The place is a goldmine."

"It was. We don't know how well it's doing now. I plan on taking Emmett with me when I go to inspect Safe Haven. If you are not in West Virginia by then, I don't mind if you tag along."

"When are you planning on going?"

"In two weeks."

Roberts would be dead by then for sure, which meant that she wouldn't be joining them. She'd seen the place, so it wasn't a big deal, and with Kian keeping an eye on Emmett, she didn't need to worry about her mate straying.

"In two weeks, I will probably be in West Virginia. But even without seeing Safe Haven again or knowing how well it's doing now, I'm sure that with Emmett back at the helm, it will get back on track."

"I'm not so sure." Kian leaned his elbows on the desk. "I will not allow Emmett to empty the accounts of new community members, and I will demand that he return what he took from the current ones. I will also disallow free labor. I don't know how profitable the place will be when people are paid fair wages for their work, and no one is being swindled out of their money."

"Emmett is not going to like giving the money back."

Kian's lips lifted in a smirk. "If he wants his flock of devoted admirers back, he will have to part with some of the money. On the upside, he will get to make more by running the new paranormal retreats. That might double his revenue."

"I think that you should talk it over with him."

"You're absolutely right. I just wanted to clear things up with you first. Do you have any objections or suggestions?"

"I didn't hear your offer yet, but I'm sure it's going to be fair. You're an honest businessman."

Eleanor actually believed that, but she said it to prime Kian to offer Emmett a good deal.

"There is one more thing that I forgot to mention. When it's time for you and Emmett to take over management of Safe Haven, Peter is going with you." He smiled. "I need someone to keep an eye on you two."

Eleanor leaned back in her chair. "Emmett is not going to like that."

"What about you? I was under the impression that you liked Peter."

"I do. But unless Peter finds a mate between now and then, Emmett's jealousy is going to be a problem."

Kian chuckled. "The guru of free love has become overly possessive?"

"You might say so."

"I'm sure you'll put him in his place." Kian rose to his feet, indicating that the meeting was over. "After you talk it over with him, I want to have a meeting with both of you."

"When?"

"Preferably today." His smile vanished. "I have bad news for Emmett, but hopefully my offer will cheer him up."

"What bad news?"

"Didn't you hear? I'm sure that by now everyone knows about Vrog."

"I heard that the team brought back Vlad's half Kra-ell father."

"Then I guess you didn't hear what happened to the rest of them."

Kri hadn't told her, maybe because she didn't know or maybe because it was classified information. "What happened to them?"

"It seems that Vrog is the only one left. He returned home from Singapore twenty-two years ago to find that most of the compound had burned and everything was gone. He dug through the ashes and found what he believes is evidence pointing to the demise of the Kra-ell males and capture of the females. He built the international school on the old compound grounds, and he's been waiting for the females to return ever since."

"Why does he think they'll come back?"

"Hope springs eternal, I guess. But after over two decades of them being gone, there is no reason to think that they will return."

Eleanor pushed a strand of her unruly hair behind her ear. "Emmett didn't like living under Jade's thumb. But it's going to be difficult for him to hear that they are all gone. Who do you think did that?"

"The two leading hypotheses are that they were either attacked by another Kra-ell tribe or that their own hybrids rebelled. Mey will go back to listen to the walls, and Vrog will give me the files that survived the fire. We might learn more."

She nodded. "I'll deliver the news as gently as I can."

Kian gifted her with another one of his rare smiles. "I'm sure that the prospect of seeing his beloved Safe Haven in two weeks and possibly staying on to manage it will cheer Emmett up."

He hadn't mentioned leaving Emmett there before, but he sure as hell didn't mean to leave him there without proper supervision, which meant that Peter was going to join him.

That wasn't good.

"With Peter, I assume?"

"Obviously, and if Roberts doesn't die by then, you as well."

"When did you decide that?"

"Right now. I originally planned on taking Emmett with me to show me around the place and introduce me to his community, but since we will need to come up with a good story for why he left and why he returned, having him leave again would complicate things."

35

VLAD

*W*endy wrapped her arms around Vlad's middle. "Do you want me to come with you? I can take the afternoon off."

"If you want."

She winced. "Can you sound any less enthusiastic?"

He cupped her cheeks and kissed her. "I'm not eager to meet Vrog. If not for my mother, I probably wouldn't even go. But she insists that I have to."

Wendy looked up at him with her warm, brown eyes. "What are you afraid of?"

He let out a breath. "I'm afraid to find out who contributed half of my genes. What if he's a terrible person?"

She grimaced. "There's no chance that he's worse than my father. You were the one who told me that I decide who I want to be, not my genetics."

Vlad arched a brow. "Did I? It's true of course. But I don't remember saying that."

"You did, among other things. Or maybe it was Bowen? I don't remember." She shook her head. "It's not important who said it, just that it's absolutely true despite what they say about nature being half of the equation. Before I met you, I thought that I was part monster, and that I should never get married and have children because of my rotten genetics. Look at me now. I'm in love, I'm happy, I'm about to get married, and if by some miracle I get pregnant, I will be overjoyed. Bottom line, even if Vrog is terrible, which I'm sure he's not because Stella speaks fondly of him, you shouldn't think that you will turn out just like him. You decide the kind of man you want to be, not your genes."

"You are so smart." He kissed the tip of her nose. "Come with me."

Her smile was radiant. "Give me fifteen minutes to get ready. I want to look nice for my first meeting with your dad."

"He's not my dad." Sighing, Vlad pushed his bangs back. "I need to talk to Richard."

"Why?"

"You saw him yesterday. He's been in a shitty mood. I think he needs a pep talk."

523

"Yeah, I noticed. It must be difficult for him. Having Vrog suddenly appear is bad enough. Then he attacks your mother and Richard fights him off, and then they bring Vrog back here. I would be upset too if it were me. Is Richard home, resting?"

"He's in the office building, going over the plans of Kian's new building project. Kian hired him to do the same thing he did for Kalugal."

"Awesome. Congratulate him for me." Wendy lifted on her toes and kissed his lips. "I'll meet you back here in twenty minutes."

"Take your time. I'm not in a hurry."

If it were up to Vlad, he would have waited a few more days to meet the sperm donor, but his mother wouldn't hear of it.

Apparently, Vrog had conditioned his cooperation with the clan on meeting his son.

As if he suddenly was so concerned.

He'd known that he'd gotten Stella pregnant, and he'd known that she wanted to keep the baby. It wasn't hard to reach the inescapable conclusion that he had a son somewhere out there, and yet Vrog had never attempted to find him.

But what if he had?

The guy wouldn't have known where to start. Stella had been just as cryptic with what she'd told Vrog about herself as he had been with her. Had she even given Vrog her fake last name?

Not that it would have helped him find her or her son. Since then, she'd changed it at least twice.

With a sigh, Vlad walked over to the office building, pulled the door open, and took the stairs to the second floor. He found Richard in Gavin's office, poring over construction blueprints.

"Vlad." Richard straightened and walked over to pull him into a bro embrace. "What are you doing here?"

"I came to see how you were doing. Wendy says congratulations on the new job."

"Thank you. And thank her for me."

"I will." Vlad glanced at the building plans. "She's coming with me to see Vrog."

"Oh, yeah?" Richard tried to feign nonchalance. "Meet the future father-in-law and all that?"

"You are the one who holds that title, Richard. You've been a rock for both of us." Vlad chuckled. "I don't want to say father figure because it's ridiculous given how young you are. But you were there for me and for Wendy when we needed help."

Richard waved a dismissive hand. "Bowen was there for her much more than I was, and now he's her stepdad."

"True, and you are her father-in-law. After all, you are mated to my mother, so the job is yours whether you want it or not."

"I want it. But Vrog is your biological father. Nothing can change that." Richard patted his still healing cheek. "Not that it's bad. The guy is as strong as two immortals, he's not ugly, and since he founded an international school that is fairly successful, he's also not stupid. There is nothing wrong with the genes you inherited from him."

That was a very grudging approval, and it had probably cost Richard to say nice things about Vrog, which made Vlad appreciate it even more.

"How is he as a person, though? Is he like Emmett?"

Richard snorted. "Not at all. Emmett is a born leader, a charmer and a snake oil salesman. Vrog is a much simpler guy, but he's honorable in his own way, which Emmett is not so much."

"Do you want to come with us?" Vlad asked hesitantly. "I'm sure Kian wouldn't mind if you took the rest of the day off for that."

"I'd rather not." Richard rubbed the back of his neck. "I can't help the rage that bubbles inside of me every time I look at him. All I can see is him holding a knife to your mother's neck, and it doesn't help that he apologized for it twice and that Stella forgave him. I can't. Not yet."

"I get it." Vlad patted Richard on the back. "If not for you, I would have torn Wendy's father's throat out with my fangs. I still feel rage every time the images of what I saw in his head flash before my eyes."

36

VROG

*V*rog couldn't sit still if his life depended on it. Well, that was an exaggeration, but anything less than death couldn't stop him from his nervous pacing.

Stella was coming with Vlad and Wendy—the pretty young woman Vlad was engaged to.

Vrog had bribed Alec to get him refreshments for his guests with one of the five gold coins he carried around with him in his pocket for good luck.

They had been part of the stash he'd found in one of the safes that had been buried under the rubble. Jade had been smart to buy gold and hide it while it had still been possible. With the advances in technology, smuggling valuables into China was difficult even for someone with mind control abilities.

Perhaps nowadays, the ability to control artificial intelligence was more valuable than the ability to control human minds. He wondered if any of Stella's clan members had that. It would explain how they were thriving despite having to hide.

When the door started to open, he held his breath, but it was only Alec with the takeout bags.

"Are you still pacing?"

Vrog nodded.

"You'll make a track in the carpet."

He glanced down at the floor. "I'm walking on the stone tiles, not on the area rug."

"Just kidding, man." Alec put down the bags on the dining table. "For the gold coin you gave me, I will also set it up nicely." He winked.

"Thank you. I'm too nervous to do it myself."

"Relax." Alec started taking the boxes out of the bags. "Vlad is a good kid. He has a heart of gold and the patience of a saint."

Something warm and fuzzy unfurled in Vrog's chest. "I bet he got that from his mother."

Alec looked at him over his shoulder. "He didn't get it from Stella. She's a hellion with mood swings galore. She's much better now that she's mated to Richard. But before that Vlad had to manage her if you know what I mean."

Vrog didn't, but he knew all about demanding females.

"It must have been difficult for her to raise a son on her own."

"No more or less difficult than it was for the other clan females. Up until very recently, there were no fathers in the clan. We had mothers, uncles, and cousins."

Vrog stopped his pacing. "Why is that?"

Alec hesitated for a moment but then waved a dismissive hand. "I don't know why they're keeping you in the dark about us. The immortal gene is passed only through the mothers, but because we are all the descendants of one goddess, we are all related and can only hook up with humans or immortals that are not her descendants. A child born to a female immortal with a human male is a dormant carrier of the immortal gene and can be activated. A child born to an immortal male and a human female is fully human and cannot be activated. That about sums it all up."

Vrog shook his head. "So you are in the same boat as the hybrid males of my tribe. You can't have long-lived children."

"If I find a dormant female who is not Annani's descendant, I can. Up until recently, we didn't find any, but lately the Fates have blessed us with several. I hope they will send one my way as well."

"Wait a second." Vrog lifted a hand. "How do you activate those dormant genes?"

Alec winced. "Sorry, dude, I can't tell you unless Kian approves it. I've already told you too much." He finished setting up the plates. "Ask him the next time he comes to talk to you."

"I will."

Vrog wasn't going to wait until Kian deigned to pay him another visit. Alec and Vernon were Guardians, so getting them to talk was difficult, but Stella, Vlad, and Wendy were civilians, and he might have better luck with them.

Except they were his family, so maybe The Mother of all Life would frown upon tricking them into revealing clan secrets to him?

Worse, what if Kian punished them for it?

There would be no tricking them into anything, then. He would just ask straight up, tell them that Kian hadn't authorized releasing that information to him, and leave it up to them whether they wanted to answer his questions or not.

When a few minutes later the door opened again, Vrog squared his shoulders, plastered an amiable smile on his face, and got ready to meet his son for the very first time.

Vernon entered first. "Your guests are here."

"Let them in, please."

"Hi." Stella walked in next, and right behind her the young couple walked in hand in hand.

Vlad was an impressive, good-looking young man, but he didn't smile. His fiancée smiled for the both of them.

"Oh, my gosh. You look so much like Vlad. Stella told us that you did, but seeing you in person. Oh, wow." She turned to Vlad. "It must be like looking in the mirror."

"That's an exaggeration." Vlad cast her a loving smile before walking up to Vrog and offering him his hand. "We meet at last."

"Yes." Vrog found his voice and shook the hand he was offered. "I want to hear all about you. What do you do? Are you in college? What are you studying?"

"Slow down." Stella put a hand on his shoulder. "We will get there. Say hello to Wendy first."

"Yes, my apologies." He dipped his head and offered the girl his hand. "You must excuse me. I'm a little overwhelmed."

"That's okay." She took his hand in both of hers. "I understand."

"Thank you." He dipped his head again. "I ordered some refreshments." He pointed to the table. "Let's sit down and have a bite while we get acquainted."

37

VLAD

*V*rog was nothing like Vlad had expected.

He seemed so human, in the way he looked and in the way he acted. In fact, he looked more human than Vlad.

The guy was nervous, excited, polite, and respectful.

If Vlad had met the guy in a coffee shop, he would have never suspected that he was an alien. Perhaps living alone among humans for so many years with no influence from his savage tribe had softened Vrog, humanized him.

"That's so thoughtful of you to order snacks for us." Wendy sat down on the chair Vrog had pulled out for her. "Thank you."

Perfect manners. Was that the Kra-ell way? Or was it just Vrog?

Wendy was overdoing it, though, trying to infect everyone with her cheerful attitude and defuse the anxious energy in the cramped living room.

Vlad had forgotten how small the dungeon apartment was, or perhaps he hadn't noticed it before. Now the walls seemed to press in on him, and there wasn't enough air for him to get in a full breath.

"So, Vlad. Tell me about yourself."

At least Vrog was just as nervous about their meeting as he was.

"I'm studying graphic design, and I work in a bakery to cover my expenses."

"He doesn't need to work," Stella said. "The clan gives every one of its members who are over twenty-five or enrolled full time in college a share of the clan's profits. Vlad started baking when he was a senior in high school, and he has continued throughout his studies."

Vrog nodded his approval. "That's admirable. We have many spoiled kids from rich families in our school. And even though the tuition is more than enough to pay for a staff of cleaners, I insist on students cleaning their own rooms and performing other chores around the campus. Work builds character."

"What made you open a school for international students?" Wendy asked.

"Originally, I thought that it would provide me with a great excuse for traveling extensively all over the world. But I discovered that I enjoyed shaping young lives, and I found it very satisfying to see my students reach success."

That was also such a human thing to say. Then again, Emmett had chosen a similar path once he got away from his tribe, so maybe it wasn't their human half that had motivated them to become teachers. Maybe once they were free of their leader and their people's traditions, they sought to learn more about themselves.

Vlad leaned back in the chair. "Did my mother tell you about Emmett?"

Vrog nodded. "The other Kra-ell hybrid that joined your clan."

"Do you know that he did something similar to you?"

Vrog frowned. "I heard that he founded a cult. That's not the same thing as running a school. We don't brainwash our students."

"Some might call it a cult, and it has cultish attributes, but Emmett really wanted to improve the lives of those who didn't fit in." Vlad glanced at Wendy. "Wendy's mother was one of his followers for many years. Isn't that a strange coincidence?"

"Indeed." Vrog smiled at Wendy. "I hope your mother was treated well by my tribesman."

Wendy grimaced. "It was a mixed bag. He's done some things he shouldn't have, but he took her in when she had nothing and nowhere to go, so I can't be mad about the things he did. Besides, even though his methods were questionable, he probably saved her life by keeping her from leaving Safe Haven."

"Forgive me, but I'm confused." Vrog glanced between the three of them. "Did Emmett keep your mother imprisoned against her will?"

"It wasn't like that." Wendy dove into a summary of what had happened to her mother, surprisingly omitting nothing from the story of abuse and healing.

When she was done, Vrog's fangs were on display, and his dark eyes flashed red. He no longer looked even remotely human or civilized.

"My apologies." He covered his mouth with his hand. "I don't let my Kra-ell side emerge often, but that story just pushed all of my buttons. I was raised to respect females, to revere them as the goddess's earthly embodiments."

Vlad shook his head. "I don't get it. Emmett claimed the same, and yet he told us that the Kra-ell females were vicious, and that they enjoyed hurting their partners during sex. I find it hard to reconcile these conflicting statements."

Vrog nodded. "Our culture is very different. But when you understand that it's all about the survival and continuation of our kind, these strange practices start to make sense. With four males to one female, human-style marriages would have resulted in many males who never got access to a female. So instead of a family of two adults and their offspring, our family is more of a tribe. Two or three females with eight to twelve males. But our tribe grew much larger than that."

"What happens when a tribe gets too large?" Stella asked.

"It's supposed to split. Jade was grooming the young generation of pureblooded females to one day become independent and take the young pureblooded males with them."

"But why the brutality?" Stella asked.

Vrog winced. "I guess that for the purebloods it's a big turn-on. Because of their scarcity, the females are in charge of reproduction, and they need to ensure that the next generation is fathered by the best males. The Kra-ell rituals and customs are all about regulating that." He smiled apologetically. "Only the most worthy get to father the next generation, and since the Kra-ell are a warrior race, worthiness is determined by brute strength."

Vlad wondered if Vrog believed in his own words. There were so many holes in his theory, and he could think of several possible methods of solving the gender disparity issue that didn't involve brutal sex. Hell, even Emmett's free love community style could work just as well if not better.

Then again, the brutality might not be a cultural construct. Maybe it was part of their physiology, and it was necessary for conception.

"Fascinating," Wendy said. "What seems strange to us might seem perfectly normal to others and vice versa."

"Indeed." Vrog folded his napkin over his knee. "I find the clan's predicament fascinating as well. With so many of its members being the descendants of one goddess, they have to breed with humans because they can't breed with each other. And then the whole thing about dormant immortal genes and their activation. I wonder when Kian will finally allow me to learn how the process works."

Vlad cast Stella a glance. "Why doesn't he?"

She shrugged. "He's paranoid. I respect the hell out of him, and I appreciate everything he has done for our clan, but sometimes he can be a pain in the rear."

Visibly tensing, Vrog leaned closer to her. "You shouldn't say things like that about your leader."

She patted his arm. "Don't worry. Kian is nothing like your old vicious mistress. I could say it to his face and there would be no repercussions."

38

EMMETT

The news Eleanor had delivered had been a hard pill to swallow. According to Vrog, Emmett's tribe was gone—the males slaughtered, and the females captured. But until they had solid evidence to indicate that they had indeed been killed, he would cling to the hope that there was another explanation.

He needed to talk with Vrog. Perhaps there were other clues that indicated an alternative explanation.

Right now, he opted to focus on the second half of Eleanor's news.

Emmett hadn't been this excited or anxious since he'd fled his tribe nearly four decades ago.

Kian must have lost his mind, but in the best possible way because he was seriously considering reinstating him as the head of Safe Haven.

Eleanor had mentioned that there were some caveats, but Emmett had been too buzzed to hear them. Hell, he would part with one of his testicles for what Kian was offering him.

Well, perhaps not a testicle, but maybe some other, less important body part he could live without.

"Calm down." Eleanor patted his arm as they entered the office building. "You need to play the game with a clear head. If Kian sees how excited you are, he will take advantage of your eagerness and offer you a crappy deal."

"Kian is a sanctimonious prick, which in this case benefits me. It will not sit well with him to take unfair advantage of me."

She huffed out a breath. "He's a businessman. And you're much less important to him than his clan. I want to say that it's human nature to look for weaknesses and exploit them, but he is not human and neither are you. Just don't let him think that you will take any deal he offers you. Play it cool."

"Yes, ma'am." Emmett leaned closer to her and took her lips in a quick kiss. "Thank you for looking out for me."

Her pinched expression softened. "I'm looking out for both of us. If we play this right, we can have a very sweet arrangement in Safe Haven. We will be in charge of our future." She winced. "Well, almost."

He frowned. "What aren't you telling me?"

"Kian wants to send Peter with you. He still doesn't trust you enough to let you fly solo, not even when I'm there with you."

Emmett stifled the growl that started down low in his belly. "Kian has a sick sense of humor."

Peter was pretending to be Eleanor's buddy, but he was an attractive male, and she was an attractive female, and Peter had a score to settle with Emmett. He might seduce Eleanor just to get back at him. On the other hand, if Peter was assigned to guard him, he wouldn't be going with Eleanor to West Virginia, and Kian would send her with another Guardian.

Except, Emmett didn't like that she would be going without him no matter who accompanied her. But that was a concern he would address later. Right now, he needed to focus on striking a good deal with Kian.

"We can make it work." Eleanor took his hand. "Come on. We don't want to keep Kian waiting."

"Is Peter going to be there?"

"I don't know. Kian didn't mention that."

They took the stairs to the second floor of the office building, and as they walked up to Kian's door, Eleanor knocked.

"Come in," Kian said.

Forcing a nonchalant smile on his face, Emmett opened the door and motioned for Eleanor to go ahead. "Ladies first."

"Good afternoon," Kian greeted them. "Please, take a seat." He motioned to the chairs in front of his desk.

"Good afternoon to you too." Emmett sat down and leaned back in a show of bored indifference. "I have to admit that I admire your decisiveness. When you decide to do something, you don't wait, you don't procrastinate, you get a move on."

"Thank you." Kian cast him a perfunctory smile. "I liked Eleanor's idea for Safe Haven, but I needed to make sure that you are trustworthy. Vrog confirming your story helped your case."

"I'm glad. So how exactly are we going to play this? After disappearing without a word for months, I can't just show up with you and your entourage and pick up from where I left off."

"I don't see why not." Kian leaned back and crossed his arms over his chest. "Given the role you played, you could make up a number of stories to explain your absence."

Emmett had thought of a couple of possibilities, one involving compulsion, and the other a good story, but he was curious to hear what Kian had come up with. "Like what?"

The guy unfolded his arms and lifted them in the air like a prophet, imitating one of Emmett's favorite poses. "You suffered a spiritual breakdown and needed to go back to your roots in the Himalayas to meditate in complete silence."

Emmett chuckled. "That's actually not bad. How would I explain you and what you want to do to the place?"

"You met me in the Himalayan mountains, where I too had retreated to meditate upon the state of the world. Our encounter was guided by The Mother of all Life, who wished us to merge our dreams for a better world and make Safe Haven a beacon of light for humanity."

Lifting his hands, Emmett clapped. "I didn't know that you were so creative."

Kian laughed. "I'm not. This was all Shai's idea. Personally, I think that The Mother of all Life is too much. Shai also suggested the spirit of Gaia as an alternative. That's what the Greeks called the goddess of Earth, or The Mother of all Life."

Kian seemed in a surprisingly good mood.

"I'm well versed in Greek mythology and many others," Emmett said. "It would seem that different cultures on different worlds all revere The Mother of all Life. It might be a coincidence, or it might not."

Kian narrowed his eyes at him. "What are you implying?"

"Nothing overly profound. It's not surprising that many cultures revere the power of nature. Still, I have often wondered whether the Kra-ell who comprised my group were the first to arrive on earth, or if there had been prior expeditions that brought their mythology with them, influencing human religions. It is also possible that your ancestors, the gods, influenced both the Kra-ell and the humans."

"The gods didn't have a formal religion, and they didn't revere The Mother of all Life. Although given their matrilineal tradition, they might have in the distant past."

Emmett nodded. "Perhaps they transferred their ancient belief in The Mother to the Fates. I'm told that many of your clan members strongly believe that the Fates guide their lives, especially in everything that has to do with finding true-love mates."

Kian winced. "With good reason, but we digress. The cover story for your absence solves only part of the problem." He waved a hand at Emmett's face. "Without the beard and the long hair, you look too young. You're supposed to be in your sixties. You need to let it grow back to how it was before."

"My hair grows fast, but not that fast. I can't regrow it in two weeks."

"Naturally. Eva can help you with that. I sent her your picture from the Safe Haven brochure so she would know what kind of wigs to order, and I told her that you will call to make an appointment."

"I'll also need to purchase a couple of gowns." Emmett looked down at his trim body. "I have to hide my fantastic physique."

Eleanor shook her head. "Or you can have Eva put you in a fat suit."

"I prefer a gown." He looked Kian in the eyes. "What exactly are you planning to do with Safe Haven?"

"Several things. I want you to start running retreats for people with paranormal abilities. It will mesh perfectly with your other self-help programs and not raise suspicion. If we get lucky, we might even find Dormants among the attendees."

"That might be more difficult to do than you think. I don't know how well the place did in my absence, but the lodge might be booked for months in advance. Also, we will need to create courses and workshops geared toward the paranormal, and that will take time."

Kian nodded. "I'm well aware of that, and I don't expect you to start doing that right away. First, we need to see if we can attract people with paranormal talents or who are interested in the subject. We might discover that there is no demand. If there is, we will then need to create a new program for them, and either alternate bookings between the paranormal and the self-actualization retreats or add another building to house the paranormal. I understand that you own a large chunk of land over there."

"I do, but most of it is not developed. It requires a lot of grading work."

Kian shrugged. "That's not a problem, and if need be, we can acquire more land. If Eleanor manages to convince the people in charge of the government paranormal program to transfer it to Safe Haven, I will probably have to build another structure to house them. I'm also thinking of building a couple of guest cabins for testing the potential Dormants."

Kian was talking as if he already owned the place, but so far, he hadn't said anything about buying it. Did he think that Emmett would just hand it over in exchange for getting to head a place that he'd founded and owned?

"You have so many exciting plans. Are you going to make me an offer to buy the place?"

Leaning back, Kian crossed his arms over his chest. "Only after I inspect it and take a look at the financials. I want to see if Safe Haven is profitable when it doesn't exploit its members."

"I assure you that it is, and I'm not interested in selling it."

As Eleanor sucked in a breath, Kian frowned. "Why not?"

"Because it's my baby. But I'm willing to share. How about we form a partnership? We can negotiate the terms after your inspection."

Kian shook his head. "I don't do partnerships unless I'm in a controlling position, especially when I invest a lot of money to expand the operations. If you don't want to sell, I can lease the place from you, but I'm not leaving you in charge."

It was Emmett's turn to frown. "I thought that was the plan."

"You will run the place as the director or chief executive officer. Naturally, you will also be its spiritual leader, but you will have to answer to me."

"What about the money?"

"You'll be given a salary, a share in the profits, and the lease payments." Kian leaned forward. "Right now, you are making nothing from the place, and all the profits are going to the Safe Haven community. So, I would say it's a good deal."

That was true, and unless Emmett reached an agreement with Kian, the guy was going to drop the plan and keep him under watch in the village. He hadn't even mentioned removing the damn cuffs from his wrists.

"How long of a lease?"

"At least fifteen years with an option to buy."

"What about the cuffs?"

"They stay on. I can't let a powerful compeller roam free."

"I'm bound by the Clan Mother's compulsion to do no harm to her clan. I have no problem with her adding another do-no-harm clause that includes humans."

Kian pinned him with a hard stare. "We both know that there are ways to circumvent compulsion. That's the deal I'm offering, Emmett. You can take it or leave it. I can find another remote location and build a retreat for paranormals there. It will just take me a little longer to get it off the ground."

Kian was bluffing, and Emmett was going to call him out on that. "Much longer. You don't have the personnel to run a place like that, and you need people who are experienced, motivated, and who keep their mouths shut." He chuckled. "You use human volunteers to run the sanctuary for the trafficking victims because you can't get clan members to work there. They are busy doing their own things or nothing at all. Giving them a share of the clan profits without demanding any work in return is demoralizing."

The wince Kian tried to stifle was most satisfying. Emmett had touched on a sore spot.

"All of that is true." Kian unfolded his arms and leaned forward. "But there is no way I'm releasing you into the world without proper precautions. I'm not going to take advantage of you financially, Emmett, if that's what you are worried about. The deal we will negotiate will include fair compensation for the property you own and for your services."

"How do I know that? You've got me by the throat. I don't have any leverage to negotiate with."

Emmett didn't really believe that, but he knew how Kian's mind worked. Wanting to prove the opposite, he might offer him an even better deal than he'd planned to.

"Of course you have leverage. I need you to do a good job running the place and covering up for the paranormal operation. You won't do that as well if you are not motivated by profit, station, and the level of autonomy I'll allow you. It's a give and take, Emmett, and it's fluid. The more I can trust you not to take unfair advantage of people, the more autonomy I will grant you."

Letting out a breath, Emmett closed his eyes. Eleanor had been right. Kian was a much tougher negotiator than he'd expected, but even though the guy was a businessman, he wasn't motivated by profits alone.

Kian really feared releasing him into the world without safeguards.

That was the price Emmett had to pay for having the ability to compel. Even a powerful immortal like Kian feared him. The only people who weren't wary of him were the immunes and those who didn't know what he could do.

That didn't mean he wasn't grateful for the gift The Mother of all Life had given him. Without it, he would probably be dead, slaughtered along with the other males of his tribe.

Besides, no gift from The Mother came without giving up something else. Emmett didn't possess even a fraction of the innate aggression of the Kra-ell males, which was one of the main reasons his father had barely deigned to acknowledge him. He was a shame to his people's warrior race—a male who preferred to read and engage in intellectually stimulating conversations than to fight.

His people were savages, and Emmett had never felt as if he belonged with them. Sometimes, he wondered if his escape hadn't actually been sanctioned, and if Jade had let him go knowingly. No one had come looking for him. No one had chased him.

"Well?" Kian asked.

Emmett opened his eyes. "We will work out a deal, but don't expect me to lease the property to you for one dollar a year."

Kian smiled. "I wouldn't dream of it."

39

GERALDINE

*A*s Shai pulled into the driveway in a huge motorhome, Geraldine opened the front door and stepped out. "What is that?"

Grinning out the open driver side window, he waved her over. "Come and take a look." He opened the door for her. "I figured that if we are taking a road trip, we can do it in style."

"It's gorgeous." It was like a small apartment, complete with a kitchen that had a full-sized fridge and a small stove, and a sitting area. There was a door in the back that she assumed led to a bedroom. "Where did you get it?"

"It belongs to the clan. Kian approved the purchase a while ago for clan members to borrow whenever they want. I was lucky that it was available."

Geraldine walked to the back and opened the pocket door. As she'd suspected, it was a bedroom suite, with a nice bathroom and a small closet.

"I love it." She sat on the bed to test the mattress. "What a great idea."

"If you are all packed, we can leave now. I already stocked it with supplies for the road."

"I made dinner." She rose to her feet and went back to check out the kitchen, "But I can pack it up, and we can stop on the way to eat it."

"I'll help you." He followed her out of the vehicle.

"How much does a thing like this cost?"

"A lot. This one was over four hundred thousand dollars."

"Oh, wow." She looked at it over her shoulder. "I would never have guessed. Why is it so expensive?"

"The interior is custom made. We bought this motorhome as is from someone who'd ordered it and then decided to sell it, which made it a little cheaper and a lot more expeditious. Usually, it takes over a year to have one of these built."

In the kitchen, she pulled the fish out of the oven and put it in a glass container. The spaghetti went into another, and the salad into a third. "Does the kitchen in the motorhome come fully equipped?"

"It does. And I filled the fridge and the cupboards." He smiled apologetically. "I probably overdid it. We are going to eat at restaurants."

"It could be fun to cook in the motorhome." She put the containers inside a carrying bag and handed it to him. "I'll get my overnight bag."

It was on the entry table by the door, and as Geraldine slung the strap over her shoulder, she took a quick look in the mirror. "I thought about using the wig."

"Why?" Shai opened the door.

"You are going to introduce me to Rhett as your girlfriend, and since you are pretending to be in your early forties, I should too." She locked the door behind him.

"You don't need to." He took the bag from her and carried both to the motorhome. "I could have a much younger girlfriend."

She followed him inside. "I thought about saying that I was forty, but if I want to mention Cassandra, which I want to, that's a problem. She's semi-famous and it's easy to find out that she's thirty-four."

As Geraldine turned to look at the house, a wave of anxiety swept through her. "What if Orion shows up when I'm gone?"

"Don't worry about it." Shai put the bag with the containers inside the fridge. "The surveillance cameras are on, and the guys watching the feed have had two days to learn who your neighbors are." He put her overnight bag in the bedroom. "If anyone comes snooping around the house, they will get him."

Geraldine sat down in the passenger captain chair and put the seatbelt on. "The village is half an hour drive from my house. How are they going to get here in time?"

"There are always Guardians on rotation in the keep. They can be here in fifteen minutes."

"He won't stay around that long if I'm not here."

"That's fine. The Guardians watching the house will activate the drone and it will follow him."

"What drone?"

"William's guys put a mini drone on your roof. It's controlled remotely through an internet satellite connection. Its battery should last until the Guardians from the keep reach Orion." He gave her an apologetic smile. "It would have been better to have a Guardian assigned to your house, but we are short on trained people. Besides, it would have been an even greater intrusion on our privacy."

"That's okay. I prefer the drone. I just wish I had known about it." She let out a long sigh. "I feel so bad about the whole surveillance thing and entrapping Orion. It's a shitty way to repay his kindness."

"I wouldn't call it kindness. At best, it was the assuaging of guilt. But what prompted the sudden change in feelings? You were fine with the idea. Did you remember more things?"

She nodded. "He always brought Cassandra and me fancy chocolates and marzipans from all over the world. I guess he couldn't bring gifts that would remind us of him, so he brought sweets that we consumed right away."

"Did he travel a lot?"

"Yeah. Being old and having a good eye for style lent itself to making a lot of money on trading in antiques. He collected them from all over."

"That's interesting." Shai turned the engine on. "I wonder if Orion had anything to do with Leo getting a job in an antiques gallery."

"Do you think that Orion got him the job?"

"If he was helping you, he might have been helping your daughter and her son, and by extension, her husband."

40

SHAI

*O*rion must have felt guilty as hell to help a creep like Leo, but then arranging a good job for him was a circumventive way to ensure Darlene's well-being.

Why hadn't she pursued a career? She had a degree from a prestigious university, and she had only one child who had left home a long time ago. What did she do with herself? Watch soap operas all day?

"Leo got the new job several months after Roni's escape," Geraldine said. "Orion wouldn't have been helping Roni by getting a job for Leo, only Darlene."

He was surprised that she remembered that. Even after the Clan Mother had restored her memories, Geraldine still had trouble remembering details. But apparently, some things registered in her mind better than others.

"Orion might have been helping them before that as well." Shai stopped and waited for the gate to open. "Leo lost his job shortly after Roni's capture. Maybe Orion couldn't help while the Feds were around." He carefully eased the large vehicle through the two arms of the open gate.

Geraldine shrugged. "All we can do is guess. I hope that once Orion shows up, we can get some answers. I just hate thinking about being the bait for his entrapment. He deserves better from me after everything he's done for me."

"Don't forget that he might have been doing it to atone for the wrong he had done you. We don't know what his story is."

"The more memories that resurface, the more fondly I think of him. He really was like a brother to me." She chuckled. "Or rather a really nice uncle who took care of me. It wasn't only treats that he gave me. He helped me financially, and he got me the fake documents that helped me stay undetected. I would have been lost without him, or worse, I would have been found." Geraldine shivered. "Imagine what would have happened if I had gotten caught, what they would have done to me. To Cassy."

He reached over and took her hand. "If he helped prevent that, then I'm grateful to him."

She smiled. "Remember that when he comes back. Be nice to him."

"I'll try."

"You'd better."

"I just hope that he shows up before next Monday."

She turned to him. "Why? What's special about that Monday?"

"Kian wants to visit Safe Haven. Do you remember what I told you about it?"

She nodded. "It's a cult in Oregon that a guy named Emmett Haderech founded. He was its guru before the clan caught him."

He arched a brow. "I'm surprised that you remember his name."

"It's unique. After you told me what it meant, it stuck in my mind." She sighed. "The true way. I wish I'd thought of something that clever for my own fake name. I often wonder why I chose Geraldine."

"It suits you." He squeezed her hand. "Anyway, Kian wants me to accompany him, and I want you to come with me. He's taking everyone on the clan's jet, and we are going to spend the night in Emmett's fancy underground bunker. It will be like a mini vacation."

"Who is everyone?"

"Syssi, the baby, Kian's butler, Emmett and Eleanor, and Kian's two Guardians."

"Why does he need you there?"

Shai shrugged. "He needs to go over the financials, and I can do that much faster than him. He's also trying to get me more involved in decision-making." He chuckled. "Kian believes that I have what it takes to become much more than just his assistant. He wants to promote me to a managerial position."

Geraldine beamed at him. "That's amazing. I'm so proud of you."

"I'm not really interested. You know what my real passion is."

"I do." She squeezed his hand. "But when was the last time you wrote anything creative?"

He grinned. "I came up with a story to explain Emmett's absence, his return, and how he met Kian. It was very creative."

She rolled her eyes. "You know what I mean. When was the last time you worked on a screenplay?"

"It has been a while."

"Then maybe you should take Kian's offer and become a manager of something. You're immortal, there will always be time for writing scripts."

"Not necessarily. What if by the time I get around to it, AI can make novelists and screenwriters obsolete?"

"Don't be silly. A computer doesn't have the creativity and never will. Just look at the Odus. They are the most advanced AI on earth, and they can only imitate, not create."

Shai lifted a brow. "I wouldn't be so sure about that. Up until Okidu and Onidu's reboots, their capabilities were limited by design. Now that they are experimenting and learning, they might evolve the same way humans did, but much faster."

For a moment, Geraldine chewed on her lower lip. "It's scary and exciting at the same time."

"I agree, but I like the way Syssi sees it. She believes that the Odus are learning like children do, and since they are surrounded by good people who treat them and each other with kindness and respect, that's what they will learn."

"I like that. She's a smart woman, and I would love to get to know her better. Maybe once I move to the village, I'll start a book club and invite her to join."

It was music to his ears that Geraldine no longer regarded the move as potential but as impending.

"If you come with me to Safe Haven, you won't have to wait. You'll have a chance to spend time with Syssi and Allegra."

Knowing how much Geraldine loved babies, he dangled Allegra as bait on purpose. She would have a hard time saying no to that.

"I would really love to come with you, and if Orion is captured before the trip, then I definitely will. But if he isn't, I can't." She smiled sadly. "I feel anxious about leaving on this less than twenty-four-hour trip to Berkeley, let alone a two-day trip to Oregon."

GERALDINE

*G*eraldine yawned and stretched her arms over her head. "You have no idea how glad I am that Rhett sleeps late on the weekends. I'm so well rested."

They'd arrived at Berkeley at three o'clock in the morning, continued driving another half an hour north of it to a Walmart, and parked there overnight. She hadn't even known that the national chain allowed that.

Shai chuckled. "A breakfast at ten in the morning on a weekend is considered very early for a college student. To wake up before noon, Rhett must be anxious to meet you."

"What's more likely is that he's excited to see the motorhome. Once you told him about it, he right away offered to come to us instead of us going to him." Geraldine got out of bed and straightened the comforter.

"He wanted to save us from Ubering to Berkeley." Shai fluffed the pillows.

"I think it was just an excuse to see this." She waved a hand around the surprisingly luxurious bedroom. "But I don't mind. Making breakfast in this tiny kitchen is part of the adventure."

The motorhome was too big to park just anywhere, so Ubering to Berkeley had seemed like a good solution. But Rhett wouldn't hear of it. They were having breakfast in the motorhome with him, and later, he would take them for a tour of the college. They would have lunch together in town, and then he'd drive them back to the Walmart's parking lot.

"Right. Do you have everything you need? If not I can get it by the time you finish getting dressed." He opened the screen and waved at the big store at the other side of the parking lot.

"No need. I'm just making omelets, and I checked last night that I have all the ingredients. But if you want to be a dear, make us some coffee while I get ready."

"I'm on it." Smiling, he kissed her cheek.

After a quick visit to the small bathroom, Geraldine pulled out the outfit she brought with her for the occasion. A pair of dark blue slacks, a red silk blouse, and a pair of red kitten mules. She looked good in it, but not young, which was precisely what she was aiming for.

When she was done, she rearranged the bed pillows the way she liked them and walked into the living area of the motorhome.

"How do I look?"

Shai's eyes blazed. "Good enough to eat."

She laughed. "You did that last night. What I want to know is whether I look like a forty-something woman."

He shook his head. "Not even close. If Rhett asks, which I hope he doesn't, you are thirty-four years old."

"That's Cassandra's age. Do I have children?"

"If you want to tell him about Cassandra, you can say that she's your sister."

Geraldine opened the fridge and pulled out a carton of eggs and a stick of butter. "It's not easy to be an immortal." She put them on the counter and pulled out an onion and a box of mushrooms. "I don't like lying, but out of necessity, I've become very good at it."

As a memory of a nearly identical conversation surfaced, she put the two items on the counter and rubbed her temple. "Orion said the same thing."

"In what context?"

"He kept saying that we were a family, and when I asked him in what way we were related, his expression turned pained, and he said that it was better I didn't know so I wouldn't have to lie about it. I remember thinking that it was an odd thing to say since he made me forget him every time he left. It didn't matter what he told me because I would forget it along with everything else. Why did he need to keep that information from me?"

"Perhaps he feared exactly what happened. That you would somehow meet another powerful immortal who would unlock those memories."

Geraldine pulled out the cutting board and peeled the onion. "That would imply that he knew about Annani, but I don't think he did. He never mentioned the clan or the Doomers. His only concern for me was being discovered by humans."

Shai smoothed his hand over his short beard. "Maybe he knew of other immortals that were not connected to the clan or to the Brotherhood, and those immortals were just as powerful as he was. He wanted to hide you from them as well."

"I don't think so." She started chopping the onion. "The impression I got was that he was very lonely, and that other than Cassandra and me, he had no one." She turned to look at Shai. "But then Darlene and Roni were his family as well, and I wonder if in addition to helping Leo find a well-paying job he also visited them."

Shai leaned against the fridge and folded his arms over his chest. "We've already decided that the next time you meet her I'm going to thrall her to reveal the truth about Leo. I might as well look a little deeper and scan her memories for Orion."

42

SHAI

$\mathcal{A}$s Rhett pulled his car up into the spot next to the motorhome, Shai opened the door and stepped down.

"She's a beauty." His son got out of the Honda Shai had gotten him as a high school graduation present. "Is she yours?"

"It's borrowed." Shai pulled Rhett into a tight embrace and clapped him on the back. "How is school?"

Rhett grimaced. "Tough. In high school, I was at the top of my class. Here, everyone is as good as me or better."

"Hi," Geraldine said from behind them.

Shai let go of his son and stepped aside. "Rhett, this is Geraldine, my partner. Geraldine, this is my son, Rhett."

"A pleasure to meet you." Rhett offered her his hand.

"Likewise." She treated him to one of her charming smiles, lifted on her toes, and kissed his cheek. "You look so much like your father." She turned her smiling face to Shai. "The girls must be going wild for your boy."

Rhett cleared his throat. "I wish."

"And you're just as modest and unaware of your masculine charms as your father. But let's continue this inside. Breakfast is getting cold."

"I thought we were going out." Rhett followed her up the stairs into the motorhome.

She looked at him over her shoulder. "What would be the fun in that?"

"Right." As he got inside, Rhett whistled. "This is bigger then my dorm room." He turned to Shai. "Is there any chance I can borrow it for the next four years?"

"Sorry." Shai clapped him on the back. "But I have to return it tomorrow."

"Who does it belong to?" Rhett sat on one of the benches flanking the small dining table that Shai had already set up for breakfast. The only thing missing were the omelets that Geraldine left in the pan to keep warm.

"My reclusive boss." Shai sat across from him.

The cover story he'd used to explain why Rhett couldn't visit him in his home was that he worked for an eccentric billionaire who lived on a secret mountain compound and didn't allow any visitors.

Rhett's lips twisted in a familiar way. "I get it that he pays you well, but you live like a recluse because of him. How did you even meet Geraldine?" He looked up at her. "Do you work for Mr. X as well?"

Putting a steaming omelet on his plate, she glanced at Shai. "Why don't you tell Rhett how we met, dear?"

They hadn't prepared a story, which they should have.

She put the remaining omelets on the other two plates, sat down, and unfurled a cloth napkin.

Shai slid next to her. "Geraldine's sister introduced us. She's dating a guy who also works for my boss."

That was close enough to the truth.

"How did that guy meet your sister?" Rhett cut a piece of the omelet and put it in his mouth.

"At a charity gala." Geraldine cast Shai a sidelong glance.

It was time to change the subject. "So, Rhett, how are your grades so far this semester?" Shai lifted the carafe and poured coffee into their cups.

Rhett finished chewing before answering. "Average, which is as good as it gets in computer science." He smiled at Geraldine. "My father studied English literature and took a few classes in business administration. It's not hard to get good grades in those."

Shai snorted. "You should have met some of my professors. At least computer science is not open to interpretation. Your program either works or doesn't. You are not graded on style, or creativity, or any other subjective criteria."

"You'd think that." Rhett reached for a piece of toast. "A program can work but still be clumsy and not elegant enough." He turned to Geraldine. "What did you study in college?"

A blush colored her cheek as she stammered, "I didn't go to college."

He nodded. "With your beauty, I bet you were a teenage model who made enough money without having to bother with that."

His son was smooth—by complimenting Geraldine on her looks, he made her feel less awkward about her lack of education.

"I was never a model, but my sister Cassandra was. She's much taller than me, and her beauty is striking and exotic. She wanted to study graphic design, but one semester of art school convinced her that it was a waste of time and money and that she could learn everything she needed online for a fraction of the cost."

"Smart woman." Rhett shoved the rest of the omelet into his mouth.

"College is not just about learning a craft," Shai said. "It's also about meeting new people and making social and business connections." He lifted his coffee cup and took a sip. "And it's never too late."

"I don't even know what subjects interest me," Geraldine said. "I like to read, so maybe I should study literature."

Shai laughed. "If you want a sure way to lose your love of reading, that's the way to go. The sheer number of books you'll be forced to read will make you not want to pick a book up for years."

4 3

ELEANOR

*E*leanor got off the phone with Kian and put it down on the coffee table. "You heard him." She looked up at Emmett who'd stopped his pacing and faced her. "He's okay with you visiting Vrog, but I have to come with you, and the Guardians in charge of him need to be in the room with us."

He nodded. "I don't mind you being there. In fact, I need you with me. And frankly, I don't mind the Guardians either. I don't know Vrog, and I have no secrets to exchange with him."

Emmett had taken the news about his people's fate too calmly. He didn't have fond memories of the compound, but still, for better or for worse, they were his family. His mother was long gone, but now he'd lost his father as well.

Pushing to her feet, she walked up to him and pulled him into her arms. "I know that you don't know Vrog, but I thought that with just you in the room, he would open up. The two of you are all that's left from your tribe."

"Vrog knows that there are surveillance cameras all over the place. He wouldn't have talked anyway."

"I'm glad that you want me with you." She pressed a light kiss to his lips. "We are a team, you and I. We've got each other's backs."

The smile he gave her was heartwarming. "Yes, we are, and I couldn't have asked for a better partner in crime and in love. You are the perfect female for me."

Lowering her arms to his waist, she leaned back and regarded him with a wry smile. "You're full of compliments today. Is that because I made it possible for you to return to Safe Haven?"

He cupped her behind and rubbed himself against her. "I don't know what I find more sexy, your knockout body or your devious mind. You played Kian better than I ever could."

She chuckled. "I wish I could take credit for planning it. The idea just formed in my head as I was trying to avoid us being sent to West Virginia. You would have hated the underground city."

"Indeed. But West Virginia is still on the table."

"Regrettably, that's true." She pushed out of his arms. "I'm just waiting for Roberts to die so I can go to his funeral and use my powers on his superiors."

"I'm coming with you."

"About that." She took out the pin holding her hair up. "I might be able to convince Kian to let you come with me to the funeral, but even that will be a difficult sell. When he suggested that I take over as director of the paranormal program, I told him that I would do it if he allowed you to come with me. He refused, saying that he couldn't monitor you inside the underground facility. That's how the idea of moving the program to Safe Haven was born. He can have you monitored there, which is the only reason he's letting you do it."

"That's not the only reason. Without me, the entire plan to move the paranormal program there falls apart. Kian needs me as the face of Safe Haven."

"I can compel everyone to make it happen."

He shook his head. "That's not how the government works. The proposal to move the program to Safe Haven will be sent over to the pencil pushers for security and financial evaluation. Since you don't have direct access to those departments, you won't be able to influence their decisions. They will check the history of Safe Haven, and if they find that I've been running the place pretty much the same way from the very beginning, they will most likely approve the move provided that it makes sense financially, and we will make sure that it does. But if they find that the place has changed management recently, they might become suspicious and less inclined to recommend the move."

"Everything you said is true, but that doesn't change the fact that Kian will not allow you to come with me to West Virginia. I hate the idea of being apart from you, but to make Safe Haven happen, I have no choice. I would probably have to stay there for a couple of months while I negotiate the move and find people in the Echelon system who I can compel to cooperate with the clan."

His eyes blazed red. "A couple of months? I can't be apart from you for so long."

"Oh, baby." She wrapped her arms around his neck. "I can't either, but it's for our future."

He shook his head. "We need to find a way to convince Kian to let me come with you. Roberts didn't live in the underground facility, right? You can insist on living outside of it and then I can come with you. He can send a Guardian to monitor me twenty-four-seven. I don't care as long as it makes it possible for me to be with you."

She smiled. "Even if that Guardian is Peter?"

"Even if it's damn Peter. I'll tolerate the bastard to be with you."

"That's sweet, but it's not going to work. You need to be in Safe Haven, and we can't let the government officials know that we are a couple. Otherwise, your pencil pushers will think that I want to relocate the paranormal program to Safe Haven to line my boyfriend's pockets."

As the light dimmed in his eyes, he sighed. "I hate to admit it, but you're right. How are we going to survive months away from each other?"

"Twice a day of video calls?"

"That's not going to cut it."

"We will figure it out somehow." She kissed his cheek. "For the sake of our future, we can suffer through a couple of miserable months."

44

EMMETT

$\mathcal{A}$s Emmett stood in front of his old cell's door, he wasn't looking forward to crossing that threshold again. It had taken a miracle and Eleanor's wits and courage to get him out of that luxurious coffin, and he never wanted to go back.

Why was he even there?

Did he really want to meet the hybrid male? He must have been a young boy when Emmett had left.

The uncomfortable feeling churning in his gut was about more than facing Vrog, though. He hadn't expected Eleanor to agree to a two-month or more separation from him, and he'd expected even less how much the prospect of that separation would affect him.

He loved Eleanor, but he wasn't in love with her. The mystical bond the immortals talked about hadn't formed between them. Theirs was a marriage of convenience, so to speak. A comfortable pairing of two like-minded people who enjoyed each other in bed and outside of it.

What more could he possibly ask for?

Emmett wasn't a believer in the fated-mates nonsense even the skeptical Kian had accepted as real. He was perfectly fine spending his life with Eleanor by his side as his lover, his partner, and his friend. It was more than he had ever imagined he would have with a female.

Her leaving on a mission shouldn't make him feel a visceral sense of abandonment, a sharp pain scrambling his insides. It should not bother him as much, and yet it did.

What did it mean?

Perhaps the bond had formed without either of them realizing it?

As the Guardian named Vernon, a fellow who Emmett hadn't met before, activated the door mechanism, Eleanor squeezed Emmett's hand. "Excited?"

"Not really," he drawled as he walked into his former cell.

A friendly smile stretching on his handsome face, Vrog pushed to his feet. "Good afternoon." He offered Eleanor his hand first. "I'm Vrog, but you can also call me James. That's my human name."

"I like Vrog better." She shook what he offered. "I'm Eleanor, Emmett's partner."

"And I'm Emmett." He shook the guy's hand. "I don't use my Kra-ell given name."

Vrog looked down at the cuffs on Emmett's wrists, identical to the ones he'd been shackled with, but he didn't comment on them. "I haven't used mine for twenty-two years." He motioned for them to take a seat. "Most of the time I even think of myself as James. Although since my capture, I've been using the old name, so it's coming back."

"Why are they keeping you here?" Emmett asked. "Do you pose a threat to the clan?"

Vrog glanced at the two Guardians seated at the dining table. "I don't, but I guess Kian needs more time to make sure that I'm harmless to him and his clan. He told me that he plans to send me back to China with a team of investigators, so my stay here is not going to be long."

"That's good." Emmett sat down on the armchair that used to be his favorite and crossed his legs. "I hated living underground, and they kept me here for months."

"I heard." Vrog cast a sidelong glance at the Guardians. "Alec and Vernon told me what you had done and why you were here for so long. I didn't know any hybrids who could compel anyone other than humans." He looked as if he had another question on the tip of his tongue but was too embarrassed to ask it.

Emmett had a pretty good idea what that question was.

"Don't be bashful, Vrog. Ask me whatever and I'll either answer or choose not to, but I won't get offended."

"How did you get free of your vow to Jade? Is it connected to your ability to compel?" Vrog shook his head. "She's been gone for over two decades, and I still can't do it."

Emmett smiled. "It is connected to my compulsion talent, but not directly. It just provided me with a loophole. I told myself that I was serving her by leaving. If I had stayed, and she discovered what I could do, she probably would have had me killed. Not an execution because I had done nothing wrong, but she would have perceived me as a threat and ordered one of the pureblooded males to challenge me to a duel. The Mother of All Life would not have approved, and Jade would have suffered the consequences."

"Clever," Vrog admitted. "What about your parents? Your friends? Weren't you afraid that she would retaliate against them?"

Emmett shrugged. "I had no friends, my human mother was gone, and my pureblooded father could go to hell as far as I was concerned."

"Who was your father, if I may ask?"

"Tuvor."

Vrog winced. "Yeah. I don't blame you. I didn't know he had a son who left. No one ever mentioned anything about you. It was as if you'd never existed."

"Obviously." Emmett folded his arms over his chest. "That would have made Jade look bad. She must have ordered my excommunication and ordered everyone to forget me. Who was your father?"

"Sybor." Given the sadness in Vrog's eyes, he hadn't hated his sire.

"I remember Sybor as one of the two semi-decent pureblooded males. The other one was Voril."

Vrog chuckled. "Jade didn't like either of them. She considered them weaklings because they weren't as cruel as the others."

"Indeed." Emmett grimaced. "That's why she loved my sire, not that she loved anyone other than herself. A better way to describe her feelings for him is that she found him adequate enough to invite him to her bed more often than any of the others. He failed to impregnate her, though, and it was one more reason for her to detest me."

45

VROG

*E*mmett's father had been a favorite of Jade, which had probably made Emmett's life even more miserable than those of the other hybrids.

No wonder he'd left.

Jade had accepted the necessity of her males fathering more children with the humans, but she hadn't liked it. She'd regarded humans as inferior, and the males she'd favored knew better than to take human females into their beds for anything other than breeding when they were fertile.

"What makes you think that the males were killed?" Eleanor asked.

Vrog sighed. He'd repeated the story several times already, and it pained him every time anew. But Emmett was a former tribesman, and even though he'd deserted, he deserved to know.

When he was done, Emmett nodded. "They wouldn't have taken those damn rings off even if their lives depended on it. I agree with your assessment that they are dead."

"What if Jade commanded them to do that?" Eleanor asked.

"They would have obeyed." Emmett twisted one of his own rings, made from gold, not from polished precious stone like the ones the purebloods had worn. "But she wouldn't have demanded it unless they were accused of treason."

Eleanor arched a brow. "And that's not possible?"

"It's unlikely," Vrog said.

"Could she and the other females have killed the males?" Eleanor asked.

"Why would they do that? They sneered at human males, and they needed the purebloods to father long-lived children."

"If the Kra-ell are related to the immortals, then the females don't need pure-blooded males to produce long-lived children. If they weren't such snobs, they might have discovered that their children with humans could have been activated."

Alec cleared his throat. "That's information Kian is not ready to share with Vrog."

"Why not?" she asked.

The Guardian shrugged. "He has his reasons. I'm just following orders."

Letting out a long-suffering sigh, Eleanor leaned forward. "So, what are your plans, Vrog? Are you going to join our clan? Or are you going to keep waiting for your bitchy mistress to return?"

He'd given it a lot of thought, and the decision was difficult—on the one hand, he had a son that he wanted to get to know, and a wedding that he wanted to attend. On the other hand, the international school he'd founded was his life project, and even though it had started as a cover, it had become much more than that.

"I have a life in China."

Eleanor waved a dismissive hand. "You have a job, and you are waiting for someone who is not coming back and who is not even worth waiting for. Here you have a son, and because of Vlad, Kian can't refuse you membership in the clan if you ask for it." She pinned him with a hard stare. "Ask for it, Vrog. You can have a life with the clan."

He looked around the small but lavish apartment. "This is very nice and comfortable, but I don't want to spend my life in here."

She laughed. "Of course not. You will come to live in the village, and you might even find a nice female to have a good life with—as her equal, not her slave." She smirked. "If you want to play kinky games in bed, you can be a slave all you like, but you don't need to play that role outside of the bedroom."

He didn't like playing kinky games, and having an immortal partner who would treat him as her equal sounded too good to be true.

The question was whether he was willing to give up the school for that. He already had a long-lived son, and although he wouldn't mind having another, that yearning had been satisfied.

"I need to think about it." He turned to Emmett, who hadn't commented on anything Eleanor had said so far. "What's your advice?"

"Same as Eleanor's." Emmett unfolded his arms and got up. "I thought I was happy as can be in my Safe Haven." He opened the bar cabinet and pulled out a bottle of wine. "I had all the women I wanted, people who worshiped me like a god, and I was making a fortune." He took out five glasses and filled them with wine. "But even though I was surrounded by people, I was lonely. I didn't have a partner. The life I built for myself was exactly the kind of life I dreamt about having before I left the compound."

He handed Eleanor a glass of wine, another to Vrog, and two to the Guardians sitting at the small dining table.

"When Eleanor and Peter showed up, and things happened the way they did, I thought that being captured and imprisoned was the worst thing that had ever happened to me." He took a sip from his wine. "Turned out that I was wrong." He stopped behind Eleanor's armchair and put his hand on her shoulder. "It was the best thing that had ever happened to me. I met a female who's my perfect counterpart, my friend, my lover, my partner. And that's worth more than the cushy life I made for myself in Safe Haven."

Smiling, Eleanor put her hand on top of Emmett's and winked at Vrog. "As you can see, my partner has a penchant for drama."

"I meant every word." Emmett took Eleanor's hand and lifted it to his lips for a kiss. "I guess my human half yearned for an exclusive relationship that would have been abhorrent to a pureblooded Kra-ell." He turned to Vrog. "Which half is more dominant in you?"

"I suppose that it's the human half. I was a young male when I was sent to Singapore, and I've spent my life among humans ever since. I don't think I could easily adapt to the Kra-ell lifestyle and its rigid hierarchy after all these years." Vrog thought of his school, and how much he enjoyed being in charge. "I won't accept being treated as an inferior again."

"Then you have your answer." Emmett finished the last of the wine in his glass. "Sell your school, and come live in the immortals' village."

"We need a school," Eleanor said. "Not right now, but in the future. Your experience might be useful to the clan."

One of the Guardians cleared his throat, probably meaning to warn Emmett and Eleanor not to say more about their village and where it was located. Or maybe the warning was about the future need for a school?

"Thank you." Vrog dipped his head. "Your warm invitation means a lot to me, but I need more time to decide, and I also need to ask Vlad what he prefers. Perhaps he doesn't want me to join the clan."

Eleanor frowned. "Why wouldn't he?"

"Stella is in a relationship with a male who hates me, and who Vlad is fond of. That might be a problem."

46

GERALDINE

*A*s Shai stopped at the gate to her community, Geraldine opened her eyes and waved at the guard. "Good evening, Karl."

"Good evening, Ms. Beaumont." He waved back and opened the gate.

They had spent a lovely morning and part of the afternoon with Rhett, touring the university and later the town. Regrettably, they hadn't had time to visit the museums or the botanical gardens, but Shai had promised her that after the Orion thing was done with, he would take her on another, longer vacation to Northern California.

Hopefully it would be soon because it was wrecking her nerves and keeping her from fully enjoying her new life with Shai. It was a shame that Rhett couldn't become a greater part of it, though, and her heart ached for Shai and the future he would have to face.

If the Fates were kind they would give them a child, and perhaps that would make things a little easier for him, but one child couldn't substitute for another, and it would always be difficult for Shai.

Geraldine knew that pain. Now that she had found out about Darlene, the guilt over missing so many years with her was a constant ache in her heart. Perhaps if Darlene were happily married with a gaggle of kids, Geraldine would have felt a little less guilty. But knowing that her daughter had a miserable life was adding another layer to the guilt.

Hopefully, Darlene could transition, and they would have eternity to make up for lost time.

When Rhett got married and had a family of his own, knowing that his son was happy and settled down would help Shai. But Rhett could never become immortal, so there was that.

Shai didn't even have the sliver of hope Geraldine had.

Shai had to make the most of the time he had with Rhett, using clever disguises and prosthetics when he visited him.

As he parked in her driveway, she covered up the wave of sadness and the tears stinging her eyes with a yawn and a forced smile. "What time is it?"

"Almost eight. Did you have a nice nap?"

There was an edge to his tone, and Geraldine wondered whether she talked in her sleep. She'd dreamt about Orion, but it hadn't been a memory.

"I did. I'm so sorry for not keeping you company. It's the engine noise. It always lulls me to sleep."

He smiled and reached to cup her cheek. "I enjoyed watching you napping peacefully until you started to frown and whimper. What did you dream about?"

Had she made those noises while thinking of Rhett?

Her eyes had been closed, so she might have drifted off into that state between sleep and wakefulness. But telling Shai her depressing thoughts would just make him sad as well. Telling him about her dream was better.

"I dreamt about Orion, but it wasn't real. I saw him walking down the street and I called after him. He looked at me over his shoulder, but there was no recognition in his eyes, and he kept walking. I started running to catch up to him, but even though he was just walking, the distance between us kept widening. When I called out his name again, he didn't even turn around, and then he just disappeared. One moment he was there and then next he was gone. I stopped and started crying, which was probably when you heard me whimpering."

"Oh, sweetheart." He unbuckled her seatbelt and pulled her onto his lap. "I'm not a psychologist, but I think that you feel abandoned by him."

"How can I feel that when I can barely remember Orion?"

"Your subconscious remembers him well enough, and that's where dreams are made."

She rested her head on his chest. "Maybe it's more about guilt than abandonment. Or perhaps it's a combination of both. When he's caught, he will blame me for setting a trap for him, and he might never forgive me."

"Makes sense." He stroked her back. "I still think that you should talk to Vanessa. "

Thankfully, the therapist had told Shai that the earliest she could see Geraldine was in three weeks. The truth was that she didn't believe a shrink could do anything for her, especially after the goddess herself had unlocked her memories. The Clan Mother was smart enough to prevent a flood of them from overwhelming her mind, and Geraldine didn't trust the psychologist to do better. In fact, she feared Vanessa would do worse.

"It's not my fault that Vanessa is so busy. I was okay with going to see her on Wednesday."

"I know. It's frustrating that she doesn't deem your case as an emergency."

"Because it's not." She lifted her head to kiss the side of his mouth. "You're just impatient. My memories are coming back slowly, just as the Clan Mother intended. At first, I was also disappointed that it didn't happen right then and there, but now I understand how smart she was not to allow that."

"You're right." He hooked a finger under her chin and kissed her.

Wrapping her arms around his neck, she kissed him back, and as he deepened the kiss and fire started low in her belly, she pushed out of his arms. "I need to shower, and so do you." She rose to her feet and stretched her arms over her head. "We can continue this conversation inside."

Amusement dancing in his eyes, he opened the motorhome's door. "A conversation, eh?"

"Or whatever else you have on your mind." Geraldine went back for her bag. "Can we wait to clean this up until tomorrow? I'm really not in the mood to do it now."

"Neither am I." He followed her to the motorhome's bedroom and lifted his own overnight bag. "Anyway, I plan to return it on Monday. I left my car in the village."

"Which means that if we want to go anywhere tomorrow, we have to take the motorhome."

Shai's grin was wolfish. "Then I guess we are not going anywhere."

47

SHAI

S hai hated that Geraldine's memories of Orion were percolating to the surface, not because they were slow to emerge, but because they were there.

On the one hand, he wanted her to remember more so he would know what the bastard had been up to, and what his motives were for being in her life. On the other hand, though, he resented the immortal's very existence and hated himself for feeling possessive and jealous like some damn caveman.

The guy had helped Geraldine over the years, and Shai was well aware that without Orion's assistance, her life would have been either much more difficult, or worse, she might have been discovered by greedy humans who would have experimented on her to find out the secret of her immortality.

But it wasn't just about that.

Even if jealousy and possessiveness were not clouding his attitude, Shai couldn't get rid of the nagging suspicion that Orion had something to do with Geraldine's so-called accident, and until he was convinced that hadn't been the case, he couldn't feel gratitude toward the guy.

As Geraldine headed to the bathroom, she cast him a look that had invitation written all over it, but he needed time to cool off and pretended not to get her meaning. "I'll whip us up something to eat while you are showering."

"Okay." She looked disappointed. "I'm not hungry, but I would love some coffee."

"I'll get the coffeemaker going." He turned around and walked out the door.

In the kitchen, he pulled out his phone and called the security office in the village.

"Shai," Morgard answered. "How was your trip?"

He'd told Kian that he was taking Geraldine on a short one-day romantic vacation, which hadn't been a total lie. They had made love in the motorhome twice, and they'd had a good time with Rhett and also by themselves.

"It was great. Was there any suspicious activity around Geraldine's house while we were gone?"

"I would have let you know if there was. Though to tell you the truth, with all the deliveries her neighbors receive, it's difficult to tell, especially with Uber Eats and Grubhub and even Amazon using private operators. Anyone can pretend to be a delivery driver. And then there are the gardeners, cleaners, pest controllers, satellite dish installers, carpet cleaners, and so on."

Shai ran a hand over the back of his head. "So what good are those cameras? Unless the guy knocks on the door and gets his face in front of the camera attached to it, we won't know that he was snooping around."

"Since he has no reason to suspect anything, we are counting on him not being overly careful. He's been visiting her for years, so he's probably grown complacent."

"I hope you're right. Thanks for the update."

"No problem." Morgard ended the call.

With a sigh, Shai put the phone on the counter and got busy with the coffeemaker.

Geraldine came down just as it finished brewing, wearing a knee-length silk robe. With the fabric draping ever so lovingly over her body, it was obvious that she wore nothing underneath.

The problem was that they were being watched, and he didn't want the guys in security to ogle her.

"Aren't you cold?"

"That's not the question I was expecting." Looking disappointed, she pulled out a chair and sat down. "What's bugging you, Shai?"

"Orion. The wait is grating on my nerves. I want this to be over already."

"You and me both. But that's no reason to brood. I come down here half naked, and you ask me if I'm cold? I'm lucky that I don't have confidence issues, at least as far as my attractiveness goes, or I would have thought that I no longer excite you."

"Don't be silly." He prowled up to her and lifted her out of the chair. Cupping her naked bottom under the robe, he commanded, "Wrap your legs around me."

When she did, he swiveled his hips, grinding himself into her and letting her feel what seeing her in that skimpy thing was doing to him. "Is that proof enough of how much you excite me?"

Her smile was pure feminine satisfaction. "Carry me to bed, big boy," she whispered throatily.

"What about the coffee?"

"It can wait." She nipped his ear, then blew into it, the tease turning his erection into a hard rod that strained his zipper.

"Feisty kitten." Kneading her bottom, he headed up the stairs.

"Don't forget the cameras," she whispered in his ear. "We are giving them a show."

"Now you're suddenly concerned with privacy? You didn't seem to care when you came down wearing cobwebs."

"Why do you think I didn't do it naked?"

48

GERALDINE

*G*eraldine clung to Shai as he carried her up the stairs, worried about the short robe revealing too much to those watching eyes in the village. Despite what he thought, she was keenly aware of them and kept her sexual innuendoes to a minimum.

It was a struggle not to run her tongue all over the strong column of his neck, to nibble at his ear and make him forget all about Orion.

The road trip and the day they'd spent with Rhett had been wonderful, and then she'd opened her big mouth and told Shai about the dream. Except, she hadn't expected him to get upset by it.

Usually, he got jealous when she said nice things about Orion, or when she expressed regret about the trap they had set for him with her as bait. But the dream hadn't been pleasant.

The truth was that she didn't know how to handle Shai's mood swings, or why he was having them. Their relationship used to be so easy, so natural, it was like winning the mate lottery. Shai should be over the moon with happiness, and so should she, but the thing with Orion hung over them like a dark cloud.

So Geraldine turned to the best tool in her arsenal, which was seduction, hoping to get Shai's mind off Orion. But with those damn surveillance cameras all over the house, she had been limited with what she could do outside their bedroom.

It was a relief to reach that sanctuary, and as Shai kicked the door closed behind them, Geraldine let loose, attacking that strong neck column with her lips and her tongue and her teeth, licking, sucking, nipping, and kissing.

When he lowered her to the long ottoman at the foot at the bed instead of the bed itself, she wondered what he had in mind, hoping it was something naughty.

Rising on her knees, Geraldine reached for Shai's zipper, but he shook his head and turned her around to face the headboard.

Well, that was a big fat clue as to his intentions.

"Don't move," he whispered against her ear.

Stifling a smile, she put her hands on the footboard and listened to him ditch his clothes.

She was still wearing the robe, but that barrier was easy to remove.

Wrapping his arms around her waist, his fingers splayed over her belly, he kissed the column of her neck, small teasing kisses that soon turned into little nips that sent shivers of desire straight to her burning core.

When one of his hands left her belly, dipping between her thighs and cupping her there, while the other slithered under her robe, closing over her breast, Geraldine bit down on her lower lip to stifle the moan rising up in her throat.

"Don't hold it in," he murmured against her neck. "I want to hear you moan, and beg, and shout my name when you come."

"What about the cameras?" she managed to ask.

"Forget them. The guys probably already muted the sound."

His fingers plucked at her nipple while his finger dipped between her folds.

Closing her eyes, she let her head drop against his shoulder and surrendered to the sensations.

"Bend down." He pushed gently on her back.

She did, pressing her chest against the footboard and sticking her bum out.

He lifted the robe, exposing her bottom, the cold air cooling the heat he'd stoked.

For a moment, he did nothing, making her wonder what he was up to, but then the tip of his shaft nudged her entrance, teasing her as he moved it up and down her folds, coating it with her wetness.

Geraldine held her breath, waiting for him to join them.

She didn't have to wait long.

Clamping one hand on her hip and the other on her shoulder, he surged inside her until he was all the way in, his chest on her back, his groin pressed against her bottom.

Then he started moving.

Slamming against the soft cushions of her butt cheeks, he pumped into her with abandon and roughness that got her fire reaching the level of inferno. When he circled his arm around her and pressed his finger to her throbbing nub, she bucked, her muscles clamping on his shaft.

As his movements became frenzied, and as he rubbed that most sensitive spot, she exploded, shouting his name and not caring who heard her, be it the neighbors or the Guardians in the security room miles away from there.

The loud hiss was her only warning before his fangs closed on the crook of her neck, the twin incision points a delicious burn that had her climaxing again.

She felt his seed erupt into her sheath at the same time the venom slid into her vein. A moment later the familiar bliss obliterated the last remnants of reason, sending her soaring on the now familiar cloud.

49

KIAN

"Good morning, Peter." Kian opened the door to his office. "You're early."

"I know." The Guardian glanced at his watch. "It's five minutes to seven. I thought you started your day at six."

"Normally I do."

Allegra had been a little fussy this morning, and he didn't want to leave before she calmed down. Syssi claimed that the baby was already aware of their routine, and that his daughter didn't want him to leave.

He didn't know enough about babies and what they should be aware of at such a young age, but in his layman's opinion, Allegra was still too young to be so observant. Then again, he had no doubt that his daughter was brilliant and developing faster than other children. Besides, he trusted Syssi's assessment.

Kian put his coffee cup down on the desk and motioned for Peter to take a seat. "How are things going for you?"

"Fine, I guess. It took some time to get used to field work again."

Kian smiled. "If you prefer, I can put you back in charge of the dungeon."

"No, thank you. I've had enough of the underground. I enjoy fresh air."

"Then you are going to enjoy your next assignment." Kian leaned back in his chair. "I have plans for Safe Haven, and since you know the place and some of the people currently running it, I want you to head that project."

Given Peter's surprised expression, Eleanor hadn't shared her ideas with him.

"What do you want to do there?"

"You know that Roberts is no longer in the picture."

Peter nodded.

"That means several things. First, someone else will be appointed as the director of the paranormal program, and second, we lost our access to the Echelon system. I came up with an idea for how to remedy the situation, and Eleanor improved on it. I want her to be the new director, which can be achieved with the help of her compulsion power and our assistance in providing her with the proper credentials. She likes the idea of heading the program, but she doesn't want to leave Emmett behind, and I can't allow him to accompany her to West Virginia. Her solution was to move the program to Safe Haven, where we can keep an eye on Emmett and also have free access to the paranormal talents in the program."

"If she can make it work, that's actually brilliant." Peter smoothed his fingers over his goatee. "But it's a big if."

"She's a compeller. She can make it happen. But first, she needs to spend a couple of months in West Virginia until things start moving. I also want her to find people working for the Echelon system and compel them to provide us the information we need."

Peter seemed doubtful, but he decided to keep his doubts to himself. "What's my part in this?"

Kian smiled. "There is a lot to be done, and I need a capable person to be the clan's representative in Safe Haven. The job requires leadership skills."

"I might not be the best person for the job. Watching over Emmett was my first command, and it was not very demanding."

"This is your chance to prove that you can be in charge of a bigger operation. Emmett knows how to run the place, and you can rely on him, but you also need to ensure that he doesn't exploit the community."

Peter grimaced. "I get it. It's the same job of being Emmett's keeper just with expanded responsibilities. Are you sure about letting him run the place?"

"This entire thing is hinged on him resuming his guru persona. He's been running the place as a spiritual retreat for nearly four decades. When Eleanor suggests moving the paranormal program to Safe Haven, it will look much better with him there than under new management. Also, no one would think it strange if the place started retreats for people with paranormal abilities. It's right up there with the other New Age stuff Safe Haven promotes."

"I see. So, Eleanor would suggest both to the decision-makers in the government to whet their appetites. A retreat for paranormals could be the perfect recruiting ground."

"You are a smart guy, Peter." Kian tapped his temple. "Neither I nor Eleanor have thought of that. The idea was for us to screen the attendees of those retreats for potential Dormants. But you are right about it being a big selling point that Eleanor can use to dangle in front of the government higher-ups."

His eyes glowing with excitement, Peter straightened in his chair. "When do you want to get a move on that?"

"I'm organizing a visit to Safe Haven on Monday two weeks from now, and I'm taking Syssi and Allegra with me, along with Eleanor, Emmett, and Shai. I thought you would go ahead of us and get it ready for our visit."

Looking unsure, Peter rubbed his hand over the back of his neck. "To be frank, I don't know how to go about it. What do I do? Do I just show up and demand cooperation?"

"More or less. I will have a document drafted that spells out an agreement between Emmett and one of our business entities. First, though, I'll have Emmett email the person in charge of the place and tell her that he's coming back and expects his place to be ready for him."

"How is he going to explain his absence?"

Kian grinned. "Shai came up with a plausible story. Emmett answered a spiritual calling to meditate in the Himalayas and revisit the limitations he had imposed on his flock—mainly the prohibition on forming exclusive relationships and having children. While meditating, he met a kindred spirit, i.e. me, and we decided to form a partnership. In exchange for my investment in Safe Haven, he will grant us the use of the land for the next twenty-five years and access to all of its facilities."

"What if after the visit you decide not to go through with it?"

Kian shrugged. "Deals fall apart all the time."

"I see that you've got it all figured out."

"I hope so."

"I have a suggestion if you don't mind."

"Go ahead." Kian waved a hand. "The more minds working on this plan, the better."

"It might be a good idea to have Bowen and Margaret come along. She spent decades in that place. She knows everyone there."

Kian nodded. "I'll discuss it with them, but I don't think Margaret will be interested. She wants to be near Wendy."

"It doesn't hurt to ask. I think Margaret will be offended if you don't."

"Right. I hadn't considered that."

It wasn't a big surprise that he hadn't taken into account Margaret's feelings, but Syssi would have mentioned it if she thought that it was an issue.

Before talking to Margaret, he needed to talk it over with her. In matters such as this, he trusted Syssi's opinion the most. Heck, he trusted her opinion on any and all topics. His mate was smart, but she wasn't opinionated, and she wasn't a know-it-all. When she decided to voice her opinion, it was only when she was a hundred percent sure about it and decided that it was worth mentioning.

5 0

EMMETT

*E*mmett had had two weeks to prepare, and he'd expected a smooth slide into his old role. He relished the return to his flock, but the guru costume felt strange, and instead of transforming him into the spiritual leader of Safe Haven, it made him feel like an actor.

An imposter.

Perhaps quality was the problem. The wig on his head was made from real hair, but it was heavy, and everything about it was off—the dull color, the rough texture, the lack of luster. The robe draping awkwardly over his body was made from synthetic fabric—a cheap imitation of the ones he'd had custom tailored for him before.

Or maybe he was just a different person than the one who'd fled Safe Haven three months ago, with Peter in his sports car and a renewed hope for the future of his people.

Damn, Emmett missed that car. He missed driving down the Oregon coast, he missed putting on a show, he missed the admiration bordering on worship of his followers, the high he'd gotten from that.

What he didn't miss, though, was the mindless debauchery he'd taken part in, or watched others engage in.

Sitting next to him in the rented limousine heading for Safe Haven was the person that had changed him from the inside out, forcing him to reevaluate his life and what he wanted to do with it.

He'd once heard a proverb about how lucky was the man who found a woman of valor. At the time, he'd sneered at it because in his mind it referenced the Kra-ell pureblooded females, and Emmett didn't consider the Kra-ell males lucky at all. He'd preferred the softness of human women, not realizing that there could be a happy medium.

Eleanor was a fighter through and through—ambitious, demanding, and assertive, sometimes even abrasive. And yet, she was soft when she wanted to be, and she wasn't cruel—never inflicting pain on him unless it was to spice things up for his pleasure.

Hell, he'd had to beg her to bite him.

Now that she knew that it drove him wild, she did it often, and he loved her even more for stepping out of her comfort zone for him.

"What are you smiling about?" Eleanor whispered.

"You." He tucked her closer against his side. "You've changed my life for the better, and you're still doing it."

Kian chuckled. "Save it for later, Emmett," he said softly, not because of any tender feelings for Emmett or Eleanor but because he didn't want to disturb the peaceful sleep of his infant daughter, who was curled in the car seat between him and his wife.

Fatherhood made the big boss much less intimidating. No man looked scary while pushing a stroller or carrying his child in a baby pouch strapped to his chest.

Still, Emmett wondered what Kian had meant by saving it for later. Had he meant it as in 'get a room,' or as in 'save the theatrical performance for the Safe Haven community'?

"Are you nervous?" Syssi asked. "You haven't given a sermon in a long time."

It had been the second one then. Syssi knew her husband better than anyone, so the meaning had been clear to her. They both thought that his expression of love and appreciation for Eleanor was nothing more than a performance.

Emmett kissed the top of Eleanor's head and smiled. "As long as I have this incredible woman by my side, I have nothing to be nervous about."

Let them chew on that.

Kian narrowed his eyes at him, but Syssi smiled. "Since Eleanor can't deliver the speech for you, I hope you have it memorized."

"Not at all. I always make them up on the spot. They sound better when they are not rehearsed, and I take cues from my audience. There is no substitute for spontaneity."

"I would have never had the guts to improvise like that," Syssi admitted. "Public speaking terrifies me, but I can handle it if I'm well prepared, and by well, I mean memorizing every word, practicing in front of the mirror, and recording myself to hear how I sound and to see how I look delivering it."

"That's a lot of prep," Eleanor said. "I also like to be prepared, but I don't bother with how I sound or look. I only care about the script." With a sigh, she leaned her head on Emmett's arm. "I need to rehearse what I'm going to say to the higher-ups to get myself reinstated. As Emmett can attest, compulsion requires very precise phrasing to work as intended."

Out of habit, Emmett glanced at Kian's left ear. His long hair covered the right, but he'd tucked it behind the other one and there was no visible earpiece in it.

He either wasn't wearing one, or William had invented a device so tiny that it was invisible. Except, a small device was no good as a physical barrier. It had to be large enough to block the compulsion sound waves from reaching the ear canal.

Emmett grinned. "I see that you finally trust me. You no longer bother with the cumbersome earpieces."

"I trust you a little more than I did before, but that doesn't mean that I'm careless." Kian motioned with his head toward the partition. "I brought Okidu along, and since he's a machine, you can't compel him. He holds the remote to your cuffs."

The guy thought that he was so smart, and even though it wasn't in Emmett's best interest to annoy the boss, he just couldn't help bringing Kian down a notch.

He smirked. "Since Okidu is programmed to obey your commands, theoretically, I can compel you to command him to relinquish the remote to me."

Kian returned with a smirk of his own. "That's not going to work. I told Okidu not to do that even if I commanded him to. He's to hold on to the remote until we are back in the village. Besides, Anandur and Brundar are both wearing earpieces, and they would stop you before you could finish the sentence."

Emmett racked his brain to find a loophole in that, but anything he came up with sounded like the retorts of a petulant teen. Instead, he decided to use the opportunity to butter Kian up. "I concede defeat." He dipped his head. "You've outsmarted me."

51

KIAN

*K*ian had never seen Emmett in action, not like that, and not live. Through his office window, he'd watched the guy proselytizing to a group of smitten clan females, and he'd heard recordings of Emmett's inspirational teachings, but he had never seen and heard Emmett while the guy was in his full costume regalia and pumped on the attention and admiration of his flock.

The result was impressive and quite entertaining. In fact, if Kian hadn't known that the essence of the story Emmett was telling with such dramatic flair had been fabricated by Shai, he might have been moved.

"The Mother of all Life called me to her." Emmett raised his arms. "She was angry at me, angry for denying her most precious gift to humanity, the gift of rebirth. I had to atone for my sin, the sin of convincing you all to go against nature and deny you the gift of children. I've spent weeks in silence, fasting, crying, praying, begging the goddess for forgiveness, until she answered me."

Emmett turned toward Eleanor, gazing at her lovingly. "The goddess sent her earthly embodiment to teach me the value of love. Eleanor taught me that there are many ways to love. For some, freedom is the only way—the freedom to choose a different partner each night, the freedom to experiment, the freedom to share their heart and body with as many as would have them. For others, this is a burden, for them, there is just one person they want to share their life with, and that's okay. There is no right or wrong in love."

As he paused, Eleanor started clapping, and soon the rest of Safe Haven's community joined her.

Riley, the one who had taken over for Emmett, had tears in her eyes, but Kian wasn't sure whether they were about the emotional impact of Emmett's 'New Way' or the realization that he would no longer share her bed.

When they'd arrived, the woman fawned over Emmett, finding every excuse to touch him until Eleanor snarled at her.

The speech continued for another hour, with Emmett gushing over the bright future of the community, the new buildings his new partner was going to erect, the new retreat for people with paranormal abilities, and so on.

At some point, Allegra woke up and began fussing, giving Syssi an excuse to leave the dining hall where the speech was delivered.

Brundar followed her outside.

Emmett smiled indulgently. "Soon, we will have many more fussy babies on our hands, and The Mother of all Life will rejoice."

Next to Kian, Anandur shifted his weight on the chair and stretched his long legs in front of him. "He's good," he whispered so low that only immortal ears could hear him. "But he needs to wrap it up. I'm hungry."

Emmett must have heard him because he smiled and lifted his arms again. "The coming months will be full of excitement. They will also be difficult. It's never easy to adjust to a new way, and the building project will disturb the community's tranquility. But no progress can be made without disrupting the status quo, and children cannot be raised in silence. Embrace these sounds. They herald a better future for us all."

In a flurry of robes, Emmett walked toward their table, leaned down, and kissed Eleanor on the lips. "You are my future," he said loud enough for everyone to hear.

As the room exploded in applause, Emmett straightened up and lifted his hand to silence his people.

"Let me introduce to you my dear new friend, Kian—the man who opened my eyes and helped me shape Emmett's New Way. Give him a round of applause."

Kian was thankful for the lack of smartphones in Safe Haven. No one snapped pictures of him as he took the spot Emmett had vacated.

"Everyone is hungry, so I'll make it short. Thank you for the heartwarming welcome your community has extended to me, my wife and daughter, and my friends. It is my pleasure to be your guest tonight, and I hope that together we will create a better future for the Safe Haven community. *Bon appétit*, everyone."

As a new round of applause erupted, several people rushed out of the dining hall, and a few moments later came back rolling buffet tables and lining them against the wall.

"I'm going to check on Syssi," he told Anandur.

The guy fell in step with him. "You're not going anywhere alone, boss."

People smiled and clapped as they passed them by, a few whispering thank you, but some didn't look happy.

Kian couldn't blame them.

They came to Safe Haven to escape the world, and here he was, a stranger who was bringing the world to them, upending their way of life, and forcing the change down their throats.

5 2

SHAI

*a*s they exited the main lodge, Shai zipped up his windbreaker. It was still mostly sunny in Southern California, but the Oregon coast was cold and breezy.

It wasn't bad, but it wouldn't have been Shai's first choice for a paranormal retreat. First of all, it was far away from their village, and secondly, the nearly permanent overcast was too glum for year-round living.

The proximity to the ocean was the place's biggest selling point.

The community building was shabby, bordering on shameful, and the lodge needed work, but the grounds were meticulously maintained.

"This place is perfect," Syssi said as Emmett opened the side gate with a card key.

His old one had been removed from the database, and when he'd asked Riley to issue him a new one, she'd done so gladly, but she had been disappointed that he hadn't invited her to join their tour of the property.

A big smile stretching across Syssi's pretty face, she turned in a circle and sucked in a long breath. "The fresh ocean breeze, the quiet, the sprawling grounds, I love it here."

Shai glanced at Kian, who didn't seem to share his wife's favorable opinion.

"It needs a lot of work," he said quietly.

Carrying Allegra in a baby pouch that was attached with straps to his chest, Kian kept his growling to a minimum and his facial expressions in neutral.

It was a bit disconcerting.

Normally, Kian was one of the easiest people to read because he never felt the need to pretend. Now that he was making accommodations for Allegra, Shai had to work harder to guess what Kian wanted.

Nevertheless, fatherhood was good for the guy, smoothing out his rough edges and making him less intimidating.

"Do you mean the new buildings?" Emmett asked.

Kian shook his head. "Everything needs to be remodeled. The decor is outdated, the community quarters are inadequate, and that's putting it mildly. The guest rooms are spartan, and on top of that, the workmanship is crap. The paint, the flooring, the tile in the bathrooms, everything needs to be replaced. I think it would be best to just demolish these buildings and build new ones."

"You're not going to recoup the expense," Shai said. "You're thinking about Safe Haven in terms of the hotels you build, but this is not a hotel. People don't expect luxury when they come to a spiritual retreat."

Kian cut him a sidelong glance. "Is suffering part of the experience? Because for what they are charged, the guests should receive better accommodations."

Shai wondered whether Kian was really that disillusioned with the place, or if it was just a negotiation tactic to get Emmett to lower his price.

"I didn't notice any major issues," Emmett said, sounding defensive. "You should listen to your assistant."

Kian pinned him with a hard stare. "You want to tell me that no one ever complained about the living conditions in the community building? Or that no guests demanded their money back after seeing their rooms?"

Emmett squared his shoulders. "There are always people who find fault with everything, and who are a pain in the butt no matter how well they are treated. Thankfully, we had only a handful of cases over the years, and I gladly refunded their money and sent them on their way."

Kian's eyes shifted to Peter. "You were a guest. What did you think about the accommodations?"

The Guardian shrugged. "The room was clean, the mattress was comfortable, and I had everything I needed. Between the classes, the workshops, and our side activities, we didn't get to spend much time in the rooms."

As they reached the beach, Syssi spread her arms. "Who cares about the rooms when they have this as their backyard?"

Kian grimaced. "I bet it's not as lovely in the winter."

Eleanor turned her back to the ocean and gazed at the main lodge. "It looks nice from here, and I like the rustic vibe. I bet Ingrid can wield her magic and transform the guest rooms into cozy havens. If she managed to do that with the dungeon cells, she would have no problem doing even better with the lodge guest rooms."

"There are cracked tiles in the bathrooms," Kian grumbled as softly as he could. "Some of the faucets are rusted, and I smelled mold. No amount of decorative magic can solve those problems."

As their group continued their discussion about what was necessary to fix and what could be improved with furniture and decor, Shai thought about the night he was going to spend away from Geraldine.

They had been inseparable from nearly the first day, sleeping in each other's arms every night, waking up together, having breakfast together.

He kept telling himself that it was only one night, but the vise on his heart refused to loosen. The tether connecting him to Geraldine pulled and tightened the further away from her he got, and the more time had passed since he'd last been with her.

It was ridiculous.

He'd seen her earlier that morning, and if he were back in California, Shai would still be in the office. But knowing that he wasn't going home to Geraldine tonight was enough to make him miss her as if he hadn't seen her in days.

How were Anandur and Brundar tolerating being away from their mates?

Was it easier for them because they'd been mated for a while, so the bond could be stretched a little further?

The bond.

Had he and Geraldine bonded without realizing it?

"What do you think, Shai?" Kian asked.

"I'm sorry. I wasn't listening."

His boss shook his head. "We were discussing splitting Safe Haven into two separate sections. The old one will continue doing business as usual, and we will build a new one that will meet our needs."

"Sounds good to me. Who is going to maintain the new section, though? The only workforce to be had out here is the community." He looked at Emmett. "Is there enough of them to run both places?"

Emmett shook his head. "We will need to get more people. Perhaps some of those paranormally talented guests would like to stay and join a community of like-minded people, and by that I don't mean Safe Haven's old community because these people are like-minded in different ways."

"A community of paranormally talented people," Syssi said. "I love it."

"You're forgetting one thing." Eleanor lifted a finger. "Someone needs to come up with a program for paranormals that will have enough classes and workshops to fill two whole weeks. Who's going to do that?"

"Margaret," Emmett said. "She's very good at creating new workshops, and she is one of us now."

"Excellent idea." Kian clapped him on his back. "She declined my invitation to join us because she has no interest in coming back to live here. But I'm sure she'd love to work on a new program for paranormals."

Eleanor pursed her lips. "Margaret has no paranormal talent and no training. How would she know what to include in those classes?"

"That's true." Kian cut a glance to Syssi. "Is it something you would be interested in?"

"I'm not qualified either. You need Amanda, but now that I'm on maternity leave, she has her hands full at the university, and soon she will become a mother herself."

He nodded. "Perhaps it's something you two can put together while on leave from the university, and Margaret can help with the final touches."

53

ELEANOR

"Being back here gives me the creeps." Eleanor sat on the bed and pulled one of her boots off.

"It's not the same room you were in before." Emmett joined her on the bed. "Besides, this is where our relationship started." He kissed her neck. "I was a goner from the first taste."

Eleanor rolled her eyes. "How romantic." She lifted her leg and pulled off the other boot. "You thought that I was tasty?"

"And sexy." He kissed her neck again. "Strong." He kissed the soft spot behind her ear. "Alluring." He nibbled on her earlobe. "Intriguing."

She couldn't think with him electrifying her skin and sending sparks of desire right down to her center.

"You're such a smooth operator." She pushed on his chest. "If you want to play, you need to take off the damn wig. I'm surprised no one noticed that it wasn't your natural hair."

He'd managed to grow a short beard over the last two weeks, the nearly black hair so soft and lush compared to the dead feel of the wig.

He smirked. "I had them all under my thrall."

"I hope you're joking."

"Of course. I don't need to use compulsion to have an audience eat out of my hand."

He was such an arrogant peacock, but he wasn't wrong. He knew how to enchant a crowd with nothing more than the power of his personality and his innate charm.

And yet, he looked at her with an expression of a boy waiting for a girl's approval.

"Are you fishing for compliments?" she purred.

"Naturally."

"You were awesome." She whipped her blouse over her head, which was the best method to render Emmett speechless.

His dark eyes blazing, he palmed her breast through her bra, but as a muffled baby wail percolated through the walls, Emmett dropped his hand and glanced at the door. "It's weird having Kian and Syssi in the room across the hallway, and Peter's room is right next to ours. The soundproofing in here is not as good as it is in the village."

She folded a leg under her bottom and regarded him from under lowered lashes. "You haven't said more than two words to Peter since we got here. You should make an effort to befriend him."

"I don't want him here."

"I know." She sighed. "But when I leave for West Virginia, it's going to be just you and him. You need to get along."

"I don't want you to go." He put his hands on her waist and lifted her into his lap. "I need to find a way to convince Kian to let me come with you. I don't even care if he sends Peter with us. It's a price I'm willing to pay to be with you."

"What about Safe Haven? You just got back. You can't leave."

He shrugged. "I can do whatever I want. Riley did a good job running the place in my absence, and she can keep doing that for a couple more months. I can tell her that you and I are working on the new paranormal retreat plan, which is true."

"About that." She grimaced. "Now everyone knows that I'm your girlfriend."

"And that's a problem?"

"Of course it is. When I campaign for moving the paranormal program here, they might accuse me of nepotism. It will look as if I want to do that here to help my boyfriend make more money."

"First of all, you are not going to campaign, you are going to compel, so it doesn't matter what they think. They will approve the transfer. And as to the ones in charge of approving the budget, they will not come here to check out the place or investigate its background for such a small project. Besides, politicians do that all the time, with complete impunity, I might add, and in amounts that make the cost of your paranormal program seem utterly insignificant."

"Yeah, I know." She pouted. "I just like being cautious and not leaving any holes in my plan if I can help it."

She also didn't like the reminder that heading the paranormal division wasn't as big of a deal as she'd made it up to be in her mind. It was a small, insignificant program that would probably get canceled if she didn't save it by compelling the higher-ups to let her run it.

Emmett caressed her back, his hands warm on her chilled skin. "Do you want me to compel the community to forget about you being my girlfriend?"

She shook her head. "Kian told you not to use compulsion on them."

"Then you can compel them. He didn't forbid you to use your power."

Casting Emmett a mock glare, Eleanor straightened in his arms. "I don't want them to forget because I don't want Riley to put her greedy little hands on you. When I'm gone, I want her to know that you're taken."

"You're not going anywhere without me."

"And you're being greedy." She wrapped her arms around his neck. "You're getting everything you wished for and more, and you are still complaining."

He sighed. "I'm not as enthusiastic about being here as I thought I would be. If you are not with me, I'd rather wait for you in the village."

"Really? How come?"

"I don't need to pretend in the village. Everyone knows my story, the good and the bad, and people still accept me. Here, I have to keep up the show twenty-four-seven. The only reprieve I get is when I'm alone with you."

54

GERALDINE

*G*eraldine clicked the TV on and started flipping through channels. When that didn't yield anything interesting, she switched to Netflix.

Surely, she could find a nice movie or show to take her mind off Shai and how much she missed him.

Usually at this time, he would come through the door, take her into his arms, and kiss the living daylights out of her. Then they would have dinner together, tell each other about their day, they would read a little before bed, and finally they would make love, usually at least twice.

Would she be able to fall asleep without him in the bed with her?

Probably not.

She couldn't even concentrate on reading, the words swimming in front of her eyes, her mind wandering this way and that.

Ugh, why hadn't Orion shown up yet?

More than three weeks had passed since the Clan Mother had released her memories, and as more of them percolated through the barrier between her subconscious and conscious mind, the more of Orion she remembered.

Sometimes, many months would pass between his visits, and other times, he would come every month, but that had been a long time ago. In recent years, after Cassandra had gotten the promotion and their finances had improved, his visits had become much less frequent.

He also hadn't engaged with Cassandra for at least eighteen years. He'd always come when Cassy was at school or at work and leave before she came home.

Orion had explained that Cassandra didn't need him, only Geraldine.

Oddly, he'd never mentioned Cassy's potential to transition. It was as if he didn't know it existed. Perhaps he and his group were like the Kra-ell, and they didn't know that Dormants could be activated.

What if he was a Kra-ell?

Geraldine shivered.

From the little she'd heard about the Kra-ell females, they were vicious and cruel, and she didn't want any of that in her genetic makeup.

No. She and Cassy were descended from the gods, not from the Kra-ell.

Ugh, she needed Orion to show up and give her the answers she needed.

Who had induced her?

Had her inducer or her immortality had anything to do with her accident?

What if her becoming immortal had been a mistake, and her inducer had tried to kill her?

What if Orion was his people's Guardian and had come to punish her inducer and help her survive?

Why hadn't he been interested in her romantically?

In all the restored memories, their encounters had been purely platonic. He'd treated her like a sister or a cousin or a good friend. Their physical contact had been limited to a quick embrace and a kiss on the cheek.

Heck, what if Orion wasn't into females?

Onegus's roommate preferred the company of other males, so it wasn't as if immortals were all heterosexual.

It might be vain of her, but Geraldine was relieved to have stumbled upon a possible explanation of Orion's lack of romantic interest in her. She hadn't met a single man yet who'd been immune to her charms, not unless he was in love with someone else or not interested in women.

Geraldine had so many questions and so few answers, and in the meantime, she was putting her life on hold.

She needed Orion to come already so she could start living her life.

His last visit had been nearly six months ago, so it shouldn't be long before he showed up again. But what if something had happened to him?

"Stop it." Geraldine clicked the TV off and rose to her feet.

In the kitchen, she put the electric kettle on and leaned against the counter as she waited for the water to boil.

As her phone rang, the one that was clan issue, her heart skipped a beat and she rushed back to the living room to get it.

"Shai," she breathed into the receiver. "I've been waiting for you to call."

"I was waiting to call you too, love. Kian dragged us all around the Safe Haven compound, inspecting every corner and grumbling about how everything needed to be remodeled. Then after dinner, he commandeered one of the offices and we worked for a couple of hours going over Safe Haven's financials. When I got back to the room, I remembered that there was no reception in Emmett's bunker, so I went back outside. I'm freezing my butt off, sitting on a rock in his backyard."

"My poor baby. Does that mean no phone sex?"

He chuckled. "Not on my side, but I don't mind watching if you want to give me a show."

"I'll save it for when you come home. It's tomorrow, right? Because I don't think I can survive one more night without you. I've been a total wreck since you left."

"Same here," he admitted. "I feel like there is a vise clamped over my heart, with a coiled string attached to it that has you on the other side. The coil can stretch, but it pulls on the vise, tightening it."

Geraldine's eyes misted with tears. "I feel the same. Do all people in love experience so much pain when they are separated?"

"Not as much, no." He was silent for a brief moment. "Those who are bonded report that it's practically impossible to be apart. It gets easier after they've been together for a while."

It took her a moment to internalize what he'd said, then it hit her, and her hand flew to her chest. "What are you saying, Shai?"

"I think that we've bonded. It must have happened gradually, that was why we didn't feel it snap into place. I talked to Brundar, Anandur, and Kian, not together of course, and each one of them described it differently. Apparently, it's not the same for every couple."

Something eased inside of her, a level of worry and uncertainty that she hadn't been aware of carrying around with her. "I love you."

"Always and forever, my heart."

55

SHAI

Shai had done everything in his power to get things moving as fast as immortally possible, hoping Kian would wrap up their visit before lunch, but his boss wasn't cooperating.

"I know you're in a hurry." Kian clapped Shai's back as they walked out of the dining hall. "But before we leave, I need to have a meeting with Emmett and Riley to discuss the declining revenues."

Last night they'd gone over the books, and provided that the information hadn't been doctored, Safe Haven was self-sufficient in that it wasn't losing money, but it wasn't making much either. What's more, revenues had been steadily declining for a while now, even when Emmett had still been in charge of the place. The sharpest drop, though, was a month after he'd left.

Hopefully Emmett's return would stop the downward trend, but unless Safe Haven got a booster shot of new blood, meaning Uncle Sam paying handsomely for the housing of its paranormal program, it wasn't likely to return to its glory days. Not that they needed it to. The objective wasn't to make money, it was to provide a safe space for the paranormally talented. If they managed not to lose too much, that would be good enough.

Shai arched a brow. "What's there to discuss? You've seen the books. The big drop was after Emmett left. Without their star showman, they had no hook. Now that he's back, things should get better."

Kian cast him an indulgent smile. "It's a management issue, Shai. The advertising continued as usual, showcasing Emmett as the main attraction even though he wasn't there, so the guests didn't know that he would be a no-show. And yet, bookings for the retreats were almost a quarter less than before. That quarter is the cream. The remaining seventy-five percent only covers the expenses."

"So what was the problem? Emmett didn't deal with any of the mundane management issues anyway. It was all done by Riley and her team."

"Riley and the others did their best because Emmett demanded it from them, and

579

I. T. LUCAS

they wanted to please him. With him absent, the motivation to go the extra mile was gone. I need to talk to them about customer service and how they respond to inquiries, but I promise to make it short."

He shouldn't have promised what he couldn't deliver.

The meeting dragged on, with Riley coming up with excuses for the poor performance, Emmett suggesting new advertising campaigns, and Kian moderating the discussion while Eleanor was punching away on her phone's calculator and throwing numbers at them.

After an hour of that, Shai tuned them out, his mind going back to last night's conversation with Geraldine.

He felt like an ass. He shouldn't have told her over the phone about the pull of the bond he felt while away from her. He should have done it over a romantic dinner, or perhaps while she was taking a bubble bath, preferably with a bottle of champagne chilling in a bucket of ice on its lip.

Perhaps he could make it up to her?

He should stop somewhere on his way home and get her an outrageous present, like a four-carat engagement ring. What woman wouldn't love a marriage proposal with a fancy ring to sweeten the deal?

Was it crazy?

Maybe. But the idea of surprising Geraldine with a ring and a proposal filled him with excitement and happiness, so why not?

He was still figuring out the details when Kian wrapped up the meeting. They said goodbye to Eleanor, Emmett, and Peter, who were staying in Safe Haven, and headed to the private airport where Charlie was waiting for them with the jet.

"What's been bugging you, Shai?" Kian asked when they boarded the plane and took their seats. "You seem distracted."

Shai wasn't about to share his romantic musings with his boss. The guy could have guessed what was troubling him from the questions he'd asked him the day before about the bond, but apparently Kian still needed to work on his emotional intelligence.

Instead of lying, Shai chose a half truth. "Frankly, I don't like the place." He glanced at Syssi. "I know that you do, but it reminds me too much of Alcatraz."

Syssi gasped. "How can you say that?"

"Just think about it. It's completely isolated, overcast most of the year, and cold. All that's missing is it being on an island surrounded by shark-infested waters."

Kian didn't dispute his observation right off the bat. Instead, he turned to look at the brothers. "What do you think?"

Anandur shrugged. "I wouldn't want to live in Safe Haven all year long, but I wouldn't mind spending a couple of months there, preferably in the summer."

"What about you?" Kian asked Brundar.

"I like it."

Of course, he did.

The Guardian would have probably turned the place into a kink club, which was actually perfectly fitting. Everything that Shai didn't like about Safe Haven was the perfect backdrop to an adult playground for those with kinky tastes.

"What's so amusing?" Syssi asked him. "You're smirking like a Cheshire Cat."

Shai folded his arms over his chest and cast a sidelong glance at Kian. "If you really want to make money on the place, let Brundar manage it."

The Guardian arched a brow. "What do I know about managing a spiritual retreat?"

"That depends on what spiritual experience you're after. I bet some of your club members reach a spiritual level of revelations while engaging in certain activities."

Covering her mouth and blushing profusely, Syssi laughed. "You have a wild imagination, Shai. You should write stories."

"He was an English major," Anandur said. "Go for it, man. A secluded retreat for the sexually adventurous. It could become a bestseller." The Guardian winked. "I even have a name for it—Kinkyland."

Kian snorted. "Knowing Emmett, he would demand part of the royalties. After all, he was the one who came up with the original idea, creating a place for those seeking free love and sexual diversity. Kinkyland is just a variation on the theme."

Anandur grinned like a fiend. "I knew it would catch on. Tell me that I'm not a genius."

"You're not," Brundar grumbled under his breath. "You're a clown."

Anandur shrugged. "I'll take it."

56

GERALDINE

*S*hai was coming home soon.

Geraldine could feel him getting closer—the tether pulling on her heart slackening a little, allowing her to breathe.

Like so many things, it was probably all in her head. She wanted to feel the bond, so she was imagining that she did.

He'd called a couple of hours ago, telling her that the plane was about to land, and also that he needed to run a quick errand on the way home. It wasn't difficult to estimate that he should walk through the door any minute now.

Ever since their conversation last night, she'd been thrumming with excitement. They'd bonded.

It hadn't happened overnight like what Cassandra had described happened for her and Onegus, but rather gradually, sneaking up on them while they had been preoccupied worrying about other things.

Shai's trip to Safe Haven had made the power of the bond evident, with both of them suffering because of the separation.

Sleeping had been nearly impossible, in part because the bed was empty and Geraldine missed Shai so much that it hurt, and in part because she'd been thinking about the bond and what it meant for their relationship.

It meant forever, for real, and she thanked the Fates for their wisdom in arranging her and Shai's pairing. The only thing still casting a shadow on their happiness was Orion, but hopefully that too would be over soon.

In the kitchen, Geraldine checked on the prime rib roast. It had been cooking for nearly three hours, and it was about ready. The dish was a bit fancy for a weekday dinner, but she felt like celebrating. Hopefully, Shai would like the roasted Brussels sprouts and glazed carrots she'd made to complement the rib roast. They weren't everyone's favorite, but they were hers and Cassy's.

When the door opened, her heart skipped a beat, and then she was running, her short-heeled mules clicking on the tiled floor.

She flung herself into Shai's outstretched arms. "I missed you so much." She clung to him.

"I missed you too." His lips found hers in a ravenous kiss that lasted long minutes.

Out of breath, she finally pushed away from his chest. "Look at us. We're acting as if we haven't seen each other in months."

"It surely felt like that." Shai picked up the overnight bag he'd dropped on the floor to catch her and took her hand. "Let's go upstairs."

Evidently, he hadn't noticed the table that was set with a white tablecloth, the candles, the wine, the crystal goblets she only used for special occasions.

Still, it was tempting, oh so tempting. But her prime rib roast had to be served as soon as it was out of the oven. Geraldine had spent hours preparing the special meal, and Shai wasn't going anywhere, not if she could help it.

She tugged on his hand. "I made a special dinner for us. It would be a shame to let it cool down and then reheat it."

He finally turned to look at the dining table. "Oh, sweetheart. Is that all for me?"

"Who else?" She pulled him toward the chair. "If you'd come a little earlier, you would have had time to freshen up, but my prime rib roast is ready right about now."

"Then we shall dine, my love." He pulled out a chair for her. "Do you have a moment to share a glass of wine with me before you need to get that delicious-smelling roast out of the oven?"

"A moment." She sat down.

Shai uncorked the bottle and poured the red wine into the two glasses, handed her one, and lifted the other. "To the love of my life."

Tears stung the back of her eyes, but she kept them at bay and smiled. "To my perfect, fated mate."

After they'd clinked glasses and sipped on the wine, Shai took her hand and brought it to his lips for a kiss. "I picked up a little something for you on the way." His other hand went into his pocket.

"What did you get?"

Geraldine's excitement ratcheted up a notch. She loved presents. It didn't even matter what it was as long as Shai spent time choosing it for her.

She hadn't expected a small velvet box, though, a box that was just big enough for a ring or a pair of earrings.

When Shai dropped on one knee, she knew for sure that the box didn't contain earrings.

"Will you marry me, Geraldine?"

As happy tears slid down her cheeks, she cupped Shai's cheek. "We are already mated, but I would love to marry you in front of our family and friends."

A grin splitting his handsome face, he lifted the small box and opened it. "I think I was supposed to do this first and ask you to marry me second, but I'm glad I didn't have to bribe you to say yes."

Geraldine gaped at the enormous solitaire diamond. "I don't know what to say."

He took the ring out of the box. "You already said yes." He slid it over her finger. "Now it's final and you can't take it back."

She wanted to tell him that he was insane, that he shouldn't have emptied his bank account to buy her this outrageous ring, but how could she?

He looked so happy, so proud to be able to give her this unbelievable engagement ring, that all she could say was thank you.

"It's beautiful, Shai. I will cherish it forever."

5 7

KIAN

*I*t was ten o'clock Thursday morning when Onegus walked into Kian's office and pulled out a chair. "Roberts died last night. Two doctors certified that he was brain-dead, and he was disconnected from life support this morning."

"When is the funeral?" Shai asked.

"Next Tuesday." Onegus pulled out his phone. "I'll text you the details. We need to get Eleanor to West Virginia."

Shai turned to Kian. "Did you decide who you want her to take to the funeral? I need to know who to order the tickets for."

"Peter is the best choice." Kian crossed his arms over his chest. "I spoke with Leon. He and Anastasia are willing to take Peter's place in Safe Haven until he and Eleanor return."

Onegus arched a brow. "Does she need Peter for anything other than accompanying her to the funeral?"

Kian shrugged. "You are the one who always insists on sending Guardians in teams. It's better that she has someone with her to watch her back."

"Eleanor is not a Guardian, and this is not a regular mission. She's a solo operator on this. If she needs Peter at all, it's for moral support."

"I want someone to keep an eye on her," Kian finally admitted. "I know that she's proven herself time and again as reliable, but having access to so much information might go to her head. Besides, she might need Peter for her other mission, which is finding people who work in the Echelon system and compelling them to give us information."

Onegus's lips twisted in a grimace. "I always feel like I don't have enough Guardians, especially now that we might be close to capturing Orion and discovering a new group of immortals." He leaned back in his chair. "Two Guardians are wasting their time babysitting Vrog, and I have people watching the surveillance feed from Geraldine's house twenty-four-seven. By now, they know all her neighbors, the license plates of their cars, where their kids go to school, and who are their gardeners and housekeepers. The problem is the damn deliveries. So many are done by Uber drivers, and if Orion is smart, he would pose as one."

"Why would he do that?" Shai asked. "He doesn't know that we are waiting for him."

"Right." Onegus cast him a smile. "But if he's old and experienced, which I suspect he is, given his powers, he's most likely very cautious."

Shai waved a dismissive hand. "He wasn't careful thirty-some years ago when he showed up with a fancy car to his weekly meetings with Geraldine." He shook his head. "I'd rather think of it as him meeting Sabina, not Geraldine. But I digress. Even I would have known not to call too much attention to myself with a flashy car, and I'm neither old nor experienced."

"But you're smart," Kian said. "Perhaps Orion is not the sharpest tool in the shed. Being a powerful immortal doesn't mean that he's also intelligent."

Shai let out a breath. "I just hope that he shows up soon, so Geraldine and I can finally move in together and have a life."

Onegus chuckled. "You're practically living together already, so I don't know what's the big deal. Is it so difficult for you to drive to and from work every day?"

Shai glared at the chief in a way none of the Guardians would have dared. "I want her in the village where I know she's safe. I'm sure you can understand that."

Theoretically, Shai was soon to become Onegus's father-in-law, so he was allowed some leeway, but he shouldn't push it. Onegus only seemed mellow and accommodating, but he was the chief for a reason.

"Is Geraldine ready to leave her house?" Kian asked. "I thought she was quite attached to it and to her human friends."

"She is." Shai walked toward the door. "Is it final about Peter joining Eleanor? I need to make the travel arrangements."

Shai seemed on edge, and Kian wondered if it was only because of the uncertainty regarding Orion, or if there was trouble in paradise.

"Unless she wants someone else, it is Peter," Kian said. "I'll call her and let you know in a few minutes." He pulled out his phone and scrolled for Eleanor's number.

"What do you want to do with Vrog?" Onegus asked as the door closed behind Shai.

"I want to send him back to China with Mey and Yamanu and perhaps one additional Guardian. I want to take a look at those files Vrog found at the site. Also, now that Mey can have free access to the entire facility, she might learn something more useful from the echoes." He checked the time on his phone. "Stella asked to speak with me about Vrog. I told her to come at nine, which is twenty minutes from now. You're welcome to stay and join our discussion."

Onegus didn't look happy. "When do you want to send them back to China?"

"That's what I'm going to discuss with Stella and later today with Vrog. He might want to stay a little longer to spend more time with Vlad."

"I hope Orion will show up before that, so my Guardians are not spread so thin. Although that might open a whole new can of worms that I'm not looking forward to catching."

58

ELEANOR

"Kian called." Eleanor entered Emmett's office and sat down on his brown, worn out couch. "Roberts died last night, and the funeral is next Tuesday."

Emmett tensed. "I suppose that you're going."

She nodded. "That was the plan all along." Except for the part that Emmett was not going to like, and there was no way she could sugarcoat it so it would become more palatable for him. "He's sending Leon and Anastasia to take over for Peter."

Emmett narrowed his eyes at her. "Why?"

"He wants Peter to accompany me to West Virginia to attend the funeral as my pretend boyfriend, and stay around to watch my back."

Emmett's eyes blazed red, making him look more demonic than ever. "I don't want you going alone with him." He pushed out of his chair and strode toward her. "Convince Kian that I have to come with you. Tell him that you're not going without me."

"He's not going to agree."

"Try." Emmett sat next to her. "I can stay in the hotel during the funeral, but we will spend the night together. He has Guardians over there, right?"

She nodded.

"If he's concerned about me running off, he can have them watch me."

She shook her head. "Perhaps you should talk to him. He might be more sympathetic toward your macho male possessiveness."

Emmett arched a brow. "You want to talk about possessiveness? It wasn't me who came up with the idea for Safe Haven. You didn't want to leave me alone in the village with all those immortal females hanging on every word I say, so you convinced Kian that Safe Haven was the perfect place for the paranormal program."

So he'd figured it out. She'd thought she'd been so clever, masking her intentions with all those excellent reasons for going to Safe Haven. But whatever, Eleanor had no problem fessing up to it. Rising to her feet, she put her hands on her hips and glared down at him. "I did that because I wanted to be with you, and I knew that Kian wouldn't let you move in with me into the government facility. And even if he did, you would have been miserable living in the underground city."

Letting out a breath, Emmett took her hand and tugged her onto his lap. "Why are we fighting when we both want the same thing?"

Her anger dissipating, Eleanor pouted. "Because from a free-love guru, you turned into a jealous alpha-hole."

"You're not any better, love." He kissed her on the lips. "Call Kian and we will speak to him together." He smiled. "I'll put on the charm."

Her suggestion that he call Kian had been sarcastic, but maybe it was actually not a bad idea. Unlike her, Emmett was a diplomat, who had a great way with people. Maybe he would be able to charm Kian into letting him accompany her.

"I'll text him." She pulled out her phone and typed up a short message. "That's less unnerving than hearing him bark at me."

A few minutes later, her phone rang.

"What's up, Eleanor? Do you have a problem with what we discussed?"

Damn, the man was intimidating, but she knew that underneath that rough exterior he had a soft heart. "Thanks for calling back, Kian. I have Emmett here with me, and he would like to talk to you. I'm putting you on speakerphone."

"What is it about? I have a meeting in a few minutes."

"Hello, Kian," Emmett said. "I'll make it short. As one mated male to another, I ask that you permit me to accompany Eleanor to West Virginia. I can't stand the thought of being away from her, and even more so, I can't tolerate the thought of her being alone with Peter. I know that you have Guardians stationed there, so you can have them keep an eye on me while Eleanor and Peter are in the field."

"The two guys stationed there are not my Guardians. They are Kalugal's men, and they have better things to do than babysit you."

"Then send one more Guardian with us."

"The Guardians also have better things to do."

Emmett closed his eyes and sighed. "I'll make it worthwhile for you."

"What are you suggesting?"

"I won't charge you anything for using half of Safe Haven to build your section of it. I'll lease it to the clan for one dollar a year for the next one hundred years, with an option to renew for another century."

Eleanor gaped at him. "You can't be serious. I will be gone two months at the most, and I will come to visit you on the weekends. You are giving up millions for nothing."

"Not millions," Kian said. "But it is a significant amount of money. I'm surprised that you didn't begin with a lesser offer to give yourself room to negotiate."

Emmett smiled. "Anything less than that would not have impressed you, and I needed to make it clear how strongly I feel about being separated from Eleanor. It's unbearable to me."

If Eleanor hadn't consciously forced her jaw to close, it would have still been hanging.

Emmett couldn't be serious. What kind of game was he playing? Why was it so important to him to come with her to West Virginia? The short separation couldn't be that insufferable because they were not bonded.

But maybe they were?

She hadn't felt any snapping into place, and although she didn't like the thought of leaving Emmett behind in Safe Haven, she didn't find it as intolerable as he did. She could survive five days without seeing him.

Could she, though?

"Fine, you can go." Kian's answer made her knees buckle. "I'll speak with Kalugal about his men watching you."

"Thank you." Emmett dipped his head even though they weren't on video call.

"And since I'm a fair man, I'm not going to take advantage of your mated bond. Our original deal stands."

If Eleanor's knees had gone soft before, now they turned into a pair of useless noodles.

Kian had said it so casually, as if it was obvious that they were mated.

Emmett smiled. "You are very gracious. Thank you."

When the call ended, she narrowed her eyes at him, "You played Kian."

"Naturally." The smile turned into a satisfied grin. "I needed to make him realize how important being with you was to me, but I knew that he was too honorable to take my offer."

On the one hand, she was disappointed that Emmett hadn't been really willing to part with a huge chunk of money just to be with her. But on the other hand, she was proud of him for being so clever and manipulative.

"What would you have done if Kian had taken the offer?"

He shrugged. "It would have still been worth it."

She slapped his arm. "You're such a liar."

"I'm not. I'm a gambler. And as the saying goes, never gamble what you are not comfortable losing. I could afford to lose the money, but I can't afford to lose you."

"You had nothing to worry about. Despite what you think of Peter, he's not interested in me, and I'm not interested in him." She cupped his bearded cheek. "Frankly, I'm starting to think that we are bonded. It didn't happen overnight like it did for some of the other couples. Instead, it grew slowly. That's why we didn't realize it was there."

"I agree." He closed the distance between their mouths and took her lips. "You are mine, Eleanor Takala."

"And you are mine, Emmett Haderech." She put her finger on his lips. "Are you ever going to tell me your Kra-ell name?"

He grimaced. "No. My father gave me that name, and it wasn't a good one. It was an insult. I created Emmett Haderech, and I like the male he became."

She hadn't known that—hadn't suspected that the proud male before her had grown up ashamed of his own name. No wonder that he'd escaped the first opportunity he got.

It also explained why they fit together so well.

Eleanor had been ashamed too—still was. She'd loved a man who hadn't loved her back and had used compulsion to keep him from leaving her. She cringed whenever she thought about that time in her life.

Except, her shame was her own doing, while Emmett had done nothing to deserve it other than being born to a human mother.

"I need to ask you something." She took his hand in hers. "If your people treated you so badly, why did you want to go back and bring Peter to them?"

He sighed. "Because if Peter could have activated their Dormants, I would have been a hero, I could have proven that I was worthy, and that my asshole of a father was wrong about me."

59

KIAN

*S*tella pulled out one of the two chairs facing Kian's desk. "I wanted to talk to you about Vrog." She hung her satchel over the back of it and sat down. "Is he a prisoner?"

"No."

"Then there is no reason to hold him locked up in a cell."

"What do you want me to do with him?"

She looked him straight in the eyes. "Let him come live in the village."

"Does he want to?"

She hesitated for a moment. "He doesn't know it's on the table. Vrog is smart enough to realize that an invitation from Emmett doesn't count because he has no authority to issue it."

Kian arched a brow. "Emmett invited him to live in the village?"

"In so many words."

"Then Emmett must not view Vrog as a threat. That's good to know." Kian leaned forward. "How is Vrog getting along with Vlad?"

Stella sighed. "They've met only twice so far. Between Vlad's part-time job in the bakery and the final project he's working on for school, he has a busy schedule."

It sounded to Kian like Vlad wasn't too eager to spend time with his biological father. He wondered if things were different for Stella.

"What about you? Have you visited him more often?"

"I was there yesterday. Vrog is lonely and worried. Despite your assurances that we are not going to keep him here for long, he wonders what your real plans are for him." She pushed a strand of hair behind her ear. "Richard threw a jealous tantrum when I went to see Vrog without Vlad. I don't want to fight with him over this, but I also can't leave Vrog all alone in that cell with no visitors and no one to talk to other than Alec and Vernon."

"I thought the three of them were getting along just fine. Alfie and Jay were supposed to take over from Alec and Vernon, but Vrog asked them to stay, and they agreed."

She rolled her eyes at him. "Of course, he asked them to stay. They are the only two immortals he's gotten to know and who treat him well. I wouldn't be surprised if he has a mild case of Stockholm syndrome, becoming dependent on the two people who are taking care of him. You need to either let him go back to his school or invite him to join the village."

Kian's temper flared at her issuing orders instead of making requests, but Stella looked upset, and he decided to let it go.

"Did you ask Vrog what he would prefer?"

Stella shook her head. "I wanted to talk to you first, so I would know whether the village was an option."

Leaning back in his chair, Kian crossed his legs. "If Vlad asks me to invite his father to live in the village, I will grant his request. But I can't allow Vrog to roam free. I don't think that he will betray us to humans, but he seemed bound by vows of loyalty to his former leader. If she somehow makes an appearance, I have a feeling he will do anything she asks of him, including betraying his own son."

Stella winced. "What if he bonds with a clan female?"

"I don't think a Kra-ell immortal couple can bond. Emmett and Eleanor seem perfectly suited for each other, but they haven't bonded yet, and they've been together long enough for that to happen."

In truth, Kian was no longer sure of that after the phone conversation with Emmett, but he suspected that the guy had put on a performance, knowing that Kian would refuse to take advantage of his desperate need to be with his mate. Emmett could have lost that bet, though, and if he was willing to put his most precious asset on the line, then perhaps he was really in love with Eleanor. Love could exist and be a powerful motivator even without the bond.

Stella pursed her lips. "You can't generalize based on one couple. It might be that they are not each other's fated mates."

"True. If Vrog decides to join the clan, we can wait and see what happens, but in the meantime, I need to exercise caution. That being said, even if he wants to join and I agree, I still need him to return to China with Mey and Yamanu first."

"And after that?"

"It depends on what I find out in those files he talked about, and what Mey hears from the echoes. If it's a dead end, I will give Vrog the option to join the clan provided that Vlad wants that. If it's not a dead end, I might need Vrog to assist in the investigation."

Kian hoped that he wasn't making a mistake. Compared to Emmett, Vrog seemed harmless, but what if it was just a very convincing act?

"Who are you sending in addition to Mey and Yamanu?"

"I don't need Jin to go, but I want them to have Guardian backup. If Alfie and Jay are not up for another trip, I'll assign two other Guardians."

"What about me? Do I get to go?"

"Do you want to?"

She grimaced. "I want to be part of this investigation, but Richard can't stand Vrog, and I'm not going without him. But if you need me to go, I will, and I'll deal with Richard's attitude."

Kian hadn't planned on sending Stella with the team, but having Richard there was not a bad idea. The guy didn't trust Vrog, which meant that he would watch him carefully and notice any signs of subterfuge no matter how insignificant.

"Your fluency in the language would be helpful to the team, but you need to talk it over with Richard. "

"I will. But you can count me in. Richard might grumble, but there isn't much he can do." Shifting on the chair, Stella adjusted her skirt. "Are you going to remove the cuffs before sending Vrog home?"

"I have no right to keep them on him when he's out of my jurisdiction and also helping us."

"But you still don't trust him."

"Obviously," Kian confirmed.

"So maybe it would be a good idea for Jin to tether him. If Vrog has been lying to us all along, he will try to contact his people as soon as he's set free."

"Do you suspect him?"

Stella sighed. "Not really, but I don't know him well enough to be sure. He might be putting on a great act."

"The same has occurred to me. I'll speak to Jin."

"What do you want me to tell Vrog?"

"Nothing." Kian straightened in his chair and pulled it up closer to the desk. "I'm seeing Vrog later this afternoon, and I can discuss the options with him." He gave Stella a slight smile. "Andrew is accompanying me. I just hope that his lie detecting abilities work on a hybrid Kra-ell as well as they work on humans."

60

VROG

*A*s Stella's clan leader explained his proposal, Vrog listened without interrupting, not out of respect and not because he didn't have questions, but because he needed time to think.

He'd spent two weeks locked up in the cell, and during that time, Vlad had visited him only twice, both times with his lovely fiancée who had done most of the talking.

Vrog had a feeling that Vlad resented him, and that he wasn't interested in getting to know him better. Not that he could blame him.

His son had probably heard from his mother about Vrog's request to abort him. If not for Stella's courage and resilience, Vlad wouldn't have been born.

"Do you have any questions for me?" Kian asked.

"How soon do you want me to go back to China?"

"Whenever you are ready."

That wasn't the answer Vrog had hoped for. "Does it have to happen soon?"

Kian let out an exasperated breath. "What are you really trying to ask me?"

The guy seemed like a straight shooter who wasn't much of a diplomat. Perhaps it was in Vrog's best interest to just say what was on his mind. "I want to get closer to my son, but he doesn't seem interested. Down here, there isn't much I can do about it, but if I stay in your village, I might be able to see more of Vlad and get to know him better."

"So you don't want to go back home?"

"I do, just not right away if it's possible." Looking at the cuffs, Vrog rotated his wrists. "Are these really necessary? I have no ax to grind with your clan. I thought I had, but I know now that I was wrong. Where would I run? And why would I?"

Kian cast a quick sidelong glance at the guy who'd accompanied him to the meeting instead of the two bodyguards he'd had with him before. Unlike the other two, though, this one wore a suit and tie and looked like he was someone important.

Kian had introduced him, but Vrog had been too anxious for the name to register. Was it Andy? Edward?

When the guy nodded, Kian crossed his arms over his chest. "You tell me."

The name suddenly popped into his head. It was Andrew.

"I have a son who is part of your clan, and who is the only long-lived offspring I will ever have. I would never endanger him."

Andrew nodded again.

What was the deal with that?

"If I let you into the village, the cuffs stay on, and you can't leave, not even to go out to dinner with Vlad. If you choose to go home, I'll have the cuffs removed when you land in Beijing."

Vrog nodded. "So that's the price of staying in your village?"

"There are other complications. We don't have guest rooms, so either Vlad or Stella would have to host you in their homes."

"Richard will never allow me in his house."

Kian didn't look surprised. "That leaves Vlad. He'll have to invite you."

Vrog groaned. "Perhaps I should just stay down here."

"That's no longer an option either. I have better use for these two Guardians than babysitting you."

Vrog felt as if the walls were closing in on him. "So my options are an invitation from Vlad to stay with him and Wendy or going home?"

"Correct."

"Can I call him?"

"Sure." Kian pulled out his phone. "I can dial his number for you."

Vrog swallowed. "I'm not ready to do this now. I don't know what to say."

"Would you prefer to ask Stella?" Andrew asked. "She could talk to Vlad for you."

Vrog shook his head. "That would be a cowardly thing to do. I'll call him a little later." He looked at the two Guardians sitting at the dining table. "Can either one of them let me use their phone?"

"Yes." Kian rose to his feet. "You have until tomorrow morning. If you don't get an invite from Vlad, I'll start organizing the team going with you to China."

That was good enough. Vrog just didn't want to have that talk with his son while Kian listened in. Getting a no, which was probably the answer Vlad would give him, would be humiliating enough without Kian witnessing it.

"Thank you. I'll call him later this evening."

"Very well." The clan's leader motioned to Alec to open the door.

Once it closed behind Kian and Andrew, Vernon got up and walked over to the bar. "Care for some whiskey?"

"I would love some, thank you."

The Guardian poured him a tall glass. "Vlad is a good kid. He will not say no."

"I don't know about that." Vrog emptied half the glass down his throat. "I have no doubt that he's a great person, but he just doesn't like me well enough to invite me to stay with him and his fiancée."

Vernon pulled out his phone. "Should I place the call for you?"

Apparently, the Guardian had figured out why Vrog hadn't wanted to call Vlad while Kian listened in.

"Give me a moment to gather my thoughts."

Vernon put the phone on the table. "Let me know when you're ready."

How was he going to phrase it? Perhaps he should just repeat what Kian had said, so Vlad would know that it hadn't been his idea? Or maybe the opposite was true, and he should claim that he wanted to stay with his son and his fiancée so he could get a taste of what having a family felt like?

Usually, Vrog was an eloquent guy, or rather James Wu was. As the head of the school, he had to be. But now he found himself lost for words.

Pacing around the small room, he rehearsed what he was going to say to his son, changing a word here, a word there, then discarding the entire thing and starting from scratch.

"You're overthinking it," Vernon said. "Just call him." The Guardian placed the call without waiting for Vrog's answer.

"Hello?" Vlad answered.

Vernon thrust the phone into Vrog's hand.

"Hi, it's Vrog."

"They gave you a phone?"

"The phone belongs to one of the Guardians. He placed the call for me. I need your advice."

"Sure." Vlad sounded surprised.

"Kian came to visit me earlier, and he gave me two options. One was to go back to China with the investigative team and help them search for more clues about my people, and the other one was to come to your village and stay for a little bit, spend some time with you and Wendy, and then go to China."

"What do you want to do?" Vlad asked.

"I would like to stay for a couple of weeks, but the problem is that the village doesn't have guest accommodations. My only options would be to stay either with you and Wendy or Stella and Richard." Vrog held his breath as he waited for Vlad's answer.

"Can't you stay with the Guardians? I'm sure some of them have a spare room in their house."

Vrog's heart sank. "Kian didn't offer me that option, so I guess it's not on the table."

Vlad sighed. "You can come stay with Wendy and me."

Vrog's relief made him lightheaded. "Are you sure? I'm a very easy guest, but you and Wendy are a new couple. I wouldn't want to intrude on your privacy."

"That's okay. Wendy says that she would love to host you."

So it was the girl's doing. He'd take it. "Tell Wendy that I'm grateful. I'll do everything I can to repay the kindness."

"Wendy says that inviting us to China and giving us a tour would be an acceptable repayment."

Vrog smiled. "Any time. I would be overjoyed to be your tour guide."

"When are you coming?"

"I suppose sometime tomorrow. Kian doesn't want to waste Guardian time on me."

Vlad chuckled. "That sounds like Kian. Wendy says that she'll have the room ready for you."

"Thank you. I really appreciate it."

"No problem. Have a good night, Vrog."

As Vlad ended the call, Vrog slumped on the couch, the phone still clutched in his hand.

"Told you that the kid was a sweetheart." Vernon took the device from him.

"Wendy is too. I don't think he would have invited me if she wasn't there to pressure him into it."

"Whatever works, man." Vernon walked over to the bar. "The important thing is that you'll get to spend time with your son."

"Yes. It is, and I plan to make the most of it."

ORION

Orion stopped at the gate into Geraldine's neighborhood, opened the window of the nondescript Honda Civic, and smiled at the guard. "Delivery for the Beaumonts. They called ahead to let me in."

Just a little pulse of compulsion was enough. The guy nodded, and a moment later the gate opened.

Nowadays there were cameras everywhere, which was why his long hair was gathered under a baseball cap, and his eyes were shielded by speciality eyeglasses that didn't correct vision but prevented facial recognition.

Orion missed the days when he could have roamed free with no disguise needed, when he could drive fancy cars and pay cash and not worry about being found out. Life was becoming more and more difficult for an immortal who needed to hide who he was and frequently change identities.

There was a car parked in Geraldine's driveway, but he knew that it didn't belong to her or to Cassandra. Geraldine didn't own one, and Cassandra always parked hers inside the garage.

Perhaps it was a new boyfriend?

Not Geraldine's, because she never brought them home, but maybe Cassandra's. It was about time that she found someone. The girl was thirty-four years old, gorgeous, successful, and nearly six feet tall, which apparently human males found intimidating. That made finding a worthy partner challenging even though she had none of her mother's limitations. Being human made things much less complicated.

Perhaps he should come later when the guy was gone. If Cassandra was dating someone seriously, Orion didn't want to interrupt their romantic interlude.

But what if the guy had moved in? What if he wasn't worthy of Cassandra?

He needed to find out who the boyfriend was, what he did for a living, and what his intentions were for Geraldine's daughter.

Parking on the other side of the street, Orion pulled a paper bag from the back seat, stepped out of the car, walked up to the front door, and rang the bell.

He knew the elderly woman who opened the door—he'd used her for the same purpose before. "Hello, Mrs. Gilbert. I have a delivery for you." A very light compulsion usually did the trick.

"Come in." Smiling, she smoothed her hand over her house dress and stepped aside.

Sometimes he wondered whether she let him in because he compelled her or because she fancied him.

He could peer into her mind, but his curiosity didn't justify the intrusion. It was enough that he was using her house to spy on her neighbors across the street.

Since neither Geraldine nor Cassandra ever bothered closing the curtains in the living room, he could see clearly nearly the entire interior of their ground floor from Mrs. Gilbert's front room window.

After instructing the woman to go back to her television show, Orion walked over to the window and looked at the house across the street from behind the sheer curtains.

Surprisingly, it wasn't Cassandra who was cuddling on the couch with a young man, but Geraldine, and the two seemed on very friendly terms.

Orion groaned. One more boyfriend that he would have to make her forget, and since she'd brought this one into her home, he would have to make him forget her as well.

Immortals could not afford to mix with humans, but Geraldine didn't know why she wasn't aging, not since she'd lost every scrap of memory in her near-fatal accident. Regrettably, he couldn't tell her again because her mind no longer worked as well as it should, and she might forget that she needed to keep it a secret.

Orion's gut churned with guilt as he watched her smiling at the young man. Even from across the street, he could see the love in her eyes. The only mercy he could afford her was to make her forget that she'd ever been in love with the man.

Cassandra must have moved out because Geraldine wouldn't have brought a man to her house while her daughter was still living with her. Except, up until his last visit, it hadn't been in the cards. Cassandra wouldn't allow herself to have a life until her mother found someone else to take care of her.

It had been a catch-22 that he was glad Cassandra had finally gotten free from, but regrettably, Geraldine's guy couldn't be allowed to stay.

6 2

GERALDINE

*G*eraldine looked herself over in the mirror and smiled. Shai was taking her out on a real date tonight, just the two of them, in that fancy-schmancy restaurant owned by one of Shai's many cousins.

Or was it an uncle?

The clan made things simple. Unless a person was their mother's sibling, which made them an aunt or an uncle, everyone else was a cousin even if they were ancient.

Normally Geraldine didn't like wearing black, but it was the best color to serve as a backdrop for the gorgeous engagement ring sparkling on her finger. The dress was curve-hugging, reached a little below her knees, and had a plunging back.

Sexy as hell was what Shai would probably call it.

With a pair of four-inch black pumps on her feet, she looked slender and tall and beautiful. The rest of her jewelry was fake diamonds, but Geraldine felt like a million bucks nonetheless.

Giving her hair one last fluff, she tucked her small evening purse under her arm and headed downstairs.

Shai rose to his feet and whistled. "I'm glad it's so dark in By Invitation Only. Otherwise, every male in the place will be drooling over you and I'll have to deal with them."

Smiling, she gave him a small peck on the cheek. "I expect you to dance with me, and do your best not to growl at anyone. I won't be the only pretty lady on the dance floor, you know."

"But you'll be the prettiest." He glanced at his watch. "Our reservations are for nine, if we leave now, we will get there too early."

"I know." She took his hand and led him to the couch. "Instead, you can tell me about the story you started writing."

He eyed her from under lowered blond lashes. "How do you know that I did?"

"I heard you clicking away on the keyboard last night, but as soon as I entered the bedroom, you closed your laptop. I know that you don't have any secrets from me, so

I figured that you started writing a new script but were embarrassed to show me your work in progress."

"You know me so well that it's scary." He wrapped his arm around her shoulders.

"Why is it scary?"

"Because it means that I'm transparent, and I can't afford to be."

She knew what he meant. "I don't think anyone other than me would have figured that out. Besides, you've been successfully hiding your relationship with Rhett for nineteen years. I don't think you have anything to worry about." She patted his knee. "Now tell me your story."

He chuckled nervously. "It's not a script this time. I'm actually writing a horror story."

She winced. "Ugh, why horror? I want to read it, and I can't stomach horror. Can you turn it into a romance?"

"It has some romance in it, or rather sex. I got the idea on the way back from Safe Haven. Kian asked me why I was brooding, and I didn't want to admit that I had a hard time being away from you, so I told him that Safe Haven reminded me of Alcatraz."

She arched a brow. "You said that it's isolated, overcast, and cold, but you didn't tell me that it reminded you of a prison."

"It was a slight exaggeration. When Brundar said that he liked it, I thought that it suited his tastes. He's part owner in a club that caters to people who are into the spicier side of sex. Then I said that Safe Haven would be the perfect location for a kink club, which got everyone talking and joking about it, and Anandur said that I should write a story about it. That's how the idea was born."

"I think it can be very interesting. But it sounds sexy rather than scary."

"Ah." He lifted a finger. "There are also unexplained murders, dark shadows slithering through the dungeons, and lots of kinky sex." Shai eyed her with a wary expression on his handsome face. "That's why I didn't tell you about it. I was afraid that you'd find it too racy."

Geraldine laughed. "If you expect me to feel scandalized by a kinky story, you don't know me as well as you think you do. I'm a lady, so you'll never hear me talk about those darker kinds of pleasures, but that doesn't mean that I'm not aware they exist. After all, my favorite genre to read is romance, and some of those books are quite spicy." She lifted her head and nuzzled his neck. "Some are about vampires who enjoy those sorts of sex games, which make them doubly spicy."

Shai glanced at the light fixture, the one that had been outfitted with a surveillance camera. "If we weren't being watched," he whispered into her ear. "I would pull this sexy dress up your thighs and have my wicked way with you."

"Oh, dear." She pretended to be shocked, covering her mouth with her hand and whispering, "Do we have time to go upstairs?"

He lifted his hand to check the time. "Regrettably, we will have to save that thought for later. We need to go."

63

ORION

$\mathcal{W}$hen Geraldine and her guy rose to their feet and headed for the door, Orion stepped away from the window.

"Goodnight, Mrs. Gilbert." He smiled at the neighbor whose house he'd used as his spying post. "I've never been here, and you've never seen me before in your life." He opened the front door and got into his borrowed Honda.

The owner of the car, an Uber delivery driver, was sitting on the couch in Orion's Airbnb, eating the Chinese delivery Orion had ordered, and watching sitcoms on the television. The guy wouldn't move from that couch until he returned and released him from the compulsion.

Driving out, Orion caught up to Geraldine's boyfriend's car and followed them until they stopped at a valet station of a restaurant that he'd heard about but had never visited.

The guy must be loaded to afford a place like that.

In days past, Orion would have thought that the young man came from a rich family, but nowadays, people in their early twenties were making millions as software developers or as influencers.

Only a decade ago, no one could have imagined that people could make a fortune from posting silly amateur videos on social media. The world was changing, shrinking, and as usual, Orion was adapting, but it seemed like he was always a couple of steps behind the technology, the politics, and the attitudes.

As an antique dealer, he had no need to explore the latest technological innovations, as a drifter with no attachment to any particular country, politics had never interested him, and as a loner, societal changes interested him only as far as they pertained to him.

Lately, though, Orion had been forced to pay more attention to what was going on in the world around him because his very survival and that of a handful of people he cared about depended on it.

He had to be much more careful.

Following Geraldine and her guy into the restaurant was too risky, and other than to satisfy his curiosity, it would serve no purpose. Instead, he snapped a photo of the license plate of the boyfriend's car and kept on driving.

He would return to Geraldine's house early in the morning to check whether the man had spent the night. If they had been living together for a while, it would be much harder to make them forget each other. They would sense the loss even if they couldn't remember what they were missing.

Orion's gut twisted with guilt.

Geraldine deserved so much better from life.

Perhaps he could allow her to enjoy her latest lover for a little longer, provided that the guy was worthy of her love.

Some of the men she'd dated in the past had definitely been unworthy, and that included Cassandra's father. The guy was a liar, a philanderer. When Emanuel had befriended Geraldine, he hadn't told her that he had a family in Ethiopia, a wife and five children. He'd lied to her, claiming that he was single, and seduced her. But it hadn't been a one-night stand like most of her encounters. Emanuel had spent the entire summer with her, and regrettably, Orion had been away the entire time. When he'd visited her again, she was pregnant, and her store of memories of the guy had been difficult to erase.

Nevertheless, it had to be done.

By erasing the bulk of her memories of Emanuel, Orion had done her a favor, saving her a lot of heartache down the line, but it was a shame that she'd liked the cheating bastard so much.

Out of all the lovers Orion had muddled and suppressed her memories of, Emanuel still remained the one she remembered best, and after several attempts, Orion had given up on trying to get rid of the remnants of memories she clung to.

The guy had been gone for years, back to Ethiopia to his wife and children. Orion hadn't bothered checking up on him, but if he was alive, Emanuel was probably still philandering despite being in his late sixties.

In his experience, humans seldom changed.

Parking a block away from the valet station, Orion considered his options. He could wait until Geraldine and her new guy finished dinner and follow them, or he could return early in the morning to Geraldine's house to check whether the guy had stayed the night.

In the end, what tipped the scales toward leaving now was the Uber driver he'd left in his Airbnb rental.

Before compelling the guy not to move away from the couch, Orion had checked that he lived alone. He also instructed him to clock out from the Uber application so no one would miss him. But if he didn't release the driver from the compulsion soon, he might have to deal with nasty cleanup.

After eating all that Chinese food and sipping on all that beer, the guy would need to answer nature's call, but because of the compulsion not to move from the couch, he wouldn't be able to get up and use the bathroom.

6 4

ORION

*S*ix o'clock in the morning was too early for food delivery. Orion had to come up with another service that would not raise the guard's suspicion.

Then again, as long as he had his special glasses and baseball hat on, he didn't need to worry about the surveillance cameras that would record his presence. Besides, there was no real reason for him to be so clandestine. Perhaps he was taking all this new technology too seriously.

After all, someone needed a reason to look at that surveillance feed, and since he wasn't planning on robbing anyone, his only concern should be the guard in the gate recognizing him from the day before, and even that could be handled with a little thrall or compulsion.

Nevertheless, he should try to look at least a little different. Another pair of glasses, a new hat, and his own rental car should suffice. The vehicle wasn't anything fancy, just a simple Chevy Malibu.

And as for the story why he was there? He could say that he was Mrs. Gilbert's nephew, delivering a prescription medicine he'd picked up for her from the pharmacy.

Satisfied with his plan, Orion donned his specialty glasses and a white baseball hat and headed out.

When he arrived at the gate, a different guard greeted him, and just like the day before, he opened the gate for Orion with the help of a little thrall.

The boyfriend's car was still parked in the driveway, confirming his suspicion that he'd moved in with Geraldine.

Like the day before, Orion parked in front of the neighbors' house, but this time he wasn't going to knock on the door.

Mrs. Gilbert was no doubt still sleeping, but he had a key. After the first time he'd used her house to observe what was going on in Geraldine's, he'd asked her for the code to the alarm and for a spare key.

Mostly, he had done so to make sure that Cassandra wasn't in the house when he visited Geraldine. She had a strong personality and a suspicious mind, and as she grew older, she'd become more and more difficult to thrall.

Besides, he wasn't worried about her.

She was a human with nothing to hide, and she didn't need his assistance. All it had taken to put her on the track to success was to give her boss a nudge in the right direction. Cassandra's talent and tenacity had been enough to take it from there.

Standing by Mrs. Gilbert's living room window, Orion couldn't see inside the house across the street because the sunlight reflected from the windows, but that wasn't what he was interested in. Since the boyfriend had stayed the night, Orion wanted to follow him when he left for work to find out more about him.

Hopefully, he wouldn't follow the guy to another house and a family.

When the door opened, the boyfriend didn't walk out right away. Standing in the doorway, he bent down to kiss her goodbye, and as she wrapped her arms around his neck, he caught the glint of the diamond ring on her finger—a big diamond, the kind a man in love gave his future bride after proposing to her.

Orion's gut twisted.

Was there another way? Could he allow her to enjoy this man for a few years?

Maybe he could compel his silence?

First, though, he needed to find out whether the man was at least decent, let alone worthy of Geraldine.

When the guy got into his car, Orion waited another minute before going out the door, locking it behind him, and getting into his Chevy Malibu.

With a heavy heart, he followed the fiancé's car from a safe distance, hoping for Geraldine's sake as much as for his own that he would not discover anything rotten about him.

65

SHAI

$\mathcal{W}$hen the gate closed behind Shai as he drove out of Geraldine's neighborhood, a prickling sensation at the back of his neck had him glance at the rearview mirror. A car had stopped at the gate, waiting for it to open again.

He'd been leaving the neighborhood through the same gate at the same time most mornings, but he hadn't seen that particular Chevy model before. It was probably nothing. One of Geraldine's nearly three hundred neighbors had gotten a new car.

Out of habit though, he glanced at the license plate, his eidetic memory taking a snapshot of the number.

Nearing an intersection, he purposely turned his right blinker on and moved into the right lane even though he needed to continue straight. There were now three cars between him and the cream-colored Chevy, and when its blinker didn't come on, Shai released a relieved breath. Just to be sure, though, he turned right at the intersection, but the Chevy continued straight.

He was becoming overly jumpy for no reason.

Why would anyone follow him?

Even if Orion showed up, he would have waited for Shai to leave and then approach Geraldine when she was alone in the house. He wouldn't follow someone who he would assume was an inconsequential boyfriend.

Unless he was jealous.

What if Orion had eliminated all of Geraldine's other boyfriends and then had done his best to erase them from her memory?

He could be in love with her, but for some reason, he couldn't be intimate with her.

Shai had never heard of an immortal male who suffered from erectile dysfunction, but then it wasn't something a male would advertise. The source of it could only be mental, though. Immortal bodies didn't develop circulation or hormonal problems.

Preoccupied with his thought, Shai had forgotten to readjust his route for the detour he'd taken. He could either make a U-turn or have the navigation system reconfigure a route for him. Stopping at the next light, he activated the system, and as he waited for it to reboot, he took a quick look in the rearview mirror.

At first, he didn't see the Chevy that was separated by several vehicles, but as the light changed and the cars started moving, he caught a glimpse of it.

It could have been a different car, but he decided not to take chances and called Onegus.

The chief answered right away as if he had been waiting for the call. "What's up, Shai?"

"I have a feeling that I'm being followed. It's a cream-colored Chevy Malibu. Write down the license plate number." He recited the combination of seven numbers and letters.

"Give me a moment," the chief said.

As he waited, Shai kept glancing at his rearview mirror, hoping to see the Chevy turn at one of the intersections they were passing through, but it kept going, following him from a distance with several cars between them.

Whoever the tail was, they weren't pros. If Shai could spot the car following him without any training, then anyone could.

"Shai." Onegus came on the line. "I think this is our guy. The security feed from Geraldine's front door caught the same car parked in the driveway of the neighbor across the street. The guy went into the house using a key, so my Guardians didn't become suspicious. I just checked, and he'd told the guard that he was Mrs. Gilbert's nephew delivering a prescription medicine she'd asked him to pick up. The guys in security should have gotten suspicious when he left Mrs. Gilbert's house a minute after you drove away, but he locked the door behind him and didn't seem hurried as he got into his car, so they didn't think it was connected to your departure. But he's following you, so there is that."

"What do you want me to do? I can take a few more random turns and check whether he's still behind me."

"If it's indeed Orion, I don't want him to get suspicious. Drive toward the village as you normally would, not too fast and not too slow, and when you get to Malibu, turn onto Red Canyon Road. We will be waiting for him there."

"That's a dead end and he will see that it is on his navigation system. Won't he find that suspicious?"

"He might, but that's the best place to trap him. I'll have two more Guardians stationed down the road in case he doesn't turn after you. One way or another, we are going to catch him."

66

ONEGUS

*O*negus glanced at his tablet, tracking Shai's progress. It had been one of the modifications Onegus had asked for when Kian had ordered the self-driving cars for every clan member. They were all equipped with trackers, so in case of an emergency they could be activated from the security office, but only when authorized by Onegus or Kian.

It was coming in handy now as he and his Guardians were lying in wait.

Orion had decided to show up at a most opportune hour—when most of the Guardians were still in the village and available to be deployed, but Onegus hadn't had much time to explain what was going on and distribute earpieces to everyone. Thankfully, his force was trained for quick response, and they were all in position and ready with minutes to spare.

Two cars with two Guardians each were waiting at the end of Red Canyon Road, while two others were idling on the side of the main road several hundred feet west of it, waiting for the Chevy to either turn after Shai or get spooked and continue straight ahead.

If the guy followed Shai into the dead-end road, they would turn around and block his exit. If he didn't turn, they would follow the Chevy until it stopped somewhere and apprehend their target there.

That's why Yamanu was in the car with Onegus. If they had to catch Orion in a public place, Yamanu would shroud the operation, hiding it from human eyes.

The Guardian leaned over to glance at the tablet. "Three minutes to showtime." He chuckled. "Who knew that one day we would be thankful for L.A.'s damn traffic. It's given us time to get ready."

Onegus nodded.

Yamanu crossed his arms over his chest. "Capturing this male should be interesting."

It was, but the uneasy feeling in Onegus's gut reminded him that they were about to entrap a guy with no proper justification.

They had no proof or even a shred of evidence that Orion had committed a crime or posed a threat to the clan. What they were about to do was unlawful, bordering on immoral.

Onegus was a lawman, not just a military commander, and he didn't like being on the wrong side of the divide.

"You look like you ate a lemon," Yamanu said.

"I don't like trapping a man just because I want to get information out of him. He hasn't committed any crimes against the clan, and as far as we know, not against humans either."

Yamanu lifted one shoulder in a half shrug. "It's very much like the situation we had with Kalugal. He hadn't done anything to us, but we wanted to find out what he was up to, so we trapped him."

"We knew that he was involved in illegal activities," Onegus countered.

"We suspected that he was making money from insider information, but as long as he wasn't enslaving humans or physically harming them in the process, that's not the kind of unlawful activity that we are concerned with."

"We didn't know whether he was enslaving humans or not. He had that enormous bunker, and we had no idea what he was doing in there. That's why we wanted Jin to tether him." Onegus sighed through his nose. "That won't be enough with Orion, though. We need to ask him questions, not just observe what he does. With Kalugal, we knew where he came from and who his men were. We know absolutely nothing about Orion."

"There you go." Yamanu uncrossed his arms. "This is a military mission, not a law enforcement operation, and you need to switch your cop cap to a helmet. We need information, Orion has it, end of story."

Onegus cast the Guardian a lopsided smile. "When you're right, you're right."

"I'm always right." Yamanu pointed at the tablet. "Here he comes."

As the circle representing Shai's car was about to turn into Red Canyon Road, Onegus switched his tablet view to the feed from the drone hovering above the intersection.

Onegus watched the cream-colored Chevy as Shai made the turn. When it slowed down to a crawl and then pulled to the curb and stopped, he was sure that the guy had gotten spooked and would keep on driving, but then the car started moving again and followed Shai onto the side road.

"Thank the merciful Fates." Onegus threw the gearshift into drive.

67

ORION

*I*t was a trap, one Orion hadn't expected, but should have.

The navigation system had clearly shown that it was a dead-end road, but he'd thought that it just hadn't been updated, as it often happened with new housing developments, and that Geraldine's boyfriend was either going home, or to inspect the work in progress.

When he noted the two vehicles behind him, Orion assumed that they were driving to the same development.

But as the car in front of him reached what appeared to be the end of the road, four burly men exited the two vehicles that had been waiting there, and the two vehicles behind him pulled to a stop, blocking his retreat.

Perhaps Geraldine's boyfriend was someone important, someone who for some reason feared for his life.

A criminal perhaps?

Orion wasn't really worried. As long as the men didn't open fire as soon as he exited the car, he would just compel them to leave, and he would have a nice little chat with the boyfriend.

After slowly opening the door, he stepped out with his arms in the air. "I'm unarmed. Don't shoot." He embedded the last part with strong compulsion, making sure that they wouldn't.

"No one is going to shoot you," a man said behind him. "We only want to talk."

Lowering his arms, Orion slowly turned around and assessed the man.

He was tall, blond, and good-looking enough to be a movie star. Perhaps this was a movie set, one that was heavily guarded for some reason.

Except, he had a feeling that it was something much worse than that. The tiny hairs at the back of his neck were tingling in alarm.

"I took the wrong turn." Orion smiled apologetically. "I didn't know that this was a restricted access road. Get back in your cars, turn around, and forget that I was ever here."

The compulsion in his voice should have worked right away.

The blond flashed him a charming smile. "Your tricks are not going to work on us." The guy pointed to his earpieces. "We know who you are and what you can do, Orion."

How could the guy block his voice and still hear what he was saying? And how did they know who he was?

Had Geraldine remembered him? Only a handful of people knew him as Orion, and only one person knew about him being immortal and the powers he possessed.

"Who are you?"

"My name is Onegus." The guy walked up to him and offered him his hand. "You have nothing to fear from us. We only want to talk."

Orion didn't take the man's hand. "Who are you?" he repeated, waving a hand to encompass the entire group. "And what do you want with me?"

"We are immortals like you," Onegus said. "We've been searching for others like us for a millennium."

Orion looked at the men with wonder, his curiosity and excitement overpowering his fear. Without his compulsion, he was defenseless against these people, but he believed Onegus that they meant him no harm. There was no hostility in their eyes or their scents, only curiosity to match his own.

"So have I. For a long time, I thought that I was an anomaly, a lone immortal cursed to walk the earth alone."

Onegus chuckled. "So you got busy creating more?"

Orion frowned. "I've never fathered a child, if that's what you mean. I'm infertile."

"You are not. Our kind has a very low fertility rate, and you should count yourself lucky that you didn't get a human female pregnant. Your child would have been human with a human's lifespan."

"Then how could I have created more like me?"

"By inducing a Dormant."

Orion shook his head. "I have no idea what you're talking about."

"A Dormant is a human who carries the immortal gene," Onegus explained. "They can be induced and transition into immortality."

The guy was contradicting himself. A moment ago, he'd said that a child born to an immortal with a human would be born human. Which meant that the immortal gene wasn't transferable unless both parents were immortal.

But he hadn't scented a lie, so there must be another explanation. "I've never met a dormant carrier of immortal genes. How would I even know that they had them?"

"What about Geraldine?" The boyfriend walked over to Onegus and stood next to him. "Did you induce her?"

"She was already immortal when I found her. I don't even know how to induce what you call a Dormant."

6 8

SHAI

*A*fter getting a pair of earpieces from Alfie, Shai had replaced his fingers with the devices. He'd listened to Onegus and Orion as patiently as he could, letting the chief do what he was good at, but Orion's answers were bullshit.

He claimed that he didn't know of other immortals, and that he'd found Geraldine after she'd been turned. Why hadn't he tried to seduce her?

The least favorable scenario Shai had come up with so far had been missing a few crucial pieces, but they all seemed to have fallen into place now.

It looked as though Orion had somehow found Geraldine after she'd been turned immortal and had compelled her into having a romantic relationship with him. But when he'd tried to get her away from her family, she'd fought his compulsion and refused.

When that hadn't worked, he'd kidnapped her, probably by snatching her up from the water when she'd gone swimming on that fateful day and putting her on a boat. She'd fought him, jumped ship, and when he'd chased after her, the terrible accident had happened, nearly killing her.

He'd managed to save her, but guilt over what had happened prevented him from compelling her to have a relationship with him again. The same guilt had also prompted him to look after her and her family ever since.

"Bastard," Shai hissed.

Onegus stopped him from lunging at the guy with a hand on his chest. "Relax, Shai. We don't know all the facts yet." He turned to Orion. "How did you find Geraldine?"

The guy shrugged. "I found her by chance."

It was such a blatant lie that no immortal special senses were required to detect it.

"Liar." Shai tried to lunge at the lying piece of shit, but once again, Onegus stopped him.

"Calm down, or I'll have to remove you from the situation. If you want to be part of this conversation, behave."

Right now, Onegus wasn't his friend and future son-in-law. He was the chief, and he wouldn't hesitate to order one of the Guardians to stuff Shai into his car and handcuff him to the steering wheel.

Shai nodded. "I'm okay."

"Good." Onegus turned to Orion. "Let's assume that I believe you, and that you happened to meet Geraldine by chance. Where was it? Did you meet her at the supermarket? Did you live in the same suburban neighborhood? Otherwise, I don't see how you could've met a suburban mother who didn't work outside her home."

Orion smiled. "I met her at one of the quilting competitions she attended. I was searching for nice, well-made quilts for an antiques gallery I own."

That could have been true, but Shai knew that it was just another lie.

What was the guy hiding?

If he knew how to detect immortals among the billions of humans, he would have also found clan members and Doomers, but he'd claimed that he'd been a solo operator.

Given the chief's doubting expression, Onegus seemed to share his opinion. "I hoped that you would cooperate and that we wouldn't need to resort to harsher interrogation methods, but regrettably, you insist on lying. Who are you trying to protect, Orion?"

Shai wanted to know that as well.

Orion was good at hiding his fear, and his voice was steady and calm as he said, "I've only ever protected Geraldine and her family."

"Why?" Onegus asked.

"Because she's immortal like me, and she has memory issues. I was afraid that she would get discovered. I had to keep shielding her."

"Why didn't you take her with you?" Onegus asked.

A shadow passed over the guy's eyes. "I travel a lot, and Geraldine was raising a daughter."

"Did you have anything to do with her accident?" Shai asked.

Wincing, Orion shook his head. "I was away when that happened. When I returned and learned that she was presumed dead, I searched for her, hoping against hope that she had survived. I found her three days after her accident. She'd washed up to shore many miles down the coastline."

That agreed with what Geraldine and Annani had told them, so perhaps that part was true.

Onegus smiled one of his cobra smiles. "I assume that Geraldine didn't have memory issues before the accident."

Orion closed his eyes for a brief moment. "She didn't."

"Did you try to take her with you before she was injured?" Shai asked.

"No. She was married and had a child." He winced. "She didn't remember them after her accident. She didn't remember anything at all, not her name, not even how to speak. She had to relearn everything from scratch."

"If you knew about her family, why didn't you return her to them?" Onegus pressed on. "Why didn't you tell her that she had a husband and a child? Did you want to keep her for yourself?"

Orion's eyes blazed with suppressed anger, but his tone remained even as he answered. "I figured that it was a unique opportunity for her to disappear. Geraldine couldn't stay around for much longer anyway, and eventually, she would have had to fake her own death and disappear. I shielded her from the anguish of it by not telling her about the family she'd left behind."

That rang true, and yet Shai's gut still insisted that Orion was playing them all and that he was mixing truth with lies to make his story sound more believable.

Onegus let out a sigh. "As lovely as it is standing out here, I think it's time to move this party to somewhere safer and more comfortable." He snapped his fingers, and before Orion knew what was happening, one of the Guardians stabbed him in the neck with a syringe.

"Don't worry," Onegus said as horror flashed through Orion's eyes. "This is only going to put you to sleep for a little while, and the worst you should expect is to wake up with a headache."

The Guardian caught Orion before the guy slumped to the ground and carried him to Onegus's car.

"Where are you taking him?" Shai asked.

"The keep."

The one nice apartment in the keep's underground was taken at the moment, and Shai debated whether putting Orion in one of the small cells was the right thing to do.

So far, he hadn't admitted to any wrongdoing, and they couldn't prove that he was guilty of any.

"Are you going to put him in one of the small cells or move Vrog to one?" Shai followed Onegus to his car.

"Kian authorized Vrog's move to the village, and he's on his way as we speak. Hopefully, Okidu will be done preparing the suite for Orion by the time we get there. I don't want him to feel like a prisoner." He put his hand on Shai's shoulder. "We might need the Clan Mother to get the truth out of him, so you need to be patient."

Shai nodded. "Should I tell Geraldine?"

"I can call Cassandra. She knows where the keep is, and she can drive her mother there. I'm sure both mother and daughter will want to see Orion as soon as possible." Onegus smirked. "I also have a feeling that he will find it much harder to lie to their faces, especially Geraldine's."

"I'll get them both. I'll tell her what he said on the way."

"Perhaps you shouldn't. Let her come to him with just what she remembers and ask him all the same questions we did. That way he will have to repeat what he told us or change his tune."

Shai ran a hand over the back of his neck. "She'll ask. What am I going to tell her?"

"Tell her precisely what I told you. She'll understand."

69

GERALDINE

*G*eraldine's hands shook as she applied lipstick.

Shai had called, telling her about Orion's capture.

Why had he followed Shai? What had he wanted to do to him?

She was terrified of the answer. What if Orion had killed all of her more serious lovers? Was that why they'd disappeared from her life so completely that she couldn't remember whether they'd actually existed?

No, that was absurd. Orion was kind. He wouldn't have murdered anyone.

Soon she would have her answers.

Cassandra was on her way, and so was Shai, and he would take them both to the keep to see Orion.

Geraldine still couldn't believe that they'd caught him, drugged him, and taken him to the clan's keep.

Hopefully, he wouldn't be too upset with her for allowing that to happen.

Hopefully, he could prove that he hadn't done her any harm.

Hopefully, they would let him go.

"What have I done?"

Her reflection in the mirror looked at her with accusation in her eyes.

"Mom, I'm here," Cassandra called from downstairs. "Are you coming down?"

"In a minute," Geraldine called back.

Taking a deep breath, she squared her shoulders, took her purse, and headed toward the stairs.

Cassandra waited for her at the foot of the staircase with worry in her eyes. "Are you okay?"

"Not really," Geraldine admitted. "But I'm holding up, and I'm readying for a fight."

"With Orion?"

Geraldine shook her head. "With Kian, Onegus, Shai, and anyone else who wants to keep Orion imprisoned. I got him into this mess, and I'm going to get him out of it."

Cassandra put both her hands on Geraldine's shoulders. "You don't have the power to fight for him, but have some faith in those men. They are not going to keep him locked up unless they have to or unless he deserves it. We don't know what part he played in your accident and everything that happened to you before and after."

Geraldine's gut clenched. "Did Onegus tell you anything?"

"No. Did Shai share any details with you?"

"He didn't. He said that Onegus asked Orion some questions and that Orion gave him some answers that they weren't sure were truthful. Onegus doesn't want me to know what those answers were because he doesn't want me to get influenced by them. He wants me to question Orion as if he hasn't been questioned yet."

"It makes sense." Cassandra leaned and kissed Geraldine's cheek. "It's going to be okay, Mom. You'll have me, Shai, and Onegus with you. You can do it."

"Of course I can." Geraldine took Cassandra's hands off her. "And I'm grateful to be surrounded by people I love and who love me back as I confront Orion. But he has taken care of me for decades, and I have to fight for him, even if my loved ones disagree."

As the door opened and Shai walked in, his pinched expression told her more than he'd been willing to reveal. Whatever Orion had told them had either been self-incriminating, untrue, or things she couldn't imagine.

"Just tell me one thing." She walked up to him. "Is it worse than what we suspected?"

"I don't know." He took her hand. "Let's put it this way. If everything he said was true, then his story matches our best scenario hypothesis. But if he lied, all the other scenarios are still possible. He didn't say anything that we haven't considered before."

"That's good to know." She let loose a relieved breath. "You looked as if you'd learned something really bad when you came in."

"I didn't." He wrapped his arm around her waist. "Are you ready to go?"

She nodded. "How long is he going to be asleep?"

"According to Onegus, he should be waking up soon. Kian is probably already there."

70

ORION

*W*hen Orion woke up, he found himself on a plush bed, his head pounding just as Onegus had warned it would.

Nevertheless, he forced his eyes to remain open and look at where he was. It looked like a hotel bedroom, with one door open to a sitting area where he could sense three males and smell freshly brewed coffee.

He desperately needed a cup.

He also desperately needed to visit the bathroom, which was behind the other open door.

At least they hadn't thrown him in a dungeon. Except, a second sweep of the place revealed that there were no windows in the bedroom, so perhaps he was in one after all.

Since there was no point in pretending that he was still asleep, Orion slid off the bed and ducked into the bathroom.

After taking care of his bladder, he washed his face, unpacked the new toothbrush that had been left for him, and brushed his teeth. There was also a new electric shaver, still in the box, a new comb, still in its plastic wrap, and a plush terry robe hung on a hook next to a towel that was the same cream color.

When he entered the living room, Onegus gave him a smile. "How is your head?" He pushed to his feet and walked over to the small bar cabinet.

"Pounding." Orion looked at the other two males sitting next to a round dining table. He recognized them as part of the team that had trapped him earlier. "I could use some coffee."

"Here you go." Onegus handed him a cup. "The boss is on his way, and he wants you sharp and alert."

"Why?" Orion took a long sip, suppressing the urge to sigh with how good it was.

"To answer his questions."

Orion sat down on the couch. "What do you people want with me?"

"Just the truth, buddy."

"And when you get it, will you let me go?"

Onegus nodded.

Orion found that hard to believe. Then again, they hadn't imprisoned Geraldine, who was exactly like him, so they had no reason to keep him.

Unless they'd used her to trap him, and it all had been a setup. Had there been someone else with her in the house? Someone keeping her from leaving?

"How did you find Geraldine? I thought that I made sure she wouldn't reveal her immortality."

"We found Cassandra first." Onegus grinned like a peacock. "She's my mate."

That was a surprise.

"Do you mean girlfriend or wife?"

"Fiancée, in human terms. Immortals mate for life."

"Cassandra is not immortal."

"She is now. I induced her transition."

"I don't understand." Orion put his empty coffee cup on the table. "You said that a child born to an immortal and a human is human. I know who Cassandra's father was, and he wasn't immortal."

"The children of male immortals with human females are born human. The children of female immortals with male humans are born Dormant, which means that they carry the immortal gene in dormant form and that it can be activated with venom."

"Venom? Like during sex? So only the female children carry it?"

"Both male and female children born to an immortal mother carry the gene and can be activated. But the males cannot transmit it to their children."

Orion took a moment to organize the information in his head, which resulted in another question. "How are the males activated?"

"Also with venom, just not during sex. They have to fight an immortal male and spur his aggression enough for him to produce venom."

"I see."

It all somehow made sense.

"How did your people find out about that? Was it trial and error?"

Onegus regarded him with wary eyes. "Let's save the rest of your questions for the boss. He should be here any minute."

"Who is your so-called boss?"

"His name is Kian, and that's all you need to know for now."

71

KIAN

*A*s Kian waited for the cell door to open, he made a mental note to do some remodeling in the underground facility. He'd never expected to be making such frequent use of the place, and this morning he'd had to expedite Vrog's move to the village to make room for Orion.

They needed at least one more apartment-style cell.

When the door finished swinging out, he strode inside, meeting the eyes of the cell's newest occupant.

As per his instructions, Orion hadn't been cuffed, and no one stopped him as he rose to his feet and offered Kian his hand.

"Kian, I assume?"

"Indeed." He shook the guy's hand. "We've been very curious about you, Orion."

"I had no idea you even existed." The guy let go of his hand and looked at Andrew.

"This is Andrew," Kian said without explaining why he was there. "And these are Brundar and Anandur." He turned to the Guardians sitting at the dining table. "You can leave. We are expecting more guests, and there isn't enough room."

Andrew's ability to detect lies didn't work as well with immortals as it did with humans, and the earpieces probably would make it even more difficult for him to read Orion. But it was worth a try.

As the two got up and walked out, Anandur and Brundar took their place.

"Who else are you expecting?" Orion asked.

"Cassandra, Geraldine, and Shai."

Orion tensed, his expression turning hard. "Do you also keep Geraldine and Cassandra imprisoned?"

"Fates forbid." Kian sat down on one of the armchairs. "Cassandra is mated to Onegus, and Geraldine is mated to Shai. They are part of my clan now." He leaned forward. "That is why I want to find out what's happened to her, and I hope you can tell us more than we've managed to figure out so far."

The tension didn't leave Orion's body, but he tried to sound bored. "Tell me what you've figured out, and I'll try to fill in the missing pieces."

Andrew cleared his throat, which meant two things. One was that he could read Orion, which was excellent, and the other was that the guy wasn't being truthful. Translation—he had no intention of telling them anything and only wanted to find out what they knew.

"I'd rather hear the entire story from you first. Everything from the day you met Geraldine to when you induced her transition, and everything that has happened since."

"I've already told your men that I didn't induce her. I just learned from Onegus how it's done."

Andrew didn't clear his throat.

Interesting. The guy had really been clueless. How was it possible?

Onegus also looked at Andrew for confirmation, and when he shrugged, Onegus's eyes widened just a fraction.

Kian debated whether to keep on interrogating Orion or wait for Geraldine's arrival. Perhaps when the guy got confirmation from her that she was indeed free and happily mated, he would be less guarded and start telling them the truth.

Crossing his legs at the ankles, Kian decided to kill time by asking questions that were not pertinent to Geraldine's case. "What do you do for a living, Orion?"

"I deal in antiques. What about you?"

"The clan owns many enterprises. We invest in new technology, building projects, precious metals, minerals, the list is long."

Orion smiled. "I'm small fry compared to you."

"You need to support only yourself. The clan has many more mouths to feed."

"How many?"

It was Kian's turn to smile. "Wouldn't you like to know. For now, that's privileged information."

"When would it become available to me?"

"When you tell us the truth, the entire truth, and nothing but the truth, and we determine that you're trustworthy."

72

GERALDINE

$\mathcal{A}$s Geraldine walked down the wide, industrial looking corridor, Shai to her right and Cassandra to her left, her heart hammered against her rib cage. They were underground, in the clan's dungeon, and guilt was swelling in her throat, choking her airway.

She was on the edge of a panic attack but refused to surrender to it.

How was she going to face Orion? What excuse could she give him for bringing him to this horrid place? Was he shackled to the wall with manacles? Were they torturing him?

Shai had laughed when she'd asked that, and Cassandra had assured her that the dungeon accommodations were more like an upscale hotel's than a prison's, but she couldn't help wondering whether they'd been telling her the truth.

"It's that one." Shai pointed to an open door that looked like something that belonged on a bank safe. It was at least a foot thick and made from some kind of metal.

All the doors on this level were like that, built to withstand an immortal male's strength.

Feeling her knees going weak, Geraldine clutched Shai's arm so tight that he winced. She forced herself to loosen her grip and let him lead her into the cell.

It was full of people, but her eyes immediately darted to Orion, who rose to his feet and started walking toward her.

The distance between them was no more than five feet, two steps for Orion, but time slowed, and she saw him approaching her in slow motion.

"Geraldine," he said her name.

"I'm so sorry." Tears streaming down her cheek, she let go of Shai's arm and flung herself at him.

He embraced her gently. "Why are you sorry?"

"You're here because of me," she whispered into his neck.

"Is that a bad thing?" He leaned back and looked down at her. "Are they mistreating you here?"

"No, they are wonderful. I love Shai and he loves me, and I'm very happy. But I remembered you, and I knew that you would come, and I told them about it, and they were lying in wait for you."

He frowned. "Why?"

"To find out what happened to me and also if there are more immortals out there. The clan has been searching for more survivors for thousands of years, but other than those horrid Doomers, they only found one survivor and several Dormants. Are there more out there?"

He shook his head. "I've also been searching."

Behind her, Cassandra cleared her throat. "Hello, Orion. I don't remember you, but I was told that you were a frequent visitor to our home when I was growing up."

He let go of Geraldine and reached for Cassandra. "I'm very proud of the woman you've become. And I'm so happy that you turned immortal. I didn't know it was even possible."

Kian rose to his feet. "Please, let's all sit down."

Geraldine glanced at Shai before joining Orion on the couch, beckoning him to sit on her other side. It was meant more as a reassurance to him than her need for his support.

She was relieved to confirm that she had absolutely no romantic feelings for Orion, but Shai needed to know that as well.

Kian's brother-in-law vacated the armchair for Cassandra, but she declined the offer and joined Onegus and the two bodyguards at the dining table.

Orion took Geraldine's hand. "How much do you remember?"

Shai had warned her not to mention the goddess. "The memories are slowly coming back. I know that you were helping me throughout the years, but I don't remember anything from before the accident."

"You were severely injured. It's a miracle that you're alive."

"Do you know how it happened?"

He shook his head. "I found you three days later. You were already healing, but you had a long way to go. I assumed that you hit your head on a rock or on a boat."

"How did you find me in the first place?" She swallowed. "Did you induce me?"

He chuckled. "You are the third person who's asked me that. I didn't induce you. You were already immortal."

"Then who did it?"

"No one." He smiled. "You were born immortal."

She frowned. "How is that possible? Even two immortal parents can only have a dormant child. No one is born an immortal."

Kian cleared his throat. "If a child is conceived by a god or a goddess with a human partner, it's born immortal."

She heard him, but she wasn't sure she'd heard correctly. "What are you saying?"

"He's saying that you are a child of a god," Orion said.

Feeling all the blood leaving her face, she turned to him. "How do you know that?"

"I know who your father is. He is my father as well, and he is a god."

73

ORION

"You are both Toven's children." Cassandra said. "And I'm his granddaughter. Oh, wow." She grinned. "Can he also blow things up with his mind?"

It was so much like Cassandra to ask that.

Orion chuckled. "No. This is a talent unique to you. I should have known that you weren't entirely human when your mother told me about the little explosions she thought you were causing. I thought that she'd imagined it."

"Didn't you feel the power swirling under my skin?" Cassandra asked.

He shook his head. "I thought that you had an explosive personality."

When several people chuckled, he glanced at Shai, Geraldine's boyfriend, who was no longer looking at him with murder in his eyes, but rather awe.

Geraldine lifted a hand to her temple and rubbed it. "I can't believe that I'm a demigoddess. Why am I not more powerful?"

It only dawned on him then that Cassandra named his father Toven.

Was that the god's real name? He'd refused to tell Orion who he really was, calling himself Herman, but he'd admitted that he'd used many names since all the other gods had perished.

Orion had studied ancient mythologies though, searching for descriptions that would match the male who had fathered him, but he didn't remember the name Toven mentioned anywhere. Perhaps his father had been a minor god whose name hadn't made it into any of the surviving mythologies.

"Well?" Geraldine reminded him that she was still waiting for an answer.

"I'm sorry." He smiled at her. "You had been suppressing your abilities even before I met you, and I encouraged that throughout the years. I didn't want you to give yourself away."

"Tell us about your father," Kian said. "What do you know about him? Where is he? How did he survive?"

"What I know about him isn't much. I know that he's a jaded bastard who doesn't care about anyone or anything. I don't know where he is because he never stays in one place for long. I didn't even know his real name until Cassandra said it, although I would like to know how she knew that. But I do know how he survived. He told me that he'd been disgusted with the proceedings in the gods' assembly, snuck out, and flew away on some flying contraption that some of the gods possessed. He hadn't known that his people perished along with a big chunk of the ancient world's population until he returned home months later and saw the devastation."

"What did he do once he found out?" Kian asked.

"Flew far away and made a home for himself somewhere else. That was all he told me."

Kian looked at the guy named Andrew, who nodded.

Was he some kind of a truth detector? He hadn't said a word other than clearing his throat when Orion had lied.

"Two more goddesses survived," Kian said. "One is my mother, and the other is her sister."

"So you're a demigod as well," Orion said.

"I'm an immortal, and that's all I am." Kian folded his arms over his chest. "I don't think of myself as a demigod. It seems pretentious."

Orion nodded. "Indeed."

He didn't like the title either, thinking of himself as hard to kill and easy to heal. His powers were useful, but they weren't godly. They were just mind tricks that even some humans could do.

Kian was still regarding him with those intense blue eyes of his. "Now that I've shared with you my clan's biggest secret, I want you to tell me how you found out that your father was a god, and how you found Geraldine. You told her that you discovered your immortality on the battlefield when you recovered from an injury that should have been fatal. Is that true?"

"That's correct. My mother didn't know who my father was."

"What about your fangs?" Kian unfolded his arms and leaned forward. "Your venom glands? Didn't you wonder what those were about?"

"When they started growing, I already knew that I was deathless. It was after that battle." He snorted. "I thought that I'd been bitten by a vampire, and I clung to that explanation for a long time. I didn't tell my mother what was going on and tried to hide those damn fangs."

"How old were you when you got that injury?" Geraldine asked.

"Fourteen."

A tear slid down her cheek. "You were just a boy."

"I wasn't the youngest. Boys as young as ten were drafted. Those were different times, dark times that I'd rather forget."

"How did you find your father?" Kian asked.

"That's a long story." He glanced longingly at the empty coffee carafe. "Can we take a coffee break? I haven't had breakfast yet either."

Kian turned to the redhead sitting at the dining table. "Can you get us pastries and sandwiches from the vending machines?"

"Sure, boss." The giant rose to his feet. "Cappuccinos, anyone?"

"I would love one." Orion smiled up at him. "If it's not a bother, with two sugars, please."

"No problem. Anyone else?"

It had been a test of sorts, to see what kind of people they were, and how well they were going to treat him. So far, they seemed like a decent bunch, and if they'd accepted Geraldine and Cassandra into their clan, perhaps they would accept him as well.

It would be nice not to be so alone, to be among others like him, and perhaps, if his luck held, he might also find an immortal mate to call his own. But he wouldn't give up his autonomy for that, nor would he ever stop searching for Toven's other children.

COMING UP NEXT
T<small>HE</small> C<small>HILDREN OF THE</small> G<small>ODS</small>
D<small>ARK</small> H<small>UNTER</small> T<small>RILOGY</small>

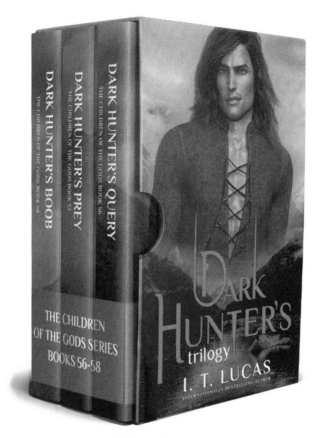

Read the enclosed excerpt

Includes:
56: D<small>ARK</small> H<small>UNTER</small>'<small>S</small> Q<small>UERY</small>
57: D<small>ARK</small> H<small>UNTER</small>'<small>S</small> P<small>REY</small>
58: D<small>ARK</small> H<small>UNTER</small>'<small>S</small> B<small>OON</small>

Dear reader,

Thank you for reading the ***Children of the Gods***.

As an independent author, I rely on your support to spread the word. So if you enjoyed the story, please share your experience with others, and if it isn't too much trouble, I would greatly appreciate a brief review on Amazon.

Click **HERE** to leave a review
Love & happy reading,
Isabell

To find out what's included in your free membership, click HERE or flip to the last page.

If you're already a subscriber, you'll receive a download link for my next book's preview chapters in the new release announcement email. If you are not getting my emails, your provider is sending them to your junk folder, and you are missing out on <u>important updates, side characters' portraits, additional content, and other goodies.</u> To fix that, add isabell@itlucas.com to your email contacts or your email VIP list.

DARK HUNTER EXCERPT

ALENA

Alena, eldest daughter of the goddess Annani, a mother of thirteen, a grandmother of seventeen, a great-grandmother of twenty-three, and a great many times over grandmother of nearly every member of her clan, gazed at her phone's screen and sighed like a besotted schoolgirl.

In her over two millennia of existence, Alena had never reacted so strongly to a male, let alone to a mere depiction of one. The portrait had been created by a talented illustrator, but it hadn't been embellished in any way. The forensic artist had merely given life to a verbal description taken from a human's memory, and Annani had attested to its accuracy.

Annani had hung the framed original in her receiving room, a fond reminder of the male's father—the god Toven, whom she'd greatly admired in her youth. According to her mother, father and son looked so much alike that they were nearly indistinguishable.

Taken by the immortal's striking looks, Alena had captured Orion's image with her phone so she could gaze at it whenever she pleased, which was often. By now, she had every detail of the drawing committed to memory—the intelligent eyes, the chiseled cheekbones, the full sensuous lips, the aristocratic nose, the shoulder-length dark hair, the strong column of his neck—and yet she still felt compelled to pull out her phone and gaze at it.

Despite being an artistic construct, the drawing looked so lifelike, Orion's face so expressive, that it made her feel as if he were looking straight into her soul.

But it was all an illusion, and getting excited over a pretty face was as shallow as it got. She was too old to be blindsided by skin-deep beauty and wise enough to know that the only beauty that mattered was the kind found on the inside.

The male was gorgeous, perfect in the way all gods and the first generation of their offspring with humans were. It didn't mean that he was a good man, or that he could carry on an intelligent conversation, or that he was the truelove mate she'd been secretly hoping for.

Alena was the eldest, and yet the Fates had bestowed the blessing of a truelove mate on her younger siblings first. She wasn't jealous of their happiness and wished them the best their eternal lives had to offer, but she wanted her own happily ever after, and she was tired of waiting.

Except, Orion couldn't be the one for her, and if he was, the Fates had a really sick sense of humor. He was a compeller, and Alena could never be with a male who could take away her will at his whim. Just imagining being so helpless and at the mercy of another made her shiver. So even though his beautiful face evoked a powerful longing and caused a stirring—the kind Alena had never experienced before—and even though she pulled up his damn picture and stared at it numerous times a day, he could never be her truelove mate.

Her one and only probably had not been born yet, or he was making his way toward her while she was letting herself get enchanted by the pretty face of another.

Alena sighed.

Hopefully, the one the Fates chose for her would have longish black hair, piercing blue eyes, and a face that looked like it was lovingly carved from granite by a talented sculptor—precisely like Orion, just not Orion himself.

Could her fated one be Orion's father? Except, Orion hadn't inherited his compulsion ability from his human mother, and Toven was probably a compeller as well.

Maybe Orion had a brother? One who hadn't inherited the ability?

After all, Geraldine was also Toven's daughter, and she wasn't a compeller.

Hope surging in her heart, Alena closed her phone and put it back in her skirt pocket.

She was running out of patience.

Supposedly the Fates rewarded those who selflessly sacrificed for others or suffered greatly with the gift of a truelove mate. Had she sacrificed or suffered less than her siblings? Was that why she was the last one left even though she was the eldest?

Kian had dedicated his life to the clan, so she could understand why he'd been granted a mate first. Amanda had lost a child, which was the worst suffering Alena could imagine, so it was only fair that she'd been the next one in line to find her fated mate. Sari had worked almost as hard as Kian to better the lives of those clan members who'd chosen to remain in Scotland, so it was also fair that she'd gotten her happily ever after.

Alena deserved hers as well.

She wasn't a natural leader like Kian or Sari, and she hadn't suffered a terrible loss like Amanda, but she was the de facto mother of the clan, and she also sacrificed a lot to keep her own mother out of trouble.

Not that any of it had been a great sacrifice or had caused her any suffering.

Motherhood was the best possible reward in itself, and traveling the world with Annani wasn't exactly a hardship either.

As Annani's companion, Alena had been an unwilling participant in her mother's crazy shenanigans, but she had to admit that most of them had been fun and not overly dangerous. She also enjoyed the babies and toddlers who arrived at the sanctuary to be kept safe until it was time for them to transition.

Life had been good to her, but she'd been doing the same thing for two thousand years, and it was time for a change.

Her only solo adventure had been impersonating a Slovenian supermodel in the hopes of luring Kalugal out of hiding.

After the fun time she'd spent with the team who'd accompanied her to New York, it had been difficult to go back to the routine. For a few precious days, she'd enjoyed being different, being her own person and not her mother's shadow.

It seemed like such a distant memory, like it had taken place in another lifetime.

The face she saw in the mirror was the same one she'd been looking at for two millennia.

Gone was the sophisticated hairstyle she'd adopted for the New York trip, replaced by her habitual loose braid, her face was free of makeup, and she wore one of her long, comfortable dresses instead of the fashionable clothes Amanda had gotten her for that trip.

Those had been given away to charity soon after she'd returned from New York.

There was no reason to dress up in the sanctuary, where everyone expected her to look the part of Annani's devoted daughter—the goddess's companion and advisor—a part she'd been playing for so long that no one could envision her doing anything else, including herself.

Not that there was anything wrong with it.

Her position at Annani's side was a duty and an honor that Alena had proudly and lovingly performed for centuries—a position that could not be filled by anyone but her.

ORION

Orion regarded the leader of his captors, noting the hard lines of Kian's face, the stiffness of his shoulders, and the sheer size of him. The guy was big, he was gruff, but he wasn't cold, and that gave Orion hope.

So far, other than the damn tranquilizer they'd knocked him out with, these immortals hadn't treated him too badly. Nevertheless, they were holding him against his will, and even though the apartment he'd woken up in was as fancy as any high-end hotel suite, it was still a prison cell.

Other than having been born immortal, he hadn't done anything to them, and they had no reason to hold him, but he was at their mercy, his compulsion ability nullified by the earpieces they were all wearing.

Without it, he was as helpless as any human, and the only way out of the situation was to cooperate with his captors and give them what they wanted, which was information about his jerk of a father.

No skin off his nose.

If they could find the god, Orion didn't care what they did with him.

Kian put his paper cup down on the table and crossed his arms over his chest. "Now that you've eaten breakfast and gotten caffeinated, I want to hear the story of how you found your father and got him to admit that he was a god."

It was clear that the guy's patience was wearing thin, but Orion needed a little more time to think. The coffee break he'd practically begged Kian for had helped ease the pounding headache he'd woken up with, but his mind was still foggy.

631

He didn't mind telling them about his father, but there were other things he'd learned from the god that he wasn't sure he should share with them.

Did it matter if they knew that he was hunting for the god's other potential children?

They already knew about his sister and niece and had accepted Geraldine and Cassandra into their clan, but had their motives been pure?

They needed new blood for their community—more genetic diversity. They might try to get to his other siblings first and draft them into their clan.

Was that so bad, though?

Perhaps they could help him with his quest.

Orion had exhausted all of the information he had, but they might have access to resources that he didn't.

Damn, if only his head would clear so he could follow one thought to its logical conclusion instead of all his thoughts jumping around in his head like bunnies on speed.

Were these people trustworthy?

Were they a force for good or the opposite of that?

Was he lucky that they had found his sister and him?

The effects of the tranquilizer were beginning to wane, but he was still having a hard time reconciling what he'd learned from his captors with what he'd been told by his father. Some of it confirmed the god's story, but there was so much more that his father hadn't shared with him.

For nearly five centuries, Orion had been convinced that he was the only immortal, an anomaly, and then he'd met his father who'd claimed to be a god—not a deity, but a lone survivor of a superior race of people who'd been annihilated by one of their own.

Herman, aka Toven, had claimed that the gods from various mythologies had been real people. At the time, Orion had doubted his father's story, had suspected that the guy was either delusional or being deliberately deceitful, but his captors had confirmed everything Herman had told him. The gods hadn't been the constructs of human imagination, and what's more, his father wasn't the only survivor.

Had his father known about the two goddesses who'd escaped the attack and chosen not to tell him?

Had he known that some humans carried the dormant godly gene and withheld the information on purpose?

"Whenever you're ready," Kian prompted.

"Can I bother you for another cup?" Orion cast the guy a pleading look. "My head feels like it's stuffed with cotton. Usually, I don't suffer from such maladies, but the tranquilizer your guy injected me with must have been incredibly potent."

Kian grimaced. "It had to be to knock out an immortal."

"I'll brew a fresh pot," Onegus said. The male mated to his niece was the head of the clan's security forces, and yet he got up to reload the coffeemaker. "It will take a couple of minutes."

Apparently, these people didn't follow strict hierarchy. The guy could have asked one of the guards to brew the coffee but had chosen to do so himself. They acted more like a family or a group of friends than a military organization, which Orion took to be a good sign as to the kind of people he was dealing with.

Next to him, his sister winced. "I'm so sorry."

He patted her knee. "My head already feels much better."

"I didn't mean the headache." Geraldine smiled apologetically. "Well, that too, but what I'm really sorry about is entrapping you. You wouldn't be in this situation if I hadn't dug into my murky past."

"Why did you?"

"Do you mean why did I want to find out about my past or why did I help the clan trap you?"

"The first one."

"As long as I was oblivious about having had another life, I was content with the one I had. But after I discovered that I had a daughter who I couldn't remember, I had to find out how it happened. But I should have just moved on." She sighed. "In part, it's your fault that I didn't. You compelled me not to leave the house for more than a day, so I couldn't start my new life with Shai in his village."

Orion nodded. "Indeed, and that means that my capture is on me, and you have nothing to apologize for." He cast a sidelong glance at Kian. "I've been careful not to get noticed by humans, but I never anticipated other immortals. Although with the advent of the modern era and the proliferation of imaging devices, avoiding discovery by humans is getting more difficult. I can rely on my compulsion ability to get out of tight spots, but I can't compel inanimate objects, and nowadays, there are surveillance cameras everywhere and everyone has smartphones they can use to snap photos with. I had to develop new tactics to avoid getting my image recorded on electronic devices."

Ironically, though, his capture hadn't been the result of technology or even his negligence. Orion had followed the best protocols he could devise. What had gotten him in trouble was precisely the thing his father had warned him against—family, people he cared about, people who could lead others to him.

His sister and her daughters were his Achilles heel.

Next to him, Geraldine shifted her knees sideways and put her hands in her lap. "I have to admit, though, that your compulsion wasn't the only reason I didn't leave the house. As much as I hated the idea of trapping you, I wanted to talk to you and not forget the conversation as soon as you left. We pieced together most of what had happened to me, but there were still so many holes in the puzzle, and I wanted answers. I needed closure."

He put a hand on her knee. "I understand. You don't need to keep apologizing."

Geraldine lifted her big blue eyes to him, so much like his own that it was like looking in the mirror. "You're my brother, but I didn't know that, and I thought that you were my inducer. Do you know how awkward it feels now that I know the truth?" She shook her head. "It gets worse. When I finally recalled our interactions over the years, I was offended that you didn't find me attractive." She chuckled. "Although, I should have known something was up because I wasn't attracted to you either." She waved a hand over his face. "If you were ugly, that would have been understandable, but you are so gorgeous that I can't take my eyes off you."

Orion had never felt comfortable with the looks he'd gotten throughout his life, either covetous from those interested in him sexually or envious and outright hostile from others, but Geraldine was his sister, and her complimenting him on his good looks didn't feel as awkward. It reminded him of his mother and the way she used to regard him with love and adoration in her eyes.

"Thank you." Absentmindedly, he reached for Geraldine's hand and gave it a gentle squeeze. "I'm curious. How did you suddenly recover your memories of me? Did your mate have anything to do with that?"

"The goddess released them." Geraldine shifted her eyes to Kian. "Is it okay for me to reveal that?"

"It's fine."

So that was how she remembered him. Orion had wondered about that, thinking that maybe her boyfriend or one of the other immortals was powerful enough to unlock her submerged memories. But it had taken a goddess to release them, which meant that the others were not as powerful as he was.

He tucked away that bit of information for later use. "Is the goddess here?" He looked at Kian. "Can I meet her?"

Kian chuckled. "The Clan Mother is very curious about you, and I have no doubt that she will want to meet you as soon as possible. She's very fond of your father and speaks highly of him."

Orion grimaced. "He must've changed a lot since she last interacted with him."

"Here you go." Onegus handed him a mug of freshly brewed coffee.

"Thank you." Taking the mug with him, Orion leaned back against the couch cushions and crossed his legs at the ankles. "Perhaps I should start my story at the beginning, many years before I met my father." He took several sips from his coffee before putting the cup on the table.

"Please do," Geraldine said. "I want to know everything about you, or at least the highlights of your life."

Now that Orion's head was clearer and his thought process faster, deciding which information to share and which to withhold became easier.

The coffee break had been a test, and it had allowed him to observe his captors interacting with each other, and more importantly, with his sister and niece.

There was no faking the loving glances between Onegus and Cassandra and between Geraldine and Shai. His sister and niece were indeed happily mated to these clansmen, which made the men his family as well.

Besides, the clan had little to gain from what he could tell them, and he didn't have much to lose.

So far, Orion's query had yielded only one result—Geraldine—and he'd been unsuccessful in locating any of Toven's other children. Perhaps he and Geraldine were the only ones, or maybe he needed help locating the others.

KIAN

"As I mentioned before," Orion began, "I was fourteen when I discovered that I was immortal."

"Hold on." Geraldine lifted her hand. "That's not the beginning. I want to know where you were born, who your mother was, and how you ended up on the battle-field at such a young age."

Kian stifled a groan. At this rate, it would be nighttime before Orion reached the part about his father, and Kian had no intentions of staying in the keep for so long.

He called his mother when Orion had been captured, but because the guy had been knocked out cold, he'd had nothing else to report. His mother was no doubt anxiously awaiting an update and getting more aggravated with every passing moment.

Besides, as fascinating as hearing about Orion's life was, he was more interested in Toven's, and even that was not as important or as fun as spending time with his daughter.

Just thinking about Allegra's cute smiles and the adorable sounds she made eased the tension in his shoulders and lightened his heart.

Orion sighed and leaned forward to pick up his coffee mug. "The man who I thought was my father was a merchant in a small town near Milan. I was born nine months after he was killed in what is known as the Great Wars of Italy or the Habsburg-Valois wars. Because of the opportune timing, no one ever suspected that the grieving widow gave birth to a child that wasn't her deceased husband's, and neither did I." He chuckled. "Although even as a small boy, I knew that I looked nothing like that fat, ruddy-cheeked man in the portrait hanging in our home's entryway. What little hair he had was light brown, and my mother was a blond." He lifted his hand and smoothed it over his chin-length raven hair. "As you can see, my hair color is nearly black."

"You have beautiful hair," Cassandra said. "Did no one wonder about the little boy who looked nothing like his deceased father?"

He shrugged. "My mother was smart. She told everyone that I was the spitting image of her cousin, and she repeated it enough times for the fib to become truth. I think that after a while, she started believing it herself."

"Did you believe the lie?" Cassandra asked.

"Why wouldn't I? I adored my mother, and I had no reason to doubt her."

Kian huffed out a breath. "You must have realized the truth after surviving the injury that should have killed you."

Hopefully, jumping ahead to that would shorten the story time.

"Not right away." Orion's lips lifted in a crooked smile. "I came up with several possible explanations, starting with a guardian angel and ending with a good witch."

"What about being bitten by a vampire?" Geraldine asked.

"That came later, after my fangs started growing. I panicked, afraid that I would become crazed with blood lust, so I packed up my things and was about to leave in the middle of the night. My mother intercepted me, and when I admitted my fears, she said that vampires didn't exist but that I might have inherited strange things from my father, who wasn't the man she'd been married to. She told me that I was old enough to learn the truth, and that if I wanted to live, I needed to keep it a secret."

"How did she manage an affair?" Cassandra asked. "I mean, war was raging, and her husband was gone. And how did Toven find her? Did he just stroll into town and seduce her?"

"I don't know. She didn't divulge any details, only that he'd been a stunningly good-looking man and very smart. I'm not sure that she remembered much more than that. When I started discovering my own powers, I realized that he must have tampered with her memories."

Geraldine tilted her head. "Do you think that Toven compelled her to be with him?"

Orion shook his head. "My father is a jaded bastard, but he's not a rapist. My mother accepted him with open arms. I know that it makes her look bad, but she'd been practically sold to her husband by her family, and the arranged marriage was a disaster. He was a terrible man, or at least that was what she claimed, and when he died, she rejoiced at finally being free and celebrated with a very handsome stranger."

"How did she remember her affair with Toven?" Onegus asked. "Did he leave at least some of her memories of him intact?"

"My mother was an artist." Orion looked at Geraldine. "Our father had a thing for creative women. Your mother was an artist as well."

Her eyes widened. "Did you meet my real mother?"

He nodded. "I did, but I'll tell you about that later. I don't want to jump all over the timeline."

Kian was still trying to understand Orion's answer to Onegus's question. "What does your mother being an artist have to do with remembering Toven?"

"Indeed." Orion smiled. "She told me that she'd drunk a lot of wine after her husband's death, and she didn't remember much about the man she'd celebrated her freedom with, but her artist's eye remembered enough of him to draw a portrait." Orion waved a hand over his face. "When I reached adulthood, I realized that I looked just like him, but that's getting ahead of the story as well. You wanted to know how I found myself on the battlefield at the age of fourteen."

Geraldine nodded.

"Quite simply, I was the only male in the household, and they demanded one from each family. My mother wasn't very wealthy, but she wasn't destitute either, and she tried to bribe the recruiters. They took her gold and drafted me anyway. Back then, a woman alone was powerless. There was nothing she could've done to prevent them from taking me."

Geraldine put her hand on his arm. "I can't imagine how terrified you were."

"I was. I just knew that I was going to die. I'd never trained with any kinds of weapons. Heck, I didn't know how to hold a pike or a crossbow."

As Geraldine's chin started to wobble and tears slid down her cheeks, Kian cast her an amused glance. "But he didn't die. That's not a ghost sitting next to you."

The redheaded guard snorted. "I disagree. We have with us the ghost of Orion's past."

DARK HUNTER TRILOGY

Includes:
56: DARK HUNTER'S QUERY
57: DARK HUNTER'S PREY
58: DARK HUNTER'S BOON

THE CHILDREN OF THE GODS SERIES

THE CHILDREN OF THE GODS ORIGINS

1: GODDESS'S CHOICE

When gods and immortals still ruled the ancient world, one young goddess risked everything for love.

2: GODDESS'S HOPE

Hungry for power and infatuated with the beautiful Areana, Navuh plots his father's demise. After all, by getting rid of the insane god he would be doing the world a favor. Except, when gods and immortals conspire against each other, humanity pays the price.

But things are not what they seem, and prophecies should not to be trusted...

THE CHILDREN OF THE GODS

1: DARK STRANGER THE DREAM

Syssi's paranormal foresight lands her a job at Dr. Amanda Dokani's neuroscience lab, but it fails to predict the thrilling yet terrifying turn her life will take. Syssi has no clue that her boss is an immortal who'll drag her into a secret, millennia-old battle over humanity's future. Nor does she realize that the professor's imposing brother is the mysterious stranger who's been starring in her dreams.

Since the dawn of human civilization, two warring factions of immortals—the descendants of the gods of old—have been secretly shaping its destiny. Leading the clandestine battle from his luxurious Los Angeles high-rise, Kian is surrounded by his clan, yet alone. Descending from a single goddess, clan members are forbidden to each other. And as the only other immortals are their hated enemies, Kian and his kin have been long resigned to a lonely existence of fleeting trysts with human partners. That is, until his sister makes a game-changing discovery—a mortal seeress who she believes is a dormant carrier of their genes. Ever the realist, Kian is skeptical and refuses Amanda's plea to attempt Syssi's activation. But when his enemies learn of the Dormant's existence, he's forced to rush her to the safety of his keep. Inexorably drawn to Syssi, Kian wrestles with his conscience as he is tempted to explore her budding interest in the darker shades of sensuality.

2: DARK STRANGER REVEALED

While sheltered in the clan's stronghold, Syssi is unaware that Kian and Amanda are not human, and neither are the supposedly religious fanatics that are after her. She feels a powerful connection to Kian, and as he introduces her to a world of pleasure she never dared imagine, his dominant sexuality is a revelation. Considering that she's completely out of her element, Syssi feels comfortable and safe letting go with him. That is, until she begins to suspect that all is not as it seems. Piecing the puzzle together, she draws a scary, yet wrong conclusion...

3: DARK STRANGER IMMORTAL

When Kian confesses his true nature, Syssi is not as much shocked by the revelation as she is wounded by what she perceives as his callous plans for her.

If she doesn't turn, he'll be forced to erase her memories and let her go. His family's safety demands secrecy – no one in the mortal world is allowed to know that immortals exist.

Resigned to the cruel reality that even if she stays on to never again leave the keep, she'll get old while Kian won't, Syssi is determined to enjoy what little time she has with him, one day at a time.

Can Kian let go of the mortal woman he loves? Will Syssi turn? And if she does, will she survive the dangerous transition?

4: Dark Enemy Taken

Dalhu can't believe his luck when he stumbles upon the beautiful immortal professor. Presented with a once in a lifetime opportunity to grab an immortal female for himself, he kidnaps her and runs. If he ever gets caught, either by her people or his, his life is forfeit. But for a chance of a loving mate and a family of his own, Dalhu is prepared to do everything in his power to win Amanda's heart, and that includes leaving the Doom brotherhood and his old life behind.

Amanda soon discovers that there is more to the handsome Doomer than his dark past and a hulking, sexy body. But succumbing to her enemy's seduction, or worse, developing feelings for a ruthless killer is out of the question. No man is worth life on the run, not even the one and only immortal male she could claim as her own…

Her clan and her research must come first…

5: Dark Enemy Captive

When the rescue team returns with Amanda and the chained Dalhu to the keep, Amanda is not as thrilled to be back as she thought she'd be. Between Kian's contempt for her and Dalhu's imprisonment, Amanda's budding relationship with Dalhu seems doomed. Things start to look up when Annani offers her help, and together with Syssi they resolve to find a way for Amanda to be with Dalhu. But will she still want him when she realizes that he is responsible for her nephew's murder? Could she? Will she take the easy way out and choose Andrew instead?

6: Dark Enemy Redeemed

Amanda suspects that something fishy is going on onboard the Anna. But when her investigation of the peculiar all-female Russian crew fails to uncover anything other than more speculation, she decides it's time to stop playing detective and face her real problem—a man she shouldn't want but can't live without.

6.5: My Dark Amazon

When Michael and Kri fight off a gang of humans, Michael gets stabbed. The injury to his immortal body recovers fast, but the one to his ego takes longer, putting a strain on his relationship with Kri.

7: Dark Warrior Mine

When Andrew is forced to retire from active duty, he believes that all he has to look forward to is a boring desk job. His glory days in special ops are over. But as it turns out, his thrill ride has just begun. Andrew discovers not only that immortals exist and have been manipulating global affairs since antiquity, but that he and his sister are rare possessors of the immortal genes.

Problem is, Andrew might be too old to attempt the activation process. His sister, who is fourteen years his junior, barely made it through the transition, so the odds of him coming out of it alive, let alone immortal, are slim.

But fate may force his hand.

Helping a friend find his long-lost daughter, Andrew finds a woman who's worth taking the risk for. Nathalie might be a Dormant, but the only way to find out for sure requires fangs and venom.

8: Dark Warrior's Promise

Andrew and Nathalie's love flourishes, but the secrets they keep from each other taint their relationship with doubts and suspicions. In the meantime, Sebastian and his men are getting bolder, and the storm that's brewing will shift the balance of power in the millennia-old conflict between Annani's clan and its enemies.

9: Dark Warrior's Destiny

The new ghost in Nathalie's head remembers who he was in life, providing Andrew and her with indisputable proof that he is real and not a figment of her imagination.

Convinced that she is a Dormant, Andrew decides to go forward with his transition immediately after the rescue mission at the Doomers' HQ.

Fearing for his life, Nathalie pleads with him to reconsider. She'd rather spend the rest of her mortal days with Andrew than risk what they have for the fickle promise of immortality.

While the clan gets ready for battle, Carol gets help from an unlikely ally. Sebastian's second-in-command can no longer ignore the torment she suffers at the hands of his commander and offers to help her, but only if she agrees to his terms.

10: Dark Warrior's Legacy

Andrew's acclimation to his post-transition body isn't easy. His senses are sharper, he's bigger, stronger, and hungrier. Nathalie fears that the changes in the man she loves are more than physical. Measuring up to this new version of him is going to be a challenge.

Carol and Robert are disillusioned with each other. They are not destined mates, and love is not on the horizon. When Robert's three months are up, he might be left with nothing to show for his sacrifice.

Lana contacts Anandur with disturbing news; the yacht and its human cargo are in Mexico. Kian must find a way to apprehend Alex and rescue the women on board without causing an international incident.

11: Dark Guardian Found

What would you do if you stopped aging?

Eva runs. The ex-DEA agent doesn't know what caused her strange mutation, only that if discovered, she'll be dissected like a lab rat. What Eva doesn't know, though, is that she's a descendant of the gods, and that she is not alone. The man who rocked her world in one life-changing encounter over thirty years ago is an immortal as well.

To keep his people's existence secret, Bhathian was forced to turn his back on the only woman who ever captured his heart, but he's never forgotten and never stopped looking for her.

12: Dark Guardian Craved

Cautious after a lifetime of disappointments, Eva is mistrustful of Bhathian's professed feelings of love. She accepts him as a lover and a confidant but not as a life partner.

Jackson suspects that Tessa is his true love mate, but unless she overcomes her fears, he might never find out.

Carol gets an offer she can't refuse—a chance to prove that there is more to her than meets the eye. Robert believes she's about to commit a deadly mistake, but when he tries to dissuade her, she tells him to leave.

13: Dark Guardian's Mate

Prepare for the heart-warming culmination of Eva and Bhathian's story!

14: Dark Angel's Obsession

The cold and stoic warrior is an enigma even to those closest to him. His secrets are about to unravel...

15: Dark Angel's Seduction

Brundar is fighting a losing battle. Calypso is slowly chipping away his icy armor from the outside, while his need for her is melting it from the inside.

He can't allow it to happen. Calypso is a human with none of the Dormant indicators. There is no way he can keep her for more than a few weeks.

16: Dark Angel's Surrender

Get ready for the heart pounding conclusion to Brundar and Calypso's story.

Callie still couldn't wrap her head around it, nor could she summon even a smidgen of sorrow or regret. After all, she had some memories with him that weren't horrible. She should've felt something. But there was nothing, not even shock. Not even horror at what had transpired over the last couple of hours.

Maybe it was a typical response for survivors--feeling euphoric for the simple reason that they were alive. Especially when that survival was nothing short of miraculous.

Brundar's cold hand closed around hers, reminding her that they weren't out of the woods yet. Her injuries were superficial, and the most she had to worry about was some scarring. But, despite his and Anandur's reassurances, Brundar might never walk again.

If he ended up crippled because of her, she would never forgive herself for getting him involved in her crap.

"Are you okay, sweetling? Are you in pain?" Brundar asked.

Her injuries were nothing compared to his, and yet he was concerned about her. God, she loved this man. The thing was, if she told him that, he would run off, or crawl away as was the case.

Hey, maybe this was the perfect opportunity to spring it on him.

17: Dark Operative: A Shadow of Death

As a brilliant strategist and the only human entrusted with the secret of immortals' existence, Turner is both an asset and a liability to the clan. His request to attempt transition into immortality as an alternative to cancer treatments cannot be denied without risking the clan's exposure. On the other hand, approving it means risking his premature death. In both scenarios, the clan will lose a valuable ally.

When the decision is left to the clan's physician, Turner makes plans to manipulate her by taking advantage of her interest in him.

Will Bridget fall for the cold, calculated operative? Or will Turner fall into his own trap?

18: Dark Operative: A Glimmer of Hope

As Turner and Bridget's relationship deepens, living together seems like the right move, but to make it work both need to make concessions.

Bridget is realistic and keeps her expectations low. Turner could never be the truelove mate she yearns for, but he is as good as she's going to get. Other than his emotional limitations, he's perfect in every way.

Turner's hard shell is starting to show cracks. He wants immortality, he wants to be part of the clan, and he wants Bridget, but he doesn't want to cause her pain.

His options are either abandon his quest for immortality and give Bridget his few remaining decades, or abandon Bridget by going for the transition and most likely dying. His rational mind dictates that he chooses the former, but his gut pulls him toward the latter. Which one is he going to trust?

19: Dark Operative: The Dawn of Love

Get ready for the exciting finale of Bridget and Turner's story!

20: Dark Survivor Awakened

This was a strange new world she had awakened to.

Her memory loss must have been catastrophic because almost nothing was familiar. The language was foreign to her, with only a few words bearing some similarity to the language she thought in. Still, a full moon cycle had passed since her awakening, and little by little she was gaining basic understanding of it--only a few words and phrases, but she was learning more each day.

A week or so ago, a little girl on the street had tugged on her mother's sleeve and pointed at her. "Look, Mama, Wonder Woman!"

The mother smiled apologetically, saying something in the language these people spoke, then scurried away with the child looking behind her shoulder and grinning.

When it happened again with another child on the same day, it was settled.

Wonder Woman must have been the name of someone important in this strange world she had awoken to, and since both times it had been said with a smile it must have been a good one.

Wonder had a nice ring to it.

She just wished she knew what it meant.

21: Dark Survivor Echoes of Love

Wonder's journey continues in *Dark Survivor Echoes of Love*.

22: Dark Survivor Reunited

The exciting finale of Wonder and Anandur's story.

23: Dark Widow's Secret

Vivian and her daughter share a powerful telepathic connection, so when Ella can't be reached by conventional or psychic means, her mother fears the worst.

Help arrives from an unexpected source when Vivian gets a call from the young doctor she met at a psychic convention. Turns out Julian belongs to a private organization specializing in retrieving missing girls.

As Julian's clan mobilizes its considerable resources to rescue the daughter, Magnus is charged with keeping the gorgeous young mother safe.

Worry for Ella and the secrets Vivian and Magnus keep from each other should be enough to prevent the sparks of attraction from kindling a blaze of desire. Except, these pesky sparks have a mind of their own.

24: Dark Widow's Curse

A simple rescue operation turns into mission impossible when the Russian mafia gets involved. Bad things are supposed to come in threes, but in Vivian's case, it seems like there is no limit to bad luck. Her family and everyone who gets close to her is affected by her curse.

Will Magnus and his people prove her wrong?

25: Dark Widow's Blessing

The thrilling finale of the Dark Widow trilogy!

26: Dark Dream's Temptation

Julian has known Ella is the one for him from the moment he saw her picture, but when he finally frees her from captivity, she seems indifferent to him. Could he have been mistaken?

Ella's rescue should've ended that chapter in her life, but it seems like the road back to normalcy has just begun and it's full of obstacles. Between the pitying looks she gets and her mother's attempts to get her into therapy, Ella feels like she's typecast as a victim, when nothing could be further from the truth. She's a tough survivor, and she's going to prove it.

Strangely, the only one who seems to understand is Logan, who keeps popping up in her dreams. But then, he's a figment of her imagination—or is he?

27: DARK DREAM'S UNRAVELING

While trying to figure out a way around Logan's silencing compulsion, Ella concocts an ambitious plan. What if instead of trying to keep him out of her dreams, she could pretend to like him and lure him into a trap?

Catching Navuh's son would be a major boon for the clan, as well as for Ella. She will have her revenge, turning the tables on another scumbag out to get her.

28: DARK DREAM'S TRAP

The trap is set, but who is the hunter and who is the prey? Find out in this heart-pounding conclusion to the *Dark Dream* trilogy.

29: DARK PRINCE'S ENIGMA

As the son of the most dangerous male on the planet, Lokan lives by three rules:

Don't trust a soul.

Don't show emotions.

And don't get attached.

Will one extraordinary woman make him break all three?

30: DARK PRINCE'S DILEMMA

Will Kian decide that the benefits of trusting Lokan outweigh the risks?

Will Lokan betray his father and brothers for the greater good of his people?

Are Carol and Lokan true-love mates, or is one of them playing the other?

So many questions, the path ahead is anything but clear.

31: DARK PRINCE'S AGENDA

While Turner and Kian work out the details of Areana's rescue plan, Carol and Lokan's tumultuous relationship hits another snag. Is it a sign of things to come?

32 : DARK QUEEN'S QUEST

A former beauty queen, a retired undercover agent, and a successful model, Mey is not the typical damsel in distress. But when her sister drops off the radar and then someone starts following her around, she panics.

Following a vague clue that Kalugal might be in New York, Kian sends a team headed by Yamanu to search for him.

As Mey and Yamanu's paths cross, he offers her his help and protection, but will that be all?

33: DARK QUEEN'S KNIGHT

As the only member of his clan with a godlike power over human minds, Yamanu has been shielding his people for centuries, but that power comes at a steep price. When Mey enters his life, he's faced with the most difficult choice.

The safety of his clan or a future with his fated mate.

34: DARK QUEEN'S ARMY

As Mey anxiously waits for her transition to begin and for Yamanu to test whether his godlike powers are gone, the clan sets out to solve two mysteries:

Where is Jin, and is she there voluntarily?

Where is Kalugal, and what is he up to?

35: DARK SPY CONSCRIPTED

Jin possesses a unique paranormal ability. Just by touching someone, she can insert a mental hook into their psyche and tie a string of her consciousness to it, creating a tether. That doesn't make her a spy, though, not unless her talent is discovered by those seeking to exploit it.

36: DARK SPY'S MISSION

Jin's first spying mission is supposed to be easy. Walk into the club, touch Kalugal to tether her consciousness to him, and walk out.

Except, they should have known better.

37: DARK SPY'S RESOLUTION

The best-laid plans often go awry...

38: DARK OVERLORD NEW HORIZON

Jacki has two talents that set her apart from the rest of the human race.

She has unpredictable glimpses of other people's futures, and she is immune to mind manipulation.

Unfortunately, both talents are pretty useless for finding a job other than the one she had in the government's paranormal division.

It seemed like a sweet deal, until she found out that the director planned on producing super babies by compelling the recruits into pairing up. When an opportunity to escape the program presented itself, she took it, only to find out that humans are not at the top of the food chain.

Immortals are real, and at the very top of the hierarchy is Kalugal, the most powerful, arrogant, and sexiest male she has ever met.

With one look, he sets her blood on fire, but Jacki is not a fool. A man like him will never think of her as anything more than a tasty snack, while she will never settle for anything less than his heart.

39: DARK OVERLORD'S WIFE

Jacki is still clinging to her all-or-nothing policy, but Kalugal is chipping away at her resistance. Perhaps it's time to ease up on her convictions. A little less than all is still much better than nothing, and a couple of decades with a demigod is probably worth more than a lifetime with a mere mortal.

40: DARK OVERLORD'S CLAN

As Jacki and Kalugal prepare to celebrate their union, Kian takes every precaution to safeguard his people. Except, Kalugal and his men are not his only potential adversaries, and compulsion is not the only power he should fear.

41: DARK CHOICES THE QUANDARY

When Rufsur and Edna meet, the attraction is as unexpected as it is undeniable. Except, she's the clan's judge and councilwoman, and he's Kalugal's second-in-command. Will loyalty and duty to their people keep them apart?

42: DARK CHOICES PARADIGM SHIFT

Edna and Rufsur are miserable without each other, and their two-week separation seems like an eternity. Long-distance relationships are difficult, but for immortal couples they are impossible. Unless one of them is willing to leave everything behind for the other, things are just going to get worse. Except, the cost of compromise is far greater than giving up their comfortable lives and hard-earned positions. The future of their people is on the line.

43: Dark Choices The Accord

The winds of change blowing over the village demand hard choices. For better or worse, Kian's decisions will alter the trajectory of the clan's future, and he is not ready to take the plunge. But as Edna and Rufsur's plight gains widespread support, his resistance slowly begins to erode.

44: Dark Secrets Resurgence

On a sabbatical from his Stanford teaching position, Professor David Levinson finally has time to write the sci-fi novel he's been thinking about for years.

The phenomena of past life memories and near-death experiences are too controversial to include in his formal psychiatric research, while fiction is the perfect outlet for his esoteric ideas.

Hoping that a change of pace will provide the inspiration he needs, David accepts a friend's invitation to an old Scottish castle.

45: Dark Secrets Unveiled

When Professor David Levinson accepts a friend's invitation to an old Scottish castle, what he finds there is more fantastical than his most outlandish theories. The castle is home to a clan of immortals, their leader is a stunning demigoddess, and even more shockingly, it might be precisely where he belongs.

Except, the clan founder is hiding a secret that might cast a dark shadow on David's relationship with her daughter.

Nevertheless, when offered a chance at immortality, he agrees to undergo the dangerous induction process.

Will David survive his transition into immortality? And if he does, will his relationship with Sari survive the unveiling of her mother's secret?

46: Dark Secrets Absolved

Absolution.

David had given and received it.

The few short hours since he'd emerged from the coma had felt incredible. He'd finally been free of the guilt and pain, and for the first time since Jonah's death, he had felt truly happy and optimistic about the future.

He'd survived the transition into immortality, had been accepted into the clan, and was about to marry the best woman on the face of the planet, his true love mate, his salvation, his everything.

What could have possibly gone wrong?

Just about everything.

47: Dark haven Illusion

Welcome to Safe Haven, where not everything is what it seems.

On a quest to process personal pain, Anastasia joins the Safe Haven Spiritual Retreat.

Through meditation, self-reflection, and hard work, she hopes to make peace with the voices in her head.

This is where she belongs.

Except, membership comes with a hefty price, doubts are sacrilege, and leaving is not as easy as walking out the front gate.

Is living in utopia worth the sacrifice?

Anastasia believes so until the arrival of a new acolyte changes everything.

Apparently, the gods of old were not a myth, their immortal descendants share the planet with humans, and she might be a carrier of their genes.

48: Dark Haven Unmasked

As Anastasia leaves Safe Haven for a week-long romantic vacation with Leon, she hopes to explore her newly discovered passionate side, their budding relationship, and perhaps also solve the mystery of the voices in her head. What she discovers exceeds her wildest expectations.

In the meantime, Eleanor and Peter hope to solve another mystery. Who is Emmett Haderech, and what is he up to?

49: Dark Haven Found

Anastasia is growing suspicious, and Leon is running out of excuses.

Risking death for a chance at immortality should've been her choice to make. Will she ever forgive him for taking it away from her?

50: Dark Power Untamed

Attending a charity gala as the clan's figurehead, Onegus is ready for the pesky socialites he'll have a hard time keeping away. Instead, he encounters an intriguing beauty who won't give him the time of day.

Bad things happen when Cassandra gets all worked up, and given her fiery temper, the destructive power is difficult to tame. When she meets a gorgeous, cocky billionaire at a charity event, things just might start blowing up again.

51: Dark Power Unleashed

Cassandra's power is unpredictable, uncontrollable, and destructive. If she doesn't learn to harness it, people might get hurt.

Onegus's self-control is legendary. Even his fangs and venom glands obey his commands.

They say that opposites attract, and perhaps it's true, but are they any good for each other?

52: Dark Power Convergence

The threads of fate converge, mysteries unfold, and the clan's future is forever altered in the least expected way.

53: Dark Memories Submerged

Geraldine's memories are spotty at best, and many of them are pure fiction. While her family attempts to solve the puzzle with far too many pieces missing, she's forced to confront a past life that she can't remember, a present that's more fantastic than her wildest made-up stories, and a future that might be better than her most heartfelt fantasies. But as more clues are uncovered, the picture starting to emerge is beyond anything she or her family could have ever imagined.

54: Dark Memories Emerge

The more clues emerge about Geraldine's past, the more questions arise.

Did she really have a twin sister who drowned?

Who is the mysterious benefactor in her hazy recollections?

Did he have anything to do with her becoming immortal?

Thankfully, she doesn't have to find the answers alone.

Cassandra and Onegus are there for her, and so is Shai, the immortal who sets her body on fire.

As they work together to solve the mystery, the four of them stumble upon a millennia-old secret that could tip the balance of power between the clan and its enemies.

55: Dark Memories Restored

As the past collides with the present, a new future emerges.

56: Dark Hunter's Query

For most of his five centuries of existence, Orion has walked the earth alone, searching for answers.

Why is he immortal?

Where did his powers come from?

Is he the only one of his kind?

When fate puts Orion face to face with the god who sired him, he learns the secret behind his immortality and that he might not be the only one.

As the goddess's eldest daughter and a mother of thirteen, Alena deserves the title of Clan Mother just as much as Annani, but she's not interested in honorifics. Being her mother's companion and keeping the mischievous goddess out of trouble is a rewarding, full-time job. Lately, though, Alena's love for her mother and the clan's gratitude is not enough.

She craves adventure, excitement, and perhaps a true-love mate of her own.

When Alena and Orion meet, sparks fly, but they both resist the pull. Alena could never bring herself to trust the powerful compeller, and Orion could never allow himself to fall in love again.

57: Dark Hunter's Prey

When Alena and Orion join Kalugal and Jacki on a romantic vacation to the enchanting Lake Lugo in China, they anticipate a couple of visits to Kalugal's archeological dig, some sightseeing, and a lot of lovemaking.

Their excursion takes an unexpected turn when Jacki's vision sends them on a perilous hunt for the elusive Kra-ell.

As things progress from bad to worse, Alena beseeches the Fates to keep everyone in their group alive. She can't fathom losing any of them, but most of all, Orion.

For over two thousand years, she walked the earth alone, but after mere days with him at her side, she can't imagine life without him.

58: Dark Hunter's Boon

As Orion and Alena's relationship blooms and solidifies, the two investigative teams combine their recent discoveries to piece together more of the Kra-ell mystery.

Attacking the puzzle from another angle, Eleanor works on gaining access to Echelon's powerful AI spy network.

Together, they are getting dangerously close to finding the elusive Kra-ell.

59: Dark God's Avatar

Unaware of the time bomb ticking inside her, Mia had lived the perfect life until it all came to a screeching halt, but despite the difficulties she faces, she doggedly pursues her dreams.

Once known as the god of knowledge and wisdom, Toven has grown cold and indifferent. Disillusioned with humanity, he travels the world and pens novels about the love he can no longer feel.

Seeking to escape his ever-present ennui, Toven gives a cutting-edge virtual experience a try.

When his avatar meets Mia's, their sizzling virtual romance unexpectedly turns into something deeper and more meaningful.

Will it endure in the real world?

60: Dark God's Reviviscence

Toven might have failed in his attempts to improve humanity's condition, but he isn't going to fail to improve Mia's life, making it the best it can be despite her fragile health, and he can do that not as a god, but as a man who possesses the means, the smarts, and the determination to do it.

No effort is enough to repay Mia for reviving his deadened heart and making him excited for the next day, but the flip side of his reviviscence is the fear of losing its catalyst.

Given Mia's condition, Toven doesn't dare to over excite her. His venom is a powerful aphrodisiac, euphoric, and an all-around health booster, but it's also extremely potent. It might kill her instead of making her better.

THE PERFECT MATCH SERIES

PERFECT MATCH 1: VAMPIRE'S CONSORT

When Gabriel's company is ready to start beta testing, he invites his old crush to inspect its medical safety protocol.

Curious about the revolutionary technology of the *Perfect Match Virtual Fantasy-Fulfillment studios*, Brenna agrees.

Neither expects to end up partnering for its first fully immersive test run.

PERFECT MATCH 2: KING'S CHOSEN

When Lisa's nutty friends get her a gift certificate to *Perfect Match Virtual Fantasy Studios*, she has no intentions of using it. But since the only way to get a refund is if no partner can be found for her, she makes sure to request a fantasy so girly and over the top that no sane guy will pick it up.

Except, someone does.

Warning: This fantasy contains a hot, domineering crown prince, sweet insta-love, steamy love scenes painted with light shades of gray, a wedding, and a HEA in both the virtual and real worlds.

Intended for mature audience.

PERFECT MATCH 3: CAPTAIN'S CONQUEST

Working as a Starbucks barista, Alicia fends off flirting all day long, but none of the guys are as charming and sexy as Gregg. His frequent visits are the highlight of her day, but since he's never asked her out, she assumes he's taken. Besides, between a day job and a budding music career, she has no time to start a new relationship.

That is until Gregg makes her an offer she can't refuse—a gift certificate to the virtual fantasy fulfillment service everyone is talking about. As a huge Star Trek fan, Alicia has a perfect match in mind—the captain of the Starship Enterprise.

FOR EXCLUSIVE PEEKS AT UPCOMING RELEASES & A FREE COMPANION BOOK

JOIN MY *VIP CLUB* AND GAIN ACCESS TO THE VIP PORTAL AT ITLUCAS.COM

CLICK HERE TO JOIN
(http://eepurl.com/blMTpD)

INCLUDED IN YOUR FREE MEMBERSHIP:

- FREE CHILDREN OF THE GODS COMPANION BOOK 1
- FREE NARRATION OF GODDESS'S CHOICE—BOOK 1 IN THE CHILDREN OF THE GODS ORIGINS SERIES.
- PREVIEW CHAPTERS OF UPCOMING RELEASES.
- AND OTHER EXCLUSIVE CONTENT OFFERED ONLY TO MY VIPs.

If you're already a subscriber, you'll receive a download link for my next book's preview chapters in the new release announcement email. If you are not getting my emails, your provider is sending them to your junk folder, and you are missing out on **important updates, side characters' portraits, additional content, and other goodies.** To fix that, add isabell@itlucas.com to your email contacts or your email VIP list.

Made in United States
Orlando, FL
06 April 2023

31849706R00359